NEW YORK TIMES BESTSELLING AUTHOR
LINDA HOWARD

wins acclaim for her sizzling historical romances . . .

"Linda Howard writes such beautiful love stories. Her characters are always so compelling."

—Julie Garwood

"An extraordinary talent."

—*Romantic Times*

. ... and for her explosive contemporary fiction that redefines romantic suspense!

"Sexy fun."

—*People*

"Will chill, thrill, and excite you. . . . A passion-filled masterpiece."

—*Rendezvous*

"Heart-pounding sensuality. . . . [A] page-turner."

—*Old Book Barn Gazette*

"Sexy, very hard to put down."

—*The Newport Daily News* (RI)

"Part romance novel, part psychological thriller . . . both frightening and funny."

—*New York Post*

"Linda Howard meshes hot sex, emotional impact, and gripping tension. . . ."

—*Publishers Weekly* (starred review)

Books by Linda Howard

A Lady of the West
Angel Creek
The Touch of Fire
Heart of Fire
Dream Man
After the Night
Shades of Twilight
Son of the Morning
Kill and Tell
Now You See Her
All the Queen's Men
Mr. Perfect
Open Season

Published by POCKET BOOKS

LINDA HOWARD

ANGEL CREEK
AND
A LADY of the WEST

POCKET BOOKS
New York London Toronto Sydney

POCKET BOOKS, a division of Simon & Schuster, Inc.
1230 Avenue of the Americas, New York, NY 10020

This book is a work of fiction. Names, characters, places and incidents are products of the author's imagination or are used fictitiously. Any resemblance to actual events or locales or persons living or dead is entirely coincidental.

A Lady of the West originally published in hardcover in 1990 by Pocket Books
Angel Creek originally published in hardcover in 1991 by Pocket Books

ISBN: 1-4165-0732-9

This Pocket Books trade paperback edition January 2005

10 9 8 7 6 5 4 3 2 1

POCKET and colophon are registered trademarks of Simon & Schuster, Inc.

Manufactured in the United States of America

For information regarding special discounts for bulk purchases, please contact Simon & Schuster Special Sales at 1-800-456-6798 or business@simonandschuster.com.

CONTENTS

ANGEL CREEK

1

Lucas Cochran had been back in town for almost a month, but it still amazed him how much the little town of Prosper had lived up to its name. It would never be anything more than a small town, but it was neat and bustling. A man could tell a lot about a place just by looking at the people on the streets, and by that standard Prosper was quiet, steady, and—well—prosperous. A boomtown might be more exciting than a town like Prosper, and people could make a lot of money in such places, but mining towns tended to die as soon as the ore played out.

Prosper, on the other hand, had started out as a single building serving triple duty as general store, bar, and livery for the few settlers around. Lucas could remember when the site Prosper now occupied had been nothing but bare ground and the only white men for miles had been on the Double C. The gold rush in 1858 had changed all that, bringing thousands of men into the Colorado mountains in search of instant wealth; no gold had been found around Prosper, but a few people had seen the land and stayed, starting small ranches. More people had meant a larger demand for goods. The lone general store/bar/livery soon had another building standing beside it, and the tiny settlement that would one day become Prosper, Colorado, was born.

Lucas had seen a lot of boomtowns, not just in Colorado, and they were all very similar in their frenzied pace, as muddy streets swarmed with miners and those looking to separate the miners from their gold: gamblers, saloon owners, whores, and claim-jumpers. He was glad that Prosper hadn't been blessed—or cursed, depending on your point of view—by either gold or silver. Being what it was, it would still be there when most of the boom-towns were nothing but weathered skeletons.

It was a sturdy little town, a good place to raise a family, as evidenced by the three hundred and twenty-eight souls who lived there. All of the businesses were located on the long center street, around which nine streets of residences had arranged themselves. Most of the houses were small and simple, but some of the peo-ple, like banker Wilson Millican, had already possessed money before settling in Prosper. Their houses wouldn't have looked out of place in Denver or even in the larger cities back East.

Prosper had only one saloon and no whorehouses, though it was well known among the men in town (and the women, although the men didn't know it) that the two saloon girls would take care of any extra itches they happened to have, for a price. There was a church on the north end of town, and a school for the youngsters. Prosper had a bank, two hotels, three restaurants (counting the two in the hotels), a general store, two livery stables, a dry goods store, a barber shop, a cobbler, a blacksmith, and even a hat shop for the ladies. The stage came through once a week.

The entire town was there only because the Cochran family had carved the big Double C spread out of nothing, fighting the Comanche and Arapaho, paying for the land with Cochran blood. Lucas had been the first Cochran born there, and now he was the only one left; he had buried his two brothers and his mother back during the Indian wars, and his father had died the month before. Other ranchers had moved in, but the Cochrans had been the first, and had bought the security the town now enjoyed with Cochran lives. Everyone who had been in town for long knew that Prosper's backbone wasn't the long center street, but the line of graves in the family burial plot on the Double C.

Lucas's bootheels thudded on the sidewalk as he walked toward the general store. A cold wind had sprung up that had the smell of snow on it, and he looked at the sky. Low gray clouds were building over the mountains, signaling yet another delay to spring. Warmer weather should arrive any day, but those low clouds said not quite yet. He passed a woman with her shawl pulled tight around her shoulders and tipped his hat to her. "Looks like more snow, Mrs. Padgett."

Beatrice Padgett gave him a friendly smile. "It does that, Mr. Cochran."

He entered the general store and nodded to Mr. Winches, the proprietor. Winches had done right well in the ten years Lucas had been gone, enough to hire himself a clerk who took care of most of the stocking. "Hosea," Lucas said by way of greeting.

"How do, Lucas? It's turning a mite cold out there, ain't it?"

"It'll snow by morning. The snowpacks can use it, but I'm ready for spring myself."

"Ain't we all? You need anything in particular?"

"Just some gun oil."

"Down the left, toward the back."

"Thanks."

Lucas went down the aisle Hosea had indicated, almost bumping into a farm woman who was fingering the harnesses. He muttered an absentminded apology and continued without more than a glance. Farming was hard on a woman, making her look old before her time. Besides, he had just spotted a familiar blond head over by the sacks of flour, and a sense of satisfaction filled him. Olivia Millican was just the type he would want when he got around to getting married: well-bred, with a pleasant disposition, and pretty enough for him to look forward to bedding her for the rest of his life. He had plans for the Double C, and the ruthless ambition to put those plans into effect.

There were two other young women standing with Olivia, so he didn't approach, just contented himself with a tip of his hat when her eyes strayed his way. To her credit she didn't giggle, though the two with her did. Instead she gave him a grave nod of acknowledgment, and if the color in her cheeks heightened a bit, it just made her prettier.

He paid for the gun oil and left, not getting the door shut good behind him before a muffled flurry of squeals and giggles broke out, though again Olivia didn't contribute.

"He danced with you twice!"

"What did he say?"

"I was so excited when he asked *me,* I almost fainted dead away!"

"Does he dance well? I swear I had butterflies in my stomach just at the thought of having his arm around my waist! It's just as well he didn't ask me, because I'd have made a fool of myself, but at the same time I admit I was powerfully jealous of you, Olivia."

Dee Swann glanced at the knot of three young women, two of whom were taking turns gabbing without allowing Olivia a chance to answer. Olivia was blushing a little but nevertheless maintaining her composure. They stood off to the side in the general store and were making an effort to keep their voices down, but their excitement had caught Dee's attention. It took only a moment of eavesdropping to discern that the gossip was, as usual, about some man, in this case Lucas Cochran. She continued to listen as she selected a new bridle. The stiff leather straps slipped through her fingers as she searched for the one that was most pliable.

"He was very gentlemanly," Olivia said in an even tone. The banker's daughter was seldom ruffled. Dee looked up again with amusement sparkling in her eyes at Olivia's unwavering good manners, and their gazes met across the aisles in silent communication. Olivia understood Dee's mirth as plainly as if she had laughed aloud, just as she understood why Dee not only didn't join them but preferred that Olivia not even acknowledge her presence beyond a polite nod. Dee jealously guarded her privacy, and Olivia respected her old friend enough not to try to include her in a discussion that wouldn't interest her and might actually irritate her.

Even as small as Prosper was, there was a definite social structure. Dee wouldn't normally have been welcome in the circles in which Olivia moved, and she had long ago made certain her friend understood she didn't want to be made an exception to the rule. Dee was totally disinterested in such socializing. Her penchant for privacy was so strong that though everyone knew they were acquainted, since they had attended the local school together, only the two of them knew how close their friendship really was. Dee never visited Olivia; it was always Olivia who rode out, alone, to Dee's small cabin, but it was an arrangement that suited both of them. Not only was Dee's privacy protected, but Olivia in turn felt a certain freedom, a sense of relief in knowing herself unobserved and unjudged at least for a few hours by anyone other than Dee, who was the least judgmental person Olivia had ever met. Only with Dee could she truly be herself. This wasn't to say that she was in reality anything less than a lady, but merely that she enjoyed being able to say whatever she thought. In their shared glance was Olivia's promise to ride out soon and tell Dee all that had happened since they had last seen each other, which had been over a month ago due to the late winter weather.

Having made her selection, Dee took the bridle and her other purchases up to the counter where Hosea Winches waited. He painstakingly tallied her selections on the ledger page that bore her name at the top, then subtracted the total from the amount of credit remaining from the year before. There was only a small amount left, she saw, reading the figures upside down, but it would last her until her crops came in this summer.

Mr. Winches turned the ledger around for her to double-check his arithemetic. While she ran a finger down his columns he eyed the group of young women still standing at the back of the store. Bursts of stifled laughter, high-pitched with excitement, made him snort. "Sounds like a fox got in the chicken house, what with all that squawking," he mumbled.

Dee nodded her satisfaction with his totals and turned the ledger back to its original position, then gathered up her purchases. "Thank you, Mr. Winches."

He shook his head absently. "Be thankful you're more level-headed than some," he said. "You'd think they ain't never seen a man before."

Dee looked back at the others, then at Mr. Winches again, and they both shrugged their shoulders. So what if Lucas Cochran was back in town after a ten-year absence? It didn't mean anything to either of them.

She had recognized Cochran when he had bumped her in the store aisle, of course, but she hadn't spoken because recognizing someone wasn't the same as knowing him, and she doubted that he had recognized her. After all, he had left Prosper shortly after her folks had settled in the area. She had been a fourteen-year-old schoolgirl, while he had been eight years older, a grown man. They had never even met. She knew his face, but she didn't know the man or much about him.

Dee made it a practice to mind her own business and expected others to do the same, but even so she had been aware of what was going on at the Double C. It was the biggest ranch in the area, so everyone paid some attention. Ellery Cochran, Lucas's father, had died a few weeks before. Dee hadn't known the man personally, only enough to put a name to his face whenever their paths crossed in town. She hadn't thought anything unusual of his passing; death was common, and he'd died peacefully, which was about as much as a body could ask for.

The matter was of only mild interest to her, on the level of hearing that a neighbor had a new baby. She had never had any dealings with Ellery, so she didn't expect to have any with his son. She had already forgotten about the Cochrans by the time she stepped out into the icy wind. She tugged her father's old coat more snugly around her and jammed his too-big hat down around her ears, ducking her head to keep the wind off her face as she walked hurriedly to the wagon and climbed up onto the plank seat.

It began snowing late that afternoon, but the swirling of the silent white flakes was one of her favorite sights and filled her with contentment, rather than restlessness at yet another delay of spring. Dee loved the changing seasons, each with its own magic and beauty, and she lived close enough to the land to become immersed in the inexorable rhythm of nature. Her animals were snug in the barn, her chores finished for the day, and she was safe in the cabin with a brisk fire snapping cheerfully, warming her on the outside, while a cup of coffee warmed her on the inside. She had nothing more pressing to do than sit with her feet stretched toward the fire and read one of the precious few books she had obtained over the winter. Winter was her time of rest; she was too busy during the other three seasons to have either the time or the energy for much reading.

But the book soon dropped to her lap, and she leaned her head against the high back of the rocking chair, her eyes focused inward as she planned her garden. The corn had done so well last year that it might be a good thing to plant more of it. Corn was never a waste; what the townspeople didn't buy, she could always use as feed for the horse. But extra corn would mean that she would have to cut back on some other vegetable, and she couldn't decide if that would be wise. By careful planning and experimentation she knew to the square yard how much she could tend, and tend well, by herself. She didn't intend to expand at the expense of the quality of her vegetables. Nor did she want to hire a young boy to help her. It was selfish of her, perhaps, but the greatest pleasure she got from her garden, other than the primitive satisfaction of making things grow, was her complete independence. She stood alone and reveled in it.

At first it had frightened her when she had found herself, at the age of eighteen, totally alone in life. When Dee was sixteen, only a couple of years after they had settled in the narrow, fertile valley just outside Prosper, Colorado, her mother, a schoolteacher, had died, leaving her daughter a legacy of books, an appreciation of the benefits of hard work, and a level head. Barely two more years had passed before her father, George Swann, had managed to get himself kicked in the head by a mule, and he died in his bed the next day without regaining consciousness.

The silence, the emptiness had haunted her. Her solitude, her vulnerability had frightened her. A woman alone was a woman without protection. Dee had dug her father's grave herself and buried him, not wanting anyone to know she was all alone on the homestead. When she had to go into Prosper for supplies she turned aside friendly queries about her father, saying only that he couldn't leave the ranch just then, and she comforted her conscience with the knowledge that she hadn't lied, even if she hadn't told the exact truth.

George had died early in the winter, and during the long, cold months Dee had grieved and pondered her situation. She owned this fertile little valley now; it was too small to support a large-scale ranching operation, but too large for her to work herself. On the other hand, the soil was lush, fed by crystal-clear Angel Creek as it poured out of Prosper Canyon and ran right down the middle of the valley. She could never remember deciding on any exact day what she was going to do with the rest of her life; she had just done what she had to as each day presented itself.

First and foremost had been the necessity of learning how to protect herself. With dogged determination each day she set out her father's weapons: a Colt .36 handgun, an old Sharps rifle, and a shiny, year-old double-barreled shotgun. The handgun was rusty with disuse, as George hadn't gotten it out of the holster where it had been hanging on a peg since they'd settled on Angel Creek. He hadn't been any good with a handgun, he'd often joked; just give him a shotgun, so all he had to do was aim in the general direction of something.

Dee had felt much the same way, but she cleaned and oiled all three of the weapons, something she had often seen her father do, and practiced loading and unloading each weapon in turn, hour after hour, until she could do it automatically, without thinking. Only then did she begin practicing with targets. She began with the handgun, because she thought it would be the easiest, and immediately she saw why George hadn't much liked it. Over any distance at all it just wasn't accurate enough to count on. She experimented until she knew the distance from which she could reasonably expect to hit within the circle of the target she'd painted on a big tree trunk. With the rifle it was much easier to hit what she aimed at, and from a much greater distance. But, like her father, she liked the shotgun best. A man up to no good might reason she wouldn't be able to hit him with a pistol, or even a rifle, and take his chances, but no man with a brain between his ears was going to figure she was likely to miss with a shotgun.

She didn't waste her time trying to build up any speed with the pistol; that was for fast draws, gunslicks looking to make a reputation, and wasn't what she needed. Accuracy was her goal, and she worked on it day after day until she felt satisfied that she was competent enough to defend herself with whichever weapon was at hand. She would never be more than competent, but as competency was what she wanted, that was enough.

The garden was something that had seemed necessary, too. She and her mother had always planted a garden and worked long hours every summer canning the vegetables for use during the winter. Dee liked working in the garden, liked the rhythm of it and the way she could actually see the fruits of her labor. Losing both of her parents so close together had stunned her with the realization that human life was temporary, and she had needed something permanent to get her through the desolation of grief. She had found it in the land, for it continued, and the seasons marched on. A garden was a productive thing, returning a bounty for the most elemental care. It eased her grief to see life coming out of the ground, and the physical labor provided its own kind of relief. The land had given her a reason to live and thus had given her life.

By early spring it was known in town that George Swann had died during the winter, and she had had to weather the storm of questions. People with no more than a nodding acquaintance would ask her outright what her plans were, if she had any folks to take her in, when she'd be going back East. She had cousins in Virginia, where she'd been born, but no one close, even if she had been inclined to go back, which she wasn't. Nor did she consider it anyone's business except her own. The townfolk's nosiness had been almost intolerable for her, for she had always been a private person, and that part of her personality had grown stronger during the past months. Those same people were scandalized when she'd made it plain she had no intention of leaving the homestead. She was only a girl, not yet even nineteen years old, and in the opinion of the townsfolk she had no business living out there all by herself. A respectable woman wouldn't do such a thing.

Some of the young cowhands from the area ranches, as well as others who hadn't the excuse of youth, thought she might be pining for what a man could give her and took it upon themselves to relieve her loneliness. They found their way, singly and sometimes in pairs, to her cabin during the summer nights. With the shotgun in hand Dee had seen to it that they had even more quickly found their way off her property, and gradually the word had gotten around that the Swann girl wasn't interested. A few of them had had to have their britches dusted with shot before they saw the light, but once they realized that she wasn't shy about pulling the trigger they hadn't come back. At least not in the guise of generous swains.

That first spring she had, by habit, planted a garden meant to provide enough for two, as that was what she had planted before, and the crops had been on the verge of bearing before she realized she would have a large surplus. She began taking what she couldn't use into town to sell it off her wagon. But that meant that she had to stay in town all day long herself, so finally she arranged with Mr. Winches that he would buy her vegetables, sometimes for cash and sometimes for credit on his books, and resell them in his general store. It was an arrangement that worked out for both of them, as Dee was able to spend more time in the garden and Mr. Winches could sell the vegetables to the townspeople—the ones who didn't have their own small garden plots—for a neat little profit.

The next year, this time deliberately, Dee planted a huge garden and soon found that she couldn't properly take care of it. The weeds outstripped her efforts to destroy them, and the vegetables suffered. Still, she made a nice profit through Mr. Winches and put up more than enough to feed herself over the winter.

The next spring, as Dee planted her third garden, a new rancher moved into the area south of Prosper. Kyle Bellamy was young, only in his late twenties, and too handsome for his own good. Dee had disliked him on sight; he was overly aggressive, riding roughshod over other people's conversations and opinions. He intended to build a great ranch and made no secret of it as he began acquiring land, though he was careful to avoid stepping on Ellery Cochran's toes.

Bellamy decided that he needed another good water source for his growing empire, and he offered to buy the Angel Creek valley from Dee. She had almost laughed aloud at the ridiculously low offer but managed to decline politely.

His next offer was much higher. Her refusal remained polite.

The third offer was even higher, and he was clearly angry when he made it. He warned her that he wasn't going to go any higher, and Dee decided that he didn't quite understand her position.

"Mr. Bellamy, it isn't the money. I don't want to sell to anyone, for any price. I don't want to leave here; this is my home."

In Bellamy's experience, he could buy anything he wanted; it was just a question of how much he was willing to spend to get it. It came as a shock to him to read the truth in Dee's steady green eyes. No matter how much he offered, she wasn't going to sell.

But he wanted that land.

His next offer was for marriage. Dee would have been amused if it hadn't been for the abrupt shock of realization that she was as disinclined to marry *anyone* as she was to sell her land. Whenever she had thought of the future she had always vaguely assumed that she would someday get married and have children, so she herself was surprised to learn that that wasn't what she wanted at all. Her two and a half years of complete independence had taught her how entirely suited she was to solitude and being her own mistress, answerable to no one but herself. In a split second her view of life was shattered and rearranged, as if she had been looking at herself through a distorted mirror that had abruptly righted itself, leaving her staring frankly at the real woman rather than the false image.

So instead of laughing, she looked up at Kyle Bellamy with an oddly remote expression and said, "Thank you, Mr. Bellamy, but I don't intend ever to marry."

It was after her refusal that some of the cowhands began to think it would be fun to ride through her vegetable garden, firing their pistols into the air to frighten the animals, laughing and shouting to themselves. If they expected her to be hiding under her bed, they soon found out, as had her erstwhile swains, how dangerous it was to underestimate her. That vegetable garden was her livelihood, and she protected it with her booming double-barreled shotgun. She never doubted that most of the cowhands were from Bellamy's ranch, but more and more small ranches were springing up, bringing in strangers who had to be taught to leave the Swann woman alone. During the growing season she learned to sleep with one eye open and the shotgun at hand, to ward off the occasional band of hoorahing cowboys who saw nothing wrong with harassing a nester. She got along just fine except for that, and she felt she could handle the hoorahing. If they ever became more than a nuisance, if she felt threatened herself, she'd start doing more than dusting them with buckshot.

It was six years since her father had died. Dee looked around the small cabin and was satisfied with what she saw, with her life. She had everything she needed and a few small luxuries besides; she had a slowly growing nest egg in the bank, credit at Mr. Winches's store, and a fertile little valley in which to grow her vegetables every year. There were two cows in the barn for milk, and a bull to make certain that she always had a yearling to provide beef. Eventually the bull and cows would be replaced by those yearlings, and life would go on. She had one horse, a sturdy animal who pulled the plow and the wagon and occasionally bore her on his back. A small flock of chickens kept her in eggs and provided a change from beef. It was all hers, and she had done it all herself.

When a woman married, whatever she owned automatically became her husband's property, subject to his will rather than hers, just as the woman herself did. Dee saw no reason ever to give up control of herself and her land. If that meant she would be an old maid, well, there were worse things in life. She was truly independent, as few women were, working her own land and supporting herself. The people in Prosper might think she was a little odd, but she was respected as a hard worker and an honest businesswoman. She was satisfied with that.

2

The trees on the Double C were finally showing new growth, a sure sign of spring. Despite the lingering chill in the air, borne on the winds sweeping down from the mountains that still wore their white winter caps, Lucas Cochran could smell the indefinable fragrance of new life, fresh and green. He had spent ten long years away from the land he loved, and now that he was back he felt as if he couldn't get enough of it, as if a part of himself that had been lost was now restored.

He had been born on this land in a mud dugout only a scant five months after his father had brought his small family west from Tennessee and settled on the broad valley that became the center of the Double C. He sometimes wondered at the courage it had taken for his mother to come out there with one baby just barely a year old and another one on the way, to leave her comfortable house and live in a hole in the ground, and all of that at a time when they were the only whites for hundreds of square miles. Those early days had been the safest, however, because the Indians hadn't yet been alarmed by the strange people moving into their territory.

Looking back, he thought that probably the '49 gold rush in California had been the beginning of the real hostilities between Indian and white. Thousands of people had poured west, and after the gold rush had ended few of them had gone home. The number of white men wandering west of the Mississippi so increased, and the tension between the two peoples had naturally increased as well. Then the Colorado Territory had had its own gold rush in '58, and the second big increase in the population of whites had pushed the situation into open warfare.

By then the Double C had grown to its present size and employed almost a hundred men, and the mud dugout had long since given way to a rough-hewn cabin. Ellery Cochran was in the process of building a big, ambitious house for his wife and family. Lucas had been fourteen that year, already pushing six feet in height and with a man's strength from a lifetime of hard work. His older brother Matthew had been almost sixteen, with all the wild impetuosity of any young male on the verge of adulthood. The two boys had been inseparable all their lives, with Matt's cheerfulness balancing Lucas's darker nature, and Lucas's level-headedness reining in the worst of Matt's adventurousness.

The youngest Cochran, Jonah, was six years younger than Lucas and had always been excluded from the close relationship between the two older boys, not from any maliciousness on their part, but because of the simple, unbridgeable distance of age. The closeness in their ages meant that Matt and Lucas had been together from babyhood, had always had each other as a play-mate, had slept together under the same blanket. Those were things that Jonah could never share, and he was largely left to his own devices. He was a quiet, withdrawn boy, always standing on the fringes and watching his two older brothers but seldom included in their rough activities. It was odd, Lucas often thought, that as close as he had been to Matt, it was Jonah's thin, solemn face that had remained clearest in his memory.

The Indians had attacked the ranch house one day while most of the men were out on the range, something they had evi-dently known. Matt and Lucas had been there only by chance, having ridden in early only because Matt's horse had thrown a shoe, and where one went, so did the other. Alice, their mother, had insisted that they eat lunch before riding back out. They had been sitting at the table with her and Jonah when they had heard the first shouts.

The Indians hadn't had any firearms, but they had outnumbered the few defenders by five to one, and it took time to reload the muzzle-loaders the Cochrans possessed. The speed of the attack, an Indian specialty, was dizzying. All Lucas could remember was a blur of noise and motion, the explosions of gunpowder in his ear, the panic as he tried to reload while keeping an eye on the Indians. He and Matt and Alice had each taken up a position at a window, and he remembered Alice's sudden scream when she had seen eight-year-old Jonah standing at an unguarded window, bravely sighting down the barrel of a pistol so heavy it took both hands for him to hold it. Lucas, the closest, had tackled his baby brother and stuffed him behind an overturned table with orders to stay there. Then he had turned back just as the front door was kicked in and Matt met an Indian warrior in a chest-to-chest clash, muscles straining, hands locked together. The Indian had held a club in one hand, a glittering knife in the other. Lucas grabbed up the pistol Jonah had dropped and whirled on one knee, trying for a clear shot, when Matt went down under the warrior's greater weight and the long knife buried itself in his chest. Lucas had shot then, his aim true, but too late for Matt.

The attack was over as fast as it had started, perhaps because the Indians had known the men out on the range, alerted by the gunfire, would be riding hell for leather for the ranch house. The entire fight had lasted less than five minutes.

Losing Matt had left Lucas like a wounded animal, unable to find comfort. His parents had comforted each other over the loss of their firstborn; Jonah, accustomed to being alone, had pulled even deeper inside himself. Lucas was the one who had been cast adrift, for he had always had Matt, and now his entire world had changed. He had truly grown up that year, for he had seen death, and he had killed, and without Matt to buffer those experiences the hard edges of his character had grown even harder.

The Civil War had started in 1861, and the army had pulled out of Colorado Territory to fight it, in effect leaving the citizens of the Territory on their own to face the increasing Indian attacks. Only the few settled towns were safe; Prosper by then had been big enough to protect itself, but the wagon trains and outlying ranches had to defend themselves as best they could. The Double C was an armed camp, but then it had to be to survive. Alice Cochran hadn't survived, but not because of the Indians; a cold had turned into pneumonia during the winter of '63, and within a week of first taking sick she was put in her grave. The second mainstay of Lucas's life was gone.

The Indian wars were even worse in 1864. In November of that year Colonel John Chivington led his Third Colorado troops against a group of Indians at Sand Creek and massacred hundreds of women and children, causing an explosion of violence that spread from Canada to Mexico, uniting the Plains tribes in the fury of revenge. Troops began returning after the end of the Civil War in '65, but the Territory was already locked in its own war.

Even with all the danger, settlers had poured west. Prosper had quickly become a busy little town, even hiring a schoolteacher, which was a sure sign of civilization. A community had to have a school as a means of attracting new settlers. Boulder had built the first schoolhouse in '60, but the people of Prosper were proud of the fact that it only took them five more years to get one, too. Lucas and Matt had been taught at home by their mother, but Jonah's schooling had been cut short by her death. For the first time in his life Jonah began attending a school at the age of fifteen, riding into Prosper every day.

Jonah never said much; he just watched. As Lucas had grown older he had regretted the lack of closeness between himself and his remaining brother, but Jonah didn't seem to want that kind of relationship. The boy lived within himself, keeping his dreams and thoughts private. Sometimes Lucas wondered what went on behind the boy's somber blue eyes, so like his own in color. He never found out.

Jonah's horse brought him home from school one afternoon. The boy clung to the saddle, an arrow all the way through his chest. Lucas had been the first to reach him, and a look of acute embarrassment had crossed Jonah's white face as he had fallen off the saddle into his brother's arms. He had looked up at Lucas, and for the first time his blue eyes weren't somber, but lit with a kind of fierce love, a joy. "I wish . . ." he had said, but what he wished had gone unsaid because he died on the next breath.

Lucas had knelt on the ground, rocking his brother in his arms. What had he wished, this young boy who hadn't had time to live much? Had his wish been something simple, a wish that it would stop hurting? Or had he wished for a girl's kiss, for his own future, for the pleasures that he hadn't yet been able to taste? Lucas didn't know; he only knew that in the last instant before death Jonah's eyes had held more life than ever before.

The Double C had soaked up Cochran blood as well as Indian blood. Cochrans lay buried in its soil. And now Lucas was the only Cochran left.

His dreams centered around the Double C, just as they always had. That was what had led to the rift with his father. Maybe if Jonah hadn't died Lucas wouldn't have felt so raw, so violent, but that was a big maybe, and he'd never let himself fret about it. The simple fact was that a ranch could have only one boss, and the two remaining Cochrans had butted heads time and again. Ellery had been content with what he had, while Lucas had wanted to enlarge.

The Double C had, after all, belonged to Ellery, so Lucas had been the one to go. Father and son had made their peace, but both knew two stallions just couldn't live in the same pasture. They regretted the break but accepted that, for both of them, it was better that Lucas lead his own life away from the Double C. They had written and even visited a couple of times in Denver, but Lucas hadn't returned to the ranch until Ellery's death.

He hadn't spent those ten years living in the lap of luxury. He had supported himself in various ways: as a cowhand, gambling, even as a lawman for a while. He knew ranch work inside out, and he was handy with a gun, but that alone hadn't kept him alive. A cool head, sharp eyes, and iron determination had served him well. Luke Cochran wasn't a man to mess with; he didn't let anything stand in his way when he wanted something. If the cost was high—well, he was willing to pay it if he wanted something bad enough. There wasn't much that could stop a man who was willing to pay the price, in blood or money, to get what he wanted, and he knew it.

But with Ellery's death the Double C had become his. It was already profitable, but he meant to make it even more so. Colorado was on the brink of statehood, which would open up a gold mine of opportunities to a man smart enough and tough enough to take them. He hadn't spent all of those ten years working at rough jobs; for the past two he had been in Denver, working with the territorial governor to secure statehood, learning how power worked, instantly seeing the vast applications of it. He had been part of the convention that had met in Denver the previous December to draft a constitution, and it was due to be voted on in July.

The value of statehood to the Double C was almost incalculable. With statehood would come settlers; with settlers would come the railroads. The railroads would make it infinitely easier for him to get his beef to market, and his profits would soar. He wanted the Double C to be the biggest and the best. It was all he had left now; the soil embraced his family in death even as it had sustained them in life. And as the Double C became richer he would work within the lines of contact he had already established in Denver. The two would feed each other: The Double C would make more money, and he would have more influence in Denver; the more influence he had in Denver, the more he could sway decisions that would affect the Double C, thus making it even richer.

He wasn't ambitious for the political aspect of it, but he needed to make certain the ranch would continue to prosper. He was willing to pay the price. The ten years out on his own had taught him some hard lessons, finishing the process of hardening that had begun in boyhood. Those lessons would come in handy now that he had an empire to build.

An empire needed heirs.

He wasn't in any real hurry to tie himself down, but he hadn't been back long before Olivia Millican, banker Wilson Millican's daughter, had caught his eye. She was pretty and cool and refined, socially adept and always well-mannered. She would be a perfect wife. A woman like her had to be courted, and Lucas was willing to do it. He liked her; he figured they would get along better than most. In another year or so she'd make him a fine wife.

But this year he'd be busy putting his plans into action.

There were so many things that he wanted to do. One of them was improving the herd, bringing in new bulls, trying new crossbreeds to produce a hardier steer without losing any quality in the meat. He also wanted to try different grasses for grazing, rather than letting the herd graze on whatever happened to be growing.

And he wanted to expand. Not too much right away; he didn't want to start off by overextending himself. But after producing a better herd he wanted to produce one that was bigger as well, and that meant more land for grazing, more water. He well knew the value of a good source of water; it could mean the difference between life and death for a herd. Many a rancher had gone under when the water dried up.

Building the ranch up would give him the solid base he needed to fulfill the rest of his ambitions. It was the first step, the most necessary step.

He had a good water source now, a small, lazily moving river that wound around the ranch. It had never gone dry that he could remember, but there had been a couple of summers when it had slowed to little more than a trickle. It had always rained before the situation became dire, but someday the rain might not come in time. Rainfall wasn't heavy in Colorado anyway; most of the water came from the snowcaps. A good year depended more on the winter snows than the summer rains, and it hadn't snowed much this past winter. A smart rancher always had more than one water source, just in case. Some streams would continue to run while others dried up.

One of the things he'd argued about with Ellery was the need for another good water source, Angel Creek specifically. Angel Creek and the river on the Double C came from the same source, a larger stream that divided in two and flowed down opposite sides of the mountain. But at the point of division the bed of Angel Creek lay lower than the other riverbed. Thus what runoff there was from the mountain during the dry weather would flow into Angel Creek, leaving the other dry until the water level in the stream rose enough to overflow into the higher riverbed.

Lucas had wanted to claim the narrow Angel Creek valley just for its water, but Ellery had refused, saying that the Double C had enough water to take care of its own, and anyway, Angel Creek was on the other side of the mountain with no good way to herd the cattle across it. They'd have to be moved *around* the mountain, and that was too much trouble. Besides, the valley was too small to support a large herd. Lucas had disagreed with his father's reasoning.

Angel Creek. Lucas narrowed his eyes, remembering how lush the valley was. Maybe it would be Cochran land after all.

He sought out his foreman. "Toby, didn't someone settle on Angel Creek some years back?"

William Tobias, who had been ranch foreman as far back as Lucas could remember, grunted an affirmative. "Yep. Nester by the name of Swann." A slight curl to his lip indicated how much he disliked even saying the word "nester."

Lucas grunted back, a scowl settling on his face. Like all cattlemen, he didn't care for nesters or the fences they put up on what had been open range. But maybe the nester on Angel Creek would consider selling. From what he'd seen of nesters, though, they were as hardheaded as mules.

Maybe this one would have more sense. It was worth a ride over to Angel Creek, at least, because he'd never know unless he asked.

A man on horseback could pick his way through any of the narrow passes, though trying to move a herd over them would have been stupid. Lucas eyed the sun and calculated that he had plenty of time before nightfall to ride over there and back, so there wasn't any point in waiting.

He wasn't optimistic about talking the nester into selling, and it put him in an irritable mood. If Ellery had listened to him, Angel Creek would already be his. Or he could have claimed it for his own before the settlers had started moving in if he hadn't been too young and hotheaded to plan ahead. Looking back and realizing what he should have done was just a waste of time.

The little homestead surprised him as he rode down the broad slope toward the farm buildings. There were only two cows and a bull, but they were fat and healthy. A lone horse in the corral looked sleek and well cared for, even if it wasn't a prime specimen of horseflesh. Chickens pecked contentedly at the ground, scarcely paying him any attention when he rode up and dismounted, tying the reins to a post while he looked around with interest. The small cabin, though roughly built, was neat and sturdy, as were the barn and fences. In the back was a plot for a large vegetable garden, the ground recently broken in preparation for spring planting, though it was still a bit early. He couldn't see anything out of place or untended, and his slim hope that the nester would sell disappeared. If the place had been rundown he would have had a chance, but this homestead was prospering. There was no need for the man to go anywhere else.

The cabin door opened, and a slim young woman stepped out onto the porch, a shotgun in her hands. Her face was calm but alert, and Lucas saw that her finger was on the trigger.

"State your business, mister."

A shotgun made him wary at any time, but he was doubly edgy facing one in the hands of a woman. If she got excited, she might accidently kill either him or his horse, or both. He tamped down a quick rise of anger and made his voice low and soothing. "I don't mean you any harm, ma'am. You can put that shotgun down."

The shotgun didn't waver. The twin barrels looked enormous. "I'll make my own judgment about that," she replied calmly. "Too many cowboys think it's funny to trample my garden."

"You don't have a garden yet," he pointed out.

"But I do have livestock to run off, so I'll keep this gun right where it is until you answer my question."

He could see the green of her eyes even in the shadow of the porch where she stood. There was no fear or uncertainty in her gaze, nor any hostility, come to that, only a certain purposefulness. A little bit of admiration tinged his anger. The nester was one lucky man to have a wife with this sort of gumption, he thought. Lucas was abruptly certain that she would hit whatever she aimed at. He was careful not to make any sudden moves as he reached up and took off his hat. "I'm Lucas Cochran from the Double C. I came over to make your husband's acquaintance, Mrs. Swann, and talk a little business with him."

She gave him a cool, level look. "George Swann was my father, not my husband. He died six years ago."

He was beginning to get irritated at being held at bay. "Then maybe I could talk to your husband. Or your brother. Whoever owns the place."

"I don't have a husband or a brother. I'm Dee Swann. This is my land."

His interest sharpened. He looked around the tidy little place again, wondering who helped her do the work. Maybe there were other women on the place, but even that would be unheard of; women simply didn't work a homestead on their own. If their men died, they went to live with relatives somewhere. He listened but didn't hear any voices or movement inside the cabin. "Are you alone here?"

She smiled, her expression as cool as her eyes, challenging him. "No. I have this shotgun."

"You can put it down," he said sharply, his irritation now plain. "I just came by to get acquainted, not to do you any harm."

She looked him over carefully, and he had the feeling it wasn't what he'd said that reassured her, but rather her own private assessment of him as a man that prompted her to lower the muzzle of the shotgun toward the floor and nod at him. "It's dinnertime," she said. "I eat early. You're welcome to join me, if you'd like."

He wasn't hungry, but he seized the opportunity and followed her into the cabin. It was only two rooms and a loft, but it was as neat inside as out. The kitchen was on the left; what he assumed to be her bedroom was on the right. There was a comfortable chair pulled over next to the fireplace with an oil lamp on a small table beside it, and to his surprise a book lay open on the table. He looked around, noting some rough, handmade shelves lined with books. She wasn't illiterate, then.

She had gone straight to the wood stove and was ladling steaming soup into two big bowls. Lucas took his hat off and sat down at the sturdy table just as she placed the bowl in front of him. A plate of biscuits was already on the table, as well as a pot of coffee. The soup was thick with vegetables and tender pieces of beef. Lucas found himself going at it as if he hadn't had anything all day.

Dee Swann sat across from him, eating as composedly as if she were alone. Lucas watched her, studying her face. She intrigued him. She didn't flirt with him the way he was used to women doing, or even seem to be aware that he was a man beyond the simple fact of identification. She was straightforward in her speech and actions, but he thought that calmness just might be a cover for the heat underneath. It was in her eyes, long and green, with banked fires in them.

At first glance she was plain, but closer examination made him realize it was an impression created by her utilitarian clothing and severe hairstyle; her black hair was pulled back and twisted into a tight knot at her nape. She had an exotic sort of attractiveness, with high cheekbones and a wide, soft mouth, but they weren't the kind of looks that were blatantly fetching. The heat of sexual arousal began to build in his loins and belly as he watched her eat, dipping daintily into the soup without any indication that she even remembered he was there.

"Don't you have any other family?" he asked abruptly, determined to make her pay attention to him.

She shrugged and put down her spoon. "I have cousins, but no one close."

"Wouldn't they take you in?"

Those green eyes studied him for a long time before she deigned to answer. "I suppose they would have, if I'd asked. I preferred to stay here."

"Why? It has to be lonesome for you, as well as dangerous."

"I have the shotgun," she reminded him. "And no, I'm not lonesome. I like it out here."

"I suppose you have plenty of men friends." How could she not have? A young, attractive woman, alone at that, would attract all sorts of attention.

She laughed. It wasn't a maidenly giggle, but the full-throated sound of a woman who knew how to enjoy herself. "Not since they learned I know how to hit what I aim at. After I peppered a few, the others decided to leave me alone."

"Why did you do that? You might have been married by

now." Her laughter made the heat intensify. Whatever her reason, he was glad she hadn't married, because he'd always made it
a point to stay away from other men's wives even when the wives
in question were willing.

"Oh, I've had some marriage proposals, Mr. Cochran. Three,
I think. I'm not married because I don't want to be. I don't plan
on ever getting married."

In his experience, all women wanted to get married. He
sipped his coffee and eyed her over the rim of the cup. "If you got
married, you'd have a man to do the work around here."

"I can handle the work just fine. And if I got married, it
wouldn't be my land any longer, it would be his. I'd rather be my
own woman."

They were sitting alone in her cozy cabin eating food she had
prepared. The conversation had without effort become far more
personal than it ever should have been on first meeting. An aura
of intimacy wrapped them, making him think of reaching out for
her and drawing her onto his knee, the way he would if she were
his woman. It was a fantasy, though, because her composed green
gaze invited nothing more than conversation. It irritated him,
because he was used to women paying him more attention than
that. Even Olivia, with her perfect manners and composure,
responded to him in the way he expected.

It was probably the last thing Dee Swann intended, but her
disinterest provoked the opposite reaction in him. Lucas had
always enjoyed a challenge, and she was certainly that; any
woman who used a shotgun to discourage suitors was bound to
keep him on his toes. Maybe she didn't need a man to work her
land, but a woman sure needed a man to take care of her other
needs. It was fine with him that she didn't want to get married,
because she wasn't the type of woman he would ever select to
be his wife. Dee would, however, he thought, make a fine bed
partner.

Lucas had gotten out of a lot of tight situations by using his
head, and he was too smart to let any of his thoughts show. He
knew that if he even hinted at anything sexual between them
right now she'd have that shotgun pointed at him faster than he
could blink. Let her get used to him first, accept him as a friend,

then they'd become really *close* friends. So he kept his face blank as he turned the conversation to his original reason for being there.

"You've gotten by okay because so far all you've had to deal with are a few liquored-up cowhands with nothing more than hoorahing on their minds. But let a man come up on you without all the yelling and shooting to warn you, and he'd be on you before you could get to your shotgun. Or a bunch of them could decide to get even with you; there's no way you could guard both doors and every window. It's dangerous for you out here," he said persuasively. "With the money you could get for this land you could set yourself up in town in any kind of business you wanted, and you'd be safe. Think about it: I'm willing to give you more than a fair price."

"I don't have to think about it," she said. "I don't want to sell. This is my home; I like it here. I tend my garden and sell vegetables in town and get along just fine. If I'd wanted to sell, I could have sold to Mr. Bellamy a long time ago."

He frowned. "Bellamy's offered to buy you out?"

"Several times."

"You should have taken his offer. You're a woman alone." He didn't like the idea of Bellamy owning Angel Creek, but he was serious about the potential danger she was in. A good-looking woman living by herself like this was just asking for trouble from any no-good passing through.

But Dee only shrugged, dismissing his warnings. "So? I'd be alone no matter where I went, so I might as well stay here."

"You'd have other people close by if you lived in town, in case you needed help. You'd be safe instead of working yourself half to death out here."

"And just what would I do in town?" she demanded, getting to her feet and placing her empty bowl in the big wash bowl. "How would I earn a living? The town doesn't need another dress shop, or another hat shop, or another general store, and the money from selling the land wouldn't last forever. There's nothing I could do except maybe take one of the rooms over the saloon, and somehow I don't think I'd be a success at that."

Luke was jolted at the thought of her working as a whore. No, he couldn't see it either. She was too proud and independent. A man didn't want a challenge when he went to a whorehouse; he wanted simple, unthinking relief. He pictured her taking her clothes off, her eyes flashing green heat in a dim room, and his blood started pounding through his body. Mounting this filly would take a strong man, but it would be worth it when he was locked deep inside her, feeling her heat, riding her hard and fast. Only a strong man would be able to handle her, keep her satisfied.

He was a strong man, and he liked a challenge. His earlier thoughts hardened into determination. He was going to teach Dee Swann that she needed a man for one thing, at least.

But because he was smart, he didn't say anything on the subject or push her anymore to sell her land. He thanked her politely for the meal, offered his aid if she ever needed it, tipped his hat, and left like a gentleman. He didn't feel the least bit gentlemanly, though, as he rode back toward the cut over the mountain. He felt tense and alive, his senses alert, his loins stirring with anticipation. No, there was nothing gentlemanly about his thoughts or his intentions; in both he was purely male, scenting female and wanting her. The only thing was, the female didn't know yet that she was being pursued, so she wasn't even running.

Dee went to the door and watched him ride away. She felt strangely disturbed and too warm; she loosened the top buttons of her blouse to let the cooling air waft over her throat. So that was Lucas Cochran. That brief glimpse of him in the general store hadn't prepared her for a face-to-face meeting. She hadn't realized that he was quite so tall, or so strongly built, or that his iron will gleamed so plainly in his blue eyes. Lucas Cochran was used to getting what he wanted, and he hadn't liked it at all that she had turned down his offer for the land.

She would bet all the money she had that he would be back.

3

Olivia Millican had spent her entire life being the perfect daughter and the perfect lady. It wasn't difficult; she was by nature both kind and composed. Sometimes she felt guilty that she had had such an easy, privileged life when she could see how so many other people had to struggle to have even a fraction of the luxuries to which she was accustomed, but she was also intelligent enough to see that neither was it her fault. Her father had worked hard to make his bank successful; any child of his would have had the same comfortable life. She tried to do what she could to help with the few small charities around town, and she tried never to be mean or rude. Her rules of conduct were simple, and she truly tried to adhere to them.

All she had ever wanted was to fall in love with a good man and have him love her in return, marry her, and give her his children. When she was younger she had never thought that it was such an unreasonable thing to expect from life; heaven knew it seemed an easy enough thing for most of her friends. She still didn't see that it was anything but an ordinary wish, yet somehow it had never happened.

She was twenty-five now, virtually an old maid, though there again her father's money was shielding her. A poor woman of twenty-five would have been an old maid; a wealthy woman of twenty-five was still "a good catch." Yet somehow, though there were good men in town, she had never loved any of them, and none of them had ever seemed to be wildly in love with her, and now just about all of those her age were married to someone else.

Except Lucas Cochran.

His name ran through her mind as she worked with her mother on the fine embroidery of a linen tablecloth, and she shivered a little. It wasn't that she disliked him; he was handsome in a hard sort of way, wealthy, intelligent, well-mannered, and certainly eligible. It wasn't her imagination that he had singled her out in some small way every time they had met since his return to town, for other people had remarked on it. He danced well and treated her with respect. Her feminine instincts also told her that after they had known each other a respectable length of time he would ask her to marry him. She was very much afraid that, because she was twenty-five and this would likely be her last chance at marriage and a family, she would say yes. But Lucas Cochran didn't love her. Despite all of the little attentions he paid her, despite the faintly possessive expression in his blue eyes whenever he looked at her, as if she already belonged to him, she knew that she aroused none of the passionate emotion in him that she had always longed for from the man she would marry.

And he was a hard man, hard in a way that her father, who had a forceful personality himself, couldn't even begin to match. Lucas Cochran would never allow anyone to stand between him and anything he wanted. Olivia knew herself to be no more a match for him than her father was; far less, in fact. Oh, he would protect her as his wife, give her children, but she would never matter any more to him than any other woman he might have chosen to fill the position. She could expect consideration but not caring, physical attention but never love, protection but not devotion.

But if she refused him, she would likely die without ever marrying and having her own family, and her woman's heart cried out for children.

"I've changed my mind about visiting Patience," Honora Millican said in her soft voice.

Olivia looked up, startled. Her mother had been looking forward to visiting her sister in San Francisco in the summer, and Olivia couldn't think of anything that would have changed her mind. Truth to tell, she'd been as eager for the trip as her mother. They seldom saw Aunt Patience. It had been almost five years since their last visit, and other than visiting her favorite relative she had also been eager to visit the glorious shops in San Francisco again. "But we've been planning it for over a year now!"

"I know, dear, but I really don't think we should leave town for several months just now." Honora smiled sweetly at her daughter, the smile that Olivia had inherited.

Olivia was both confused and disappointed. "Why ever not?"

"With the attention Mr. Cochran has been paying you? It wouldn't do to be gone so long and let some other young woman gain his attention."

Olivia bent her head over the embroidery to hide her expression, which she knew must reveal the leap of panic she felt. Had she also been hoping against hope that this time she would meet someone special in San Francisco? "You talk as if it's a foregone conclusion that he intends to propose," she said, though she thought it was herself.

Honora said placidly, "Of course he does. Why, everyone can see it in the way he looks at you."

"He isn't in love with me," Olivia said, raising troubled eyes to her mother.

But Honora didn't look in the least disturbed. "I admit Mr. Cochran isn't one to wear his heart on his sleeve. But why else would he pay such attention to you?"

"Because I'm the banker's daughter," she replied. "I'm presentable, and I was schooled back East."

Honora put down her needle and frowned, her interest now wholly engaged. "That's a remarkably cynical outlook, dear. What makes you think Mr. Cochran isn't interested in you for yourself? You're a beautiful young woman, even if I do say so myself."

Olivia bit her lip, knowing that she didn't have any solid reasons she could put forth for her statement, only intuition. She didn't want to cause Honora any worry. Her mother tended to fret to excess if any ill wind of health or humours blew on the two people she loved most in the world, her husband and daughter. It was both a source of security, knowing herself so well loved, and a sense of responsibility that she should do whatever she could to keep Honora from being upset.

So she made herself smile at her mother and say, "All the same, I'm not certain it wouldn't do Mr. Cochran some good to think about me meeting so many good-looking men in San Francisco."

Honora's face cleared, and she began to chuckle. "I see. You don't want him to feel too sure of himself. Wonderful idea! But all the same, I don't think we should go off for the entire summer this early in the relationship."

Olivia stifled a sigh. She had hoped that Honora would think it such a good idea that the decision not to go to San Francisco would be reconsidered. Now she knew that she would have to tell her mother all of her fears and uncertainties in order to change her mind, and Olivia wasn't willing to do that. For one thing, she wasn't certain that she wasn't simply being foolish, fretting over "love." No other young woman in town would hesitate a minute if given the opportunity to marry Lucas Cochran—well, except for Dee, but Dee was different. Another reason was that Olivia was a naturally reserved person, respectful of the privacy of others simply because she needed it so much herself. Not even to her mother could she reveal her inner fears, because Honora would then find it necessary to confide in Olivia's father and perhaps even in certain of her friends in town; in short, it would soon become common knowledge.

Both of her parents would become so upset and make such a fuss that she simply couldn't face it. She was their only child, having been born after Honora had miscarried twice, and they had showered her with all of the devotion that should have been shared with a houseful of children. They wanted only the best for her; nothing else, in their eyes, was good enough. She would do anything to keep them from knowing how unhappy she was.

So she bent her head over the embroidery and said nothing else on the subject, pushing her unhappiness to the back of her mind as she listened to Honora's placid chatter about the upcoming social. Prosper had a rather active social life for a town its size, with various small parties and entertainments arranged throughout the year. Late each spring the women of the town put on a large picnic and dance, and everyone in the area was invited. The women in town took turns organizing the affair, and this spring was Honora's turn. The older woman was in her element, planning and organizing, delegating, double-checking and triple-checking each detail. For weeks her conversation had consisted of how well or ill things were going, and today was no exception. Olivia listened patiently, offering advice whenever asked but for the most part providing only an audience, which was really all Honora wanted.

As often as not, when Honora began reviewing her plans and accomplishments she eventually remembered some little detail that had to be taken care of immediately, and that day was no exception. She abruptly dropped the embroidery hoop to her lap and said, "Oh, dear."

The moment of crisis was so predictable that Olivia smiled with gentle amusement even as she asked, "Is something wrong?"

"I completely forgot to arrange with Beatrice Padgett for us to use her punch set! I can't believe it slipped my mind like that."

"I'm sure she takes it for granted that her punch set will be needed," Olivia comforted. "After all, she's the only person in town who owns over three hundred punch cups."

"Still, it would be terribly rude not to *ask* her, just to *assume* that her possessions are available for our use. I'll write her a note right now," Honora said, putting the hoop aside and rising to cross to her writing desk. "Do you have a moment to spare to take it to her, dear? I simply have too much to do this afternoon, though I'd love to visit with Beatrice, but you know how she talks. It's practically impossible to get away from her once she gets started."

"Of course," Olivia said, gladly putting her own embroidery hoop aside. She was very good at needlework, but that didn't mean she enjoyed it. "I think I'll go for a ride while I'm out." She wanted to be alone for a while; maybe a brisk ride would banish her melancholy, which lingered as a hollow feeling deep inside despite her efforts to push it away. Or maybe she would visit Dee. As soon as she had the thought she realized that was exactly what she needed. Dee's implacable logic always went straight to the heart of a matter, and she always said exactly what she thought. Olivia needed that kind of clear thinking right now.

She went upstairs to change into her riding habit while Honora set about writing. By the time she came back down the stairs Honora was folding the note.

"There," she said, tucking the paper into Olivia's pocket. "Take your time, dear, and do tell Beatrice that I'm sorry I couldn't come myself, but I promise to visit her soon to go over all the plans for the social."

The Millicans kept their two horses in the livery, so Olivia walked first to the Padgett house, which took only five minutes. But it was the truth that Beatrice Padgett liked to talk, and it was over an hour before Olivia was able to leave. Beatrice insisted that she come in for tea to the point that continued refusal would have been embarrassing, so Olivia found herself once again sitting and listening, with nothing more required of her than an occasional nod or comment.

It was an enjoyable hour, though, because Beatrice was a genuinely likable woman, friendly and without malice. Olivia had often thought that Beatrice and Ezekiel Padgett were something of a mismatch. Beatrice, in her late forties, still retained enough beauty for one to see that she had once been quite something. She was a warm woman given to hugs and pats, freely affectionate and exuding a soft, rather voluptuous sensuality. Ezekiel, on the other hand, was tall and dour, seldom smiling, his face too rawboned for handsomeness. Olivia had wondered how they could live together in any sort of harmony, though she had once seen Ezekiel look down at his wife's face when he thought them unobserved, and his expression had softened almost to tenderness.

So love did grow even in unlikely marriages, perhaps had been there from the beginning, at least on Beatrice's part, for why else would such an affectionate woman have married such a dour man? It was plain to anyone why Ezekiel would have married Beatrice, even without love, so Olivia didn't consider that.

Perhaps she was foolish to worry about marrying Lucas. Maybe they would grow to love each other as much as Beatrice and Ezekiel did, as much as her own parents did.

But no matter how she tried, she simply couldn't imagine such a look on Lucas's face as she had seen on Ezekiel's.

Dee looked out the window when she heard someone riding up and smiled when she saw it was Olivia. It had been too long since they'd had a chance to chat, but now that the weather was better Olivia would come to visit more often. She poured two cups of coffee and walked out on the porch to greet her friend.

Olivia dismounted and took the coffee with a smile of thanks as they sat down on the porch. "I thought winter was never going to end," she sighed. "I've wanted to come out several times, but the weather never cooperated."

"From what I heard in Winches's store, Lucas Cochran's courting you."

That was Dee, going right to the point. Olivia's tension eased a little. It was a relief to talk to Dee because there were no social inanities with her, no need for a polite social mask or worry that Dee might be shocked at anything she said. Not that she was likely to say anything shocking, Olivia admitted ruefully to herself. It was just that it was nice to know one *could*.

"It seems so," she said.

"Seems? He either is or he isn't."

"Well, he hasn't actually said anything. It's just that he's paid attention to me."

"Enough attention for people to start talking about a wedding?"

"Yes," Olivia admitted, unable to hide the misery in her eyes.

"Do you love him?"

"No."

"Then don't marry him," Dee said with a finality that suggested the matter was closed.

"But what if he's my last chance?" Olivia asked softly.

"For what?"

"To get married."

Dee sipped her coffee. "Do you really think you'll never meet anyone else?"

"It isn't that. It's just that no one has ever fallen in love with me, and maybe no one ever will. If I can't have love, I'd still like to have a family. He truly may be my last chance."

"Well, I'm probably not the best person to come to for advice," Dee said, and she chuckled. "After all, I've already turned down three men. He came out here the other day, by the way. Cochran, that is. He wanted to buy Angel Creek."

The thought of that was interesting. Lucas was accustomed to having things his way. Olivia could just imagine what he'd thought when he'd met Dee, who could be as intractable as a rock wall when she chose.

"What did you think of him?"

Dee grinned. "That he'd make a dangerous enemy. And that no one tells him 'no' very often. He doesn't take it well."

"And you enjoyed telling him."

"Of course I did." Mischief gleamed in her green eyes as she glanced at Olivia. "He could use taking down a peg or two."

"I don't think he'll give up," Olivia warned.

"No, he won't."

Dee looked as if she positively relished the thought of thwarting Lucas, and not for the first time Olivia wished she could be more like her friend. Dee wasn't intimidated by Lucas, or by anyone. There was a kind of inner strength to her, a surety that most people didn't have. Olivia didn't feel certain of anything, with her longing to have a family at odds with her fear of marrying someone she didn't love. She couldn't imagine Dee ever feeling that kind of uncertainty. Dee would simply make up her mind one way or the other, and that would be that.

"I think Lucas would ride roughshod over me if I married him," Olivia said, and she bit her lip.

Dee thought about it, then nodded. "Probably."

That blunt assessment startled Olivia into a spurt of laughter. "You didn't have to agree!"

"Oh, you aren't weak," Dee explained, smiling a little. "It's just that you're too gentle to fight him when he needs to be fought. But cheer up. Maybe you'll meet someone in San Francisco you really want to marry."

"Mother's canceled the trip. She didn't think it would be smart to leave Lucas for such a long time while he's showing so much interest. Of course, Lucas may not have any plans to marry at all, and I could be worrying over nothing." The thought popped into her head that Dee would make Lucas a much better wife than she herself would, and she almost blurted it out but stopped herself in time. Dee would look at her as if she were crazy if she said such a thing.

But it was true. In both temperament and character Dee was a fair match for Lucas; both of them were so strong that they would completely overshadow anyone who wasn't just as strong. The only thing was, Dee wasn't the least interested in getting married.

Nevertheless, the idea lingered.

On the way home Olivia detoured by the bank to tell her father hello. Just as she stepped up on the sidewalk the door to the bank opened, and Kyle Bellamy came out, flanked by two of his men. He removed his hat as soon as he saw her.

"Miss Millican, how are you today?"

"Fine, thank you, Mr. Bellamy. And you?"

"Couldn't be better." He looked down at her, giving her his self-confident smile. No doubt about it, Kyle Bellamy was a good-looking man, and he knew it. His dark hair was thick and curly, his eyes light brown beneath black brows, his smile white and straight. Moreover, he was tall and muscular, and his ranch, though nowhere near the size of the Double C, was prosperous and growing. For all that, something about the man made her uneasy.

He made no move to continue on his way, and Olivia's innate good manners came to the fore. "I hope you're making plans to attend the spring social. It won't be long," she said.

"I wouldn't miss it." He gave her his white, wolfish grin. "Especially if you're going to be there."

"Just about everyone in town will be there," Olivia replied, neatly sidestepping his comment, which was personal enough to make her feel uncomfortable.

"I'll look forward to claiming a dance with you." He tipped his hat again and stepped past her, followed by both of his men.

As the second hired hand passed he, too, tipped his hat, surprising Olivia into darting a quick look at his face. She had only a fast impression of black hair, darkly tanned skin, and black eyes warm with admiration before he was past her, but the impact was strong enough to freeze her in her tracks, a little stunned.

Surely she had mistaken his expression. After all, her glance had been so quick. No, surely the man hadn't looked at her with *tenderness,* the way Ezekiel looked at Beatrice. How could he, when he didn't even know her? But the fact remained that his look, imagined or not, had made her heart beat a little faster and her skin feel a little warm.

She entered the bank, smiling politely and returning the greetings of those who spoke to her on her way into her father's office. Wilson Millican rose on her entrance, beaming his welcome. "Your mother's had you running another errand, at a guess," he said, and he laughed as their gazes met in perfect understanding. "She's enjoying this as much as if she were sixteen again and this was her first party."

"She'll swear she never wants to be involved in the planning again, but by the time next February rolls around she'll be fretting to get started."

They chatted for a few minutes, with Olivia telling him about her visit with Beatrice. She didn't want to take up too much of his time, so she kept her visit short. She was rising to her feet when her curiosity got the better of her, and she said, "I stopped outside to talk with Mr. Bellamy for a few moments. Who were those two men with him?"

"Two of his cowhands, Pierce and Fronteras, though from the looks of them I'd say they were handier with a pistol than a rope."

"Gunmen?" she asked, startled. "Why would he need gunmen?"

"Now, I didn't say they were gunmen. I said they looked like they'd be handy with their pistols, and maybe they are, but then a good many men around here are good hands with a firearm. As far as I know, Bellamy's cowhands are just that, cowhands." He patted her arm in reassurance, though he wasn't too certain of his own words, especially when they concerned the two men that had been with Bellamy. One thing was certain, though, and that was that he wouldn't want either of those two men anywhere near Olivia. She was too fine a person to associate with that type of man. None of the ranch hands caused any trouble in town other than the normal drinking and fighting sometimes, but as a father he couldn't be too careful of his daughter's well-being.

"Which one was which?" Olivia asked, still driven by her curiosity.

"What?"

"Which man was Pierce, and which was Fronteras?"

"Pierce has been with Bellamy for a couple of years now. He's a quiet man, never says much. The dark, Mexican-looking man is Fronteras. Guess he is Mexican at that, though he's tall for one. Must be mostly Spanish."

He was a Mexican. She felt a little surprised at herself for not having realized that at a glance, though he *was* tall, as her father had noted. Then she was even more surprised by her own curiosity about a man whom she had never even met, because passing on the sidewalk certainly didn't constitute an introduction. It wasn't her usual behavior, but then she was upset by her increasing sensation of being caught in a trap. She didn't know what she could do to escape, or even if she wanted to escape. All she knew was that she felt on the verge of panic.

"A man could do worse than marrying a banker's daughter," Kyle Bellamy mused. "Especially one who looks like Olivia Millican."

Pierce grunted in reply. Luis Fronteras didn't say anything.

"She's his only child. When he dies she'll get everything. Or rather her husband will."

"I heard Cochran was courting her," Fronteras murmured.

Kyle shrugged his shoulders. "That doesn't mean I can't pay attention to the lady, too."

He sipped his whiskey, thinking about Olivia Millican. Why not? He had as much chance with her as anyone else, maybe more. Women had always seemed to like him. He liked a bit more spunk in his women than Olivia seemed to have, but she was pretty and rich, and in Kyle's experience money made up for a lot of shortcomings. He was doing all right with money right now, but he had learned the hard way not to count on everything staying all right. Having Wilson Millican's money would make his life a whole lot more comfortable. He'd start his own courting of Olivia and give Cochran something to think about.

He was on his second whiskey, savoring both the biting, smoky taste of the liquor and his mental image of marrying Olivia Millican, when Tillie sauntered over to him. He leaned back against the bar and enjoyed the sight, because Tillie had a walk that could make a man's privates stand at attention even if he had a lot more than two whiskeys in him.

Tillie was something, all right. He'd met her for the first time about ten years back, in New Orleans. She'd been all of fifteen then, he guessed, remembering how fresh and wild she'd looked. He grinned, thinking that he was probably the only person in town who knew that her name was Mathilde. He called her that sometimes, when they were in bed together, always earning a long warning look from those heavy-lidded eyes of hers. It was all right with him if she chose to be Tillie the saloon girl; he just didn't want her to forget that he knew where she came from.

Of course, she knew more about him than anyone else, too, but he didn't worry about it. Tillie had never tried to use the information to get money out of him. She was oddly accepting of her life in a two-bit saloon in a small town, her rich brown eyes full of a half-weary, half-accepting worldliness. A man never felt as if Tillie was judging him; she simply took him as he was and expected nothing else.

A lot of the men in Prosper, including the married ones, had found their way into Tillie's embrace. She was generous even when her time was paid for, giving at least the appearance of affection and sometimes even her passion.

Kyle never expected anything less than full participation from her and never let her give less. Sometimes she wanted to hold back from him, but he'd known her a long time, knew exactly how to make her squirm and buck beneath him, and in the end she would always give him what he wanted.

She looked more like twenty than twenty-five, he thought,

admiring her creamy skin and dark mahogany hair. She was still slim, still supple, her breasts full and upright.

She leaned against the bar, her mouth voluptuous with invitation. "Kyle," she murmured in greeting.

He didn't need much encouragement. His name in that soft drawl was enough. He set his glass down and took her arm. "Upstairs."

She blinked at him in mocking surprise. "Well, hello to you, too. Nice day, isn't it?"

He ignored her light sarcasm and continued propelling her toward the stairs. He gave an abrupt flick of his hand to Pierce and Fronteras, letting them know that he'd be a while and they could do whatever they wanted.

Luis Fronteras watched Bellamy disappear up the stairs with his arm around Tillie's waist before returning his attention to the beer in front of him. Pierce sat down at a table with him, silently nursing his own beer. That was normal for Pierce, who seldom said more than three words in a row.

Luis was irritated by the small pang of jealousy he'd felt watching Bellamy and Tillie go upstairs together. Not because of Tillie, though God knows she was a head-turning woman, but just because of the simple fact there was a bond between the two of them, even if it was comprised mainly of plain sex. It had been a long time since he had felt kinship of any sort with anyone. Ten years, in fact. Ten years of drifting, of occasionally relieving his sexual urges with a willing woman but never giving her any more of himself than the use of his body. At first he had needed the mental and emotional solitude, then it had become habit, and now it felt impossible to change even though he sometimes wanted more. More . . . what?

More women? He could have a woman anytime he wanted. Luis had a gift for pleasing women, and he knew it. Mainly it was that he liked everything about women, even their tempers and jealousies and plain contrariness, and what woman could resist being so frankly appreciated? To Luis it was simple: He was a man, therefore he loved the ladies. They were the most delicious creatures he could imagine. Women had flocked to him from the time his voice first began to deepen.

But he wasn't interested in a multitude of women. Right now he was interested in one woman: the blonde Bellamy had spoken to outside the bank. Miss Millican, the banker's daughter. Olivia. He had liked her quiet composure and pretty face as well as the shape of her bosom beneath the prim cut of her riding habit.

He hadn't liked the idea of Bellamy courting her, using her just to get his hands on her father's money. A woman deserved more than that, especially one who looked as sweet as Olivia. It wouldn't bother Bellamy at all to use her, but Luis had unerring instincts when it came to women, and something told him that such callousness would destroy her.

There was already sadness in those pretty blue eyes. He had caught only a glimpse of it, but it had been there. Something was making her unhappy. Bellamy would only make her even more unhappy.

He'd like to kiss those sad shadows out of her eyes, hold her and pet her and tell her how very lovely she was. A woman always needed to know that she was appreciated.

He smiled cynically to himself. He was a drifter and a Mexican, too handy with a gun for his own good. She was the banker's daughter, and it looked like she would have her choice between the two richest ranchers in the area. There wasn't much chance Miss Olivia Millican would ever even know his name, let alone let him hold her.

4

Somehow Dee wasn't surprised to see Lucas Cochran riding toward her three days later. It was still early in the morning; she was outside with a pan of chicken feed, scattering it to the clucking fowl grouped around her skirts. "Mr. Cochran," she said in greeting when he was close enough to hear her.

He didn't dismount but leaned down to prop his forearm on the saddle horn as he watched her strew the feed. "Good morning," he said. "I was on my way into town and thought I'd ride over to check on you."

Her eyes were bright in the strong morning sun, and greener than any he'd ever seen before. "I don't remember saying anything that would give you the impression I needed to be checked on, Mr. Cochran," she said with more than a little sharpness. She had painstakingly taught herself how to be independent and resented his implication that she wasn't capable of taking care of herself.

"Call me Lucas," he said. "Or Luke."

"Why?"

"Because I'd like for us to be friends."

"Not likely."

He grinned, enjoying her starchiness. It was refreshing to be around a woman who didn't cater to him and defer to his every opinion. "Why not? Looks to me like we could both use a friend."

"I like being alone," she replied, tilting the pan upside down and slapping it lightly on the sides to knock loose the last few grains of feed. She crossed to the small back stoop and hung the pan on a nail driven into the wall. Lucas walked his horse behind her as she strode swiftly to the barn, her skirts kicking up with each step. She wore only one petticoat, he decided, eyeing the brisk sway of that blue skirt. And a thin one at that.

He ducked his head down to enter the barn, automatically closing his eyes for a second so they could adjust to the dimness, and watched as she efficiently ladled feed to the single horse and two cows.

She was damn good at ignoring him, he saw, and he began to get a little irate at her manner. Then he remembered that it was her farm, and she hadn't invited him. His horse stamped a hoof restively as she fetched a stool and positioned a milk bucket under one of the cows. Lucas sighed and dismounted, looping his reins over a rail. The other cow needed milking, too. "Got another bucket?" he asked.

Streams of milk were already hissing into the bucket in time with the motions of her hands as she turned her head to him. Those green eyes had a dangerous look to them now. "I don't need any help."

"I can see that." His irritation was growing, and it echoed in his voice. "But did you ever think about accepting an offer of help, not because you couldn't handle it just fine yourself but because the chore would get done faster with two people working at it instead of just one?"

She considered that, then gave a brief nod. "All right. There's another clean bucket in the tack room there, to the right. But I don't have another stool. You'll have to squat."

He fetched the bucket and patted the cow on her fat sides, letting her know he was there before he slid the bucket under her. He squatted down and wrapped his strong fingers around the long teats, then pulled with the rhythmic motion that, once learned, was never forgotten. Hot milk splashed into the bucket. His mouth moved in a wry grin as he thought how glad he was none of his men could see him now.

"Have you always been such a hedgehog?" he asked in a tone of casual interest.

"I reckon," she replied in the same manner, and he grinned again.

"Any particular reason for it?"

"Men."

He snorted. "Yeah, we can be real bastards."

He wasn't certain, but he thought he heard a chuckle. "I wouldn't dream of disagreeing."

"Those lovesick swains of yours must have been persistent," he said, hazarding a guess.

"Some of them. But it wasn't love they had on their minds, and we both know it. It seems like men just naturally see a woman alone as fair game."

There wasn't another woman in town who would have said that to him, but then he had already realized at their first meeting that Dee was blunt in her speech and frank in her opinions. He felt a slow burn of anger at the thought of other men trying to seduce her, or maybe even just catch her alone when they wouldn't bother with pretense of seduction. The knowledge that he was determined to seduce her himself didn't moderate his temper. For one thing, he didn't intend to dishonor her; no one but the two of them would ever know what went on between them. He wasn't a raw kid who felt the need to boast about his women in order to impress others with his masculinity. For another thing, damn if he didn't respect her for what she had accomplished out there. It had taken a lot of hard work, but she hadn't flinched from it, rather had risen to the challenge and gloried in it. The pristine condition of the farm was a true measure of her fierce spirit.

His voice was tight with that possessive anger when he said, "If anyone else bothers you, let me know."

"I appreciate the offer, but it's something I have to take care of for myself. You might not always be around; they have to know I can defend myself, that I don't need to rely on anyone else."

Her logic was unassailable, but he didn't like it. "I can make certain they never come back."

"The shotgun tends to be persuasive," she said with humor in her voice. "There's nothing like buckshot in his backside to make a man reconsider an idea. Besides, I'm not sure I can afford to have you as a protector."

He didn't pause in his milking, but his brows drew together and his head came up. "Why not?" he demanded sharply.

"Folks would think we were sleeping together." When he didn't reply to that, Dee continued to explain. "The men around here pretty much leave me alone now because I've convinced them I don't want *any* man. But if they thought I'd let one man in my bed, then they would think I was available, and they'd take even less kindly to being turned down than they did before. It would get nasty, and I'd probably have to kill some of them."

His strong hands had emptied the cow's udder, and he lifted the bucket away, rising to his feet just as Dee finished milking. Her cheeks were flushed with her exertions as she slid the bucket away and stood, stretching her back. Lucas leaned down, picked up the other bucket, and walked out of the barn toward the house, leaving her to follow. Her brows rose at the way he made himself so at home on her place. It was obvious he was used to being the boss. Then she shrugged; he was being helpful, so it would be petty of her to complain that he was too self-confident about it.

He waited on the back stoop for her to open the door. "What do you do with this much milk?"

"Most of it goes back to the animals in their feed," she admitted. "I churn it for butter, drink some of it, use it in cooking."

"One cow would do."

"With two cows I get two calves a year that are butchered as yearlings. You had some of the beef in the soup you ate the other day. And this way, if one of the cows dies, I still have milk." She wrestled the churn out and tied the straining cloth over it. "I don't guess one cow more or less matters much to you."

"Not when I have a couple thousand heads of beef on the range." He tipped one of the buckets and slowly poured the milk through the straining cloth, then emptied the other bucket.

Dee picked up the coffeepot and shook it. "There's more coffee left. Would you like a cup?"

Lucas was too smart to push her this early in their acquaintance, but being around her was fraying his patience, and he decided not to linger. "Not today. I need to get on to town, then back to the ranch. Thanks for the offer, though."

"You're welcome," she replied gravely. "And thank you for your help. I promise not to tell anyone you milked my cow."

He looked sharply at her, and though her expression was bland he could see a gleam of laughter in her eyes. "You'd better not."

She actually smiled then, and his body responded immediately. Damn, she was something when she smiled!

She walked out on the porch with him and leaned against a post while he returned to the barn, then walked out leading his horse. She watched him mount, noting the play of muscles in his arms and shoulders and the way his pants pulled tight on his buttocks and thighs. The brim of his hat shadowed his face, but she could still see the intense blue of his eyes.

"See you," he said, and he rode off without looking back.

She tried, but she couldn't stop thinking about him as she went about the rest of her morning chores. She knew plain enough why he'd come over the first time, since he'd been honest about wanting to buy the land, but why had he ridden so far out of his way this morning? At first she had been expecting him to make a grab for her, but he hadn't said or done anything the least suggestive, and she admitted to herself that she was just a tad disappointed.

Not that she would have let him kiss her. After all, the man was intending to marry Olivia. But Olivia didn't want him. Dee knew how much her friend wanted to fall in love and have a family, that she was worried she would never have the chance. And Olivia wasn't even certain Lucas had any intentions of marrying her. After meeting him the second time Dee was certain that he wasn't the man for her gentle friend.

It had been nothing less than the truth that she couldn't afford for anyone to think she was available, and it was likewise true that she wasn't interested in marrying anyone. None of that, however, negated a third truth: She was human, and she was a woman. She had liked talking to him this morning, liked his company. He talked to her as an equal, giving her a subtle but delicious sense of freedom because she didn't have to censor her words or behavior for him. Most men would have strongly disapproved of the things she had said, but Lucas had seemed to enjoy the frankness of their conversation. And despite herself she had responded to him as a woman, her skin growing warmer, her breath coming quicker. If he *had* reached for her, would she truly have pushed him away? She was honest enough with herself to admit that the temptation was there.

She was a bit embarrassed by her own duplicity. No matter that she had told him she wasn't interested in men, no matter that she told herself she neither needed nor wanted his admiration of her as a woman; she was very much aware of him as a man, and it hurt her ego a bit that he didn't seem the least bit attracted to her. Then again, why should he? He was Lucas Cochran; he could have any single woman in town, and probably quite a few of the married ones. He was not only very good-looking, he was almost overwhelmingly male, tough and strong and sure of himself, mentally as well as physically. She could read plainly in his eyes that he could be ruthless, and that a person had to be either reckless or a fool to stand in his way.

She, on the other hand, wasn't anything special. She saw it in her mirror every morning when she washed her face. She was a woman who worked hard, and who was more inclined to spend any extra money on books than to buy clothes or luxuries for herself. There was nothing refined or delicate about her, though she did suppose she was fairly intelligent and better educated than most, the latter point due to her mother having been a teacher and instilling a love of books in her early in life. They were two characteristics that equipped her well to manage her own life but made her particularly ill-suited to be content under anyone else's rule.

There was nothing in her for a man like Cochran to desire, and it was foolish of her to wish it were different.

Lucas never deliberately sought out Olivia except at social functions where they would have met anyway, for he saw no reason to solidify any relationship between them when it would be at least a year before he had any real time to devote to courting and marriage. Nor did he ever feel any great need for her company; she was pretty and pleasant, but she didn't fire his senses. As he rode into town that morning after leaving Dee, however, he not only made no effort to see Olivia, he was downright reluctant to meet her even by accident.

He liked Olivia; she was sweet and kind, a true lady. He could even imagine taking a great deal of pleasure in bedding her. What he couldn't imagine, however, was ever feeling aroused to the point of madness with her. When he thought of heated sex, of sweat and twisted sheets and fingernails digging into his back while he reveled in a female body beneath him, that body was Dee's, the face was Dee's, and it was long black hair that lay tangled on his pillow. Dee would never docilely accept him; she would fight against his domination, her hips thrusting back at him. She would claw and twist and fiercely seize her own pleasure. And afterward, lying exhausted, she would watch him with those enigmatic green eyes, daring him to take her again.

He couldn't even think of Olivia with those images of Dee burning in his mind. He wanted her with an urgency that surprised him. He had desired women before, some passionately, but the mere thought of a woman had never made him feel as if he were on fire. And he hadn't even so much as touched her hand yet! But he would, and soon. He couldn't wait months to have her, or even very many weeks.

He gritted his teeth against a hard surge of arousal. The way he felt now, the time remaining to Dee's chastity could be measured in days, and even that was too long. He wanted her now; he was as hard and fractious as a stallion ready to mount a mare in heat.

Instinctively he knew that Dee was a virgin, even though she had lived alone for five years. Her innocence both hindered and helped. She would not immediately recognize the seriousness of his seduction and wouldn't know how to control her responses to him, which certainly gave him an advantage. But her innocence also meant he would have to restrain himself, to make certain she had been pleasured even before he entered her, and his control was already under a great deal of strain. Once he had her naked in his arms he would be near madness with the need to penetrate and find his ease within her. If he lost control and gave her only pain, she would fight like a wildcat the next time he tried to touch her.

No, no one in his right mind would ever categorize Dee as docile. She was a wildfire, while Olivia was as cool and contained as a mountain lake.

He stopped in at the saloon even though it was earlier than he liked to drink; maybe a beer would dull the ache in his groin. At that hour the saloon was almost empty, with only one other customer, who sat slumped sipping a whiskey with his back to the batwing doors as if the light hurt his eyes. Lucas recognized the signs of a hangover and left the man alone.

The bartender was polishing glasses, not paying any attention to him after serving him a beer. The two saloon girls were playing cards together in a half-bored, half-lazy fashion, spending more time talking than playing.

After a while Tillie, the red-haired one, got up and sauntered over to Lucas. Though his senses were too focused on black hair and green eyes for him to react to Tillie's lush beauty, he admired the sensuousness of her walk. She didn't just walk; she swayed, she glided, she undulated. It was a movement so completely female that even the man with the hangover followed her with his bloodshot eyes.

"Good morning," she drawled, sitting down at his table. Her accent was distinctly Southern, lazy and soft-sounding. She tilted her head at the other man. "He's got a reason for drinking, but you don't look like you're having a hard morning."

He was having a hard morning, all right, in one sense of the word. "Just passing the time."

"Or maybe you came in here for another reason." Now her voice was even softer, slower, more inviting.

"I'm not in the mood for a woman," he said abruptly.

Tillie gave a warm laugh, sitting back in her chair. "Oh, I think you are, sugar, but I'm not the woman, and that's exactly what your problem is. You've got that angry, hot-and-bothered look that a man gets when a woman doesn't lie down for him the minute he thinks he wants her."

"A man never gets that look around you, does he?" Lucas countered.

"Not often, sugar, not often. Well, if you're not in here to drink, and you don't want to go upstairs, why don't you join Verna and me in a poker game? We get bored just playing each other."

But he wasn't interested in a card game either, and he shook his head. Tillie sighed sympathetically. "Then there's nothing I can do for you, Mr. Cochran, other than wish you luck."

"I don't need luck," he growled, getting up from the table. "What I need is patience."

Tillie's soft laughter followed him out of the saloon.

Olivia lingered in the dry goods store until she saw Lucas exit the saloon and head back in the direction of the Double C. It was cowardly of her to hide from him when he had never been anything but polite, but the possibility of meeting him in the street with innumerable eyes looking on had made her feel slightly ill. She wouldn't have been able to say a coherent word to the man, what with wondering about the whispering and conjecturing going on behind all the storefront doors. Nor had he looked to be in a particularly good mood. Even from a distance she had been able to see the dark scowl on his face. If Lucas was overwhelming when he was in a good mood, how much more intimidating would he be in a temper? She didn't want to find out.

5

Maybe if Dee hadn't been so tired it wouldn't have happened, but she had spent the morning replowing the garden, breaking up the huge clods of dirt into smoother soil, suitable for planting. The first few days of garden work were always the hardest on her, for her muscles had grown softer over the comparatively lax winter months. So when she climbed into the barn loft to fork down more hay for the livestock perhaps she wasn't as alert as she normally would have been, and maybe her reflexes weren't as fast. For whatever reason she didn't see the cat, and she stepped on its paw. The cat squalled; startled by the noise, Dee lurched backwards and misjudged her step. She hurtled out of the loft to land flat on her back on the ground, her head hitting with a soft thud.

For a long, agonizing moment that seemed like an eternity she couldn't draw air into her lungs, and she lay as if paralyzed, stunned with pain, her sight growing dim. Then her insides decided to work properly, and she inhaled greedily despite her aching rib cage.

It was another several moments before she felt able to take stock of herself. Her arms and legs moved without undue pain, and her sore ribs felt more bruised than broken. Her head was throbbing dully. If the ground hadn't been covered with a thin cushion of straw, she had no doubt she would be in much worse shape than she was.

The cat leapt out of the loft and meowed at her in rebuke, then disappeared around the corner.

She staggered to her feet and managed to finish feeding the animals, but when she went back to the house she could barely climb the steps. Cooking seemed too much of a bother, so she didn't. She merely cleaned herself up with a sponge bath and gingerly brushed out her hair. Her head ached too much for her to be able to tolerate the tight braid she usually put her hair in for sleeping; she winced at the thought. It was all she could do to pull on her nightgown and crawl into bed.

She didn't sleep well because every time she moved in her sleep her aching muscles protested and woke her up; but when dawn came, and she opened her eyes for good, she was relieved to find that the headache was gone. She would have been in a fine mess if she had sustained a concussion, but thankfully that didn't seem to be the case.

Still, when she tried to get out of bed she sank back with a stifled cry as a sharp pain laced around her ribs. She lay there panting for a few minutes before gathering herself and trying again. The second attempt was no more successful than the first.

She was loath to try again, but she knew she couldn't simply lie in bed all day. For one thing, she had natural needs that had to be attended to.

The third time she didn't try to sit up but rather rolled off the bed and landed on her knees, which probably added to her collection of bruises. She leaned against the side of the bed with her eyes closed, trying to summon the strength and determination to stand. Fortunately, getting to her feet was less painful than sitting up had been, but the effort still made her turn pale.

She managed to take care of her more urgent needs and gulp down several dippersful of water, for she was very thirsty, but the simple act of removing her nightgown defeated her. She could not raise her arms to lift it over her head. Even if she could, she wasn't at all certain she would be able to dress herself properly.

But the animals needed caring for, and it wasn't their fault she had been so stupid and clumsy as to fall out of the loft.

She had been lucky that in the six years she had been alone she had never before been ill or hurt. Knowing that she had no one else to rely on, she had always been extremely careful, even to the point of holding a nail with a long pair of tongs rather than risking hitting herself on the hand with a hammer. She had done everything she could think of to make her surroundings and her habits safe, but none of her precautions had kept her from stepping on that cat.

Even if she managed to get down the steps and wore her nightgown to the barn, how would she feed the animals? She couldn't lift her arms, much less heavy buckets of feed.

She was so furious at herself for having been careless that she could barely think. It didn't help that each movement brought a renewed onslaught of pain.

Her legs were stiff and sore, but she rather thought that was from the unaccustomed exertion of plowing. Her back, however, seemed to be one massive bruise from shoulders to hips, and her ribs ached with every breath she took. She tried to sit and found that she couldn't. She considered simply falling onto the bed, but the thought of what she would have to endure when she tried to get up again kept her from doing that. Standing seemed to be her only recourse.

But the spring morning was chilly, and she was growing cold standing there barefoot, wearing nothing but a nightgown. The coals in the fireplace would catch if she could place a fresh log on them, but that, too, was beyond her. It looked as if she would have to go back to bed to keep warm, regardless of the pain it would cost her to get up.

When she heard the drumming of hoofbeats her first thought was that she had to get the shotgun, and she moved too quickly. The resulting pain shut off her breath, and she froze with a stifled moan.

"Dee!"

The shout made her almost weak with relief. It was Lucas. She would swallow her pride and ask him to take care of the animals today; surely by tomorrow she would be able to do it herself. Painfully she moved to the window just in time to see Lucas heading toward the barn to look for her.

"Lucas," she called, but he didn't hear her.

She went to the door, holding her breath against the jarring of each step, then stared in frustration at the bar she had automatically dropped across the door when she had come in the night before. She tried to lift her arms but found that even if she forced herself to bear the pain there was a point beyond which her muscles simply wouldn't work. That point, unfortunately, came before she could get the bar raised out of the braces.

"Dee? Where are you?"

He came out of the barn and headed toward the back of the house. Panting, Dee bent her knees and wedged her shoulder under one end of the bar, then straightened. The heavy bar bore down onto her sore flesh like an axe cutting into her, but she couldn't think of any other way of getting the door open, so she ground her teeth together and ignored the tears of pain that burned her eyes. The bar slid out and hit the floor with a thunderous clatter.

Lucas heard the noise and paused, then turned back toward the house, certain that the sound had come from there. Caution made him put his hand on the butt of his pistol.

She managed to pull the door open and stood wavering with one hand gripping the frame for support. "Lucas," she called. "I'm in front."

He came around the side of the cabin and took the steps with two long strides, dropping his hand from his pistol when he saw her. "Why didn't you answer?" he asked in irritation, then he stopped as he got a good look at her.

She was swaying slightly as she stood in the doorway, while her right hand, held down at her side, clutched the frame so tightly her fingers were bloodless. She was barefoot and wore only a plain white nightgown, long-sleeved and high-necked, as demure as a nun's habit except for the fact that he could see the darkness of her nipples beneath the cloth. Her heavy mane of hair was loose and tousled, hanging down her back in a black tide. At first glance she seemed perfectly all right, and his body was already responding to her improper attire, but almost immediately he realized that her face was white and that she was holding herself stiff and motionless.

"What's wrong?" he asked, reaching for her because she looked as if she would collapse at his feet. Alarm made his tone rough.

"No, don't touch me!" she cried in panic, shrinking away from his hand. The movement brought more pain, and though she bit her lips to keep from crying out, a moan sounded low in her throat. When she had control of herself again she said, "I fell out of the barn loft. I'm too sore to do anything."

"Come back inside and let me shut the door," he said. He didn't make the mistake of trying to help her, even though she could barely move. He suppressed a strong urge to yell at her because if she didn't insist on living by herself and doing a man's work she wouldn't be hurt, but that would wait. He entered behind her and closed the door, then crossed to the fireplace and quickly added a couple of logs, using the poker to stir up the coals.

"When did you fall?" he asked curtly, turning back to her.

"Late yesterday afternoon."

At least she hadn't been lying helpless for days. It had been a week since he had seen her, so she could easily have been injured all of that time.

He tossed his hat aside and knelt on one knee beside her. "This will hurt, but I'm going to check for any broken bones. Just stand there as still as you can so I can get it over with."

"I don't think there's anything broken," she protested. "But I'd be grateful if you'd take care of the animals today. I'm just bruised, so I'll be able to take care of them tomorrow after I get the soreness worked out."

"Don't worry about the animals. And I'll see for myself if any bones are broken or not."

His mutter was rough, his face grim. He had decided what he was going to do, and she knew she wasn't in any shape to stop him. Dee clenched her fists as he put his hands under her nightgown and ran them up her legs as briskly and efficiently as if she had been a horse. His probing fingers were necessarily less than gentle, and she sucked in her breath as her sore muscles protested. He looked up, blue eyes narrowed, at her intake of breath.

"My legs are just sore from work," she gasped in explanation.

His hands went higher, to her thighs. The hem of her night-gown bunched over his arms. His touch was hot, his callus-roughened palms and fingers hard on her silky skin. She was acutely aware of her nakedness beneath the thin cotton, and of the heat of his big body as he crouched so close to her that her thigh was practically nestled into the curve of his broad shoulder, and his face was almost against her belly. "Stop," she whispered.

He looked up, and she saw that he was enraged. His eyes looked like blue fire. "Stop, hell," he snapped. "You can forget about your modesty, because this damn nightgown is going to have to come off."

"No."

He rose to his feet with savage grace. "That's what you think."

She lifted her chin in a stubborn movement. "I can't take it off. I've tried, but I can't raise my arms."

He glared down at her, then abruptly pulled his knife from his belt. She couldn't move fast enough even to begin to evade him. He grasped a fistful of cloth in the front of the gown, pulled it out from her body, inserted the knife point, and sliced upward. The garment gaped open.

Dee made a futile effort to grab the edges together again, but in her present condition she was no match for him. He simply brushed her hands aside, then pulled the nightgown off of her shoulders and down her arms. The material caught for a moment on the curve of her hips, then slid downward of its own accord to pool around her feet.

Panic and humiliation combined to engulf her in an enormous flood. A strange gray mist obscured her vision, and her ears began to ring.

"Goddammit, don't faint," Lucas barked, putting his hands on her waist to catch her in case she did. "Take a deep breath. Breathe, goddammit!"

She did, because pride refused to allow her to faint like a

ninny. The sickening gray mist faded, and she focused on his face, set in lines of pure rage. A strange sort of relief spread through her, because his anger gave her something to concentrate on.

"Don't swear at me, you bastard! You cut my clothes off of me!"

His hard fingers clenched her waist as he fought the urge to shake her. Only the knowledge that she really would faint if he did kept him under control. Damn her, didn't she know when to quit fighting? She was hurt, and someone had to take care of her because she couldn't do it herself.

But color had rushed back into her white face, and that curious panic was gone from her eyes, which had darkened to emerald with her anger. Despite his own temper he almost grinned, because if she were well enough to be angry she probably wasn't hurt too seriously. Besides, Dee's anger was exhilarating, intensifying her color and reassuring him of her strength. If he had cut a nightgown off of any other woman he knew, he'd have been faced with screaming hysterics. But Dee had sworn back at him and matched his anger with her own even though she was as helpless as a kitten.

"Shut up and let me see what other damage you've done to yourself," he said, thrusting his face close to hers.

Dee swayed on her feet, painfully aware of her bareness as the cool air brushed over her skin, but she couldn't fight him, couldn't run from him, couldn't even manage to wrap herself in a blanket. She loathed being helpless, but reality made her admit that she was. He was looking her over good, and she moved her hands in an automatic attempt to shield herself. A flush pinkened her torso and face.

"For God's sake, I've seen naked women before," he snapped, putting his hands on her rib cage and forcing his attention to the tracing of each rib, probing for breaks.

"I don't care what you've seen," she snapped back, carefully not looking at him. If she didn't watch him examining her, she might be able to preserve some small mental distance. "*I've* never been naked in front of a man before."

"I'll pull off my own clothes if it'll make you feel better."

"Lucas!"

"Dee!" he mocked in the same tone of voice, then he brushed her hair back over her shoulders. The thick mane had veiled her breasts, which were now revealed to be high and creamy, conical in shape, lushly rounded and tipped by small pink nipples. His stomach muscles contracted, and a rush of blood to his groin made his shaft thicken. Damn, she was pretty, all slim and firm and rounded in exactly the right places. He grimly tightened his control, but his nostrils flared at the sweet warm scent of her, and his fingers ached to slide into the notch between her legs. If she hadn't been hurt . . .

He fought for sanity. If she hadn't been hurt, she wouldn't be standing naked under his hands now. She would be outside doing her chores, encased in clothing, her wild tumble of hair sternly twisted into a knot. But she *was* hurt, and he had to remember that.

Her collarbones were straight, without any telltale lumps to signal breaks, and she didn't flinch at his firm touch even though he carefully watched her face for any sign of pain. He felt her neck and told her to turn her head from side to side, which she did with some care but no great difficulty. Then he walked around behind her, gathered the great mass of hair which fell to her hips, and looped it over her shoulder.

He swore softly between his teeth.

"I figure I'm bruised," Dee said, staring into the fire. "I landed on my back."

Her shoulders appeared to have taken the brunt of the fall, because a great black and purple welt stretched from shoulder blade to shoulder blade. Her lower back was also bruised, the discoloration extending down to the twin dimples of her buttocks.

Gently he checked her ribs and found them sore but not broken, as was the case with her arms. All things considered, she was lucky to have escaped with such minor injuries.

He began thinking of all the things that needed to be done. "I'll fix you some breakfast," he said. "Do you want to go back to bed or sit here by the fire?"

She turned her head and gave him a baleful look. "I can't sit around like this."

"I don't object. The scenery looks good from my view, except for the strange colors." He lightly patted her bottom, taking care not to touch her bruises.

She moved jerkily, painfully away from him, and he was briefly ashamed of himself for teasing her when she couldn't fight back. He went into the bedroom and pulled a blanket off the bed—a double bed, he noted—then returned to her and folded it snugly around her. She hugged it to her with a look of intense gratefulness and relief, and he realized how difficult it had been for her to be unclothed in front of him. He wanted to kiss her and tell her that it would be all right, that soon she would be accustomed to him, but it was never good tactics to let your adversary know your plans in advance.

He helped her to the big, well upholstered chair before the fire, but sitting down was something she had to do at her own rate. When at last she was as comfortable as she could get he turned his attention to the wood stove.

Cooking was something he had learned by necessity, and he was competent with the basics. He put on a pot of coffee, deftly made a pan of biscuits, and sliced bacon to put on to fry. After satisfying himself that the stove wasn't too hot, he went outside and gathered enough eggs for breakfast. He had eaten some biscuits and cold beef before riding over, but now his stomach was demanding more.

When he returned to the house Dee was still in exactly the same position she'd been in before he'd gone outside. The blanket had slipped away from her bare feet. He went over and knelt down to cover them, wrapping them more securely in the folds.

"Thank you," she said. Her frustration with herself was plain in her eyes.

He patted her knee. He knew how being sick or hurt grated on the nerves. The few times in his life that he had been confined to bed, even as a child, he had raised such hell that everyone around him had breathed a sigh of relief when he began to mend.

He finished breakfast, put everything on the table, and returned to her chair. "I'm going to pick you up," he said. "I'll put my arm around the middle of your back, where you aren't so sore."

"I have to get dressed," she said irritably. "I can't eat with this blanket wrapped around me."

He slipped his arms around her, one across her back and the other under her thighs, and lifted her easily. His muscled back and arms barely felt the strain. "I'll take care of the blanket. Don't worry."

By the time he had her settled her cheeks were hot again, because by necessity the repositioning of the blanket had caused her breasts to be exposed. When he finished she was wrapped in a roughly fashioned toga, with her right arm and shoulder completely bare. She found that if she moved carefully, she could feed herself by moving her arm only from the elbow down. It was movement from the shoulder that was excruciating.

"Do you have a bathtub?" he asked, taking generous portions for himself.

"I use a washtub."

The washtub would have to do, Lucas thought. It wouldn't be as comfortable for her as a bathtub that she could recline in, but he would manage.

As soon as they had finished eating he redeposited Dee in her chair before the fire, then cleaned up the dishes and hauled in buckets of water to begin heating on the stove. "I'm going to feed the animals while the water's getting hot," he said, and he left the cabin.

Dee tried to find a more comfortable position. Tears of frustration prickled her eyelids, and angrily she blinked them back. She refused to let herself bawl like a baby despite her predicament.

Only part of it was because of the pain and helplessness, which was galling enough. Her nakedness in front of Lucas was more distressing to her, assaulting her modesty and adding to her sense of vulnerability. It would have been bad enough with any man, but when Lucas looked at her she felt as if he were stroking her in all of her private places.

It was an hour later when he returned to the house. He replenished the fire, then dragged the big washtub inside and positioned it in front of the fireplace. Dee watched as he carried in more water and began filling the tub, then dumped in the hot water until steam was rising.

"All right, in you get," he said, rolling up his sleeves.

She clutched the blanket tight with her fist, gazing longingly at the steaming tub. A long hot soak would be heaven for her sore muscles, just what she needed, but her nerves had been stretched almost to the limit by her nudity before him that morning. "I think I can manage on my own," she said. It would hurt, but she would bear the pain for the pleasure of that wonderful hot water.

For an answer Lucas tugged the blanket free and pushed it aside.

"Damn you," she said between clenched teeth as he lifted her.

"For once, would you just shut up and let me help you?" Her stubborn independence made him angry all over again, but he handled her carefully as he knelt and lowered her into the water. She sucked in her breath at the heat of it but made no more protest. Her common sense told her that at this point it would be a wasted effort.

He left her sitting in the water while he found two strips of toweling. He folded them and placed one on the edge of the tub behind her head. "Lie back and let your head rest on this," he ordered. "Get your shoulders underwater."

Gingerly she did as he said, wincing at each movement. He placed the other towel across the rim at her feet and lifted her legs out of the water, resting them across the towel. Then he brought more hot water and slowly poured it in until the water level rose almost to the edge.

Dee closed her eyes against the picture she knew she must make, lying there in the clear water, completely nude like a wanton.

The sight of her was making it difficult for Lucas either to move or to sit, with his hardened shaft cramped beneath his pants as it was. Her breasts bobbed gently in the water, making him think about sliding an arm under her back and lifting her up so that he could take those sweet nipples in his mouth.

Though her eyes were closed and he couldn't read her expression, he knew that the redness of her cheeks wasn't due entirely to the heat of the water. He ran his fingers through the length of hair hanging down the side of the tub to pool on the floor. "Don't be embarrassed," he murmured. "You're too pretty to be ashamed of being naked."

Dee swallowed but didn't open her eyes. "You shouldn't see me like this."

"Even though you're hurt? Don't be silly. If I were shot in the leg, do you think you wouldn't have to take my pants off so you could tend to me?" He continued to gently stroke her hair. "You're just damn lucky I came by today. What would you have done on your own? What about the animals?"

"I don't know," she admitted, then honesty prodded her. "I'm grateful to you, truly, but this is—it's scandalous."

"If anyone knew about it," he agreed. "But it's between us, and no one else is going to know. I suppose I could have gone into town and tried to get some woman to come out here and take care of you, but I'm strong enough to pick you up without hurting you. And I like looking at you," he admitted quietly. "If you weren't hurt, I'd be trying to get between your legs." He paused. "Are you afraid I might force you while you're helpless?"

She did open her eyes then, her look somber and searching. "No. You wouldn't force me. You aren't that type of man."

His mouth twisted wryly. "Sweetheart, don't put it to the test when you're in good shape again. I'm so hard right now my guts are hurting."

No man had ever talked to her like that before, but she had seen the animals mating and knew what he meant. And when it came down to it, she felt more comfortable with his bluntness than if he had pretended to scruples she couldn't trust.

He kept her in the tub for almost an hour, dipping out water when it cooled and replacing it with hot water fresh from the stove. Her skin was red and wrinkled when he finally lifted her out and stood her, dripping, on the rug. She found that some of the soreness had eased, and she could move her arms a bit more. He dried her with one of the towels, his hands moving over her bare body with excruciating attention. Then he carried her back to the bed and placed her face down on it.

Dee bit her lip and kept her cries locked inside while he

firmly rubbed a strong-smelling liniment on her aching muscles. The resulting heat was almost worse than the original pain, but again she held back her protests.

Sweat beaded Lucas's forehead when he was finished. He asked, "Do you have any of your pa's shirts left?" He had had almost all he could endure. If he didn't get her covered up, he might end up on that bed with her despite his best intentions. Her soft round buttocks, creamy white and perfect, would feel wonderful against his lower belly, or cupped in his big hands.

"No, I got rid of all of his things."

Damn. He stood and pulled his own shirt free of his pants, then unbuttoned it. Like most shirts, it only buttoned halfway down, and he pulled it off over his head. "You should be able to get into this," he said, straightening the garment and placing it on the bed before helping her to her feet again. Then he knelt and held the shirt for her to step into, and he worked it up her hips. The position brought his face very close to her soft body, and his breathing grew quicker.

He guided her arms into the sleeves and eased the cloth into place. The shirt engulfed her, hanging almost to her knees, the sleeves dangling past her hands. He buttoned it, then rolled the sleeves back until her hands emerged. "There, you're decent again," he said with a strained look on his face.

Not quite, since her lower legs were still bare, but she was painfully grateful to him for the covering. The shirt was warm from his body and carried his scent. She felt surrounded by him, and the sensation was remarkably pleasant.

She found herself staring at his chest. It was broad and muscled and hairy, the dark curls crisp-looking against his tanned skin. He evidently spent a good bit of time working without his shirt. "How will you explain going home without your shirt?" she whispered, not raising her eyes.

"I don't reckon I have to explain," he drawled. He was the boss. He could wear a shirt or not, as he damn well pleased.

She was still looking at his bare torso with helpless fascination. "Look at me," he said, putting a finger under her chin and tilting it upward. Her lashes swept open, and those deep green eyes fastened on him. He moved closer, bent down, and closed his mouth over hers, forcing her lips to part and using his tongue. He didn't trust himself and quickly released her, stepping away from the enticement of her firm body beneath the thin shirt, but the kiss was enough to make her eyes go dark with shock.

"You're safe for now," he said. "But when you're healed, things will change. I'll be coming after you, and it won't take me long to get you."

6

Dee felt much better the next day, though still not able to lift her arms more than a few inches. Lucas showed up again shortly past dawn, and they went through the same routine, with him cooking for her and taking care of her chores. Afterward he insisted that she soak in hot water again, and this time was far more embarrassing than it had been before. She wasn't in as much pain and therefore was even more acutely aware of her nakedness. So was Lucas. She could see it in his clenched jaw and the sweat glistening on his brow.

She had lain awake a good bit of the night, going over and over what he had said. As accustomed as she was to defending her virtue with a shotgun, it had still rattled her to find that Lucas had the same intentions as all those others who had come slipping around. What made him far more dangerous to her was the fact that knowing it didn't rouse her to contemptuous anger, as was the case with the others, but rather made her heart beat a little faster. It frightened her to admit that she *wanted* Lucas to want her, but it was the truth.

So what was she going to do about it? Let a man into her life after fighting so hard to achieve independence? Have an affair with him, when it would destroy her respectability if anyone found out about it? *Betray Olivia?*

Nor could she ignore the possibility that what he really wanted was Angel Creek. He no doubt planned to exploit her vulnerability to him to convince her to sell out. After all, buying the land had been the reason he had first sought her out.

What she knew about sex was only what she had seen in the barnyard, when the bull mounted one of the cows. She knew what happened but had had no idea of the fierce physical attraction between a man and a woman until Lucas had come riding up. His kiss, as brief and hard as it had been, had shown her that there was a great deal more to mating than she had suspected. She had foolishly thought she would be able to keep him from kissing her, but she had not only let him, she had wanted more. She had felt the burn of physical desire for the first time, and it tormented her, for her body had felt out of her control.

If Lucas wanted the land, he also wanted her. She wasn't so naive that she didn't realize the significance of the bulge in the crotch of his pants, even if he hadn't so bluntly admitted his intentions. It weakened her to know that the torment was mutual.

After he had dried her and clothed her in another of his shirts, brought specifically for that purpose, he silently put her back in bed and left the cabin, his boot heels thudding on the porch. When he returned half an hour later he was back in control of himself, but his blue eyes still held signs of his bad temper.

"I don't think you should come by tomorrow," Dee said, pulling the sheet to her chin. "I'm much better today, and the soreness will leave faster if I work it out."

"Trying to get rid of me?" he asked. "It won't work."

She turned her face away from him. "What about Olivia?" she asked quietly. "She's my friend."

She couldn't see him, but she could feel his fierce gaze fasten on her. He didn't show surprise at her words. He just said, "What about her?"

"The talk is that you're going to marry her."

"I'd thought about it," he admitted, his temper fraying. Did she think he would be there if he had committed himself to another woman? "But not lately. We certainly as hell don't have any sort of understanding between us. I'm a free man."

She plucked at the sheet, still not looking at him. "It would probably be better if you didn't come by tomorrow anyway."

"If you weren't such a damn idiot, you wouldn't need for me to come by," he growled, glad that she had provided him with an excuse to release his temper. Being around her, with her either naked or only partly clothed, had strained his control to the limit. He felt half-mad with the need to have her.

"I know," she said, readily accepting the blame, which only made him angrier. "I try to be so careful, but that time I wasn't."

"You shouldn't be pitching down hay in the beginning!" he yelled. "You shouldn't be working this farm by yourself! Why can't you move to town and be a normal woman, instead of trying to prove that you can make it all on your own when it's pure insanity that you'd even want to?"

Dee looked at him then, her eyes narrowing in a dangerous, catlike way. It wasn't in her to simply take his attack in silence, so she didn't. "What I want to know is why you think it's any of your business," she said in an even tone. "I appreciate your help, but that doesn't give you the right to tell me how to live."

"You know what gives me the right." He walked over to stand by the bed, glaring down at her. "You know it's going to end only one way."

"I believe that's still my decision."

"When the time comes, you're going to lie down and open your legs for me," he said savagely. "Don't try to fool yourself."

She tried to lift herself up on an elbow, but her shoulders and arms were still too sore, and she fell back with a stifled moan. This further evidence of her own physical helplessness, however, didn't mean that she thought he was right. "Then I see only one solution: Don't come back here, because you aren't welcome."

"Are you going to use the shotgun on me?" he taunted, leaning down so close that she could see the glittering depths of his eyes. "Then take your best shot, sweetheart, because I'll be back."

She lashed out in retaliation. "You overestimate your charm. I'd always wonder what you really wanted, me or Angel Creek."

"Both, sweetheart," he said, and he crashed his mouth down onto hers. It was a rough kiss, and she tried to bite him, but he jerked his head back, then returned to kiss her even harder. His fingers clamped on her chin and held it down so he could enter her mouth with his tongue. Dee clawed at his arms, but with her limited range of movement it was a wasted effort. He held her down and ruthlessly kissed her until she felt the coppery taste of blood in her mouth. He tasted it, too, and the pressure eased. He sucked her lower lip into his mouth and stroked it with his tongue, soothing the hurt.

He unbuttoned the shirt she wore and opened it, baring her breasts. Her breath caught in her throat as his hard, warm hand closed over one of the soft mounds.

"This is what it would be like between us," he muttered. "Hot and wild. Think about it, damn you." His thumb rubbed her nipple into a tight peak, and her entire body clenched from the pleasure and pain of it. He cupped both breasts, holding them high and together, and buried his face against them. His hot breath washed over her, then he took one nipple between his teeth, drawing it into his mouth with a strong sucking motion. Incredible heat shot through her, and she whimpered, her hips writhing a little.

As if that were a signal he released her breast and stood, his face dark and taut with both anger and physical need. "I can make you go wild," he said. "Remember that when you think about using the shotgun on me."

He walked out, leaving her lying on the bed with her shirt unbuttoned and spread open, her bare breasts heaving with the violence of the response he had stirred in her. A moment later she heard him ride away. "Damn you," she whispered, and she would have shouted it if she thought he might hear her. She was shaking with anger—or was it from the empty torment he had aroused in her body? Perhaps it was both, though the whys didn't really matter.

She had never before been vulnerable to a man, but she was to him. That was the most frightening thing she had ever faced in her life, far more frightening than being left alone to fend for herself. She had never doubted her ability to survive, but she was terrified of what Lucas could do to her.

Losing first one parent and then the other had shaken her to the core. She had been afraid, so horribly afraid, but she had had to go on. She had been forced to recognize, with brutal swiftness, how fragile life was, how easily it could be taken. She had pulled deep inside herself, unwilling to trust her emotions to anyone else because she simply couldn't bear any more pain and couldn't take the risk of losing someone else she loved. Devoting herself to the garden had saved her sanity, given her a sense of life again, because the earth was so giving. It, at least, was eternal. It would be there long after she herself had died. She could trust the warm soil, the cycles of the seasons, the renewal of life each spring. Except for Olivia, she hadn't even been tempted to let anyone close to her again.

And now Lucas was shattering her mental wall of remoteness. He could destroy not only the life she had built for herself but her very self-respect. If she let him mean too much to her, he could reduce her to someone she would despise, without will or spirit, willing to do anything to keep him happy. Wanting him hadn't blinded her to his nature; Lucas was strong and arrogant, ruthless when it came to getting what he wanted. He wanted her, and he wouldn't listen to any of her refusals. It wasn't that she feared he would force her, for his own ego wouldn't let him do that, but rather that she would lose her own will to tell him no.

He had demonstrated to her very aptly how weak she could be when he wanted to make love to her. And he hadn't even done that much—kissed her, and touched and kissed her breast—but she had been on the verge of pleading with him for more. It was humiliating to realize he could handle her so easily.

Though anger had motivated her to tell him not to come back, now that she had calmed down she realized it was only common sense, and the best thing for her. The question, though, was if Lucas would obey.

She had her answer early the next morning when she heard hoofbeats approaching. She looked at the shotgun but admitted that it was a futile threat, right now at least. Though she had managed to dress herself in a fashion, she still wasn't capable of lifting the heavy weapon and firing it with any sort of aim.

Without knocking he opened the front door, which had been left unbarred for the past two days. Dee turned from the stove to look at him, a stinging rebuke on her lips that she forced herself to swallow; after all, the door had been left unbarred for that precise reason.

It gave her no small measure of satisfaction to see his black eyebrows snap downward in a scowl when he saw her standing at the stove turning bacon with a fork.

"You shouldn't be doing that."

"I told you, I'm feeling better. I can manage this."

"But not putting on your shoes," he observed, looking down at her bare feet.

She had tried but hadn't been able to bend down far enough to pull on her stockings or shoes. It was also true that she still wore his shirt, but it served well enough as a blouse. She had struggled until she had donned her underdrawers, a petticoat, and her skirt and tucked the shirt in. After two days of being bare or almost so, the heavy clothes had given her a certain sense of comfort.

He tossed a small package on the table. She looked at it, then lifted her brows inquiringly at him. "It's a nightgown. To replace the one I cut off of you."

She was glad that he had thought of it, for she only owned two. "I'll wash your shirts and return them."

"No hurry." He was watching her so intensely that she began to feel uncomfortable and had to resist the urge to check if all of her buttons were buttoned. But he only reached out to take the fork from her hand and said, "Sit. I'll finish this."

Lucas was very aware of the short pause before she did as he said, and he didn't relax until she was safely sitting down. He had ridden up to the cabin with every nerve alert, waiting for a shotgun blast at any second. He had pushed her too hard and too far the day before, and he knew it. With most women—hell, any other woman—he would have expected nothing more than a temper tantrum at worst, and more likely tears or sulking. But Dee was likely to do just as she said and greet him with buckshot. Which was, he thought grimly, just what he deserved for having been so stupid. He had been thinking with his gonads, not his brain. Just because he had been hot and hard and frustrated he'd let his temper get the best of him.

After breakfast he knelt and slipped plain white stockings on her feet, smoothing them up her legs and tying the garters just above her knees. After the past two days such a service didn't even bring a blush to her face. Then he laced her into her sturdy work shoes, and his face became grim again as he thought of the dainty cloth slippers she could wear if she didn't insist on working like a horse. This time, however, he had sense enough to keep his mouth shut.

He took her outside to walk around, her first trip past the cabin door since the morning after she had fallen. She insisted on inspecting the garden plot she had plowed, and she told him what she planned to plant. "Corn, of course, and peas. I had good luck selling squash last year, so I'll add another row of it this time. Here I'll make the beds for the onions and carrots, and a few pepper plants. And I think I'll try potatoes this year. Mr. Winches always has them, but I imagine he pays a pretty penny having them shipped in."

Her eyes were shining as she looked at the plot of raw earth; she saw green food-bearing plants, plants that fed her through the winter and gave her a means of living. Lucas looked at the same earth and thought of the work she would have to do, first planting, then the daily battle with weeds and insects, and finally the harvesting days, when she would have to work the hardest, for she would not only be doing her normal chores but working in the kitchen to put up in canning jars the vegetables she would need over the winter. A farm woman didn't have it easy at the best of times; a farm woman on her own was likely to work herself into an early grave. Unless she had sense enough to sell out.

Dee was strong, her slim body lithe and well muscled, but eventually the work would get to be too much for her. Lucas looked down at her, with her hip-length hair flowing down her back and her exotic face lifted to the morning sun, and he swore to himself right then that he would get her off the farm before it killed her or made her old before her time. He'd have to fight her every inch of the way, but that would keep him on his toes.

Before he thought, he bent his head and kissed her, his hands on her waist to pull her close against him. Her green eyes widened with surprise, then slowly fluttered shut as her mouth opened gently for him. Her lips were soft and full, the lower one still slightly swollen from his roughness the day before. He treated her with more care now, keeping the pressure light even though his tongue probed sensually. This time she tilted her head and met his advance with first a hesitant touch, then a tender searching with her own tongue that made his senses reel. His hands tightened momentarily on her waist, then he slid one arm behind her while his other hand moved up to close surely over her breast.

Immediately she tried to pull away, a protest sounding in her throat. Lucas held her, his long fingers kneading the rich flesh, rubbing at her sensitive nipple. "I'm not going to do more than this," he muttered as his mouth moved roughly down her throat. "Just relax and let me make you feel good."

He made her feel too good, Dee thought in despair, and it all happened too fast. One kiss, one touch, and she wanted him to do everything. She even wanted to open her legs to that hard length she could feel pressed against her belly, and that would never do, because it would be such an enormous error to give Lucas that sort of hold over her.

She couldn't push at him, but she found enough strength, enough sanity, to turn her head away and say, "No, Lucas. No. I don't want you to do this."

"Liar," he said, but he raised his head. His lips were shiny from kissing her, the set of them a little cruel. She was totally at his mercy and she knew it, but she wasn't certain he had any mercy. If he chose to continue making love to her, she would not only give in, she would join in, even beg him if necessary.

"I'm not lying," she insisted before he could kiss her again. Honesty impelled her to add, "I didn't say that I don't want you. I said that I don't want you to treat me like this."

"Even in that, you're lying." But he slowly let her go, and that was what she had intended.

She felt as if all of her clothes were awry; it was disturbing to look down and find that nothing was disturbed after all. All of the turbulence had been inside.

"You wouldn't do this if I were anyone else." Her voice was low as she made the charge. "You wouldn't treat Olivia like this."

She remembered the day she had first seen him since his return, how civil he had been to Olivia and the giggling young women grouped around her. He would never handle any of them the way he had been touching her.

Lucas's gaze sharpened. "Like a woman, you mean? Maybe you're right. But don't accuse me of treating you like a whore, damn you, because we both know different."

"A whore is what people would call me."

"How would anyone know? What's between us is private."

There was nothing more to be said, it seemed. She turned to go back to the house, and he fell into step beside her, his strong hands helping her up the steps when her back muscles protested. He kissed her again, then left her to attend to the chores.

She was alone that night when, more out of curiosity than for any practical reason, she opened the package that contained the nightgown, as she was still confined to sleeping in his shirt. The garment that was revealed had nothing in common with her practical white sleepwear, not even intent, for surely this wasn't meant to be worn *in* bed, merely *to* bed, where a lover's eager hands would remove it.

She trailed her fingertips over the sheer silk, noting the exquisite workmanship. The part of her that appreciated the luxuries of life marveled at the beauty of it, and at how well the pale, shimmering pink would complement her coloring, but the practical part of her was furious with him for depriving her of something she had needed, and trying to replace it with this highly impractical gown. Of course there was no mistaking his intention—that she would wear the gown for him.

He would have made her less angry, she thought, if he had bought *two* gowns, one to replace the gown he had destroyed and this bit of froth for his own amusement. Let him think what he liked, but she truly needed another warm nightgown.

She said as much to him the next day, starchily adding that she might as well continue wearing his shirts, which at least had sleeves. He grinned at her, a devilish glint in his blue eyes. "I like you in either one," he said.

It was two more days before she was well enough to dress herself completely and do the chores, albeit with much less dexterity and speed than normal. The last day, having made a deliberate effort to be up and about early, she was already milking one of the cows when Lucas arrived. He said nothing, merely helped her finish with the milking, then carried the milk inside for her. Both of his shirts had been washed and neatly ironed and were folded on the table for him.

He went outside and came back in with another package. "Just to keep you warm when I can't," he said, grinning as he tossed it to her.

She opened the package, half afraid this choice would be even more inappropriate than the other. But the soft white cotton gown was all she could have asked for, long-sleeved and high-necked. The bosom was set with tiny tucks, and the buttons extended down almost to the waist. She would be able to step into it, she realized, and she gave him a truly warm smile for his consideration. Her shoulders and arms still protested if she pulled anything on over her head.

"I wonder what Mrs. Worley thinks about you buying so many nightgowns," she mused, trying to picture that stern lady's face when Lucas purchased the silk confection. Come to think of it, where *had* he bought the silk nightgown? She couldn't think of any merchant in Prosper who carried such goods. He would have had to special order it from the East, or from San Francisco, and certainly he hadn't had enough time for that.

"Mrs. Worley doesn't think anything about it," he replied maddeningly. "The cotton gown was my mother's."

He didn't say where he had gotten the silk, she noticed.

He had been ignoring his own work to attend to her, and now that she was on her feet again he would have to spend the next several days seeing to business. "I won't be able to check on you for a while," he warned. "For God's sake, be careful."

"I am careful. After all, that's the first accident I've had."

"And it could have been your last, if it had broken your neck."

"What? And deprive you of a reason to complain?" she said sweetly. "I'd never do that."

"The spring picnic and dance is next week," he said, thinking ahead and ignoring her jab. It was such a busy time at the ranch, with all the spring branding and castrating to be done, that the picnic would probably be the next time he'd see her. "If I don't get by before then, I'll see you there."

"I doubt it," she said. "I don't go to the spring dances."

He stopped and gave her one of those grim looks of his. "Why not?"

"Why should I?"

"To socialize with your neighbors."

"If I did that, someone"—meaning some man—"would assume that I wanted to be friendlier than I have been in the past. It seems easier not to encourage anyone."

"You could spend your time with the women."

She laughed out loud at that. "What poor woman wants me to monopolize her time? People go to have fun with their friends, or to flirt, and I don't qualify for either. Besides, this is a busy time for me, and I really can't afford to waste an entire day doing nothing, especially since I've lost so much time this past week."

He scowled down at her, angered that she allowed herself so little in life. He had been looking forward to dancing with her, to feeling her long, strong legs brushing against his. In the hurly-burly of the day, no one would be paying any attention to them. "I want you to go," he said. "Put on your best dress and for once forget about the damn farm."

"No," she said. No more excuses, no reasons, just no.

Lucas didn't take rejection well. "If you aren't at the picnic," he said, "I'll come looking for you."

7

The day of the picnic dawned with perfect weather, the sun rising in a glorious display of cream and gold on the snow-capped peaks of the far mountains. Olivia was awake to see it, for it seemed there were a hundred last-minute details that needed to be seen to. That was always the case, but in the past she had enjoyed the excitement of preparation; this year it was all she could do to present a serene face to her parents and friends. She dreaded the day, without having any one solid reason for doing so. Perhaps, she thought, it was that she had given up hope. Always before the future had loomed before her with its great golden promise, but in the past months she had lost her faith in that promise.

It wasn't that a proposal from Lucas seemed imminent; in fact, in the last few weeks she had begun to wonder if she had only been imagining his intentions. In some indefinable way she no longer felt that intense will focused on her. It was silly, because when they had met, which was seldom, he had been exactly the same: courteous, protective, occasionally even flirting a little, but taking care not to overwhelm her.

Though she couldn't help feeling relieved, she was saddened almost beyond bearing at the very real possibility that she would never have her own family. She could just picture herself ten, even twenty years in the future, quietly sitting beside Honora with their heads bent over tiny embroidery stitches, while her hair grayed and wrinkles appeared at her eyes and throat, and her body lost its firmness. Her parents would be sad, too, because there would be no grandchildren for them to cherish.

It was as if her life had slipped by while she wasn't looking, and now she was left with empty hands. And empty arms, she thought, mourning the tiny babies she had wanted but seemed destined never to have.

So she went through the motions, sheer determination keeping a smile pasted on her face, and by midmorning the Millican carriage had joined a parade of buggies, wagons, carts, people on horseback, and a great many even walking, all making their way to the large meadow just outside of town where the picnic was always held.

It was a truly perfect spot, with enough trees to provide shade for those who sought it, yet plenty of open space for the youngsters to play. A good many people were already there, and by lunch all but a few people from within a fifty-mile radius would be wandering over the meadow, with nothing more serious on their minds than seeing friends and enjoying the picnic, an entire day with nothing to do.

Except the women always had plenty to do, Olivia thought. There was the food to be seen to, the children to be watched, games to be organized. The men, of course, stood about in groups talking and laughing or perhaps organizing their own contests of strength or skill. An impromptu horse race wasn't unknown. The women soothed the normal array of wounds and tempers from both children and men, until sometimes Olivia wondered if there was much difference between the two groups.

Practically the first person she saw was Lucas, his tall, powerful form easily spotted in the crowd. He was wearing brown pants and a white silk shirt, his brown hat shading his eyes from the bright morning sun, and he caught her attention more easily than those men who had dressed in their best suits. As he approached she noticed how his dark hair curled down over his collar. He reached them with a murmured greeting and began helping to unload the small mountain of food they had brought in the carriage.

She wondered uncertainly if she had been wrong about his intentions after all and thought she would go mad with this see-sawing back and forth. All of it was in her own mind, of course, so she had no one but herself to blame. Was he interested or not? If he was, did she want him to be, or not? If he asked, which would be worse, to accept or to refuse?

When all of the food was safely arranged on a quilt spread beneath one of the trees Lucas tucked her hand in the crook of his arm. "Do you want to walk around and see everyone?" he asked.

She could scarcely refuse with her mother beaming at them, and she tried to make herself relax as they strolled slowly about.

When he returned her to the same spot an hour later it was without anything personal having been said between them. To her relief, he had treated her as an undemanding friend.

Lucas truly liked Olivia, but during the long walk his attention had kept slipping to the knots of people they passed, and he'd been aware that he was looking for a small, queenly head with a wealth of black hair, or a woman who moved with a long, free-swinging stride that made her skirts kick up in a way that definitely wasn't ladylike. He was sure all of those excuses she had given for not attending had been just that—excuses—and he fully expected her to be there. What woman could resist the chance to flirt and have fun?

"Have you seen Dee Swann?" he asked Olivia absently, still surveying the constantly moving throng of people.

Olivia lifted her brows a little at the casual way he said Dee's name, and her eyes sparkled with quickly veiled interest. "No, I haven't. I doubt she'll be here. She never comes."

"I told her to come. I mean, I think she needs to get away from that farm. . . . I heard she fell out of the loft and hurt herself week before last."

"Oh, no," Olivia cried. "How bad was she hurt?"

Lucas didn't stop to think that Olivia sounded more distressed than such news would merit from a casual acquaintance. "Heard she was bruised up pretty bad. But she's back in fighting form now."

Olivia's interest heightened. Even though she was worried

about Dee, she realized how uncomfortable Lucas was, as if he'd accidentally said more than he should have. Indeed, from whom would he have heard that Dee was injured? Olivia knew perfectly well how isolated Dee was. It was obvious to her that if Lucas knew her friend was injured, it was because he had seen her himself, visited her, maybe even tended to her. She remembered the stray thought she had had about how well Lucas and Dee would suit. Perhaps . . .

"She should be here," he said again, and he was scowling.

Lucas didn't accept that Dee really wasn't going to show up until lunchtime. He kept expecting to spot her in the mingling crowd until finally he realized that she wouldn't be with a crowd of people even if she did attend the picnic; she would be on the outskirts watching, her deep green eyes as enigmatic as a cat's. He couldn't imagine her enjoying a cozy gossip or giggling with a group of girls.

On the other hand, he wouldn't have been the least surprised if she had come sauntering up at the last minute, knowing he'd been getting angrier and angrier with every passing second, wearing her most arrogant expression and daring him to say anything.

But finally he realized that she wouldn't be there, and his anger continued to build in him. He kept it tightly controlled and forced himself to act as if he enjoyed the food he ate, when in truth he hardly knew what he put in his mouth. *Damn* her, why hadn't she come? He knew now that she wouldn't attend the dance either.

He also knew he wasn't going to let her ignore him.

Dee was nearby, for she had broken the hoe handle and had driven the wagon into town to purchase a new one, only to find the general store closed for the day.

She felt like a fool. Of course the Winches family, like everyone else, was at the picnic.

She shouldn't have expected anything else. The streets were deserted. Everyone in town seized the opportunity to relax and enjoy the day.

It would mean another trip to town to replace the hoe handle, but there was no help for it, and she was too practical to stand around fretting. Weeds could be pulled up by hand as well as chopped down by hoe. So she turned the wagon around and headed back home. The only other people in town, she noticed, were the two saloon girls, who of course weren't welcome at the town's social events. Both of the women sat outside on the sidewalk, something they would never have done if the town hadn't been temporarily deserted.

One of them, the redhead named Tillie, waved to her, and Dee waved back. "Good day," she said.

What must their lives be like? Dee wondered. They had to be painfully lonely, though they were almost never alone. Her own situation was the opposite, for she was often alone and enjoyed it.

"May I walk with you?"

An air of heavy content had settled over the crowd as the huge quantities of food mingled with the afternoon heat to make everyone drowsy. More than a few were actually dozing on the quilts brought from home. Olivia had been strolling aimlessly about, smiling at friends but not stopping to talk. Lucas had left soon after eating, and since then Kyle Bellamy seemed to have been everywhere she turned. He had been very polite, but she just couldn't warm to the man. His eyes were too bold, and he was too persistent. She had finally been driven to keep walking, for if she stopped he soon appeared at her side.

She was startled by the soft, deep voice behind her and turned to find the Mexican, Fronteras, watching her with a smile in his black eyes.

She hesitated, remembering that he worked for Bellamy, and that she didn't know him.

"Of course, if you don't want to, I understand," he said.

She was stricken as she realized he expected his invitation to be refused because he was a Mexican. Her sympathetic heart squeezed a little, and she found herself saying, "Of course I'll walk with you." At least Kyle wasn't likely to catch her as long as she kept moving.

He fell into step with her. For once her impeccable manners seemed to desert her, and she could find nothing to say. They had walked for perhaps a minute when he said, "My name is Luis Fronteras."

"I'm Olivia Millican." Silence fell again. Finally in desperation she blurted, "Are you Mexican?" Immediately color flooded her face. Of all the things she could have said, why had she said that? She wanted to bite her own tongue.

"I was born in Mexico," he said with a lazy smile, not the least bothered by the question. "I suppose that makes me Mexican, though I haven't been there since I was a child."

Indeed, he spoke just like everyone else she knew, without a trace of an accent. "Have you lived in the area for long?" She wouldn't necessarily have met him even if he had, for the banker's daughter didn't move in the same social circles as a cowhand.

"Do you mean in Colorado itself, or here around Prosper?"

"Both," she said, interested. It sounded as if he had traveled a great deal, and she had always wondered about how it would be to live a nomadic life.

"I've wandered through Colorado several times over the years. I spent several years down in New Mexico Territory, and some time up in Montana and further west, around the Snake River." He looked thoughtful. "I've been to California a time or two, so with all the crisscrossing I guess I've been in about every part of the country west of the Missouri."

"You can't have spent very long in any one place." He was tall, as tall as Lucas, she noted. It made her feel small to walk beside him, and protected. She darted a look at the big revolver in the holster tied down to his right thigh. He wore the weapon casually, as if he was never without it. Was he more of a gunman after all, rather than a cowhand?

"I've drifted a bit." For a while he had thought New Mexico would be his home, but that dream had died under a stallion's murderous hooves. He had been so empty after burying Celia, as if part of him had gone into the grave with her. After a long time he had realized that he still lived, but it wasn't the same. Life had a way of going on regardless; he didn't know when the mourning had ceased, only that it had. He remembered Celia now as a bright smile and almost piercing sweetness, but he couldn't quite form her features in his mind. Ten years had passed, and in those ten years he had traveled a lot of ground, held a lot of other women in his arms.

"I've often thought I'd like to travel," Olivia said, looking up at the sun through the shifting pattern of leaves overhead as light breezes stirred the limbs. "To not see the sun set in the same place two days in a row."

She could scarcely have said anything more unexpected. Luis looked down at the delicate oval face and tried to imagine her going days, weeks without bathing, with a thick layer of dirt and grime coating that white skin, and found it utterly ridiculous. And who would ever expect her to sleep rolled in a blanket on the ground?

"You wouldn't like it," he stated positively. "Insects, dirt, bad food, not enough water, and never able to get a sound sleep. That's what it's like to live on the trail."

Her lips moved into a smile. "Ah, but there are other ways to travel. Imagine going by train from city to city, letting the rails rock you to sleep at night. Perhaps I wouldn't want to do it forever, but I would like to try it."

There was a little of the adventuress in that ladylike soul, he thought with appreciation. He'd like to travel the country by train with her. They would have a sleeping compartment, and at night he would enter her and let the train rock them to completion, rather than to sleep.

Some children were chasing a ball, shrieking with laughter as they shoved and slipped across the field. Luis stopped, his hand on her arm, until the children tumbled safely by, then slowly they resumed their walk.

Olivia felt oddly at ease with him, and she couldn't really say why, because they had only just met and hadn't really talked of anything, but there was something about him that made her relax. Perhaps it was the small things, the way he adjusted his long stride to match hers, or the care he had taken not to let the children collide with her, but she felt safe. Of course, most men were courteous in those ways, but with this man it felt like more than mere courtesy, as if it were his very nature to protect her.

"Do you have family nearby?" she asked.

"I don't have any family at all, or at least none that I remember. I guess that's why I've drifted the way I have."

"And you've never been married?" She immediately said, "I'm sorry, I shouldn't pry."

"I don't mind answering. I was planning on marriage once, but she died. That was ten years ago."

"Do you still love her?" *Why* couldn't she control her unruly tongue? She had no business at all asking him such personal questions, but she couldn't seem to stop herself. She felt her face heat at her rudeness, but he treated the question as easily as if it were about the weather.

"In a way." Thoughtfully he continued, "Celia was a wonderful person, truly worth loving, and I still love the person she was. But I'm not still *in* love with her, if you understand the difference."

"Yes, I do." Olivia was astonished at the relief she felt.

They came to a small stream and walked along it until they reached a log that had been placed across it. Olivia looked back at the picnic, blinking in surprise at how far they were from the others. Only a few people were visible from where they were, most of the townsfolk hidden by trees and brush and the curve of the meadow.

"Perhaps we should go back," she said a little nervously.

Luis stepped up on the log and held his hand out to her. "And perhaps we shouldn't. The explorers would have taken forever if they had never ventured out of the sight of the crowd."

She bit her lip, then cautiously placed her hand in his and let him help her up onto the log. She couldn't believe she was doing this. Olivia Millican had never done anything as outrageous as wandering off with a strange man; but then, she thought a little rebelliously, Olivia Millican had always longed to travel. Perhaps it was time to start paying attention to the secret Olivia. After all, she felt perfectly safe with Luis.

The log rolled unsteadily as they made their way across it, but fortunately they needed only a few steps to cross, and then Luis was clasping her waist in his strong hands and lifting her the rest of the way. She felt as if they had crossed a huge obstacle to their explorations, rather than a small stream. She didn't think she had ever been in this area before.

They walked beneath the trees, and Luis pointed out different kinds of birds to her. She was enthralled, for she had lived all of her life in towns, and the limit of her knowledge about birds was that she could tell a robin from a crow. Behind them the sounds of the picnic faded completely away, and she could hear only the birds and the wind rustling in the trees, their quiet steps, and their voices. He was holding her hand, his strong fingers wrapped securely around hers, the heat and roughness strangely reassuring. She ought not to let him hold her hand, she thought, but she didn't do anything to stop him. They should return to the picnic. She said nothing.

They were as alone as if miles from town, wandering deeper and deeper into the forest. She wondered if her parents were worried but knew they would simply think she was with friends.

The rich smell of the forest satisfied something deep inside her. The contentment shone out of her face as she looked up at him with a luminous smile, and without thought Luis reacted to that sweet femininity, pulling her into his arms and bending to her mouth.

Instinctively he kept the contact light, feeling the softness of her lips and letting her respond at her own rate. Olivia did so by degrees, beguiled by the tenderness of the touch and the hard warmth of his body. Her forearms, which had been resting on his chest while she subconsciously decided if she should push him away or not, slid up, and her hands laced around his neck as her body made its own decision. It felt so good to be held by him like that, so she snuggled closer. His taste was intriguing, so she instinctively parted her lips to taste him more, and that was all the encouragement Luis needed. He put his hand on the back of her head and held her while he deepened the kiss, first gliding his tongue over her lips, then slipping it inside when she didn't protest. He felt the little start of surprise she gave, but it was followed immediately by sweet yielding.

Olivia was dizzy from the pleasure of kissing him. She had been kissed a few times before—she was, after all, twenty-five years old—but no one else had ever kissed her with an open mouth, inviting her to part her own lips. She shivered with delight at the sensation of his tongue first touching lightly, then moving deep inside her mouth. She jerked at the unexpected invasion, expecting it to be awful, but the swift rise of intense, heated pleasure instead had her pressing closer to him.

"You're so sweet," Luis murmured against her mouth as he slanted his head and returned for more of those hungry, invading kisses.

She had never felt passion before, never suspected that any man could make her feel that way. She had never before let any man hold her fully against him, her breasts crushed into his chest. It felt wonderful, she thought dimly. Her breasts ached, and that hard pressure seemed to ease them. Another ache was growing in her, deep in her belly, and she couldn't understand it or find ease for it.

He raised his head, staring down into her dazed blue eyes. His own eyes were hot with need. He was breathing hard, but so was she, her soft breasts heaving. Luis recognized all the signs of an aroused woman, but he also plainly saw the innocent bewilderment behind the passion.

He hadn't brought her out here for this, he told himself. He had watched her for a long time, noticed how she kept trying to evade Bellamy, and had impulsively asked her to walk with him. But now they were alone, and he hadn't been able to resist that sweet mouth.

He could have her now. He could lower her to the moss-covered ground and have her skirt up before she fully comprehended what she was doing. As inexperienced as she was, she wouldn't have an inkling how to control her own desires. But a hasty seduction would likely be the only time he would ever have her; he knew women well enough to know that afterward she would go to any lengths to avoid him. That wasn't what he wanted. She was so sweet he wanted to lose himself in her time and again, and the only way to do that was to be patient and truly win her.

He realized all of that but couldn't bring himself to let her go without tasting even more of her. He began kissing her again, tightening his arms around her and positioning his hardness against her soft mound. He felt the gasp she gave, took it into his mouth, and kissed her beyond her alarm. Slowly he sank down to his knees, taking her with him.

Boldly he put his hand on her breast, squeezing it through the cloth, but that wasn't enough. He wanted to feel her warm, naked flesh. Olivia arched away from the touch, her eyes flying open.

"Don't be frightened," he crooned, lulling her with more kisses, stroking her breast and ribs.

"You—you shouldn't do that."

"This is part of making love. Does it feel good?" Some women found it painful rather than pleasurable, so he was always careful to ask.

"Y-yes," she stammered. "But that isn't the point."

"What is the point, then?" He continued kneading her breast, and he found her tight little nipple with his thumb. She gasped again as he rubbed it, and hot color tinted her cheeks.

"That—that we shouldn't be doing this." She closed her eyes, involuntarily concentrating on the wonderful sensations.

"Do you want me to stop?"

"No," she moaned. Then her nails dug into his shoulders. "Yes. We have to."

"Not quite yet," he whispered, and he slipped his hand inside her bodice. Olivia gave a pleasured cry at the searing heat of his palm on her naked breast. Her nipple was very hard, thrusting eagerly forward. Swiftly he opened her dress so that both breasts were bare, then bent her back over his arm and took one of the succulent little buds into his mouth, circling it with his tongue before pulling at it with a hard sucking motion.

She shook and shuddered, straining against him, soft little cries coming from her open mouth. The ache low in her body had grown beyond her control, and she writhed with it, her hips moving, asking for something she couldn't identify. Luis felt the movement and knew exactly what she needed, but now wasn't the time. He forced himself to be content with teaching her just part of the pleasure he could give her.

Her breasts were small and milky white, the nipples pink and delicate. She quivered every time he rubbed them, luring him to complete what he had started. It took all of his willpower to resist, to bring her down gently by pulling the edges of her dress together again and holding her close, kissing her and murmuring to her, telling her how much he wanted her and how he ached, knowing it would make her feel better if she knew that he wasn't unaffected by this.

Still, her pale face flamed with embarrassment when her senses returned. She pushed his hands away and began fumbling with her dress, trying to restore it to decency.

"Don't be ashamed," he said. "You're beautiful."

"How can I not be ashamed?" she asked in a strangled voice. "You're a stranger, and I've let you—" She broke off, unable to put into words the depth of her disgrace.

"We aren't strangers now," he said in a quiet voice. "Olivia, look at me, darling."

She shook her head, so he caught her chin and firmly tilted it upward. "Do you think I can't respect you or I wouldn't have touched you like that?"

The distress in her eyes was his answer. He leaned forward and gently kissed her. "I touched you, darling, because I want you so much I couldn't help myself. I stopped because I *do* respect you and want to see you again."

She surged to her feet, her face red. "Oh, no!" she cried involuntarily.

He caught her hands when she would have run from him. "Because you think this will happen again?"

Olivia could barely stand still, so great was her distress. Tears swam in her eyes. "We must never—"

"Don't expect me to stay away from you, because I can't. And I'll kiss you again every chance I get. Eventually we'll make love, Olivia—yes, we will," he said sternly when she began shaking her head. "Forget that I'm just a drifter and you're the banker's daughter, and remember how it felt with my mouth on you, because it will be much better than that, darling. Much better."

8

Dee was drawing a bucket of water when Lucas rode up that afternoon. Her heart slammed against her breastbone at the sight of him; it had been over a week since she had seen him, and it was alarming how much she had missed his high-handedness. The battles with him made her feel more alive than she ever had before because she could be herself while she was fighting him, and nothing she said would shock him.

He swung down from the horse and looped the reins around the rail. "I told you I'd come after you," he said grimly, walking toward her.

Dee hefted the bucket of water with a warning glint in her eyes. "And I told you I wouldn't go to the picnic. I have my reasons, and I'm not going to ruin things just to satisfy one of your whims."

His eyes glittered with an unholy blue light, and he kept on coming. "I've been wet before," he said.

Maybe the water wasn't much of a deterrent, but the bucket was heavy. Dee swung it at his head, soaking both of them as the water sloshed out. He ducked, and she quickly shifted position, drawing back for another swing.

"You leave me alone," she warned.

"There's no way in hell," he retorted, and he grabbed for her.

Dee ducked, and the wooden bucket caught him on the shoulder. He stopped, swearing while he rubbed the place she had hit. Those blue eyes narrowed on her. "You'd better knock me out this time," he said, and he lunged.

She took him at his word and tried her best to knock him in the head, but this time he didn't let the heavy bucket stop him. It banged against his back as he dived under her swing, and before she could dodge away he jammed his broad shoulder into her midsection, then lifted her. He straightened with her dangling over his shoulder and strode purposefully toward the house.

Furiously she discovered that she was helpless in that position. Her kicking legs were anchored by his left arm, and the only target she had for her fists were his legs and buttocks. Since it was the only thing she could do, she bit him.

He roared with mingled pain and rage and slapped her bottom with all his strength, which was considerable. Dee cried out at the burning impact, then tried to bite him again. He twisted, dumping her off of his shoulder onto the back stoop, then immediately grabbed the back of her collar and used it to drag her into the house.

As soon as he released her she jumped to her feet and sprang at him. "You little bitch," he said admiringly, and he laughed as he evaded her fists, taking hold of her arms and instead forcing her back against the wall.

Dee fought with the intent to win, and that meant using whatever means she could. She was severely hampered by the way he held her arms, so she resorted to kicking, trying for his crotch. His laughter stopped abruptly when her foot landed on his thigh, far too close for comfort, and he solved the problem by crushing her up against the wall with his body.

"Now fight me," he panted.

She tried, twisting and heaving, but with the wall behind her and his heavy body pressing her from the front she had no room to do anything more. She kicked, and he used the moment of motion to force his legs inside hers. With another quick move he had her lifted off her feet, his muscled thighs holding hers apart while he ground his pelvis against her.

She stopped fighting, because it was useless and would only increase the heavy pressure of his erection between her legs. She leaned her head back against the wall, panting. "Damn you, let me go."

Instead he lifted her higher and hungrily closed his mouth over her breast. The wet heat penetrated her layers of clothing, and she felt her nipple tighten, pebbling under the onslaught of his tongue. Desire mingled sharply with anger until she wondered if they weren't the same thing after all.

He released her arms so he could pull at her blouse, and without that support her weight dragged downward, pressing her even harder against his groin. A heavy surge of pure need shook her, making her cry out, and she clenched her hands in his hair rather than using her new freedom to fight him off. Her blouse ripped under his savage hands, then his fingers locked in the top of her shift and jerked, subjecting it to the same fate. He cupped her naked breasts in his hands and pushed them together, his beard scraping her soft skin as he sucked at first one breast and then the other.

She twisted, crying out again. Lucas drank in the sound, roughly kissing her while he continued massaging her breasts. There was no stopping this time; he had to have her, had to satisfy the burning, untamed hunger in both of them. He worked his hand under her skirt and untied her drawers, dragging them down over her buttocks.

Dee stilled as she felt her underwear slipping down; her head turned away, and her eyes closed. She had been totally naked in front of him before but had not felt so bare as she did now, so vulnerable. He moved back a little from her and let her legs come together, and the cotton drawers slithered down her legs to pool around her ankles. "Step out of them," he whispered, and mindlessly she did.

The heavy weight of his body returned to lie against her, holding her to the wall. His hands were still under her skirt, on her naked flesh, kneading her buttocks and stroking her thighs, and finally covering her mound.

She held her breath, not even daring to breathe in her agony of anticipation and need. His hand moved slowly, one long finger slid-

ing down into the slit of her soft folds. The lash of pleasure was
almost cruel, and so strong that she bucked in his arms. He held
her, that one finger moving mercilessly back and forth. He sank it
a little way into her, and she almost screamed from the shock, yet
her legs opened wider to allow him to do whatever he wanted. She
squirmed, her nails digging into his shoulders as his wet finger
returned to find the small nub at the top of her sex and roll it back
and forth, this time shattering her control and making her scream.

"God, you're beautiful," he muttered, watching her skin flush
with desire. She was unutterably wild and glorious, with her head
tilted back and her bare breasts heaving from the force of her
breathing. She had blazed up like wildfire, burning beyond her
control, just as he had known she would.

She was wet silk between her legs, so soft and hot he thought
he might explode just touching her. He held her securely and
eased his finger into her again, probing deeper, using his thumb
to rub her and keep her hot so she wouldn't object to his penetration. She jerked, whimpering, and her internal muscles tightened on his finger to hold it so snugly he almost groaned aloud,
thinking how tight she would be on his shaft. He couldn't enter
her very far before he met the surprisingly firm resistance of her
maidenhead, and he knew that this initial act wouldn't be very
easy for either of them.

His hand had brought her close to orgasm, and she squirmed
wildly against him, seeking release from the terrible, exquisite
tension. "Easy, easy," Lucas whispered against her mouth as he
pushed his thigh between her legs, shoving it high and hard
against her. The heat of her burned him even through his pants.
"Let me show you how."

He put both hands on her hips and began rocking her against
his thigh. She shuddered and moaned and couldn't stop, the low
gasping sounds growing louder as the aching need intensified.
The hard thigh between her legs both eased the ache and made it
worse, so that she didn't know what to do. She began sobbing
and beat at him with her fists, but he merely pushed her higher
so that her toes were off the ground and she forked his leg. His
hard hands kept her hips moving in that maddening rhythm, and
she couldn't take it any longer, she couldn't, until it felt as if

every muscle in her lower body clamped down and convulsed and her senses exploded in a storm of sensation. The great waves of ecstasy washed over her one after the other and finally passed to leave her as weak as a kitten, barely coherent and limp in his hands.

Lucas lowered her to the floor and stretched her out, his face hard with his own passion as he tore his pants open. If he took the time to carry her into the bedroom she might recover enough to begin fighting him again, and he had to be inside of her or go mad. Nothing was easy with Dee, and certainly not her denouement; having tested the strength of her maidenhead, he knew it would hurt her, and Dee didn't take kindly to being hurt.

He shoved her skirt to her waist and spread her legs, then settled between them. She made a low sound deep in her throat, and her slim legs came up to clasp his hips. Lucas set his mouth on hers, feeling the sleepy parting of her lips and the slow glide of her arms around his neck. He drank in the sweetness of her response even as he reached down and guided his shaft to the small, soft opening and pushed inside. He did it with a strong, even stroke, not pausing at the internal resistance but not being rough with her either. He could almost feel the shock reverberate through her body as it absorbed his penetration, the virginal walls tightening about him as if to prevent him from going deeper, and it felt even better than he had imagined. She was hot and wet and impossibly tight, the sensation racing along his nerves.

Then she screamed. It was a sound of mingled pain and fury, and just what he had expected. Some women would lie docile beneath a dominating man, but not Dee. She exploded into movement, her entire body heaving and bucking in an effort to dislodge him from inside her. Everything about it maddened her: the burning pain as he forced his way into her, his weight as he held her down, the very penetration of her body. She couldn't accept it; she mindlessly struggled against that domination, against the invasion of herself.

Lucas held her down with all of his weight and the iron strength of his arms and legs, letting her fight it out until she became accustomed to his length inside her. Her fierce struggle moved her on him almost as if he were thrusting, and he ground his teeth as he held himself as still as possible. Sweat sheened his skin as he waited for her to tire, for the pain to lessen, for her to begin to feel the pleasure of a man's fullness stretching her and probing deep. She was naturally voluptuous, and he had already shown her the heights of physical enjoyment; she wouldn't be able to deny herself for long. He hoped.

That point came gradually. She was already tired from both their previous struggle and her climax; he could feel her muscles relax, against her will, for she would almost immediately tighten them for renewed rejection, but the pauses between struggles grew longer until the struggles finally ceased. She lay still beneath him, breathing hard, her eyes closed against the naked triumph in his.

He kissed her forehead and smoothed the tangle of hair back from her face. "Is it still hurting?" he murmured against her temple.

She moved restlessly, and her hands settled on his sides as if she couldn't decide whether to embrace him or push him away. "Yes. I don't like it." Then honesty compelled her to add, "But it doesn't hurt as much as it did at first."

"Just lie still for a little longer, sweetheart. If it still hurts then, I'll stop."

She was silent, and her breath continued to slow. Lucas shifted against her, luxuriating in the feel of her enveloping him. Sweat trickled down his back.

"Damn you, you knew it would be like this, didn't you?" Experimentally she flexed her inner muscles around the burning shaft that had invaded her, relaxing a bit when it didn't result in pain.

Lucas tensed and groaned. "Jesus. Sweetheart, please, don't move."

"You're crushing me," she said in a low voice. "Couldn't you at least have put me on the bed?"

"We'll get to the bed," he promised, brushing her lips with his. For now, he thought, the floor was just fine.

She opened her eyes. Her gaze was solemn and questioning. "What you made me feel before—doing this will make me feel the same?"

"If I do it right. If you want me enough."

She gave a little laugh and lifted her knees alongside his hips. "Oh, I want you."

"Enough?"

She knew what he was asking, and her somber green eyes met his intense blue ones. "Yes. Enough."

He moved slowly, thrusting inward until his entire length stretched her. Dee gasped, her body arching upward, and just as slowly he withdrew. "You don't want me to stop?" he asked, just to make sure.

Her hands clutched at his sides. "No." Her voice sounded strangled, "Oh, no."

"I don't know if I can hold back long enough to satisfy you this time," he said with grim honesty as he began moving in a strong rhythm.

For answer she locked her strong legs around his hips and lifted herself up to him, offering her body, as generous as he had been in first taking care of her. That was all it took. He began moving into her with a powerful rhythm, and she accepted him, welcomed him. With a stifled shout he went rigid, then shuddered violently and convulsed with the force of his seed spurting from his body.

An hour later they lay naked in the bed, exhausted and almost asleep. Scarcely had they recovered from the first lovemaking than he had grown erect once again, and that time he had carried her to the bed and finished stripping their clothes off. She had found that making love could be a slow tangle of bodies, hot and languorous, that carried them to the same conclusion.

He had drawn it out, building her arousal so high that when the crest finally broke she had been wild with it, so that she had inevitably carried him to the same heights. He had made love to his share of women, but none of them had ever engrossed him the way Dee did. He was fascinated by the changes passion wrought in her body, from the hardening of her nipples to the moistening of her sweet little female channel. She was a she-cat in bed as well as out, giving just as fiercely as she took. He had known making love to her would be a challenge, but he hadn't known it would be both tiring and exhilarating, like riding and conquering a tidal wave until it subsided into gentle breakers on a beach.

He felt a cold twinge of panic as he lay there. Making love to anyone else after having had Dee would be like giving up the bite of whiskey for the sedative effects of heated milk. Because he didn't want to think she had ruined him for anyone else he willed the idea and the panic away, but it kept returning.

There was no way he could be satisfied with Olivia now. Before meeting Dee he had been certain in his mind that Olivia was the wife he wanted, a gently bred woman who knew how to hostess a large dinner, who would be at ease with politicians and million-aires. He had planned to acquire her just as he had planned to acquire more land, but in one short afternoon those plans had been turned to ashes. Thank God he had held back and hadn't actually asked Olivia to marry him; she deserved a lot more than a husband who couldn't get another woman out of his mind.

He thought of Denver and the political maze he would have to negotiate to build the power base necessary to influence decisions the way he wanted. There would be receptions and dinners, endless maneuvering taking place with the socializing. He was willing to do that to build the Double C into an empire, maybe to pave the way for one of his own sons to be governor, but he had pictured Olivia at his side during the endless social functions, her cool, polished manner perfect for the situation.

Now when he brought up the image he found that the woman didn't have a face. No matter how hard he tried, he couldn't imag-ine Dee there. He couldn't see her catering to the comfort of a self-important politician; she would be more likely to skewer him with that rapier tongue of hers. No, she didn't fit in at all with the life he had planned for himself, even supposing she would be willing to try, which she wasn't. She had made it plenty clear that she liked her life the way it was, thank you, without anyone to tell her what to do. Sometimes—hell, most of the time—he wanted to grab her and shake some sense into her, but at the same time he grudgingly gave her the respect she deserved. It took a strong-willed woman to accomplish what she had, and she wasn't likely to submit that will to any man's.

So where did that leave him? Right where he was, he thought, and he didn't like the idea. He had learned not to make assumptions where Dee was concerned. Just because he had made love to her twice didn't mean she would regard him as her lover, that she wouldn't fight him next time. And even if she didn't put up a fight about that, she would still resist with every stubborn inch of her against allowing him into any part of her life beyond that.

But for now she was sleeping in his arms, and he was exhausted from a physical satisfaction that went bone deep. He held her closer, made utterly content by the feel of her warm, sleek body lying naked against him, and he drifted off to sleep himself.

The sun was going down when Dee woke. For a moment she was totally disoriented, without any sense of what time or what day it was. She never slept during the day, but from the angle of the sun she knew it wasn't dawn. She was too groggy to make sense of it until she woke up enough to realize that she wasn't alone in the bed. That in itself was startling, for she had never before shared her bed with anyone, but then full reality hit her with stunning force. She was in bed with Lucas, and they were both naked because he had made love to her.

She didn't feel ashamed; her nature was too elemental for her not to be aware of the naturalness of the act. But she did feel a strong need to retrench her position, to reestablish herself as an individual after the mindless giving of her body. It was as if he had taken over control of her when he thrust his thick shaft inside her. She had fought against the natural domination of it even as her traitorous flesh had begun shivering with delight around him.

She shifted cautiously, feeling the unaccustomed soreness in her thighs and loins, and the movement made her aware of the stickiness between her legs. Another wave of reality hit her full in the face. Twice Lucas had emptied his seed deep inside her. He might have made her pregnant.

As women had done for thousands of years, she counted the days until her next monthly flow. It would be over two weeks until she knew, two weeks of fear and worry, because her life would be impossible if she were to have a baby.

Lucas pulled her closer and lazily cupped her breast, his big hand possessive. She hadn't realized he was awake until he did so, and she quickly looked up but immediately lowered her gaze from the hard, gleaming triumph in his eyes.

"What are you thinking?" he asked, his voice a deep, lazy rumble against her hair.

"That we can't do this anymore." She looked up at him again, her expression a little haunted.

That look on her face stilled his automatic rise of anger. "Why not, sweetheart? You liked it, didn't you?" He stroked her hair back from her face.

"You know I did," she said steadily. "But now I might have a baby."

He paused, a slight frown gathering his brows. A baby. In the savage delight of possession he hadn't given a thought to the possible consequences.

"When will you know?"

"About two weeks. A little more."

He stroked her breast, enthralled by the satiny texture of it. She was his now, damn it, and he wasn't going to give her up. "There are ways to keep you from getting pregnant."

"I know," she said tartly. "All I have to do is stay away from you."

He smiled and kissed her, his mouth rough on hers. "Other than that. I'll get a sponge for you."

She was instantly curious. "What do you mean? How can a sponge keep me from having a baby?"

"I don't know how it works, I just know it does. It's just a little sponge, and you soak it in vinegar and put it up inside you."

Her cheeks flamed, and she jerked upright, away from his exploring hands. He laughed and grabbed for her, wrestling her back down on the bed. She wasn't fighting in earnest, only huffy and embarrassed by the notion, and he grinned as he subdued her.

"How did you learn about anything like that?" she snapped, glaring at him. "It's a whore's trick, isn't it?"

"I imagine whores would know about it, but other women use it, too." He didn't answer her question about how he knew about it. He'd had some wild times in New Orleans and other places, but she didn't need to know about them.

Dee turned her head away from him because she knew full well he had learned about such a thing from other women. Part of her was relieved that there was a solution, but part of her, like a child, wanted to retreat to the way things had been before this afternoon, when she had been unaware of the way her body could respond to his, before she had felt his hard length plunging into her. Things had changed, and she couldn't change them back.

The question, of course, was if she really wanted to change them. She felt as if she had leapt headlong over a cliff in the dark. It was frightening, taking her to places she hadn't known before. If she truly wished the changes undone she would have to wish Lucas out of her life, wish he had never ridden up to her door, and she couldn't do that. As infuriating as he was, as determined to have his way, he made her feel more than she had ever imagined possible.

She was very much afraid she had fallen in love with him.

9

Olivia had to force herself to attend the dance that night. Lucas was absent, and she knew people were whispering about it, but his absence was the only bit of relief she could find. Because of their strange talk about Dee, Olivia suspected he had gone out to the farm. She mentally crossed her fingers, for if Dee were ever to marry it would have to be to a man like Lucas, someone as strong as she was. Dee would totally cow most men; she could never be happy with someone who didn't match her in strength. Olivia wondered if perhaps she was wishing away her own last chance to be married, but at least she wouldn't be faced with the nerve-racking decision of whether or not to accept Lucas if he proposed. Now it looked as if he wouldn't, and she was glad.

But Lucas wasn't her real concern. All she could think about was what had happened in the woods. She didn't know how she had gotten through the day. Her nerves felt so frayed she thought she would scream if she had to smile at one more person. She couldn't look her mother in the face. Honora had raised her to be a good, decent woman, yet at the first opportunity she had let a strange man lead her into the woods and take liberties with her. Not just kisses; she had once supposed a kiss to be a daring thing, but now she knew the respectful pecks on the lips she had received before had been as chaste as a brother's. She had not only accepted Luis's tongue into her mouth, she had delighted in it, actually participated. No wonder he had thought he could touch her breasts! He must suppose her to be as immoral as the saloon girls, for she certainly hadn't conducted herself as a lady ought.

She could barely attend to any of the conversation around her, so she became even quieter than usual, her face pale with distress. Everyone was having such a good time that no one noticed, except for Luis, standing on the edge of the crowd, watching her.

It so unnerved her that when Kyle Bellamy approached and asked her to dance Olivia had placed her hand in his before she realized what she was doing.

His hand on her waist drew her closer to him than she wished to be; after this afternoon she was acutely aware of a man's body. She wondered with sudden horror if Luis had bragged to his boss about his success with her. Would that be why Kyle assumed he could hold her so close?

She stiffened in his arms. "Mr. Bellamy, please."

"I'll please you in any way I can."

She couldn't decide if the remark was suggestive or merely flirtatious, and at the moment she didn't care. "You're holding me far too close."

He immediately loosened his grip and let her move back. "I apologize," he murmured, but his smile made her suspect he wasn't sorry at all.

Kyle danced well, his movements strong and sure. Under any other circumstances she might have put aside her instinctive uneasiness about him and enjoyed the dance, but tonight it was impossible. She could only pray it would be over soon.

"Would you like to walk outside with me?" he asked. "It's a pleasant night, and the air is stuffy in here. I confess I've been wanting a chance to talk to you, to get to know you better."

"Thank you for the offer, Mr. Bellamy, but I'm tired from this afternoon and would rather sit in here."

"Then perhaps I may sit with you?"

She didn't know what to say. She couldn't be rude to the man, but she had no desire at all for his company.

"I plan to go home soon," she said, desperately improvising.

"Then may I sit with you until then?"

God, he was persistent! What else could she do but say yes?

When they were sitting down he kept brushing his leg against hers, and Olivia twisted a bit to the side to prevent the contact.

"I'd like to call on you tomorrow," he told her.

Her guilty conscience made her feel certain now that Luis had told him, and he obviously expected to enjoy the same liberties! She could think of only one excuse, and she hastily used it. "I don't think that would be proper, Mr. Bellamy. I have an—an unspoken agreement with Mr. Cochran. I'm sure you understand."

"If it's unspoken, then I assume you're still a free woman," Kyle said boldly. "And I don't see Cochran here tonight."

"No. He—he had business elsewhere."

"A man who would desert a lovely woman like you doesn't deserve her."

Luis watched the byplay from across the room and could easily imagine the conversation he couldn't hear. He didn't like the way Bellamy was leaning so close to Olivia, and from the frozen expression on her face she didn't care for it either but didn't know how to stop him.

Olivia glanced in his direction and froze. She couldn't help looking his way, and every time she did she found him watching her. Her distress grew, because she imagined his black eyes held disdain. After all, what else could he think after the way she had behaved?

What Luis was thinking was that he should have known she would suffer under a massive load of guilt, and he ached to comfort her. Poor darling, she really had no idea about the physical side of life. Olivia had been raised too conventionally and was herself too ladylike by nature for it to be any other way. She didn't even know how to rid herself of Bellamy's unwanted attentions.

Luis looked around, and his gaze settled on two of the Bar B's ranch hands, men he knew to be hot-tempered. They were almost always contesting each other in one thing or another, and tonight was no exception. The object of their competition tonight was a pretty little farm girl whose face was flushed with pleasure at so much male attention.

Luis eased his way through the crowd. Both men held drinks in their hands, supposedly punch, but he knew the drink was well laced with whiskey. In the jostling crowd it was easy to reach out and bump one man's arm enough to make him spill the contents of the cup all over the farm girl's best dress.

He quickly moved back out of the way, blending into the crowd and listening to the growing sounds of altercation he left behind him. The man who had spilled his punch was accusing the other of deliberately pushing his arm. The disagreement erupted into a full-scale fistfight before he could make his way back across the room.

Kyle scowled with annoyance when he saw that the combatants were two of his own men. He said something to Olivia and left his seat, swiftly crossing the room. It wouldn't do his standing in the community any good if his men were so rowdy, and Luis knew that Bellamy was very proud of his respectability.

Luis looked at Olivia's pinched expression and silently berated himself. He had almost pushed too hard that afternoon, so now she was remembering her shame rather than the pleasure of his kisses. It would take all of his charm to repair the damage.

He made his way through the crowd toward her. She saw him before he could reach her and immediately spun away, retreating from him.

She was afraid of him! Luis was thunderstruck at the realization. No woman had ever before feared him, so why did it have to be this particular woman who ran from him, this woman whom he wanted as he had never before wanted anyone?

Her action angered him. He was a man, instinctive and possessive, and he intended to claim Olivia as his without examining the whys and wherefores of it. He increased his pace and caught up with her before she could reach the safety of her mother's side, stopping her by the simple means of putting his boot down on her skirts. She jerked to a halt and threw him a pleading look over her shoulder, but she had the choice of either staying where she was or having her skirt torn off.

"Dance with me," he said, only for her ears. "Please."

"No!" She gasped the refusal. She was so distraught that she couldn't be in his arms again without somehow betraying herself.

"Then walk outside with me."

"No!" This time the refusal was tinged with horror. Another invitation to do something improper! How *could* he ask her to walk with him again, after what had happened that afternoon? But that was probably the reason he asked, she thought bitterly. He expected to find her as easy again.

Luis put his strong hand on her arm and turned her. "Go outside, Olivia. Now."

She hadn't heard that hard, commanding tone from him before, and it silenced her. Numbly she let him guide her out of the meeting hall where they always held the annual dance, and down the steps.

The cool air washed over her hot face as he led her across the street and into the shadow of a huge tree. She could still hear the music and the laughter, the cacophony of conversation from a multitude of throats at once, but it was all muted and far away now, overlain by the sounds of the night.

"What do you want?" she whispered almost fearfully. She tried to free her arm, but he tightened his grip.

"I want you to stop looking as if you expect to be stoned to death," he retorted angrily.

Olivia's spine stiffened at his tone. She wasn't given to temper, but that didn't mean she wouldn't stand up for herself if she felt under unjust attack. "I'll look any way I please," she retorted, embarrassed that the best she could think of was such a childish reply. She was at a disadvantage, having had little experience with arguing.

Apparently he noticed it, too, for his grasp eased, and a faint smile teased the corners of his mouth. "Remind me someday to teach you how to fight," he said. "What you should have said was something that would make *me* feel guilty, too."

She bit her lip, immediately reminded of her own lack of

decorum. "Why should I?" she asked, the words troubled. "What happened was my fault. I never should have gone with you."

"Ah, darling." He laughed softly and enfolded her hand, carrying it to his mouth. He delicately licked one of her knuckles, and she trembled. "Don't take all the blame on yourself when my shoulders are so much broader. I at least knew what I was doing."

"I'm not a child, Mr. Fronteras." She was irritated that he evidently thought her so stupid she hadn't been aware of the inappropriateness of going off alone with him. "Of course I knew what I was doing."

He still looked amused. "Did you? I don't think so. If you'd had any experience at all, you wouldn't be so upset now. Has anyone else ever kissed you?"

She knotted her fists. "Of course," she said indignantly.

"Really? How?" He sounded skeptical. "Closed-mouth pecks that didn't even give you a taste?"

Abruptly she realized the absurdity of what she was doing, trying to convince him of experience she didn't have when she had been worried that he would think exactly that of her. She jammed her fingers against her mouth to stifle her laughter, and Luis grinned, too.

"That's better," he said. He gently caressed her cheek. "What happened today is what happens between two people who are attracted to each other. It isn't shameful, though it certainly should always be private. Do you think your friends haven't felt a man's touch on their breasts? I assure you that most of them have."

"Most of my friends are *married*," she pointed out. "I assume that married people are—are more free with each other," she finished carefully. She could feel her face heating at his bluntness.

"Some more than others," Luis drawled, thinking of the poor souls who probably did no more than ruck up their nightshirts and finish within five minutes. Poor men? Poor ladies! "But you can bet that they made love at least a little even before they married."

"I don't think so," she said, disconcerted at the idea.

A couple of cowboys left the meeting hall just then, their joking voices loud in the still night air. Luis put his arm around her waist and drew her to the other side of the tree, out of their sight. She felt the rough bark against her back and leaned thankfully against the sturdy support.

"Of course they did. It's so enjoyable, after all."

She was finding it difficult to keep the point of the argument in mind. "Enjoyable or not, Mr. Fronteras—"

"Luis."

"—I should never have allowed you such liberties today, and I'm ashamed of myself for such behavior."

"Moralistic little darling," he said tenderly.

"I am *not* your darling! Please don't call me that."

"But you are. You just haven't admitted it yet."

She took a deep breath, trying to compose herself and reorder her thoughts. "Our relationship is far too casual for me to permit such incidences between us, and I won't allow it to happen again—"

He put both hands on the tree, bridging her rib cage and effectively hemming her in. "Don't," he said quietly, interrupting her. "Don't make statements you'll then feel obliged to live up to."

"But I must," she replied just as quietly.

Luis drew a deep breath. He couldn't allow her to turn him away. It wasn't just the protectiveness she stirred in him, or the desire, it was the overwhelming need to have her for himself. He couldn't just seduce her; Olivia would consider herself "ruined" and would never marry, just to keep her sordid secret. She was sweet and honorable and deserved better.

He felt as if he were only slowly beginning to understand his own mind, but suddenly he knew what he wanted. He wanted Olivia, and he would do whatever it took to get her.

He leaned close to her. "No, there's no need. My intentions are honorable. There's nothing to fight against, unless you dislike me so much that you only want me to go away, and I don't think that's the case. Even if it were, I wouldn't go," he finished with iron determination.

Her breath caught. She tilted her head back against the tree, looking up at his lean face revealed by the moonlight spilling down through the gently shifting leaves. She was so stunned that she groped to order her thoughts.

It was almost impossible to comprehend. He wanted to *marry* her? That surely was what he meant by "honorable intentions." Yet how could he? He was a drifter, by his own admission. He had no home. Though she had dreamed of travel, there had always been an image of home in the back of her mind, the center to which she returned. "Home" wasn't her parents' house in those dreams, but a warm, welcoming home she had made with the man she loved. They would have children, so of course there had to be a home. How could she even consider marrying a man who couldn't provide that?

"Nothing to say?" he asked with a wry smile. "You don't love me yet, Olivia Millican, but you will. I won't give up until you do."

Then he leaned down and began kissing her, and her breath caught all over again, for if his kisses had been thrilling that afternoon, they were even more so now that she knew what to expect. She had the brief thought that she should resist, but she ignored it. She didn't want to resist, she didn't want to think about what she should or shouldn't do; she wanted to enjoy, to seize this moment of pure pleasure.

She found that having once traveled a road, it's difficult to keep your feet from turning down it again. His bold hand searched her breasts, burning her with his heat, and she couldn't find the inclination to refuse him. Instead her own hands stroked up his muscled back, kneading the hard flesh with delight as she learned the differences between his body and hers. She found his black hair thick and silky as she ran her fingers along the nape of his neck. He shivered a little, and her heart leapt at the knowledge that her touch excited him.

A thick groan broke from his throat, and he eased away from her, his breath coming loud and heavy. "Go back inside," he said, "or we'll do more than kiss, and this isn't the place for it. Tomorrow is Sunday, so I won't be working. Will you go for a ride with me?"

She couldn't think. What would she tell her parents? They wouldn't approve of her riding with anyone they knew nothing about, much less a Mexican drifter.

He seemed to realize all of that without her saying a word, and he smiled bitterly. "Of course not," he said, answering the question for her. "I understand. I should have thought before asking you such a question."

"Luis," she said hesitantly, "it isn't—" But it so obviously *was* that she broke off in midsentence.

"It is. But when you love me, it won't matter." He kissed her again, lingeringly, then caught her shoulders and turned her back toward the meeting hall, toward music and lights and laughter. "Go on, go back, before your pretty dress gets all mussed up. But if you decide to go riding tomorrow, try the north road. I'll be riding there myself around two o'clock."

He gave her a little push, and her steps carried her automatically back to the meeting hall. She stepped inside and was engulfed in warm air and noise. She was still dazed and couldn't concentrate, but the crushing burden of guilt seemed to have fallen away. She didn't know what to think. It seemed as if in a matter of a few hours the course of her entire life had been rerouted, and she didn't know where she was going.

How odd that she had felt despair at the thought of a marriage proposal from Lucas, who could give her everything in the way of material wealth, yet the thought of marrying Luis, who could give her nothing but adventure, made her feel shivery and excited, even frightened, but never despairing. Luis was right in saying that she didn't love him, for she barely knew him and was too cautious to plunge headlong into anything— wasn't she? Yet she hadn't denied him, hadn't turned him down flat as she was sure she should have. Instead she had let him kiss her and fondle her, after swearing to herself that it would never happen again. And she couldn't get his proposal out of her mind.

He hadn't actually proposed; he had just said that his intentions were honorable, a curiously formal phrase from a drifter.

She saw Kyle Bellamy making his way toward her, and she quickly reached Honora, who was flushed with pride at how well everything had gone during "her" year.

"I'm going to go home, Mother," she said quietly.

Instantly Honora blinked and frowned, switching her attention from the dance to her only chick. Olivia could almost feel the motherly concern being focused on her.

"Are you feeling ill, darling?"

"I have a headache, and the noise is making it worse." It was the most time-worn excuse in the world, but Olivia wasn't accustomed to lying to her mother and couldn't think of anything more original.

"I'll get your father to walk you home." But right before leaving in search of Wilson Honora gave her daughter such a look of sympathetic concern that Olivia sighed, knowing her mother was thinking the same thing everyone else was. It would be all over town tomorrow that she and Lucas had had a fight, or something else that would explain why he wasn't at the dance and she was leaving early with a headache.

She would have to tell her parents that she had mistaken Lucas's intentions, that he was after all only a good friend. They would be disappointed, but she couldn't let them continue to look on Lucas as her suitor. Not tonight, though. She had far too much on her mind.

Wilson dutifully walked her home, and Olivia went straight upstairs to bed. She lay in the darkness and thought of all that had happened that day. She remembered the way Luis's mouth had closed over her tender breast, and she blushed, clasping her hands over the suddenly throbbing mounds. She should never have let him—

But she had.

She shouldn't go riding tomorrow, she thought. Whatever she did, she shouldn't go anywhere near the north road. She told herself that and knew she wouldn't listen to her own advice.

10

The town was still quiet from the picnic and dance the day before when Lucas rode in the next afternoon. Church was already out, and people had gone to their homes to rest off the aftereffects. It being a Sunday, when few men could justify stopping by the saloon for a drink, the establishment was occupied only by a few cowhands who had no duties for the day.

Both of the saloon girls were sitting and talking with the drinkers, as that encouraged them to drink more. Tillie looked up and smiled her slow smile at Lucas, and he gave a little jerk of his head. Her eyebrows rose, then she murmured a few words to the cowboy whose table she had been gracing and excused herself.

When she had sashayed close enough Lucas said softly, "Let's go upstairs."

Tillie looked amused. "You still have woman trouble?"

"Upstairs," he repeated, not wanting to say anything where they could be overheard.

She walked in front of him, leading him up the narrow stairs. Lucas could feel eyes boring into his back and smiled wryly. If they only knew why he was there!

Tillie's room was small, most of the space taken up by the double bed, though there was a washbasin and a dresser crammed into one of the corners. It was surprisingly clean and sweet-smelling.

She sat down on the bed and crossed her elegant legs. "Do you want anything special?" she asked in that slow, warm voice, and despite himself Lucas couldn't help thinking that her "special" might be almost enough to kill a man.

"A favor," he said.

She laughed aloud. "Somehow I knew my luck wasn't running true today. Well, maybe another time. What can I do for you?"

"Do you have any of the little sponges that keep women from conceiving?"

Those enormous brown eyes twinkled at him, and he grinned back, at ease with the request. Tillie wouldn't ask questions and wouldn't gossip, and her amusement was without malice.

She got up and sauntered over to the dresser. "So your woman troubles are over. You didn't strike me as the kind of man who would let it go on too long anyway, so I'm not surprised." She hummed a little as she opened a door and extracted a hand-painted ceramic box. "How many do you need?"

It was his turn to laugh. "I don't know. How many *do* I need? Isn't one enough?"

She giggled, a sound rich and musical. "Here, take three. You know—just in case."

He snorted as she put the three small round sponges in his hand, but the smile still played around his hard mouth.

"Just soak one in vinegar," she instructed. "I suppose you know what to do with it, because it's a sure bet your lucky woman doesn't."

Lucas shook his head in amusement at the thought of the fight he would probably have getting Dee to use these. Then again, he was always surprised by the battles she chose to fight and the ones she ignored, so it was possible she wouldn't say anything at all.

Tillie's dark eyes were suddenly serious. "You take care of that woman, Lucas Cochran," she said sternly. "It wouldn't do at all for folks to find out about you and her, not after all the trouble she's had from some of the men around here."

Lucas's head jerked up, his eyes narrowing dangerously. Tillie held up a placating hand. "Word won't get out from me," she said.

"How did you know?" His voice was silky smooth and deadly. "Did anyone see us?"

"Relax, no one knows but me. I just happen to know who wasn't at the picnic yesterday, and word got around about how you left early. She came into town yesterday morning, to the general store, but it was closed. I was sitting outside and saw her. She waved at me. I've seen her before, and she's never been snooty. She's a straightforward woman, with more grit than just about any two men put together."

"She does have grit," Lucas said.

"There's been lots of talk about you and the banker's daughter," Tillie said. She looked him up and down, then shook her head. "I never could see it. You need someone meaner than that, a woman who can stand up to you without blinking an eye."

Lucas smiled. "Tillie," he said, "you know too damn much about people."

"I've had a lot of time to study them."

He put the little sponges in his pocket. "How much do I owe you?"

"They're on the house. Next time I order some from New Orleans, I'll let you know so you can get a supply."

He leaned down and kissed that exquisite mouth, lazily taking his time about it because she was so damn beautiful. When he straightened she blinked and said, "My, my. I haven't been kissed like that since Charles Dupré—never mind. Are you sure the sponges are all you want?"

He cupped her chin and kissed her again. "I'm sure," he said. "I need to save my strength."

She gave a wonderful, lusty laugh. "I guess you do. This is going to just destroy my reputation, us up here laughing like jackasses and you going back downstairs within five minutes."

He grinned at her as he opened the door. "No, it'll be my reputation that's ruined if I couldn't last more than five minutes."

She fluttered her lashes at him as she passed by. "If I ever got my hands on you, you might *not*."

Lucas was in a good mood as he rode back to the Double C. The sponges in his pocket provoked a big temptation to swing east and visit Dee, but he resisted it. She would be too sore for making love again, and he wasn't all that certain of his self-control.

Thunder rumbled in the distance, underscoring his decision to go home. He looked upward but saw only deep blue sky. The storm clouds must still be beyond the horizon, he thought. They needed a good rain, since the snowpacks on the mountains weren't as deep as they should have been, but he sure hoped he got to the ranch before the storm arrived.

Luis looked upward at the same rumble of thunder. Olivia kept her attention on the ground before her as her mare carefully picked her way over some rough ground. "I hope it rains and settles the dust," she said.

He hoped it rained for more basic reasons. It had been too long since they had had even a brief spring shower, and the water holes were getting a little low, especially since it was just May. But as much as the rain was needed, he hoped it held off for another couple of hours. He didn't want his time with Olivia cut short.

She had been distinctly nervous when he had ridden up beside her, so he had restricted himself to conversation and the quiet enjoyment of her company. She had slowly relaxed, and now the strain was gone from her face. As much as he wanted to hold her again, he wanted more for her to feel at ease with him. It was time for her to get to know him better. Besides, there were some things he wanted to know about her, too.

"Is there an understanding between you and Lucas Cochran?" he asked quietly, watching her face.

"No," she replied. "He's never spoken of marriage, and neither have I, though everyone just assumed that he would."

"Don't you want him to? He's a powerful man, and from what I hear he's going to be even bigger than he is now."

"I like Lucas, but he's just a friend." How good it felt to be able to say that! From the way he had acted the day before, she was certain he was fascinated with Dee. "If he *had* asked me, I don't know what I would have said."

"Because he's rich?"

"No. I know I've been raised with luxuries, but I don't think I've ever expected them as my due. But I'm twenty-five, and I'm afraid that if I don't marry soon, I never will, and then I'll never have my own family."

"I'm thirty-two," he said. "I've begun to think that I want to have a family, too."

She gave him a quick look and blushed.

"Why haven't you married before?" He quietly soothed his horse when the animal shied as a blossom blew in front of it. "I know you must have had offers."

"No. No one ever asked. Somehow I just never fell in love with anyone, and evidently no one fell in love with me either."

"I was serious about what I said. About my intentions."

"I know," she whispered. She sighed. "Why have you drifted?"

"It's always seemed the natural thing to do." He looked up at the sky again, but it was still clear. He wondered if he could explain it so she would understand. "I've always been good with a gun. I've never hired it out, but when a man is fast with a six-iron it tends to make most people uneasy around him. And sooner or later someone thinks he's faster and wants to prove it. No town wants to have a fast gun settle down there, because it draws other guns. For a while I worked for the Sarratt brothers down in New Mexico, and I could have stayed there, but then Celia died, and so did my reason for staying.

"After a while, moving on seems like the natural thing to do. It has its own lure, to see what's beyond that mountain range, then the next one, then the next one. Always a new place and new faces, and sometimes nothing but a huge empty world with me right in the middle of it, just me and the horse and the sky. I've gone weeks without seeing another human being. And sometimes, when I'm in a town, I miss that."

"But you hired on with Mr. Bellamy. Do you intend to stay?"

"I hired on to rest from the trail for a while and earn some money doing it. I've been here almost two months now, and so far I'm content. I like the town. It's the kind of quiet, sturdy town I like."

She noticed that he hadn't answered her question but didn't

feel that she had the right to press him further. What would it take to induce him to settle down? she wondered. Marriage? He hadn't said so, and she would be foolish to assume that such was his intention, perhaps almost as foolish as she would be to consider marrying him at all.

But he fascinated her in a way no one else had ever done. She glanced at his dark, lean face, admiring his wonderfully chiseled features. There was an obvious aura of danger about him, but she never felt threatened. Instead, when his warm, dark gaze touched her, she felt infinitely admired and . . . safe, as if he would forever stand between her and anything that would harm her.

Thunder rumbled again, closer this time. He looked regretful. "We'd better turn back."

Common sense agreed with him, but she felt like shaking her fist at the sky. Why couldn't the rain have held off just another hour or so? The storm might even bypass them completely, but they couldn't depend on that.

Smiling at the disappointment on her face, Luis reined his horse closer to hers and leaned over to kiss her lingeringly. Her lips parted for him without hesitation, so sweetly that it was all he could do to break away. He might not have if his horse hadn't sidestepped nervously, away from such close contact with her mount.

One kiss would have to be enough, he thought, or they would likely get caught by the storm anyway. They reined the horses around and started back.

"I don't know when I'll get back to town," he said after a while, "but I'll see you when I do."

She started to ask him how he would contact her but kept silent when she realized how insulting the question would be, for it would imply that he wasn't good enough simply to come to her house and ask to see her. Yet weren't they going out of their way not to let anyone see them together precisely because they both knew her parents would object?

She should tell them, she thought, and let them know that she . . . what? Was considering marrying Luis? Without knowing where or how they would live? Honora would make herself ill with worry. Her parents were indulgent rather than dictatorial, so she didn't fear they would forbid her to see Luis; she was twenty-five, not a giddy seventeen-year-old to be locked in her room. But it would upset them, and she didn't want that.

So it seemed as if she could either have them upset or continue to sneak around as if she were doing something wrong, and neither choice appealed to her. The only solution was to stop seeing Luis entirely, which she discarded at once as unacceptable. In one short day he had shattered the pall of gray desolation that had shrouded her for so long, and she felt wondrously alive, her heart pounding with excitement whenever she was with him.

She had always done exactly as a lady ought, living contentedly within the boundaries of convention. This was the only time she had ever stepped outside those boundaries, and she found it exhilarating. If she was condemned for it, then she would simply have to deal with it, for she found that the need for his company was as compelling for her as drifting had been for him.

Dee looked up when she heard the patter of rain on the tin roof, the sound quickly increasing to a soporific drumming that drowned out all other sounds. With the rain came a chill, but she didn't want to light a fire, so she got a quilt from the bed and sat down in her big chair with it wrapped around her. The warmth of the quilt comforted her.

She had been reading, but the book no longer interested her. She laid her head back and closed her eyes, letting the rain-induced drowsiness wash over her.

Lucas hadn't been back today. She had been jittery all day long, expecting him to come riding up with that intense look in his eyes that she now knew to be desire. He was arrogant enough to expect her to lie down with him whenever he wanted her, but she hadn't made up her mind about the situation.

She loved him. Since she had unwillingly admitted to herself the source of her agitation whenever she was around him, she had analyzed the situation from every angle and accepted that there was no easy solution to it. By loving him she had made herself vulnerable, and she would eventually be hurt by it. He didn't love her, which was the only thing that would have made him equally vulnerable and kept their relationship balanced. Loving him hadn't blinded her to the truth: Lucas was a hard man, one who was ruthless in getting his own way. He wanted her physically, he even cared for her to some extent, but that wasn't at all the same thing as love.

It would be better for her if she stopped the relationship cold, but she didn't know if she could. Lucas wouldn't give up without a fight, and she doubted her own ability to resist him. She wanted him with a deep, primitive strength that frightened her, knowing as she did that it was beyond her control.

There was always the chance that her feelings would lessen over time, as she grew to know him better, but she didn't think so. His character would always challenge her, both infuriating and invigorating, but never boring. She had always been protected from love because she had never met a man whose will was as strong as hers until Lucas. He would fight and laugh and love with her, and she would fall more and more in love with him.

Despite his assurance that there were ways to prevent conception, she knew that she would be at risk every time she made love with him. Bearing an illegitimate child, no matter how beloved, would destroy her standing with the townfolk. She cherished the respect she received now because only she knew how hard she had worked to earn it. Some people might not like her, and probably most of them thought her odd, but no one could say that she wasn't respected.

So she had to consider the possibility of pregnancy, and she ached deep inside in a way she never had before. She was intensely female, vital, and earthy, and thinking about his children shattered her old self-contentment and made her aware that there was something else that she needed in life, something so much a part of herself that she wondered a little numbly how she hadn't known this truth about herself long before this. She wanted children, wanted to feel them growing inside her, wanted to hold greedy little mouths to her breast, wanted to watch them grow and prosper and someday bring their own children to her to be rocked. She wanted Lucas's children.

Perhaps if she became pregnant, he would want her to marry him.

She shied away from the thought as soon as it occurred. She

didn't want to be married, not even to Lucas. A woman became a man's property as soon as she became his wife. Dee wasn't afraid that Lucas would ever mistreat her, but she couldn't bear the thought of losing the independence, the acknowledgement of herself as someone to be dealt with, that she had worked so hard to establish. Her land would become his without his having to pay one cent for it.

Thinking about it, she decided that he would be certain to want to marry her if she became pregnant, because Lucas would want his child, would in fact do whatever was necessary to make certain the baby bore his name. And she thought him capable of marrying her in order to get Angel Creek. She couldn't bear it either way, because she wanted to be loved for herself, wanted for herself, not because of a child inside of her or the land she owned.

She sat wrapped in the quilt long after the rain had stopped, long after the sun had gone down, her eyes open and somber as she looked at the various choices she could make. All of them would bring her pain, and because she loved him she would accept that pain in order to have whatever time with him she had been allotted.

11

The rain the day before hadn't been enough to raise the levels in the streams or watering holes, but the fresh spring grass was vibrantly green and abundant, and the air was washed clean of dust. Lucas was tired and sore after a day of branding calves, but whenever he lifted his head and looked around him he felt a deep sense of peace. All of the land that he saw in every direction was his, and he had never wanted to be anywhere else than right there. He loved it with every particle of his being, and he wouldn't hesitate to kill to protect his home, as he had done before, or to die in the effort. He was willing to spill both blood and sweat on the ground to make it prosper.

When the last calf of the day was branded and had been released to run bawling back to its mother Lucas stood and stretched, turning from side to side to work the kinks out of his back. He eyed the sun; it was only an hour until sundown, not enough time for him to get back to the house and change out of his filthy clothes, then get over the narrow pass leading down to Angel Creek before dark. He could go the long way around, taking the road to Prosper and then cutting back toward the mountains, but the ride alone would take him over two hours, and it was possible someone would see him riding toward Dee's place. He wasn't going to have people whispering about her behind her back, so that option was out. But he needed her with a deep, burning ache that had grown worse as the day passed and wouldn't get any better until he was with her again, sliding deep into her silky body, feeling her wrap those strong, graceful legs around him. He looked again at the sun, thinking of taking his chances over the pass, then finally realized that it would be stupid to try. He would have to get through another night without her.

He had spent only the one afternoon with her, yet he craved her with the ferocity that drove the addicts in the San Francisco opium dens to their pipes. Losing his brother Matt had been hard, and since then he had been essentially alone in spirit because he had taught himself to need no one, to be complete unto himself; but now he had to deal with a nagging sense of incompletion, as if he had left part of himself down at Angel Creek. The notion was ridiculous, and he scoffed silently at himself. No one could mean that much to anyone else. It was just that Dee wasn't like other women he had known, and her differences were what intrigued him. He wanted her, that was all. It was a challenge to get past all of those thorns to the wild-honey sweetness of her.

He wondered with disgust when he had taken up lying to himself.

Thunder boomed, and he looked at the sky for the third time. His foreman, William Tobias, evidently thought he was looking for signs of rain and said, "I don't think that one's going to come our way. Sounds like it's headed for the mountains." The gangly sun-dried man leaned over to spit. "Sure do wish we'd get a hard spell of rain. We ain't dry, but I'd like to have more water in those holes before summer gets here."

Lucas thought of the pure, never-ending water of Angel Creek and felt the old irritation with his father rise up within him. That land should have belonged to the Double C for a long time, but due to his father's lack of judgment it was now in the hands of a stubborn woman who was likely to work herself to death rather than listen to reason.

But if his father had bought Angel Creek all those years ago, Dee's father wouldn't have settled there, and he would never have met Dee. Lucas frowned, trying to balance the pleasure of owning Angel Creek against the excitement of making love to Dee. The frown changed to a wry smile. Angel Creek wasn't going anywhere; he'd get it eventually. Maybe he was just as glad that it had been unsettled when George Swann had brought his family west.

He and the foreman stood watching the storm clouds low on the horizon as they drifted away toward the mountains. The late afternoon thunderstorms were a frequent occurrence during spring and early summer, so both men expected they would get their share of rain.

Resigned now to the fact that he wouldn't get over to Dee's after all, Lucas mounted his horse and started back toward the house. If he knew Dee, she had probably decided that he intended to visit only when he needed sex and would have the shotgun in her hands the next time he showed his face.

He realized that he was grinning as he rode home. Damn if getting her wouldn't be worth a load of buckshot in his ass!

Dee stepped outside the next morning just as dawn was turning the sky a glowing, translucent pink. She had reached for the feed pan as soon as she had stepped onto the stoop, but now she withdrew her hand without touching it, her eyes on that wonderful sky arching above her, around her, surrounding her with the glow.

The peace of the morning enfolded her. She turned away from the chores that awaited her and walked silently toward the meadow, her senses drinking in the colors and fragrances of the new day.

The long meadow was filled with graceful spring grass, the morning dew covering it with diamond glitter. A profusion of wildflowers spread before her eyes as far as she could see, a riot of blues and pinks and purples dotted with cheerful yellows and the occasional cluster of crimson clover, the dark red clover heads nodding as if they had to entice the industrious bees who found their sweet scent irresistible. She wandered among them, the dew wetting her faded skirt to the knee, but she didn't notice and wouldn't have cared if she had. Some days were magic and were to be savored. The chores would always be there; this dawn was fleeting and would never be duplicated.

The sky overhead gradually changed from pearly pink to opalescent and finally to a great, shining golden bowl as the sun finally emerged and bathed the meadow in radiance. Birds sang almost deliriously, and the silver rush of water in the creek sounded like a thousand bells.

She walked down to the creek and watched the crystal water dance over the stones. Her blood sang through her veins, and her heart was full. This was her home, and it was paradise.

"Dee."

She heard her name, though it hadn't been loudly spoken, and turned to look at him. Lucas stood some twenty feet away, his glittering eyes narrowed with some unnamed emotion, his face hard and intent. He was perfectly still, his big, muscled body locked in place; he never took his gaze off her, and the force of his lust hit her like a massive wave. Her body reacted automatically to his presence, immediately growing warm and heavy, her skin abruptly becoming too sensitive for the touch of her clothing. Her breasts swelled and ached, and her loins tightened.

She looked like a primitive goddess, and Lucas could hardly catch his breath. She stood next to the creek, surrounded by wildflowers, and the exotic face turned toward him was as serene and dreamy as the dawn itself. He had never seen her like that before, all defenses down, simply a woman exalted by the dawn.

His whole body expanded until he felt as if his skin would burst, and he was dizzy with the rush of his blood. His sex throbbed violently, and he knew he had to be inside of her.

He never remembered crossing the ground between them, only that she didn't move, and then she was within his grasp, her body firm and rich, her mouth inexplicably shy beneath the savagery of his. He carried her down, crushing her into the wildflowers, and shoved her skirt to her waist. The barrier of her drawers maddened him, and he stripped them away with rough hands, her pale thighs naked and vulnerable in the morning sun. He was so swollen with need that he cursed under his breath at the difficulty of unbuttoning his pants. Then he was free. He opened her soft folds with one hand, revealing the small opening, and with his other hand he guided himself to her. He looked down at the broad head of his sex poised against the delicate opening, and his testicles tightened painfully. He thrust into her, groaning aloud with the shattering relief of her tight, silky wet channel clasping his aching length and soothing him with both pleasure and the promise of more.

Dee accepted his heavy weight with slender arms wrapped around those powerful shoulders, accepted the fierce drive of his loins slamming into her, accepted his masculinity and lust and welcomed all of it. She felt almost unbearably stretched and possessed, but there was a bright glory to it, and she reveled in it. Her head rolled slowly back and forth in the dew-fresh grass as her entire body gave itself over to him.

She climaxed abruptly, the sensation exploding in her loins and making her legs tremble around him. Her cries lifted into the crystal air, and her back arched as he reared back on his knees with a guttural roar. His own climax swiftly followed, his head thrown back and his neck corded with the force of his convulsions. He gripped her slender hips and held her tightly locked onto him until the last spasms had eased, until he was emptied of his fever.

Afterward he was silent, and so was she, as he got to his feet and rebuttoned his pants. He bent and picked up her discarded drawers, then lifted her into his arms and carried her back to the cabin. She let her head rest on his shoulder, her eyes closed. There still didn't seem to be anything to say.

Lucas was shaken by the power of the surge of lust that had overtaken him. He had taken her without preliminaries, without gentling her body into arousal, but he hadn't been able to hold back. At that moment nothing had existed in the world but the two of them and his maddened need to have her. By rights, he thought, she should be trying to get to her shotgun rather than lying so still and quiet in his arms.

He sat down in one of the kitchen chairs and cradled her on his lap, his hands stroking her soothingly as if he could give her the consideration now that he hadn't been capable of earlier. Dee sighed with gentle pleasure, her nose turned against him so she could inhale the clean, warm scent of his body.

"Did I hurt you?" he asked, his voice rough-edged.

She stirred a little, then settled in his embrace once more. "No." His intrusion into her body had been shocking, but there hadn't been pain, only primitive joy.

She didn't seem angry, either, but lay in his arms with the sensuous lassitude of a thoroughly loved woman. Of all the reactions he had expected, this voluptuous yielding hadn't been one of them, and it was all the more beguiling because he was taken by surprise. This was one reaction he didn't think he would ever tire of.

"I brought the sponges," he said wryly, his mouth quirking with an ironic smile. He hadn't even given a thought to them, and in any case he couldn't have restrained himself.

She opened her eyes and gave him a heavy-lidded stare. "Did you think they would do a lot of good in your pocket?" she asked. Then she sat up with curiosity on her face. "What do they look like?"

He maneuvered her and stretched out his leg so he could get his hand in his pocket, and he withdrew the small sponges. She looked at them lying in his callused palm, picked one up, and squeezed it between her fingers, then gave it back to him. "They're just regular sponges," she said, visibly disappointed. He grinned a little, knowing that she had been expecting something far more exotic and frankly wicked.

"I know. I expect it's the vinegar that does the job."

"Well, it's too late now."

"But it won't be the next time."

She gave him another of those green, heavy-lidded looks. "Unless you come at me again like the bull on one of the cows."

"Since the next time isn't very far in the future, I think I can promise that," he said.

"I have to do the chores."

"I'll help."

They were back in bed within the hour, their naked bodies twining with the steadily building tension. The small vinegar-soaked sponge sat in a dish next to the bed. When neither of them could wait a minute longer he showed her how to insert the sponge, his long fingers reaching deep inside her and almost carrying her to completion without him. They made love until they were both exhausted, and Lucas pulled the sheet up over them just before he dozed off, his arms wrapped protectively around her slender form. He was contented all the way to his bones.

When they woke up he wanted to make love to her again. He was startled when she tried to squirm away from him. "I don't want to," she said fretfully.

"Damn if you aren't the most contrary woman I've ever seen," he muttered. *"Why* don't you want to?"

She shrugged, her mouth sulky. "I just don't want you holding me down again right now."

He ran his hand through his hair. God, why had he been surprised? The wonder was that she hadn't done something about it before now, but of course she was too inexperienced to know.

"Then you get on top," he said.

Interest sparked in those green eyes. He could see she was intrigued by the idea of controlling their lovemaking, and therefore controlling him. He wanted to laugh out loud but thought she might change her mind if he did. Personally, he loved lying on his back and letting a woman ride him, and his imagination went wild as he pictured Dee's rich breasts swaying over him.

"I don't know how," she said.

His hands were persuasive as they moved over her, enticing her closer. "I'll show you," he said. Just thinking about it had already made him hard and ready.

She loved it, too. By the time she settled astride him, sinking down to envelop his shaft, his hands were locked on the headboard above him as he strained to control himself. He was gasping, his eyes closed from the pleasure she had wrought. She had seduced him that time, her mouth tender on his mouth and chest, her breasts brushing against his stomach and loins as she swayed over him. He thought of other things he would teach her, but right now he had all he could handle. Of course she loved it; she was enthralled by having him at her mercy, if he could call it that. It was more like torment, delicious, searing torment.

Dee moved slowly, rhythmically, her eyes closing as her own hunger built. This was pure ecstasy, she thought, and she knew that she would never regret these moments no matter what happened. It wasn't the physical pleasure that was so precious, but the link between them that was forged by that pleasure. She felt herself dissolving and cried out, unaware that he had reached his peak just ahead of her; then she fell forward onto his chest in exhaustion.

By the time he left late that afternoon she knew that for her, at least, the link between them would never be broken.

12

June came in hot and dry. It was particularly frustrating because almost every afternoon thunder would echo from the mountains, and dark clouds would tantalize them with the possibility of rain; but the clouds would slide away, and if they ever released their moisture, it happened on the far side of the mountains, and Prosper got none of the runoff.

Each day dawned as hot and clear as the one preceeding it, and Lucas began to worry, even though the Double C still had good water. There was no telling how long a dry spell would last, and it wasn't just the water holes that were drying up; the grass was getting dry and brittle, with no new growth to replace the grazed areas. The cattle were having to graze farther each day, then returning to the creeks and water holes for water. They were daily growing leaner, and each day they had to cover even more ground. He didn't like it, but there wasn't a damn thing he could do about it. Admitting that didn't sweeten his temper.

After going without Dee for two weeks he rode over to Angel Creek one day, leaving a lot of work undone because another minute without her was one minute too long. He was restless and irritable, not just because of his sexual needs but because he couldn't get her out of his mind. No woman had ever invaded his thoughts like that, getting in the way of his work, interfering with his sleep. His desire for her hadn't cooled; he wanted her more than ever, his hunger all the more intense because it had to be hidden, even from his own men. If the men ever wondered where he went, they never asked. He suspected they all assumed he was seeing Olivia, and of course they would never make joking remarks about a lady the way they would if the woman was less than respectable. It enraged him that anyone would consider Dee less deserving of respect than Olivia, but he couldn't say anything without making Dee a target, so he had to keep his mouth shut.

Dee was sitting on the front porch placidly rocking when he rode up, and she made no effort to get up to welcome him. She was probably mad at him, he thought with a sigh, but then he decided that she wasn't. If Dee had been angry, she would have let him know it. It was more likely that she was just taking it easy in the shade.

He put the horse in the barn where it was cooler, and as he walked back to the house he noticed how green everything was, when everywhere else the grass was turning brown and the tree leaves were limp. Angel Creek was a lush oasis in comparison. He stopped and looked around. Her garden was thriving, and as far as he could see up the valley the meadow grasses were green and resilient. He could hear the quiet rush of the water in the creek, the sweet, cold, crystal-clear mountain water that fed this little valley and made it thrive.

The valley wasn't big enough to support all of his cattle, but if he owned it, then it would be a safeguard against drought. Enough cattle could survive there to keep him from being wiped out. Indeed, keeping some cattle there would even help those heads left on the Double C, because they would get what grass and water there was to be had.

Dee was still rocking when he stepped up on the porch and sat down beside her. Her eyes were closed, but her foot maintained the slow, steady movement of the chair.

"I'll give you five thousand dollars for Angel Creek," he said.

Those inscrutable green eyes opened and regarded him for a moment before her thick black lashes swept down again. "It isn't for sale."

"Damn it," he said irritably. "That's twice what it's worth."

"Must not be," she reasoned. "Since you offered five thousand, then it's worth five thousand."

"Seven thousand."

"It isn't for sale."

"Would you be sensible about this?"

"I am being sensible," she insisted. "This is my home. I don't want to sell it."

"Ten thousand."

"Stop it."

"What are you going to do when you're too old to work the land? This is hard work, and you won't be able to keep doing it. You're young and strong now, but what about ten years from now?"

"I'll let you know in ten years," she retorted.

"Name any kind of business you'd like to have, and I'll set you up in it. You're not going to get that kind of offer from anyone else."

She stopped rocking and opened her eyes. Lucas watched her intently, his pulse speeding up now that he had finally aggravated her out of her cool demeanor. It was like deliberately prodding a tigress to attack, but he was tired of that blank refusal even to discuss selling Angel Creek. He might not win, but she'd at least listen to him.

"That's not as interesting as the offer Kyle Bellamy made," she said with soft mockery.

He felt a spurt of anger. He could just imagine what Bellamy's offer had been. When he'd first met Dee he hadn't liked it that Bellamy was also interested in buying the land, but now he disliked even more the thought that the man had wanted Dee.

"I can just imagine the offer he made," he said sarcastically.

"I doubt it." She gave him a smile so sweet he was instantly wary. "He asked me to marry him."

This time Lucas didn't feel a spurt of anger, he felt a huge rush of it, so hot that his entire body seemed to expand and burn. His pupils constricted to tiny black points. "Not if I can help it," he said in a voice so flat and toneless she wasn't certain he'd said anything at all.

"It was my decision, not yours. I turned him down, of course."

"When was he here?" Murder was still in his eyes.

She shrugged. "Before you ever came back to town."

Some of the anger faded as he realized that it wasn't a recent event. But if Bellamy ever came back to Angel Creek, it had better be to say good-bye.

"I don't want him here again," he said flatly, just in case she was in any doubt.

"I didn't invite him in the first place." She added thoughtfully, "I didn't invite you, either. Isn't it strange? The poor men who could have used a homestead just wanted me for sex; you and Bellamy have plenty of land, but you want more. I'd have to say that Bellamy wants it more than you do, since he offered marriage."

Lucas tensed, every instinct alert. "Is that what it would take?" he asked, carefully feeling his way. He felt as if he were treading through quicksand, where one misstep would be a disaster. He realized that he was holding his breath, waiting for her answer.

Dee didn't look at him, but out across her land. "Getting married would be even worse than selling out," she said. "I'd lose both my land and my independence. Of the two, selling it would at least let me stay independent."

Sharp disappointment thudded in his chest. Until he felt the force of it he hadn't realized how much he had wanted her to say yes, that she would be interested in a marriage proposal from him. Shock froze him in his chair. He had known since the first time he'd made love to her that she had ruined his plans to marry Olivia, that he couldn't marry Olivia while he still wanted Dee so fiercely. He couldn't imagine Dee consenting to be the mistress of a married man, nor would it be fair to Olivia. And Dee had made her opinion of marriage plain the first time they'd met. Until now he hadn't really thought of marriage to her because she didn't fit in with his plans; he had been prepared to marry her as a necessity if she should become pregnant, but the subject had never come up between them, and it had just been speculation on his part that she would marry him even then. Now he had brought it out into the open, and her refusal had hit him squarely between the eyes. He wanted Dee as his wife, and not because she would fit into his plans. If anything, she would make things harder.

But with her he could laugh and fight and not have to worry about hurting her feelings if he snapped at her. Dee would give back as good as she got. And in bed she was wild and natural, giving him complete freedom of her body without embarrassment and exploring him in the same manner. He would find some way to make her fit into the mold he wanted.

He'd marry her in a minute if she'd have him, but Dee didn't want to marry anyone. Marriage would make her feel caged, and she couldn't tolerate that.

"Then take the money," he said, not looking at her because he was afraid she would read too much in his eyes. "It's enough to invest, so you'll always have enough to live on. That way you'd still be independent, and you wouldn't have to work yourself to death on the land. Hell, you could even buy more land, if that was what you wanted."

"But it wouldn't be Angel Creek," she said softly. "I love it here. I fell in love with it the first day I saw it." And it had given her a reason to live. In exchange for its healing bounty she was its caretaker, its guardian. Sometimes she felt a superstitious fear that she was like a plant that would die if uprooted from the soil of this small valley.

And she would never love any man as much as she loved this damn place, he thought savagely. He would rather have had Kyle Bellamy as a rival than Angel Creek, because he could fight Bellamy, but how could he fight the land? He remembered the look of dreamy ecstasy on her face the morning he had come to her in the dawn and found her out in the meadow, and sharp jealousy pierced him as he realized it had been for the land, for the wash of golden sunlight, for the crystal flow of water, and not for him.

The hell of it was, he loved the Double C just as fiercely. He couldn't condemn her when they were so much alike. That was why he was so relaxed with her, because she matched him strength for strength. But damn it, it wasn't like he'd be asking her to move to another country.

He stood up and held out his hand to her. "Let's go inside," he said abruptly. He needed her. God, how he needed her.

But she didn't take his hand, just gave him another of those cat looks. "If you rode all the way over here just for that, you'll have to be disappointed. I'm having my monthly."

He *was* disappointed but felt no inclination to leave. Even if he couldn't make love to her, he needed her in other ways. He kept his hand extended. "Then come sit on my lap and drive me crazy," he said.

Her face brightened with interest, and she put her hand in his. She was always willing to drive him crazy.

But as it happened they spent more time talking than snuggling. He had been serious about her sitting on his lap, so that's what she did, both of them in the big chair in front of the fire. He told her about his breeding plans for his herd, about his expansion ideas, how he planned to use the politicians in Denver to further his ambitions. The citizens of Colorado were supposed to vote to ratify the state constitution on the first of July, and it would then go to the federal government for a vote to admit them to the Union. He told her what statehood would mean, and she sat up to frown at him.

"I don't know if I want crowds of people coming out to settle. I like it the way it is now."

"It's progress, honey. With more people we'll get more businesses, and more railroads. Railroads are the key. Colorado can't be completely civilized without them."

"What difference does it make?"

"Money," he said simply. "You can't do anything without money."

"But I don't want things to change." She nestled her head back on his shoulder and said pensively, "I don't like change."

"Everything changes." He combed his fingers through her long hair and pressed a kiss to her temple. She turned her face into his throat, and he held her tighter, as if he could protect her from the changes that were inevitable for them both.

It had become customary for Olivia to go riding every Sunday afternoon. Sometimes she would return without seeing

Luis, her disappointment carefully hidden behind her calm demeanor. But most of the time he would join her at some point. She seldom saw him at any other time, for his duties on the ranch kept him busy. The days between those stolen Sunday afternoons crept by at a snail's pace, while the few hours she spent with him were gone almost before she knew it. She was so obsessed with seeing him that she even neglected to ride out to see Dee and felt guilty because she had so much to tell her.

She couldn't seem to think of anything other than Luis. Her heart would begin hammering as soon as he appeared at her side, making her feel as if she would suffocate in the heat. She had already ceased wearing the fitted jacket of her riding habit, but convention insisted that she keep her blouse firmly buttoned all the way up to her throat and the sleeve cuffs fastened at her wrist. The unusually warm weather was uncomfortable, and her physical reaction to Luis made it seem even worse.

She would often look at the open throat of Luis's shirt and envy men the freedom of their clothing, but it wasn't long before the smooth brown skin visible in that open neckline would distract her from the details of clothing, and the heat would intensify.

Luis saw the way her gaze would linger on his open shirt and the flush that would soon climb to her cheeks. Though she didn't realize it, she was becoming more accustomed to the physical desire between them, and as each Sunday passed without anything more than kisses she was becoming hungrier. She was innocent, but she was a woman, with a woman's needs. The day would come, and soon, when her desire and curiosity would grow too strong, and she would reach out for him. He only hoped it would be soon, for the frustration was killing him. He had never waited so long for a woman before, but then no other woman had been Olivia.

As June progressed the heat became even more oppressive, and riding during the afternoon was almost unbearable for both riders and animals. On a Sunday afternoon toward the end of the month Luis found a spot of intense shade under a stand of big trees and reined in his horse, dismounting with the fluid, catlike grace she found so fascinating.

"Let the horses rest," he said, reaching up for her. "We'll start back when it cools down some."

Olivia was more than glad to rest in the shade. She patted her face with her handkerchief and sat down under a tree while Luis gave the horses a little water, then tied them with long lines so they could graze. That done, he sat down beside her and placed his hat on the ground, then wiped his face with his sleeve.

"Do you want some water?" he asked.

She laughed, amused that he had taken care of the horses before offering any water to her. "Is there any left?"

"I brought a full canteen." He plucked a blade of grass and tickled her nose with it. "Always take care of your animals first. They'll keep you alive."

"Since we're less than an hour from town, I think we'll make it before we run out of water," she said gravely, then she laughed again.

He looked up at the blue bowl overhead, and the searing white sun. "If it doesn't rain soon, the water situation could really get desperate. The creeks on the Bar B are almost dry, and I imagine the other ranches are in the same shape."

"I hadn't realized things were that bad," she said, ashamed that she hadn't thought of it. "Are the wells going dry, too?"

"So far, no, but they could."

All of the ranchers, big and small, kept their money in her father's bank. If they went broke, then the merchants would lose money, too. She had always imagined the bank as permanent, but in a flash she saw that it depended on the solvency of the people who used it, which could never be guaranteed. Prosper itself had seemed invulnerable to the vagaries of boomtowns, as firmly rooted as any of the cities back East, yet could it survive if a drought destroyed the ranches? People couldn't stay if there wasn't any way to make a living. Shops and stores would close, neighbors would move away, and Prosper would die.

Everything people built was so fragile, at the mercy of weather or disease or just plain bad luck, and survival was no more than a matter of chance.

She looked up at the sun with both fear and worry in her eyes. Luis was sorry he had mentioned the growing dry spell, for there was nothing that could be done. He was a fatalist; life had taught him to accept what couldn't be changed, and he had learned early that either you survived or you didn't. If a drought destroyed Prosper, then he would roll up his bedroll and saddle his horse, and when he left he would take Olivia with him. Life was too short to fret over changes. He could be just as happy with her sitting at a campfire as he could in a house with a roof over his head.

But she was already fretting about the people she knew who would be hurt by a drought, and he wanted to pull her head down to his shoulder and protect her from those worries. Instead he stretched out on the ground and pillowed his head on her lap, nestling down on the softness of her thighs.

The pressure of his head made her lower body tighten in reaction to his nearness. Olivia held her breath, almost overcome by the sensation flooding her. Her breasts began to throb and swell, yet at the same time she felt oddly protective toward him. Tentatively she touched his damp black hair, then smoothed it away from his forehead. He sighed as if in relief. Once she had touched him there seemed to be no reason why she shouldn't continue, so she began tracing the lines of his face with her fingertips.

His eyes were closed. "Umm, you smell good," he murmured, turning his face toward her. With his head on her lap he could smell the warm, female scents of her body, and he was growing hard.

Olivia smiled, thinking of the perfume she had applied that morning, glad that he liked it. She had even dabbed a bit between her breasts, feeling wicked as she did so. She wondered what he would do if she leaned forward so that her breasts were closer to his face. Would he nuzzle against her in search of the elusive sweet scent?

But she didn't dare, and regretfully she wished that ladies didn't always have to be retiring and genteel, to let the men take the lead. For that matter, ladies weren't even supposed to think of such things!

She looked down and saw that he was watching her and smiling, and she realized that she had heaved a sigh. "It's so hot," she said quickly, by way of explanation.

"Yes, it is. Why don't you unbutton your collar and roll your cuffs back?"

If she did, her immaculate starched blouse would be decidedly rumpled when she returned home, but she was feeling stifled, and baring her arms would bring a small measure of relief. She ignored the first part of his suggestion and briskly unfastened her cuffs, turning them back several times so her forearms were bared.

"That's good," he said, then he lifted his hand to the buttons at her throat.

She stilled, her blue eyes darkening as his strong, lean hand slowly released each tiny button in turn. Her collar loosened, and fresh air seeped in to cool her heated skin. His hand moved down past her collarbone. "That's enough," she said, trying to sound casual.

"Is it?" He didn't stop but unbuttoned the next one, then the next. And the next. The weight of his hand was lying between her breasts now, brushing them with every movement. His eyes held a hooded, sleepy sensuality. His mouth looked full, his lips slightly parted as if he waited for a delicious treat.

The beginning swells of her breasts were exposed, then the lacy edging of her shift. Slowly his fingers moved downward all the way to her waist, leaving her blouse gaping open in their wake. She sat very still, hardly even daring to breathe.

He shifted more onto his side, facing her. Slowly he pulled her blouse free of her waistband, then spread it open. Her lovely breasts were covered only by the thin cotton shift, her nipples clearly peaked beneath it. He traced both of them with a light fingertip, loving the delicacy of her, then moved closer and lifted his head just a bit to close his lips firmly around one of them.

Olivia bit her lip, her eyes closing at the feel of his mouth clamping down on her nipple. His mouth was hot and wet, and his tongue curled around the tip, stroking it through the damp cotton. Then he began to suck, and the rhythmic pulling started a fire that ran straight to her loins.

They were utterly silent. She heard the horses stamping nearby, the chomping of their big teeth on the grass. A small breeze rustled the leaves overhead, and insects droned lazily in the heat. He suckled her with a complete lack of urgency, not caressing her in any other way.

Until Luis, she hadn't known that a man would ever want to put his mouth on her breasts. She had thought of suckling babies but never imagined that such a maternal act could, with a man, be so erotic. The strong mouth working at her breast couldn't be mistaken for an infant's sweetness, nor could the rasp of his beard-roughened cheek against her soft skin. The secret flesh between her legs was throbbing in rhythm with the pull of his mouth, and she leaned helplessly forward to give him better access.

He responded by taking her deeper into his mouth. Her shift was so wet now that it might as well not have been there, but suddenly it was maddening. Frantically she shrugged her shoulders, letting the straps fall down her arms.

"Be still," he whispered around her nipple.

"No—wait. Here." She whispered, too, lifting her hand to push the loosened shift down over one breast, baring it. She guided the nipple back to his mouth and whimpered softly at the exquisite pleasure of his lips on her nakedness. She cradled his head in her arms and held him to her, suffused with warmth and desire.

Her body delighted in the sensations it was feeling, both subtle and intense. When he finally sat up away from her she made a low sound of regret, but he hushed her with a finger on her lips. "You'll like this, too." And he pulled off his shirt, revealing a broad, muscled chest with a diamond of soft, curly black hair stretching from nipple to nipple.

Olivia reached out to circle her fingertips around the tiny points, marveling at how different they were from hers. They hardened instantly, and she looked up in surprise to see a taut expression of enjoyment on his face. "They aren't so different after all," she murmured, stroking them again.

He put his hands over hers and guided them over his chest. "No, not so different. I love it when you touch me. I want to feel your hands on my bare skin. It feels the same to me as it does to you when I touch you."

His hands left hers, but she didn't move them. She liked it too much, liked the feel of his muscled body under her fingers. She slid them along his rib cage and let them lie there for a minute, enjoying the way his chest expanded and contracted with each breath. His stomach muscles were hard and flat, but the skin on his belly was silky smooth, indicating his vulnerability. Back at his chest again she felt the strong, steady pounding of his heart. His shoulders were wide and sleek and hard, the skin gleaming like satin in the sunlight. He was beautiful. Without thinking Olivia touched her lips to the tender skin just beside the shoulder joint, her tongue lightly tasting the faint saltiness of perspiration. Luis shuddered, and his hands closed hard on her waist, drawing her against him.

Incredibly, she had forgotten that her blouse was open and one breast bare. The warm, hard pressure of his chest against her brought a sharp cry from her, and slowly he turned her from side to side, rubbing her breasts on his hard body.

"Luis. *Luis!*"

"What is it, love?" he asked softly. "Do you want more?"

She dug her fingernails into his upper arms, gasping with the delight of it. "Yes," she said. "Please."

He laughed a little at her impeccable manners even when they were both so aroused it was all he could do to keep from taking her completely. Only his acute instinct about women held him back, for though he could easily seduce her, she wouldn't yet give herself to him out of love. And it was love he wanted from her, not the knowledge that he was skilled enough as a lover to make her body ready before her mind was. When she was truly ready she would let him know. Until then he was prepared to suffer excruciating torment in order for her to discover how much sheer enjoyment she could have with him.

He removed her blouse and let it drop to the ground, then slid the straps of her chemise all the way down and drew her arms free. The soft cotton draped around her waist, leaving her upper torso completely bare. She was blushing a little, her porcelain skin glowing. Shifting to his knees and drawing her up, too, he put his arms around her so that their bodies were together from shoulder to knee and began kissing her. He could feel her shiver with delight as her soft breasts flattened against the hard plains of his chest, feel the instinctive, startled recoil of her hips away from him as soon as she felt his arousal, but then shyly she returned. Her hips sought his, undulating gently as she instinctively searched for the most comfortable position, which was of course the most intimate. He groaned deep in his throat as she finally settled with her soft mound cradling his hardness, her legs parted slightly to make room for him. He thought that she might very well kill him with her own innocent brand of seduction.

"I want to lie naked with you," he murmured. "Every night, love. When you marry me I'll teach you everything a man and a woman can do together, and you'll enjoy every minute of it."

Olivia buried her face against his chest. He hadn't phrased it as a question, thereby relieving her of the necessity of answering. But he had said it so positively, as if he had no doubts she would marry him. Did *she* have any doubts? She didn't know. She was frightened of the sort of life he might expect her to lead, wandering about the country, but at the same time the thought of it excited her. She didn't know if she loved him, but she did know she could barely exist through the week, that she felt truly alive only on the one afternoon a week when she was with him. And she very much wanted him to show her everything about love-making.

Since meeting Luis she no longer had any doubts about the bond between Beatrice and Ezekiel Padgett. It was the sweet, hot bond of the flesh, the shared delights when they were together in bed. And would she, Olivia, ever settle for anything less now that she sensed what awaited her?

"I think I love you," she said, lifting her face to his. "But I'm not certain. The thought of marrying you frightens me almost as much as the thought of *not* marrying you. Would we go away from here? Would I have to leave my family?"

"Almost certainly," he replied, not lying to her. His heart was pounding as he realized how close he was to having what he wanted. Her lovely face was troubled as she thought of leaving the secure home she had known all her life. "We would have wonderful adventures together, making love beneath the stars, or taking a train wherever it might happen to go. And we would have babies, love, and a home where they could grow up safe and secure. Do you think your parents would like to keep their grandchildren occasionally while we take to the trail for a while?"

She laughed shakily, her mind whirling with the images he had described, but she couldn't answer the question about her parents. They would be horrified at the thought of their beloved only offspring marrying a drifter. They both wanted so much for her and would be terribly hurt and disappointed. They loved her, and she didn't think they would reject her no matter whom she married, but tears swam in her eyes at the thought of causing them pain. Still, she couldn't go on forever as she had been these past weeks, and neither could Luis.

She looked up at him with tear-wet eyes that held both pain and a promise. "I'll give you my answer soon," she whispered.

Dee walked out on the porch and held out a glass of cool lemonade to Olivia, who sat on the very edge of the rocking chair, keeping it tilted forward on the rockers. She studied Olivia's face, thinking that she had never before seen her friend as edgy as she was now.

"What's wrong?" she asked.

Olivia sipped her drink, then rolled the glass back and forth in her hands. She watched the motion of her own fingers as if fascinated. "I think I'm in love," she blurted. She drew a deep, shaky breath. "With Luis Fronteras. And I'm scared."

"Luis Fronteras?" Dee asked blankly. "Who's he?"

"He works for Kyle Bellamy. He's a Mexican. A drifter."

Dee gave a low whistle of astonishment and slowly took her own seat. This was like a queen taking up with a commoner.

"He wants me to marry him," Olivia continued.

"Are you going to?"

The look Olivia gave her was agonized. "I can't bear the thought of not seeing him again. But it will hurt my parents so, and I don't want that either. I don't know what to do."

Dee wasn't sure what advice to give her. She knew how important family was to Olivia, and she also knew how impossible it was to stay away from the man you loved, even when your common sense told you to.

"What is he like?"

"Gentle," Olivia said, then she frowned. "But I think he can be dangerous, too. It's just that he's always gentle with *me,* even when he's—" She broke off, and her face turned pink.

"Aroused?" Dee suggested helpfully, grinning when Olivia's flush deepened.

"Is Lucas gentle when *he's* aroused?" Olivia retorted with spirit. "And don't tell me you don't know, because I won't believe you. At the picnic he couldn't stop looking for you, and he left right after lunch and never came back. I've thought right from the beginning that he'd be perfect for you," she finished smugly.

"Perfect?" Dee said in disbelief. "He's overbearing and arrogant, and he—" She broke off, because she couldn't lie to either herself or Olivia. "I love him," she finished flatly. "Damn it."

Olivia threw herself back in the rocking chair with a whoop of laughter, sloshing the lemonade over the rim of the glass. "I knew it, I knew it! Well? Has he asked you to marry him?"

"He asked if marriage would be the price for Angel Creek. Not exactly the same thing." Dee managed a crooked smile. "The fact that I love him doesn't mean that he loves me."

"Well, he does," Olivia replied. "If you could have seen him at the picnic! He kept trying not to let it slip that he'd been seeing you, but he couldn't talk about anything else."

Dee went still. "He told other people about me?"

"No, he was just talking to me," Olivia reassured her. "He came here after he left the picnic, didn't he?"

"Yes."

Olivia cleared her throat, good manners wrestling with her curiosity. Curiosity won. "Does he . . . I mean, has he tried to . . . you know?"

"Make love to me?" Dee clarified in her blunt way.

Olivia flushed again but nodded.

"He's a man."

Dee evidently felt that her bald statement was explanation enough. Olivia decided to agree with her. "Do you like it when he touches you?" she asked in a rush. "I mean when he touches your . . ." She stopped, appalled at what she had been about to say. What if Dee hadn't permitted Lucas such intimacies? With her question she had practically admitted that she and Luis . . .

"Stop blushing," Dee ordered, though her own cheeks were growing warm.

"He has, then. Well? Did you like it?"

Confused, Dee wondered just what Olivia was asking and what part of the body she was thinking about. Caresses, or the actual sexual act? Then she shrugged, because the answer was the same regardless of the question. "Yes," she said.

Olivia closed her eyes on a sigh of relief. "I'm so glad," she said. "I thought I was wicked, even though Luis said everyone . . ." She stopped herself again and opened her eyes. She had never before had such an opportunity, and she felt giddy with the freedom. "Does he take your blouse off when he touches you there?"

Dee was beginning to feel harassed. "Yes."

"Has he ever taken the top of your shift down? So that he can see your—er—breasts?"

"Yes."

Though her face was bright red, Olivia wasn't about to stop. "Has he ever kissed you there? Like a baby, I mean, only different. Well, maybe it's the same—"

Dee erupted from her chair. "For God's sake!" she yelled, goaded beyond endurance. "If you must know, he's stripped me naked and done everything there is to do! And I enjoyed every minute of it!" She struggled with herself for control and took a deep breath. In a more moderate voice she said, "Maybe not every minute. It hurt the first time, but it was worth it. Though I do like it better when I'm on top."

Olivia's mouth moved, but no sound emerged. Her eyes were so huge they eclipsed her face. She shut her mouth.

They stared at each other in silence. Dee's lips twitched first. She gulped, then bent double as she shrieked with laughter.

Olivia pressed her hand to her mouth in an effort to stifle the unladylike sounds that were bubbling up, but it was a useless effort. She guffawed. That was the only word for it. The lemonade spilled in her lap.

When the hysterical fit of laughter had subsided into giggles they wiped their streaming eyes and struggled for composure. "Come inside and sponge your skirt," Dee said, her voice still shaky with mirth.

Olivia stood and followed her into the cabin. "Don't try to change the subject," she warned, and her shoulders began shaking again. "I want to know *all* about it. If you think I'm going to let a chance like this go by, you're crazy!"

"Ask Luis," Dee replied maddeningly, and it set them both off again.

13

Kyle Bellamy kicked at the dry creek bed, then looked up at the cloudless sky. It hadn't rained in six weeks. It might not rain for another six weeks. They didn't normally get that much rain anyway, but then they didn't usually need it because of the runoff from the snowcaps. But there hadn't been as much snow during the past winter, and now they weren't getting even the normal amount of rain. Who knew how long it would last? Droughts sometimes lasted for years, turning what had been fertile into wasteland. He'd never thought it would happen here, but hell, no one ever settled where they thought there'd be a drought.

He felt an almost sickening sense of panic. He had sworn that he'd make something of himself, something respectable, and he'd been close enough to taste it. Now the damn weather was turning it into dust, literally. The *weather!* Of all the ways he could have been done in, of all the things that could have caught up with him, it was the weather that would bring him to his knees.

There was only one creek left running now on the Bar B. When it dried up his cattle would die. Without the cattle he wouldn't have the ranch, wouldn't have the money to restock, because he'd just spent all of his capital to add to the herd. Damn, why hadn't he waited? But he'd wanted the ranch to expand, and now he was in danger of losing everything. He wouldn't be able to pay his men's wages, would end up as nothing . . . again.

God, he'd been so close. He had thought the years when he'd had to steal food to survive were finished. He had buried his memories of the little boy who lived in the streets of New Orleans and was sold into prostitution at the age of ten. He never let himself think about the man he had killed when he was just twelve, to escape the horror. He had thought he'd never again have to cheat or lie. All he'd wanted was to be like respectable folks everywhere, to be welcomed into people's homes and treated like someone who counted. He'd had that in Prosper. Only Tillie had known him when he had lived with scum, had lived *like* scum, and she would never tell. He and Tillie were alike, two misfits whose backgrounds couldn't bear close scrutiny—for different reasons—but he had chosen the path of respectability, and Tillie had chosen to be as unrespectable as a woman could get.

He had planned to marry, have kids, do all the normal, respectable things and wallow in the doing of them, for that was what he had never before had. His dream had come true for a while, yet now he could see it slipping away from him. Even his plans for Olivia Millican didn't seem to be going anywhere. He called on her, paid all sorts of attention to her, but she still remained maddeningly indifferent to him. Damn it, the banker's money would have made all the difference to him.

Now, unless it rained soon, all of his plans were going to be just like the ground he walked on: dust.

He had racked his brain trying to think of ways to beat the drought. He had thought of building long troughs and filling barrels with water from the well, then hauling the water out to the troughs. But he had too many cattle; they would go mad at the scent of water and trample one another trying to get to it, knocking the troughs over. He couldn't dump the water into the water holes, because the ground was so dry it would just soak it up. Hell, he probably didn't even have enough water in the well to fill more than a couple of barrels anyway. The water table had to be low, too.

Why had he bought more cattle? If the herd was smaller, there would be more graze and water to go around.

Maybe he could sell off part of the herd. They were too thin; he'd lose money if he did, but not as much as he'd lose if they all died. But he was afraid they wouldn't survive the cattle drive to a railhead, either.

He wasn't the only one who was hurting. People in town were getting by fine and would be all right as long as their wells held out. But the other ranchers were all in the same fix he was in; the only creek still running that he knew of was Angel Creek, and he didn't guess it had ever gone dry.

It could have been his. It *should* have been his. He'd never thought the Swann woman would be so stubborn about selling, but she wouldn't even talk about it. He'd even asked her to marry him when it had become obvious she wasn't about to sell, but she'd turned that down, too. The only time in his life he'd asked any woman to marry him, and she hadn't even hesitated before refusing. The funny thing was, by then the land hadn't been his only reason for asking. Dee Swann was a damn fine-looking woman, with those witch-green eyes, and she was respected in town. Maybe not well liked, but they sure respected her. And she was tough enough that she didn't give a damn if they liked her or not.

She was sitting in that rich little valley with all of that water, not doing anything but raising that garden of hers and letting all the rest of the land lie fallow. It was wonderful grazing, the vegetation fed by the creek even when there wasn't any rain, and it was going to waste.

After she had refused to marry him he had followed the creek out of the valley, thinking that maybe he could divert it toward his land. To his surprise the creek bed had veered sharply to the east and dissipated at the foot of the mountains, seeping underground through porous rock to emerge again only God knew where. It came from the mountains and went back to the mountains, detouring only through that little valley and creating some of the best land he had ever seen.

The Bar B had been good land—not as good as Angel Creek, but good ranch land. In the four years he'd been there the rain had come regularly and the water holes had stayed fresh. He'd always worried more about the winters than about the summers, afraid a blizzard would wipe him out, but instead there hadn't been enough snow this past year, and the runoff hadn't been sufficient. Now one rainless summer was destroying a lifetime of dreams.

He mounted his horse, his handsome face drawn as he looked around. Everything still looked green, but it was deceptive. The vegetation was dry and brittle, making a faint crackling sound whenever a breeze stirred. He would have railed at fate if it would have done any good, but he had learned while still a boy in the muddy streets that the only help to be had was what he could provide for himself. Cursing, as well as praying, was a waste of breath.

There was only one person he could talk to about it, only one person who would understand what it meant to him. Not even the other ranchers could know how hard this hit him. Since it was still early afternoon he counted on the saloon being almost empty, and when he got there he found it was. Tillie wasn't in sight, though, and he scowled at the thought that she might be with a customer. Verna, the other saloon girl, was propped against the bar chatting with the bartender. She straightened when she saw Kyle walk in.

"Is Tillie upstairs?" he asked, ignoring the look of disappointment on Verna's face. He imagined she heard that question too often. It couldn't be easy for her, being essentially in competition with Tillie for what business Prosper could provide. Knowing Tillie, though, she probably often sent men Verna's way.

"She went over to the hat shop," Verna replied.

Kyle got a shot glass of whiskey from the bartender and sat down to wait, but he wasn't a patient man, and it quickly got on his nerves. Hell, what did he care if the townspeople saw him walking with Tillie? He was going to lose the ranch, so what did his carefully cultivated respectability matter? When it came down to it, he'd been born a gutter rat and would die one, no matter how hard he tried to change things.

When he found her Tillie was just leaving the shop, a hatbox held in her hands like an offering. She never gave any indication in public that she knew him, and now she started past him without even glancing in his direction. Kyle stopped her, taking the hatbox from her hands and tucking it under his arm. "I'll walk you back to the saloon."

She lifted her eyebrows in surprise. "You shouldn't be seen with me like this. None of the mamas will want you courting their daughters."

"I don't give a damn," he said under his breath.

She began strolling down the sidewalk. "After all the work you've done to make a place for yourself here?"

He didn't want to talk about it on the street. His emotions were too raw, his disappointment too strong.

Not many people were out stirring around in the heat, but he saw heads swiveling to watch his progress down the street with Tillie. It would be all over town by nightfall that Kyle Bellamy had been parading around town with one of the saloon girls, as brassy as if he didn't know any better. And he simply didn't care. What he cared about was his ranch, and the lack of rain. Let them pass judgment if they wanted. He was sick and tired of the whole charade, pretending to be a gentleman when he didn't have a genteel bone in his body.

The saloon was blessedly cool after the harsh glare of the sun. The bartender didn't pay them any mind as they started up the stairs. Verna watched them go with a hint of envy in her expression.

When they were in her room Tillie sat down before her mirrored vanity and slowly began removing hat pins from the delicate froth of velvet and veiling that had been perched on her head. She never visited any of the shops while dressed in the immodest, brightly colored dresses she wore in the saloon. The dress she had on was as demure as any of the dresses the good wives of the town wore to church, but it had probably cost considerably more. Tillie's taste in clothes ran toward the expensive. The bronze fabric was wonderfully flattering to her complexion. He reached out and fingered her sleeve, thinking that her love of good clothes was probably the last remnant of her former life.

"Open that hatbox for me," she said. Her rich brown eyes held a mixture of excitement and satisfaction. Tillie adored hats.

Kyle obeyed, taking the top off and lifting out a small bit of fur and velvet. The hat was a dark burgundy color, the fur was black, and a dashing little black plume curled around the edge. The half veil was attached to the hat with twin cascades of dark red rhinestones. It looked ridiculous in his big hand, but Tillie set it on her head and angled it over one eye, and it was immediately transformed into a masterpiece.

"Miss Wesner does such good work," she purred, turning her head from side to side in sublime satisfaction. "I designed the hat, and she made it exactly as I described it."

"And now you have to have a gown made to match it."

"Of course." She met his eyes in the mirror and gave him a slow smile. She must have seen something in his face, because the smile faded and she briskly removed the hat, swiveling to face him. "What's wrong?"

"The drought," he said simply. "I'm losing the ranch."

She was silent. She knew what drought meant, knew that nature was both fickle and merciless.

"I only have one creek still running, and it's low," he said. "When it dries up the cattle will start dying. I tried, but I've lost."

"You've started over before. Do it again."

"Why bother? I'm beginning to think I should have stayed with the cards. At least then I could do something about a run of bad luck."

Tillie shook her head. "You'd have gotten killed. You're a good cheat, but you aren't that good. I could always spot you."

He pinched her chin. "Only because you're so damn good at it yourself, darlin'."

Tillie shrugged, saying nothing. Kyle examined her exquisite face, searching for some sign of the life she had led in either her skin or her expression, but she looked as serene as a nun. She hadn't changed much at all from the days of her girlhood in New Orleans. "Why don't you go back?" he asked suddenly. "You could do it. No one would have to know."

She didn't move but subtly withdrew anyway, her expression going blank. "Why would I want to go back?"

"Your family is one of the richest in Louisiana. Why would

you want to live like this, in one room over a saloon, when you can have a mansion?"

"I couldn't tolerate it when I was a girl," she said gently. "The rules, the restrictions, being treated like a brainless doll. I've been on my own a long time now, making my own decisions, good or bad. How could I go back, even if my father would allow me in the house, knowing that at best it would be just the same? At worst, he would keep me locked up so I couldn't damage the family reputation any more than I already have."

"Does your family know where you are?"

"No. They think I'm dead. I arranged it that way."

"Then your father could be dead by now, and you wouldn't know about it."

"I occasionally get news from New Orleans. He was still alive six months ago. I don't wish him dead," she said, smiling at Kyle. "He's my father. He isn't a wicked man, just very strict, and I couldn't live like that. It's best this way. But why are we talking about me when we should be discussing your plans?"

"I don't have any. I tried, and I lost."

"It isn't like you to give up," she chided.

"I've never wanted anything this much before. I can't imagine working up any interest in anything else."

She touched his cheek in sympathy, her slim fingers cool on his skin. "It could rain tomorrow. Or the day after. And I have money. I can always stake you to get you going again."

He shook his head. "You'll probably need it. If the ranches go under, so will this town. You'll have to set yourself up somewhere else."

"Things haven't gotten that bad yet. I always hope for the best."

"But prepare for the worst." Over the years he had run into her in different places, and at varying degrees of prosperity. He had seen her ragged and hungry, but even then she had always been planning, never wasting what little money she had. They had even thrown in together for a while, living off his winnings at cards, always ready to dodge out of town if anyone spotted his light touch with the pasteboards. They had huddled together under one thin blanket on frigid nights during the worst of their luck and spent three whole days and nights making love in a soft hotel bed once when they had hit a lucky streak.

Then they had gone their separate ways, for some reason he no longer remembered. Likely she had just had her own plans, and he had had his. He hadn't seen her again until they had both wound up, by sheer coincidence, in Prosper. But maybe it wasn't such a big coincidence, for they had both been looking for the same thing: a quiet, steady little town. They had both worked boomtowns and knew it was no way to live. Boomtowns were too violent. Security was better.

"If you change your mind about the money," she said, "all you have to do is ask."

"I know."

He felt a surge of desire for her. He never tired of making love to Tillie. They had known each other for so long, made love so often, that they were entirely comfortable together. He knew just how to touch her and did so, reaching out to fondle her breast with the exact degree of pressure that she liked. She inhaled sharply, her eyes darkening. "Well," she said. "I see your spirits have revived."

He took her hand and placed it on the front of his pants. "That isn't a spirit, but it sure has revived."

"Darling," she purred, "it's never been dead."

They undressed leisurely, pausing often for kisses and unhurried caresses. She started to go down on her knees and take him into her mouth, but he stopped her because, despite his slow pace, he felt that would be more than he could stand, and he wanted it to last longer than that. He put her on the bed and made love to her, using the advantage of his intimate knowledge of her to take her to the peak twice before he allowed himself release.

Afterward, as they lay quietly together, he felt a small measure of contentment. He might lose the ranch, but after all, he still had Tillie. She had always been there when he needed her. He only hoped he had been as good a friend to her as she had been to him.

14

Kyle was drunk even though it was only early afternoon. He seldom allowed himself the excess because men who drank too much often said too much, and he wanted to keep his past life just that, in the past. But there were some occasions that seemed to call for drink, and watching his ranch die qualified as one of them.

Besides, he didn't have anything else to do, unless he wanted to ride out and look at the land drying up. If he wanted to see water, he'd have to ride all the way over to Angel Creek.

Now that was an idea, he mused. Maybe if he offered the Swann woman even more than he had before, she'd accept this time. Not that he had the money, but she didn't know that. All he needed was her signature on a bill of sale. He'd start moving his cattle in and worry about the money later. Like the old saying went, possession was nine tenths of the law.

That was what he'd do. He'd offer her so much money she'd have to be stupid to turn it down.

He wasn't so drunk that he couldn't ride, and soon he was on his horse. At least he was doing something, and that was a relief. It was the helpless waiting that drove him crazy, but patience never had been his long suit.

Entering the Angel Creek valley was like traveling to a different part of the country. Where the ground was cracking with dryness on the Bar B and the pastures were turning brown, here the earth was softened by the underground moisture, and the meadow grasses grew tall. It even felt cooler. He reined in, thinking in confusion that it couldn't *actually* be cooler, but then he decided that it really was. He frowned until the slight breeze on his face told the story. The valley acted like a funnel to the breezes coming down from the mountains, sweeping the cooler air downward. It was still hot, but not as hot as it was everywhere else.

The Swann woman came out on the porch when she heard his horse, and she had that damn shotgun in her hands, just the way she had the other times he'd talked to her. She'd never threatened him with it, but he'd never been able to forget it was there, either.

She stood as proud as any of the high-nosed New Orleans ladies of his youth, even though she worked the soil like a man and her clothes were plain and old. Hell, Tillie dressed better than she did. But her head was held high on her slender neck, and those witch-green eyes were rock steady. "Mr. Bellamy," was all she said in greeting.

He didn't dismount. He just leaned forward, resting his arms on his saddle horn. "I'll double my last offer for this place."

She arched her brows, and he saw the gleam of amusement in her eyes. "Your last offer was marriage. Are you saying you'll marry me twice?"

He wasn't in the mood for sarcasm. "I need this land. I need the water. My cattle are going to die if they don't have water, and you have just about the only good creek for a hundred miles or more."

Dee sighed and looked at the cloudless blue sky. Why couldn't it rain? "I'm sorry, Mr. Bellamy, but I won't sell to you." She did feel sorry for him; she felt sorry for every rancher, big and small, and every farmer. But she couldn't take care of them all, couldn't parcel out the water that ran through her land.

Kyle reined his horse around and rode away without another word. He was so angry he couldn't speak anyway. Damn her! She just wouldn't listen to reason. She was using only a little more than an acre of the land and letting the rest of it go to waste, but still she hung on to every inch as if it would kill her to let it go. For the sake of her piss-ant vegetable garden his cattle were going to die.

No, by God, they weren't.

He was almost sober by the time he got back home, but his anger hadn't abated, and neither had his savage determination.

One of the cowhands was coming out of the barn. "Get Pierce!" Kyle yelled. "And Fronteras!"

The two men were out on the range, so it was late when they finally trudged up to the house where he waited. "We start rounding up the cattle tomorrow," Kyle said. His voice was abrupt and still angry.

Pierce slowly nodded, as if he had to consider the idea before giving it his approval.

Luis was curious. "Where are we taking them?"

"Into the Angel Creek valley."

Pierce said, "That Swann woman's place?"

"I talked to her today," Kyle replied, knowing that they would assume she had given him permission to graze his cattle on her land.

Pierce nodded again. "Valley's small. You want all of the cattle?"

"Yes." The cattle would quickly overgraze, but at least they would have water. His mind was made up. No matter what Dee Swann said or did, his cattle were going into that valley.

Rounding up the cattle wasn't easy. They didn't want to leave what little water they had and tended to stray every chance they got. Everyone on the Bar B worked all the daylight hours the next day and got up before dawn on the second day to start again. The men felt as if they'd grown to their saddles.

It was late morning of the third day before they began moving the herd, and they reached the mouth of the little valley in the middle of the afternoon.

Dee had gotten up early that morning to weed the garden before the heat got bad. She couldn't remember it ever being so hot before, and the plants were beginning to show it. They were growing, but she was afraid the crops were going to be stunted, burned by the sun.

The ranchers had to be in bad shape. She hadn't been into town for the past few weeks, but the last time she had gone everyone had been talking about how dry it was, and how it was hurting the grazing. Kyle Bellamy had been desperate when he'd ridden out to try to buy her land, and sympathy stirred in her as she remembered his face.

She wondered how Lucas was doing. She had seen him only once since the time he had tried to talk her into selling out; it had been just after the vote to ratify the constitution, and he had been jubilant over that, but tired from work and worried about the lack of water. She had wanted to assure him that everything would be all right, but the words would have been useless. How could she assure rain?

If the drought continued and his cattle died, would he ever forgive her?

She straightened and looked at the sun, already feeling its heat though it was still early in the morning. Her chest felt tight. She had no control over the weather, but she did have Angel Creek.

Lucas wanted her land. Like Kyle Bellamy, he had even offered marriage in an effort to obtain it. Every day since then she had lived with the knowledge that he hadn't wanted her for herself, but for the land. It lay cold and heavy in her breast, and time only seemed to make it grow heavier. It didn't help that she had realized the basis of his attraction to her right from the beginning, because like a fool she had fallen in love with him anyway. She couldn't even let herself attach any importance to their lovemaking, for Lucas was undeniably lusty by nature, and she thought any willing woman would have sufficed for his needs.

Sometimes she thought about riding up to the Double C and telling him that she had changed her mind, that she was willing to marry him if he was still interested. She would play the scene through in her mind right up to the part where he accepted; then her pride would reject the idea, and she knew she would hate her-

self if she did it. She had always planned to live alone, enjoyed
living alone. She still did enjoy her life, but for the first time she
wanted more.

She wanted Lucas. It wasn't just physical, though she yearned
for the smell and touch of him, for the release given by his driving
possession. She wanted more. She had never had an entire night
with him, only a few stolen hours. She had never faced a dawn
after sheltering the dark hours in his arms, or watched him shave.
She wanted years of thunderous arguments; living with a man like
Lucas would keep her on her toes. He would ride roughshod over
a woman who didn't stand up to him. It was a kind of strength she
had never before seen in a man; she was used to doing the intimidating. Lucas not only matched her, he gave her an unspoken
compliment by not holding himself back as if she were a frail
flower who would collapse under the storm of his temper.

If he married her in order to get Angel Creek, she would have
those years she coveted, but she wouldn't have his love, and she
wouldn't have self-respect.

Yet she loved him, and he needed her. Rather, he needed her
land.

She looked at her garden. The plants were strong and green,
just beginning to bear fruit with the long summer weeks of ripen-
ing ahead. Despite the lack of rain they were flourishing, fed by
the creek that kept the rich soil moist.

Perhaps Lucas could move some of his cattle into the valley. A
fence could be built around the cabin and garden to protect
them. He couldn't bring the cattle over the pass, but it would
only take a couple of days to bring a herd around the base of the
mountain. She saw no reason why he wouldn't agree to the plan;
the cattle could even winter there.

If necessary, if he refused to accept the favor, she would sell
Angel Creek to him. It would be like selling part of her heart, but
she couldn't stand by and let his cattle die when she had the
means of preventing it.

Accepting that was a blow that made her eyes sting as she
looked around at her home. Saying that she loved it only
scratched the surface. Over the years as she had worked the soil,
coaxed life out of it, she had found a contentment that went

deeper than love. It wasn't just the satisfaction of making things grow, it was everything about Angel Creek, the utter perfection of it. Her soul had taken root there, sinking deep into the earth. She could live in other places, but none would ever be like this, where she so completely, overwhelmingly *fit*.

Yet for Lucas she would give it up.

He had such big dreams, such towering ambitions. He'd achieve them, too, if the Double C survived this drought. Colorado was on the verge of statehood, and he was on the verge of putting his plans into action. He deserved the chance to do it. Men like Lucas were different from other men; he was a leader, a man who got things done.

She had never been to the Double C, never been up to the narrow pass Lucas used to enter the valley. Except for her trips into town she hadn't strayed from Angel Creek since the day her family had first settled on it. Even if she had been familiar with the way to the Double C she wouldn't have gone, for the mere fact that she had visited Lucas Cochran would be so out of character for her that immediately her relationship with him would have been suspected. Regardless of that, she would go to the ranch and tell him her decision.

After all, it was the way she lived that had necessitated secrecy, for anything less than a spotless reputation would have endangered her. A woman alone couldn't take too many precautions. But if she lived in town, she wouldn't have to be so careful. She and Lucas could be discreet about the extent of their intimacy, but they wouldn't have to conceal their relationship entirely. That was assuming, of course, that they would even have a relationship after Lucas had gotten what he wanted from her, namely Angel Creek.

It was afternoon, and the sun was searing when she finished her chores and went inside to wash off in cool water. Now that she had faced what she had to do in order to live with herself she was restless, filled with impatience to get it over with. Maybe Lucas would accept her offer to graze his cattle in the valley, and she wouldn't have to uproot herself. If he insisted on buying the land, she wanted to get it over and done with, like a dose of bitter medicine.

After washing she changed into clean clothes and stood for a minute looking around. The next couple of hours would decide if she lived here or not, and for a moment the idea of leaving was so hard to bear that she let her head drop forward as she fought tears.

Then a sound made her lift her head, listening. That sounded like cattle bawling. And thunder; she thought she heard thunder. Hope rising, she went to the window and bent to look out. Not a cloud in sight. The bull and both cows were placidly grazing, but she still heard cattle bawling, or something that sounded like it.

She stepped out on the porch, her head tilted to the side as she listened curiously. Her gaze settled on a cloud of dust that was rising above the trees, and she stared at it blankly for a moment before an expression of horror crossed her face. She darted back inside, got the shotgun, and crammed her pockets full of extra shells.

The first of the cattle came into view. Knowing she didn't have a moment to waste, she put the shotgun to her shoulder and fired just over their heads, hoping to spook them the other way.

The cattle milled around in confusion, excited by the smell of water but nervous at the boom of the shotgun. She shot the other barrel and quickly reloaded, her heart pounding so hard in her chest that she felt sick. If the cattle got into the garden, they would destroy it.

"Put the shotgun down," Kyle Bellamy yelled. He rode toward her, a rifle in his hands. "The cattle are going through here."

"Not on my land," she replied fiercely. The valley was narrow, and the cabin was close to the mouth of it; he'd have to herd the cattle right between the cabin and the barn, and the unprotected garden was right behind the cabin. What the cattle didn't trample, they'd eat.

The herd hadn't turned. She fired again, and this time she aimed low enough to hit the cattle. At that distance the buckshot stung without doing a lot of damage, and the cattle bawled in panic, turning sharply away from both the noise and the pain.

The leading edge of the herd turned back into the others. She shot a fourth time, and they began bolting.

A rifle cracked, and the wood behind her splintered.

She dodged back into the cabin and slammed the door, hurriedly ramming shells into the shotgun as she did so. With a quick swing of the barrel she knocked the glass out of the window and shot again.

Cursing with every breath, Kyle shot back. "Get the cattle!" he yelled at his men. "Goddammit, turn them around."

Some of the men were already trying. Others had drawn their pistols at the sound of gunfire. They all knew about the Swann woman, knew she tended to greet people with a shotgun. She'd even peppered a few men who'd tried to keep company with her, the bad-tempered bitch. She shouldn't treat people like that. If the boss was intending to give her a taste of her own medicine, that was fine with them. Sporadically at first, then with increasing regularity, they began shooting at the cabin.

Luis reined his horse off to the side, his lean, dark face taut with anger and his hand on his pistol butt. He didn't know what the hell had gotten into Bellamy, but he didn't intend to make war on a lone woman.

He was good with a pistol, but not good enough to take on twenty men in a blood lust. For a split second he considered killing Bellamy, then realized that wouldn't stop it. He didn't have a lot of time to get help before the sons of bitches either killed the woman or overran her cabin and raped her; he'd seen enough blood lust to know that it wouldn't make any difference to them which it was.

The cattle were stampeding wildly, panicked by the gunfire, maddened by the smell of water. A thick cloud of dust billowed over everything, cutting visibility. Luis went with the cattle, yelling to agitate them even more, then finally broke free to turn his horse toward Prosper.

He rode the animal hard even in the heat, and it was white with lather by the time he reined it to a halt in front of the marshal's office. He jumped down, his booted feet thudding on the sidewalk as he shoved the door open. The office was empty.

The most logical place to look was the saloon. If the marshal wasn't there, someone would likely know his whereabouts.

But the marshal was nowhere in sight when he entered the saloon. "Where's Marshal Cobb?" he asked of anyone in the saloon.

"Don't rightly know," a man said. Luis recognized him as a shopkeeper.

"I thought I heard he's visitin' his daughter up Denver way for a few days," another said. "You got trouble?"

"Bellamy's trying to run his cattle into the Swann woman's valley," Luis said curtly. "There's shooting going on, and it'll be either a raping or a killing if it isn't stopped."

Everyone in the saloon was silent. Luis looked around at the men, but none of them were jumping to help. "Since the marshal's gone, are any of you willing to help that woman?"

Eyes shifted away. For the most part the men in the saloon at that time of day were townsfolk, merchants and clerks. They hadn't cleaned their weapons in years. If a bunch of rowdy cowhands had gone wild, they weren't going to stick their noses into it, at least as long as it stayed out of town. It wasn't like Dee Swann was a friend or anything; she always kept to herself.

Ranchers would have had weapons handy and been willing to help, but there weren't any ranchers in the saloon. They were too busy during the day doing what they could to keep their cattle alive. Luis turned away in disgust, his dark eyes going cold.

"Wait," Tillie said, hurrying toward him. She stepped out on the sidewalk, her hand on his arm. She looked pale. "Lucas Cochran on the Double C will help."

"She doesn't have that kind of time," Luis said harshly.

Tillie's brown eyes were huge and anguished. "Then you go back and help her, and I'll ride to the Double C."

Luis gave a brief nod, already turning away. "You'd better hurry."

He cut overland, pushing his tired horse hard and coming in from the side. He could still hear gunfire, which meant that the woman was holding her own. Despite his grimness his mouth twisted in a grin. She must be a real hellcat. A woman like that deserved all the help she could get.

He left his horse and worked his way the last hundred yards on foot, choosing a thick stand of trees for cover. Bellamy and his men had pretty well settled in their own cover and were taking their time squeezing off shots at the cabin. Some kept trying to work their way around and catch her from behind, but the cabin was in a large clear area, and there wasn't a lot of cover for them to use. The woman was a good shot. She was using a rifle now and was moving from window to window.

Luis considered his strategy. He didn't care about keeping either his identity or his position hidden; his only objective was to help the Swann woman prevent them from overrunning her cabin, or maybe turning the cattle back onto her land. It might even help if Bellamy's men knew he was helping her; though he had lived a calm life in Colorado, his skill with a pistol was well known. It might make some of them reconsider if they knew he was waiting for them.

Time was both their ally and their enemy. If he and the woman could hold off long enough, the Double C men would be able to get there. If aid didn't arrive by nightfall, then Bellamy's men would be able to reach the cabin undetected.

With that in mind, he cooly began choosing his targets. His purpose wasn't to keep them pinned down, but to rebalance the odds in his favor as much as he could. If a man was dead or severely wounded, then you didn't have to worry about him even in the dark. His mouth moved into a thin, cold smile. Hell, he'd spent enough time in Colorado anyway.

Tillie didn't take the time to change into riding clothes or to ask permission to borrow the nearest horse. By the time Luis was galloping out of town in one direction she was galloping in the other. Her garish short skirt made it possible for her to ride astride, though her legs were bared from the knee down. She glimpsed several shocked faces as she raced out of town but didn't spare a thought for the picture she made.

Her heart was pounding as hard as the horse's hooves on the packed earth. Oh, Kyle! she thought. Why had he done it? She would have lent him the money; no one would ever have known, and he could have kept his ranch, kept his dream of being a prosperous, respected rancher. Now he had attacked Dee Swann, and the townspeople would never forget, never accept him. It didn't matter that he had done it out of desperation; he would be condemned. And if Lucas Cochran didn't get there before Dee was raped or murdered, Kyle would be hanged.

The saddle leather rubbed raw patches on the insides of her tender thighs, but she didn't dare slow down, not when every minute counted. It would take Lucas a long time to get to Angel Creek anyway, maybe too long. At least Dee had Fronteras helping her now—unless they were both killed.

The horse began to tire. Panic welled up in her, but she refrained from kicking the poor beast. If she killed it by running it too hard in this heat, she would never reach the Double C in time. But the urge to hurry beat within her like bird wings until her head echoed with the refrain, *Hurry, before it's too late.* Too late for Dee, too late for Kyle . . . too late for herself.

Then she saw the ranch buildings. The Double C ranch house was two-storied, with a white-columned porch wrapped all the way around it. She didn't pull on the reins until she reached it, and the exhausted horse stumbled clumsily.

"Lucas!" she screamed even as she slid from the saddle. "Lucas!" She ran up on the porch and pounded on the door with her fist.

"Here! Tillie, I'm over here."

She turned and saw him striding up from the barn, his long legs eating up the distance. She ran down the steps and sprinted across the yard toward him, screaming the entire way. "You've got to get down to Angel Creek! They've gone crazy, they're shooting at her, trying to take the land—"

She reached him, and he grabbed her arms to halt her. His blue eyes had turned to ice. If hell had been cold, it would have looked like his eyes. "Who is it?" His fingers bit into her soft arms. She gasped for breath, and he roughly shook her. "Damn it, who is it?"

"It's Kyle," she said, still gulping air. "Kyle Bellamy. He's desperate—the Bar B's water is almost gone."

Lucas turned, roaring for everyone to get their rifles and saddle up. Every man within hearing ran to obey. Lucas sprinted for his own mount. Tillie ran after him, her red taffeta skirts kicking up and showing her petticoats.

"Luis Fronteras is helping her," she yelled. "He rode into town and sent me after you, then he went back."

Lucas gave a brief nod to show that he'd heard. The tight sense of panic in his chest eased a little as he realized Dee wasn't facing Bellamy and his men all alone.

He swung into the saddle, and Tillie grabbed his leg. "Don't kill Kyle," she begged frantically. "God, Lucas, please don't kill him. I love him. Please, please don't kill him, promise me."

Lucas looked down at her, that icy look still in his eyes. "I can't make any promises," he said. If Bellamy had harmed Dee, he wouldn't see another sunrise.

Lucas put spurs to his horse, riding hard for the pass that would get him to Angel Creek faster than any other way. Tillie stood in the yard and watched the men ride out, and tears slowly tracked down her dusty face.

15

Dee crouched beneath one of the front windows. She had discarded the shotgun in favor of the rifle, for accuracy, but she was running out of shells. She had prepared for a lot of things, but never for a siege, and that's what this was.

At least they hadn't turned the cattle. Maybe the men hadn't tried but had turned their attention to her. After all, if she were dead, then they could move the cattle in without trouble.

She didn't know how long it had been going on because one of the shots had hit her clock, and she had no idea what time it was. Late afternoon. The sun was red and low in the sky. Come dark, they would approach the cabin, and she wouldn't be able to cover all the windows. She had already blocked the bedroom door so that even if anyone crawled through the bedroom window he wouldn't be able to come up behind her without her knowledge.

She gripped the rifle as she carefully watched for someone to make a careless move and show himself. The wood stock was slippery, and she wiped her hand on her skirt, but it didn't seem to help. She looked down and saw that it wasn't sweat on her hand, but blood. Some of the flying glass had cut her arm.

She was tired, deathly tired, but she didn't dare rest for even a minute. She was thirsty but couldn't even cross the room for a drink of water.

There. A slight movement, a hint of blue. Dee carefully sighted down the barrel and squeezed the trigger, not even hearing the sharp crack as the rifle fired. She saw a brief commotion of movement and knew she'd hit someone.

Immediately another volley of shots struck the little cabin, gouging out long splinters of wood, ricocheting off the wood stove. She flattened herself on the floor as a bullet zinged across the room, gaining herself more cuts from the shattered glass that covered the floor. There wasn't a piece of glass left in any of the windows.

Quickly she sat up, swinging the rifle around. One man darted from cover, and she fired, sending him diving back. Damn, she'd missed him.

It would be dark soon. She had to do something, but there was nothing she could do. If she fired without seeing a target, she would waste her bullets, but if she simply waited, they would win anyway.

She wiped her bloody hands on her skirt again. God, she was bleeding all over from cuts. Her clothes were soaked.

She didn't care. She was thinking with an awful clarity. Those men were in a blood lust, and if they didn't kill her outright, they would each take a turn raping her. And she knew she would rather die. They would not violate her body, the flesh that she had shared only with Lucas—not while she drew breath. Her instinct was to fight, and she supposed it was too late now to start going against her instincts. If she had to die, she intended to take as many of those bastards with her as she could.

She scrambled to her knees, put the rifle to her shoulder, and began firing. The rifle was a repeater, so she shot until it was empty, then hastily reloaded and began firing again. Return fire tore into the cabin.

The window frame splintered, and she fell back with a stifled scream. Her left shoulder burned like fire, and she glanced down to see a long, thin sliver of wood protruding from it. She tried to pull it out, but her fingers were too slippery to hold it. Since there was nothing she could do, she put it and the pain out of her mind.

Luis had attracted a lot of attention once Bellamy and his men had noticed they were being fired on from two positions. He had been hit twice—once a shallow burn on his left bicep that he had ignored, the second time in his right side. The wound hadn't hit any internal organs, but it had bled like a son of a bitch. He had pulled off his bandanna, pressed it over the long gouge, and resumed firing, but soon the blood was streaming down his hip and leg.

He had to have more pressure on the wound. He transferred the pistol to his left hand and pressed his right elbow hard against his side. A wave of dizziness made him shake his head in an effort to clear his vision. If Cochran didn't get there at once, it would be too late. The woman was still shooting, but it would be dark soon, and he was losing too much blood to be able to help her.

Lucas split up his men, sending some of them to circle around behind Bellamy while he and the rest of them approached unseen down the slope, keeping the barn between them and the line of fire. Because of the large clearing around the cabin none of Bellamy's men had been able to work around to the side, and Dee was concentrating all of her fire to the front, where they were using the trees as cover. The surge of relief he felt when he heard her firing steadily made him feel weak. They were in time. Damn, what a woman!

He had to wait until his men who had flanked Bellamy had made their move, then his group began firing from the side. Bellamy didn't have a chance under the savage crossfire of the Double C men. Lucas realized that Dee was still shooting; she didn't know what was happening and was likely to kill some of his own men if she wasn't stopped. "I'm going into the cabin," he yelled. "Keep their heads down."

He ran toward the back stoop under the protection of a hail of bullets, but someone spied him anyway, and a bullet kicked up dust just in front of him. With all the lead flying it wasn't healthy for a man to stand and politely knock at a door; Dee would probably cut him in half with the shotgun anyway before she knew who he was. He leapt up on the back stoop and hit the door at a dead run, driving his muscled shoulder into it and sending it crashing back against the wall. Dee was at one of the front windows, and she scrabbled clumsily around, screaming as she fired the rifle. His heart clenched in pure terror when he saw her covered in blood, but he didn't pause for even a second. He dived to the floor, rolling to the side and coming up to lunge for her. She was still screaming as she swung the rifle at his head.

"Dee!" he yelled, grabbing her. "Goddammit, it's me, Lucas!" He wrested the rifle out of her bloody hands and tossed it aside, then wrapped his arms around her.

She shrieked, trying to throw herself backward even as she pounded at his face with her fists. Her eyes were wild, the pupils shrunk to tiny pinpoints.

"Dee!" he roared again, just trying to hold her still. She was hurt—God, she was hurt, and he didn't want to cause her any more pain, but he had to calm her down. He wrestled her down to the glass-covered floor, pinning her with his heavy weight. "Dee," he repeated, saying her name over and over. "Look at me. It's all right. I'm here, and I'll take care of you. Look at me."

Slowly she stilled, more from exhaustion than comprehension. She was quivering from head to foot, but at least she had quit fighting him. Her wild eyes were fastened on his face as if she were trying to make sense of what was happening. He kept talking to her, his voice low and soothing, and finally she blinked as understanding dawned. "Lucas," she murmured.

He was there. He was really there. She was conscious of relief, not so much because she was safe but because she could rest now. She was tired, so very, very tired, and oddly cold. The pain that she had held at bay for so long finally caught up with her as she let her tired muscles relax. She heard herself make a strange moaning sound, and her body loosened into total limpness. Her head lolled on the plank flooring.

Lucas could barely breathe. She was drenched in blood, her clothing soaked, even her hair matted with it. For the first time he noticed a long sliver of wood stuck in her shoulder, and he felt sick. As gently as he could he released her and got to his feet. He kicked the furniture she had piled against the bedroom door away and jerked a blanket from the bed, shaking it to make certain it didn't have glass on it, too, then replacing it. Returning to the other room, he lifted Dee as carefully as possible and carried her to the bed.

He looked around for a lamp, but they had all been broken. He examined her as thoroughly as possible in the dim light, his heart pounding as he looked for gunshot wounds. A bullet had creased her left hipbone, and she had that wicked splinter in her shoulder, but all of her other wounds were cuts from the broken glass. She was covered with them—small cuts on her scalp and face, her neck and shoulders and arms. Taken separately, her wounds were not serious, but there were so many of them that she had lost a dangerous amount of blood. Her lips looked blue, and beneath the blood her skin had a chilling translucent quality to it.

He heard his own voice swearing low and savagely as he tried to halt the bleeding, but he wasn't aware of what he was saying. Such minor wounds, and she might yet die.

He heard booted feet crunching on the broken glass, and William Tobias appeared in the doorway. "She all right, boss?"

"No. She's lost a lot of blood. Get the wagon hitched up. We've got to get her into town."

"That Mexican, Fronteras, caught a couple of bullets. He's lost a right smart amount of blood, too, but I reckon he'll be all right. About five of the Bar B men need burying, some more need patching up. There was about thirty of the bastards after her. We hurt 'em the most, I reckon."

Lucas nodded, not taking his attention from Dee. "Hurry up with that wagon."

William left to see to it.

Lucas started to remove the long splinter from her shoulder but decided to leave it. Blood was oozing around it, but if he pulled it out the wound might start bleeding heavily, and she didn't need to lose any more blood than she already had. He carefully wrapped the blanket around her and lifted her.

William pulled the wagon right up to the porch just as Lucas

stepped outside with his burden. His men were standing around
with their weapons trained on the Bar B men, the look on their
faces saying that they wished someone would try to get away.
The wounded were sprawled on the ground; the dead had been
left where they lay.

"Where's Fronteras?" Lucas asked as he gently placed Dee on
the wagon bed. She didn't move.

"Here."

"Put him on the wagon, too."

Two of his men lifted one of the wounded and laid him on the
wagon. Lucas saw the Mexican's dark eyes open. "Is she all
right?" he asked huskily.

"She's hurt," Lucas replied, his voice tight. "Fronteras, you
have a place on my ranch for the rest of your life if you want it."

Luis managed a semblance of a smile, then his eyes closed
again.

"Will, get them to the doc. I'll be along in a few minutes."
Lucas stepped back. William nodded and slapped the reins
against the horse's back.

Slowly Lucas turned his head to look at the Bar B men.
Killing rage was bubbling in his veins, and it was cold, ice cold.
Kyle Bellamy stood with his men, his head down and his arms
hanging loose at his sides.

Lucas wasn't aware of moving, but suddenly Bellamy's shirt
was knotted in his big fist. The man looked up, and Lucas's powerful right arm cocked back, then drove his iron-hard fist into
Bellamy's face.

He had never before taken joy in fighting, but he felt savage
satisfaction every time his fists thudded into Bellamy. He beat
the man to the ground, then pulled him up and beat him some
more. He kept seeing Dee's blood-soaked body, and he hit
Bellamy even harder, feeling ribs crack as he drove his fists into
the man's sides and midsection. Bellamy made no effort to fight
back, merely raising his arms to try to block some of the blows.
That didn't incline Lucas toward mercy.

Finally Bellamy pitched forward and lay still, and one of the
Double C men caught Lucas's arm as he started for him again.
"No point in it, boss," the man said. "He can't feel a thing."

Lucas halted and stared down at the motionless man at his feet. His face was unrecognizable, but Lucas didn't feel the satisfaction of vengeance. His rage was so deep that even killing Bellamy wouldn't ease it.

He hadn't promised Tillie that he wouldn't kill Bellamy, but he owed her. If she hadn't ridden her heart out to reach him, Dee would have died alone in her cabin. He let his hands drop.

"What do we do with them?" one of the men asked.

Lucas growled. There wasn't any use in taking them into town; they hadn't broken any of the laws within the marshal's jurisdiction. Unless he was willing to string them all up right now there was nothing to be done. "Let them go," he said.

He looked at the Bar B men, and his voice was almost a snarl when he said, "Get off this land, you bastards, and take your scum with you. If any of you ever feel brave enough to attack a lone woman again, I swear to God I'll make you think hell is paradise compared to what I'll do to you before you die. Is that clear?"

The Bar B men answered with sullen mutters. Lucas went to his horse and mounted. If he didn't leave, he was likely to kill them all anyway.

It was full dark, and the moon hadn't yet risen, but the light from the countless stars was enough to let him see the road. He rode as fast as he dared and caught up with the wagon just before it got to town.

Doc Pendergrass and his wife, Etta, swiftly went to work on Dee. Luis Fronteras had been put in another room, and he was deemed less critical since he was still conscious and Dee wasn't. Lucas was pushed from the room as soon as he had placed Dee on the table, and he paced back and forth like a caged animal.

Tillie slipped in the door. Though the saloon would be busy now that it was night, she was wearing a dark green dress with long sleeves and a high neckline rather than the short, gaudy outfit she wore when working. Her face was very pale, but her expression was calm. "Did you get there in time?" she asked.

Lucas took off his hat and ran his hand through his hair. "Yeah. I hope. She's cut up pretty bad from the glass where they shot the windows out, and she's lost a lot of blood."

"But they didn't—"

"No. She was still holding them off when we got there."

He hadn't realized how taut she had been until he saw her subtly relax. Her enormous brown eyes never left his face. "Kyle?" she whispered.

"I beat the hell out of him."

She flinched, then controlled herself again. "Thank you, Lucas."

He shook his head. "No. She'd be dead now if it hadn't been for you."

"And Luis Fronteras. Is he all right?"

"He's hurt, but he'll make it."

She stood with her head bent for a minute, then sighed and straightened. She squeezed his arm in a gentle caress before she left.

It was over an hour before Doc Pendergrass came out, and he firmly shut the door behind him when Lucas started forward. "I got all the bleeding stopped," Doc said. "Etta's cleaning her up now."

"Is she conscious?"

"Not really. She roused up a little a couple of times but drifted out again. Sleep's the best thing for her right now. I'll tell you more after I take care of Fronteras."

Lucas sat down with his elbows propped on his knees and his head hanging forward. He needed to see her, to reassure himself that she was all right.

It didn't take the doctor as long with Luis as it had with Dee. He was out again in fifteen minutes. "Stitched up and sleeping," Doc said tiredly. "He'll be all right, probably up and around in a couple of days."

"What about Dee?" Lucas asked in a hard voice.

Doc sighed and rubbed his eyes. He was a slim, good-looking man in his early forties, but right now weariness made him look ten years older. "There were a lot of cuts. She's had a bad shock to her system. She's going to be a very sick woman for several days, feverish and weak."

"I want to take her to the ranch. Is it safe to move her?"

Doc looked up in surprise, then comprehension showed in his

face. Like everyone else in town, he had thought Lucas connected with Olivia Millican. Lucas Cochran and Dee Swann . . . well, well. "No," he finally answered. "Not for a couple of days, maybe longer. It'd be better for her to stay here with Etta to look after her anyway."

Lucas's face was hard. "When she's well enough to travel I'm taking her to the ranch." There was a part of him that wouldn't relax until he had her safe under his roof. Until the day he died he would never forget how he had felt when he had first seen her soaked in her own blood.

16

Luis was hurt. Olivia didn't hear about what had happened until the next morning, when Beatrice Padgett visited and was relating, in shocked tones, the events of the day before to Honora. ". . . and one of Mr. Bellamy's men, a Mr. Fronteras—I believe he must be a Mexican—decided to help Dee hold them off, and he was shot, too."

Olivia made a muffled sound of shock. Honora and Beatrice looked toward her, and Honora quickly got to her feet at the sight of her daughter's white face. "Sit down, dear," she said, urging Olivia toward a chair. "It's horrible, isn't it?"

But Olivia pulled back, her eyes full of anguish. "Where—where is he?" she gasped. "Mr. Fronteras. Where is he?"

"Why, at Dr. Pendergrass's, of course. Mr. Cochran took both him and Dee to the doctor's to be tended," Beatrice answered. "That saloon girl, the one called Tillie, fetched Mr. Cochran to help. Isn't that the strangest thing? I wonder why she rode all the way out to the Double C."

Olivia whirled and ran from the house, ignoring Honora's alarmed cry.

Luis! Beatrice hadn't said how seriously he was hurt, but it must be bad if he was still at the doctor's. For the first time in her life Olivia forgot about decorum and dignity; she snatched her skirts up and ran, her heart thudding in a sick panic. It was three blocks to Dr. Pendergrass's office. She darted around people on the sidewalks when she could and shoved past them otherwise. By the time she reached the office her hair was falling down and she was gasping for breath, but she had never cared less for her appearance.

She shoved the door open and stumbled inside. The first person she saw was Etta Pendergrass. "Where is he?"

Etta immediately assumed that there was an emergency. "I'll get him, dear. He's just in here checking Mr. Fronteras—"

Olivia bolted past her into the room she had indicated. Dr. Pendergrass looked up at her precipitous entrance and leapt to the same conclusion his wife had. "What's happened, Olivia?" Surely only a serious accident or illness concerning one of her parents could prompt Olivia into such uncharacteristic actions.

But Olivia didn't answer. Her hands flew to her mouth as she stared at Luis, lying on his left side, his upper torso bare. A large white bandage was located at his waist. Tears swam in her eyes, blurring her vision. "Luis?" she whispered, her voice begging. Let him be all right, she prayed silently. Please let him be all right.

He shifted gingerly onto his back, his dark eyes narrowing at her white face. "Would you let me speak to Miss Millican in private?" he asked the doctor in a tone that commanded rather than requested.

Dr. Pendergrass arched his brows a little and said, "Of course." He left the room, closing the door behind him.

Luis held out his hand, and Olivia ran to him. She touched his face, his chest, his shoulders, whispering incoherently while tears slid down her cheeks. Holding his left hand to the bandage on his side, he struggled to a sitting position. "I'm all right," he soothed, pulling her close to him and kissing her hair. "It's just a flesh wound. I'm stiff and weak, but it isn't serious."

"I just heard," she stammered, clinging to him. "I'd have been here last night if I'd known. Why didn't you have someone send for me? *Why?*"

Using his thumb, he wiped her cheeks. "And let everyone know?" he asked gently.

She struggled to control her breathing. "Well, they know now," she blurted. "I ran through town like a madwoman."

He was silent a minute while his hand rubbed her back in comfort. "I could think of something as an excuse if you want."

Olivia stilled with her head on his shoulder. He wasn't going to take advantage of the situation to force the issue. He had said it was her decision, and he was standing by that. But could she go back to pretending she didn't care about him? Just hearing that he'd been hurt had stripped away the last film of doubt from her mind. Why was she dithering when she felt that way about him? She had never been a silly person, but she had certainly been acting silly the past couple of months. Her greatest dream had come true, and she had been afraid to accept it because Luis Fronteras wasn't a landed gentleman. She was worse than silly; she was a snob.

Slowly she lifted her head, her damp blue eyes locking with his dark ones. A soft smile trembled on her lips. "No, I don't want you to lie for me," she said in as steady a voice as she could muster. "What I want is to marry you, Luis Fronteras."

His dark eyes were piercing, and he held her chin so that she couldn't look away. "Are you sure? Make very certain, Olivia, because once you say yes I won't let you go no matter what happens. I'm not a gentleman. I keep what's mine, and I'll fight as dirty as I have to to keep it."

She framed his face with her hands and leaned forward to kiss him. "Yes," she said. A smile broke like the sun coming up, bathing her face in radiance. "Yes. Yes yes yes yes *yes*. How many times do I have to say it before it's official?"

His dark brows arched, and he locked her in his arms. "It's official," he said. "We'll get married as soon as possible."

"Mother will want me to be married in the church. It'll take at least a month to get everything arranged."

"A month!" he growled. Then he warned, "Don't be surprised if your parents refuse to have anything to do with me."

She felt sad at the possibility but faced it. "If they do, that's their loss." Nothing would stop her from marrying Luis.

Somehow it no longer mattered that she didn't know how they would live, or even where. She would be with him, and that was all that mattered. She loved him. It was a simple truth, and she wondered why it had taken her so long to recognize it.

She had learned in a few horrible moments that morning how swiftly fate could step in and perhaps take him away forever. Before another minute passed she wanted to give him the gift of her love. She said it simply. "I love you."

His pupils flared until his eyes were black and bottomless. "And I love you. We may not live in a big house, but I'll take very good care of you."

"I'm sure you will." A blush rosied her cheeks, but her gaze remained steady. "In all the ways that matter."

He had the most devilish grin she had ever seen, and the power of it almost made her heart stop. "Yes, darling, in that way, too."

He had to kiss her, and it was even more potent than it had been before, because now she felt no need to draw back. She gave him all of her response and the complete freedom of her body. It was only his stifled groan when he moved too abruptly that made them realize where they were and draw back.

Her concern, which had abated when she had seen that he wasn't mortally wounded, returned full force. Now that she had calmed down she could see how drawn and pale he was, and the dark circles beneath his eyes. "Lie back down," she urged, pressing his shoulder with her hand.

He obeyed because he was as weak as a kitten. Olivia settled the pillow under his head and drew the blanket up to his chest, then sat down beside him with his hand clasped in hers. She couldn't bear to be separated from him just yet. "What happened?" she asked. "Who shot you?"

"In that kind of gunfight it doesn't matter. So many people were shooting there's no way to know."

"But what *happened?* Why did it happen?"

"Bellamy decided to drive his cattle onto Dee Swann's property. The Bar B doesn't have much water left, and I guess he was desperate. Desperate people do stupid things." Luis sighed tiredly. "I thought she'd given him permission, but she hadn't, and she shot to spook the cattle, turn them around. Bellamy seemed to go mad. He started shooting at her, and some of the men joined in."

"And you helped her. Do you even know her?" She was filled with admiration for what he had done.

"No, but she was a woman alone, and it was her land. She was in the right." He decided that it might not be smart to tell his future wife that he had a deep and lasting fondness for women in general, and there was no way he could stand by and let a woman be terrorized. Not that Dee Swann had seemed frightened, he reflected with admiration. She had faced Bellamy like an Amazon.

"Dee's a wonderful friend," Olivia said softly. "Thank you for saving her life. I heard some of the men in town wouldn't try to help her, I think probably because she keeps to herself and doesn't seem to need anyone, but that's just an act. I'm glad you were there when she *did* need someone's help. I only wish you hadn't been hurt."

"I didn't do it by myself. If Tillie hadn't gone after Cochran, and he hadn't got there as fast as he did, Dee and I would both be dead."

Olivia stroked his hand, loving the strength in his lean fingers. "I'll ride out to help her get the cabin straightened up."

Luis's face tightened. "She isn't at the cabin. She's right here. Doc says she's cut up pretty bad and lost too much blood. He's been up with her all night, and now fever is setting in. He's worried about her."

Olivia turned white and jumped to her feet. She hadn't even asked if Dee was hurt! Her mind had emptied of everything but Luis when she'd heard he had been shot. "Oh, my God," she said, and tears slipped down her cheeks. Luis reached out a steadying hand, but she whispered, "I have to go to her." She ran from the room.

Her friend lay silent and motionless except for the faint rise and fall of her chest. The only color in her face was from the livid cuts that marred her skin. Dee had always been so vital that Olivia almost didn't recognize her lying so still. She had never imagined anything could bring Dee down.

Etta was sitting by the bed, keeping a cold cloth on Dee's forehead. Olivia could see the worry plain in her eyes.

"Has she been awake?" Olivia asked, agonized.

Etta shook her head. "She hasn't stirred since Lucas brought her in last night."

Olivia swiped at her wet cheeks. "You must be so tired you can hardly sit up," she said. "I'll sit with her while you rest."

Tillie rode out to the Bar B. Though there was activity around the ranch house, there was a strangely abandoned feel to it. All of the men looked exhausted, even those who hadn't taken part in the fight, for they had been chasing the scattered cattle for most of the night.

"Where's Mr. Bellamy?" she asked one of them.

"In the house, ma'am."

She knocked, but no one answered, and after knocking a second time she opened the door. "Kyle?"

There was no answer. She walked through the downstairs and found it deserted, then went upstairs. Kyle's bedroom was on the left. She tapped on the door, which was ajar, then stepped inside.

He lay on the bed, fully clothed except for his boots. His shirt bore reddish-brown stains. She walked over and stood beside the bed, looking down at him. Compassion turned her eyes black. He had tried to clean his face, for a stained cloth lay on the floor, but dried blood still caked one of his nostrils and was splotched in his hair and on his neck.

His poor face was so swollen and misshappen she could barely recognize him. Both eyes were blackened and puffy, his nose was broken, and huge knots distorted his cheekbones and jaw.

"Kyle," she said softly.

He shifted a little and groaned. One of his eyes opened a slit.

"I'll get some water and clean you up," she murmured,

bending over him so he could see her without turning his head.

He sighed, then muttered, "Ribs." His mouth was so swollen that the word sounded mushy.

"Your ribs are hurt?"

"Yeah."

She touched his arm. "I'll be right back."

She got what she needed from downstairs and returned to his bedroom with her supplies. He didn't look as if he had moved an inch.

She took a pair of scissors and deftly cut his shirt off of him, then probed his ribs. His midsection was mottled with black and purple bruises, testimony to the power of Lucas Cochran's fists. As gently as possible she probed his ribs, searching for breaks. He cried out when she touched a certain place, but she couldn't feel anything out of place and decided they were only cracked.

"Your ribs need to be wrapped," she said. "Kyle, darling, you'll have to sit up. I know it hurts, but I can't do anything with you lying down."

She gently coaxed him into a sitting position, supporting him as much as she was able, but Kyle was a big man, and she didn't have enough strength to give him much aid. When he was sitting unsteadily on the side of the bed she wrapped a wide band of cloth around him, pulling it tight. He groaned but then gave a sigh of relief as the tight wrapping supported his ribs and kept them from moving.

While he was sitting up she washed his face, taking care to use only the lightest touch, then cleaned the blood from his hair and neck.

"Thirsty," he mumbled.

She got him some water. He took a cautious sip and rinsed it around in his mouth, then spat it out into the bowl, turning the water inside an even darker red. Then he slowly drank the rest of the water.

"If you can stand up, I'll undress you," she said, but he couldn't. She helped him to lie down and struggled until she had wrestled the rest of his clothing off, then covered his nude body with a sheet. "Sleep," she said. "I'll stay here with you."

She was as good as her word. She held his hand while he slept, and every time she looked at his face her eyes blurred with tears. She knew she had done the right thing, but that didn't make it easy.

She loved him so much, had loved him for years. He thought it was only coincidence that they had both settled in the same area, but she had found out where he was and left her luxurious house in Denver, where she had been the pampered mistress of a very wealthy man, without a backward look.

He had wanted respectability so much. She knew how he had grown up and knew how he had wanted to put all of that behind him. Kyle wasn't a bad man, though he could easily have been, considering what his life had been like. It was just that the ranch and what it represented had come to mean so much to him; he had lost all perspective when it had been threatened, and now he had destroyed the reputation he had worked so hard to build.

But he was alive, and that was all that mattered to her.

It was late that night before he woke again, and she supported him while he used the chamber pot. He asked for more water but didn't want anything to eat. He went back to sleep.

By morning he was more alert, and Tillie fed him some bread softened in milk. When he indicated he didn't want any more she knew she couldn't put if off any longer.

She had learned to face everything in life without flinching, especially the hardest parts, so now she didn't look away from him. "I couldn't let you kill Dee Swann," she said. "People may never forgive you for what you did, but if she had been killed or raped, you'd have hanged. I'm the one who got Lucas Cochran to stop you."

His left eye was swollen completely shut, and his right eye would open only a slit. Carefully he looked up at her, his gaze devoid of anger. He just looked empty. "I had to do it," he said, the words indistinct. "The water . . . but it didn't work. I didn't mean to hurt her. But I lost. I lost it all."

"No," she said fiercely. "You haven't lost it all. You're still alive, and that's what matters most. Even if this ranch turns to dust, you'll be able to start again. Maybe not here, but there are other places. I have money, and you've always been able to win at the card table. We'll get by."

"We?" he asked. His one good eye didn't move from her.

"Yes, we. We make a good team."

Almost imperceptibly he nodded.

17

Lucas stood beside Dee's bed, looking down at her. Despite her fever her face was deathly pale.

"Has she woke up?" he asked Etta, and his voice was harsh.

The doctor's wife gave him a concerned look and shook her head. "But that isn't surprising. She's very sick, and rest is the best thing for her." She dipped a cloth in cool water, wrung it out, and placed it across Dee's forehead. Dee never stirred.

Lucas wearily rubbed his eyes. It had been almost two full days, and she still hadn't so much as opened her eyes or said a word. After losing so much blood how could she have any strength to fight the fever?

Beneath the nightgown Etta had clothed her in Dee's shoulder was covered by a bulky bandage. He suspected that the shoulder wound was the main source of the fever, but Doc said that he'd cleaned it good and that it was no more inflamed than any of the cuts. It was just that all together her wounds had been a tremendous shock to her system. Added to that, she had exhausted herself trying to fight off the Bar B men. Recovery would take time.

But she was so damn still. Even when she had fallen out of the loft she had still been full of spirit despite the fact that she could barely move. Dee was a fighter, but how could she fight when she wasn't conscious? He was so used to her strength and fierceness that this utter helplessness, this complete absence of her fire made him sick with fear.

In his mind she had always been formidable as both foe and lover. It was a shock to look at her now and realize that she was both smaller and more fragile than he'd ever imagined. He'd always thought of her as a tall woman, even though he knew he could look down on the top of her head; it was the impression that she gave, the way she carried herself, the arrogant tilt of her head, her towering pride—all of these combined made him see her as larger than she truly was. She was of only medium height, if that, and her bones were as slender as a child's. He was stunned at how frail she looked.

He was full of rage at what had happened to her, a rage that burned far deeper and hotter than the anger he'd felt when she had fallen out of the loft. None of it would have happened if she lived like other women. On a rational basis he knew that it wasn't her fault, that accidents happened, that she wasn't to blame for Kyle Bellamy's murderous stupidity. But for as long as she lived out at Angel Creek things like this would happen, her fault or not. The land invited greed with its very perfection, and there would always be someone who thought he could take it away from her. And being herself, Dee would always fight rather than try to protect herself by running.

It was the water that made the Angel Creek valley what it was, and water that was the cause of all this.

He stared down at her, lying there as still as death. If he didn't do something to stop it, the next time really might kill her.

He nodded to Etta and strode out, his face set in lines of grim determination.

The root of it all was the water. Without it the valley would lose its value. Dee wouldn't have any reason for clinging to it, and she would have to live a more reasonable way. There wouldn't be a reason for anyone to shoot at her, or for her to work like a man.

He rode back to the Double C and told William to get ten of the men and some shovels and be ready to ride in fifteen minutes. Then he went to the storeroom and got a couple of sticks of dynamite, in case they were needed.

He already knew how the creek forked up in the mountains, sending most of the water down the east side of the range and into the valley. It had been years since he'd been up there, but he could see in his mind just how the creek beds split. With any luck he'd be able to take away the one thing that made Dee's land so valuable.

God, she'd be mad, but there wouldn't be anything she could do about it. Since it would be his fault that the land had lost its value he would give her the same amount he'd already offered her, and she wouldn't have any choice but to take it and move to town. Eventually she would cool down, and then he'd start courting her again, out in the open this time. He figured by Christmas he'd have her talked around to marrying him, because she couldn't deny the fire between them any more than he could. They'd make love and babies and probably fight like two wildcats tangled up in a pillowcase, and they'd enjoy every minute of it.

They found the gap in the mountain where Angel Creek forked and the lower creek bed cut to the east. "Just look at that water," William said, shaking his head. "Straight from the snow-caps."

Lucas walked the bank, examining the fork. Up there it was big enough to be called a river, and it still flowed strong and clear, deep enough that there was some overflow into the fork that ran down onto his property, though it had been greatly reduced. If he could dig the western creek bed lower at the fork, then the water would divert onto the western side of the mountain.

He pulled off his boots and waded out into the western fork, catching his breath at the icy water. He dug his toes into the soft silt and cursed because just under the thin layer of silt was bedrock. He moved up and down the fork and found the same thing. There was no way they were going to dig through rock, and the dynamite fuse wouldn't burn under water.

He waded out again and stood looking at the water, thinking. The only way to blow that bedrock was to dry out the western fork.

He got a shovel and hefted it in his gloved hand. "Start digging," he told the men. "Pile dirt here at the fork and divert all the water to the east."

"Boss, that'll dry up our water completely," William said, looking at him as if he'd lost all of his senses.

"Temporarily," Lucas said. "When it's dry I'm going to blow the bedrock and lower the creek bed."

William turned back to the river and studied it, then a grin spread across his weathered face. "You're gonna turn that water our way."

"I sure am."

"Dee Swann ain't gonna like it worth a damn."

"I'll handle Dee Swann," Lucas said.

It took them three days. They dug up shovelfuls of dirt and packed the west fork, closing it off. The river swung happily eastward, emptying all of its crystal water into the Angel Creek valley. When the west fork was dry Lucas drilled holes in the bedrock and set the dynamite in it, then strung a long fuse and lit it. He and the men ran like hell for as far as they could before the dynamite blew with a thunderous explosion that shook the ground beneath their feet.

The explosion destroyed the earth dam they had built, and the river split once more, water tumbling down both sides of the mountain. The majority of the flow now went down the west side.

"Close off the east fork," he said. "I want a dam packed so solid that not even a trickle goes down the east side of the mountain. We'll seal it off with clay."

The force of the water would erode the dam, and he'd have to have it repaired regularly, but that would be a small price to pay for peace of mind. At least he'd be able to sleep at night without worrying about Dee's safety.

By late afternoon of the third day the eastern fork was blocked.

Despite his exhaustion he had been riding into town every night to see Dee. Olivia and Etta had been taking turns sitting with her, and the worry etched on Olivia's face made him break out in a cold sweat every time he thought about it. The night before Dee had awakened briefly for the second time, but the fever still hadn't broken. Four days of a high fever had taken a visible toll on her body, wasting away flesh she hadn't needed to lose. She had recognized him, whispered his name. Lucas had held her hand and talked to her, but she had slipped back into sleep almost immediately. Olivia had touched his shoulder in comfort. "She'll be all right," she said, her voice breaking a little. "She has to be."

He was bone tired, but he couldn't let a day go by without seeing her, whether she knew he was there or not. It was as much for himself as for her that he went into town that night. Every time he saw her he was convinced anew that he had done the right thing, the only thing that would protect her. He didn't delude himself that she would take it well when she found out what he'd done, but by God, he'd never again have to see her lying so deathly still.

This time, however, Olivia looked up with a smile when he entered. She held a finger to her lips and motioned him back out of the room, following him and carefully closing the door behind her. "The fever broke," she said, beaming. "She ate a little bit of soup, then went back to sleep."

Relief washed through him like a flood. He was still exhausted, but he felt a hundred pounds lighter, as if lead weights had dropped from his shoulders. "Did she talk?"

"She asked for water, but if you mean did she carry on a conversation, the answer is no. She's still very sick, Lucas, and weak. She won't get over this in a couple of days. Dr. Pendergrass says it will be three or four weeks before she'll be strong enough to look after herself."

He didn't even have to think about it. He knew exactly what he wanted. "I'm taking her to the Double C tomorrow."

Olivia gaped at him. "You can't do that!"

"Yes, I can. It'll be quieter there than it is here, with people going in and out."

"But she's a woman!"

He lifted his eyebrows at her. "Believe me, I noticed."

"But that's why she can't stay with you."

"She almost died. She's sure not in any shape for what you're thinking," Lucas said bluntly, bringing a blush to Olivia's cheeks. "I'll take care of her, get her back on her feet. And I'm not asking permission, Olivia, I'm telling you what I'm going to do."

Olivia took a deep breath and tried again. "You don't have any women out there on that ranch. Who's going to bathe her, change her clothes? I've already talked with Mother about taking her home with me. Surely you can see that she can't possibly go out to the ranch." Her voice softened. "She's my best friend, Lucas. I know how much she means to you. I'll take good care of her, I promise."

He looked at her sharply. "Dee told me you two were friends, but—"

"Best friends," Olivia repeated. "I feel a bit smug because I thought from the beginning that the two of you were perfectly suited for each other."

Lucas cleared his throat. "I think I owe you an apology, Olivia. I know nothing was ever said between us, but I gave you and everyone else the impression that I intended—"

She put her hand on his sleeve. "No apology is needed. I like you very much as a friend, but I never wanted anything more. You didn't either, really. Besides, I'm very much in love with someone else."

"Do tell." He lifted his eyebrows. "Who's the lucky man?"

"Luis Fronteras."

"Hell!" he said in surprise, then he apologized. "Sorry. He's doing all right, isn't he? I've had so much on my mind I haven't asked."

"He's staying at Lindfor's Hotel now. He's almost recovered."

He gave an approving nod; he couldn't fault Olivia's selection, even if Fronteras wasn't the type of man he'd ever thought would appeal to her. A hard look came into his eyes. "Some folks might have something to say about him, whether it's their business or not. I owe him a debt I won't ever be able to repay, so if you need my help in anything, all you have to do is get in touch."

"Thank you, Lucas." She rose up on tiptoe and kissed his cheek. "I'll remember that. And I'll take good care of Dee for you."

His face changed, his eyes glittering stubbornly. "I know

you would, but I haven't changed my mind. I'm taking her with me."

"You have to consider her reputation," Olivia said in exasperation. "People will talk."

His smile was chilling. "If they're smart, they won't."

"Well, they will. You can't take care of her like that."

Her reasoning gave him pause. He'd intended to do those intimate things for Dee himself, but letting the entire town know was something else. He adjusted his plans but didn't change his mind. "I know you'd take care of her, but I want her with me. I'll hire a woman to help. Sid Acray's oldest girl would be glad of the money." Not only did he want Dee close by, but if she was at the ranch he could control who saw her. That way she wouldn't hear about what he'd done to Angel Creek from anyone else but him, when he decided it was a good time to tell her.

Olivia saw from the expression in those hard blue eyes that he wasn't going to be swayed. He wanted Dee Swann on the Double C, and that's where she'd be. Well, she had wished for Lucas and Dee to get together, and she had gotten her wish. Even with Sid Acray's daughter for a chaperon the townfolk would be scandalized if they didn't get married.

She gave him a stern look. "Do you plan on marrying her?"

"Just as soon as I can talk her around. But don't tell her," he cautioned. "Maybe I can surprise her into saying yes if she hasn't had time to think about it."

They smiled at each other in perfect accord.

Lucas was back the next morning with a buckboard, the wagon bed padded with quilts. Etta Pendergrass was severely aggravated with her husband for not telling Lucas that Dee was too sick to be moved, but he refused to lie just because his wife was shocked by what she considered a scandalous idea. Dee was very ill, but she would recover just as fast at the Double C as she would in town. Besides, he wasn't fool enough to try to stop Lucas Cochran when he'd made up his mind to do something.

Dee was awake when Lucas entered the room, her eyes dull but aware. "Lucas," she whispered.

He wanted to snatch her up and crush her to his chest, but

she was so very frail that he restrained himself. Instead he picked up her hand and stroked her fingers. "I'm taking you home with me," he said.

She nodded and managed a little smile. He wrapped her in one of the quilts he had brought and carried her out to the buckboard. A small knot of people gathered on the sidewalk, murmuring among themselves. The Acray girl, Betsy, climbed into the back to watch over Dee on the trip back to the ranch.

Doc Pendergrass, Etta, and Olivia followed him out. "Just make sure she eats and doesn't try to do too much too soon," Doc told him. "She won't feel like getting out of bed for another week or so at least, but rest is the best thing for her."

"Betsy will take good care of her," Lucas said, mindful of the people listening. He was filled with satisfaction. The circumstances weren't what he would have liked, and there were some bad storms ahead, but for now Dee would be right where he wanted her—under his roof.

He handled the buckboard carefully on the trip to the ranch, taking twice as long as it would to ride it on a horse, but he tried not to jostle Dee in case her shoulder was more painful than he realized. It was nerve-racking trying to see every rough spot in the road, listening for even a change in her breathing. When at last the ranch house came in sight he heaved a relieved sigh.

He reined in the horse at the porch and stepped over the seat into the wagon bed, going down on one knee beside Dee. "Run inside and turn back the covers on the bed," he told Betsy. "Her bedroom is upstairs, the second door on the right."

Betsy jumped down and scurried to do his bidding. She was only seventeen and thoroughly intimidated by Lucas, though he'd tried to put her at ease. But there was something about him that made some women nervous, so he put it out of his mind.

Dee was awake, though there was still that disturbing lack of expression in her eyes. It was as if she saw and understood but just couldn't muster the strength to care about anything. "Tell me if I hurt you," he said as he slid her on the quilts to the edge of the wagon bed so he could lift her without jostling her any more than necessary. He jumped down and gathered her in his arms, holding her close against his chest. He had carried her before and knew how much lighter she was now. His heart gave a big thud as a remnant of fear lashed him. The loss of blood had come so close to killing her that he didn't think he'd ever recover.

Betsy was standing beside the bed when he carried Dee in. He placed his precious burden down and unwrapped her from the quilt, then settled the covers over her. "Do you want anything to eat?" he asked. "Or to drink?"

"Water," she said.

Lucas glanced at Betsy, who scurried to the water pitcher sitting nearby.

"Whatever you want, just tell Betsy," he said, stroking her cheek. "Sleep as much as you want. All you have to do now is get well."

He dropped his hand and turned to leave, but she said, "Lucas," and he turned back.

"The cattle," she whispered. "My garden—"

Even now she was worried about that damn garden! He controlled his spurt of anger to give her the assurance she needed. "They didn't get in it. You stampeded them all the way back to the Bar B."

A slight smile spread over her colorless lips. Betsy brought the glass of water, and he moved so she could support Dee's head and let her sip. By the time Dee signaled that she had had enough and Betsy let her head rest on the pillow again Dee's eyes were closing with fatigue. Lucas quietly left the room.

He would have only a few weeks until she regained her strength and he'd have to tell her about the water. He meant to make the most of his period of grace to strengthen the bonds between them while he could. As soon as she was well enough to do without Betsy she would be all his.

It was the custom in the Millican family to spend the evening together after dinner, reading or sewing or just talking. Even when Olivia was a little girl she had been included in that intimate time, her parents always making her feel that her childish contributions to the conversation were as important as theirs. After losing their other children Wilson and Honora had doubly appreciated the preciousness of their daughter and had devoted themselves to making her life as perfect as they possibly could. The harmony of those after-dinner hours had always been a part of her life that Olivia loved, and she feared that she was about to ruin it. Luis had offered to be with her when she told them, but she had declined. If there was any unpleasantness, she didn't want him to hear it. It was ridiculous to protect him, but part of her reasoning was based on diplomacy. It would be easier for him to get along with her parents at a later date if there weren't any memories of harsh words between them.

Strangely enough, there didn't seem to be any gossip. Honora and Beatrice had both been discreet about her behavior when she had learned Luis had been hurt. Etta and Dr. Pendergrass had evidently not said anything either about the way she had flown to Luis's bedside. Olivia almost wished there *had* been gossip so she wouldn't have to introduce the subject so abruptly.

There didn't seem to be any other way to do it, however, so she took a deep breath and said, "Mother, Papa, I have something to tell you." Her mother turned to look at her expectantly, and Wilson put his paper down. "I've fallen in love, and I'm going to be married."

Their eyes rounded with surprise, then Honora clapped her hands and jumped up. "That's wonderful," she cried, laughing excitedly. "I just *knew* Mr. Cochran would propose, though I did wonder when—"

"Mother, no," Olivia interrupted. "It isn't Lucas."

Both their faces had been wreathed in smiles, but now their expressions went blank with surprise. "Not Lucas?" Wilson asked with a perplexed frown. "But he's the only one who's been courting you, except for Bellamy, and of course you'd never have anything to do with him. Everyone in town thought—"

"Everyone but the two people involved," Olivia replied gently. "Lucas is a friend, but we've never been in love."

"But if it isn't Mr. Cochran, then who is it?" Honora recovered from her surprise and was fairly quivering with curiosity.

"Luis Fronteras."

Again their faces went blank. Honora sank into her chair. "Who?" she asked in bewilderment. The name was familiar, but she couldn't place it. And it sounded . . . foreign.

"Luis Fronteras. He worked for Mr. Bellamy. He's the man who helped Dee until the Double C men could get there."

"A gunman?" Wilson was incredulous. "You say you're going to marry a Mexican gunman? Olivia, that's ridiculous. Why, you don't even know him."

"A Mexican!" Honora's eyes rounded with shock.

"On the contrary, I know him well." Olivia met their gazes. "I've been riding with him every Sunday. And I love him."

Wilson folded his paper and tossed it aside. "That's impossible. You have absolutely nothing in common with a man like that. Why, he'll never settle down and provide you with a home."

"Perhaps where I live won't be like this," Olivia admitted. "But this isn't an impulsive decision. I've thought about it for a couple of months. I could marry a man who could give me a big house and a lot of clothes, but I wouldn't be one tenth as happy with him as I would be in a tent with Luis. I want to have a family with him, and I trust him to take care of me and our children. What does it matter if he isn't rich?"

"You'll find it matters a great deal when you have to do without." Wilson shook his head. "We've always done our best to shelter you, so you don't have any real idea of the kind of life you're proposing to lead. Darling, you deserve much more than he can give you. You couldn't survive."

"Of course I can. Don't you see, he *loves* me. And I love him. That's what I need, what I've always wanted more than anything else. Not to marry a rich man, but to marry a man I love."

"Absolutely not," Wilson said sternly. "I forbid it. You're just infatuated with him and have no idea what you're talking about. I realize he's a romantic sort of figure, especially after the way he helped Dee, but you need stability to have a good marriage, not a gun sharp who'll always be looking over his shoulder."

"Oh, Papa," Olivia said sadly. "I'm not asking your permission. I love you and Mother very much, and I want you to be at my wedding, but I'll have it whether you're there or not. I know you're concerned for my safety, and everything you've mentioned has made me think, too. But Luis is more than all those things you've said. He's a good, honorable man. Look at the way he risked his own life to help Dee, to use your own example! None of the fine, upstanding citizens in the saloon could find it in their hearts to give help when he asked for it, but you wouldn't be kicking up such a fuss if I wanted to marry any of them. Please don't turn against Luis because he isn't the type of man you've always thought I would marry. He's exactly the type of man who will make me happy, and I want you to be happy for me."

"You want too much." Wilson's face and voice were both stiff. Honora was quietly weeping.

"I'm sorry you feel that way, but it won't change my mind."

18

Olivia lay sleepless long after the house was silent that night. The grandfather clock downstairs chimed midnight, but she was wide awake. She had hated the scene with her parents, hated their unhappiness, but it hadn't changed her mind. She had never been as certain of anything in her life as she was of Luis.

At first the scraping noise didn't register, as accustomed as she was to the tree limbs outside her window brushing against the glass. Then she realized that the sound was that of her window being raised, and she leapt from the bed with a scream lodged in her throat.

"Don't run," Luis said in a low voice. "It's just me."

"Just you!" Her knees shook, then buckled a little. She grabbed for the bedpost. "Are you trying to frighten me to death? Don't ever do that again!" But even in her fright she kept her voice to a fierce whisper.

He chuckled. "Yes, ma'am. I hope this is the only time I ever have to climb through your bedroom window."

She was much struck by that fact. "Yes, what *are* you doing climbing trees so soon after being shot? What if you opened the wound again?"

"I didn't. It was just a little wound, after all. I feel fine." He put his hand on the back of her head and kissed her. "I couldn't wait until morning to find out if I have to wait a month for a fancy church wedding, or if we can do it a lot faster."

She put her hands on his biceps, drawing strength from the hard warmth of his body. "We can get married as soon as you want," she said, and despite herself there was sadness in her voice.

He kissed her again, his mouth tender. "I'm sorry, darling. I know you wanted them to be happy."

"Yes, I did. But I found that I'm selfish enough to want my own happiness, too." With a little sigh she went into his arms; feeling them fold around her was like coming home. As he gathered her close she abruptly realized how thin the barrier of her nightgown was, allowing her to feel the heavy buckle of his gun belt and the extra cartridges shoved in the little loops, even the buttons on his pants. The last was so evident because of the heavy bulge behind them.

Once she would have been mortified had a man held her so close she could feel his body, but Luis had spent months accustoming her to his touch, teaching her the pleasure of physical love. A thrill went through her at the knowledge that he desired her, and without thought she moved her hips against him.

He slipped one hand down to her buttocks and urged her closer, bending his knees a little to bring them together. She sighed at the adjustment of their bodies.

Luis angled his head to fit his mouth on hers. Now. The time was now. She had made her choice, and he wasn't going to wait even one more night before making her his. Perhaps a gentleman would wait until they were married, but he wasn't a gentleman—he was a man who wanted his woman. The marriage rites were for society; the most basic vows would be sealed with their bodies.

She was no longer frightened by his kisses, or by his hands on her body. She shivered with delight whenever he touched her breasts. He led her through those things he had already taught her, feeling the delicious tension beginning to tighten her muscles. He unbuttoned her nightgown and slid his hand inside to stroke her satiny breasts, and she gave a soft moan as her nipples tightened.

He stepped back and unbuckled his gun belt, letting it drop to a chair. Then he pulled off his shirt.

Olivia moved to him, fascinated by the faint gleam of light on his smooth skin. It was too dark to see his expression, but she discovered that she didn't need light; she knew him, knew his wide shoulders and hard chest, his muscular abdomen. The bandage at his waist was a small splotch of white, and seeing it made her ache anew. She kissed him, brushing her lips across his chest to find his little nipples. "I love you," she whispered, her breath warm on his skin.

He tilted her head up and settled his mouth on hers, his tongue slowly entering and teasing. His hands swept across her shoulders, and the nightgown dropped to her waist, held up by the curve of her hips. Before she could do more than draw a quick breath he pushed it past her buttocks, and it dropped to the floor around her feet.

She stood frozen, her frightened eyes lifting to his face, and now she wished that she had light so she could see him. No, she didn't. She was naked, and if she could see him, he could also see her. She realized that he could see her very well, the paleness of her skin visible even in the darkness.

Her bareness was shocking. Her hands fluttered downward to shield her sex, and with inexorable gentleness he caught her wrists and moved her hands to her sides. "Have I ever hurt you?" he asked with his lips at her temple.

She began to tremble. "No," she whispered.

"I'm going to make love to you tonight. You're going to be completely mine. Do you know what's going to happen?"

She tried to think, tried to prod her stunned mind into coherency. "I . . . not really."

"Have you ever seen animals mating?"

"N-no. I mean yes. I saw a pair of dogs once." And she had been painfully fascinated before the impropriety of what she'd been doing had occurred to her, and she had rushed away in embarrassment.

Luis smiled against her hair. His innocent darling. "The concept is roughly the same," he said, soothing her with light caresses on her back and hips. "You've felt how I get hard when

I'm with you. To make love I put my shaft inside you, here." And he moved his stroking hand to the front of her tightly clenched thighs, sliding one finger into the soft folds.

She jerked wildly, and he caught her to him with one strong arm. "Stop that," she moaned. "You mustn't." Her trembling had increased, and she felt weak, the muscles in her legs shaking and threatening to go limp. She couldn't believe that he was touching her between her legs, or that it was causing a violent firestorm to race along her nerves. She felt unbearably heated, her skin so sensitive that his touch almost made her cry out. Only the dim knowledge that she had to be quiet kept her from screaming aloud at this painful ecstasy. He had aroused her before, given her pleasure that had left her aching for more, but nothing had been like this. It was as if before he had given her only water to taste, and now he was giving her full-bodied wine. There was simply no comparison.

"Let's lie down, love," he coaxed, kissing her again. She stood rigid, and he persuasively rubbed his finger on the tiny nub between her legs, keeping his touch feather-light because she was so new to it all. She trembled again, and he felt the strength go out of her legs. He lifted her onto the bed and quickly removed his boots and pants. His entire body was aching with anticipation as he lay down with her.

She felt dazed by what was happening. He was seducing her, and she was helpless to stop it. She didn't want to stop it. But she felt as if she were on a runaway train that was going faster and faster, totally out of control, and she couldn't jump off.

She felt his hard length jutting against her hip, and without thought she reached down to move it. As soon as her fingers closed around that alien flesh she jerked her hand away. Luis moaned, his hips arching a little. "Touch me," he murmured roughly, his breath coming fast. "Please. I've wanted to feel you holding me—"

She hesitated, for it seemed impossibly bold and wicked. But so had everything else he had taught her, and she loved it all. Shyly she folded her fingers around him again, and in the next moment she was fascinated by the feel of him, hardness covered by silky smooth skin. She felt the first faint edging of fear, for she didn't see how he could possibly enter her as he had said.

He moved over her, levering her thighs apart with his.

It took all of her self-control to lie still. Her hands twisted in the sheet.

He sensed her distress and soothed it with low whispers of reassurance and kisses that lingered. He fondled her breasts and kissed them, and soon the tension eased out of her muscles. Her legs relaxed so that they were no longer clamped on his. His talented fingers searched out the softness between her thighs, and the petals opened like a flower blooming. She made a soft sound, and her head rolled on the pillow.

He stroked her to passion, entering her with his fingers while using his thumb to keep her aroused. She arched and twisted, her body instinctively seeking his. He rubbed her to the very edge of completion, then removed his hand and guided his manhood to her opening.

Again she went still, though her chest was heaving. He leaned closer, letting her cradle his weight. The force of it pushed him a little way into her.

She closed her eyes, her entire body trying to draw back from him. He was inside her just enough for pain to threaten, and what she felt warned her that it would be true pain, not just discomfort. "It hurts," she whispered.

"I know, darling. But it's just this first time."

She lay beneath him, feeling the pressure as he eased deeper into her. She could feel her inner channel opening and painfully stretching to admit him. She felt a deeper stretching, and he was hurting her, the pain hot as her maidenhead tore to let him forge deep into her body.

He held himself still to let the pain abate. His shoulder was wet with her tears, and he set about soothing her even though his manhood was throbbing painfully. The soft clasp of her inner muscles was maddening, luring him toward a satisfaction he couldn't let himself have just yet.

The only true way to soothe her was to take her to the peak he denied himself, to show her the ultimate pleasure that was the reward for enduring this initial pain. His own climax would have to wait, for nothing was so important as giving her ease. He slipped his hand between their bodies and found her soft nub again, coaxing it from its protective folds with a whisper-light touch, luring Olivia back into passion. He pleasured her with hard-won patience, not trying to take her swiftly to climax but instead letting the pleasure build so that she felt first a gentle relaxing of her muscles, then the slow return of arousal. Only when her hips began to lift against his hand and initiate the movements of lovemaking did he increase the pressure and speed of his stroking fingers.

Olivia had been bitterly disappointed by the pain of his penetration even though Dee had said that the first time hurt. All of her previous lessons in sensuality had been full of heated pleasure, and despite her fear she had trusted him to make this final surrender as completely enjoyable as all the rest of it. Instead there had been pain, and the harsh shock of having her body invaded. But his experienced touch was bringing back pleasure so fast and so strong that it swept over her in waves. She surged beneath him, trying to take him deeper into her because somehow that had become part of the ecstasy; she locked her legs around his and writhed in increasing passion. Luis groaned aloud at the movement of her body on his length, trying to hold back, trying not to thrust hard and deep when every fiber in him needed to.

She cried out, and he put his hand over her mouth. She stiffened and shuddered, and he felt the soft internal shivers that heralded the onslaught of her peak. He couldn't stop himself then; he began to thrust, and in only a few seconds he followed her into mindless pleasure. The force of it emptied him and left him unable to move, sprawled heavily on top of her.

She moved her hand slowly down his back, luxuriating in the feel of his strong muscles. She felt dazed and dreamy. So there was pleasure after all, a pleasure so intense that she had thought she might die of it. She didn't regret that he hadn't waited until they were married, only that he hadn't completely seduced her before. This new intimacy was overwhelming in both the pleasure it afforded and the bond it had forged. She felt more utterly his than she had ever thought she would feel with a man, and more possessive of him than she had known was possible. She loved him, but this bond of their bodies was more primeval than that.

After a long while he stirred, lifting himself from her body. "I have to go," he said sleepily, "or I'll still be here in the morning, and that would have your father looking for a shotgun. I'll come for you at about ten. Will that give you time to pack?"

So it would be that soon. He had claimed her and saw no reason to wait even a couple of days for their marriage.

"Yes," she said, and she kissed him. "Where will we stay? Or will we be leaving town immediately?"

He didn't hear any hesitation in her voice, only curiosity. She truly didn't care where they stayed. Suddenly he felt like laughing out loud, exulting in the fate that had given her to him. "We'll stay in the hotel for a while until we decide what to do."

"So I won't need to pack all of my clothes right now?"

He grinned. "Well, I guess I can safely say that you won't need any nightgowns."

No, she wouldn't. She smiled as she watched him dress. She would have Luis to keep her warm. It was the most delicious future she had ever imagined.

She was calm when she went downstairs to breakfast the next morning. "Luis is coming for me at ten," she said. "We'll be married this afternoon."

Tears welled in Honora's eyes, and she hastily blotted them away. "There's no need to be so hasty, dear. Won't you think this over for a little while longer?"

Olivia put her arms around her mother. "I have thought it over. I love him, and that isn't going to change. The only reason to wait would be if you and Papa wanted to give me a wedding."

Wilson sighed heavily and got up from the table. "You can't expect us to celebrate your marriage to a man like Fronteras."

"I wish you would, but no, I didn't expect it."

He bent his head, staring unhappily at the floor. Most of his objection was based on how unsuitable Fronteras was for Olivia, but part of it was an unwillingness to lose his daughter. He would have missed her at any time, but the parting would have been easier if he had been assured he was giving her safe-keeping into reliable hands. Olivia deserved better than a life of insecurity.

She had always been the perfect daughter, adorable as a child, sweet and loving. She had never shown any wildness, had instead been precociously responsible and levelheaded. He knew doting parents never thought anyone good enough for their children, but it was painfully obvious that Olivia was marrying far beneath herself.

She was his only child, the light of his life. She would inherit his money. Was that why Fronteras was marrying her? Did he expect to be supported by his father-in-law? Olivia certainly deserved better than that. But she tended to see the best in people, and it wouldn't occur to her to be suspicious of Fronteras's motives. Wilson hadn't accumulated his wealth by being a fool. He knew a lot of men who had married because of money; he didn't want that to happen to Olivia.

He hadn't wanted to meet the man at all, but now he decided to delay his departure to the bank; he had a few things he wanted to say to Luis Fronteras.

Luis arrived promptly at ten, driving a buggy he had rented from the livery stable. Olivia, watching eagerly for him, felt her heart swell when she saw that he hadn't made any effort to impress; he wore his customary pants and shirt, a bandanna knotted at his neck, his gun belt buckled low on his lean waist and tied to his thigh. He looked exactly like what he was, and she loved him for not trying to put on a false front. Luis didn't need to impress anyone.

She opened the door and stood waiting for him, her face radiant with happiness. Luis smiled as he walked toward her, his dark eyes alight. The memory of their lovemaking shimmered between them, and Olivia's breath caught.

"I'm ready," she said, indicating the two cases behind her.

As Luis bent to pick them up Wilson opened the door of his study and cleared his throat. "I'd like to speak to you, if I may."

Honora came down the stairs, wringing her hands at the sight of the cases. Her eyes were red-rimmed.

Luis straightened, his dark face calm. "Of course."

Wilson stood aside and indicated his study. "In private."

"Papa," Olivia said, her tone alarmed.

"Hush. This is between us."

"No, it isn't!" she cried, stepping forward. "I'm involved, too."

Luis touched her arm, smiling down at her. "It'll be all right," he softly assured her. Then he walked into the study, and Wilson closed the door behind them.

He turned to face the banker. Perhaps Olivia had expected to leave without this confrontation, but Luis had known better. The man was concerned about his daughter; hell, Luis wouldn't have thought much of him if he hadn't been. If he could settle any worries, he was willing to try—it would make Olivia happier, and he would do anything to accomplish that.

Wilson drew himself up. "I'll give you five thousand dollars to leave here and never see my daughter again."

Luis's eyes narrowed, and a dangerous gleam entered them. "No" was all he said.

"If you think that marriage to my daughter will make you rich—"

"Stop right there. Don't even say it." His dark eyes were cold with anger. "I'm marrying Olivia because I love her. If you're worried about your money, then keep it. I don't want it or need it." Without another word he walked past the banker and left the room.

The sight of his face made Olivia's heart skip a beat, and she rushed to him, catching his arms in a grip so tight her nails dug into his flesh. "Luis?" she whispered, frightened.

His expression softened as he looked down at her. "Don't worry," he said. "We can leave now."

Behind them they could hear the study door open again. Honora took a quick step forward as if she could keep them from walking out the door. Then she stopped, her anguished gaze locked on the man who was taking her beloved daughter away. Luis glanced up at her, his usual warmth toward women entering his eyes. He could understand Honora's distress and would willingly have done anything he could to alleviate it, except for leaving Olivia behind.

He crossed to the stairs and took Honora's hand. "I promise you I'll take good care of her," he said.

Even through her pain Honora responded to him, her fingers tightening around his; she clung to him as if for comfort. "But where will you live?" she wailed.

He shrugged. "Wherever Olivia wants," he said simply. "But wherever we are, I promise we'll bring the grandbabies to see you once a year, without fail."

Grandbabies! Honora's mouth opened and closed without making a sound. Her chest swelled with emotion. Grandbabies! Her own beloved Olivia's children.

And this man loved Olivia, truly loved her. Honora had been so worried, but now she could see it in those deep eyes. Well, of course, she thought suddenly. How could anyone not love Olivia? He might not be a stalwart pillar of the community, but he was a strong man, and sometimes that was better security than an uneventful life. More than anything she wanted Olivia to be happy, and, looking at this man, she was suddenly certain that he would make that happen.

"Do you think you could wait for me to arrange a wedding?" she asked.

"Honora!" Wilson said, shocked.

Luis gave her a devilish grin, one that made Honora's heart beat a little faster. "I'd rather not," he said. "But I'd be honored if you would stand up with us this afternoon."

"I . . . why, yes," she said, flustered. She gave Wilson a beseeching look. "Of course we'll be there. I wouldn't miss Olivia's wedding for anything."

"Honora!" Wilson said again.

She turned toward her husband. She seldom gainsaid him in anything, but what did men know about other men? It took a woman to know what another woman needed. "Don't 'Honora' me! Can't you see that he loves her?"

"Of course he does," Olivia said confidently. She smiled at her parents, her eyes shiny with tears. "What more could you want for me?"

Only the moon, Wilson thought, his chest painfully tight. But more than anything he didn't want to lose his beloved daughter, didn't want her to feel unwelcome in his home. Olivia had always been levelheaded, so why didn't he trust her judgment? It looked like the only thing he *could* do. His own eyes felt suspiciously moist, and he cleared his throat. "You're right. You have what's important. We'll be at your wedding, darling. Like your mother said, we wouldn't miss it for anything."

He and Luis shook hands, and though the look he gave Luis was hard, there was understanding between them. Honora began crying again, but this time her tears were much happier. Though she would miss Olivia dreadfully, she had always looked forward to this day.

And, of course, she always cried at weddings.

19

Dee got carefully out of bed and walked to the window. Sometimes she felt a dreadful sense of unreality and needed that view to reinforce in her mind where she was. There was a large block of time she couldn't remember; her last vivid memory was of crouching on the floor of the cabin and holding the rifle to her shoulder. After that there were only snippets of impressions until about a week ago, when she had awakened one morning and felt truly awake, though horribly weak, and the contrast between her last memory and her present situation was so sharp as to make her feel lost.

She hadn't asked questions, so she still didn't know exactly what had happened. She needed to know, but the need wasn't urgent. She would find out later, when she felt stronger. It was as if the immense weakness of her body had sapped her mind's energy, too; she didn't want to talk, didn't want company, she wanted only to sleep. She emerged briefly from the cocoon of sleep whenever the demands of her body grew too great, and as soon as the problem was solved—be it thirst or hunger or a need for the chamber pot—she drifted off to sleep again.

The periods of sleep were growing shorter, however, and for a few days she had been moving around the room with Betsy Acray's support. This was the first time she had gotten out of bed by herself, and though her legs were wobbly she was pleased that they supported her. It was a small milestone. If she had been presented with the task of walking down the stairs, she couldn't have done it, but as she felt not the slightest desire to go down-stairs she didn't care.

She was in Lucas's house. She wasn't certain how she had come to be there. He visited her at least twice a day, in the morn-ing and again at night. When he asked her a question she made an effort to answer, but the effort was apparent, and the answers were monosyllabic, so he didn't try to carry on a conversation. Sometimes when he looked at her she could see volcanic rage in his eyes and she wondered what was wrong, but the rage didn't seem to be directed at her, so she didn't feel it was worth the effort to find out.

It was the first time she had ever seen the Double C, and the contrast between the way Lucas lived and her own home was sharp. She had seen only this one room, but as it was a guest room the rest of the house was probably even grander. The bed was an immense four-poster, the linen sheets so smooth they felt like silk. The wood floor had been sanded to a satin finish and then polished, and a thick rug covered it to cushion her feet. There was an enormous wardrobe, a chaise longue upholstered in silk, a graceful cherrywood desk and chair, and a mirrored dressing table with a small bench. A big, comfortably upholstered chair had also been brought in for Betsy.

She had never felt inferior before, but Lucas's house made her feel that way. He would be at ease with women who wore silk dresses and perfume and jewels, while she milked cows and plowed and got dirt under her nails. He must have wanted Angel Creek very much to have been willing to marry her to get it. What would he have done after the wedding? Bought her a house in some city and sent her away so she wouldn't embarrass him?

She felt ashamed of herself for even thinking that. Lucas had been kind, taking her into his home while she recovered. He had never said or done anything that indicated he thought he was better than she; it was her own depression that brought the thoughts to mind. But seeing the Double C—as much of it as she could see from her window—and this room had made her realize how wide the gulf was between them.

"Oh!" Betsy said sharply from the doorway. "Miss Dee, you got up by yourself!"

Dee turned from the window. Betsy was carrying a tray with her noon meal, which meant that she had slept several hours after eating a few bites for breakfast.

"I'm going to get fat," she mused. "All I'm doing is sleeping and eating."

It was the first unnecessary thing she had said in the time Betsy had been taking care of her, and the girl threw Dee a startled glance as she hurried to deposit the tray on the desk and lend a supporting arm. "Miss Dee, you need to eat all you can. You're as thin as a stick."

Well, that was comforting, Dee thought wryly. Betsy was leading her toward the bed, and she rebelled. The bed was wonderful for sleep, but she had had enough of both sleep and that bed.

"I want to sit up and eat," she said. "The desk will do just fine."

Betsy looked worried, but Dee refused all attempts to change her mind. By the time they had crossed the room to the desk she felt as if she had run ten miles; her legs were trembling as she sank down onto the chair. Still, it was an accomplishment, and she would have to push herself if she ever expected to regain her strength.

Her meal was simple, a bowl of broth and a biscuit. She wondered why people thought that starving a sick person would help her get well. She was even more disgusted when she realized she couldn't eat all of it.

Still, it was time to make a change. "Who does the cooking here?"

Betsy still hadn't adjusted to a patient who was talking after two weeks of almost total silence. Her eyes were huge as she said, "His name's Orris, ma'am."

"Tell Orris that I appreciate his trouble, and that for dinner tonight I'd like to try just a little meat and potatoes in the broth. I won't be able to eat much, but it's time to start trying."

"Yes, ma'am," Betsy said.

"And are there any books in the house?"

"I don't know, ma'am. I ain't looked around." She had been too terrified of Mr. Cochran to risk his ire if he'd found her snooping around his house.

"Well, ask Orris or someone else. I'd like to have something to read, and I don't care what it is."

"Yes, ma'am."

"Are any of my clothes here?"

"No, ma'am."

"Then tell Lucas to get them. I'm tired of nightgowns."

Betsy's eyes rounded with horror at the thought of telling Mr. Cochran to do anything. Dee said, "Never mind. I'll probably see him as soon as you will, so I'll tell him myself."

Betsy slumped with relief. "Yes, ma'am." It had been a lot easier when Miss Dee hadn't done anything but sleep.

Dee's brief foray had exhausted her, but at least she still felt awake. She would have liked to continue sitting in the chair, but common sense told her it would be best to go back to bed before she toppled over. As she settled back down she looked toward the window. The sun was bright and hot, and she needed that brightness. After the dark weeks the sun told her that she was well and truly on the mend.

When Lucas came in to see her that night his eyes glittered with satisfaction. "I heard you've been sitting in the chair today."

She put aside the book she'd been reading. It was dull, but better than looking at the walls. She went straight to her request. "I need some of my own clothes. Would you get them from the cabin, or send someone else for them?"

He sat down in the chair and stretched his long legs out, crossing them at the ankle. "There's plenty of time for that."

She gave him a long warning look. "I don't intend to do anything more than sit in this room. I'm just sick of nightclothes. I can sit in regular clothes as well as I can sit in this." She tugged at the nightgown's long sleeve.

"Why go to all of the effort to change clothes when you're still spending so much time in bed?"

"Are you going to get the clothes or not?"

"No."

"Then get out and leave me alone," she snapped.

He threw back his head with a roar of laughter. Relief poured through him like sweet water, as delicious as when her fever had broken. These two weeks of withdrawn silence had been pure torment, because the frail woman lying so quietly in bed hadn't been the Dee he knew. This was his Dee, tart and headstrong, and he was going to love every minute of the next few weeks, with her totally in his control.

He got up and leaned over her, bracing his hands on either side of her hips. "You can't make me," he said. His eyes were alight with mirth.

Those green eyes narrowed dangerously. "Not right now, no."

"Not ever. When I've cared to fight with you I've won every time. No matter how much you dislike it, I'm stronger than you. And this is my land; what I say goes. You'll get your clothes only when I think you're strong enough to need them."

"I won't ever get that strong," she said sweetly, "if I don't eat."

He straightened with a scowl. She was herself again, all right. She was just contrary enough to refuse to eat, and her health was too precarious for that.

"All right," he growled. "I'll get your damn clothes. But I want your word that you won't try to go downstairs by yourself."

She gave him an impatient look. "I've already said I didn't intend to leave this room. I'm not stupid. The only way I could get down the stairs would be if I fell down them."

"That's exactly what worries me."

"Then you're worrying for nothing."

He glared at her, aware that she hadn't exactly promised anything, but equally aware that if he pushed her she would only get more obstinate, and they would end up in a battle of wills. If she showed good sense in what she tried to do, he'd let her set her own pace, and the only way to find out was to let her do it.

"What kind of shape is the cabin in?" she asked.

He wished she hadn't asked until she was stronger, but there was no use in trying to evade the question. "All of the windows are broken, the back door is splintered, a lot of things inside were shattered or are full of holes."

Her lips tightened. "The bastards. Have you checked to make certain Bellamy didn't run his cattle back in there?"

"He hasn't," Lucas said with certainty. There wouldn't be any point in it now, with Angel Creek dry, but Dee didn't have to know that yet. He wasn't going to tell her until he had to; he intended to use the next weeks to spoil her rotten and bind her to him.

"Will you check on it for me?"

The anxiety in her voice made him feel guilty. He leaned down and kissed her forehead. "Of course."

He was so delighted that she was talking again that he was reluctant to leave her. He sat on the bed, talking and teasing, trying to make her eyes flash angrily again, until Betsy came in and gave him a shocked look. He sighed, chafing under the necessity of observing at least a semblance of propriety. He'd be glad when Dee was well enough to do without Betsy so he could send the girl home.

Dee set herself to recovering her strength, carefully pushing herself more and more every day. Lucas brought her some of her own clothes the next day, and though they looked out of place in the luxury of the bedroom she felt relieved to be wearing something other than a nightgown. It made her feel she was truly on the road to recovery. She hadn't lied to Lucas about her intentions; she kept to her room, slowly walking back and forth, forcing herself to stay up for longer periods each time. As she became more active her appetite returned, and her face no longer looked so pale and drawn.

Lucas began to devote more time to keeping her entertained, knowing that boredom would drive her to test her limits faster than anything else. He brought a big selection of books upstairs for her, and at night he taught her how to play poker. To his delight she already knew how to play chess, no doubt one of the benefits of having a schoolteacher for a mother. Playing with her kept him alert. Her philosophy in chess was the same as it was in life: She was aggressive and determined. The trouble was, he could never predict which battles she would choose to fight or when she would simply use defensive strategies. They were so evenly matched that more often than not the games ended in a draw.

She had been at the Double C for three weeks when she descended the stairs for the first time, to eat a real meal at a real table. Lucas kept his arm firmly around her and his attention focused on each step, ready to catch her if she should falter. She gave him a cool look that said she wouldn't let herself be so weak and walked steadily to the table with her head held as arrogantly as any ancient queen's.

The occasion signaled that Betsy's usefulness had come to an end, and he wasn't sorry to see it. He suspected that she hadn't been much use the past week anyway, that Dee had been riding roughshod over her. Little Betsy was helpless against Dee's iron determination, and ridiculously worshipful. Every time she opened her mouth it was "yes, ma'am" until the two words ran together into one. If she decided to emulate her new heroine when she returned home, poor old Sid Acray would have the devil's own time controlling his newly headstrong daughter.

So Betsy was sent home the next morning, with Lucas's sincere gratitude for her help and generous wages in her purse. She cried as she hugged Dee and left with tearful admonitions to "be careful!" wafting back to them.

Lucas chuckled as he watched the buckboard disappear down the lane with Betsy still waving. Then he turned to take Dee's arm and walk with her back into the house. "Well, sweetheart, you're on your own today, so try not to get into any trouble. Orris is in the kitchen if you need any help, and I'll be back this afternoon."

She sighed. "I have to admit I've been looking forward to the solitude. I'm not used to having someone hover over me twenty-four hours a day."

He looked down at her and smiled as he felt the familiar tug of desire in his groin. Tonight he was going to do something about it. She still looked so frail that a good puff of wind would knock her off her feet, but she was stronger than she looked. She was regaining her weight, and translucent color glowed in her cheeks and lips. He had searched through his mother's old clothes and found a few light day dresses that were so plain they hadn't had any particular fashion to date them; Betsy, who had proved able with a needle, had hemmed and tucked until the dresses fit Dee, who was wearing one of them today. The flimsy, pale yellow lawn cloth suited her, as did the way she had caught her heavy tresses high on the back of her head, baring the delicate nape of her neck. As soon as they were inside he bent and pressed his mouth to that innocently sensuous groove, and he felt the shiver that ran through her.

Her clothes weren't all he'd fetched from the cabin. The little sponges lay in a box in his bedroom.

Dee felt his arms close around her and caught her breath in painful relief. She hadn't realized how much she had missed being held, how alone she had felt. She had quickly become accustomed to his touch, to feeling his hard body warm against her, and the lack of physical contact had depressed her. He hadn't even held her or kissed her during all the time she had been at his ranch except for passionless pecks on the forehead, and she hadn't cared for those at all. Lucas's nature wasn't passionless, and neither was hers.

She turned into his embrace, letting her head rest in the hollow of his shoulder. "Tired?" he asked, rubbing his hand over her back.

"I'm always tired. I just try to ignore it."

He lifted her in his arms and carried her upstairs, where he deposited her on the chaise longue and arranged a pillow behind her head. "Don't ignore it. Rest when you need to. You'll get your strength back faster that way."

"I don't have a lot of time," she said. "It's been a month. The garden will be overgrown with weeds, and everything will be getting ripe in a week or so. I *have* to get strong enough to work."

He stroked her cheek, then let his hand drift downward until it covered her breast. "Get strong enough for this first," he said.

Her heavy black lashes drooped. "You can do all of the work."

"I intend to." He leaned forward and kissed her, his mouth slow and hot, his hand heavy on her breast as he leisurely kneaded her. "But I'd like for you to be awake."

She laughed, then sighed at the deliciousness of his touch. "I think I can manage that."

He left her with a wink, and she closed her eyes, letting herself drift. With the night to look forward to, she had no intention of exhausting herself during the day.

Lucas rode over the pass to Angel Creek that day. His own land had revived with the rush of water, renewing enough of the grazing so that the cattle would survive; they were leaner than he liked, but they were not starving to death or dropping dead from dehydration. The change in Dee's valley was painful. It was still green, but the vegetation was brittle. The sight of her cabin made his jaw clench. It had been such a tidy, sturdy little place, and now it was almost destroyed. The walls and roof still stood, but the wreckage of the windows and the contents testified to the amount of firepower that had been directed at her. It was a miracle that she had survived. If she had been any less of a woman, she wouldn't have. It was as simple as that. She had seen to her own survival by teaching herself how to shoot, and by being smart enough to stay behind cover.

He walked out back to the garden and stood looking at it for a long time. The plants that had been so lush and promised such a rich bounty of crops had shriveled in the dry heat. Dee had worked so hard, and it had come to nothing, by his own hand. The creek bed was completely dry, and the valley was strangely silent. It had been perfect, and he had deliberately destroyed it. He would do it again, for it was the only way he could force Dee into a safer life. That didn't mean he didn't regret the change. Angel Creek had been special. Now it was nothing.

He had had Dee's livestock taken to the Double C, except for the chickens, which could survive on their own. They had already disappeared, lured out of the valley in search of insects and water. The valley was abandoned, and the cabin showed signs that squirrels and other small critters had begun nesting inside. He looked in the barn and found spare lumber and nails, so he boarded up all the windows and reset the back door in its frame. Dee would be upset enough without finding the cabin taken over by animals.

The valley bothered him. He was glad to get back to the ranch, which was alive and busy.

20

Lucas came into her bedroom that night as she was brushing out her hair. He took the brush from her hand and pulled it through the long strands, easing out the tangles until it streamed down her back like black silk.

She watched him in the mirror, her heartbeat settling into a heavy thud. He was shirtless, and the muscles in his torso flexed with every movement. He was so intensely masculine that even performing that very feminine chore for her didn't detract from his virility, but then only a man as self-confident as Lucas would have been so completely comfortable performing it anyway.

She wore the filmy pink gown he had brought her when she had fallen out of the loft. The thin straps barely hung on her shoulders, and the low-cut bodice lay loosely on her breasts, inviting a man's hand to slip inside. The fabric was just transparent enough to torment with what it didn't reveal, though she knew her nipples were plainly visible through the cloth.

Lucas's attention was focused on the mirror, and she watched the way his face changed, hardened, as he looked at her breasts. "It's been a long time," he murmured. Though the time could be measured in weeks, it had still been too long. He was beginning to think that even a day without her would be too long. He put the brush down and placed his hands on her shoulders, his rough fingers gliding over her smooth skin. He paused as he felt her thinness, the frailty of her collarbones.

Dee knew what he was thinking and let her head drop back against his abdomen. Their eyes met in the mirror. "This is the second time you've taken care of me," she said.

"And I hope the last."

She smiled, remembering how difficult it had been for her to accept his help that first time. But she had learned that she could trust his strength, and that had made this time of convalescence easier. If it had been anyone but Lucas caring for her, she would have forced herself to return to Angel Creek long before she was well enough. But he had said he would look after it for her, and she trusted him with her life as well as her valley.

She caught his hands and carried them to her breasts, closing her eyes in pleasure at the contact. "I won't break," she said huskily.

He picked her up and sat down in the big upholstered chair with her on his lap, her legs draped over the chair arm and her back supported by his left arm. "I don't have much control," he admitted, his voice a little thick. "If I lie down with you, I won't have any."

"Do you need it?" she asked. She gave him a slow smile. "You could always make it up to me an hour from now."

He laughed roughly. "I'm trying not to tire you out too much. I'm not going to make love to you all night long."

"Pity," she said.

"Yes, isn't it?" Slowly he brushed his mouth against hers, lightly touching his tongue to her lips. She slid her hand around his neck and moved closer, firming the contact. He obliged, slant-ing his head and deepening the pressure, gliding his tongue inward to meet hers. It had been so long that the onslaught of sensation was a little overwhelming, a little frightening, as if it were all new again.

Knowing that she was his, that he had the complete freedom of her body, went to his head faster than whiskey. He had meant to take his time, but the thin silk barrier over her breasts was intolerable, and he pulled the straps down her arms with two quick movements. She gasped a little as the bodice drooped to her waist, then she freed her arms from the straps and leaned back against his arm, offering him unobstructed sight and touch. He took advantage of both, cupping a soft mound in his palm and lifting it slightly as his thumb rasped over the nipple, making it tighten and stand erect. He pinched it lightly, enjoying the firm resilience.

"Lucas."

"What?" The word was absently spoken.

"I don't need a lot of attention."

He looked up and noticed the color in her cheeks, the way her breathing had hastened. "It's been a long time for me, too," she said, strain evident in her voice.

He held her gaze and slid his hand up her thigh, pushing the gown high and baring her legs. When he reached the notch between her legs he expertly slipped his fingers in, sliding them along the soft folds. Dee's body jerked, and she let her legs fall open. "Don't close your eyes," he whispered when he saw her lashes start to droop. "Keep them open. Look at me."

She blinked, trying to focus, but her expression was dazed. He touched her soft opening and lightly circled it with his fingertips. She couldn't help it; her head fell back over his arm as her entire body tightened, the heated sensation coiling through her. He let her lie back with her head dangling backwards and removed the support of his left arm, leaving her lying across his lap like a sacrifice.

She felt helpless lying like that, totally at his mercy. She was bare except for the nightgown twisted around her waist, and totally boneless, unable to sit up even if she had wanted to. He pushed her legs further apart, and cool air washed over her sensitive flesh, telling her how exposed she was to his gaze. She heard a low, throbbing moan and knew it was hers.

"Are you ready for me?" he whispered, and he slid one big finger into her.

She arched and cried out, the hot tension radiating from her loins in waves. He moved his finger in and out, stimulating her almost beyond sanity, making her writhe on his lap in helpless, mounting ecstasy.

She was like fire, out of control and rapidly escalating toward climax. "Not yet," he said urgently, sitting her up and turning her so that she faced him, sitting astride his lap with her legs spread. He tore at the buttons of his pants. "Not yet. I want to be inside you, sweetheart, I want to feel you come."

"Hurry," she moaned, her hips undulating in search of the hot pleasure he had taught her.

He grunted as he freed his swollen organ and held it braced for her, his other hand on her buttocks bringing her forward, sliding her onto his shaft. She almost screamed at his hard, fierce heat penetrating deep into her. His big hands closed on her hips, and he moved her up, down, up again. The second downward stroke was all she required, and she was lost, submerged in the shimmering wave of sensation that caught her and tossed her in its upheaval, sending her inner sheath into spasms and making her soft muscles clamp down on him. He threw back his head with a harsh groan, fighting his response, but it was too late for him, too. He heaved upward, his fingers bit into the soft flesh of her hips as he ground her down onto his manhood, penetrating as deep into her as he could go, and his hot seed erupted with a force that convulsed him.

They calmed slowly, small aftershocks of sensation erupting along their nerve endings and prolonging the pleasure. Fatigue settled on Dee like a heavy blanket, and she slumped forward, her face buried against his throat, unable to move.

Lucas held her cradled in his arms. He felt pretty damn weak himself. He rubbed her back, luxuriating in the aftermath of release. "Dee? Honey, are you all right?"

She made a noise, but nothing that resembled words.

He gripped her arms, holding her back a little from his chest. She was utterly boneless. "Dee? Damn it, answer me."

"Leave me alone," she mumbled.

He eased her back down onto his chest, stroking her hair away from her face. "Do you want to go to bed now?"

"Mmm."

He smiled and closed his eyes. God, it felt good to hold her, to feel her safe and warm in his arms. It felt good to thrust into her and let go of his control, to feel the deep linking.

He shifted her in his arms so she was lying sideways again and awkwardly pulled up his pants with one hand while he supported her with the other. She looked blissfully asleep and didn't stir even when he got to his feet. He placed her on the bed, removed the nightgown, shed his own clothing, put out the lamp, and got into bed beside her. He settled her against him, feeling the contentment now that she was where she belonged. If he had his way, she'd never spend another night away from him.

He normally woke before dawn, and the next day was no exception. He was achingly hard. Dee stirred against him, and he mounted her, sliding into her with a total lack of haste.

This time it was slow, almost leisurely. She responded drowsily, and he tried not to make any great demands on her. The demands of her own body, however, eventually dispelled her lassitude, and she began moving under him with increasing urgency. The morning sun, already hot, was rising over the mountains by the time they relaxed, mutually replete.

Realization of what he had done hit him like a poleax. He propped himself up on his elbow, his hand going to her belly. "Damn it, we didn't use the sponges."

Her eyes opened, and they looked at each other in silence. He didn't say, "If you get pregnant, we'll get married," because she didn't respond well to ultimatums, and that's essentially what the statement would be. What he said was, "If we had a kid it would have to be a pure hell-raiser," and a slow grin spread across his face as he contemplated the idea.

"Don't look like that," she grumped.

"Like what?"

"Like the idea tickles you."

"It does. Just think what a fighter a son of ours would be."

"It would serve you right if you only had girls," she announced, "and every one of them was just like you. Just think of all the young men prowling around."

The idea was mind-boggling. He fervently hoped he never had any daughters, because he didn't think his heart could bear up under the strain, especially if they were anything like their mother. Dee didn't know it yet, Lucas thought to himself, but she was going to be the one having his kids.

* * *

Two days later they had visitors at the Double C. Dee was sitting on the porch, and Lucas, who had made a point to stay close by since she had truly begun recovering, was in the barn. He walked up to the house when he saw a pair of riders approach.

Dee got to her feet and walked to the steps. One of the riders was Olivia. Betsy had been full of the gossip about Olivia marrying a Mexican gunman who just happened to be the very same man who had risked his life to help Dee during the fight with the Bar B men, of which he had been one. All of that had confused Dee, because she hadn't known anyone was helping. It certainly explained why she had been able to hold them off for so long, however. And she had never even met the man whom Olivia loved.

But she was about to meet him, for the man riding with Olivia was tall and lean and darkly handsome, and the way he wore his gun said that he was very proficient with it. She looked at him curiously and felt a little shy.

"Oh, Dee, you're looking so well," Olivia said warmly as she slid from her horse. With a small sense of shock Dee realized that Olivia had been riding astride, something she would never have suspected her of doing. It was something that she herself did all the time, but Olivia was different.

"I feel fine," Dee said, smiling as she went down the steps. "I don't have my full strength back, but every day I'm a little stronger."

They hugged each other, aware as they did so that their lives had changed over the course of this summer and would never again be the same. Olivia's eyes misted over, and Dee bit her lip to keep her control.

Luis dismounted and stood beside Olivia, his dark eyes surveying Dee with obvious approval. She felt herself blushing a little and was surprised at herself. There was something in that very male look, which was in no way insulting, that made her soften. "This is my husband," Olivia said with pride. "Luis Fronteras. Luis, this is Dee Swann, my best friend."

Dee held out her hand, but instead of shaking it Luis folded her fingers tenderly in his and carried them to his lips. "Miss Swann, you were amazing with that shotgun. It was something to see."

Her hand still tingled where he had kissed it. She looked down at it in amazement, then back up to Luis. "I owe you my life," she said simply. "Thank you."

"Thank Mr. Cochran," Luis said, nodding toward Lucas, who was striding toward them. "If he hadn't arrived when he had, I think we would both be dead."

Lucas shook Luis's hand and kissed Olivia's cheek. "Congratulations," he said to Luis. "You have a wonderful woman for a wife."

"I think so," Luis said peacefully.

"Come inside and have something cool to drink," Dee invited. "It's too hot to stand around out here."

Lucas put his hand on Dee's elbow as she went up the steps. She was feeling the effects of the heat far more than anyone else, which indicated how far she was from complete recovery.

There was iced tea to drink, for Orris had been making it for Dee. Lucas and Luis each took a glass, and their eyes met ruefully, but they didn't say anything. Dee and Olivia, of course, saw nothing unusual in drinking tea.

"I wanted to see for myself that you were recovering," Olivia said to Dee, "and to tell you and Lucas good-bye. Luis and I are leaving tomorrow."

"Where are you going?" Dee asked. "Will I ever see you again?"

"Of course you will! We won't be gone forever. We're going to go to St. Louis and take a train ride." A look of ecstasy came into Olivia's blue eyes. "We're going to go as far as the tracks will take us. It's something I've always wanted to do."

Dee thought about it. She had always thought of traveling as what you had to do to get to a definite destination; she had never considered traveling just for the sake of traveling. If that was Olivia's dream, she could scarcely have picked a better husband for herself. She wished them all the happiness in the world.

Lucas and Luis were talking quietly, and without being able to hear what was said Dee knew they were discussing what had happened at Angel Creek. Their faces were too serious for it to be otherwise.

"Bellamy hasn't been seen in town," Luis said. "Opinion is

pretty strong against him." He eyed Lucas. "I heard you beat the hell out of him."

"I tried hard enough," Lucas replied grimly.

"Tillie has been staying out at the Bar B with him, taking care of him."

"She loves him," Lucas said. "I don't understand it myself, but she does."

"Yet she still rode out here to get you to stop him."

"And she was crying the whole time. She begged me not to kill him. I guess I would have if it hadn't been for her. If Dee had died, I'd have killed him anyway."

"Is Dee truly all right?"

Lucas glanced over at her. "Stronger every day. She'll want to go back to Angel Creek pretty soon."

Luis grimaced. He knew what Lucas had done, because he'd heard rumors and had ridden out to Angel Creek himself to see if they were true. He hadn't told Olivia, knowing that she would be very upset on Dee's behalf. His dark eyes were grave. "I don't envy you, my friend, when she finds out."

Lucas grinned. "It'll be interesting for a while, but she'll eventually see reason."

"If she loves it so much," Luis said, "she may be too hurt to see anything but the pain. You took a big risk."

"And I'd do it again," Lucas said quietly. "I'd sow every acre of it with salt if that was the only way I could keep her safe."

21

Dee woke up and stretched lazily, deliciously aware of Lucas next to her in the bed. They had slept together every night for over two weeks, and she had cherished every moment of it because she knew it couldn't last. She lay in the early-morning darkness and faced the knowledge that the time had come for her to go home. She was fully recovered; there was no need to stay and every reason for her to leave. She had so much work to do that she didn't know if she would be able to handle it, but she had to get started or lose her entire garden. Vegetables wouldn't wait indefinitely without spoiling.

Lucas stirred and reached for her, tucking her in close against him. "I'm going home today," she said quietly.

He stiffened beside her, then got up and lit the lamp. His beard-roughened face looked harsh in the mellow light. "Why?"

"Because it's my home. I can't stay here forever. People are already talking, not without good reason."

"You could marry me."

She looked both rueful and sad. "You don't have to offer. Kyle Bellamy's sense of timing couldn't have been worse. I had just decided to let you graze your cattle in the valley, to get you through the drought. From what I've seen, though, you're still in good condition. You don't need Angel Creek."

"You don't either," he said roughly, stricken by her offer. Damn her generosity; she made him feel doubly guilty. "If you hadn't lived out there, none of that would have happened."

"It doesn't matter now. I just wanted you to know that you don't have to marry me to have access to the valley."

"Marry me anyway." His eyes were fierce. "You know it isn't just Angel Creek I want."

"I know." She thought of his ambitious plans, his fine house, and knew that she was out of place. "You want the Double C to be an empire. I can't be part of that, Lucas. I couldn't bear it in Denver, not even temporarily. I would make you miserable. People would ridicule you because of me. I'm not very good in social situations," she said with a wry smile that did nothing to ease his expression. She tried another way to make him understand. "When—when my parents died I was terrified. All of a sudden I had no one, and I thought I might die, too, because I had no reason not to. But I had the land. Somehow, living there, making things grow—it helped. It isn't just that I love it, but that I need it. Angel Creek valley doesn't belong to me nearly as much as I belong to it."

"Damn the valley!" His outburst was violent. He thrust his fingers through his dark hair, wishing it could have been put off for another week. "There's nothing out there now. I diverted the creek."

Dee blinked at him, not certain she understood. "What?"

"I diverted the creek. Angel Creek is dry now. Your valley isn't worth a hill of beans without water."

Dee got out of bed, her face blank with shock, her mind reeling from the enormity of what he'd done. She reached for her clothes.

"I'd do it again," he said harshly. "I would have eventually done it anyway, to keep the ranch going. Come hell or high water, I'll do what I have to do to protect the Double C. But that damn valley was going to get you killed, and you're too stubborn to admit it. Without it you'll be safe, you can sleep without having to keep one eye open. I did what was necessary."

She didn't look at him as she finished dressing. She spoke slowly, still feeling numb from the shock. "Then you should understand that I'll do whatever's necessary to keep my garden."

He lost control of his temper in the face of her obstinacy. "Forget the damn garden!" he yelled. "You don't need it. I'll give you the money you would have earned from it."

She straightened and faced him. Her eyes were terrible in their glittering clarity. "Keep your money, Cochran. I told you the day I met you that I wouldn't make a good whore, and nothing's changed."

It was worse than a nightmare, because she could wake up from a nightmare. She had imagined the garden overrun with weeds, the vegetables overripe. She could have salvaged something from that, put by enough to get her through the winter even if there wasn't enough to sell at the general store.

What she saw was the complete opposite of the overripe bounty she had expected. The vegetables had literally withered on the vine, seared by the heat, deprived of the water that had nourished the earth. The ears of corn hadn't filled out. When she examined the stunted ears she felt only a few dried kernels beneath the husks.

Angel Creek was dry, and the valley was turning brown. She walked out into the meadow, the one that had been full of wildflowers that glorious dawn when Lucas had made love to her lying on the soft meadow grasses. There were no flowers now, no sweet, rich scents to delight her.

Without the rushing whisper of water the valley was eerily quiet. She walked up the creek bed. She could see it was dry, but somehow she had to verify it. How could she mourn unless she truly understood the depth of what had happened there?

And Lucas had done this to her, deliberately destroyed her home.

She wanted to feel the energizing rush of anger, clean and hard, but this went beyond anger. She felt numb, as if a part of her had ceased to live.

She went back to the cabin and stared at the boarded-over windows. That would also be Lucas's doing, she guessed. She supposed she should be glad he had made the effort.

The cabin was in ruins, but remembering the barrage of bullets that had assaulted it, she hadn't expected anything else. She had been prepared for that. It was the death of the valley that shook her to the base of her soul.

Work had always soothed her, so it was a good thing she was facing such a mammoth chore. She hardly knew where to begin in the cabin. So much had been damaged, and little of it could be salvaged. She swept out all of the broken glass, then drew up a bucket of water and spent an hour on her knees trying to scrub the bloodstains from the floor.

It took an hour before it registered. Water. She sat back on her heels and looked at the water bucket. The well was still good.

Hope ran wild, making her giddy. Dropping the scrub brush, she dashed out to the garden and walked down the rows, examining each plant.

The corn was totally lost; it was too dependent on water during the growing stages. But what about the beans and tomatoes, the onions and squash? Some of the plants had been sturdier than the others and still had life in them.

She ran back to the well and dropped the windlass, listening for the life-giving splash as it hit water.

All of her determination centered on the well. It took more strength than she had ever realized to draw up a bucket of water, and she was trembling after she had done it three times. Three buckets of water, at half a bucketful to each plant that looked as if it had a chance at survival, equaled only six plants. The intensely dry heat seemed to suck it out of the ground almost as fast as she poured it on, but she was careful to pour at the base of the plants so the root systems could get as much as possible.

The sun was too hot. She paused and looked up at it, wiping her face on her sleeve. It was wasting water to pour it out in this kind of heat. Nighttime would be better; the plants would get more of it that way, and she would be able to work more comfortably in the cooler hours.

With that decision made she returned to the cabin and the work there. The results were discouraging. There was so little left that didn't have a bullet hole in it, even the pots and pans. Her iron skillet had survived, of course, but other than that she found only two pots that were usable. Even her biscuit pan was a casualty, and the coffeepot had so many holes in it that it resembled a sieve.

But no matter how useless it seemed she didn't let herself stop. If she stopped, she would think about Lucas, and she would break. She would sit down and howl like a lost child. If she could just stay busy and numb, she would be all right.

She had become soft during the past weeks. When the night finally cooled it was all she could do to force herself to move instead of collapsing in bed, as her body kept insisting she do. Everything was too dry for her to risk carrying a lamp out to the garden, so she worked by starlight.

She found that after a while she became so numb that she no longer felt her exhaustion. She hauled up bucket after bucket of water and trudged to the garden to empty it on what seemed like endless rows of plants.

It was some time after midnight when she realized she had been standing at the well in a stupor, holding an empty bucket in her hand. She didn't know how long she had been standing there.

Her legs felt as if they had lead weights attached, and her hands had no feeling. She was so tired she couldn't lift her feet. She went back to the cabin, fell facedown on the bed, and didn't stir until noon.

That first day set the pattern for the days that followed. She tried to sleep as much as possible during the day, and at night she hauled water to the garden. She didn't think about it, didn't try to assess her progress, she just did it. She knew that if she ever stopped she would have no hope left.

Eight days after she had left, Lucas rode over to Angel Creek. It was late in the afternoon, but cooler than it had been in weeks. He figured eight days had been long enough for her to stew; now they could have a thunderous fight and clear the air.

Every day he had resisted the urge to check on her, to ride out there and see if he could talk sense into her. Damn, he missed her. He hadn't had nearly enough time with her. It would take a lifetime to satisfy him.

The first thing he saw when he rode up was Dee carrying a bucket of water out to the garden and carefully pouring it around the plants.

Anger seared him. That damn garden! He should have pulled

the plants up by the roots and burned them. Why couldn't she see how useless it was?

He strode to meet her as she walked back to the well. She would have gone past him without even glancing at him, and his temper erupted. He jerked the bucket out of her hand and hurled it across the yard. "What in hell are you trying to do?" he yelled. "Kill yourself?"

She pulled her shoulders up very straight. "Thanks to you," she said softly, "I'm having to water my garden by hand."

"Goddammit, Dee, it's too late!" He grabbed her arm and dragged her over to the garden. "Look at it!" he raged. "Open your eyes and look at it! You're pouring water on dying plants! Even if you could get some of them to bloom again, winter will be here before they can bear."

"If I don't have a garden, then I don't eat," she said. She tugged free of his grip and walked over to pick up the bucket.

He followed her and kicked it away from her outstretched hand. "Don't pick it up," he said with clenched teeth. She had been almost back to normal when she had left him, now she was noticeably thinner, and dark circles lined her eyes. Her face was pallid and drawn. "You've lost," he said. He put his hands on her shoulders and shook her. "Damn it, you've lost! It's over with. There's nothing left out here worth having. Get your clothes, and I'll take you home."

She jerked away from him. "This is my home."

"This is *nothing!*" he roared.

"Then *I'm* nothing!" she suddenly shrieked at him.

He tried to regain his control, but his voice was iron hard when he spoke. "You have two choices. You can take the money I offered you for the land and live in town, or you can marry me."

She was taking deep breaths, searching for her own control. Carefully she said, "Why would you want to buy worthless land? I don't want your conscience money, and I won't take charity."

"Then we're getting married."

"Those are your choices, not mine." Her hands were knotted into fists. "If I won't take your money to ease your conscience, you can bet I won't marry you for the same reason. My choice is to stay on my land, in my own home."

"Damn it, you'll starve out here."

"My choice, Cochran."

They faced each other like gunfighters. In the silence that stretched between them they heard a deep rumble, and a cool wind played with her skirt.

Lucas lifted his head, a frozen expression on his face. He sniffed, catching the unmistakable scent of dust and rain.

Dee looked up at the bank of dark clouds advancing toward them. The sky had been clear for so long that she stared at them in stupefaction. Rain clouds. Those were actually rain clouds.

They saw it coming, a misty gray wall sweeping down the slope. Within a minute it had reached them, slapping at them with scattered raindrops so big that they stung when they hit and made little dust rings fly up from the earth.

Lucas took her arm and propelled her up on the porch; they reached it just as the rain became a deluge. Thunder boomed so loud that the ground shook.

They stood in silence on the porch and watched the rain blow in sheets. It became apparent that it wasn't going to be a brief summer thunderstorm as the rain settled down to a hard, steady downpour.

He had seen it before and knew it for what it was. It was a drought-buster, the signal of a change in the weather, and just in time, too. None of the surrounding ranches had gone under, but another week would have seen cattle dying. Everyone had survived the drought.

Everyone but Dee.

The hard rain would replenish the ground water and refill the wells. It would save ranches and herds, bring grass springing back to life. Runoff from the mountain would fill Angel Creek again, but it would only be temporary. The valley would revive, but it would be too late for her, too late for the garden. When it was all said and done, everyone had made it through the drought except her.

She turned and walked into the cabin, quietly closing the door behind her.

She hadn't cried before, but now she did. She had kept herself under strict control, forcing herself to work automatically instead of thinking, but she could no longer keep the thoughts at bay.

Lucas could not have chosen anything designed to hurt her more. She had fought so hard for her independence, had carefully carved out a life for herself that she had loved, and he had destroyed it. If it had been Kyle Bellamy, she could have understood it; she could have been angry and hostile, she would have done what she could to prevent it, but she wouldn't have been so totally stunned by betrayal. It wouldn't have devastated her emotions if she hadn't loved Lucas, but she did. Even now she loved him. And he had demonstrated more clearly than she could ever have imagined that she meant nothing to him at all.

Lucas stood outside the door and listened to her crying, the sound mixing with that of the rain until sometimes they were indistinguishable, or perhaps they were the same.

He had never imagined Dee crying. He had never imagined that the sound of it would tear at his soul and leave it ravaged.

He had never imagined that he could hurt her, and now he knew just how stupidly arrogant he had been.

22

Lucas remembered what Luis had said: If Dee loved Angel Creek so much, she would be too hurt to see beyond the pain. He had known she loved it, but he had disregarded her feelings, assuming that he knew what was best for her. The truth was, he had done what was best for himself, not only in securing water for the ranch but in trying to manipulate Dee so that she had no choice but to marry him. Not once had he considered that losing Angel Creek would break her heart, though he should have; he loved the Double C in the same way. He loved it so much that he would never, ever forgive anyone responsible for destroying it.

But he had done exactly that to the woman he loved.

He had been so arrogant that he had blithely assumed living on the Double C would more than compensate her for losing Angel Creek. He had assumed that she would merely be angry, and that he would eventually be able to wear her down.

He should have remembered her deep, fierce passions, and the way she had looked that morning when he'd found her in the meadow, her face so radiant it had hurt him to look at her. He had discounted the strength of her love and made the worst mistake of his life. How could he convince her that he loved her after he had deliberately smashed the very foundation of her life?

Everyone was jubilant about the rain, almost giddy as they watched water holes refill and streams begin to run. Even the Bar B had managed to get by. Lucas felt savage as he watched it rain again the next day, and the next. It had all been for nothing, everything that Dee had endured. Bellamy had attacked her for nothing. He, Lucas, had destroyed Angel Creek valley for nothing. Fate and nature had mocked them by sending the rain just in time for the ranchers, but far too late for one woman.

He had her bull and two cows returned to her, and he bought some chickens to replace the ones that had left when he'd diverted the creek. He didn't take them himself because he didn't think she would be glad to see him under any circumstances just then, and maybe never.

Dee forced herself to go through the motions of living. She was too stubborn to let herself give up, but she did everything automatically, without hope or purpose. As Lucas had so caustically pointed out to her, she had been wasting her time pouring water on dying plants. None of them had recovered enough to bear.

No matter how she looked at it, she was in a hopeless situation. She still had some of last year's bounty that she had canned, but not enough to last through the winter, unless she could live on milk and eggs. She didn't have enough money to repair the cabin and buy food, too, but she wouldn't be able to stay in the cabin through the winter without repairing it. If she repaired the cabin, she would starve. Every alternative she explored brought her to a blank wall.

Unless she could find a job, she didn't know how she could live through the winter. And even if she did, what about next year? Could she manage a large garden without Angel Creek to nourish it, relying only on what rain came? Perhaps, though it would inevitably mean watering by hand again. A lot of families got by like that. But families were just that, families. By definition there were at least two people to share the work. Though she was strong, she knew her limitations. If she tried to grow a garden as large as she normally did, she would wear herself down trying to tend it, and exhaustion led to clumsiness, which led to accidents.

She could grow just enough for herself and manage to eat. But there wouldn't be any money for repairs, or for clothes. Not that she had that many clothes now, she thought, picturing her utilitarian garments, but she had always been able to replace them as they had worn out.

If she found work, she could survive, but it wouldn't be much more than that. She wouldn't be able to garden, wouldn't have the time.

She had loved it so. The rich scent of the earth in the mornings, the cool, silky feel of the dew, the tangible rewards of harvest, the almost blissful satisfaction of seeing the life and bounty that, with her care, the earth had given so generously. There had been a sublime rhythm to the seasons. She had followed nature's timing, renewing in the spring, flourishing in the summer, harvesting, then lying dormant through the long winters. No matter what she did now, it seemed she had lost that, the very thing she had most loved.

But people all over the world faced shattering disappointments, even tragedies, and went on with their lives. Time was inexorable. She had to either cope or give up. She knew how to do the first, but not the second.

The first person she went to see about a job was Mr. Winches at the general store. He peered sharply at her. "What's that?"

"A job," she replied calmly. "It doesn't matter what. I can do your books, put up stock, sweep the floor."

"I can do all that myself," he grumped.

"Yes, I know."

He was still staring at her. He chewed on his lip. "Sorry about what happened to your place. Guess that's why you're here."

"Yes."

He sighed. "Wish I could help you, but the plain fact is it would be stupid for me to pay anyone to do what I can do myself. The store just ain't big enough to call for it."

"I understand," she said. "Thank you."

She didn't even feel disappointment, because it was exactly what she had expected. If she did get a job, no one would be more surprised than she would.

She tried the dry goods store, but Mrs. Worley was just managing to support herself. An employee was out of the question. It was the same situation at the hat shop.

She walked up and down the streets, going into every business. The bank didn't need any more clerks. The two restaurants were family-owned, and hiring anyone to help meant a family member would be left with nothing to do. Likewise at the two hotels. It was a fact of life. In a family-run business the jobs went to family. She had known the situation before she began asking, but she asked anyway on the off chance that someone might be laid up and unable to work.

The one seamstress in town didn't need any help. Most women did their own sewing; there just weren't enough people in Prosper who paid to have their sewing done.

Dee even asked about cleaning houses, and Mr. Winches let her put a notice up in his store. No one contacted her. The people who could afford to have someone do their cleaning already had someone to do it.

What she had told Lucas when she had first met him was the literal truth: The only job for her in Prosper was in one of the rooms over the saloon.

The one asset she had had—the land—was worthless now. She might be able to give it away, but no one was interested in buying it. She knew that Lucas would give her his guilt money in exchange for the deed, but it would be nothing more than disguised charity, because he certainly didn't need it. He had plenty of water—the sweetest, clearest water imaginable, inexhaustible. He had the Angel Creek water.

It wasn't called Angel Creek over on that side of the mountains. She didn't know if it even had a name. It wouldn't have the same character over there, for the Double C was wide grazing land, and the effects of the water would be muted. In her narrow little valley it had been miraculous, creating a small paradise. That was why it had been called Angel Creek. She had never thought of it as just a cut in the ground with water running through it; Angel Creek had been alive, with its own personality, its mystery, a full partner in the bounty her garden had produced. She grieved for it as if a person had died.

If there was anything she had it was pride, yet as the days

passed she was forced to the realization that she might yet have to swallow that pride and accept Lucas's money. There was nothing for her there, but she would be able to start again somewhere else.

Lucas! She still couldn't let herself think about him. The pain was still too fresh, too enormous. She lived every day with the knowledge of it, but she didn't take it out and examine it, or try to understand it. It was simply there. As long as she could ignore it she could function, but if she ever let it out it would destroy her.

Her body, whose rhythms were as inexorable as the seasons, told her that she didn't carry his child.

She should have been relieved.

Yet, against all logic, she had hoped. A baby now would be a disaster for her, but still she had hoped. Those two unprotected times with him had been her last chances to conceive. She no longer cared about her reputation, if any of it was left; she would have loved his baby with all of the fierceness of her nature, just as she loved him. She wouldn't hurt so much if she didn't love.

It took Dee a moment to recognize the woman who rode up to her cabin. She wore a stylish riding habit and an impossibly chic little hat with a plume curling around the brim and sat gracefully sidesaddle. But the dark red hair was the same, and the liquid brown eyes. It was Tillie, the saloon girl who had ridden to the Double C for help. Dee supposed she owed her life as much to Tillie as she did to Luis Fronteras or Lucas. They had all played their parts.

The two women faced each other. "Good morning," Dee said quietly. "Would you like to come inside?"

Tillie dismounted and walked up on the porch. It was the first time in ten years that she had been invited into a respectable home. The cabin was humble and severely damaged, but not many people would have asked her inside or even greeted her civilly.

"Thank you for what you did."

Tillie gave a little smile. "It was only partially for you. I couldn't let Kyle destroy himself that way."

"I heard you're living on the Bar B now."

"Yes. We're getting married. But we may not stay in this area. I don't imagine folks will ever forget what happened, or forgive him. It's lucky both of us are good at starting over. And thank *you*. You could have stirred people up against him even more, but you didn't."

"There didn't seem to be much point in it. Lucas almost killed him." Colorado was a state now, she realized, but statehood hadn't changed the way folks handled things. If there was a dispute, people settled it without bringing the law into it. Kyle had received more punishment than the blows from Lucas's fists; he was virtually an outcast, his reputation destroyed.

Looking around the cabin, Tillie said, "You'll be starting over, too. I came to offer you some reparation for the damage. I know I can't make up to you for what happened to your place, but it will help you get by."

Starting over. Dee's heart thumped. How could she start over? "Kyle didn't cause this," she said. "Oh, he's the cause of the damage to the cabin, but Lucas Cochran is the one who ruined this valley."

"He wouldn't have done it if it hadn't been for Kyle," Tillie said gently. "It was a hard decision, and a hard thing to do, but then Lucas is a hard man. He knew that as long as you had Angel Creek there would be someone trying to take it away from you, and you'd always be in danger. So he took away the only reason anyone would have for wanting the valley. He did it to protect you."

A look of utter desolation came into Dee's eyes. "I would rather have taken the risk."

"*Lucas* couldn't have risked it. He loves you too much."

Dee said slowly, "When I walk outside, what I see doesn't look like an act of love."

"I know. Like I said, it was a hard thing to do. It was hard for me to ask Lucas to help you that day, knowing that Kyle might be killed because of me. Not many people would have seen that as an act of love, but it was. I would have done anything to have stopped him, even if he had hated me for it."

"I don't hate Lucas," Dee said, and it was the truth.

"But can you forgive him?"

"No. Not now. Maybe not ever. I just feel empty, like a huge part of me is gone. But it isn't a matter of forgiveness, it's a matter of living. Right now I'm not very interested."

Tillie had seen that look before in other women's eyes, even in her own eyes on occasion. It was the look of someone who had nothing to lose. That kind of bleakness went deep, and if the person ever recovered, she was different, changed in ways that were hard to understand.

"I brought the money with me," Tillie said briskly, changing the subject.

"I don't want Kyle's money."

"It isn't his, it's mine."

Dee looked at her in surprise. "All the more reason not to take it. You shouldn't have to pay; you aren't responsible for any of this. If anything, I owe you for saving my life."

"But Kyle's debts are mine," Tillie insisted. She smiled wryly. "It's part of loving someone."

"Thank you, but no." She might eventually have conquered her pride and accepted Kyle's money, she thought, because this was partially his fault, but it was out of the question to take money from Tillie.

Tillie hesitated. "I hear you've been looking for work in town."

"Yes, but there isn't any."

"Then take the money. I can afford it, and you need it."

Dee thought about the money and starting over, but it wasn't money she needed; it was water. She went still, staring at Tillie as if she had never seen her before. What was wrong with her brain? Anything that had been done could be undone. A creek that had been diverted once could be diverted again.

She must have been in a stupor from shock, from the pain of Lucas's betrayal. It was the only excuse she had for sitting there instead of *doing* something about the situation. She had never been one to sit and rail at fate; she rolled up her sleeves and took matters into her own hands.

She felt alive for the first time since Lucas had told her what he'd done, the old glitter returning to her eyes.

Watching her closely, Tillie said, "What? What is it? Do you have an idea?"

"I do. And there's something you can do to help me."

"Anything. I'm at your disposal."

A slow smile broke over Dee's face. "Can you get me some dynamite?"

Always interested in an adventure, Tillie went with her when Dee followed the creek bed up into the mountains to the source. It wasn't an easy trip by any means; Dee was certain there had to be an easier way, but she didn't know what it was.

They both wore pants, which was a good thing because several times they had to proceed on foot, leading their horses. They climbed and skirted and detoured, sometimes losing sight of the creek bed and having to work their way back to it. But when they reached the fork it was unmistakable. The earthen dam curved across the east fork, sending all of that beautiful water down onto Double C land.

Dee stared at the structure that had killed her farm. If Lucas had needed the water to survive, she would have built the dam herself, a handful of mud at the time. She had been willing to sell the valley to him. But *damn* if she would let him destroy something so beautiful, something that she loved so much, just because he thought he knew what was right for her better than she did!

"Have you ever used dynamite?" Tillie asked.

"No."

"Oh, my God."

"Don't worry. I asked in town. The blacksmith used to do some mining and showed me how it's done."

"Do you just light the fuse and throw it on the dam?"

"No. I'm going to plant it on the east side of the dam, at the bottom of it. That way, when it blows, it'll lower the creek bed, too." She understood very well the dynamics of what Lucas had done, and she was going to do the same thing.

It took her a while, using a knife, to gouge out two holes in the hardened clay. She wedged the sticks of dynamite in and stretched out the long fuses. She had taken the precaution of burning lengths of fuse so she could time how long it took to burn a foot, and she estimated how long the fuse would have to be to give her time to get safely away from the blast.

"You'd better start on down the mountain," she said to Tillie. "I'll give you five minutes before I light the fuses."

"I'd like to watch," Tillie said. "I came this far. I want to see you do it. I'll leave when you do."

They looked at each other and grinned.

Dee lit the fuses.

They ran for their horses, swung into the saddle, and rode for all they were worth. Dee silently counted the seconds.

Lucas was walking along the creek bank, looking at the water rushing along, oblivious to the battles that had been fought over it. It was deeper than he'd ever seen it before, in some places deep enough to swim.

He wondered if it was worth it.

Dee had been going from door to door in town, asking for work rather than coming to him. The irony of it was that he was the one person who couldn't deny her anything, and she would rather die than ask him.

He had hoped, despite everything, that she would come to him, that she would cool down enough to realize that he'd done it to protect her. But it wasn't a matter of temper, it was a matter of a hurt so deep that she was still reeling from it.

And it was pride. There had never been a prouder creature born than Dee Swann. That didn't make it easy to love her, but if she had been less proud, less fierce, she wouldn't have been the same person, and he wouldn't have loved her to distraction. If she hadn't been so strong, she wouldn't have been able to match him in strength of will, and he couldn't have loved her otherwise. She was exactly what he needed, a true mate.

But he had struck hard at that pride, and at the independence that was such a large part of it. Dee *would not* forgive him for Angel Creek; she couldn't do that and remain the same person. He had expected—demanded—that she be less than the person she was. She had to have the freedom of independence; it fed something within her, was part and parcel of the spirit that made her so strong. How had she put it? Angel Creek didn't belong to her as much as she belonged to it.

If he forced her to come to him, to surrender her pride, it would kill something within her.

The only chance he had was to give it back to her, that independence and pride. She would never come to him except as an independent woman with her dignity intact. She would always insist on maintaining that independence, on keeping some part of herself separate. How could he blame her for that when he was the same? He would never subordinate himself to anyone else, and neither would she. She might be his partner, but never his dependent. He had never wanted it otherwise, but it had taken losing her to make him realize it.

He looked at the water again. Precious stuff, but not as precious to him as Dee.

She had turned down his marriage proposal even after he'd told her it wasn't because of Angel Creek. At the time he'd been so angry that he hadn't thought about it, but suddenly it hit him. Even if he somehow made it up to her for Angel Creek, she still wouldn't marry him. He had told her all about his plans, how he intended to make the Double C an empire by using his money to influence political decisions. He had talked about the social functions in Denver, the balls and receptions he and his wife would have to attend because deals had a way of being made in social settings. He had been thinking of Dee at his side, had actually been arrogant enough to think he could make her over into a proper little socialite.

But Dee couldn't live that way, and she knew it. It wasn't just that she wouldn't enjoy the life; she had to be outside, free, unfettered by the suffocating rows of buildings and the unending rules of society. Had he truly been so blind that he had imagined she would fit in just because that was what he wanted? She had never asked him to change. How could he have been so stupid as to expect it of her?

He thought about all of his plans, his ambitions, and he weighed them on a mental scale. He had wanted influence only because of the Double C.

But hell, he was already rich. And Dee would bring much more to the ranch than his ambitions ever could. She would bring herself, her spirit, the children they would have.

He had to choose, and with blinding clarity he knew that there was no choice at all. He would take Dee over any amount of power or influence he could ever hope to build. He would sign the Double C over to her completely if that was what it would take to get her back. He wanted her as his partner for life.

His partner.

He blinked, astonished at the idea that had come to him. It just might work. It was the only thing he'd thought of so far that would even begin to make it up to her.

He heard the boom, low and rumbling, that came from the mountains. He looked up, expecting to see clouds, but the sky was clear. He didn't know where the thunder had come from.

Thunder, hell! Abruptly he realized exactly what it was. His mouth fell open, and he stared at the mountains. Then, helplessly, he began to laugh.

He should have expected that she would do something about the situation. That big boom was a signal that she was back in fighting form.

It was the next day when Dee heard a horse being ridden right up to the cabin. She looked out and saw Lucas swinging down from the saddle. She had expected him the day before and wondered what had taken him so long.

She picked up the shotgun and walked out on the porch. "What do you want?" she asked without preamble.

He stopped with his boot on the first step, warily eyeing the shotgun. "Now, Dee. If you were going to use that, you should have done it the first time I saw you. It's been too late ever since then."

She smiled. "It's never too late to correct a mistake."

"Exactly." He jerked his head toward the sound of running water, where Angel Creek once again flowed clear and deep. "Who set the charges for you?"

She jerked her chin up. "I didn't need anyone to do it for me. I did it myself."

Lucas stared at her, aghast. His heart almost stopped as he thought of the danger she had been in. Damn it, didn't she know how unstable dynamite was? He hadn't even considered that she had done it herself, though now that he thought about it he realized that he should have expected it. When had Dee ever asked anyone to do anything for her?

"Are you crazy?" he yelled, his face flushing with anger. "You could have been killed!"

She gave him a scornful look. "I suppose you think I didn't know what I was doing."

"Did you?" he shot back.

She lifted her eyebrows at him. "Evidently," she drawled. "I'm still here."

He felt like banging his head against the wall in frustration, and then suddenly he laughed, because he hoped she would be driving him crazy like that for the rest of his life. Maybe he was already crazy, because he could swear he'd seen a glint of amusement in those witch-green eyes. She loved making him lose control.

"Tillie helped me," she volunteered.

"Tillie!" He took off his hat and wiped the sweat off his forehead with an agitated motion. "Jesus." But it made sense. Tillie would do it because she would feel obligated to atone for Kyle's sins. In this instance, Lucas knew that his own transgression had been much greater than Kyle's, even though he had done it out of love.

Dee gave him a challenging look. "If you build another dam, I'll just blow that one up, too."

"I don't intend to build another dam," he said irritably. "Hell, I should have blown that one up myself. I just didn't think of it in time."

Startled, Dee stared at him. "Why would you do that?"

"Because I was wrong." He gave her a level look, their gazes locking. "Because I didn't have any right to build it in the first place. Because I'd do anything to get you back."

She had never seen his eyes so blue, so determined. Her heart began thumping in her chest, but she didn't dare let him see it.

He moved up one step, and she brought the shotgun up. "Stay right there," she warned.

He didn't even look at the shotgun. "Will you marry me?" he asked.

Involuntarily she glanced toward the creek.

"No, not because of that damn water," he snapped. "Keep this valley. I don't need it. What I need is you. I'll have papers drawn up so that the valley remains yours, and I'll sign the Double C over to you. Just marry me."

Dee was astounded by the offer. Her arms went limp, letting the shotgun waver and the barrel point downward. Before she could take another breath Lucas was on the porch, cautiously removing it from her hands and setting it aside.

"What did you say?" she asked dazedly.

"I said Angel Creek will stay your personal property, yours to do with as you see fit without any say-so from me. I don't know why I didn't think of it before. And I'll give you my ranch. I'll give you whatever you want if you'll just say yes."

She had never imagined he would say anything so astounding. He simply couldn't mean what he was saying. "But . . . *why?*"

He drew a deep breath; it was damn hard to put himself on the line, staking everything he had and his future happiness against her answer. "Because I need you, sweetheart. I need a wife who'll knock me in the head when I try to ride roughshod over her, and you're the only one who has ever dared. I've lost count now of how many times I've asked you to marry me, but let's get one thing straight right now: I've never asked you because of this valley or the water. I asked you because I love you. Is that clear?"

She couldn't think of anything to say. She gaped at him, her mind as blank as a chalkboard that had been wiped clean.

"I said, is that clear?" he barked.

"You can't want me," she blurted.

"Why the hell can't I?"

"Because . . . because I'm not what you want," she sputtered. "You're going to spend a lot of time in Denver, and I couldn't live like that. People would make fun of me. I wouldn't fit—"

"No, you wouldn't," he agreed maddeningly. "To hell with Denver. I'd rather have you."

"I can't ask you to give up—"

"Goddammit, you aren't asking me to give up anything!" he roared, at the end of his patience. "I know what I want. Now answer my damn question!"

She blinked and tried to gather her scattered thoughts. "I don't want the Double C," she said. "I wouldn't marry you because you offered me land."

Lucas threw his hat on the porch and considered stomping it. Instead he seized her arms and shook her. "Then forget the damn land," he said, his teeth clenched tight. "Just say you'll marry me."

It began unfurling slowly, a bloom of joy swelling inside her chest, and she tried to contain it. If she didn't, she'd be in danger of bursting. He meant it. Incredible as it was, he meant it. He would never offer to part with an inch of his beloved Double C unless he thought it was the only way he could convince her to marry him, yet he had offered to give her the entire ranch. He loved her, and the hot look in those blue eyes told her that he didn't feel even a tinge of regret for giving up his ambitions. He had made up his mind, and when Lucas Cochran made up his mind about something no one could change it.

"All right," she said.

He shook her again. "All right, *what?*"

She began to laugh. "Yes," she said.

"Yes, *what?*" God, she would make him a raving maniac before the year was out.

She gave him a smile of blinding sweetness. "Yes, I love you, too. Yes, I'll marry you. But not because of the Double C or any other reason, except that I love you. Was there anything else?"

Lucas hauled her against his chest, his arms so tight that her ribs were constricted. He closed his eyes as tears burned. He had gambled his entire life on this and had been in terror that she would refuse him. "God, you're stubborn."

"I know," she said placidly, the words muffled because her face was against his chest. "As stubborn as you."

"I meant it about Angel Creek. It stays yours. You need it, sweetheart. I didn't understand before." He kissed her hair. "As new owner of the Double C, you're one of the richest women in the state."

She lifted her head and gave him a blinding smile. "No," she said.

"Of course you are. I know how much the ranch is worth, damn it."

"I don't want the Double C."

"A deal's a deal."

"Not until I say 'I do' it isn't. I won't take the Double C. You need it just the way I need Angel Creek." Her hands crept up his back. "This doesn't have to be a surrender, you know. Why can't it be a partnership?"

"Hell, I don't care," he said impatiently. "Just as long as you marry me."

She felt surprisingly peaceful. "It doesn't matter whose name is on the papers as long as I can still come here," she said, and with a start she realized that it was true. Angel Creek was hers even if the title had Lucas's name on it. She trusted him, and because she did she wouldn't have to fight to maintain her independence. The respect he gave her as a person was a measure of her true independence, and that was all she'd ever wanted. Marrying him couldn't change that at all.

"That's what I realized about the Double C," he admitted. "The name didn't matter. Having you mattered, and the land would still be there. But we'll do it however you want," he said, tilting her face up for a hard kiss. "It can be your legacy to our kids, if you want."

Her entire body rippled with pleasure at the thought of the hours of lovemaking that would be necessary to get those kids. Lucas absorbed the movement, his own body responding.

"We'll fight a lot," he said, thinking of it with anticipation. He could barely wait.

"That's almost certain."

"And make love when the fighting's over."

She drew back to give him a long, green look. "That remains to be seen."

"No," he said, lifting her in his arms. "It doesn't." He strode down the steps and over to the creek bank, where the crystal water of Angel Creek swirled and glittered just as it had before, but with a certain giddiness to it, as if it were glad to be back. With a deep shout of laughter he tossed her into the water, then jumped in himself. It was cold, but they didn't care. Shrieking with laughter like a child, Dee jumped on his back and forced him underwater again, and they grappled together until the laughter died and something else came into his deep blue eyes.

He pulled her up on the bank and covered her there, shoving her skirt up and stripping her wet drawers away, then unbuttoning his pants and tugging them down only as far as was necessary, because he couldn't wait a minute longer. He linked them with a hard, single thrust, groaning as the tight heat of her body enveloped him. This was nothing less than paradise.

Dee's legs embraced him, then loosened. She pushed at his shoulder, and he rolled, taking her with him. She sat up and pushed her wet hair out of her eyes, and he caught his breath at the look of ecstasy on her face. It was the same exalted expression he'd seen there one dawn, and he had put it there. With the bright sky behind her and her eyes as green as emeralds, she was the most beautiful thing he'd ever seen, and she was his.

"We're getting married tomorrow," he said.

She leaned forward to kiss him, her mouth tender. "Whatever you say, darling," she purred.

He wasn't fooled for a minute.

EPILOGUE

Kyle and Tillie Bellamy eventually sold the Bar B and moved back east. Dee received one letter from Tillie saying that they were happy and were considering a move to New Orleans. She never heard from Tillie again.

Luis and Olivia Fronteras traveled for two years, then to her parents' delight returned to Prosper and bought land just west of the Bar B. Though Wilson Millican was never certain just how his son-in-law supported Olivia, they always seemed to have money and he didn't think he should inquire too closely. Olivia was happier than he'd ever seen her, and that was all he asked. He never would have imagined his sedate daughter as having a streak of adventure in her, but he had to admit it suited her. Then, in swift procession, Olivia presented her husband with three daughters. She couldn't have made him happier, because Luis was always delighted to be surrounded by females.

Lucas and Dee Cochran had five children. Three boys came first, hell-raisers just like he had predicted. The next two were girls, and by the time the oldest one was a year old Lucas was worrying. His baby girls were so much like their mother that he knew he wouldn't draw an easy breath for the rest of his life.

He and Dee fought and yelled and made up. The house rang with noise and passion. He wouldn't have had it any other way.

A LADY of the WEST

Dedicated to two wonderful friends,
Catherine Coulter and Iris Johansen,
for a lot of intangibles, such as support,
encouragement, laughter, and memories.
Thank God for Houston, Texas, February 1985.

A man in a passion rides a wild horse
—Benjamin Franklin

Beward the fury of a patient man.
—John Dryden

PROLOGUE

The land itself was extraordinarily beautiful, which was perhaps why the earliest humans to settle on the continent chose to live there. Twenty-five thousand years later, give or take a century, it would be called New Mexico, a name that failed utterly to suggest the magic of the pristine alpine forests in the north that were dotted with cold, crystal clear lakes, and graduated to rolling grasslands and solitary mountain cones. The air was so clear it soothed both the eyes and the brain, and the sunset skies were always filled with color.

The first people to live in New Mexico were what the white man would later call Indians, and they flourished for thousands of years in the beautiful land. But when the Spaniards came with their armored warriors, steel lances, and fierce horses to unearth the gold buried in the rich land, they claimed the earth itself for their faraway king. As a reward to the intrepid settlers, the Spanish kings gave them land grants, pieces of paper that declared ownership of the wild land they attempted to tame.

One of these early Spanish settlers was Francisco Peralta, a tall, quiet man with fierce green eyes. He marked out the boundaries of what he would call his, and defended it with his blood. He built an adobe house and sent to Spain for the gently born woman who had agreed to be his wife.

They had only one child, a son. But what a son he was! Juan Peralta extended the boundaries of his father's land, he mined gold and silver, raised horses and cattle, and so became wealthy. In his turn he took a bride from Spain, a woman who fought beside him during Indian raids and who bore him three children, a son and two daughters. For his family, Juan Peralta built a new house, far grander than his father's. His was a harmonious design with arched doorways, cool white walls, and dark earthen tile floors. Fragrant flowers bloomed in the courtyard.

Juan's son, named Francisco after his grandfather, worked even more wealth out of the *rancho*. But his delicate wife died only six months after the birth of their first child, a daughter. The grieving husband never remarried and cherished his daughter, Elena, as the most precious thing in his life.

By that time, 1831, Americans were wandering all over the West, spreading out from Texas. Most of them were trappers and mountain men, some adventurers. There weren't many at first, but more and more of them came, hard, restless men who were careless of the great beauty of the land. The Peraltas looked down on these crude Americans, and Francisco forbade Elena to speak to any of them.

But one of the Americans, Duncan Sarratt, didn't care a snap of his fingers about Francisco's edicts. When he saw dainty Elena Peralta, he fell in love. Worse, Elena fell in love with him, too. Francisco raged, he threatened, he tried to intimidate both his daughter and the American. But he had given Elena too many years of loving indulgence for her to take his threats seriously. She *would* have her American.

So she did, and they married with Francisco's reluctant permission. Not being a stupid man, however, he quickly saw that Duncan Sarratt was, perhaps, just what Elena had needed to protect her inheritance. The green-eyed American was a man who knew how to fight and how to protect his own.

Francisco didn't live long enough to see his grandchildren born. He died the next year, 1832, and Duncan Sarratt became ruler of the Peralta lands. He grew into such an absolute ruler that he became known as "King" Sarratt. It followed, as easily as night follows day, that the high valley became known as Sarratt's Kingdom.

The heirs to the kingdom were born: a son, Jacob, and two years later another son, Benjamin.

The boys grew up in the elegant adobe house built by their great-grandfather. They played games on the cool dark tiles, dangled by their hands from the courtyard balconies, wrestled and fought like two tiger cubs, and learned to love every inch of the kingdom that would be theirs.

But in 1845 the Americans fought a war with Mexico. It didn't touch the Sarratts much at first, as far north as they were. But one result of the war was that Mexico ceded to the United States that great and lovely land the Americans designated as the New Mexico Territory. With a whisk of a pen, the Sarratts were living on American soil.

The United States didn't recognize the laws and grants of the government it had replaced. The old Spanish landowners had been living on their granted land for a hundred years or more, but suddenly their homes were legally up for grabs. They could retain their land by filing on it, but most of them didn't know that. Duncan Sarratt, living in relative isolation in his huge valley kingdom, didn't know it. It didn't make much difference; anyone trying to take Sarratt's Kingdom away from him would have to fight to the death to do it.

The sound of gunfire woke the boy. He rolled from his bed and reached for his pants; the year was 1846, and at thirteen he had been doing a man's work on the ranch for the better part of two years. Whatever the trouble was, he didn't intend to hide from it under the bed like a kid.

He heard people running, and shouts echoed in the house as well as outside in the courtyard. He could hear his father's voice yelling orders. The boy stamped his feet into his boots and ran out into the hallway, tucking his nightshirt into his pants as he went. He collided with his younger brother, who had just bolted from his own room. He steadied the younger boy, who asked, "What's wrong?"

"I don't know." He started down the hall with his brother at his heels.

They heard an explosion of gunfire downstairs, inside the

house. There was a moment's silence, and then more shots followed, thundering, echoing through the high-ceilinged rooms. The boys automatically ducked to the side.

"Duncan!" Their mother, Elena, bolted from the bedroom she shared with their father. Raw terror was in her voice as she called out to her husband, who was downstairs. She stared at her sons, then grabbed them to her. "Stay here," she commanded.

At thirteen the boy was already taller than his mother. "I'm going to help him," he told her, and turned toward the stairs.

"No!" She seized his arm. "Stay here! I *order* you to. Take care of your brother. I'm going downstairs to your father. I'll find out what's going on and come back to tell you. *Promise me!* Promise me you'll stay here!"

"I can take care of myself." Her younger son thrust out his jaw. He was as fierce as his brother. She stared at him for a second, trailing her hand down his face. "Stay here," she whispered, and ran.

They had never disobeyed a direct order from their mother. They stood in the hallway, anxious because they didn't know what was happening and furious because they wanted to be a part of it. The booming sound of pistol shots and the crack of rifle fire vibrated through the big house. There were shouts and curses from below, footsteps running, glass shattering.

Then a scream splintered through the noise. It rose to a shriek, then fractured into a raw, deep wail. It was their mother.

The older boy bolted for the staircase, but an abrupt sense of caution kept him from hurtling down the steps. He threw himself to the floor, and eased his head around the railing so he could see what was going on.

A man lay sprawled in the entrance foyer, only the top part of his body visible from where the boy lay. Even though half the face was gone, the boy could tell it was his father. An icy feeling of disbelief began spreading through his body. His mother had thrown herself on her husband's body and was still wailing in that awful way. As the boy watched, a man reached down and grabbed his mother's arm, dragging her away from the body. As he did so, the lamplight fell across his face. The boy froze. It was Frank McLain, one of his father's men.

"Get the kids, too." McLain's voice was low, but the boy heard him. "Make sure they're dead."

Elena shrieked and threw herself at him, her nails scoring his face. McLain cursed, then drew back his fist and hit her on the side of the head, knocking her to the floor. "Get the boys," he said again, and bent to the woman.

The boy scrambled backward and grabbed his brother. "Run!" he hissed.

The house was their home; they knew every inch of it. Knowing that their rooms would be the first places searched, they went instead to the corner back bedroom, the guest room, which had a small balcony over the inner courtyard.

"I'll go first," the older one whispered, and swung his legs over the side of the balcony. He gripped the black iron railing and eased down until he was hanging above the ground, then let go. It was only about a six-foot drop, one they had made many times in their rowdy games. He landed as lightly as a cat and immediately blended into the dark cover of the shrubbery that grew close against the walls. There was a quiet thump, and his brother joined him.

"What's going on?" the younger boy whispered.

"Pa's dead. It was McLain who did it. He's got Mother."

There was still sporadic gunfire, as people loyal to Duncan Sarratt and the Peralta family tried to fight. The boys crept around the wall, staying in the shadows. Their rifles were in the study, where they put them each day after carefully cleaning them. They had to get them. The inner ice was still spreading through the older boy; he kept seeing his father sprawled on the dark floor, with half of his face missing.

Their mother's screams grated through the cold night air.

They crawled in through the kitchen door. Inside, their mother's screams were louder, hurting their ears. She was still in the foyer, and they could hear thickly muttered curses, too.

The boy knew, and he went even colder. He was thirteen, and he knew. He rose to his feet, moving as silently as a young panther. He saw a gleam of steel on the kitchen table, and his hand automatically closed on the long-bladed kitchen knife.

The screams were only moans now, and growing weaker.

When the boy walked into the foyer, he saw McLain rising to his knees between Elena's legs, pulling out of her body. His pants were open and lowered over his buttocks, his shrinking penis glistening wetly. His pistol was still in his hand. With a faint smile, he put the barrel to the woman's head and pulled the trigger.

An inhuman howl clogged the boy's throat, but he was ice clear through now. He threw the knife, his aim sure, practiced through many hours of play. McLain saw only a movement in the shadows, and he dodged to one side, just enough that the blade went through his shoulder instead of his heart. He bellowed for help and struggled to his feet just as the boy's weight hit him, knocking him back to the floor. The jarring impact made him scream in pain, and the cold floor scraped his bare ass. The boy jerked the knife free, and the bloody blade slashed downward, toward the man's exposed privates. McLain screamed and tried to roll away. The movement of his body deflected the knife enough that it gouged a shallow slit in his upper thigh. With a feral snarl, the boy withdrew the blade and tried again, this time with a low, sideways movement of his arm. The knife gleamed both silver and scarlet, then McLain knew hot, burning, choking agony as the steel sliced into his ball sac.

He shrieked, mad with pain and fear. He rolled and tried to kick, but his legs were tangled in his lowered pants. He'd never known terror before, but now it congealed his blood. He couldn't stop screaming as he tried to evade that slashing knife. In the flickering light he could catch only glimpses of the boy's face, and it was wild.

"I'll cut your goddamn cock off and feed it to you," the boy whispered savagely, and McLain heard him even over the shrill hysteria of his own screams.

A shot deafened them, and the boy was slammed sideways. The knife clattered to the floor, but the boy wasn't down. He scrambled awkwardly toward the kitchen, and the other boy, the younger one, darted forward to help him.

"Kill them!" McLain shrieked, clutching his bleeding balls with both hands. "Kill those little bastards!" He rolled on the floor, his britches still around his knees, and hatred for that

Sarratt whelp swelled in his throat until he nearly choked. He whimpered, too terrified to move his hands and see what kind of damage the knife had done, but blood was dripping from between his fingers, and he realized he could bleed to death. Still whimpering, shaking, he lifted one bloody hand and moaned aloud. His penis was still there, but the left side of his sac was a mangled mess. He didn't know if he'd lost his left testicle or not.

God damn him, the bastard had nearly castrated him! He'd wipe the face of the earth clean of Sarratts, he'd skin that boy and leave him for the buzzards. But even as he thought of all the things he wanted to do, McLain knew he'd never forget the choking terror and pain, the humiliation of rolling on the floor, his britches down, while that knife darted and slashed.

The boys lay in the small cave they'd discovered five years before, on the northern edge of Sarratt's Kingdom. The pain roiled through the older boy, shaking him, making him grind his teeth together in an effort to stifle his moans. His brother lay still, too still, beside him. The older boy whimpered from the effort it took him to lift his arm and put his hand on his brother's chest, to feel the rise and fall of his breathing.

"Don't die," he whispered into the cold darkness, though he knew the younger boy was unconscious. "Don't die. Not yet. We've got to kill McLain."

His younger brother had taken a bullet high in his left side. The older boy didn't know how they had managed to escape, but like wounded animals they had crawled away into the darkness. He himself had two wounds, one in his right thigh, another through the fleshy part of his waist. Blood drenched his shirt and pants, and he could feel himself weakening, his head becoming light from the pain and blood loss.

Dimly he realized they might die here.

"No," he said, and touched his brother's still form again. "No matter what, we have to get McLain. No matter what. I swear it."

1

Major Frank McLain stepped into the sun and watched the buggy approach, his eyes narrowed with anticipation.

She was finally here.

Fierce, gloating satisfaction filled him. He'd never been good enough before, but now a damned Waverly would be his wife. Her mother was even a Creighton—Margaret Creighton—and the girl had the Creighton looks herself, all pale, calm elegance, and aristocratic bones.

Victoria Waverly. Before the war her family would have spit on him. Now she was marrying him because he had money and all they had were empty bellies and impeccable bloodlines. The war and the hunger it had created were the world's greatest equalizers. The Waverlys and the Creightons hadn't blinked twice at marrying their daughter to him in exchange for a more comfortable life.

He could barely wait. He'd wrenched this land from the Sarratts with blood and death and pure guts, and made it his; he now owned more land than any plantation owner in the South ever had, made his name one to be reckoned with in the territory, ran more cattle and employed more men than anyone else around, and still something had been lacking. He'd never gotten what he'd wanted more than anything else in his life, and that was a lady at his table, a true aristocrat to share his name. There had never been any hope of it before, but after the war he'd gone back to Augusta, back to the town where he'd grown up as poor and despised white trash. He'd searched there for the perfect woman of his dreams, and he'd found Victoria. His heart beat faster just thinking about her. He had waited four months for her to arrive, and now she was here. They would be married that night.

One of the men standing behind him shifted to get a better look. "Who's that in the buggy with her?"

"Her little sister and her cousin, Emma Gann, came with her," McLain answered. He didn't mind that Victoria had brought some family with her. He kind of liked the idea of having them under his roof. Men from all over the territory would probably come to court them. White women were still a rarity, and true *ladies* were as precious as gold. He had a pleasant moment's thought of the alliances he could forge with advantageous marriages for the two young women. By God, he'd build an empire that would make the Sarratts look like two-bit dirt farmers. Twenty years had passed since he'd killed the last of them and taken the land, but he still hated the name. Duncan Sarratt had always looked at him as if he were trash, and that bitch Elena had acted as if he'd dirtied the air she had to breathe. But he'd gotten both of them, made them pay, and now he lived in the Sarratt house. No, goddamn it, it was *his* house, just as it was his land. There were no Sarratts anymore. He'd made sure of it.

The half dozen men standing behind him were, in a way, just as eager for the buggy to roll to a stop. Oh, there were some white whores in Santa Fe if they wanted to ride that far, but all of the women on the ranch or anywhere nearby were Mexican. The few white women in Santa Fe who weren't whores were the wives of soldiers, or the odd rancher's wife. These women coming in now were supposed to be good women, but only the Major's wife would be off limits. Hell, they all knew him. If he wanted to plow his wife's sister, he'd do it and not think twice. So they watched the approaching buggy with hot eyes, wondering what the women would look like, not that it mattered.

Will Garnet spat on the ground. "The Major is acting like a

fool over this woman," he muttered. "Ain't no split-tail born worth this much fuss."

The few men who heard him agreed, but didn't say anything. Only two men on the spread were immune to the Major's rage, and Garnet was one of them. He was in his early forties, with dark hair graying at the temples, and he had been with the Major from the first. He was the foreman and did pretty much as he wanted, with the Major's blessing. They all walked lightly around him, except the man standing a little away from their group, his posture relaxed and his eyes cold under the brim of his hat. Jake Roper had only been on the ranch a few months, but he, too, seemed immune to the Major's anger.

They had all been hired as cowpunchers or wranglers, but it was a fact that some of them had been hired more for their handiness with a sidearm than for their bulldogging ability. A man who had made his fortune the way McLain had needed to keep an eye out for his enemies. Not only that, but a spread as big as his was vulnerable to rustling and lightning raids by the Comanche. So McLain had built his own private army of gunmen, and Jake Roper was the fastest. Even the other gunhands tended to steer clear of him. Garnet might have a mean streak in him a mile wide, but Roper was ice clear through. Garnet might backstab a man, but Roper would squash out a life with as little thought as if he'd stepped on a bug.

Roper himself had little interest in the women. The Major was making a fool out of himself, but it didn't bother Roper. He gave his boss a sidelong glance, but all his contempt was hidden behind his cold eyes. This fancy, high-nosed Southern *lady* wasn't so special, not if she was marrying McLain. He had a good idea what she was in for. But she'd chosen to come here; she could damn well make the best of it.

When the buggy reached the front of the house, it stopped and McLain stepped forward. He lifted his arms to help one of the women down. "Victoria!"

She stood, but instead of allowing McLain to lift her from the buggy, she placed a gloved hand on his forearm and stepped down. "Major," she said calmly, and lifted back the veil from her bonnet.

Roper's first impression of her face was that it looked like it belonged to a bloodless porcelain doll, very correct and passionless. Yep, a lady, all right, all the way down to her lace drawers—and God forbid any man should see them. Her hair was light brown, what he could see of it, and her voice had been low. That was a blessing; shrill, screeching women disgusted him.

The next woman to alight, also with a gentle hand on McLain's forearm, was a bit on the plain side, with dark brown hair and brown eyes. But Roper thought she had a sweet smile. He eyed her consideringly. He figured this was the cousin.

The next one didn't wait for assistance, but jumped to the ground with a small gurgle of delight. She tugged her bonnet off, and whirled it by its strings. "Oh, everything's beautiful," she breathed, looking around with wide eyes.

Standing beside Roper, Garnet stiffened and swore under his breath. She was a young girl rather than a woman, but she was stunningly beautiful. Her hair was a golden blond mass, and she had big, dark blue eyes. Roper figured a girl like that was going to cause a lot of trouble among the men on the ranch. The little sister was just too pretty to leave her alone.

"Garnet! Roper!"

Both of them stepped forward, faces blank. The Major was beaming like an idiot as he turned toward them. "Victoria, my dear, these are my two right hands. Will Garnet is my foreman and Jake Roper makes sure we're all safe here. Boys, say howdy to my intended, Miss Victoria Waverly."

Victoria's eyes showed nothing as she gracefully held out a slim gloved hand to the foreman. "Mr. Garnet," she murmured.

"Ma'am." His hand enclosed hers, and he looked her up and down in a way that made her draw back nervously. She met his gaze and was made even more uneasy by his eyes, which were flat and expressionless, like a snake's.

She withdrew her fingers as quickly as possible, resisting an urge to wipe them on her skirt. Instead, she turned to the other man. "Mr. Roper."

She looked up at him and froze. His hat was pulled down low over his eyes, but she could still see them glittering coldly at her. He slowly, deliberately lowered his gaze to her breasts and stared

at them for what seemed an eternity to her, before raising his
eyes to meet hers again with contempt.

Roper ignored her outstretched hand and merely lifted the
brim of his hat. Victoria dropped her arm and turned away, her
discomfort intensified. If Garnet's manner was offensive, this
man was frightening. His face was still, yet he had looked at her
with such obvious disrespect that it shook her. No one, not even
the Yankee soldiers, had ever looked at her like that.

It took all her self-control to appear calm as she turned to the
man she had come three-quarters of the way across the continent
to marry. "If you don't mind, Major, we'd like to freshen up now.
The dust is terrible."

"Of course, of course. Carmita! Show Miss Victoria and the
girls where they can wash." His voice was harsh when he spoke to
the servants, and Victoria gave him a quick glance. She had been
raised to never be rude to a servant. But the short, round,
middle-aged woman who answered the Major's summons wore
an expression of perpetual good nature.

"Please, this way," she said with a warm smile.

Victoria turned to find her cousin, Emma, close behind her,
but her sister Celia had wandered off toward the corrals. Victoria
called to her, and as the girl skipped back, her face aglow with
delight, Victoria didn't miss the way most of the men were looking at Celia. Men everywhere looked at Celia with pleasure, but
this was different. They watched the girl the way a cat might
watch a mouse.

Victoria ushered Celia into the house ahead of her, wondering
desperately if she had done the right thing in bringing the girl
with her. At least in Augusta she wouldn't have had to deal with
these threatening strangers.

Emma fell into step with Victoria, and her cousin's fine dark
eyes mirrored her own uneasy impressions. "Those men . . ."
Emma murmured.

"Yes," Victoria said.

The huge house was Spanish in style, the walls made of thick,
whitewashed adobe. Coolness enveloped them as they stepped
inside, and Victoria's spirits lifted as she looked around. The
walls were clean and white, the spacious rooms were enlivened

with colorful rugs. On the second floor Carmita led them past the first door on the right but opened the second, and beckoned Victoria forward. "Your room, señorita," she said.

Victoria was pleased by what she saw. The floor was of dark wood, and a curtained, four-poster bed was set against the left wall. On the right was an enormous armoire. There was a washstand bearing a simple white pitcher and bowl, and a mirrored dressing table for her toilette. Under the window was a chaise longue, and across it was folded a cream-colored blanket. "It's lovely," she said, drawing a huge smile from Carmita.

Celia whirled around the room, sending her skirts flying. "A room of your own!" she crowed. She and Victoria had shared a room for as long as she could remember, and this was an unimaginable luxury to her. "And Emma and I will have rooms of our own, too, won't we?"

Victoria looked at Carmita, who nodded. "Yes, of course," she told her sister as she smoothed a golden strand of hair from Celia's face. No, there was no way she could have left her in Augusta with their parents, who were bitter and joyless after the death of their only son in the war. Celia needed laughter and sunshine, and she gave it back in abundance. But she was a fragile, vulnerable girl. Like a hothouse bloom, she needed careful nurturing to flourish.

"May we see my room next? Please, may we?"

Her enthusiasm was contagious, and Victoria found herself laughing with the others as they trooped down the hallway. "How many rooms are there in the house, Carmita?" she asked.

"Fifteen, señorita. Eight downstairs, seven upstairs."

"You are the housekeeper?"

"*Sí*. There is also Lola, the cook, and my daughter, Juana, who helps me in the house."

Victoria had caught a glimpse of a black-haired young woman when they arrived. "Was it Juana I saw at the stables?"

Carmita's face hardened. "No, señorita. That was Angelina Garcia. Juana does not go to the stables."

"What does Angelina do?"

Carmita only shrugged, and didn't explain. Victoria made a mental note to ask again about this Angelina.

The rooms assigned to Emma and Celia were identical, square and plain, but possessing simple charm. Celia bounced on each double bed in turn, ecstatic at their good fortune, and even Emma's eyes held a fragile hope that things were looking better at last. Victoria tried to muster some of that same sense of optimism, but instead her heart could manage only the slow, heavy beat of dread. She had to marry Frank McLain, and only desperation had brought her to this pass. He had been outwardly kind, but she doubted she would ever be able to make herself feel comfortable with him.

At the thought of marrying him, a shudder shook her. He was barrel-chested and thick-necked, like a bull, though he wasn't very tall; the combination made him appear brutish. Victoria felt suffocated at the idea of sharing a room with him.

She had brought Emma and Celia with her thinking that at least they would have food and clothing enough to be secure. The war had reduced them, quite literally, to starvation, and the Major had seemed their only hope. But after meeting those men—Garnet and Roper—and seeing the others standing back with their awful interest in Celia, she had to doubt her wisdom in taking her cousin and sister from Augusta.

Roper had stared at her with contempt in his cold eyes. She shivered and decided she would stay far away from the man. She was glad he hadn't taken her hand when she'd offered it; she was glad he hadn't touched her. Yet she wondered why he had looked at her like that, as if she were trash. Never in her twenty-one years had anyone done that; she was a Waverly, her mother was a Creighton, and both families could trace their roots back several centuries to English nobility. Before the war, they had been at the top of the social pyramid. Before the war . . .

Before the war, she reminded herself, a lot of things had been different. She straightened her shoulders. She had lost the privileged way of life she had been born to, the luxuries, the comfort and protection of wealth. She had gone from having it all to having nothing, but she had coped. She had kept her head high even when she was hungry, even when her dresses were threadbare and she shivered with cold, when her only pair of shoes had holes in the bottom. Dresses and shoes had never been the sum of her existence, so she had never mourned for the loss of them.

What the war had done was shatter her family, taking a cousin here, an uncle there. Emma's fiancé had been killed the first winter, and the echo of sadness had never left her eyes. Emma's mother, Victoria's mother's sister, had died in '63. Her cousin had come to live with the Waverlys. Then Victoria's adored older brother, Robert, had been killed in the Wilderness campaign. After that she had also lost her parents. They still lived, after a fashion, but their hearts had died.

Victoria had always known that Robert was the magic one, the center of the family, but she'd never been jealous of him, because she had dearly loved him, too. She and Celia had been loved, or at least she had thought they had been. But with Robert's death, her parents had grieved until there was nothing left to give their daughters.

She thought of the home she'd left, of her parents locked in bitterness for what was lost, and knew that she couldn't have left sixteen-year-old Celia there alone. Celia was different and sometimes others grew impatient with her. All of her life Victoria had stepped between Celia and trouble, and she wasn't going to stop now.

Carmita interrupted Victoria's thoughts as they left Emma's room by saying, "The Major, he said the wedding would be tonight. You have your dress, yes? I will get the wrinkles out."

Tonight! A chill ran through Victoria. "Tonight? Are you certain?"

The housekeeper looked puzzled. "Of course. He has sent for the padre. He told me this himself, this morning."

Victoria said nothing more but went with Carmita back to her room, where the trunks had been delivered. With Emma's assistance, they sorted through everything until they found the dress (paid for with the Major's money) that Victoria had brought to be married in. Carmita took it off to be steamed.

Silently Victoria began putting her clothes away in the armoire. Emma joined her, efficiently folding and hanging.

After a moment Emma said, "You know, you don't have to go through with it. We can always go back home."

Victoria leaned against the armoire. "How can we? Do you

truly think the Major would pay our way back? No, I agreed to the bargain, and I'll keep it."

Emma paused in the folding of a delicate lawn nightgown, which had also been purchased with the Major's money. All of their clothing was new and had come from him, even their underwear. Emma's eyes were worried. "Have we made a mistake in coming here?"

"I hope not. I pray not. But those men downstairs . . . the way they looked at Celia—"

"Yes. I saw."

Victoria walked to the window. The land was beautiful, incredibly so, but alien to everything she had known. She had expected a calm, peaceful ranch, and instead she sensed an undercurrent of violence she couldn't explain. "I feel uneasy," she murmured. "Those men are so threatening. That sounds silly, doesn't it? But I didn't expect them to be armed."

"The territory is still a dangerous place. I expect most men are armed."

"Yes, of course. It's just so different from home. The Yankee soldiers were armed, but that was expected."

"And they didn't look like the gunslingers we've heard so much about."

"Or read about in that dreadful dime novel Celia bought in Texas."

The two young women looked at each other and smiled, remembering the lurid descriptions that had had Celia wide-eyed. Emma's common sense calmed her, but Victoria couldn't entirely dismiss her own uneasiness. A faint blush rose to her cheeks as she returned to the chore of unpacking, and she darted a quick glance at Emma. Her cousin was two years older than she, and had been engaged. Perhaps she was in possession of more information than Victoria was.

"I wonder if he will sleep in here?"

Emma looked around. "It doesn't seem likely. If he intended for you to share a room, wouldn't he have put you in the room he already occupies?"

Relief almost made Victoria's knees go limp. "Yes, I should have thought of that."

"Perhaps that door connects with his room." Emma pointed.

Victoria walked to it and twisted the knob. It opened into another bedroom, obviously occupied. She quickly shut it again. "I'd thought it was to the privy."

At least now she knew they definitely wouldn't share a room, thank God. But that wasn't all that worried her. She busied herself hanging the sensible skirts and shirtwaist blouses she'd insisted on having for everyday wear. "Do you know what will happen tonight?" she asked in a low voice. "Afterward—when we're alone."

Emma's hands stilled, and she bit her lip. "Not really. Didn't Aunt Margaret tell you before we left?"

"No, except to say that I must do my duty. That's all very well, if I only knew what my 'duty' was. I feel so stupid! I should have asked. You were engaged; what did Aunt Helen tell you?"

"I suppose she thought she would wait until right before the wedding, for she never told me anything. The things I heard in school—"

"Yes, I know. I imagine I heard the same things, but I can't believe they are true. The only thing I really know is that married people may sleep in the same bed." *And have babies.* She barely contained a shudder at the thought. She didn't want to have the Major's children; she couldn't even bear for him to share her room.

Emma bit her lip again and thought of Jon, her fiancé. After they had become engaged, he had often kissed her in what she knew must be an improper manner, but it had been so wonderful she had gloried in it rather than rebuking him as she ought. He had held her tightly and touched her breasts. He had used his tongue while kissing her, though at first she'd been shocked. And when he'd held her so tightly against him, she had felt a hardness in his trousers, and she had instinctively known that it pertained to what happened between a man and his wife, that mysterious, fearsome unknown they'd whispered about so avidly in school.

Jon. The long years since his death had eased the brutal grief, but not the yearning. She had loved him, but more than that he had begun awakening her physical senses in a way that left her feeling her aloneness even more keenly than she would have.

Still, she knew that she would rather be alone than be the one who married Major McLain.

Victoria was truly the only family Emma had left, for she had never been close to her aunt and uncle, and Celia, though happy and lovable, would never be able to share the memories of growing up together as she and Victoria did, or the responsibilities of adulthood. She clenched her fist and looked at her cousin, who had agreed to marry Major McLain in order to protect her family. For all her air of fragility there was steel in Victoria, and fierce determination. Emma knew more than anyone that it was Victoria who had somehow managed to keep them all fed these past two horrible years when no Southerner had had enough food, Victoria who had bartered and economized, who had spent hours laboriously tending a small vegetable garden in the backyard. Now her cousin needed information, and no matter how embarrassing the discussion was, Emma decided to give it to her.

She cleared her throat. "Jon—used to touch my breasts."

Victoria was very still, her eyes wide and troubled. She tried to imagine the Major touching her there, and shrank from the idea.

"And he used to get hard. His—his privates would get hard." Emma looked down at her clasped hands and couldn't look up again. "I think a husband does something between a woman's legs with his privates, and that's what makes a baby."

Victoria felt as if she couldn't breathe. Dear God, did she have to let the Major rub his privates against hers? He would have to lift up her nightgown, and he would have to be unclothed. . . . Nausea made the back of her throat burn, and she swallowed. The horrible image of his thick, brutally strong hands on her breasts, pulling up her gown, made her whirl away and clench her fists.

Emma stared at her hands. "Of course, Jon never did anything to dishonor me," she murmured. "But I wish he had. I liked it when he kissed me, and touched me. I wish he had done the rest of it, too, and perhaps I would have had his child."

They had been so strictly raised that for Emma even to think such a thing was scandalous, but Victoria couldn't feel shocked. Emma and Jon had been in love, and for them to do that even

unblessed by marriage seemed far less obscene than the proposal
that she do the same thing with the Major inside the marital
bonds. With that realization, she felt the truth of Emma's aloneness and moved to touch her cousin's shoulder.

"I won't feel as frightened now, knowing. Thank you." She
made her voice firm.

Emma gave her a little smile. "I don't know that much. Most
of it is guessing. I suppose we should have asked."

"Much good it would have done us. Can you imagine Mother
saying even as much as you have?"

Emma hesitated. "Will you tell me?" She blushed. "I mean,
when you know for certain."

Respectable women never talked of such things, but Victoria
nodded. She didn't feel daring, only desperate. She and Emma
would have to bolster each other and work together to protect
Celia, who saw good in everyone and therefore knew neither danger nor caution.

Victoria looked around the room. It was pleasing in its simple
colors, larger and airier than she was accustomed to, as were all
the rooms in the house. Tonight she would become a wife and
would no longer be Victoria Waverly, but Mrs. Frank McLain.
Someday she might be a mother. This, it seemed, was to be her
role in life, and her duty was to fill it impeccably.

She had been raised to be first a perfect lady and then a perfect wife, an ornament on a man's arm and a capable mistress of
his house. In her world women were gentle and graceful, charm-
ing and concerned only with a woman's activities. A wife always
deferred to her husband. She would try to be the lady she had
been raised to be, try to always be gracious and proper. She knew
nothing else she could do; there was no backing out, so she might
as well make the best of it. Many women had married men they
didn't love and led fulfilled lives; Victoria was certain she could
do the same.

But when she thought of the coming night, she couldn't stop
shivering.

Will Garnet couldn't get the little blonde out of his mind.
Her glowing face was perfect, and he bet her breasts would be

nice and round, instead of drooping like Angelina's. Hell, Angelina would lie down for any two-bit saddle tramp who had the price, so there wasn't anything special about her. Now, that little blonde . . . she was a virgin for sure, she had that look about her. Garnet wanted to be the first. He wanted to see that beautiful little face when she got it for the first time; he bet she'd like it, after she got used to it some. Not like her cold stick of a sister. The boss wouldn't be getting anything in his bed except a poker.

Garnet cast a sidelong glance at Roper, who was sitting at the table in the bunkhouse. He didn't have much use for the man, and he knew the feeling was likewise, but they would both be at the wedding. Boss's orders, just to make certain no trouble interrupted the ceremony. Garnet grunted and spoke to the gunhand. "The boss's woman ain't much, is she? But, damn, that little sister sure makes up for her."

Roper was cleaning and oiling his big .44s, and never looked up.

Familiar anger rose in Garnet. If Roper wasn't so damned fast with those guns, he'd have kicked his ass a long time ago. But nobody pushed Roper, not even the Major. If it had just been that, a bullet in the back would have taken care of him. The thing was, any back-shooter would have to make *damn* certain Roper was dead, and most of the men thought Roper wouldn't go down that easy. He'd only been on the ranch a few months, and they still didn't know much about him, other than he was damn good with horses, snake-quick with a gun, and as cold-blooded and deadly as a rattler. It was in his eyes, those cold, clear, emotionless eyes.

Roper never let his guard down. Even now, while he was cleaning his .44s, he only unloaded one at the time. Nor were they his only weapons; a big Bowie knife, all fourteen inches of it, rode in a scabbard at his left kidney, and another knife, this one thin and balanced for throwing, was in his right boot. Those were the only ones Garnet knew about; he figured the gunslick had at least one more hidden somewhere on his body.

But what really made the men wary of Roper was the way he'd killed Charlie Guest a couple of months back. Guest had always had more mouth than sense and was a bad-tempered bully on his good days, so Garnet really didn't give a damn that Roper had killed him. It was the way he'd done it. Guest had taken a dislike to Roper and started mouthing off at him, and got even madder when the gunhand had ignored him the way he was doing Garnet now. Then Guest had made the mistake of going for his gun. He'd never made it. Before he could even clear leather, Roper had been on him, moving so lightning fast that Garnet still wasn't quite sure what had happened.

Roper had dropped Guest to the bunkhouse floor and planted a knee in his back. He'd hooked his left arm around Guest's neck and pushed on the man's head with his right hand. They'd all heard Guest's neck pop like a chicken's. Without even breaking a sweat, Roper had left the dead man lying on the floor and gone back to what he'd been doing like he'd never been interrupted.

The dead silence in the bunkhouse had been broken when one of the cowpunchers blurted, "Why didn't you shoot him?"

Roper hadn't looked up. "He wasn't worth a bullet."

The Major liked having a man like Roper in his employ; he felt it gave him a certain stature. Garnet didn't like the way the Major was depending more and more on the gunslick, but was helpless to do anything about it. Nobody on the ranch was going to take him on after what he'd done to Guest.

Goaded by his silence, Garnet snapped, "That little blonde's mine."

Roper flicked a glance at him. "Fine."

Somehow, the indifference stung Garnet. Nothing touched Roper. The man wasn't human; he didn't even use Angelina's services. Garnet had begun to think something was wrong with Roper in that way until they'd gone into Santa Fe and Roper had holed up with a woman the entire three days they'd been there. The fool woman had watched him leave with a dreamy look in her eyes.

Just under his breath Garnet said, "One of these days, gunslick, I'll get you under my sights."

Roper lifted his head and smiled in a way that didn't change the expression in his eyes at all. "Any time."

2

Victoria's dress was white, long-sleeved and high-necked, and had one of the new slim skirts she had seen the Yankee ladies in Augusta wearing. Celia oohed and ahhed over it, when she wasn't whirling around in her own new blue dress.

Emma brushed out Victoria's waist-length hair, skillfully wound and secured it up on her head, and pulled several strands loose at the temple to soften the look. Emma's calm face helped. Victoria's hands were steady as she affixed a tiny spray of seed pearls in her hair. "How does this look?" she asked.

"It looks wonderful!" Celia was full of admiration. She adored Victoria and was happy that she looked so pretty in her new dress. Celia didn't begin to understand what this wedding meant to her sister. Victoria tried to pretend the occasion was as happy as her sister believed it to be.

"It does look wonderful," Emma said more quietly. Her dress was also blue, a shade that went extremely well with her pale skin. Her mass of dark hair had been wound into a smooth coil on the back of her head. Her eyes met her cousin's in the mirror, and Victoria managed a small, reassuring smile.

Carmita knocked and put her head in the door, smiling broadly as she took in the three young women. "The Major is ready, señorita. You look very pretty!"

Victoria rose to her feet. "Thank you." She managed a smile for Carmita, also. Just before they left the room, she took one more look around it. She would not be a Waverly the next time she stepped through this door. A white silk and lace nightgown lay across the bed, and she quickly looked past it.

The men were gathered in what she assumed was a parlor. She saw McLain, the priest, Father Sebastian, and the two men she had met that afternoon, Garnet and Roper. Victoria quickly walked to the Major's side, not letting her gaze touch either of the two hands as she gave them a polite nod. Roper stood a little in her way, but he didn't move, and she had to go around him to keep her skirts from brushing his legs. She could almost feel the scorn in his eyes as he watched her.

The Major was beaming as he took her hand and tucked it in the crook of his elbow. "You look beautiful," he said heartily. "I sure am getting my money's worth." She controlled a flinch.

To the priest McLain said, "Get on with it."

The wedding ceremony was brief, too brief for Victoria's peace of mind. In only a couple of minutes they were man and wife. McLain turned her to face him and pressed his wet mouth on hers. Victoria kept her lips firmly together and her mind blank as she willed herself not to shudder. She drew back as quickly as possible and turned away, meeting Roper's eyes as she did so. For the first time she noticed he wasn't wearing his hat, and she could clearly see his face. His eyes were clear and cold, his expression so contemptuous she almost stepped back. Why did he hate her so much?

The thought made her lift her chin as imperiously as any Creighton or Waverly had ever done; this man was a common thug, a hired gun. She gave him back stare for stare.

Roper's lips twitched into a humorless little smile, and he gave her a brief nod, as if in recognition of her nerve. Still, it wasn't until he turned away that she felt herself released.

The Major rubbed his hand down her arm, accidentally letting his fingers touch her hip. Victoria started, but forced herself to smile at her new husband. It was just that she was so nervous, she told herself, and she didn't really know him. Once she had a chance to relax, everything would be all right.

"What did you think of your bedroom, girl? Right nice, ain't it?" The Major's tone was somehow leering, but he seemed anxious for her approval.

"It was lovely," she replied, glad she could be honest. "I'm sure I'll be very comfortable. The chaise especially is a nice touch."

He squeezed her hip again. This time, however, she was looking at him and saw the glitter in his dark eyes when he did so. Now she knew it wasn't accidental. Such a public caress shocked her, and the look in his eyes frightened her a little.

"Later," he said with a wink, "you'll like the bedroom even more."

She couldn't reply. The thought of the coming night was almost enough to paralyze her, if she let herself dwell on it. So she forced it from her mind and somehow got through the evening.

It was a strangely silent gathering, with only the Major talking and everyone else answering him in monosyllables. Emma, bless her, kept Celia close to her side. Victoria tried to smile at the appropriate times and contribute some polite conversation over the dinner Lola served, but she was too tense to do more than go through the motions of being a gracious hostess.

McLain kept touching her. Victoria noticed Garner kept watching Celia. And Roper, whose eyes made her shiver, kept watching her, but now his expression was unreadable.

She wished desperately that she had never agreed to marry McLain. She thought hers was the most dismal wedding supper she'd ever attended, and felt a small spurt of amusement because she was the most dismal person attending it. The amusement quickly died, however, when McLain stroked her arm with the gloating possessiveness that made her feel sick. She felt as if he were flaunting her before the two other men.

For a moment her distress was so powerful that she had to look away, and found herself staring at Roper again. His cold eyes met hers, then flickered to McLain. When he looked back to her, she was mortified to see a faint understanding. That he should know she was dreading the night, and what McLain would do to her, was unbearable.

She went white, then red, then white again. She wanted to

run from the table, and clenched her hands tightly together. She had never before had any idea that a man might be imagining her with her nightgown pulled up, but she was certain Roper was thinking just that. Every ounce of modesty she possessed was outraged.

The only thing to do, of course, was to pretend not to notice him. It was rather like closing one's eyes and pretending to be invisible, but it was better than nothing.

Roper watched the color build and recede in her face, and realized the cause; he even felt faint pity. She wasn't a cold and passionless doll, after all. She was frightened—justifiably so, though she couldn't know that. McLain had a reputation for being rough and hasty with women. Nor was he particular in his choices, though this time, it seemed, he'd gotten himself a lady. Bad luck for the lady.

Roper realized he didn't like the idea of McLain rutting on her. It made him furious with himself, but there it was. McLain wouldn't appreciate her pale delicacy, nor would he take the time to give her pleasure. She was too fine for the bastard. She had guts. Damn few men had ever stared at him like that, challenging him with a look. People usually didn't want to look at his face, for some reason; they would only glance at him, and quickly look away. But this pale, slender woman had stood as steadfast as a rock and matched him look for look. She had acted as if she were a queen and he the lowest of her subjects. The thought of it caused a spurt of anger that surprised him. Roper seldom let himself feel any emotion, and he especially didn't want to feel any for McLain's wife.

But there it was. Anger. Respect. Desire. God, yes, desire. He shouldn't feel any of it, he couldn't afford to feel any of it. He'd have to do something about her, sooner or later, and he didn't need his mind clouded by all these unwanted thoughts and emotions. He couldn't let himself soften at all, not now.

Deliberately he looked at the little sister. She was undeniably lovely, and the expression in her dark blue eyes was both sweet and happy, though there was an elusive quality about her he didn't understand. Maybe she was simpleminded. Not stupid, just simple. She was just a beautiful child.

But looking for a distraction didn't help. He turned back to McLain's wife, and the images of hate rose up again in his mind, though he kept his face carefully blank. McLain, murdering his father. McLain, raping his mother and then putting a bullet in her brain. McLain, stealing the land that had been in his mother's family for over a hundred years. McLain, sending the young killer, Garnet, out to hunt down and kill two boys, and damn near succeeding. McLain, living in the cool, gracious house where Roper had been born, back when this whole valley had been called Sarratt's Kingdom.

Jacob Roper Sarratt had returned. He'd come to kill McLain and take back the valley. Until today, that was all he wanted.

Now he wanted McLain's wife, too.

Victoria sat propped against the pillows, clad in her long-sleeved, high-necked white nightgown. She was cold, deathly cold, all the way down to her bones, but she couldn't shiver. Her body felt heavy, incapable of even that tiny movement. Her heart was beating in a slow, ponderous rhythm that threatened to choke her.

Emma had wanted her to leave her hair down, but Victoria had insisted on braiding it as usual, explaining that the tangles were horrendous if she left it loose. The truth was, Victoria didn't want to look too attractive to the Major. It was a small defense, but one she felt would help her in spirit if not in fact.

The bedcurtains were drawn back and tied to the four posters. The room was illuminated by three candles set in the graceful silver candelabra on the dresser, and Victoria wondered why the room was lit with candles instead of an oil lamp, which gave off more light. There had been lamps downstairs. She would ask Carmita tomorrow.

Tonight, though, perhaps it was best that the room wasn't brightly lit. Perhaps she should even snuff the candles. She considered it, and was about to throw the covers back when the connecting door opened and the Major entered her room.

She froze. He was wearing a dark robe, but below the hem his legs were hairy and bare. His bull neck and thick shoulders looked even more odd in contrast to the spindly size of his calves.

But it was his face that most terrified her. He wore such an open expression of gloating anticipation that she wanted to die. Dear God, what was he going to do to her?

He walked to the side of the bed and removed his robe, exposing a white nightshirt that came down to his knees.

"Well, girl, are you ready?" Again, his voice had that leering tone.

She managed to make an assenting noise, but it was a lie. She would never be ready.

"Lie down, then. Did you expect to do it sitting up?" He laughed.

She could barely move, but managed to shift her position so that she was lying flat on the mattress. He got into the bed beside her and leaned up on one elbow. Victoria's muscles tightened even more. He had brown eyes, she noticed. His heavy jaw was darkened by a shadow of beard, and she could smell a sweet, cloying scent about him. Lying this close to him, she was overwhelmed by the mixture of cologne and sweat, so much so that she had to struggle to prevent herself from gagging. Desperately she tried to remind herself that he seemed clean enough, he was just a rather heavy man and naturally sweated.

He bent and pressed his mouth to hers. She could feel the clammy sweat on his upper lip. Revolted, she tried to press her head deeper into the pillow to escape him.

Oddly, the kiss seemed to excite him. He began breathing faster, and his beefy hands jerked at her nightgown. Victoria clenched her fists and tried to prepare for the exposure. At least they were still under the sheet.

But when the nightgown was about her waist he kicked the thin sheet away and rose up on his knees. Victoria closed her eyes, so humiliated she could barely think. He was looking at her *there*, something she couldn't remember anyone ever doing before. It was shocking enough that he should see her bare legs, but for him actually to look at her triangle of hair was horrible.

The sound of his heavy breathing was the only noise in the room. He put his hand on her bare leg and she jumped. "Feels good, does it?" he panted. "Just wait, there's more."

She couldn't bear more. It couldn't get worse than this. He

pulled her legs apart, and nausea churned her stomach. Dear God, he was actually looking between her legs. In all her nightmares she had never imagined this.

He shifted so that he was kneeling between her spread legs. She felt him touching her there, rubbing his fingers over her, and suddenly he pushed one thick finger into her. Her eyes flew open and she went rigid as pain tore through her body. She was dry, and his rough finger felt like sandpaper as it ripped apart the delicate tissues of her hymen. The pain and the idea of what he was doing were finally too much, and she dug her heels into the bed in taut rejection of that horrible penetration, her muscles locked.

With his other hand he had pulled up his nightshirt and was rubbing and pulling at an ugly, veined thing. Victoria looked at him in horror as she suddenly realized what he was going to do. She hadn't thought she could get any stiffer, but she could feel her muscles pulling even tighter, her body going as rigid as a board. He was cursing for some reason as the ugly little sausage rolled limply in his hand.

Abruptly he let himself down and pushed it against her, and Victoria gagged.

McLain barely noticed her stiffness. It was what he expected; she was a *lady*, not a whore like Angelina. It was his own unresponsive flesh that held his attention, infuriating him. Dammit, he'd never had this trouble before! Despite his wound, he'd always been able to hump any woman he could get beneath him. But now his organ remained flaccid, no mater how vigorously he pulled at it. Frantically he pushed it against her, hoping that the feel of her would get him hard. He grew more panicked and furious with every passing second as nothing happened.

And then he realized she was lying frozen beneath him, just like that Sarratt bitch Elena had done. The demon that had tormented him for twenty years, that lurked inside him always waiting for a chance to leap out, smiled evilly. Once again out of the recesses of his mind came the hellish memory of pulling out of Elena and the shining knife abruptly slashing at him. He remembered the terror, the sick helplessness he'd felt with his pants around his knees as he rolled on the floor, trying to escape that darting knife. And once again he felt the sharp pain and horror of steel cutting into him.

He jerked away from Victoria, cursing and limp. Furious, humiliated, but above all else lost again in that remembered horror, he left the bed and stamped into his own room, slamming the door behind him.

For a long time Victoria lay as he had left her, with her nightgown up around her waist and her body rigid. The only sound she could hear was her own rough, sobbing breaths. When she did move, it was to shove her fist against her mouth to stifle the hysterical sounds that welled in her throat.

She couldn't bear it. If this was what being married entailed, she simply couldn't bear it. The wrenching loss of modesty, the pain . . . how could any woman ever endure this? She felt shattered by the intrusion into her body, and terrified because she knew he hadn't finished it, though she didn't know why. She only knew he had been trying to put that—thing—into her as he had put his finger. She had never dreamed her very body would be penetrated, never dreamed such things were possible or that men's bodies were so different from women's.

Slowly, her movements stiff and jerky, she slid from the bed. She wanted to wash and she had to blow out the candles. She wanted to hide in the dark and pretend this had never happened but she knew she couldn't. Her hands were shaking as she wet a soft flannel in the cool water and drew her nightgown up again. She pressed the wet cloth between her legs to soothe the ache and was startled to find it came away stained with blood.

She stood with her head bowed for a long time, trembling. If this was what her life was to be like, she must somehow find the strength to endure it. For Emma and Celia, she had to endure it. For her parents. This was the sort of bargain women had made for centuries, and she would find the strength to keep her end of it.

Knowing that she was only one of many was little comfort, because she was appallingly alone. She couldn't retreat and say, "No, I don't like this, I'm going home." She couldn't run to Emma and sob out her fears like a child. There wasn't even the security of her home, of familiar rooms and streets, familiar people. This huge, elegantly simple hacienda, so alien from her home in Augusta, was where she would live for the rest of her life. She hoped that in time it would become home. But now she knew she had no hope at all that she would ever become accustomed to the Major.

At length she blew out the candles and felt her way across the dark room, to crawl between the sheets and lie for long hours, shivering and trying to muster her courage. She did eventually find some measure of control. If it wasn't courage, perhaps it would do.

She got up early, having only dozed fitfully, and dressed in one of the simple skirts and shirtwaist blouses she had brought. After pinning up her braids, she slipped quietly from the room. She didn't want to wake the Major. She hoped to find Carmita in the kitchen. Victoria had an urgent question that had been tormenting her all night, and Carmita would know the answer. It would be difficult to voice such a question, but she was learning that difficult didn't mean impossible.

As it happened, Carmita, Lola, and Juana were all in the kitchen, gossiping cozily. The friendly chatter of rapid Spanish halted when they noticed Victoria in the doorway.

"Señora," Carmita said, smiling broadly. They were all smiling at her. Belatedly Victoria realized they expected a blushing bride. She did blush, though not from happiness.

She said, "Please, Carmita, may I talk with you for a moment?" Despite her efforts at control some of her despair must have shown for Carmita stopped smiling and rapidly came to her side.

They walked out into the courtyard, so pretty with its multitude of yellow roses. Victoria pretended to look at the roses, fingering some of the velvet petals. She said, low, "If my questions embarrass you, please don't feel you have to answer. It's just—I don't have anyone I can ask, except for you."

Carmita looked puzzled. "Of course, señora."

Victoria flushed again. "Carmita . . . when a man—that is, what does a man—how are babies made?" She was beet red by the time she finished, and felt utterly helpless.

Carmita gaped at her. Victoria hurriedly turned away, but Carmita laughed and put her motherly arms around the tense young woman. Her brown eyes were warm. "No one thought to tell you the way of things? Poor señora! Yes, sit down, and I will tell you about men and babies."

She did, very succinctly, and Victoria heaved an inner sigh of relief. It was as she had thought, the man did enter a woman's body and there emptied himself of his seed, which sometimes resulted in a baby, though not, Carmita said with heartfelt thanks, every time. The Major had not done that to her, so she would not be having his baby. At least, not yet. She didn't know what had gone wrong last night, and she knew he could return to her bed at any time. They had a lifetime together for him to consummate the marriage. But for today, at least, she was safe.

Another question occurred to her, and she said diffidently, "How does a woman know if she is to have a baby?" She knew they didn't have to wait until they grew big, because she had known several women who had announced their expectancy long before there had been obvious evidence.

Carmita patted her arm. "Your monthly bleeding won't come, señora."

Victoria considered that. Her monthly cycle was so regular she always knew to the day when to expect the onset. It appeared she would have a reliable means of telling, if the worst happened.

"You will also cry a lot, and sleep a lot, and feel so sick that no food stays down," Carmita continued cheerfully. "When you do feel like eating, you will want strange things that, of course, Lola will not have, and someone will have to go to Santa Fe to buy it. That's the way of it. When I carried my Juana, I felt as if I had to have oranges, every day. Señora, I don't like oranges, but every day I ate them, five and six a day. Then Juana was born, and I didn't like oranges anymore."

Victoria sat in the courtyard after Carmita had returned to the kitchen, enjoying the early-morning coolness and the bright sun, calming her frazzled nerves. She had survived the night, as horrible as it had been, and the new day was fresh and sunny. If the coming night brought a repeat of the horror, well, she would survive that, too.

She thought about the things Carmita had told her and wondered why well-bred young women were kept so abysmally ignorant of such basic facts. She would far rather have known what was going to happen, as unpleasant as it had been, than to have suffered in the dread of the unknown, which had made it just that much worse. Her mother had known what she would face, yet had left her in ignorance. Victoria found that hard to forgive.

She would tell Emma. Not about the Major's failure, but the true facts of what men did to women in the marriage bed. She would tell her how babies were made and how a woman knew if she were pregnant. And later, if Celia were ever to think of getting married, Victoria would tell her, also.

She thought of the way Garnet watched Celia, and bit her lower lip. Now she knew what he wanted, and she was more determined than ever to keep Celia away from him.

Roper. He, too, had known what the Major would do to her.

Stunned, she realized that every man knew all of this, that only women were kept ignorant. This was what men did to fast women, to prostitutes. The realization put a different slant on every memory she had. The dances and socials and picnics she had attended had all been a part of the ritual leading up to the marriage bed, and bared bodies, and all of her young beaus had known what would happen. How many of them had looked at her and imagined her with her nightgown rucked up to her waist?

In retrospect she felt very indignant. The system of carefully perpetuated ignorance seemed to her rather like throwing lambs to wolves. She had been prepared for the indignity but not the total loss of modesty or the pain. She thought she would not have been so blindly terrified if she'd had a realistic idea of what to expect. But now, she thought with a wave of depression, she fully knew what her marriage to the Major would be like.

Roper paused by the gate to the courtyard, his attention caught by the young woman sitting so still, with her hands folded in her lap. The bright morning sun glinted on her hair, picking up the gold in it. He realized that her hair was dark blond, not the brown it had appeared before.

She sat staring at nothing, motionless. He knew she couldn't have had a wonderful night, yet her pale face revealed none of it. She might have been a statue, except for the way the light breeze played in the loose tendrils of hair at her temples.

His mother had sometimes sat in the courtyard, when she could find a spare minute in her busy days. Elena had been warm and vibrant, always ready to laugh with her sons and husband. The young woman who sat there now was cool and controlled, with a face as blank as marble.

He felt faintly contemptuous of her for marrying McLain. He felt disgusted with himself for wanting a woman McLain had touched. But the sight of her made his chest tighten, and blood rushed to his loins. He knew her stillness masked her pain and fear, and he admired it. He wanted her for that cool control. He wanted to shatter it with warm passion, he wanted her naked and vibrant and alive with need for him, he wanted her to claw at his back and arch her hips against him. He wanted to snatch her up and take her far away from here, because she was so out of place around men like McLain and Garnet, even himself. Their lives were stained with blood and violence, and it would inevitably touch her. He didn't see how he could prevent it.

He had stared at her too long; she turned her head, sensing his presence, and their eyes met across the courtyard. Without haste, every movement graceful, she rose from the bench and returned to the house. Roper clenched his fists at being dismissed by her, but too much was at stake for him to lose control now. His time would come.

The Major came to her room again that night. Victoria made no sign of protest, but lay with her arms at her sides. Again, McLain expected her to behave no differently.

He was desperately afraid of another failure, of again losing himself to those terrors of the past. McLain crouched between her opened legs and frantically tried to beat life into his unresponsive sex. The more afraid and humiliated he felt, the harder he tried, and nothing happened. All the while she lay there like a damned statue, reminding him of Elena, as if the woman had risen from the dead to torment and punish him.

He swore and rolled off of the bed and returned, trembling, to his own room. Cold sweat trickled down his face and barrel chest. The damn bitch had emasculated him, finished the job that Elena and her bastard had started!

His worst nightmare had become reality. God, he'd wanted her for so long, all of his life. Not her in particular, but someone like her, a lady to show the world he was someone important. She was perfect; a woman of impeccable bloodlines, manners, and breeding. She made Elena and that damned Sarratt look like white trash. She was finally his, and he couldn't take her.

He laughed soundlessly, a little insanely. He had his lady, all right, but he couldn't do a thing about it.

He thought of her white-skinned, perfect body and broke out in a sweat again at the thought of touching her and finding his manhood limp and useless.

In a thousand nights during the past twenty years he had awakened to hear himself whimpering, and found his hands cupped protectively over his privates. A thousand nightmares had been filled with a scarlet-stained knife and a boy's hate-twisted face. In his dreams he couldn't escape and the knife finished its job. The reality had been bad enough; he'd walked spraddle-legged for weeks and his left testicle was drawn and withered. He'd lived in hell until he had recovered enough to find out if he was still capable of humping a woman, though he never let anyone know how desperate he'd been. After finding out that he *was* still capable, he took to bragging that he was more man with only one ball than most men were with two. But bragging hadn't kept the nightmares away.

But that wasn't true anymore. His greatest fear had been realized. He couldn't get an erection.

She was so dainty and pristine, so untouchable. Frank McLain sat in the darkness of his room and tried to work things out in his mind, find some sort of explanation for the humiliating failure of his flesh. Goddammit, he'd never had any trouble humping a woman before, once he'd recovered from the knife wound. Only this one.

So it had to be her fault. It wasn't him; it was something about *her*. Maybe ladies weren't for screwing. He had his lady for ruling over his house, his lady to dress in fancy gowns and show off in Santa Fe. With her culture and background, there was no limit to how high he could rise in the territory. That was why he'd married her. Hell, he didn't care if he got any brats on her; he didn't give a damn about leaving all of this to some snot-nosed kid who probably wouldn't have half of his own strength. This was *his,* won with his guns and brains and guts. He was undisputed king in this part of the territory, and now he had his queen. He had what he wanted. Let her keep her knees locked; women like her were made to be treated like dolls, cosseted and protected, showcased in all their finery and jewels.

That was what was wrong. He just hadn't understood before. He'd take care of her like she was royalty given into his protection, untouchable and untouched. When he wanted to hump somebody, he'd go to the kind of women he was comfortable with, women who squirmed and squealed and liked it.

Like Angelina Garcia. She was just a whore, but she liked it any way a man could give it to her. McLain thought of the times he'd plowed her himself and to his enormous relief felt his manhood begin to stir. Yeah, that was what it had been all along. There wasn't anything wrong with him, it had been his wife.

He jerked off his nightshirt and hurriedly dressed. He had to have a woman, a real woman.

Angelina had a room in the small building where the houseservants once lived, back when the damn Sarratts had kept enough servants to button up their britches. Most of the building was used for storage now; Carmita, Lola, and Juana used two rooms just off the kitchen. Angelina wasn't much on keeping her room neat; it was always strewn with clothing and food, and stank of sex. She was greedy; she wanted several men a day, and if they didn't come to her she went to them. She was flamboyantly beautiful, with a lush body, long black hair, and flashing dark eyes. As he hurried across the dark ground, McLain thought of what he was going to do to her and grew fully hard.

He could barely wait. A thin line of light showed beneath her door. He pushed it open and Angelina turned her head sharply at the intrusion. She was naked, lying under a patched, yellow sheet, and she wasn't alone. One of the cowpunchers lay naked and groggy beside her.

Angelina was at first astonished to see him; after all, he'd only gotten married the night before. Then a slow, self-satisfied smile curled her lips.

"Get out," McLain said to the cowboy.

The man stumbled to his feet and awkwardly got into his britches and boots. He too was astounded that the Major was there. The tale would be all over the ranch by morning.

Angelina lolled against her pillows, letting the sheet fall to the side so that her large breasts were revealed. "So," she said in a purring voice. "Your grand lady can't satisfy you?" It wouldn't take much, as she knew from experience. The Major was too fast, but she always praised him as if he were the biggest and best stud she'd ever had. Angelina was shrewd enough to know she had a good thing here, and the best way to keep it was to butter up the boss.

McLain grunted as he unbuttoned his pants. "She couldn't even get it hard," he muttered, and from that, and his haste, Angelina understood exactly what had happened. She wanted to laugh, but knew she had too much to lose if she shared the joke with others, even later. She stifled her smile and instead stretched out her arms toward him.

"She must be a cold fish, then," she purred.

McLain freed his erection and lowered himself. "Bend over," he panted, already near climax at the thought. "I want to do it that way."

3

The dull, endless chores of domesticity had a settling effect, Victoria mused. It had been a week since her marriage, a week in which she had thrown herself into the duties of running the household in an effort to make herself too busy to think. She admitted that the larger portion of her growing serenity was due to the Major's continued absence from her bedroom, but mending had its own soporific effect. She stifled a yawn.

Emma chuckled. "Here we are, about to doze in the sun like two doddering old tabbies." She took two more tiny stitches, then smothered her own yawn.

"It's so pleasant here," Victoria said. She was coming to appreciate more and more both the weather and the landscape of her new home. It was June; the sun could be quite hot at noon, but the air was dry. The result was wonderful, after the humidity of the South. The nights were chilly and crisp, perfect for snuggling under blankets.

"Especially here, in the courtyard. I don't believe I care if this hem is mended." Emma replaced the skirt in her basket, looking enormously satisfied with the decision. She yawned again. "But I *do* believe a nap is necessary."

"Siesta must be contagious."

"It seems to be. Not that they're totally foreign to us.

Remember when we used to take naps before evening dances?"

"A long time ago." Victoria looked down the past five years.

"Yes." They said no more about the days past. Neither of them liked to discuss it. The changes brought by war had been too violent, the difference in their lives too complete. Too many people had died.

Emma got to her feet and Victoria did also, her brows knit as she realized she hadn't seen her sister in at least an hour. "I think I'll look for Celia," she said. "She didn't tell me where she was going."

"And wherever Celia is, Mr. Garnet will be close by," Emma said grimly.

Victoria wondered how Garnet attended to his job when he seemed to spend so much of his day lurking around Celia. He hadn't made any untoward moves, but his constant hovering made Victoria uneasy. If she found him near Celia again, she would inform the Major of his foreman's behavior, although she grimly suspected he was fully aware of it.

"Shall I come with you?" Emma asked.

It was tempting to accept her offer. Victoria often felt as if she needed support, and she knew Emma would stand unflinchingly by her side to face anything. But Emma, for all her willingness, was sensitive enough that conflict could upset her to the point of nausea. So Victoria smiled and shook her head. "No. She'll be in the stable, as usual. I'll just tell her we need help with the mending."

"If only she understood," Emma said.

"If she did, she wouldn't be Celia."

Rather than go through the house, Victoria left the courtyard by the rear gate. The ranch buildings were spread in a semicircle about the house, with the smithy to the right, the springhouse far in the rear, a couple of storage buildings, and two bunkhouses, the stable, an enormous barn, and various corrals extending to the left. It was almost a hundred yards to the stable; by the time she reached it, she wished she had put on a bonnet. The sun was deceptively hot on her bare head.

The stable, in contrast, was cool and dark, and redolent with the earthy scents of horses, oiled leather, and hay. Temporarily blind, she stood for a moment just inside the door, letting her eyes readjust to the dim light. When she could see again she quickly spied Celia at the far end of the barn. Celia had climbed halfway up the door of a huge corner stall and was leaning over it with her hand outheld.

Victoria recognized the horse. It was Rubio, the Major's prize stallion. He had boasted about the horse at length, taking delight in the tales of its kicks and bites as if they were admirable. The stallion had killed the Mexican who had been taking care of him the year before. Seeing Celia like that, so close to the big animal, made Victoria's heart stop. She took a step forward but didn't call out, not wanting to startle the horse.

A man came through the open doors at the other end, a black silhouette painted against the bright sunshine. Even without seeing his features, Victoria recognized Garnet. She hurried her step.

Rubio neighed warningly as Garnet approached. The horse withdrew to the back of the stall, stamping his feet and snorting.

Celia turned to the man and said, "You've scared him! He was just about to take this sugar from my hand."

Garnet hadn't seen Victoria even though she was no more than twenty feet away when he put his hand on Celia's leg, then slid it up to her hip. "Let me help you down."

Celia laughed, a silvery sound. "I can get down by myself."

Angered almost beyond control, Victoria still managed to keep her voice even. "Of course you can. Let's go back to the house; I need help with the mending."

Always amenable, Celia gathered her skirts and jumped to the hay-strewn floor. "I forgot about the mending," she said apologetically. "I was just talking to Rubio." She turned back to the stall. "Isn't he beautiful?"

He was beautiful, and savage. He was a big horse, superbly muscled, dark red in color. Victoria would have been as enthralled as Celia if it hadn't been for his eyes; they held not just spirit, but a viciousness that chilled her. The horse was a killer, but Celia saw only beauty.

"Yes, he's beautiful," Victoria agreed. "Why don't you run ahead and wash your hands before we start the mending?"

"All right." Celia happily left the barn, humming to herself.

Victoria turned back to Garnet, and inwardly braced herself against the hostility in his expression. She kept her voice cool. "Mr. Garnet, I shall tell you this only once: stay away from my sister. Don't touch her again."

He sneered and took a step toward her. "Or you'll do what?"

"I'll tell Mr. McLain you've been neglecting your duties and pestering Celia."

Garnet laughed, a brutal sound. His eyes were dark pits. "Now, that really scares me. He'll tell you to mind your own business, *Miz* McLain. I run this ranch, and the Major knows it. He can't get along without me."

"I can." The emotionless voice came from the open double doors behind Garnet. "I can get along without you just fine, Garnet. In fact, I like the idea."

Garnet whirled, and a spasm of hate twisted his features. If he had been angry before, now he was furious. "This is none of your business, Roper."

"It is if I make it my business." He hadn't moved from the doorway. With the light behind him it was impossible to see his face, but Victoria found that it wasn't necessary; his voice, flat and cold as it was, stated his intent. "Leave the girl alone."

"So you can have her?"

"No. I don't want her. But you're not going to have her, either."

Garnet's right hand moved, but Roper moved faster. The big revolver was in his hand before Garnet touched the butt of his. Victoria hadn't even seen Roper's hand move. Garnet froze, and even in the coolness of the stable a sheen of sweat covered his face.

"Pass the word," Roper said flatly. "Everyone leaves the girl alone."

Just for a second Garnet froze, unwilling to retreat. Watching him, Victoria saw the exact moment when he realized he didn't have any choice, if he wanted to live. He turned and stalked off. Victoria quietly exhaled a breath she hadn't realized she'd been holding. She forced herself to look at Roper as he stepped farther into the stable, though she wanted to flee like Garnet. "Thank you."

He said, "You made an enemy."

Wryly, she answered, "So did you."

He watched the way the small amusement tilted the corners of her lips upward. "That was nothing new between me and Garnet. One of us will kill the other before it's over."

"So you did it just to annoy him?" For some reason that angered her. She thought of leaving, but didn't. She didn't even step back when Roper walked so close by her that his legs brushed her skirt.

"What difference does it make, as long as it keeps him away from your simpleminded sister?"

Her fists knotted. "She's not!" she hissed. "Celia reads and writes; she's as intelligent as most. She's just . . . different." Temper burned in her cheeks. "Don't you dare call her simpleminded."

"Different, how?"

How, indeed? How did you explain a near adult who still had the innocence and glee of a child without using the label of simplicity? Celia was as fey and otherwordly as a wood nymph. It was as if she was so sensitive to everything that she had to block out the darkness of life in order to survive, leaving her with only sunlight. Victoria sought for the words. "She . . . doesn't see ugliness, or evil. She expects everyone to be as open and good-natured as she is."

He snorted as he swung a saddle down from the railing. "That's worse than simplemindedness. That's plain stupid, and out here it'll get you killed." He towered over her, and as Victoria refused to step back in retreat she was forced to tilt her head back to look at him. Their eyes met and a strange little frisson of fear raced down her spine. His eyes glittered under the low brim of his hat, and she saw that they were a clear, dark hazel green. He was so close to her that she could see the black specks in his irises, so close that she could smell the sweat on his skin, and feel the heat emanating from him. Her skirts were brushing his dusty boots, and she didn't care. She felt paralyzed as she stared up at him, held immobile by a strange, frightening excitement that knotted her stomach and set her heart to pounding. All of her life she had associated the scents of shaving soap and cologne with men, very civilized smells that she had thought pleasant and nothing more. Yet now the hot, primal smell of Roper's sweaty skin was making her weak, making her think she might have to have support just to stand.

He shouldn't be that close to her. She knew it, yet she couldn't retreat.

"Get on back to the house," he said. His lips barely moved. "You don't belong out here."

She didn't know if he meant the stable or the entire territory, but she suspected he meant the latter. She squared her shoulders and said, "Thank you again, Mr. Roper." She left with as much dignity as she could summon. Had he sensed her shameful, illogical response to his closeness? He angered her and frightened her, but something about him touched a primitive part of her that she hadn't known existed, a part that she knew she must suppress.

She shaded her eyes with her hand as she emerged into the bright sunlight again, and paused when a flash of color caught her attention. To her left lounged a voluptuous young woman, with a thick mass of black hair spilling down her back. She had large dark eyes, lush red lips, and she was brazenly displaying the deep cleft of her full breasts under a white blouse worn off her shoulders. She obviously wore no petticoats beneath her skirt. The young woman met her gaze insolently, her dark eyes raking down Victoria's neatly coiled hair, starched long-sleeved, high-necked shirtwaist, and prim blue skirt.

This was the woman Victoria had seen on her arrival, whom she had taken for Carmita's daughter. What had Carmita said was her name? Victoria had an excellent memory for names, and she produced it after only a short moment. The woman was Angelina Garcia, a remarkably lovely name for a woman whose own beauty was as vivid as that of an overblown rose.

Since she obviously didn't work in the house, Victoria assumed that she must be married to one of the men. She wondered where they lived. She approached the young woman with a smile, determined to be friendly even though Angelina's manner wasn't welcoming.

"Hello," she said. "I'm Victoria Wav—McLain." She wondered if she would ever be accustomed to her married name.

The woman regarded Victoria for a moment longer in sullen silence, then tossed back her long black hair. "I'm Angelina."

"I saw you the day I arrived. I apologize for not speaking to you before now. Which one of the men is your husband?"

Angelina laughed, a sound of deep satisfaction. "None of them. Why should I marry?"

Not married? That was confusing . . . unless she lived with someone without benefit of marriage? Victoria felt her cheeks heat at her mistake. The poor girl, what an unstable, humiliating existence. But Angelina didn't act humiliated; she seemed positively gloating. Her eyes were alive with it.

In that instant Victoria knew she should walk away and return to the house where she was insulated from these people who were so very different from her. A lady would never dream of talking with a woman of ill-repute, which Angelina obviously was or she would never live with a man not her husband. Nor would a lady have confronted one of her husband's employees in the stables, as she had just done. But perhaps she was less of a lady than she'd thought, because she didn't walk away from Angelina.

Instead she said, "You have a man?" It was an inelegant question, but she didn't know how else to phrase it.

Angelina laughed again, a gloating sound that grated. "I have many men. All of them are my men. They all come to me—including your husband." Again the laugh, and the dark eyes glittered with spite. "He came back to me the night after your wedding! We all thought that was very interesting, no?"

White-faced, Victoria at last turned and walked away, but it was too late. The woman had scored her victory. Humiliation blinded her, and she didn't see the man until she walked into him. His hard hands grasped her shoulders to steady her, holding her soft body so close to him that her breasts were against his ridged abdomen.

It was Roper, leading his horse across the yard. She was too distressed to realize he could easily have avoided her and instead had deliberately put himself in front of her. She backed up, not looking at him. "I beg your pardon," she said tonelessly.

Roper glanced to where Angelina still lounged against the

wall, smirking her triumph, and guessed what had happened. The shock was plain on Victoria's white face.

He felt an unaccustomed impulse to comfort. "Don't pay any attention to Angelina," he said. "She's a vicious little bitch." He wanted to put his arm around her, feel the softness of her against him again. God, she had smelled so clean and sweet. A fire smoldered low in his belly, swelling his groin.

If anything, Victoria went even whiter, but she lifted her head with a proud motion and stepped away from him. "Thank you, Mr. Roper," she said steadily. "I'm quite all right."

He watched her walk away again, then went over to Angelina. She straightened, her red lips assuming a seductive smile. It was wasted on Roper; Angelina had been trying to get him into bed with her since he'd come to the ranch, but he wasn't interested. Angelina couldn't believe any man could be unresponsive to her beauty, and Roper had resisted her longer than any man she'd ever wanted. But it was not, she thought, because he didn't want her. He was jealous of all the others who enjoyed her favors, she was certain. He was just being difficult. She didn't mind; it made him more attractive in her eyes, and she was certain that sooner or later he'd come to her. His difficultness would make his surrender that much sweeter.

She thrust her breasts out for him, but he didn't even glance down. His cold eyes never left hers. "What did you say to her?"

"The fancy lady?" Angelina shrugged and pouted. "Nothing. I don't like women. I like men." She tried another smile on him.

Neither his expression nor his tone changed as he repeated, "What did you say to her?"

Many men before her had felt afraid when Roper spoke like that. Angelina felt a chill and straightened with a jerk. "I told her that the Major came to me the night after her wedding," she replied sullenly, then insisted, "It was the truth! You know that."

He did know it. Everyone on the ranch knew it and had snickered about it, joking that the Major's high-nosed lady must have near frozen him to death, and Angelina had had to thaw him out. Roper had been glad that McLain hadn't found any pleasure in his wife's bed, glad that she hadn't clung to him in ecstasy. He was sure Victoria hadn't been spared her husband's attentions, but he'd been relieved to think that, though the Major would occasionally bed Victoria out of duty, Angelina would still bear the brunt of McLain's perversions.

But what had it done to Victoria to discover that her husband had deserted her for a whore's bed one day after their wedding, and that everyone on the ranch knew it? She was a proud woman, and while she couldn't care about McLain, his actions must have wounded her all the same. No woman would like being the butt of raunchy jokes and sniggers, but for a woman like Victoria . . .

To Angelina he said, "McLain's mighty proud of his wife."

She spat on the ground. "If he cared about her, he wouldn't have come to me." She started to say that McLain hadn't been able to do it to his wife, but caution stilled her tongue. No man liked for it to be known that he'd failed so intimately; McLain would likely have her killed if she told.

"She's his wife, like Rubio's his stallion. What do you think he'd do if you let his stallion go, or if his wife left because of you?"

Angelina blinked her great dark eyes, for the first time realizing that her gloating triumph hadn't been very smart. She wasn't intelligent but she was cunning in her self-interest. She remembered how the Major had bragged for months about the real Southern lady coming to marry him, and shivered, thinking of how brutal the Major could be at times, when it seemed as if he enjoyed sex more if he could hurt her in some way. She knew he liked to hurt her, and she didn't want to provide him with any excuses to do so.

Her lips trembled, and she moved closer to Roper. "Will she tell him?"

He was unmoved by her distress, for he'd noticed that she took advantage of her nearness to rub her breasts against his arm. "She might," he said to make her worry about it, and mounted his horse before she could rub anything else against him.

Roper shook his head at himself as he rode off. He was a hard man; he'd seen his father murdered, his mother raped and killed when he'd been only thirteen years old. Roper had killed his first man when he'd been fourteen, when the man had tried to rob the two boys of their pitiful store of food. For twenty years the brothers had worked for their revenge, biding their time, gathering money and making plans. Nothing had been allowed to stand in their way. Nothing had mattered but putting Frank McLain in the ground and reclaiming their heritage. Roper kept his nose out of other people's business and expected them to keep theirs out of his. That was why it was so out of character for him to interfere, and he'd done it twice in a matter of minutes, all for the same woman. What did he care if Garnet got in the little sister's bloomers? He'd never have interfered if Victoria hadn't tried to face Garnet down, but she had, and he hadn't been able to stand by and let Garnet abuse her. He was the one man on the ranch Garnet wouldn't stand up to, but now he'd have to watch his back every minute.

All for a woman. He'd had women since he was fifteen, but they were always casual encounters that had never meant more to him than the temporary easing of his sexual needs. He loved women, though he'd never been *in* love; he loved their softness, the sweet musky scent of their skin, their lighter voices and smaller bodies, the clinging of their hands around his strong neck and the way their legs locked around his hips, their soft cries as he gave them pleasure. He always tried to please his woman, no matter how casual the bedding; it was a reflection of his own strong, sure sexuality that he enjoyed the act more when the pleasure was mutual.

But of all those women, he'd never wanted one the way he wanted Victoria. It was more than physical, though God knew that was strong enough and getting stronger. He wanted to see her smile. He wanted to protect her. He didn't know what made her different, but she was. She was also forbidden to him. She was a lady, and the wife of his enemy. He had blood on his hands, and would have more: the blood of her husband.

He found that it didn't matter. He thought of the way she'd lifted her chin with evident pride even though she had just been slapped in the face with her husband's infidelity. He thought of the way she protected her sister, and of the way she looked him full in the face when so few people did. She was alone and vulnerable, trapped in an unhappy marriage, but she had courage.

Damn it, why didn't she go back to Augusta where she belonged? Maybe if she was out of his sight, he wouldn't think about her, and she couldn't threaten his plans.

Victoria went straight to her room and sat on the chaise, forcing herself to take slow, deep breaths to calm herself. She had never before felt so angry and humiliated. Gradually she realized that she was angry because of the humiliation, not because she had learned that her husband had been unfaithful. She didn't care that the Major had gone to another woman; in fact, she was grateful, if it would continue to keep him away from her.

But the public nature of his betrayal upset her deeply. He had gone to that—that *whore*—barely twenty-four hours after their wedding, and everyone on the ranch knew it. She wouldn't have believed Angelina's word, but she'd seen the truth in Roper's usually impassive eyes.

The house staff knew, of course. The ranch was a small world in itself, so insular that everyone knew what everyone else was doing. No wonder Carmita had been so solicitous this past week.

She was Victoria Madelyn Marie Waverly; her mother was a Creighton. She had learned that lineage and tradition counted for little without money behind it, but pride had been bred into her as surely as the aristocratic bones of her face. Her husband had offended her in a way that no woman could forgive, exposing her to public humiliation. She also had to live with the galling knowledge that she had no means of recourse. Her husband did not love her, did not desire her, so she had no power in his life. She could threaten to expose his impotence, but it wasn't in her nature to publicly humiliate him. So she could only sit and let the realization creep into her that she could do nothing. She would have to continue as if she didn't know anything about it and therefore force everyone else to ignore it, too, at least in her presence.

But she was still outraged at Angelina's presence on the ranch. Though now she understood the whispers she'd heard as a girl about men who had kept fancy women on the side, she knew that the mistresses and the wives were always kept well separated. Again, she would have to ignore it, for if she tried to force

Angelina to leave, everyone would know that she was aware of her husband's infidelities and would think she was acting out of jealousy. To be thought jealous of her husband and that whore was unbearable, and so she would let things remain as they were.

A soft tap on her door distracted her, and Celia poked her head in. "I thought we were going to do the mending." There was no accusation in her voice, only puzzlement.

Victoria forcefully composed herself and patted the chaise. "Come sit with me for a moment." As difficult as it might prove to be, she knew she had to try to make Celia understand why she must stay away from Garnet, from any man who tried to touch her. Given the realities of the world they now lived in, Victoria knew this was a duty that could not wait.

Celia happily sat down beside her sister. She had something on her mind she wanted to ask her sister. She had complete faith in Victoria. She loved and trusted Emma, too, but it was her sister who had washed and bandaged her skinned knees, who had patiently answered all of her questions, soothed her after bad dreams, and returned her love unstintingly. She twirled a strand of her blond hair and mustered her courage. "Do you think the Major would let me ride Rubio? I *so* want to!"

Victoria was startled, and worried, because Celia often acted on her desires. "I don't think he would, darling. Rubio is a stallion, and stallions aren't used for pleasure riding. They're too strong-willed and dangerous."

"Mr. Roper rides him. I've seen him." Awe and envy mingled in Celia's tones.

Something deep in Victoria tingled at the mention of his name. "I'm sure he just rides Rubio to exercise him. And Mr. Roper is a man, sweetheart. He is much larger and stronger than you are."

Celia thought a minute, admitting the truth of that. But she wanted to ride Rubio so much that she couldn't let it go. "I'm a good rider, aren't I?"

"It's been a long time since any of us were on a horse." Another change wrought by war; all of the horses had been taken by the armies. "I suspect we're all sadly out of shape and practice, and you were just barely off of ponies when we lost the horses."

Celia looked so forlorn that Victoria hugged her and stroked her bright hair. "Would you like it if I asked the Major for horses we could use for pleasure riding? It would be good for us to get some exercise. Emma and I used to ride for hours." A faint wistful note crept into her own voice, and Celia immediately forgot her own disappointment as she rushed to give her own sort of comfort to Victoria.

Comfort took the form of a cheerful smile and a rush of enthusiasm. "Could you? I'd like that so much!"

"Then I'll ask the Major tonight." Victoria paused, trying to gather her thoughts. She still had to explain Garnet to Celia. She took a deep breath. "Sweetheart, I want to explain something very important to you." Celia nodded, her expression becoming serious.

"Mr. Garnet—" She paused again, frowning a little. "Mr. Garnet is an evil man. He would like very much to hurt you. You must be careful. Don't let him touch you or catch you alone."

"Hurt me? How?" Celia still didn't look alarmed, merely interested.

Victoria had been afraid that Celia wouldn't take the warning at face value, but would want details. Finding the words was more difficult than she'd imagined. "There are—things—that a man can do to a woman that will hurt her."

Celia nodded. "Hitting hurts," she said.

"Yes, it does. And he might hit you, to make you do these other things that would hurt you even worse."

"What things?"

There was no way out of it. She inhaled deeply again. "He would pull up your skirt and touch you on—on your privates."

Celia jerked upright, her young face indignant. "I'll be damned!" she said. She'd heard one of the cowpunchers say that, and liked it. All of the best words were forbidden, it seemed, so she said them only in her head, but that one had slipped out in her surprise.

Victoria almost laughed. She knew she should scold, but she was too relieved at Celia's vehement reaction. "Yes," she said. "Exactly."

Celia was still huffy. "I'll hit him if he even speaks to me again," she declared.

"You must try your best not to be alone with him. And please be cautious with the other men, too. I don't trust some of them." It was an odd feeling, but some of the Major's employees seemed to be just what they were, cowhands, while others seemed— meaner, and somehow disassociated with ranch work.

"Mr. Roper?"

Again Victoria felt that funny little jolt, and an even funnier feeling spread behind it. "No," she said slowly. "I think you'd be very safe with Mr. Roper. He even warned Mr. Garnet to leave you alone."

Celia gave a decisive nod. "I like Mr. Roper."

Victoria hugged her sister again, feeling much better now that she knew Celia understood at least part of the danger. It was odd how safe she felt in telling Celia that Roper wouldn't harm her, would in fact protect her, when she herself didn't feel that safe with him. Her heart had begun pounding again. She remembered the hot smell of him, the hardness of his body when she had col- lided with him, the way his hands had held her. She felt weak and strangely warm. She would take her own advice and avoid him as much as possible.

4

The Major was in a good mood that night, and Victoria didn't betray by either word or manner that she had talked with Angelina. Instead, she listened to him talking expansively over dinner. She nodded and smiled at all the right places.

She waited patiently, and when the right time finally presented itself in a small pause, she said, "I've been thinking how much I'd love to start riding again. All of us would. Do you think you could select some nice mounts for us? You have some lovely horses, and I know you would make good choices. Though not, of course, if you need the horses for ranch work." Her face revealed none of her thoughts as she gave him a small smile, one that managed to be reserved despite its surface warmth. He wasn't sensitive enough to tell the difference and beamed at her compliment to his equine knowledge.

"Of course, my dear." He patted her hand. "I should have thought of it myself." He'd tell Roper to pick out three mounts suitable for ladies. No one on the ranch knew horses better than Roper.

Emma's quiet face had its own glow at the thought of riding again, and Celia all but bounced in her chair. "When I've practiced and I'm really good, may I ride Rubio?" she asked.

He laughed at her foolishness. "You'll never be strong enough to control Rubio," he said, boasting of the horse's strength. "You just stay with the quiet nags, and let the men handle Rubio."

Just as quickly as that the brightness was gone from her small face, but she didn't argue. Celia seldom argued about anything. She looked down at her plate and pretended to concentrate on her food.

For once Victoria was glad the Major was so heavy-handed, because she was terrified Celia would take it into her head to try to ride the stallion. She picked up her spoon again and thanked him for the use of the horses, then made a commonplace remark to Emma, who had been trained in the same social graces and immediately picked up the conversation.

McLain looked around him at the three genteel, pretty-mannered women, and swelled with pride.

Victoria knocked on Celia's door, but no one answered. Worried because her sister hadn't recovered her spirits all evening, she opened the door and looked in, expecting to find the girl soundly asleep. Her heart sank when she saw the empty bed. Quickly she crossed to Emma's room, hoping that Celia was visiting with their cousin. Her knock brought only a nightgown-clad Emma to the door.

"No, I haven't seen her. I thought she was in bed," Emma said in reply to Victoria's anxious query. "I'll get dressed."

Celia had a lifetime habit, when upset, of finding a hidey-hole and burrowing into it. The refuge had never been in her own bedroom, but always in a smaller, tighter place, as if she needed the security of closeness. In the past Victoria had never been alarmed, but they were no longer in their old home.

Emma reappeared in little more than a minute wearing a plain skirt and shirtwaist, with a shawl knotted around her shoulders and her hair haphazardly pinned. "Do you remember the time the two of you were visiting us, when we found her in the chicken coop?"

Celia had been all of three at the time, and brokenhearted because she had been scolded. At other times she had been found in the storm cellar, a closet, under a bed, or a buggy, burrowed in hay (again, when they were visiting Emma), and once, when she was small, under a washtub. After an hour or two she would emerge sunny-tempered again, so they had ceased to look for her unless she was actually wanted for something.

They swiftly searched the house and found nothing. Victoria even poked her head into the Major's room; he had gone out after dinner, so she knew he wasn't in there. Neither was Celia. Carmita and Lola were sitting around the kitchen table and Lola said that she hadn't seen the señorita since dinner.

"Perhaps she is talking to the . . . the—" Lola stopped, frowning as she tried to think of the English word she wanted.

"The man who sells things from his wagon," Carmita said.

"A tinker?" Victoria asked.

They both smiled at her. "*Sí,*" Carmita said, relieved. "The tinker."

"I didn't know a tinker was here."

"He arrived just before dark, señora. He and his daughter. They are spending the night."

Victoria and Emma looked at each other. A tinker, being new to Celia, might attract her like a cat to catnip. "Where is the tinker's wagon?" Emma asked.

"Next to the bunkhouse, señorita."

The bunkhouse, where the men slept. Victoria hurried out the door. It was unthinkable that any of them would attack Celia, yet at the same time she thought Garnet capable of anything. Unbidden the thought intruded of asking Roper for help, and she flinched from the idea as if it had stung her.

Emma kept pace beside her and they both slowed as they neared the bunkhouse, with the hulking shadow of the tinker's wagon beside it. Through the small window they could see the men sitting around a couple of small tables, or lying on their narrow cots. Nothing unusual seemed to be going on. Victoria was even more reassured to see Garnet playing cards at one of the tables. There was no one at all around the tinker's wagon.

"Let's separate," she said, keeping her voice low so the men wouldn't hear. "I'll look in the stables and barn."

"We didn't look in the courtyard; I'll go there, and check the blacksmith shed on the way." Briskly Emma set on her way, and Victoria turned in the other direction.

Now that she was alone, the darkness seemed oppressive. Her heart began to beat faster as she quietly approached the long stables and entered. Most of the stalls' occupants were dozing, though a couple of horses put their heads over the top rails and whickered at her. She patted their velvet noses as she passed by, reassuring them. It was too dark inside for her to see much more than their large dark shapes, but all of the stalls were occupied and there was nowhere else in the long, low building for Celia to find a nook. No, the barn was far more likely. The barn was also where Rubio was stabled, away from most of the other horses because of his tendency to fight.

She opened the barn door just enough to slip through, and this time her way was lighted by a single oil lamp hanging on a post at the far end, close to Rubio's stall. The stallion, though, was quiet. Victoria could hear him making small rustling sounds as he shifted his feet.

She also heard another sound, the words indistinguishable but the timbre soft and definitely female.

If Celia were in the stall with Rubio . . .

On no account must she startle the horse. She lifted her skirts to keep them from dragging on the straw and quietly slipped nearer to the small pool of light.

She heard a groan and more rustles. Then a man's voice, unmistakably deep. The woman again, this time sounding as if she were in pain.

A chill coursed through her entire body. Celia?

She went closer, and the rustling noises were louder. She was still in the black shadows when she realized they weren't coming from Rubio's stall, but from the opposite side of the barn, where there was a small, unused box stall. The edges of lamplight were just spilling through the open rails, and she edged still closer, her heart in her throat because she was afraid it was Celia. Yet she didn't rush forward, and when she was close enough to see into the box, she was glad she hadn't.

The first glance told her that the woman in the straw wasn't Celia; she had a mass of dark hair. Nor was it Angelina. She didn't know the woman. She felt relief, then shock as she realized exactly what she was seeing. Such were her own experiences with sex that she almost screamed, thinking the woman was being raped. Then another firestorm of recognition went through her, and she had to jam her fist against her mouth to keep from making an outcry anyway. She saw two things simultaneously. First, the woman, far from being raped, was clinging to the man and encouraging him with whimpering, pleading words in Spanish. And, second, the man was Jake Roper.

The knowledge was like a blow to the chest. Air left her lungs in a rush, and she could only hang there, unable to move or breathe. The most incredible, unreasonable hurt filled her, and she tried to turn away, to leave quietly. She didn't want to see this, couldn't bear it—

But her legs still wouldn't work. Her muscles were frozen, and she could only stare helplessly, taking in details she didn't want to see.

The woman was naked except for her skirt, which was twisted around her waist. Victoria could tell that much, even though the shadows cast by the single lamp covered the lower halves of their bodies. Roper's shirt was off, revealing a powerfully muscled torso that glistened with sweat as he moved over his partner, the muscles tightening and flexing with his movements. The woman was clinging to his broad shoulders, her head thrown back and her eyes closed. Victoria stared at Roper's face, which she could see better than the woman's. It was tense and concentrated with fierce sensuality.

The woman gave a low cry and thrashed wildly for a minute, locking Roper within the grip of her arms. He held her firmly and began moving even faster. Moments later, a deep groan of pleasure sounded in his throat.

A sheen of tears blurred Victoria's vision, and she bit her lip to hold back a sob. The small pain in some way released her, and she took a step backward.

Like an animal scenting danger, Roper's head came up, and he stared right at her.

It was only a second, yet it lasted an eternity. His face was dripping with sweat, the skin still pulled taut in the immediate aftermath of orgasm, his eyes fierce and his hand already on the heavy pistol that lay next to him in the straw. Victoria stood with her fist held to her mouth, her eyes wide and glittering with tears. She knew that he saw her, even in the shadows. She knew she couldn't stand there another minute, pierced by that strange pain. Her limbs stiff, she forced herself to step more deeply into the shadows, one step at a time, until she could no longer see them. Finally she was able to turn and hurry from the barn, no longer caring about silence, wanting only to get away.

Infuriated, strangely shaken, Roper lifted himself from the woman and hitched his pants back up. She was still lying on the straw, her lush breasts glistening with sweat. Those breasts had excited him just a short time ago, but now all he wanted was to get away from her, and she deserved better than that. Damn it, he couldn't even remember her name. She'd made it plain, from the moment the tinker's wagon had pulled in, that she was interested in him. He'd taken her at her word. It was just a little diddling, not meaning anything to either of them except for the physical relief.

But Victoria had seen them. He thought grimly that the sex she'd had with the Major was probably starched and restrained, done in the dark with her nightgown pulled up only as much as was necessary. She had probably never dreamed of such things as nearly naked bodies rolling in the hay, sweating and straining toward completion.

Thinking of what she'd seen made him feel ashamed. He tried to push the unfamiliar emotion away, but it stubbornly refused to go. Damn, he wished it hadn't happened, wished Victoria hadn't had that stricken look in her eyes, wished that he could go after her and explain that it didn't *mean* anything. He wondered if she would understand that, or if she'd even care. But she'd looked at him as if he'd hurt her in some way she barely understood, and he was powerless to comfort her.

The woman—what was her name? something like Florence— was languorously sitting up, her face still dreamy. Not Florence . . . Florida? Florina, that was it. She stretched, lifting her arms to better frame her heavy breasts with their dark brown nipples, and eyed him with a kittenish sort of sensuality that made him feel hemmed in. He ignored her unspoken invitation for even further dallying and stuffed his shirttail into his pants.

"You'd better get on back to the wagon before your father misses you," he said in a flat tone.

She pouted, but began cleaning herself. "He is already drunk and asleep."

"He might wake up."

"Even if he did, he wouldn't care."

Roper strongly suspected that her "father" wasn't related to her at all, but it meant nothing to him one way or another. People got by as best they could. When she had dressed, he assisted her to her feet, gave her a kiss, patted her on her round bottom, then sent her on her way. As soon as she was out of sight, a black frown settled on his face.

Damn it to hell!

Victoria ran to the house, panting and near tears. Just before she reached it, Emma came to meet her.

"I found her," Emma reported, her tone amused. "She wasn't in a hidey-hole at all, she was in the courtyard counting stars."

Victoria forcibly regained control of herself and blinked the stupid tears away. Why on earth was she crying? It had been something of a shock, of course, seeing that, but nothing tragic. She wrenched her mind back to Celia, and received another shock when she realized that she'd forgotten her. It wasn't like her at all to be less than conscientious, and the lapse bothered her almost as much as what she had seen.

She took a couple of deep breaths to calm herself, gratefully aware that Emma would think her state of upset due to Celia. "Sometimes," she managed to say in a painfully even tone of voice, "I'd like to shake her."

Emma chuckled, and hooked her arm through Victoria's. "If you did, you'd spend the next month making it up to her, so there's no point in it," she said cheerfully. "Celia is Celia."

Victoria knew that. Celia never changed, thank God. But when she sought the sanctuary of her room a little later, Victoria stared at her own pale, oval face and wondered why the changes inside hadn't shown themselves on the outside. She still looked much as she had at the age of sixteen, but now she had known war and hunger, desperation, a loss of dreams, and the ugliness of a man's sexuality. For a moment, thinking of the horrible touch of the Major's hands, she felt nauseated again. Then another picture intruded, and the nausea changed to a moan of pain.

Jake Roper. His body rippling with muscles in the dim light and his hard face taut with pleasure. That woman's hands clinging to his shoulders, her head thrown back in ecstasy. For all the violence and power of their coupling, there had been a gentleness in the way he'd handled the woman.

Victoria buried her head in her hands. God, she was so foolish! Roper was nothing but a hired killer; she had had a few moments conversation with him, had briefly felt his body against hers in an accidental collision, and she was jealous—*jealous!* But not of him, she fiercely told herself. Never of him! She, a Waverly and a Creighton, was jealous of a tinker's daughter for the pleasure in her life. That wasn't much better, but she could bear that thought easier than the other.

She heard the Major moving about in his room, and she froze in dread that the connecting door would open. When the seconds passed and the door remained closed, she slowly relaxed and began to get ready for bed.

But when she was lying between the cool sheets, she couldn't sleep. She couldn't get the picture of Roper out of her mind; every time she closed her eyes, she saw his muscled body surging rhythmically. So *that* was exactly what went on between men and women. That was what the Major had tried to do to her. Knowing the basics hadn't enabled her to picture the scene in her mind, but now she could.

Her heartbeat was slow and heavy. Her body felt weighted down, and hot. She wondered how she would feel if it were Roper in the next room, Roper who opened the connecting door. She would lie there in bed waiting for him, and her body would feel as it did now, heavy and waiting. Again she saw him with that woman, but the picture changed and she was the woman clinging to him.

She turned onto her side, aghast at what she had been thinking. A lady never even thought such things about her husband; to think them about another man was scandalous. But her body ached, and she pressed her thighs tightly together in an effort to find relief from the shameful feeling. Her eyes burned with tears again. *Damn* Jake Roper!

Jake Roper damned himself. He lay in his bunk listening to the snores of the sleeping men around him and stared at the ceiling. He had made two serious mistakes, and now he had to deal with them. First, he should never have allowed Victoria Waverly to marry McLain. He could easily have had her kidnapped on the way and held her until he'd finished his business with the Major, but hindsight was as useless as it was clear. Or he could have killed McLain before Victoria arrived, and solved a lot of problems. Instead he had chosen to wait for his moment, to stay true to the plan he and Ben had decided on. Now it was too late to keep Victoria out of it.

His second mistake was in letting her get under his skin.

It wasn't as if she'd even tried. She wasn't a flirt; she was as straitlaced as a nun. She'd probably slap his face if he tried to kiss her. He grinned a little as he thought about it, though the grin was wry because he knew he was going to try it very soon. After what she had seen that night, he'd be lucky if she didn't claw him like a wildcat.

First chance he got, he was going to send a telegram to Ben and tell him to gather the rest of the men and head toward the ranch. But it could be a few weeks before he could get to Santa Fe and another month to six weeks before Ben could get here. Say, two months. Two months left until the culmination of twenty years of planning. The broad valley, once known as Sarratt's Kingdom and now simply as Kingdom Valley, would be Sarratt property once again, returned to its rightful owners—

—if he could convince Victoria to marry him. Force her, if necessary.

Damn it, he should have prevented the wedding, but he hadn't realized the implications until it was too late. With McLain dead, the kingdom would belong to his widow, Victoria. The only way to bring it back under Sarratt ownership was to marry her, as a woman's property became her husband's. So Jake would have to marry her.

It was amazing that one young woman could, with her mere presence, wreck twenty years of planning. Not that those plans hadn't changed a lot over the years anyway. As boys, their dreams of revenge had been wholesale destruction of McLain and all his men, of everyone living on the ranch. But as they had grown older, the plan had changed. There were no doubt innocent people living on the ranch, people who had had no part in McLain's treachery, people who had begun working there only after the slaughter and had no idea what had happened. For all their grim focus on revenge, the Sarratts weren't murderers. Killing McLain and his men was one thing, more like killing rabid dogs than taking a human life. But years had passed and there had to be new people hired, servants, women, maybe even children. An attack like the one McLain had used wasn't feasible to them any longer.

Twenty years. They had drifted for twenty years, not aimlessly, though it might have looked that way. Anywhere they could find work, they had taken it and begun saving their money dollar by hard-earned dollar. They had dug in mines, hired out their guns, worked as ordinary cowhands. Jake had trained horses, Ben had gambled, using their own particular skills. They knew they would need money to implement their evolving plan.

So twenty years had passed. He was thirty-three now, not a thirteen-year-old boy wild with grief and rage. The rage still burned, but it was under control. An eye for an eye . . . he didn't want McLain's eyes, he wanted his blood for his father's blood, his mother's blood. The bastard was living in the Sarratt house, sleeping in Duncan Sarratt's bedroom, walking daily across the tiled foyer where he had raped and killed Elena. It ate at Jake, seeing McLain walk into that house every night. Only his iron control kept him from getting out of bed and walking across to the house right now. It would be so easy; he could climb the stairs, go into the bedroom, and lay his gun barrel against McLain's temple. A little squeeze of the finger, and it would be over. But it would probably be over for him, too, and that wasn't his plan. He and Ben were going to own the valley again, so it had to be legal. Not only that, he was reluctant to see Victoria in bed with McLain; the very thought made him angry, and sick.

The plan they had settled on was for Jake to hire on at the ranch, find out how many men were left from the original bunch that had attacked them, and who they were. While he was doing that, Ben would be hiring good men they could trust, men who were standing ready to assume their new jobs. When Jake had arrived and seen the situation, he knew they'd have to replace a good two-thirds of the hired hands. The hired guns would go; Jake had no use for them. He didn't expect any of them to interfere, as they had no real loyalty to McLain. He also figured about half of the regular cowpunchers would drift away, for their own reasons. Some wouldn't like working for the Sarratts; some would be afraid too much attention would be turned on the ranch, and they would want to remain unknown. Jake didn't question a man's motives; he had some things in his background that couldn't stand too much light on them, either.

So Ben had men standing ready to take up the jobs that would be left vacant, and Jake had identified the men who had taken part in the raid. Charlie Guest had been one of them, and Jake had enjoyed killing him. He'd deliberately done it in a manner that was sure to make the others wary of him. That left five: McLain, Garnet, Jake Quinzy, Wendell Wallace, and Emmett Pledger. Wendell was going on seventy and was almost blind, so Jake discounted him as a threat. Garnet was a back-shooter. Quinzy wouldn't turn a hair at much, but neither would he put his life on the line for McLain or Garnet. Quinzy looked out for himself first. Pledger, on the other hand, was mad-dog mean and cold-blooded into the bargain, willing to kill for the pleasure of it.

When McLain had murdered the Sarratts and stolen the ranch, the only form of law had been the United States Army, which had more than had its hands full with the Navaho and the Mexican Army. Law had existed only in the immediate vicinity of the army, and then only army law. General Kearny hadn't concerned himself with the small, bloody wars being fought all over the vast new territory for control of huge tracts of land. McLain was as smart as he was murderous; first he'd killed the Sarratts, then legally filed on the land.

It was supposed to have been just as simple for the Sarratts. Kill McLain and take over the land. He'd had no heirs; the land would have reverted to the government and been available for filing. This time it would be the Sarratts doing the filing.

It would even be legal. There was no law against killing a man in a fair fight. Jake allowed himself his own cold smile when he thought of it. With his own men in place to protect him from a bullet in the back, he'd face them one by one in a gunfight. Until the end of the war there had been no such thing as a quick draw, but with thousands of ex-soldiers pouring westward it was a skill that had quickly developed within the past year. Hell, McLain's holster still had a flap on it. Jake had cut the flap off of his and practiced for hours to develop both speed and accuracy. McLain wouldn't stand a chance. The only one who came close to him in speed was Quinzy, but he tended to hurry his shot and often missed the first time. Pledger was more accurate, but slow. Garnet was respectable in both speed and accuracy, but Jake was faster and he knew it. He should be able to take them all without trouble. If not, Ben would finish the job.

Only now the ranch would belong to Victoria.

He wondered what he'd have done if McLain's chosen wife had been ugly or ill-tempered or a whiny idiot. He couldn't kill an innocent woman, but he didn't think he could force himself to marry a woman like that, either. Victoria, on the other hand, was just right to be the mistress of Sarratt's Kingdom. He hated to admit it, but McLain had chosen well. She was a lady, she had courage, and she didn't simper.

Marriage wasn't such a bad idea. He'd never considered it before, but once he and Ben had the kingdom back, it would be time to settle down anyway. Jake figured Victoria would do for him, circumstances being what they were.

Victoria sat upright with a jerk, clutching the sheet to her chin while her body went cold. The Major stood in the open door, outlined by the light coming from his room. Dear God, she couldn't bear it again. . . .

"I been thinking," he announced, his words slurred, and with horror she realized he was drunk. She could smell the stench of alcohol from across the room. " 'Bout them horses you and the other gals want. Ain't no horses on the ranch fittin' for ladies, they're all work horses 'cept for Rubio. We'll go into Santa Fe to buy some fancy ridin' horses, and maybe find some of them fancy saddles ladies use. That's what we'll do, we'll go to Santa Fe, and let all those bastards get an eyeful of my womenfolk."

He laughed and lurched farther into the room. "They'll be so jealous they can't stand it," he predicted, and seemed to take great pleasure from the thought. "Yessir, when they find out you three ladies are up here, I'll have men from all over the territory sniffin' around. Not no trash, mind you, but men who mean something, and they'll all be beggin' to court them other two gals, especially that fancy little sister of yourn—*yours*," he corrected himself, and laughed again. "We'll leave in the morning. I can't wait to see their tongues hangin' out like hound dogs in a pack."

He took another step toward her, and suddenly she knew that she'd do anything, even run screaming from the house, to prevent him touching her again.

"If we're leaving in the morning, we'll have to get up early," she said, fear making her voice sharp. "We need all the sleep we can get. I'll see you tomorrow, Major, bright and early."

He stopped, weaving back and forth on his feet. She waited, holding her breath. Then he said, "We need sleep. Good thinkin', sugar. You ladies need to rest a lot, you ain't used to life on a ranch, or on a trail, either."

"Good night," she said, and lay back down, tucking the sheet around her. Then she bit her lip and called, "Major?" as he turned to go. "I—thank you for the horses. It's very generous of you."

"Nothin's too good for my wife," he said with heavy self-satisfaction.

It wasn't until he'd left the room and closed the door behind him that she relaxed. She didn't know if he had intended to try again to bed her, but just having him that close had been almost more than she could bear. If he had actually tried to do to her what she had seen Roper doing to that woman—

The remembered image flashed in her mind again, tormenting her. Damn him! Why should she care what he did? "I *don't,*" she whispered into the darkness, and knew that she lied. God help her, she did care. She was horrified by the admittance. She was married; Jake Roper and every other man, except her husband, was forbidden to her. There were only two classes of women, good women and bad women. For a woman to consort with any man except her husband, in any way except socially, was for her to cross the line between good and bad. For her even to think of Jake Roper in such a manner was sinful.

But propriety had given her a husband she despised, and sin or not she couldn't rid her mind of the insidious weakness of thought that brought to the fore, again and again, Jake's form and narrowed, glittering green eyes.

She hated him. He made her lust, and she hated him for it. Lust was an ugly, shameful thing, but she was beginning to know its power. It made her feel hot and restless, her body heavy and aching; it kept her from sleep and tore at her conscience. Because she couldn't handle it any other way, she took her desperation and formed it into resentment against the man who had, without even trying, brought her to this pass. How he would laugh, in that sneering way, if he knew!

After leaving Victoria, McLain stood in his bedroom, swaying a little as he thought. He'd been drinking, so maybe that was why he'd had the thought that this time he'd be able to get hard if he tried it with her again. He shuddered, remembering the two times he *had* tried. By God, no way he'd risk that again.

But he needed a woman, something to keep him from going to sleep and having that damn nightmare again. It was coming more and more often lately, robbing him of sleep and wearing him down.

Angelina. He snickered at the thought of having to kick another cowhand out of her room. Hell, what did he care? He liked the idea of making another man crawl off of her so he could crawl on. Showed 'em who was boss.

He quietly left his bedroom, taking exaggerated care that he didn't slam the door. The house was dark and he held onto the banister to keep from stumbling over his own rather unsteady feet. Just as he reached the bottom step he saw a flash of white out of the corner of his eye, and terror chilled him. He could feel his scalp prickling as his hair lifted. Sarratt was back! The flashing knife—maybe it was a ghost—

Then the white moved again and he saw that it was a woman in a nightgown, moving past the doorway of the dining room, walking toward the kitchen. His terror changed immediately to anger against whoever had scared him like that, and Angelina was forgotten as he walked toward the dining room.

"Who's there?" he snapped. By God, he'd teach her to wander around like that at night, scaring him. It was one of those Mex women, probably Carmita; she was always poking her nose in every cranny of the house.

The woman was already in the kitchen. She came back to the doorway just as he entered the dining room. "Señor?" she asked in a timid voice.

Now that they were in the same room, he could see her well enough to identify her. It was Juana, the young one. Her long dark hair was streaming down her back. The plain white nightgown was long-sleeved and high-necked, but his eyes narrowed as he looked her over.

He'd been intending to give her hell, but abruptly changed his mind. "What're you up to, gal?" he asked in a smooth tone as he approached. "Walking around in the dark like this."

Juana took a step back. "I'm sorry, señor," she blurted. Her dark eyes looked huge in the faint light. "I was going back to my room."

"What were you doin'?" he demanded. "Maybe slippin' out to meet some cowhand?"

She vigorously shook her head. "No, señor. I—I carried a book back to your study. I read them, sometimes. I apologize, señor, I won't get one again without your permission."

"Forget the damn books," he said, his tone becoming thicker. He put his hand in her hair, twisting the heavy dark locks around his wrist. "You can read all the books you want if you'll be nice to me."

Juana tried to draw back. "Señor?" she asked in a quavering voice.

"You know what I mean." He jerked her to him and ground his mouth over hers. Terrified, Juana raised her fists and began to pound at him, but her efforts were useless. He had the strength of a bull.

He laughed soundlessly at her as he clamped his hand over her mouth and forced her down to the floor. "If you scream, I'll throw you and your nosy mother off the ranch." He grunted as he unbuttoned his britches and jerked up her nightgown. Juana tried to hit him again, and he balled up his fist and hit her in the head. She whimpered with pain.

He kneed her legs apart and thrust into her. She bucked once, then lay still. She was dry, but he kinda liked that; made her feel tighter. He'd wanted to do this for a long time; he thought of the Mexican servants as belonging to him anyway. Now the pleasure was doubled for him because he was so relieved to find he still had the power and virility to force a woman, even if he couldn't force his wife.

When he was finished, McLain climbed off and nudged Juana with his boot. "You say anything about this, gal, and you'll regret it." Feeling satisfied that his threat would keep her in line, he returned upstairs and fell into bed. Angelina could wait.

Whimpering, Juana curled into a ball. The pain in her lower body was so bad she could barely move, and her head was throbbing. It was over an hour before she could get up, and then she walked like an old woman, bent over and hobbling. At night, she noticed, blood looked black.

5

Jake looked both left and right as he left the telegraph office, but saw no one he knew. As capital of the territory, Santa Fe was bursting at the seams and no one paid any attention to one more dusty cowhand. The streets were crowded with bonneted women, men in blue army uniforms, prosperous merchants in their tailored suits, rough ranchers, shopkeepers, saloon bartenders, politicians, children darting and playing, and untold numbers of dusty cowhands. He was hidden in their swarming midst.

He settled his hat lower on his forehead to shade his eyes and began walking up the street. It was past noon, when McLain had told Victoria they would look at a string of horses. The Major had asked Roper to help in the selection, and he was looking forward to the excuse to stand close to Victoria and watch her evade his eyes. She hadn't looked at him square in the face since the night she'd caught him with Florina. Right from the first she had met him stare for stare, bolder than most men, but now she tried not to even acknowledge his presense. He was going to have to do something about that.

About twenty horses were milling about in two adjoining corrals. Celia was perched on the railing with her bonnet dangling down her back by its strings, and enthusiastically pointing out the horses she liked. From what he could tell, she had narrowed her favorites down to about half of the herd. Victoria and Emma were standing a little back from the fence, watching the horses and occasionally asking questions of the beefy man standing beside them, who evidently owned the herd. McLain was leaning on the railing with Garnet beside him. Several more McLain men were close by.

Emma pointed. "I like that one," she said decisively, and McLain signaled that her choice be separated from the herd.

Jake looked the horse over. It was a stocky, strong-looking gray gelding with calm eyes, and it didn't fidget when it was cut from the herd. For a lady's mount, it was a good choice. When the Major noticed he'd arrived and caught his eye, Jake nodded his approval.

Celia squealed, and Jake saw Victoria give her sister a loving, amused look. "This one!" Celia called, pointing to a showy chestnut with cream-colored mane and tail.

The beefy man transferred his chew of tobacco from one cheek to the other. "He's not real well-mannered, miss," he said gruffly.

Jake walked up beside Celia and rested his arms on the top railing while he looked over the horses. "What you want," he said in a quiet voice, "is a horse with good strong legs and one that don't look like it'll shy every time a rabbit crosses its trail." The girl loved horses, but from what he'd seen she hadn't had much experience with them. She was attracted to the fancy-colored animals regardless of their temperament, but what she needed more than anything was a horse with a placid disposition.

He pointed out a dark brown horse with one white stocking. "Now, look at that horse," he said. "It's got good strong shoulders and legs, and a deep chest. That means it's got good lungs. That horse could carry you all day and all night without getting tired." It was also as calm as the horse Emma had selected.

Celia tilted her head a little to the side as she studied the animal. "He isn't very pretty," she said.

"It's a mare," Jake corrected. He looked at the beefy man. "How about bringing that dark brown mare with the stocking up so the lady can meet her."

A simple rope bridle was fashioned on the mare's nose, and she willingly walked over to snuffle at Celia's shoes and skirts before nuzzling at her hand. Celia giggled, a sound like liquid sunlight, and stroked the mare's neck.

"She's dusty, but a good brushing will make her shine," Jake said.

The mare blew through her nose, sounding as if she agreed, and Celia was won. She turned a beaming smile on Jake. "I want this one," Celia said, still patting her new friend's neck.

Jake glanced at Victoria and caught her watching him. For the first time she didn't jerk her eyes away as if she couldn't bear to see him. Pushing it, Jake walked up to her and tipped his hat. "Mrs. McLain. Miss Emma."

Victoria was a little pale, but she met his gaze. "Thank you," she said in a low voice, nodding toward Celia.

"No thanks needed, ma'am. Do you need any help picking out your own horse, or have you already made up your mind?"

Victoria had, but she looked blindly at the horses again. He was standing so close that she could feel his warmth at her shoulder.

"Let Roper pick one out for you," McLain said. "He knows his horses."

"I already know which one I want. The tall mare with the blaze. The dark chestnut." She felt stifled by Roper's nearness and stepped forward until she reached the railing.

To her dismay Jake moved forward, too, under the guise of looking for the mare. His left shoulder crowded her and immediately he put his left hand on her waist. "Steady, ma'am," he said, as if she had stumbled.

He took his time removing his hand. He was standing between her and the Major, blocking her from McLain's view with his own body. Victoria shuddered and stepped sideways. Her skin burned where he had touched her.

The beefy man transferred his chew again, eyeing the mare in question. "I don't know, ma'am. She's only about half broke to the saddle, and tends to be a touch headstrong."

Jake looked at the mare and his eyes narrowed with interest. No doubt about it, that was a damn fine horse. She was big for a mare, as big as most stallions, and she had fire in her eyes. She was strongly built, but her lines suggested speed, too.

He rubbed his jaw. "How old is she?"

"Three. Ain't never been bred."

"Too wild looking," McLain announced. "I don't want my wife risking her neck on some half-wild nag."

Victoria pressed her lips together and looked away. Jake realized she wouldn't argue with McLain, just as he realized she badly wanted the mare. He rubbed his jaw again and motioned with his head for McLain to walk a little bit away with him.

"That mare is a fine-looking piece of horseflesh. Just look at her. Tall and strong, and full of piss and vinegar. Think of the foals you'd get by putting Rubio on her."

McLain thought and looked at the mare again. His eyes gleamed. "That's an idea, Roper. I'll buy her, but pick out some other nag for Victoria."

"Why not give this one to her? She's in love with the horse. She'd think a whole lot more of this one than any other horse here, and be more appreciative."

"You heard the man, the damn horse ain't good broke."

"Hell, that's no problem. I can have her settled down in a couple of weeks. All of them will need work with a sidesaddle anyway, before they'll be fit to ride."

McLain pursed his lips, watching the mare toss her head. Roper was right; that was a fine-looking animal. He almost rubbed his hands together in glee as he thought of the quality of foals she'd drop. He was going to buy that horse, but putting Victoria on her was something else.

"I don't know," he said. "Victoria's a lady, not a Mexican wench who'll throw her leg over a donkey. She might not be able to handle a horse like that."

Jake's eyes gleamed and he turned his head so McLain couldn't see. "Let me work with Mrs. McLain, and I'll have her the best damned horsewoman in the territory. Buy her one of those fancy riding habits like the women wear back East, and people all over will talk about her and that mare."

If there was anything that swayed McLain, it was the idea of someone else envying him. He laughed heartily and said, "By

God, that would be a picture, wouldn't it? All right, Roper, you teach that mare some manners and my wife how to ride."

He'd said it loud enough for Victoria to hear, and she blanched. My God, what had Roper said to him? She already knew how to ride! There was no need for Roper to give her any lessons. But she didn't say anything, because the most important thing was that the Major was going to buy the mare. She had been fond of the horse she had regularly rode before the war, but something about this magnificent animal tugged at her. The mare was as fierce and arrogant as any stallion, not flashy, but confident in her own strength and speed. She had heart, and Victoria wanted to share in her freedom. When they got back to the ranch she would make it plain that she didn't need any riding lessons.

She was still exhausted from the bone-crushing journey, as they had only arrived in Santa Fe the day before. Moreover, they had been invited to a party at the governor's house that night. She needed both to rest and to escape from Roper's company. "It's getting late, Major. We need to return to the hotel to get dressed for the party."

The Major checked his watch and scowled. "Damn. I need to see someone this afternoon. Roper, escort the ladies back to the hotel. Garnet, you come with me."

She inhaled to voice a protest, then let her breath out with rueful acceptance. For whatever reason, fate was conspiring against her in her efforts to avoid Roper. All she could do was be so gracious that no one would suspect how his presence disturbed her.

His eyes gleamed dark green as he took her elbow in his right hand and Emma's in his left, as if he knew of her discomfort and enjoyed it. Celia danced along behind, beside, and in front of them, her bright presence masking Victoria's silence. Emma made the usual small talk, leading Victoria to wonder if no one but Roper saw her agitation. Did she hide it so well, even from Emma?

The hotel was three stories tall, and the Major had booked their rooms on the top floor so they wouldn't be bothered by the coming and going of the other guests. Emma and Celia shared a room next door to Victoria's room, and beyond that was the

Major's. Victoria was devoutly thankful that there was no connecting door. She had slept better in the hotel room than she had since the day she'd been married.

Emma and Celia entered their room first, and Victoria firmly disengaged her arm from Roper's grip. "Thank you for your escort, Mr. Roper," she said in polite dismissal as she retrieved her door key from her bag.

"You're very welcome, Mrs. McLain," he replied in solemn tones. He took the key from her and opened the door, then put his hand on her back and forcefully ushered her inside.

Victoria whirled to see him shutting the door and locking it again, from the inside. Her heart lurched as she faced him. "Please leave, now, and I won't say anything about this."

He took off his hat and ran his hand through his dark hair. "About what, Mrs. McLain?" he asked softly.

"About—this. Forcing your way into my room."

"Have I touched you? Insulted you? Kissed you?"

Her heartbeat was even faster now. Her palms were damp, and she put her hands behind her back. "No," she whispered. Something occurred to her, and she lifted her chin. "You're doing this for revenge, aren't you? Because I—I accidentally intruded the other night in the barn. I apologize, Mr. Roper. It was completely unintentional."

A corner of his mouth kicked up in a little smile. "You sure got an eyeful, didn't you? But you must have liked what you saw, because you didn't leave, you stood there until the end."

She blushed painfully, and he gave a low laugh. How could she explain that she'd been frozen, unable to move? She couldn't tell him how pain had lanced through her or how fiercely jealous she had been.

"I've got a deal to offer you," he said, watching her intently. "I won't say anything around the ranch about you watching me with Florina if you'll give me that kiss you're so terrified I'll take." He knew the risk he was running by being in her room, but he couldn't pass up the opportunity to have her to himself for just a few minutes. Let her start getting used to the idea that there was something between them, and accustom her to his lovemaking.

Now she went pale, and for a minute she felt as if she might faint. "You—you want me to *kiss* you?"

"Yes, ma'am, I do. I've never had a lady kiss me before. I want to know if you taste any different, if your lips are softer." He looked as if he were wickedly enjoying her agitation. "I want a long, slow, mouth to mouth kiss."

"I'm married!"

He shrugged. "So?"

So, indeed? She looked at him wildly. Did all men feel that way about the marriage vows? Her husband had broken his easily enough. Kissing Roper wouldn't be infidelity in act, but it would be in spirit. She thought of the distasteful way the Major had put his mouth on hers, but the thought of kissing Roper like that wasn't distasteful at all. It was deeply, primitively exciting and it frightened her because she should never even think such a thing, let alone act on it.

"I can't," she whispered.

He smiled again, and she shivered. "Oh, I think you can," he murmured, slowly advancing. "Just think of what the men would say if they knew you had watched. They'd get a real hoorah out of it, and they'd laugh every time they saw you."

She backed up a step. "Mr. Roper—"

"Jake."

"You don't know what you're asking of me. I—"

"I think I do." He moved again, his hand shooting out to catch her arm and prevent her from retreating further. "I'm asking you to kiss me the way a woman kisses a man. Nothing else. Just a kiss."

She couldn't believe how hot his hands were. If he were that warm all over, what would it feel like if he— She jerked her thoughts to a standstill, appalled at herself. She stared up at him.

"That's all?" she whispered. "Just a kiss."

"That's all."

"It's blackmail."

"Yes."

It was sinful and she knew it, but sin has been sweet from the beginning of time. The temptation to taste him was so powerful she was shaking with it, and it was forbidden. She was a respectable married lady; she should cleave only unto her husband—

—who cleaved unto any cheap slut who would have him.

She felt paralyzed, mesmerized. His eyes were glittering down at her, so close that she could see the tiny golden striations around the black iris, blending into forest green tinged with blue. She could feel his breath on her face and knew that, sin or not, she was going to let him kiss her.

His left hand slid around the small of her back and urged her closer. Immediately Victoria's hands flew up to clutch his biceps in faint alarm and protest, but she said nothing. The swell of his muscles under her palms left her unwillingly beguiled and weaker than she wanted to be.

He pulled her closer, inch by inch, until their bodies touched. Victoria inhaled a quick breath, shattering inside at the powerful intimacy of this simple contact. He was so warm and hard, his muscled body supporting hers; he held her so close that she could feel the buttons of his shirt digging into her breast, the buckle of his gunbelt cutting into her abdomen, and his strong thighs rubbing against hers through the fabric of her skirt and petticoats.

Her heart was slamming painfully against her rib cage as she waited, then he bent his head. His mouth, warm and firm, touched hers for a moment, then lifted. Was that all? She felt faint with relief that it had been as uncomplicated as that, though still very improper.

He frowned down at her. "Not like that."

"Like what?"

"That wasn't the kind of kiss I want."

She stared at him. "What other kind is there?"

He looked momentarily startled, then his eyes narrowed. It was possible, he realized. Women like her thought they should endure rather than participate. McLain certainly wasn't a man to make her realize she should enjoy it. Roper was going to enjoy making this aspect of her education about life in the West his responsibility.

He cupped her jaw in his right hand. "Open your mouth this time," he ordered.

She looked aghast. "Open my—"

He quickly took advantage of the opportunity and covered her parted lips with his own. She made a quick sound of panic in her throat and tried to jerk away from him, but he locked his arm around her waist.

Victoria stared up at him with wide, frightened eyes. She sensed violence in him, as if he wanted more from her and was determined to get it. He had said just a kiss; had she been a fool to believe it would stop at that? She pushed against his arms in a futile effort at escape.

His right hand tightened on her jaw and his hard fingers exerted heavy pressure on her chin. Against her will, she felt her clenched teeth part and suddenly his tongue was inside her mouth. Shocked, astounded, she froze, and in that moment of immobility she became aware of his mouth moving over hers, of the warm stroke of his tongue inside her mouth. A strange heat began moving through her body, weakening her so that she had to cling to his arms to even stand upright. Both the heat and the weakness were insidious, creeping through her to undermine both her determination to keep this under control and her certainty that she could. In his embrace, with his mouth on hers, she was certain of nothing but the growing upheaval of her senses. This pleasure was wicked, and increasingly seductive. Her eyes drifted shut.

She had expected to give him one kiss, but that wasn't what happened. His mouth returned to hers over and over again, and both of his arms were around her now, crushing her to him. If she had ever had control of this situation, it was gone now.

He could have done anything with her, and she would have been helpless to stop him. Only the abrupt intrusion of someone pounding on the door made him swiftly release her and step back.

Victoria swayed, and panic shot through her as she realized someone had caught Roper in her room with her. She went white. If it was the Major— She couldn't finish the thought, because it was too horrible to contemplate.

Roper moved swiftly to the door, his right hand on his pistol butt.

"Wait!" Victoria said in an agonized whisper.

He gave her a brief glance. "It's next door," he said sharply. "Some drunk is trying to get into your sister's room." He opened the door and stepped into the hall.

Victoria flew to the doorway just as Roper said, "You planning on beating that door down, Pledger?"

Victoria recognized the man, though she'd never spoken with him. He'd been surly all the way to Santa Fe, and the other men hadn't associated with him much. His eyes had the mean look of a vicious dog, and she had unconsciously avoided him. Too late she realized the mistake she was making in letting him see her with Roper.

He turned on Roper with a snarl, but when his gaze lit on Victoria his lips twisted into a nasty smile. "I do declare," he mocked. "Playing patty-cake with the boss's wife? Bet he'd be real interested to know that, wouldn't you say?"

Jake considered the situation, and his eyes narrowed. It couldn't be much better, just him and Pledger facing each other. He could kill the bastard now just as well as later. Now that he'd sent the telegram to Ben and his brother was on his way, there was really no reason to wait. In fact, there was no way he could let Pledger walk away, not after he'd seen Jake come out of Victoria's room.

Smiling a little, Jake moved closer to the man. "Why don't you go to the saloon and hire a whore to scratch your itch," he suggested softly. "Leave the ladies alone."

Pledger hooted. "Just like you did, Roper? I've always wanted me some of that *refined* stuff. You just go back to diddlin' the boss's wife, and I'll try out that purty little sister, and neither of us will say nothin' about the other. How about that, pard?" He sneered and spat on the floor at Roper's feet.

Roper was smiling. Victoria saw it only from the side, just a small curl of the lips, but it chilled her. She stood in the doorway, watching with a sort of horrified fascination.

Jake's walk was easy and relaxed, so relaxed that Pledger didn't react until it was too late. "Stop right there," he said, and moved his hand toward his gun butt. Just as the last word left his mouth Jake kicked him between the legs, holding back just enough on the kick that Pledger wasn't felled. As it was, he sagged to the side, gagging as he grabbed his crotch.

Pledger straightened painfully, his eyes wild in a white face. "You son of a bitch," he said, and grabbed for his gun.

He had just cleared leather when Jake's first slug punched a hole in his chest and slammed him backward against the wall. Reflex jerked Pledger's finger on the trigger and for the second time the narrow hall shuddered from the thunder of gunfire. Pledger's bullet went through the floor and lodged in a wall on the second story.

His eyes, already glazing, were full of hate as he slid sideways to the floor.

Jake held him in his sights, hammer already cocked back again. If Pledger so much as twitched, the second slug would be between his eyes. No way was he going to live to say as much as a single word to anyone.

But Pledger's last breath sighed out of him as his pants stained with the release of his bladder. Jake eased the hammer down on his gun.

Emma and Celia had been too frightened to open their door before, but the sound of gunfire followed by that immense silence stirred Emma to action. She jerked the door open and stared in confusion at Roper, then down at Pledger. "Oh, God," she said.

Celia's frightened face poked out beside her, and the girl's beautiful eyes rounded with shock when she saw Pledger's body.

Jake turned his head and looked at Victoria, who was still frozen in the doorway. Their eyes met, his hard and green, hers almost gray with shock. In that moment she was more frightened of him than she had been of Pledger.

They had no time to say anything. Booted feet were running up the stairs, and a crowd of men erupted upward into the narrow hall. Jake punched out the empty shell and replaced it, then returned the pistol to its holster. He looked remarkably unconcerned as people crowded around, overlapping questions with comments.

One man nudged Pledger's boot with his own. "Ugly son of a bitch. Who was he?" Then he noticed the three women standing there and swallowed. "Beg yer pardon, ladies."

None of the women seemed to have noticed. Victoria was still staring at Jake, her face white. Jake reached out and took Emma by the arm, bending down to talk low in her ear. "Take Mrs. McLain back into her room. She saw the whole thing, and she looks a mite shocked."

Emma looked swiftly at Victoria, then back to Jake and nodded. "Help me with Victoria," she said to Celia. Victoria found herself taken in hand and ushered back into her room, the door firmly closed on the ugly scene in the hallway.

She sat down and folded her hands in her lap, holding herself inside. She felt numb. A man had just been killed in front of her, and despite all she had seen during the war, nothing had been as brutal as that. Jake had been so . . . casual about it, as if the taking of a life was nothing to him. And the smile on his face still made her shiver in reaction.

Celia sank down onto the floor and put her head in Victoria's lap. The girl was shocked and silent.

Automatically Victoria smoothed the bright blond hair, as she had been doing since Celia's childhood. Emma sat down on the bed, as quiet as Victoria.

"Did you hear what he said?" Victoria asked.

"Some." Enough, Emma thought, to know that Jake Roper had been in this room with Victoria. Enough to know that Roper had *had* to kill Pledger to keep him silent. Not that she thought for one minute that Victoria had betrayed her marriage vows; for one thing, there hadn't been time, and for another, Victoria was too inherently honorable.

But Jake had in fact been in here alone with her, and Emma had accurately pegged the Major as a mean, violent, petty man who would, she was afraid, judge Victoria by his own standards— which was to say, none at all. For Victoria's sake, Emma was prepared to back whatever story Jake offered.

Fifteen minutes later the Major and Garnet arrived, having been fetched from a saloon by a breathless youngster with the news that there'd been a shooting at the hotel and the Major's wife was involved. The boy hadn't known anything other than that garbled message. They had both been on their way upstairs with a couple of the saloon's soiled doves, and the Major was in a foul mood from the interruption.

"That's two of our men you've killed, Roper," Garnet said, eyeing the tall, muscular man before him with suspicion.

Jake shrugged. "He went for his gun first. A man braces me, I don't ask if he's serious or just funning."

"You *say* he drew first." Garnet's eyes were alive with hate.

McLain looked from one hired gun to the other, his eyes wary. He had remained alive because he was shrewd if not intelligent, and Garnet's suspicious attitude alerted him. Fights were common among a bunch of men, but Roper was *killing* men with whom he was supposed to be working. It did make a man stop and wonder.

"Garnet's got a point," McLain said, eyeing Roper closely. "There any witnesses?"

"Mrs. McLain saw the whole thing." Jake sounded bored. "Ask her."

"I'll do that." McLain stomped to Victoria's door and slammed his heavy fist on it. "Victoria!"

Emma snatched it open, and the three men entered. Celia rose from the floor and Victoria got to her feet, too. She was still pale, and she didn't look at Jake.

"Roper says Pledger drew on him first. Is that so?" McLain growled.

Victoria clenched her cold hands in her skirts. "Mr. Pledger went for his weapon first, yes."

"What I want to know is what you and Pledger were doing up here," Garnet said.

Suspicion darkened the Major's face. Steeling herself, Victoria lifted her chin. "Mr. Roper walked us back to the hotel, at the Major's request."

"I'd seen them to their rooms and gone back down to the lobby when I saw Pledger slip in, like he was trying to be sneaky." Jake took a tobacco pouch out of his pocket and leisurely rolled a cigarette. "I followed him, found him up here trying to break into Miss Emma and Miss Celia's room. Don't guess I have to tell you why. I tried to get him to go back downstairs with me, but he refused and went for his gun."

"You saw this?" McLain asked, cutting his eyes to Victoria.

"Yes." She agreed to the lie with her own. She didn't look at Jake.

McLain looked at Emma. "Is that true? Was Pledger trying to get into your room?"

At least Emma didn't need to lie. "He was beating on the door and saying . . . ugly things. We were afraid to open it."

Jake lounged back against the doorjamb, his eyes narrowed to sleepy slits as he surveyed the others. "I did what I had to do to protect the women. That's what you wanted, isn't it, Major?"

"Of course," McLain snapped.

"Then what's the problem?"

"I'll tell you what the problem is," Garnet said, stepping closer. "The problem is you killing two of our oldest hands. Pledger and Charlie Guest had been with the ranch for years."

Jake smiled. It was the same expression Victoria had seen just before he'd killed Pledger. "I could always make it three," he suggested in a silky tone.

"That's enough damn killing!" McLain yelled. "Back off, Garnet. It riles me to lose Pledger, but I sure as hell don't want my two best men killing each other over him."

"Sure, boss." Garnet stepped back, but his expression remained hate-filled.

Jake wasn't surprised that Garnet had backed off so easily; face-to-face wasn't his style.

McLain put on his best smile. "The party tonight will be just the thing to make you ladies forget about this," he said. "The governor can't wait to meet you, since word's out that I have the three prettiest women in the territory. Every man in Santa Fe will be trying to dance with you tonight."

Victoria seized desperately on that excuse. "My goodness, I'd forgotten about the party! We'll have to hurry. Run along, gentlemen—" She made little shooing gestures with her hands. "Oh, Major, could you have the hotel send up hot water to both rooms?"

"Of course, my dear." He patted her on the cheek. "Dress up in your fanciest dress—give these yokels something to gawk at."

When the three women were alone again, Victoria visibly sagged. "I don't know if I can bear even the thought of a party," she said in a stifled voice. "Dear God." But she forced herself to straighten and took deep breaths to compose herself. "I suppose we'll have to go and make the best of it. Celia, dear, are you all right?"

"Yes." Celia looked unusually grave, but her dark blue eyes were steady. "Jake had to kill him, to protect us. I'm not sorry."

Victoria felt sick. Yes, Jake had killed to protect, but had he done it for Emma and Celia, or to conceal his own indiscretion with Victoria?

There was a hardness in him that terrified her, yet she was inexplicably drawn to him. Try as she might to avoid him, fate kept twisting their lives together, forcing them to share sordid secrets that created an unwilling intimacy between them, and now they were sharing lies.

Yet she had stood in his arms and let him kiss her in a way so improper and shattering that she could scarcely bear to think about it. She was another man's wife! To do what she had done had been betrayal, but at the time she had gloried in it. She had enjoyed the scent and taste of him, the feel of his strongly muscled body against her, thrilled to the power of his arms.

She had even dreamed of him. And that was, perhaps, an even greater betrayal.

6

Victoria excused herself and sought out the ladies' convenience, needing to get away just for a moment from the chatter and social smiles, and from the unexpectedly harrowing nearness of blue uniforms. It was silly, because the war had been over for a year, and in the meantime she had certainly become used to the sight of blue uniforms on the streets of Augusta. But never before had she been required to meet Union soldiers socially. She had no hate for them and wasn't bitter, as so many Southerners were, but when the first Union officer had bowed over her hand, she had felt afraid, as if they were still foes. The soldiers certainly did nothing to calm her already frayed nerves.

She had used rigid control to survive the evening. She hadn't allowed herself to think of the gaping hole in Pledger's chest, the ugliness of death, the boneless sprawl. Nor had she let herself remember the vile things he had said or the chilling way Jake had smiled. Most of all, she had blocked from her mind the hot, endless moments she had spent in his arms. It shouldn't have happened and must never happen again. She had to forget it forever.

The hallway was deserted, and though two lamps illuminated it for the benefit of the guests, the light seemed dim, absorbed by the rich but rather dark patterns of the wallpaper and carpeting. She longingly thought of the simple white walls and clear, uncluttered lines of the hacienda. If she enjoyed her marriage half as much as she did that house, she would have been very happy indeed.

The convenience was at the back of the house. As she passed an open doorway, it was filled with a dark, massive figure. She was startled but not frightened, merely thinking it another guest. An arm stretched out of the shadows and grabbed her, jerked her into the room, and only then did she become alarmed. She inhaled jerkily to scream, and the man clapped his hand over her mouth.

"Damn it, don't scream," he muttered.

The simple recognition of his voice twanged at her nerves. She jerked her head away from his hand. "What are you doing? You shouldn't be in here! How did you get in?"

"I'm here because the Major doesn't go anywhere without backup. I've been walking around outside, keeping an eye on things. This door was open, and I could see in through the window. From the parade of ladies going up and down the hall, it didn't take much brain to figure out where they were going."

"So you sneaked in the back door?"

"Crawled in the window."

"And grabbed the first woman who came by?" She was incensed and thought she might still scream. He hadn't let go of her, his fingers were still hooked around her waist, and the way he was holding her so close made her uneasy.

"No, I waited for you." He let go of her and walked to the open door, which he eased shut without even a click. "I wanted to talk to you."

Without the light coming from the hallway, the room at first seemed totally dark. She moved closer to the windows, both to put some distance between them and to see better. She lifted her chin. "What do we have to talk about?"

"Pledger."

She flinched a little at the name. "You killed him. What more is there to say?"

"Plenty. Don't let your high-nosed conscience push you into confessing. Pledger was dirt. He murdered and raped, and enjoyed it."

"Like you enjoyed killing him?"

He was silent a moment, then gave a low, harsh laugh as he moved toward her, into the light from the windows. "Yeah, I enjoyed it. I felt like I was doing a good deed."

Victoria clenched her hands. "You killed him to keep him from telling the Major that you were in my room. You shouldn't have been in there at all; it's my fault a man is dead, and I lied to hide why he was shot."

"Not much else you could do."

"Is a life, even his, so cheap? What could have happened if you hadn't shot him, if he had told? You'd have been fired and the Major would have been angry with me, but that would have been his right—"

"Wake up," he snapped, still keeping his voice low. "This isn't about a job! McLain would have told Garnet to get rid of me, and he wouldn't mean just throw me off of the ranch. But even if he didn't kill me, if he just fired me, where would that leave you? Where would it leave your little sister?"

"Celia?" Victoria stared up at him, trying to see his features in the faint light.

"If I'm gone, who'll keep Garnet away from the girl?"

She hadn't thought of that. She felt dizzy, as if she had almost walked off a cliff and seen it just in time. Good or bad, and for his own reasons, Jake Roper was the only protection Celia had—or, come to that, she herself had. He had killed to protect them. But why? She didn't delude herself that he cared anything about her; how could he? He didn't know her. True, he had kissed her, but she was learning that didn't necessarily mean anything to a man.

Whatever she saw in his cold green eyes, she was certain it wasn't tenderness. His reasons for protecting them were his own. She felt as if she were being used, but she couldn't see how. She had no power, no influence for him to hope to exploit.

She inhaled. "I won't say anything," she said, her tone stifled.

"Just make sure you don't. What about your cousin? Did she hear what was said?"

"I think so, but Emma would never say anything."

"And Celia?"

"She won't tell, either."

"Can you trust her?"

Her anger was immediate, but she tamped it down. He didn't know Celia, couldn't understand that her peculiar characteristics in no way indicated an untrustworthiness. But perhaps her anger was because all her emotions were so close to the surface tonight. Because of that, she restrained her immediate retort and instead merely replied, "Yes."

"Make sure she understands."

"She already does, Mr. Roper." She said it through her teeth, her control slipping a bit.

"Jake."

She stepped back. "I think not. This afternoon was a mistake, one that won't be repeated. It would be best if we—"

"It won't, huh?" He almost laughed, but instead took her by the shoulders and pulled her to him. He wrapped his arms around her, forcing her into full contact with him from knee to breast. "Do you think I wanted to be attracted to you? I didn't, and I don't like it, but that's the way it is, and I'll be damned if I let you treat me like I'm invisible."

Uselessly she shoved against his chest then turned her head to the side as his mouth lowered. He caught her chin and was bending to her again when there was a faint scratching at the door, and Emma said in a low voice, "Victoria?"

Jake released her as Emma opened the door and slipped inside, swiftly closing it again.

Victoria drew herself up, sharply aware of what Emma must be thinking.

Emma carefully navigated the dark room until she was standing before them. "You had been gone too long, so I came looking for you," she said in her quiet voice. "I heard your voices when I passed the door. We'll go back in together, and no one will think anything of it." To Jake she said, "I didn't have the opportunity earlier to thank you for what you did, Mr. Roper. I'm deeply grateful."

Tears stung Victoria's eyes. Dear Emma. Her love and loyalty, her support, never wavered.

"No thanks are necessary," Jake said.

"Perhaps not, but then you weren't on the other side of that door." Emma put her hand on Victoria's arm. "Give us time to get back to the party before you leave."

Amused, he said, "I'll go out the same way I came in, through the window."

"Be careful, Mr. Roper. And thank you again, whether or not you think my gratitude is deserved."

They left together and when they were in the hall, Victoria gave a low, shaky laugh. "I still need to use the convenience."

"Of course."

Emma didn't say anything else until they were returning to the party. Then she whispered, *"Be careful."*

Victoria shuddered. "I hope the situation never arises again," she said, and hoped that Emma understood she had no intention of becoming embroiled in an unsavory relationship with Jake Roper. He frightened her, even though she felt this sordid physical attraction for him. He made love as casually as he wiped his boots, and he killed the same way.

She ignored the sudden chill she felt and pasted a bright smile on her face as she and Emma rejoined the party.

That goddamn Roper was up to something.

Garnet didn't know what it was, but he felt more and more uneasy as he thought about Pledger. He lay in his bed in the hotel, his booted feet crossed carelessly on the white bedspread, smoking in the dark while he thought about it. Pledger had been a mean son of a bitch, but he hadn't been stupid, and the fact was it was plain stupid to draw on Roper. Yet Pledger had done that very thing and earned himself a pine coffin. Roper's explanation had made sense right up to the part where Pledger drew on him.

It had been an easy life on the hacienda, but maybe it was time to be thinking about changing things. There was trouble in the air that he couldn't identify, but he could feel it. Maybe the Major was losing his grip on things. Maybe it was time for a stronger hand.

He smiled, a cold little smile. Yeah, maybe that was it. The Major was so damn impressed with Roper's gun that he wouldn't hear of getting rid of him, so maybe the thing to do was get rid of the Major. That would put Roper out of a job, neat and simple. Garnet would be rid of him without trying to get the drop on the son of a bitch. Once Roper left, the little corn-haired gal would be all his; her high-falutin' sister wouldn't be able to do a damn thing about it.

Hell, no, that wouldn't work. Roper was too friendly with the Major's wife. Kill the Major, and *Roper* would be the one who stayed to comfort the grieving widow and her pretty sister.

The solution was pretty simple. It didn't take him longer than a second of consideration to settle on it. All he had to do was kill the Major's wife as well as the Major. He'd have to figure out some way to do it so no one could put the blame on him, but it could be done. On a ranch the size of the kingdom, there would be plenty of opportunities. The bitch had helped him by getting this bee in her bonnet about riding. There would be lots of times when she'd be all by herself, with no one else within sight or earshot. Garnet was a fair shot with a rifle; it would be no trouble a'tall to put a bullet in her head. Then the Major, and after that it would all be his.

Garnet lay in the darkness, so satisfied with his plan that he could almost taste it, so impatient to feel the little yeller-haired gal beneath him that he had to reach down and rub his aching loins. The best part of his plan was that he wouldn't have to do *nothing* about Roper—he could just fire him!

Garnet was like a great many people in that he used himself as the measure by which to judge others, which was what had kept him alive for so long. He automatically expected the worst of someone, and because of that he was extraordinarily wary. Trust was alien to him. He believed himself to be safe with the Major only because he knew too much and had made the Major dependent on him, which was the only smart thing to do. Garnet's one weakness was that he was blind to the possibility of someone else's greater sense of purpose. If it were Garnet who lost his job, he would pack his saddlebags and leave, so he expected Roper to do the same. It never occurred to him that Jake might be so enraged by the death of the Major's wife that he'd stay, because Garnet himself would never risk his life for a woman, especially a dead one. Nor did he know that Roper had another, more compelling reason for remaining on the Kingdom Ranch.

So he lay in bed and planned, so hungry for the power that was within his grasp that he couldn't sleep. He kept rubbing slowly at his crotch, thinking of both the ranch and Celia Waverly, until they became intertwined in his mind. He could have easily left his room and found a whore, but a strange hot compulsion kept him in bed. He didn't want to stick it in some gaudy, cheap-smelling whore; he wanted to stick it in Celia, and nothing else would satisfy him.

The return trip to the ranch was just as arduous as the journey to Santa Fe had been. They spent most of it in the bone-racking buggy, lurching over rocks and into holes, and choking on dust kicked up by the riders in front. The only comfort was late in the day, when they stopped to make camp. The heat began to cool, the dust settled, and they could stretch their legs. While the simple meals were being prepared, Jake worked with the three new horses and Victoria's gaze was often lured in that direction. She told herself it was just to watch the animals, but Jake's deep voice drifted on the quiet air like velvet, instructing, soothing, praising. Against her will, it worked the same spell on her as it did on the horses.

Celia's dark brown mare was the fastest to pick up on the proper behavior for a horse wearing a sidesaddle, a fact which pleased the girl and made her even prouder of her mount. She named the mare Gypsy, a name that was considerably flashier than its bearer, and lavished the animal with attention. Jake figured the mare would be ready to ride by the time they reached the ranch, but didn't say anything to Celia because he knew she would immediately start demanding to ride out by herself. It was better if she didn't know until the others could go with her.

The gray gelding Emma had chosen didn't present many problems, either, but Victoria's mare was another story. The beefy man had lied, she wasn't even half-broken to the saddle. What's more, she didn't like it. She tried to bite him every time he put the saddle on her back; she blew up to keep him from tightening the cinch (a trick she abandoned after he kneed her the first few times she did it); and she wasn't above a well-placed kick. He didn't even try mounting her; he figured that was going to be a real battle and didn't want to start it until he had her in a corral where she couldn't run away if she managed to throw him. When he didn't have the saddle on her she was as affectionate and playful as a child, but the saddle just plain made her mad. She plain made him mad, too, but he told himself ruefully that it was his own fault for volunteering to train the horses. He'd get her gentled for Victoria if it killed him, and he thought it just might.

Victoria herself was acting as if he were made of thin air, looking right through him. He let it pass, because he had plenty of time once they got back to the ranch. Much as she tried to deny it, she liked the way he touched her. So he watched her with hooded eyes and bided his time.

They arrived at the ranch late the following morning. The Major strode into the house yelling for Carmita, leaving the women to get down from the buggy unaided. Jake swung down from his horse and reached the buggy in time to help Emma. Celia, of course, had already jumped down and raced off. Emma smiled at him and murmured a thank-you. Jake turned back to reach for Victoria, and his eyes locked with hers for a second before she looked away. But he'd seen enough to read her reluctance to let him touch her. He smiled grimly and grasped her around the waist, rather than simply giving her his hand to help her balance. Swinging her to the ground, he said, "Ma'am," politely, and touched his hat.

"Thank you, Mr. Roper." Her voice sounded a bit strained.

"I'll be working with the mare tomorrow morning, ma'am, and you need to be there."

She'd gotten only two steps away; she stopped and turned back. "Why is that?"

"If I do all the work with her, ma'am, she's going to think she's my horse. Don't reckon you want that, do you?"

Victoria stared at him. Common sense told her that all she required was a good horse for riding; what difference would it make if the mare was fonder of Jake than of her? Then anger roiled in her, not lessened at all by the knowledge that she was reacting exactly as he wanted. It was *her* horse and she didn't want just a mount; she wanted the mare to give her the equine version of friendship. It would forever eat at her if the horse went more willingly to Roper than to her, and if that was small of her, then so be it.

She looked away. "What time?" She kept her voice calm, as if it didn't matter.

"Ten. That'll give you time to sleep late, get rested up."

He knew she was tired. The knowledge softened something inside her, something that she couldn't allow to soften. She tried not to let his casual solicitude touch her, but it did. For whatever reason, Jake was protective of her and she was forced to acknowledge that it *did* matter. She wanted to go into his arms and let her head rest on his shoulder, just for a moment.

Her face was flushed as she walked into the house, but thankfully that could be put down to the hot sun. Emma was standing in the entrance foyer removing her bonnet and gloves. From the back of the house came the Major's muffled shouts as he discovered something that displeased him. Celia ran down the stairs with a quick drumming of her heels and would have dashed past had Emma not stepped in front of her.

"Goodness, where are you off to in such a hurry?" Victoria asked as she began removing her own bonnet.

"To the stables. Jake said he'd teach me how to curry Gypsy."

Emma's mouth curved in amusement. "Don't you think you should change out of that dress into something more suitable?"

Celia shrugged. "A dress is a dress."

"There are old dresses and new dresses; old dresses are better for currying horses."

Celia looked down at her dress, then said, "All right," and darted back up the stairs.

Victoria laughed. "She'll never appreciate the difference."

"She missed so much, didn't she?" Emma mused. "The parties, the dances, the flirting. Can't you just see how all the boys would be clustered around her?"

The smile faded from Victoria's face as she placed her bonnet and gloves on the table. "What will happen to her, I wonder? She's so trusting. I want her to find someone wonderful to love, a

man who's gentle and will cherish her as much as she deserves."
She continued in a low voice. "I worry, because I haven't seen a
man like that out here."

Emma said, "For any of us." She had loved Jon, and grieved
for him, but her fiancé had been dead a long time now and she
was still young. She, too, wanted to find love, marry, and have a
family. She admitted to herself that she'd come out here with
high hopes, for Victoria's marriage had signaled an end to hunger
and poverty, and she had dreamed . . . vague, romantic dreams of
handsome cowboys, virile, adventurous men who had taken on
this wild country and won. Instead, they were isolated on the
ranch, which seemed to hide a layer of ugliness and hatred
beneath the beauty. With few exceptions, the men were hostile
and leering.

Nor was Victoria's situation better; if anything, it was worse.
Emma shuddered at the thought of being married to the Major,
of having to submit to him in bed if he chose to visit her. The
idea would have been unthinkable if they'd still been back in
Augusta, but now Emma wouldn't think one whit less of Victoria
if she took what comfort she could from Jake Roper. He was a
man, not a loathsome slug like the Major. He was too much man
for Emma's taste, but Victoria was stronger than she, perhaps
even strong enough for someone like Roper.

McLain stomped to the front of the house. Both women
moved out of his path, and he passed them without a word, his
face dark with a scowl as he climbed the stairs. Neither of them
dared ask him what was wrong.

McLain slammed the door to his bedroom and kicked a chair
across the room. He'd asked about Angelina's whereabouts first
thing, and Lola, with a smug look, had told him that Angelina
had gone off with one of the hands that morning and wasn't
back yet. He was enraged; not only was she not there when he
wanted her, but he knew damn sure the cowhand wouldn't be
doing any of the work he was supposed to be doing. The goddamn whore! He'd teach her a lesson when he got his hands on
her.

There was nothing he could do about it now, however, and

that made him even angrier. Maybe that girl Juana . . . naw, hell, he'd had her once, and she hadn't been any better than his fist. Not as good, because she'd just lain there and sniffled. He didn't even consider taking his wife to bed; his mind shied away from that possibility to the extent that the thought never formed. He was bothered enough with his haunting fears of the Sarratts; in fact, his nightmares and jumpiness seemed to be getting worse lately, as if the ghosts were closing in for the kill. He sure as hell didn't need his stiff lady wife reminding him of Elena. The sound of Victoria entering the adjoining bedroom unnerved him to the extent that he left his room as quickly as he'd entered it.

He stood in the hallway, red-faced with anger and looking for a scapegoat. The cheerful sound of humming at first made him even angrier, and then he noticed that it was coming from Celia's room, where the door had been left slightly ajar. Now *there* was a beauty, prettier even than Angelina. And she wasn't as all-fired proper and straitlaced as her sister. She just might like having a man if she tried it. The more the Major thought about it, the more he liked it. Celia was a Waverly, too, after all; she just wasn't a lady in the same way that her sister was. He knew Victoria would be busy for at least five minutes changing out of her traveling clothes. He balanced caution and temptation by tiptoeing down the hall until he could see through the narrow crack between door and jamb.

Celia was in her petticoats and chemise, still humming as she selected one of her older dresses from the armoir and slipped it on over her head. It had the advantage of buttoning down the front, which was why she had chosen it, and she bent her head to the task.

McLain watched her, struck by the golden creaminess of her bare shoulders and arms. She had nice big tits, too, with the dark centers plain under the thin cotton chemise. The sunlight streaming through the window illuminated her hair, and he had the uncharacteristically fanciful thought that she looked like an angel. God, she was a beauty! And a little hoyden, not like Victoria at all. Certainly nothing like Elena. The ache in his loins had intensified while he stood watching her, and he thought about what it would be like to have her. He'd have to keep it secret from Victoria, but he thought he knew a way to accomplish that.

He glanced furtively down the hall, then back at Celia. She was nearly finished dressing, so he slipped away as carefully as he had approached. His heart was pounding with anticipation.

He went downstairs to the library and took an opened bottle of bourbon from the desk drawer. There was a glass in the drawer, too, but he ignored it and tipped the bottle to his mouth. The liquor burned down his throat, a pleasant warmth that matched the one in his gut. By God, here was something to look forward to! He drank once more in celebration of his own cleverness. The only thing was, he'd have to make sure Victoria didn't find out. She was high-nosed enough that she'd pack up and leave if she found out he was diddling her little sister, and the humiliation would be unbearable after all the strutting and bragging he'd done in Santa Fe about his patrician wife. He could always lie about it, of course, but there were so many people on the ranch that someone would blab and the truth would get out.

But he was confident he could bed Celia all he wanted, and the girl would never tell. She was a simpleminded little idiot. All he had to do was threaten her somehow. . . . He mused about it for a minute, trying to think of something that would scare her. Finally his face split into a grin. That was it, by God! He'd tell Celia that if she ever told, he'd hurt Victoria. He thought about saying he'd kill Victoria, but thought that might be pushing too hard. The girl might panic. The beauty of the plan was that it was a lie, but she was so simple she'd believe anything he told her.

He'd have plenty of time to put his plan into action, too. Buying those horses for the women had been a stroke of genius. Since they didn't know their way around, they wouldn't go far by themselves, but he could always tell Roper to go with them, give him orders to show them the ranch or take them to someplace far enough away that he knew they'd be gone a couple of hours. From what he'd gathered, Celia didn't ride well enough to make that kind of trip, so she'd have to stay behind. Then she'd be his.

If that didn't work, he'd manage something else. Bribe her with a promise to ride Rubio, maybe, and get her away from the house. He was in a fever of anticipation, thinking of it. Celia wasn't a whore like Angelina; she'd be all tight and fresh . . .

He squirmed in the chair and took another swig of bourbon. Roper would have to hurry up and get those damn horses trained.

Another sip emptied the bottle. With a disgusted curse, he shoved the empty bottle across the top of the desk, dislodging some papers, and a silver glint caught his eye.

He froze, his insides clenching. When he finally managed to move, his hand was shaking. With a jerk he pushed the papers completely to the side, uncovering what he'd only glimpsed.

A knife. The blade was sharpened to a razor edge.

It wasn't his. He hadn't left it there.

His eyes darted left and right. He was afraid to move, afraid to look behind him. He strained his ears for any sound that would indicate someone was in the room with him. And then his mind went over the edge.

Sarratt!

The bastard boys weren't dead, or their ghosts had come back to get him. He had to watch out for them now.

He didn't pick up the knife. He couldn't. His thighs clenched together protectively.

Maybe he wouldn't understand what the knife meant. Juana stared at the closed door, her eyes burning with hate. It didn't matter if *he* knew; she knew, and she meant it. If he ever touched her again, she would kill him. The hate had festered inside her since the night he had raped her, and she hadn't forgotten. She would never forget.

"Why did your sister marry McLain?"

Jake hadn't meant to ask the question, and he was furious with himself for letting it slip out. But it had been nagging at him; he needed to know. Celia looked at him over Gypsy's back as she continued to stroke the curry brush over the horse's shoulder and sides. For a moment there was a very old look in her dark blue eyes. "So we wouldn't be hungry," she said after a moment.

Of all the answers he might have anticipated, that wasn't one of them. He narrowed his eyes at the girl. "Hungry?"

"We didn't have any food or money. The Major said he'd give a lot of money to Mama and Papa if Victoria would marry him. So she did."

The simple explanation hit Jake hard. Victoria had practically been sold; she hadn't married McLain to help herself, but to help her family.

He didn't ask anything else, and Celia brushed in silence for several minutes before she looked at him again and asked, "When can I start riding Gypsy?"

"In another week, about."

"Why so long?"

"I want to make certain she understands how she's supposed to act when her rider is sitting sidesaddle."

"Why do I have to have a sidesaddle? Why can't I have a saddle like yours?"

"Because ladies don't ride astride." He personally thought sidesaddles were stupid and dangerous, but if he told her that then he'd have to explain why she had to use one anyway and he didn't want to get involved in that kind of discussion with her.

If he'd known Celia better, he'd have realized that she didn't drop a subject until she understood it. "Why don't ladies ride astride?"

He pulled his hat lower over his eyes. "Because their skirts would be pulled up and show their legs."

"Then why don't women just wear pants like men do?"

"Because that would show their legs, too."

Her head popped up over Gypsy's back. "No more than it shows men's legs," she said indignantly. "How are women's legs different from men's legs?"

Jake reflected on how easy it was to get backed into a corner. He thought of a lot of answers he could give her, but settled on a literal one. "They're prettier."

Her head bent as she evidently surveyed her own legs, hidden though they were by her blue skirt. "But if they're prettier, why hide them?" she asked, now totally perplexed. "It seems to me that men should wear skirts to hide their legs if they're ugly, and women should wear pants."

His lips twitched again, but he controlled his laughter. "Men have to do a lot of heavy work," he pointed out. "They couldn't do it if they were hampered by skirts, now could they? Can you imagine the Major wearing a dress and branding steers? He'd catch his petticoat on fire."

Celia giggled. Another thought occurred and she narrowed her eyes at him, which made her look like a ferocious kitten. "Women wear skirts while they're cooking."

"Men are clumsier than women. Women can manage skirts; men would get their big feet tangled in all that cloth and fall down."

"Sometimes I do, too. That's why I think I should wear pants."

He surrendered, and did the only thing a man could do. "Why don't you ask Victoria about it?"

Celia sighed regretfully. "No, she'd never let me."

She returned to brushing Gypsy, and Jake watched her with a little smile. She was delightful; he could see why Victoria was so fierce in protecting her. He could even see why she had let herself be married off to McLain; after all, she didn't know what kind of bastard the man was, and she'd done the best she could to provide for her family. Privately Jake thought that their father must be a weak, lily-livered son of a bitch to sell his daughter to a man twice her age, but that didn't make his daughter any less a lady.

Celia and Emma would become Jake's responsibility when he married Victoria. He realized that he'd probably have a lot more of this kind of conversation with Celia and didn't know whether to laugh or groan. At least he could always send her to Victoria when the topic got too much for him to handle. Maybe he could get her to ask Ben some of her questions. It had been a long time since he'd seen his brother discomfited; he looked forward to it.

Victoria patted the mare's neck and murmured to her. The horse liked all the attention and kept nudging Victoria with her head to encourage her to continue.

"What are you going to name her?" Jake asked as he worked the bridle on over the mare's head and eased a light bit into her mouth. She didn't mind either the bridle or the bit, and mouthed the metal without any trouble. It wasn't until he put the saddle on her that she began acting up. He wondered what in hell she'd do when he climbed on her back.

"I don't know." She had thought about it, because they had always named their animals, but she hadn't been able to think of a name that seemed suitable for the mare.

"Name her something that means ill-tempered, vicious, and contrary," Jake muttered.

Victoria couldn't help the sudden smile that lit her face. "She's none of those things!"

"Just wait until she takes a nip out of *your* leg." He looked down at her bright expression and felt his loins tighten. One way or another, this damn horse was a godsend, forcing Victoria to spend a lot of time with him. He intended to use every minute of that time making her aware of him. Lady or not, she was a woman beneath those clothes, and she liked it when he touched her.

"You'd better step out of the way, or you might get that nip now," he warned. He waited until Victoria moved away before settling the saddle on the mare's back. The horse whipped her head around, but he was too fast and her teeth snapped on air.

Victoria laughed, and the sound clutched at Jake's chest.

"You might think it's funny, but you're not riding her until I can get her broken of all her bad habits," he said. The mare side-stepped away as he tried to tighten the cinches, and he cursed her luridly, not bothering to apologize to Victoria for his language. She'd probably hear a lot worse by the time her precious horse was fit to be ridden.

"Why aren't you putting a sidesaddle on her?" she asked.

"Because I've got to ride her, and there's no way in hell I'm going to try it with one of those things."

Victoria laughed again. It was funny, watching the mare shift away from him; if a horse could have expressions, then the mare was definitely enjoying what she was doing. Jake just kept at the task until he had the cinches as tight as he wanted. He called the mare names that Victoria had never heard mentioned in polite company, but he was never rough with her. When he finished he patted her neck, and contrarily she turned her head to nuzzle his chest.

"You damn contrary cayuse," Jake murmured, then took the reins in his hand and said to Victoria, "Climb up on the fence. I'm going to try riding her, and I don't think she's going to like it."

Victoria complied as the men who happened to be nearby all wandered over to prop their arms on the fence and call encouragement, insults, or advice to Jake.

"You won't last ten seconds, Roper."

"Stay in the saddle—"

"Give that hoss a ride—"

"Show these jackasses how it's done— Pardon me, ma'am."

"Hope you like dirt, Roper, 'cause you're about to get a mouthful of it."

"I don't doubt that none," Jake replied, grinning at the razzing. "It wouldn't be the first time." He set his hat firmly on his head and fit his left boot into the stirrup, then swung into the saddle with one easy motion.

For a second the mare stood stock still, as if she couldn't believe there was actually someone on her back. Then she exploded into motion, first up on the back legs, then twisting and coming down with her head low. She bucked and jumped and corkscrewed, and tried to brush him off against the fence. The men were yelling, and clouds of dust enveloped them.

The mare twisted again and came down hard, her hindquarters lifting. Jake came off over her head and landed with a thump. The men laughed and shouted suggestions. He heard Victoria laugh, and the sound rippled through him on a wave of pleasure even though he was spitting dirt out of his mouth. Jake eased into a sitting position. The mare had settled down as soon as his weight had left the saddle, and ambled over to nudge him.

"You goddamn scrub," he said softly as he climbed to his feet. "You've got to learn how to behave, so the lady can ride you. You won't get me off this time; I'm gonna ride you until you're so tired you can't jump, and then I'm going to teach you some manners."

He took up the reins again and was back in the saddle before the mare knew what he was doing.

She had tired a little from her first effort at unseating him, but she wasn't ready to admit defeat. With fire in her eyes, the mare sunfished and corkscrewed; she tried everything, but the man on her back didn't fly off. She ran straight for the fence and swerved only at the last second, and one of the men jerked Victoria backward off the fence, out of harm's way.

"Sorry, ma'am," he said, never taking his eyes off the man and horse.

"That's quite all right. Thank you."

"Yes, ma'am."

The mare tried several more times to brush him off, then just began running around and around the corral. Her speed didn't slow. "I'm taking her over!" Jake yelled, and pulled her head around until she was headed directly for the fence. Her powerful hindquarters bunched, she lifted, and was clear with plenty of room to spare. Jake's hat flew off, but he stayed in the saddle. He bent down low over the horse's neck. When she got that temper worked off, her training could start. Letting her run was the best thing he could do. At this point it was the only thing.

"Guess we'll have to build the fence higher," one man commented.

Victoria watched man and horse receding in the distance.

"When will they be back?" she wondered aloud.

"When that hoss tires out, I reckon."

She looked at the man who had spoken. He was the same one who had jerked her off the fence when the mare had veered in her direction. She felt embarrassed that she didn't know his name and felt that she should thank him again for his action. She held out her hand. "I'm indebted to you, Mister—?"

"Quinzy," the man said. He looked at her hand, then wiped his own on his pants before taking hers. "Jake Quinzy, ma'am."

"Thank you, Mr. Quinzy, for acting so swiftly. I was taken off guard and couldn't have moved out of the way on my own."

He pulled his hat down lower over his eyes. "It was my pleasure, ma'am."

Like so many of the other men, Jake Quinzy wore his holster tied low on his thigh. His face was weathered to the texture of old leather, with myriad lines radiating around his eyes, and there was a touch of gray in his sideburns, but he was as lean and muscled as any of the young men. His eyes, a curious grayish-brown, were emotionless as he studied her from under the brim of his hat.

How was she supposed to act with men like this? She had no idea what type of life he had led, what kind of man he was. Yet he was still standing there and the countless hours of having good manners drilled into her compelled her to make conversation.

"I admit, I feel rather jealous of Mr. Roper," she said with a smile. "I had hoped to be the first to ride the mare."

"It's best someone else works the kinks out of her," Quinzy replied. "You might get hurt if she threw you."

"My goodness, I've been thrown before!" She laughed, remembering some of the spills she'd taken and the bruises suffered. "Everyone who rides has parted company with his saddle, I imagine."

"Yes, ma'am, I reckon that's so."

Quinzy had chores to do, but he remained standing beside Mrs. McLain, letting her lead him in small talk. He seldom had a chance to talk to a woman like her. She fascinated him; she was as tidy as a Sunday-school teacher and a sweet smell lingered in the air around her. Her skin was pale and smooth, and she had been soft under his hands when he'd put them on her waist to pull her down from the fence. She was so different from him that he felt like a great, rough, clumsy bear in comparison. Garnet called her a high-nosed, hoity-toity bitch, but Quincy thought she was calm and dignified. He decided Mrs. McLain was one thing he didn't need to be taking Garnet's advice about.

The mare ran like the wind. Her powerful muscles bunched and expanded as her hooves pounded the earth. Jake settled into the rhythm, his legs holding her, his hand trying to coax her to respond, but she ignored him and he finally decided to let her run until she couldn't.

Her stamina was amazing. He was a big man, but she acted as if she didn't feel his weight at all. Long after most horses would have been exhausted, her long legs still worked effortlessly. He sensed that she was no longer running from temper, but from the sheer joy of running, and admiration for her filled him. God, what a horse! She was a fit mate for Rubio, as outstanding a mare as he was a stallion. The foals they would get from her would leave all other horses in their dust.

On the other hand, the Major might have been right, as much as he hated to admit it. She might be too much horse for Victoria to handle. She was as strong as most stallions, though Rubio had her beat when it came to sheer power.

Gradually she began slowing, first to a canter, then a walk. He patted her neck, his admiration plain in his voice as he praised her. She wasn't even blown; she was tired, but her gait was still steady, and she tossed her head in a show of spirit.

"That's a good girl. God, you can run! Are you ready to head back home now?" She stopped and he let her rest for a minute, but he didn't dismount. She was just contrary enough to take off without him. When her breathing had slowed, he squeezed her with his legs and lifted the reins. She snorted, shook her head, and ignored him.

Jake swore softly and nudged her with his heels. She tried to bite him. It looked like he had a long day ahead of him.

It was two hours later when they returned to the ranch. By then she was responding to some of his signals, but ignoring others. He kept his temper under control and his hands light on the reins. Despite all the problems she'd given him, she was a magnificent animal. She still had enough energy left to prance as they approached the corral, to demonstrate that he was on her back only because she allowed it.

Victoria was nowhere in sight, but she'd evidently left orders that she be called as soon as he returned because she walked up while he was still unsaddling the mare. She'd changed out of her riding habit into a dark blue skirt with a high-necked shirtwaist blouse that had a hint of lace at the throat and sleeves. She looked as cool as the winter snows, while he was hot and dusty and had a headache from being out in the sun so long without his hat.

"How did she do?" she asked, stroking the mare's nose.

"It was a draw," he muttered. "I won on some things, she won on others."

He was as sweaty as the horse and his face was streaked with dirt. He was exactly the rough type of man that she'd always avoided, but she didn't return to the house as she knew she should. Instead she watched him take care of the horse, and the sight of his strong, tanned hands and forearms, bared by his rolled-up sleeves, fascinated her.

"I've thought of a name for her," she said, because she couldn't think of anything else to say.

"I've thought of a few myself," Jake grunted.

"Sophie."

He grunted again, a sound that didn't express either approval or disapproval. "Sophie it is, then."

"I didn't want to name her some common name like Princess or Duchess, or a mythological name. Just Sophie." She stopped, a little tense because she wanted him to like her choice.

"It'll do." He led the horse into a stall and fetched a bucket of water for her, then fed her. He slapped her darkly gleaming rump, and she shifted sideways just enough to jostle him.

Victoria laughed and he looked up, a half-smile twisting his lips. "I heard you laughing when she tossed me."

She didn't look guilty. Her eyes twinkled at him. "It was funny. She looked so proud of herself."

He closed the stall door and propped his arms on top of it. He was so close to her that she could smell his sweat and feel the heat of his body. Before she could put some protective distance between them, he reached out and brushed the backs of his fingers across her cheekbone. "I didn't mind," he said softly. "I like hearing you laugh." She didn't laugh enough, he realized. He wanted to gather her close and protect her, give her a world where she could laugh more.

His touch confused her. She looked away and searched for some way to change the subject. Sophie was the most obvious excuse available, so she said, "Can she run?"

"Can she run," he repeated softly, awe in his voice. "She's so fast and strong that maybe it isn't a good idea for you to ride her."

Victoria stiffened. "I'm a very good rider, and she's my horse."

"She's headstrong and stubborn, and so strong that if she decided to bolt you wouldn't be able to hold her."

"I repeat, she's my horse and I'll ride her."

"Come to think of it, you do have a lot in common with her," he said, his gaze intense as he looked at her. "She's proud, contrary, and kicks up a fuss about a man riding her, but she'll like it once she gets used to it and settles down some."

Victoria turned white and fell back a step from the look in those hard, level green eyes. There was no mistaking his meaning and no mistaking the way he was looking at her. "No," she whispered. "Don't say that." She lifted her skirts to leave, but he grabbed her arm and pulled her closer to him.

"Running away won't make it any less true."

"Mr. Roper, please let go of me."

"Jake," he said. "Don't call me Mr. Roper like I've never

kissed you and you haven't kissed me back. And maybe I don't want to let go of you. Maybe I want another kiss."

"Hush!" She looked around desperately, terrified that someone would see or hear them. For God's sake, why was he doing this? Any number of people could walk in. He'd killed Pledger to keep the man from telling that he'd seen Jake coming out of her room, and now he was deliberately jeopardizing that same secret.

"No one's around." He smiled a little grimly and released her. "Don't look so scared. You're not going to have to scream 'rape' to protect your reputation. I'm not going to throw you into a stall and flip your skirts up, even though the idea is mighty pleasing, *Miz* McLain."

"Jake, please." He might think her proud, but she would beg if necessary. "I'm not that sort of woman. I'm sorry if I gave you that impression—"

"The impression I got is that you're a woman who doesn't know how much pleasure your body can give you—"

"*Pleasure!*" she said in a stifled tone of disgust.

He was pleased at this confirmation that she didn't enjoy her marital duties with McLain. It still grated at him that she slept with the bastard at all, but he couldn't stand the thought of her enjoying it.

"Yeah, pleasure." His voice was rough and low. "Don't make the mistake of thinking that having me inside you would be the same as having McLain."

The color washed into her face as she remembered the shameful dreams and fantasies she'd had about him, and she felt as mortified as if he'd been able to read her mind.

She began backing away. "This isn't right," she whispered. "We can't—"

"That's right, run away. Like I said, that won't change anything. I'll see you in the morning. Ten o'clock."

She hurried back to the house, her face burning. She'd tell the Major that she wanted someone else to train the horse. But what excuse could she give for wanting Jake replaced? She couldn't do anything that might result in him being fired; he was the only protection she could provide for Celia.

There was nothing she could do. She was caught in a spider web of circumstance, and she couldn't tear free without endangering Celia.

So she was there at ten the next morning, her face carefully composed and blank. Jake was already mounted on Sophie and was patiently walking her around the corral, teaching her the commands every well-mannered horse should know. Except for giving Victoria a piercing look when she first walked up, he ignored her and concentrated on the mare.

The sun was hot, and a trickle of perspiration made an itching path down her spine. She rubbed the back of her neck, which was beginning to prickle despite the floppy-brimmed hat she'd borrowed from Carmita that morning. Why did he want her out here if he was going to do all the work with the horse?

"Did you have any trouble with her this morning?" she finally asked.

"A little. She wanted to jump the fence and run like she did yesterday. But she didn't try to bite me when I saddled her, so we're making progress."

"How long will it be before I can ride her?"

"Depends."

"On what?"

"On how she acts, and how fast she learns."

"Mr. Roper, it's very hot out here. I have better things to do than just stand in the sun letting dust settle on me."

He reined Sophie in and stared at her. "All right. Let's change saddles on her and you can start doing some of the work. But I don't want to hear any squalling if she throws you."

Victoria's heart leaped at the thought of getting to ride her beautiful horse, and she smiled at him. "I don't 'squall' when I'm thrown."

"Then let's see how good you are."

He led Sophie to the stable and unsaddled her, throwing the saddle on his own horse. He nodded toward the tack room. "Your saddle is in there. Get to work."

If he thought she wouldn't know how to go about saddling a horse, he'd soon find out differently. Victoria found one of the new side saddles the Major had bought in Santa Fe and a saddle blanket, both of which she carried to where Sophie was restlessly shifting about.

"Watch her teeth," Jake warned.

Victoria patted Sophie and talked to her before positioning the blanket on her back. The mare turned her head and watched every move. When Victoria lifted the saddle, the horse shifted but didn't move out of reach. She allowed the saddle to be put on her back and finally turned her head away as if bored while Victoria tightened the cinches.

Jake had already finished saddling his own horse, a big gelding, and he came over to boost Victoria into the sidesaddle. She waited for him to cup his hands for her to step into, but instead he clasped her around the waist and effortlessly lifted her. Startled, Victoria grabbed his shoulders for balance, her fingers digging into his heavy muscles. He plopped her in her seat and held her there, narrowly watching Sophie for any signs of rebellion.

Victoria steadied herself with a deep breath and hooked her right knee around the pommel while she found the stirrup with her left boot. Sophie glanced around, curious at this much lighter weight and strange seat, but she seemed to accept them.

Jake swung into his saddle. "She has a real tender mouth, so keep a light touch on the reins. All she needs is a nudge with your heel, but don't kick her. That riles her up."

Victoria obeyed, and found that she had to give Sophie only the smallest hint of direction with the reins. They walked out of the stable into the hot sun and halted in the yard when the Major hailed them. "Fine-looking horse," he enthused as he approached. "Yep, she'll give us some fine foals when we breed her."

Victoria stiffened. This was the first she'd heard about breeding Sophie. Eventually, yes, she wanted a foal from the mare, but Sophie was still young and there was plenty of time. She wanted to be able to enjoy her new mount first. "I don't want Sophie bred yet," she said firmly.

The Major didn't even look at her. He was still examining Sophie, beaming over her. He slapped the horse's neck a little too hard and the mare took exception to it by dancing away. Jake's hand shot out to aid Victoria in controlling the animal, and Victoria murmured softly to settle the horse down.

The Major put his hands on his hips. "You were right, Roper. The foals we'll get from her will show up all the other horses in the territory," he said, as if Victoria had never spoken at all. Her lips tightened, but a wife didn't argue with her husband in public. There would be time later.

"She's strong and fast," Jake agreed noncommittally.

Still McLain stood there, his eyes narrowed and sort of glittery. "Uh—where are you going on your ride?"

"I thought we'd head toward the river, then circle around to the north a little."

McLain nodded. "How long you think you'll be gone?"

Jake's face was impassive, the way it always was when he was talking with McLain. It was the only way he could keep his hatred from showing. "Maybe a couple of hours."

"Take your time, take your time. There's a lot of ranch to see." He finally stepped back, but not before slapping Sophie's neck again. The horse neighed in protest and reared a little. Again Jake reached out protectively to aid Victoria, this time to catch her in case she came off the saddle. But Victoria remained firmly seated and settled Sophie down nicely herself. By the time the horse was quiet, McLain was striding back toward the house without even a glance in their direction.

The bastard. Jake's face was grim as he watched him leave.

They walked the horses across the yard, then kicked them into an easy canter. Jake watched both Victoria and Sophie, but the former was indeed a good horsewoman and the latter seemed inclined to behave. He relaxed and let himself begin to enjoy the ride. It was a beautiful summer day, and the woman he planned to make his own was beside him. Things like that could go to a man's head.

The river was about a mile from the house, a broad, shallow ribbon that glittered and gulped. "Why wasn't the house built closer to the river?" she asked. She thought it would have been the sensible thing, to be close to a water supply. There was a small creek that ran just behind the house, but it would disappear in dry weather.

"See how shallow it is? It floods every spring from the runoff." He pointed to the north, on his left. "See that stand of cottonwoods on the riverbank? The river is about waist deep there. That's where we take our baths, in the summer, anyway."

The men bathed in the river? She felt ashamed of her ignorance, for she had assumed that they had bathtubs for their convenience. If she had thought, she would have realized that it would have been a never-ending job to haul and heat enough water for as many men as worked on the ranch.

"How many men are there?"

"A little over a hundred."

"That many? I wouldn't have guessed."

"Only about half of us are at the hacienda at any given time. The others are out at line shacks or on the ranch. The ranch is over half a million acres."

She was astounded by the size. No one had bothered to tell her before, and she was too shy to ask, in case it sounded like avarice on her part. But she had trusted Jake enough, and what he'd told her boggled her imagination. The thought of being surrounded by so much space frightened her, but she also felt a sense of exhilaration. She looked back in the direction from which they'd come, but the hacienda was hidden from view by both a thick stand of trees and the lay of the land. Except for Jake, she was alone, more alone than she could ever remember being before. There was the sun and the earth, the river, the wind, the magnificent horse beneath her, and it felt wonderful. She couldn't wait until she could begin riding on her own, and said as much.

He snorted. "Woman, use your common sense! You can't go riding out here alone, not ever."

She started to snap that she'd do whatever she pleased, but her common sense did indeed assert itself as she realized he knew much more about this wild, beautiful land than she did. So she said calmly, "Why?"

"The hacienda has been here for a long time, but that doesn't mean the land is civilized. If you get tossed off out here and your horse runs away, it means a helluva lot more than walking a half-mile to a neighbor's house. There aren't any neighbors. There are bears, mountain lion, and snakes to watch out for. Not only that, there are occasional Indian raids on the cattle, though it isn't as bad now that the Navaho are on the reservation. They'd steal your cattle while you were looking at them. There are drifters wandering through, and some of our own men aren't fine, upstanding citizens, in case you haven't noticed. It wouldn't do for you to be caught out here on your own."

"When will you have Emma's and Celia's horses trained? Then I'll be able to ride with them."

"Celia's horse has been ready, but I haven't told her because she'd be hell-bent and determined to take off on her own." They shared a look of complete understanding, and Jake smiled ruefully. "She's already been pestering me to let her ride astride like a man."

Victoria looked horrified. "What did you tell her?"

"I told her her skirts would get in the way, and she'd have to ask you for permission anyway." His eyes were bright with amusement.

"Thank you very much," she said tartly, but couldn't help smiling. "What about Emma's horse?"

"Miss Emma's gelding won't be any trouble, either. It was just this lady I was worried about."

"She's behaving perfectly."

"So she is. It makes me nervous."

Victoria threw back her head and laughed, exposing her white throat and dislodging the hat; it dangled down her back, suspended by the cords from her neck. Still chuckling, she reached back to retrieve it.

Jake couldn't stop looking at her; she was so bright and happy, the way she should be. He felt that odd clenching in his chest again, then it eased into a throb.

He reined in and dismounted. She stopped laughing and looked at him in surprise as he came around and lifted her from the saddle. She grabbed at his shoulders, trying to stiffen her arms and hold herself away from him, but he let her slide down his body until her boots touched the ground. Her habit skirt caught on the buckle of his gunbelt, exposing her white petticoat.

Her face flamed and she tried to jerk backward, but his hands were still on her waist and he pulled her against him as he bent his head.

He wasn't rough with her. His mouth was warm, the intrusion of his tongue slow and sweet. Victoria trembled, but she had experienced his kiss before and the temptation to know it again was too powerful. Her arms went around his neck and she welcomed the penetration of her mouth with shy, uncertain movements of her tongue against his. He shuddered, his arms tightening around her, and wonder filled her that she could make this man, dangerous as he was, feel the same hot, uncontrollable pleasure he aroused in her.

He stroked his hands up her back, and she arched into him like a cat. Jake quickly took advantage of the instinctive offering of her body and closed his hand over her breast. Victoria jerked, her eyes flying open. No one had ever touched her there; she tried to tear away from him, but he easily controlled the motion and continued his gentle caress.

"Stop!" she whispered. His hand burned her breast even through the layers of clothing, eliciting a shameful tightening in her nipple. She knew she shouldn't let him do this, knew she should never enjoy it, but she did. The hot pleasure intensified and a soft moan caught in her throat.

He reached up and removed his hat, then let it drop in the dust beside them. The sun glinted on the green in his narrowed eyes. "Why do you want me to stop?" he asked, his voice low and rough. His breathing was fast, his body taut.

"It isn't right." The excuse sounded feeble even to her own ears, but it was the excuse that had been drummed into her since the day she had gone to long skirts and left childhood behind. She had never before imagined that it would be so weak against the impulses of her own body.

Jake's expression didn't change as he stared down at her. "It doesn't get any righter, sweetheart." The truth in his own words struck him. He had held a lot of women, but none had felt as perfect in his arms as she did; none of them had made him feel *at home.* It was amazing how he could feel both so comfortable and so aroused at the same time.

"We have to stop." She knew she should withdraw her arms from around his neck and push him away, but there was something so primitively satisfying in standing there in the bright sun, in his arms, feeling the heat of his body and inhaling the scent of his skin, that she couldn't bring herself to step away.

"In a minute." His voice had roughened again, and her heart jumped as he bent toward her. Her strength was washed out on the tide of warmth that filled her, and her head fell back. He trailed biting kisses down her exposed throat, then back up to her mouth. He touched her other breast, and the same tingling assailed her again. A heavy ache began forming deep in her lower body; she squirmed unconsciously, her hips writhing against his, and he made a rough sound as he dropped his arm to circle her hips and grind her into him, rubbing the hard ridge of his manhood against her soft mound.

It had been nasty with the Major. With Jake, she wanted only to cling, blindly seeking more of this fevered pleasure. Her hands slid up into his sun-warmed hair, and she pressed her palms against his head to hold it down where she could take more of his kisses. His taste was heady, a mixture of coffee and tobacco, and his breath filled her, a mingling no less intimate than that of his tongue probing hers.

Sophie shifted impatiently, bumping into them. Jake raised his head. "You sorry jackass," he said hoarsely.

Victoria was breathing in fast gulps. She stepped back, her hands pressed to her face. In another minute she would have been lying down in the dust for him. That sure knowledge was so at odds with the way she had always thought of herself that she felt devastated; she had to admit to her own weakness now. She wanted Jake Roper in a carnal way she could no longer deny. She had been savagely jealous when she'd seen him making love with the tinker's daughter, just the thought of him made her heart beat faster while his presence pitched her to a state of intense awareness that was almost painful.

Dear God. She loved him.

She had always thought the state of love required long acquaintance with someone, a sure knowledge of personality and a basis of friendship. Now she knew that it could be forged from a base of lust, that liking wasn't necessary and that long-held standards crumpled before it.

His hair was tousled, his lips swollen, and his expression hard as he still dealt with his own arousal. He leaned slowly down to pick up his hat, as if every movement had to be careful. After he adjusted it on his head, he said, "I'll be damned if I apologize."

"No," she agreed in a whisper.

"It won't be the last time." He reached out and trailed one finger down her pale cheek. "You're gonna be my woman, but it won't be in the dirt, with the sun burning this pretty white skin. We'll be in bed, Victoria, with the door locked, and we won't have to worry about anyone interrupting."

The years of her mother's training shouted at her to deny his arrogant assumption that she was his for the taking, but she couldn't. She couldn't lie to herself, couldn't hide behind strictures that no longer held sway out here in this rough, wild land. She wanted him; she wouldn't pretend otherwise, even though it wouldn't, couldn't, happen.

She moaned inwardly and managed to whisper, "I can't. I'm married."

"Married!" He hissed the word. "You're married to a whoring, murdering bastard. How do you think he got this hacienda? Do you think he *paid* for it? He murdered the family it belonged to, the Sarratts; he raped Elena Sarratt before he put a bullet in her head. That's the man you want to be faithful to, the man who was in a whore's bed the day after you married him."

His words were like blows. Nausea twisted her stomach and she stumbled to her knees, bent over from the waist, gagging and heaving.

His face grim, Jake got his canteen and tugged his handkerchief free from his throat, then poured water over it. After capping the canteen, he knelt beside Victoria and gently wiped her face. She took the handkerchief and pressed it to her cheeks, trying to deal with the sickness that still roiled in her at the thought of such a man touching her. "How do you know about that family—the Sarratts?" she finally asked in a muffled voice.

"Word gets around." He held the canteen out to her. "Take a drink of water."

She swished water around in her mouth before spitting it out on the ground, then drank. She should be mortified, vomiting and spitting in front of a man, but somehow that seemed a petty concern after what Jake had just told her. She lifted her head and stared at him with shadowed eyes. "I can't stay here," she said flatly. "I'll get Emma and Celia and leave. I can't stay in the same house with him."

Jake cursed at the idea of her leaving. "No," he said.

She clutched his arm. "But I can't stay."

"You have to stay. I'm here, Victoria. I'll take care of you."

"What can you do? You're not in that house with him, you don't have to take your meals with him and look at his face, listen to him—"

"It won't be for much longer," he said. He hadn't wanted to tell her that much, but she had reacted more strongly than he'd anticipated to the truth about her husband.

Her dazed eyes focused on him. "What do you mean?"

"I mean that I've heard some rumors, and that's all I can tell you. Trust me, Victoria. Stay. I'll take care of you."

His green eyes burned into hers. For a moment she was as frightened of him as she was sickened at the thought of the Major; there was something hard in his eyes, as if he would stop at nothing to get his way. Yet he was the man she loved, dangerous as he was. If she left, she might never see him again. Pain clenched her heart at the thought.

"All right," she whispered. "I'll stay."

8

She could barely look at the Major that night at the dinner table. The food was tasteless in her mouth. She couldn't stop thinking what Jake had told her about *her husband* raping and killing that poor woman. She was cold with revulsion, her thought processes slowed by the grisly images that occupied her mind as plainly as if she'd actually seen it happen.

She took a sip of water. "This is an old house. Who owned it before you?" As soon as she heard the words she was appalled at herself. Why had she said that? Shock was making her stupid.

McLain stiffened and his ruddy face turned a curious gray color. "Why do you ask? Who's been talkin' about it?"

The only thing she could do now was pretend casual curiosity. She was aware of Emma's sharpened interest, but didn't dare look at her cousin. "No one. I was just wondering about the house. How old is it?"

He looked around the room with furtive eyes, as if assuring himself there was no one lurking in the shadows. "I don't know. You sure no one said anything about it?"

"Yes, I'm sure. It's Spanish missionary architecture, isn't it? It's lovely, and it must be at least two hundred years old. Don't you know?"

McLain took one more quick look around the room. No one had been talking about it; hell, there wasn't anyone left alive who knew about it except for Garnet, Quinzy, and Wallace, now that Roper had given Pledger his entry into hell. She was only asking because the house was old; Southern aristocrats like her put a lot of stock in old things.

"It's about that, I guess," he muttered, and wiped his forehead with his napkin.

"What was the name of the family who owned it before?"

"I don't remember." He said it too quickly.

Juana had entered with Lola to clear the table and heard Victoria's question. She shot the Major a hate-filled look and said, "Sarratt, señor. The family's name was Sarratt."

He bolted to his feet, his face flushing with rage. "Don't mention that name to me, you goddamn bitch!" he roared, sweeping his plate to the floor with a quick motion of his thick arm. "Get out! I'll kill you! Goddamn it, I'll teach you to meddle in things that're none of your goddamn business—"

Juana ducked as he reached for her, but he grabbed her arm and slapped her across the face with all his considerable strength. Lola shrank back, her fists crammed against her mouth to keep her wails stuffed inside. Juana was screaming and would have fallen from the force of the blow if he hadn't been holding her by the arm. Celia shrieked, her face white, and Emma was rising to her feet.

Icy rage exploded in Victoria. She could gladly have struck her husband down in that moment had she the means at hand. She lunged forward as he lifted his arm to strike Juana again and caught him by the wrist, her fury giving her sufficient strength to thwart him. *"Mr. McLain!"* Her voice was cold and ferocious. Her blue eyes looked almost colorless as she stared at him, like ice pools around tiny pinpoints of black.

For a moment she thought he would strike her, too, he was so enraged at being balked in his intention to punish Juana. He turned on her with a snarl, but she stood her ground, her face white and her jaw set.

He froze, staring at her as the red color drained from his face. Slowly he let his arm drop.

"How dare you." She had to push the words through her clenched teeth; they were scarcely more than a hiss. "Those are neither the words nor acts of a gentleman. You have shamed and embarrassed me." Instinctively, she settled on the attack that would hit him at his most vulnerable point, his pretensions of respectability. Puny though it was, it was the only weapon she had against him.

He reddened again and darted a look at Emma and Celia, who were both staring at him in horror. Damn! The way the girl was looking at him now, she wasn't likely to let him get close enough to touch her, much less bed her. And Victoria was staring at him as if he'd just crawled out from under a rock, her patrician nose pinched in disgust.

It was all that Mex bitch's fault, throwing up the Sarratts to him, making him lose control. If he'd ever been able to find the hole that snot-nosed Sarratt whelp had crawled into when he died, he'd have spit on the carcass. But maybe he wasn't dead . . . He thought of the knife in his library again, which reminded him of that flashing knife and the boy's hate-filled eyes.

He felt as if his skin were swelling, as if he might burst. He looked at the silently accusing women, and their stares were like more knives, flashing in the darkness. He whirled and stormed from the room, walking so quickly he was nearly running.

Juana's sobs were quiet but they echoed in the silence left by McLain's exit. Victoria put her arms around the girl. "I'm sorry," she whispered. "I'm sorry."

Juana sobbed brokenly.

"Are you hurt?" Victoria asked.

The question affected Juana strangely. She gulped her sobs, raised her bloodshot eyes to meet Victoria's concerned gaze and said in an unsteady voice, "He'll hurt *you*."

"No, he will not." Victoria straightened, her blue eyes fierce. Things had changed; she wouldn't tolerate that monster's presence in her bedroom if he did happen to try . . . *that* again. She would scream the house down, she would vomit if he dared touch her. She would leave, take her family and leave in the morning.

But Jake had said to stay. He'd said he would take care of her. He had said it might not be for much longer.

What had he meant? That he was making plans himself to take them away from here?

The thought terrified her, but she knew she would take the chance. Running away with another man would brand her forever no matter what the circumstances were or the fact that her husband was a murderer. She would be ostracized from polite society, and the thought of it made her go cold, but what did that mean out here? Not as much as the thought of Jake. He frightened her, he infuriated her, but he made her feel so alive that she ached with the force of her own blood coursing through her body. To be with him without the benefit of marriage would cast her soul into mortal danger; to be without him would condemn her to death in life. He had become more important to her than her own life, and that, more than anything else, was what frightened her.

She calmed Lola; Juana herself had become rigidly dry-eyed and held herself away from comfort. "The Major won't do anything," Victoria assured them. She hoped she wasn't lying. Here was another responsibility; she would have to make certain they didn't suffer for her actions. She wondered how Jake would feel about having an instant household of six women, and smiled wryly. Whatever his plans, she was sure he wasn't prepared for *that*.

"Return to your duties," she said soothingly, patting Juana's shoulder. "I promise he won't do anything, and if he tries, scream for me."

Lola put her arms around Juana, who stiffly allowed the embrace. The red imprint of McLain's hand was turning into a dark bruise on Juana's face. Lola led her into the kitchen.

Celia's face was shuttered, she who was the most open of people. "I'm going to bed," she murmured, and fled the room.

Emma turned to look after the girl in astonishment and started to follow her, then stopped and turned back to Victoria. "Come up to my room," she said. "We can talk there."

Upstairs, they both seated themselves on the bed to talk as they had been doing since they were children. "Why did that happen?" Emma asked, going straight to the heart of the matter.

Victoria clenched her fists as she remembered what Jake had said; now she knew beyond any possible doubt that every horrible word of it was true. "Jake told me that the Major stole this ranch from the Sarratt family, by killing all of them. He said that the Major raped the woman—I don't remember her name—and then shot her in the head."

Emma turned white at Victoria's even-toned statements. "If it's true—" she gasped. "My God, you actually asked him about the Sarratts—"

"I wanted to see how he'd react." Her eyes burned. "My husband is a murderer, a rapist, and a thief. It was true, everything Jake said."

"What are we going to do?" Emma got up and began to pace the room. "We can't stay here, but how are we going to leave? I doubt Major McLain would lend us the money and use of his buggy. We'll have to think up some reason for going to Santa Fe again, and we'll leave from there, somehow."

"I can't leave. Not yet."

Emma gaped at her. "Why? You said yourself, he's a rapist and a murderer! How can you stay?"

"Jake—Jake asked me to stay."

"Ah." With that one syllable Emma signaled her understanding of everything. She paused, thinking through their situation. When she finally spoke, it was to say softly, "Victoria, you know I'll give you my support in any way you need it. You've always been the strong one, the one who somehow kept us all fed when there was no food. We might not even be alive today if you hadn't had the courage to sacrifice your happiness to marry the Major. But how can we stay? Why doesn't Jake simply leave with us?"

"I don't know." Anguished, Victoria stared at her cousin. "Perhaps he's planning to take us away; he only asked me to stay and said that it wouldn't be for long."

"Do you trust him?"

"Do I have any choice? He's the only protection we have." She could have trusted him if she thought he was doing it out of regard for her or even out of a sense of right and wrong, but she still had the uneasy feeling that he was doing it for his own reasons, and that they had nothing to do with justice or herself at all.

McLain was sweating profusely, his eyeballs moving swiftly back and forth beneath his closed lids. In his dreams he had just withdrawn from Elena's limp body when a hideous figure leaped at him from the black shadows in a corner of the room. It was the Sarratt whelp, with a wolf's head and glowing yellow eyes; instead of hands he had long, white, curving claws. He swiped at the Major's exposed genitals with those claws again and again, and in his dream McLain was screaming and rolling all over the room, but his body lay heavy and still in the bed, with only his hands twitching. The boy was tearing at his throat with dripping fangs, and the yellow eyes were glaring at him so close that McLain could see his own reflection in them. The claws finally reached his groin, and he screamed madly as his manhood was torn from his body—

He came awake with a jerk, his eyes flying open as he stared in terror around the dark room, expecting the hellish figure to leap on him from the corners. The shadows were expanding, pressing down on the bed. He couldn't move. He could only lie there, sweating, waiting for his own horrible death. His heart raced and the stench of his fear-sweat filled the room. The silence was unbroken by anything except his own labored breathing.

He was still after him. The bastard hadn't died. He was still out there, with his flashing knife, waiting for his chance, waiting to catch him alone, waiting . . .

Finally McLain summoned enough courage to stumble from the bed and light a candle. The frail, solitary flame illuminated only himself and cast the remainder of the room into even deeper shadows. He needed more candles, more light. An oil lamp—yes, that was what he needed. A couple of oil lamps.

His hands shaking, he found three more candles and lit them, putting them around the room to diminish the shadows. He wanted more, but he couldn't make himself open his bedroom door to go downstairs and get them. What if the Sarratt whelp was waiting, crouched, on the other side of the door?

He'd just wait until daylight and make sure he had lamps in here before another night fell. If he just had enough light, there wouldn't be any shadows for the whelp to hide in and he would be safe.

Jake patted Sophie's rump as he walked behind her to let her know he was here, but he was still ready to leap out of the way of a well-placed kick. He didn't trust her manners that far. He noticed that she was showing signs of coming into season, and he decided not to ride his own horse on today's outing with Victoria. It would be safer if he rode another mare, for both Victoria and himself.

"You got that damn mare settled down yet?" McLain asked, walking up behind him.

Jake glanced at the man, noting his red-rimmed eyes and unshaven jaws. He looked as if he'd been drunk all night. The cold hatred that lived inside Jake hardened more, as it did every time he looked at McLain. "She'll do," he said. He didn't add that he doubted she would ever be docile; Sophie's spirit would always burn too hot for that. She would always be contrary and arrogant, and love to run. "She's coming in heat."

McLain grunted. "Try her out with another stallion tomorrow morning. If she's ready, put Rubio with her."

Jake gave a short nod. McLain shifted his feet. "You taking Victoria for a ride this morning?"

"I don't know." Every muscle tensed. He didn't want to talk about Victoria with McLain. He hated hearing her name come from the man's filthy mouth, hated knowing that she bore the McLain name.

"Show her around the ranch," McLain said abruptly. His eyes were glittering.

Jake shrugged. "Sure." McLain's insistence was a bit strange, but it was too convenient for Jake to worry about it.

"I'll send her out. Why don't you show her North Rock? She'd like that."

"The Rock's about a two-hour ride."

"You said she's a good rider; she can make it." McLain turned and hurried to the house. Jake's eyes narrowed as he watched him leave. This *was* strange. It was almost as if McLain were throwing Victoria at him, but for what reason?

Maybe that episode in Santa Fe with Pledger had made him suspicious; maybe McLain thought he could catch Jake being too familiar with his wife, and give him a reason to put a bullet through his head. No one would say a word about it; a man had a right to protect his family. The whole idea sounded just like something Garnet would think up.

Jake saddled Sophie and another mare; in less than half an hour Victoria appeared wearing her riding habit. She looked pale, but bright spots of color burned in her cheeks. She didn't look at him as he lifted her into the saddle.

"Where are we going?" she asked once they were away from the house.

"No place in particular. Just riding." The last place he was going was to North Rock.

"I didn't want to ride today."

He eyed her consideringly. She seemed more upset now than she had the day before. Damn her lady's conscience; whenever she had time to think, it undid whatever progress he'd made with her. Anger, still close to the surface after his meeting with McLain, roiled inside him. He'd be damned if he'd let her back away from him again. "Because of what happened between us yesterday?" he asked in a hard voice.

"Nothing happened!" She bit her lip, ashamed of her swift disclaimer because it wasn't true. Hiding from what she felt wouldn't make it go away.

"The hell it didn't, lady," he snapped, reining the mare he was riding closer to Sophie.

She finally cast him a quick, desperate glance. His green eyes were glittering dangerously under the shadow from his hat brim. "I know," she said, and swallowed. "I'm sorry. It's just—" She swallowed again. "I asked him last night who owned the ranch before him. He wouldn't answer, and when Juana said the Sarratts had owned it he became violent and hit her." The words were jerky, her voice strained. "It's true, what you said, or he wouldn't have acted like that. I can't stand being here, living in the same house with him. How much longer will it be, Jake? Are you going to take us away from here? I'll go anywhere you want if we can just leave."

She stopped her tumbling flow of words, waiting for him to tell her that they would leave soon. But he was glaring at her and the silence was filled only by the sound of the horses' hooves and breathing, the jingling of bits and creak of leather. She floundered in a sea of agonized embarrassment. Had she so completely misread him? Had he not meant, after all, that he'd take them away?

"Don't mention the Sarratts to him again." Jake's voice was as hard and dry as an empty riverbed.

Victoria went even whiter. She lifted her reins and nudged Sophie with her heel, urging her to greater speed. With Sophie, it didn't take much urging. She leaped forward as if propelled by a spring, and Victoria was glad of the mare's excess of spirit. She wanted nothing more than to get away from Jake Roper, from having to look into his face and see her own stupidity.

Jake cursed and spurred his horse after her. If the mare he was riding hadn't been a quarterhorse bred for speed over the short distance, he wouldn't have overtaken her as quickly as he did. When he drew even with Victoria, he leaned over and snatched the reins from her hands, easing Sophie to a slower pace. "Don't try that again," he snapped, angered by the risk she had just taken. She didn't know the speed of which Sophie was capable, or how headstrong the mare was.

"Or you'll do what?" she shouted, shoving at his arm. "Let go!"

He gritted his teeth. "Victoria, settle down," he said with sorely strained patience, trying to hold on to his temper.

Even through his anger, he was a little amazed at her defiance. From the first, she had dared him when even armed men walked softly around him. The lady might be straitlaced, but she wasn't a coward.

She dropped her hand and turned her face away from him. "I apologize." Dear heaven, how many times was she going to have to apologize to him today? As mortifying as it was, she might as well face it. "I misinterpreted your words yesterday. I thought you meant that we—" She stumbled to a halt, unable to find a phrase that left her any dignity.

All he could see was the pale curve of her cheek. "You didn't misinterpret a goddamn thing," he said low.

The look she gave him was so uneasy that he wanted to take her in his arms right then, but they were still too close to the house. He'd be a fool to take that kind of a risk, especially now with Ben on the way. If he just remained patient, he'd have both her and the ranch, but the strain was so intense that his powerful hands were knotted into fists. "Let's get farther from the house," he muttered. "I know a place we can go."

Her heart thudded painfully against her ribs, but she followed him. He was as much an enigma to her now as he had been the first day she'd met him, and she was terrified that she was putting not just her life but also Emma's and Celia's in his hands. He was a gunfighter, a man who made a living by dispensing death. She couldn't read his thoughts, couldn't feel that she knew him as anything other than unpredictable. But she would rather be with him and in danger than live a safe life without him.

They rode without speaking at an easy pace for half an hour. They were in a lovely, narrow valley, carpeted in yellow snakeweed. A crown of aspens stood on top of the hill, waving gently in a breeze they couldn't feel down in the valley. Jake led them toward the aspens.

When they were among the trees, he reined in and dismounted. "No one can see us in here," he said, reaching up to clasp her waist and lift her down. He didn't add that the high ground made it hard for anyone to approach unseen, either, no point in scaring her when his suspicions might be unfounded. His first urge, feeling her slim body in his hands, was to pull her close and take his fill of her. Her faint, sweet scent teased him. His loins hardened and grew heavy to the point where he almost didn't care that now wasn't the time or the place. It wouldn't take long to flip up her skirt if that was all he wanted, but he wanted more than a few minutes of rutting. He wanted all of her, he wanted to drown himself in her sweetness, wanted it too much to risk ruining his plans by pressing her too hard.

He carefully tied Sophie's reins to a tree limb, though he trusted his own mount to remain with just a ground tie, letting the reins drag on the ground. Victoria still avoided looking at him, at least until he reached out and took her hand, carrying it to his mouth for a brief kiss. Then she gave him a brief glance full of distress, and he wondered what she was thinking. He'd never before met a woman who had such a multitude of prickly morals, like a cactus. She was still living in a fantasy world ruled by courtly manners; what did it take to open her eyes and make her realize that life in the West was rough and the only rule was to stay alive by any means necessary?

"Let's sit down," he suggested, and with his boot scraped together a mound of pine needles. She sank down on the pile, carefully arranging her skirt to cover her low, dainty boots. He sprawled beside her and propped himself on his left side so his right hand and arm were free.

"I'm making some plans," he said after a minute. "I'll get you away from McLain, but it'll take a little time."

She picked up a stick and drew it through the dirt. "What about Emma and Celia?"

"Them, too." No problem at all, he thought. Of course, she didn't know that his plans were to replace McLain, not to leave.

"How long will it be?" she whispered. "I can't bear it much longer."

"I don't know exactly. You'll have to be patient until it's time." It was almost intolerable, letting her walk into that house as McLain's wife, and if it was that bad for him, how must Victoria feel? But she had to for now. He'd make it up to her afterward, when the ranch belonged to him and Ben again.

She turned her head away from him, wondering how he could ask that of her if he felt even half as strongly about her as she did about him. The hard answer to that question, she was afraid, was that he didn't. Pain squeezed her insides, but she kept her eyes dry and her chin steady; whining wouldn't do any good. If he didn't love her, then he didn't love her. At least he wanted her enough to be with her, which gave her the chance of eventually winning his love.

Jake caught her chin in his gloved fingers and turned her face toward him. "Don't pout," he said with a hard edge in his tone. "I'm doing what I can and you'll just have to be patient."

"I'm not pouting," she said.

"Then stop turning your head away from me."

She looked at him directly then, blue eyes steady under her level dark brows. "I don't know anything about you, or understand anything. I think I'm entitled to a certain amount of worry."

His mouth tightened. "I don't rightly see how you can say that after yesterday. There's something between us, Victoria. Whether you 'understand' it or not. Why the hell else would I put myself out to help you?"

"I don't know. That's what worries me." She saw a flicker of expression in the dark green of his eyes, but it was gone before she could read it. "You keep so much of you hidden, no one can get to know you. I feel as if I'm putting myself in your hands without knowing anything about you."

"You know I want you."

Her blue eyes looked bruised. "Yes," she said. "I know that."

He wanted to feel her skin and he impatiently pulled off his gloves, then touched her face again. His fingers delved into her hair, while his thumb stroked the velvety texture of her cheek. The sunlight filtering through the trees dappled her hair; he trailed a strand through his fingers, picking out shades ranging from palest gold to auburn to light brown. Her skin looked almost translucent, while her eyes were shadowed with secrets he couldn't fathom. A surge of lust heated him so fully that he broke out in a sweat. God, he had to have just a little of her, a taste, a feel, or he'd explode.

"Don't worry about anything," he muttered, hooking his hands under her arms and pulling her toward him. "I'll take care of you. Just trust me, and don't say anything to anyone." His mouth closed over hers, and Victoria found that while he was holding her, at least, she didn't worry about anything at all.

Celia heard someone coming and quickly scrambled into her hiding place in the loft, afraid that it was Garnet trying to catch her alone as Victoria had warned her he might. She was as agile and silent as a cat as she stretched out to press her eye to a crack in the floor.

It wasn't Garnet, she saw; it was the Major, slowly walking

the length of the barn and peering in all the stalls. "Celia," he softly called, his tone cajoling. "Are you in here? I've got something I want to show you."

She didn't move, except for closing her eyes to blot him out of her sight. She could barely stand to look at him anymore; there was something about him that she found repulsive, though she couldn't have explained exactly what it was. It was as if there was a dark cloud surrounding him, a darkness of evil. At first she had tried to like him, for Victoria's sake. But she'd failed and now it was all she could do to tolerate even being in the same room with him.

"Celia," he called again. "Come here, girl. Let me show you something."

A cold chill ran over her body. She didn't move as she watched him leave the barn, his head swiveling as he looked for her. She would stay hidden until Victoria returned.

The Major had said they were riding to North Rock, but Garnet was a fair hand at tracking and from what he saw they weren't even heading in the same direction as the Rock. He followed carefully, making certain he didn't chance upon them before he knew it. They had ridden into a valley and he hesitated to follow them there; they would be able to see him from any vantage point. Taking the chance that they would return the same way, he picked his spot, hiding his horse below a small crest and choosing a huge clump of boulders the size of a small house as his own hiding spot.

He kicked a few small pebbles out of his way and sat down. With his rifle resting in a small notch in the rock, his hat tilted to keep the hot sun out of his eyes, he waited.

Sophie shied restlessly when Jake settled Victoria in the saddle, and he briefly considered putting her on his own mare instead. But after her little sideways dance Sophie settled down. "Keep a good grip on the reins," he said as he swung into his own saddle. "She's flighty today."

Victoria leaned down to pat the satiny neck. "She seems all right."

"She's coming in heat."

Victoria blushed. "Oh," she said faintly.

Jake led the way out of the trees, bending low to avoid limbs and keeping a sharp eye on Sophie to make sure she didn't try to brush Victoria off. Sophie mouthed the bit impatiently, not liking it that the other mare was in front of her. Without waiting for Victoria's instruction, she lengthened her stride until she was half a neck in front and plunged out of the treeline with every intention of taking the run that had been denied her.

Victoria held the reins steady, pulling back enough to let Sophie know she wanted her to slow down but not enough to hurt her soft mouth. The mare snorted, shaking her head at the pressure. Jake kneed his mare up beside her. "Can you hold her?"

"Yes. She wants to run. Why don't we let them have some fun?"

Remembering how Sophie could run, he shook his head. "This horse can't keep up with her. Just hold her in; we'll let her run one day when I'm riding my stallion."

Several things happened simultaneously. Sophie, impatient with the restraint, reared a little and twisted away from Jake's mare. Victoria was slung to the side, but managed to retain both her seat and the reins. Jake cursed and leaned forward to grab her bridle as a sharp crack split the air ahead and just to the right of them.

Victoria barely registered a swift buzzing sound when Jake lunged from his horse, his momentum taking him clear across Sophie and knocking Victoria to the ground with him. She landed on her back and for a moment saw nothing but black and scarlet spots. Just as her vision began clearing, Jake grabbed her and jerked her roughly across the ground to a clump of bushes. "Stay here," he snapped.

She hadn't any choice; she couldn't manage to move with any coordination. In a daze she watched him run for his horse and jerk the rifle from its scabbard. Then, bent low, he ran back to her.

"Are you all right?" he asked, not looking at her. He was scanning the rest of the valley.

"Yes," she managed to say, though she wasn't certain. She noticed the red stain on the light blue of his shirt, and shock propelled her to a sitting position. He'd been shot! Someone was shooting at them.

"Let me see your arm," she said, scrabbling for the handkerchief in her skirt pocket.

He didn't look around. "It's all right, just a burn. It didn't go in."

"Let me see," she repeated stubbornly, getting to her knees and reaching for him.

He pushed her down and gave her a brief, cold glare. *"Stay down.* He could still be watching."

Victoria set her mouth and hooked her fingers in his belt, then tugged. He lost his balance and sat down beside her. "Damn it—"

"He might shoot you again! You're a larger target than I am."

Jake's eyes were like splintered ice. "He wasn't shooting at me. If that damn horse hadn't shied, you'd be dead."

She stared blankly at him. Why would anyone want to shoot her? "Someone was probably hunting." That had to be it; she couldn't imagine, couldn't let herself think that it was anything else.

He grunted. "Any hunter who's that piss-poor of a shot is going to die from hunger. There's no way two people mounted on horses look like a couple of deer or anything else but what they are." He pulled his pistol from the holster and handed it to her. "Do you know how to shoot?"

She had handled single-shot dueling pistols; during the war it had seemed wise to know something about weapons. She closed her hand around the worn handle and lifted the heavy weapon. "Some," she whispered.

"Then shoot anybody you see, except me," he instructed. Then he was gone, slipping around the clump of bushes and out of sight.

She sat immobile, alert to every small sound. His mare was peacefully cropping grass a short distance away, but she couldn't see or hear Sophie. Birds called, insects hummed, and a light wind sifted through her hair. It was almost an hour before she heard him call, "It's clear." She scrambled up to see him walking toward her, leading Sophie.

"Whoever it was is gone," he said. "He shot from those big rocks. Must have waited for a while, from the signs. Just one man, and his tracks head straight toward the river." Tracking would still be possible, if he had the time, but he didn't. He had to get Victoria back to the ranch. He'd look around afterward, but by then whoever had done it would have had plenty of time to wipe out his tracks.

She insisted on checking the seeping burn on his upper arm and tied her handkerchief around it. Her cheeks were pale but she hadn't screamed or gotten hysterical even when he'd knocked her out of the saddle. Her hair was straggling half down her back, she was dusty from head to boot, and her skirt was torn. She didn't look much like a lady now, but the steel in her backbone was unbowed. He didn't know who had tried to kill her, but he was damn sure going to find out. Then there'd be one bastard less on this earth.

9

Jake walked into the dining room while they were eating dinner. He didn't look around, because he hated to see this house and know that McLain lived in it. He looked straight at Victoria, his face grim, and knew by her expression that she hadn't said anything about what had happened. He didn't know why, but it wasn't his concern.

"Somebody shot at Mrs. McLain today," he announced abruptly to McLain, who had looked up in surprise at his entrance. "If her horse hadn't shied she'd have been killed."

McLain's face turned dark red. "Shot at her! There ain't nobody on the ranch who'd shoot at *my* wife."

"I found where he waited. Somebody tried to kill her. No mistake."

Celia was very still in her chair, her gaze unreadable but riveted on McLain. "It was the Sarratts," she said in a small, clear voice.

McLain jerked, then swiped his plate to the floor with a motion of his thick forearm. He half-rose to his feet, his eyes bulging from his head as he glared down the table at the girl. "It ain't the goddamn Sarratts!" he bellowed. "They're dead, all of them!" His voice was both fierce and desperate, too, as if he didn't believe his own words. He slammed his fist down on the table, making their plates and glasses jump and rattle. "That god-damn Duncan Sarratt and his bitch of a wife, they're both dead, and their two half-Mex whelps with them! They're dead, I tell you!"

Jake controlled the urge to put his pistol to the man's head right now and be done with it. Hate blinded him to the Major's obvious fear. The strength it took to control his rage left Jake so raw he could barely speak. "I don't want the women out riding until I find whoever it was. I went out this afternoon and trailed him as far as the river, but it got dark before I could find where he left the water. I'll try again tomorrow."

"Find him," McLain said, breathing heavily to control his rage. "And kill the son of a bitch."

Jake nodded at the women and left as abruptly as he'd entered.

McLain was still blowing air like a bull, his bloodshot eyes fastened on nothing. Victoria quietly excused herself and hustled Celia out of the room. When they were out of earshot, she grabbed her sister's arm. "Why did you say that?" she whispered fiercely. "You saw how he got last night when Juana mentioned their name!"

Celia looked up, her expression raw. "I hate him. I wanted to see him afraid, like he was last night. I hate him!" She tore loose and ran up the stairs to her room, where she slammed the door.

Emma was standing behind Victoria when she turned around; her cousin's face was white and drawn. She was shaking. She looked at Victoria with something close to terror in her fine eyes. "Why didn't you tell me?" she asked in a taut voice. "My God, someone tried to kill you!"

"And failed, though Jake was wounded in the arm. I didn't want to worry you." Nor had she wanted to talk about it. Beneath her surface calm, she felt frightened and vulnerable. Something was going to happen and she didn't understand what or why; she only sensed the increasing instability of their lives.

"We have to leave here," Emma said.

"I can't!" Victoria started to speak again, then motioned with her head for Emma to follow her. She didn't want to take a chance on anyone overhearing them talk. They went to Emma's room and firmly closed the door. Victoria walked to the window. "We went over this last night. I can't leave without Jake."

Emma sat down on the bed and clasped her hands. "Do you love him?"

It sounded as shocking now as it had the first time she'd said it to herself. She was a married lady, a Waverly from Augusta; he was a hired gun, a man who killed without a flicker of emotion. It was still shattering to realize how little any of those things mattered. "Yes."

"Does he love you?"

"He—he wants me."

It was hard to evade Emma. "But does he love you?"

"No." The admission filled her with pain. She had seen lust in his eyes, but not love.

"Then how can you afford to risk your life to stay near him?"

"Would you have left Jon?" Victoria asked in a choked voice. "Even if you had known that he didn't feel the same way about you as you felt about him, could you have left him?"

Emma's lips trembled and she stared down at her hands. "No," she finally said. "No, I couldn't."

"Then you know why I'm staying. You and Celia can leave, go back to Augusta."

"I won't leave you, either. And you know there's nothing for us back in Augusta."

And maybe nothing here, in this wild, hard, beautiful land, except death at the hand of someone who had some reason for wanting her dead. Out here, it seemed, that reason didn't have to make much sense.

"If something happens to me, I want your promise that you'll take Celia and leave immediately."

Emma stared at her, white-faced. "Don't let anything happen," she whispered in reply.

After leaving Emma's room, Victoria tapped on Celia's door. She found her sister sitting quietly by the window, staring out at the courtyard. She didn't look up and smile as she usually did.

Victoria put her hand on Celia's shoulder, wondering what

had happened to take the happiness from her eyes and leave behind that strange remoteness. "Is anything wrong?" she asked in a gentle tone.

A shiver racked Celia's slender body. "He was calling me," she whispered. "Like you'd call a cat. It scared me and I hid in the loft. I watched him through a crack in the floor, sneaking around, looking in all the stalls and calling my name. I hate him. I wish the Sarratts would kill him."

Victoria's throat was tight with fear. "Who?" she asked. "Garnet?"

Celia looked up at her, dark blue eyes fierce with mingled fear and hatred. "No. The Major."

Victoria lay awake that night, too tense to sleep. She simply couldn't keep her eyes closed. She stared at the ceiling, wondering if she was making the right decision in staying, if she had any right to subject Emma and Celia to such danger. But did she have any choice? Lying there sleepless, she swore an oath: if the Major touched Celia or hurt her in any way, she'd kill him herself.

The connecting door opened, and her entire body went cold. She turned her head to look at the thick-set figure swaying in the doorway. Dear God, no . . .

"Is he in here?" McLain asked, slurring the words. The stench of whiskey emanated from him.

She wet her lips and eased into a sitting position. What did he mean? Had someone seen Jake kissing her? She stared at him, tensing her muscles to jump up and run if he came any closer. "Who?"

"Sarratt. That damn basserd. Is he in here?"

She could barely understand his words. "No." Her throat was tight. "No one is in here. You can see."

"He's trying to kill me, an' he'll kill you, too, jus' to get even with me. Nothin' a Sarratt would like better than to get his hands on my woman." He sounded almost boastful as he swayed back and forth, a willow in an invisible wind.

"The Sarratts are all dead. You said so."

He laughed, a strange, cackling laugh. "Yeah, but mebbe not.

Mebbe not. Never could find the boys' bodies. Did you know that? Never did find their bodies. If Sarratt's back, he'll kill us all in our beds, especially you. That's jus' where he'd like to find you. Yep, in a bed. He'd enjoy plowin' you and listenin' to you scream, just the way his mama screamed. . . . You sure he's not in here?"

Her throat was dry; she had to swallow before answering. "I'm certain."

"He won't be able to sneak up on me," McLain muttered as he backed into his own room. "I'm keeping a sharp eye out for him, and the lamps lit. Yeah, lots of lamps . . . no shadows." The door closed on his mutterings.

He had gone mad. Victoria stared at the door. She couldn't believe that he had a conscience, but his murderous past was coming back to him, twisting his mind. Even knowing he was insane she couldn't stop a chill; if it were true that one of the Sarratt sons had survived, she could understand that he would stop at nothing to wreak his vengeance on McLain, to destroy him and his family as he had destroyed the Sarratt family.

Someone had shot at her today. If it hadn't been for Jake . . . if Sophie hadn't acted up at just that moment . . .

Was someone trying to kill her as vengeance against McLain? She could easily imagine him having enemies.

He'd never found the boys' bodies.

If one of the Sarratts had survived, would he hate McLain enough to destroy an entire family, as McLain had done? Hate enough to deliberately set out to kill McLain's wife?

She shivered, because she knew the answer was *yes*.

The next morning Jake put Rubio in the pen with Sophie. The big red stallion squealed as he caught the mare's scent, and shoved his nose at her hind quarters. His erection was already jutting out from his body. Sophie danced nervously away, though she had stood still not half an hour ago while another stallion sniffed at her. Jake cussed her contrariness, but in a rueful, accepting tone. He'd already hobbled her front feet, so she wasn't going anywhere.

Rubio squealed again, this time angrily, and nipped the recalcitrant mare to teach her who was boss. Sophie's head whipped around and she nipped back, enraged. Rubio tried to mount her and she jerked away, neighing with fright. Had she been a wild horse she'd have been running across the hills in an effort to save her maidenhead, and the stallion would have run her down. Hobbled in the pen, though, Sophie didn't have much chance.

Rubio reared again and caught her arched neck with his teeth as he penetrated. Sophie screamed, shuddering under the stallion's weight and impact, but now she stood still for him as her instincts dictated.

Victoria heard the mare scream and concern puckered her brow. She put aside her sewing and walked to a window, but the angle was wrong and she wasn't able to see anything. Curious as to what was causing the uproar, wondering if Sophie was getting the best of Jake again, she went out on the patio and looked toward the barn.

Rubio was out of his stall and was attacking Sophie. Sheer panic shot through her and without thinking she began running toward the pen. She had always known that horse was a killer; something inside her went cold every time she saw him—

Then she saw Jake watching calmly, and a few of the other hands standing around. She saw Rubio biting Sophie's neck, saw the lunging thrusts of his hindquarters, and stopped as if she had hit a wall. Dear God! They were mating! Her beautiful, spirited mare was being mated to that vicious killer. It revolted her as much as the thought of McLain climbing into her own bed.

"Stop it!" She hadn't meant to yell, but the words burst out of her.

Jake turned his head. Victoria was standing halfway between the house and the stable, her eyes wide with horror. She began running toward him.

Some of the men were standing around to lend aid if needed, and he scowled as he realized he didn't want Victoria watching the horses mate, with the men watching her. He left the pen and strode toward her, catching her arms when she tried to bolt past.

"Stop him!" she gasped, trying to pull free of his grip. "Get him off her!"

He shook her a little, swinging her around so his body blocked her view of the horses. "I can't stop it. What's wrong with you?"

Her face was white, her eyes huge as she stared up at him. "I didn't want her bred," she said in a strangled tone. "You *knew* that. Not now. Especially not to *him!*"

Her missishness irritated him; it was common sense to put the best stallion on the best mare to get the best foals. His hands were rough as he turned her around and began forcing her back toward the house. "Did you think we'd breed her to some scrub?"

His fingers were biting into her arms; he was almost dragging her in his haste to get her inside, out of the sight of the other men. Some deeply possessive instinct was outraged that they had seen her witnessing a sexual act, even one between two animals. He didn't stop until they were on the patio. "Get back in the house. You shouldn't have come out here."

His total lack of understanding was like a slap in the face. She didn't expect sympathy, but she did expect at least an acknowledgment that she had a right to feel as she did. She pulled away from him and turned her head from the sights and sounds of the two horses mating. "I thought she was *my* horse," she said in a small, clear voice. "I didn't give permission for her to be bred."

"I suggested breeding her to Rubio before the Major ever bought her," Jake said impatiently. "That's the only reason he bought her, not to give you a pleasure mount. I talked him into letting me train her for you; otherwise you'd be riding something like Emma's gelding. We decided yesterday to put Rubio in with her. This isn't hurting her, and you'll have a fine foal out of her."

"No, I won't." Her eyes were clear and stark as she stared at him. "The *Major* will have a fine foal from her." Her back was rigid as she turned away from him to go into the house.

He clamped his hand on her shoulder and jerked her back around to face him, angered by the way she'd turned her back on him. "Stop acting like a fool. This isn't your precious South; we can't afford to let a good animal go to waste. Did you really think she was bought only for you to ride?"

Victoria lifted her chin, pride keeping her hurt from her face. She wouldn't have been so upset if it had been any stallion other than Rubio, but he'd scoffed at her objections to the horse. Her voice expressionless, she said, "I suppose I did. After all, Emma's gelding hasn't been used for ranch work, nor has Celia's mare."

"They aren't the same quality as Sophie." He tamped down his impatience and tried to get her to see reason. There was just no sense in this kind of behavior. "Like I said, this isn't hurting her. When I've found whoever shot at you yesterday and it's safe again, we can go riding just like before."

Her expression didn't flicker. "I'm afraid not, Mr. Roper," she said, and once again turned to enter the house. "I don't have a horse."

So it was Mr. Roper again, was it? Anger burned in his gut as he stalked back to the corral. The horses were finished, but none of the men would approach Rubio and Sophie was acting up whenever one of them got close to her. The unfamiliar situation had made her nervous, and a nervous Sophie was a biting Sophie.

Still fuming, he put Rubio back in his stall, patting the muscled red neck and telling the stallion what a good job he'd done. Rubio snorted, his ears back a little. Jake didn't turn his back on the horse as he left the stall and shut the door. If the foal's temperament was a mixture of sire and dam, he thought dourly, they might as well shoot it when it was born because no one would ever be able to ride it.

Sophie moved awkwardly away from him, lifting her hobbled feet high as if trying to step out of the rope. She had blood on her neck where Rubio had bitten her; it was black against her dark chestnut coat. Damn him, the stallion was always rough on a mare. Jake murmured soothingly to Sophie until she finally stood still and let him approach. He patted and stroked her, watching the wild look fade from her eyes. When he bent down to remove the hobble, she butted him affectionately with her head.

Damn it, was everything female just naturally contrary? He wanted to give Victoria a good shaking. She'd acted as if she would never be able to ride Sophie again and had taken it out on him.

Patience. He just had to have patience. But it was hard, and getting harder.

During the days that followed, Victoria didn't leave the house. Neither did Celia nor Emma. The three women passed the time with the mundane chores of everyday life, giving each other strained, silent looks but carrying on with an outward air of calm. What else could they do? Hysteria wouldn't solve anything.

Celia remained close to her sister and cousin, instinctively seeking the safety of their company. She could barely remain in the same room with the Major long enough to take her meals.

McLain looked increasingly awful as the days passed. His eyes seemed permanently red and swollen, his face haggard and unshaven. Victoria doubted that he was bathing, because a persistent sour smell clung to him. She could hear him at night, pacing on the other side of the door and muttering to himself, and the sound made her shiver. He was mad. She couldn't manage to feel any pity for him; this punishment seemed all too fitting to his crimes. But she did fear what could happen when he made the final descent and reality no longer had any meaning for him. He could convince himself that one of the Sarratt boys was in a room with them, and start shooting. Or, even worse, he might decide that she was the Sarratt woman, the one he had raped and murdered, and reenact his deed. She would rather be killed outright than endure his touch.

She didn't know how much longer she could bear it. The days were spent close to the house, making certain Celia was always watched, unable to ride out as she longed to do. The nights were also spent watching the connecting door, listening to the Major's increasingly crazy mutters and bursts of laughter. The very air was full of menace and she was helpless to escape it, because it was outside as well as in. No matter which way she turned, there was danger.

* * *

Narrow-eyed, Garnet watched McLain. The damn fool was going crazy, talking to himself about the Sarratts coming back to kill them all. Things hadn't worked out as he'd planned. He'd missed his shot with the woman, and since then she hadn't been riding at all. Damn Roper, too, while he was at it. Garnet had sweated until he'd been able to reshod his horse, knowing Roper had looked real good at the hoofprints leading away from the failed ambush. Now he couldn't get a shot at the woman, and McLain was getting the men all stirred up with his howling about Sarratts coming back from the grave to get them.

Maybe he should do what he'd originally planned and just kill the Major. At least it would shut him up. Only problem was he couldn't do that until he'd found some way to get rid of Roper. Garnet never allowed himself to think that he was actually afraid of Roper, he thought of it as caution, because the man was cat-quick with a gun and as mean as a wounded grizzly. Will Garnet prided himself on not being afraid of no man walking, but he also prided himself on being smart enough to know there were some people you just didn't mess with. Roper was one of them.

Jake Quinzy halted beside him, also watching the Major reel back toward the house. Quinzy spat in the dust before he spoke. "Major's gettin' spooky. I been here a long time, but I been thinkin' maybe it's time to be movin' on."

Garnet sneered. "That crazy talk about the Sarratts scare you?"

Quinzy spat again. "Don't reckon." His eyes were cold slits. "Don't reckon I like workin' for no crazy man, neither."

Garnet didn't like telling anyone his plans, but he needed Quinzy's gun. "The Major might not be around much longer."

Quinzy grunted and rolled that around in his mind. "You thinkin' of takin' over?"

"Don't see why not, do you?"

"No skin off me." He paused. "Unless you plannin' on hurtin' Miz McLain. Guess I'd have to part with you on that."

Startled, Garnet looked at him. He couldn't remember Quinzy balking at anything before. But now wasn't the time to

re's going to be some shooting when we take the ranch,"
ated out. "There's a chance the women might be hurt."

if I can help it. When we have some backup, I'm going
McLain out, make him face me. If I go up against him
u and the men watch the others, there shouldn't be any
oting."

ld it right there." Ben moved around to face his brother.
not going up against him alone."

makes sense."

e hell it does. This is my fight, too, and I'm going to have
tand around while you take all the risks."

he darkness Jake couldn't see Ben's face, but he didn't
. There was no way he could keep Ben out of the fight.
t. How long will it be before the men get here?"

w days, maybe a week. Lonny will push 'em hard."

eek at the most. Everything in Jake tightened at the
of it finally ending. He wanted McLain dead so much it
e wouldn't even let him be buried on Sarratt land. A
hen the land would be theirs again—and Victoria would

cLain's going loony," he said, rubbing the back of his neck.
tired, but every nerve in his body had been jumping since
en Ben ride up. "There's no way of telling what he'll do.
arted running around and babbling about the Sarratts
back—"

stiffened. "Well, hell, he's right, but how did he know?"
e doesn't. That's just it. Every time something happens, he
lobbering and muttering about the Sarratts getting him. If
dies, he thinks it's been poisoned. If he hears a shot, he
it was fired at him."

ooks like the bastard's sins are coming home to roost, after

he point is when we move we'll have to move fast. We'll
come in at night quiet and slow. Most of the men are out
he herds at any one time, so we'll only have to deal with
a third of them here at the house. We'll take the
ouse first, and we'll have to do it without any shooting.
those men are taken care of, we can get the house. McLain

buck him on it. Instead he said, "I got plans for the little sister,
not Miz Roper. Good plans." He laughed.

Quinzy chuckled, too. "Yep, she is right purty, ain't she?
Reckon the fuzz a-tween her legs is as yeller as her head?"

Just thinking about it made Garnet start breathing faster.
That was something else he was mad about; he hadn't seen Celia
leave the house in days. The women were holed up inside like
Injuns were attacking or something.

"When you plannin' on makin' your move?" Quinzy asked.

"Don't know." Now he wished he hadn't said anything,
because if he didn't do something it would make him look like a
coward. On the other hand, he couldn't do anything until he
could get at the Major's wife.

So all he could do was wait it out.

A lone, dusty rider approached the ranch late one afternoon,
slumping in the saddle with fatigue. Angelina Garcia was the first
to see him and her eyes brightened at the thought of having a
new man, but she didn't move from her languid slump against
the barn wall.

The next one to see the rider was one of the gunhands. He
nudged Garnet, pointed out the stranger to him. Garnet looked
without much interest; it was just another down-at-the-heel
wrangler, one of the thousands who had poured west after the
end of the war, drifting and looking for work.

Jake watched the man ride in and made no effort to speak or
attract his attention. Time enough for that later. What the hell
was he doing, riding in here like this? If anyone noticed their
resemblance, people would get suspicious. But when the rider
turned his head, Jake stifled a grin as he saw that the man had
grown a short, dark beard. Smart.

Work was what the man asked about, and Garnet considered
it. He didn't have to ask the Major every time he hired a cowpuncher because they tended to drift out as often as they drifted
in. But, as dirty and tired as he was, this man didn't have the look
of a cowpuncher. Maybe it was his eyes, cool and guarded; maybe
he just looked a mite too comfortable with the iron strapped to
his hip, the handle worn smooth with use. If he guessed right, this

was a gunnie, maybe on the run. They could always use another gun, but the Major liked to look them over himself. Of course, the Major had been acting so loony lately, Garnet would be surprised if he could talk sense.

To hell with the Major. What he liked wouldn't make a difference much longer, anyway. "Yeah, find a place to bunk down," Garnet said. "You any good with that piece you're wearin'?"

"I'm alive," the man said flatly as he swung down from the saddle.

"How're you called?"

"Tanner." He offered just the one name, and Garnet didn't ask if it was the front or the back one. Hell, it probably wasn't his real name, anyhow.

Tanner took care of his weary horse before seeking any sort of comfort for himself. He watered and fed the animal, brushed the dust from its coat, and put it in an empty stall. Slinging his saddle onto his broad shoulder, he went in search of the bunkhouse.

Like all of the buildings except the wooden barn, the bunkhouse was made of thick adobe, so it was cool in the summer. Regardless of that, weather permitting, a lot of the men preferred to sleep outside rolled in their blankets. Tanner had his choice of empty bunks. They didn't look too dirty, and he didn't much care. He was so tired he thought he'd probably be able to sleep standing up. Figuring there wasn't anything he could do or find out that wouldn't wait until morning, he pulled off his boots, slid his .44 under the thin pillow, and went to sleep. He didn't feel the lumps in the mattress.

It was a little after midnight when he woke, feeling human again. Not wanting to disturb the men nearby—including Garnet, he saw—he silently slid the .44 back into his holster. Patting his pockets for the makings of a cigarette, he carefully rolled, licked, and lit it with a straw he'd stuck into the stove. He then picked up his boots and tiptoed out like a man who just wanted a smoke in the middle of the night. Outside, he pulled on his boots and started wandering around, smoking and looking at the stars. It was a moonless night, but that made the stars just that much brighter. It was the kind of night when sound carried for long distances.

He walked to the corral and leaned [...] finished the cigarette. Only then did [...] check on his horse, which was dozing [...] ing, he next visited the barn.

"About time you woke up," a low vo[...] look at his brother.

"Anyone around?" Ben asked in an [...]

"No." Jake had waited through the [...] tain no one entered the barn. Still, he [...] into the building, away from the do[...] stamped a hoof, a signal that he didn't [...]

"What the hell's going on?" Ben felt [...] temper in his voice. "Your telegram said [...] sible, that things had changed. I starte[...] we've hired, then left the rest of it to Lo[...] to get them here pronto, and I lit out. I d[...] into the ground, then I get here and every[...] ured they'd found out who you are." He [...] halfway expected to find his brother d[...] knew the consequences if anyone four[...] before their men got there to back them [...]

"The Major has got himself a wife."

"So?"

"So when he dies, she inherits."

Ben was silent as he absorbed what thi[...] "Shit," he said.

"Yeah. She's a lady, young enough to [...] cousin and little sister live here now, too."

"So what're we going to do? We c[...] woman."

"No, but a widow can remarry."

Again Ben was silent, thinking it throug[...]

"Can you think of any other way?"

"No, but there's another side to it, too. [...]

"Yes," Jake said. Victoria was still pou[...] horse, but he'd held her in his arms and fe[...] response often enough to know he could m[...] he wanted.

sleeps in the big front bedroom." It had been their parents' bedroom. "We'll go in quiet and bring him out." Victoria would be in the bedroom, too, he thought. He didn't want to see her in bed with McLain, but he'd do whatever he had to do, even if it meant killing McLain in front of her.

Ben nodded. "We can't take a chance on anyone seeing our men, then. I'll leave in a couple of days to meet them. But once I leave, I won't be able to just wander back in without making Garnet suspicious. I'll hold the men at Parson's Pass. We can't move without knowing if you're ready or not, so you'll have to come tell us."

Jake didn't like the idea of leaving the ranch even for the four days it would take to get to Parson's Pass and back, but there was no other way. The women would just have to do what they'd been doing anyway and stay inside the house.

"This is the one and only meeting we can have," he said. "It's too risky; someone might see us together. From now on you don't know me."

Ben yawned. "Never saw you before in my life, feller," he said as he walked away.

10

"Who's that?" McLain asked suspiciously, looking at the new gunhand.

"Says his name's Tanner."

"Where's he from?"

"He didn't say, and I didn't ask." Garnet moved a step away from McLain; the man stank of sour whiskey.

McLain's eyes were even redder than usual, the pupils contracted to tiny points. "Get rid of him. I don't want any strangers around here. He might be one of Sarratt's spies."

"Don't be so goddamn stupid," Garnet snapped, abruptly out of patience. "We killed the little bastards, remember? I put lead in both of them."

Once McLain would have turned on him like a rabid wolf for talking back, but now he only wagged his head. "We never found their bodies. We looked, but we didn't find them."

"They're dead, I'm telling you! Shot up the way they were, no food or water, no way of getting to a doctor, there's no way they could have lived. You're worrying about damn ghosts and it's spooking the men."

McLain peered at him with owlish concern. "If they died, why didn't we ever see any buzzards? The buzzards would've found 'em even if we couldn't."

"They're *dead*," Garnet hissed. "It was twenty years ago. You think they wouldn't have been back long before this if they'd been alive?"

There was no logic that could penetrate McLain's feverish certainty. "They waited until I got married. Don't you see? They want to kill my wife, the way I killed theirs."

"You didn't kill their wives, you killed their mama." Garnet thought he would explode with frustration. The idiot couldn't even think straight!

"But they can't kill my mama, so they're going after my wife!" McLain shook his head at Garnet's lack of understanding. "They're doing it because she's mine, see? But they won't get *me;* I'm keeping a lookout for them, every night, waiting. The bastards are gonna try sneaking up on me, but they'll be the ones surprised because I'm waiting for them."

"Jesus." Garnet looked at the man and shook his head, seeing the futility of arguing. He'd worked for McLain all these years because the Major had been even dirtier and sneakier and more brutal than he was himself, but now all he saw was a loony, stinking old man. McLain's deterioration had happened quick, but Garnet felt neither sympathy nor loyalty for him. While McLain had been strong, Garnet had run with him. Now that he was weak, Garnet planned to destroy him with no more compunction than he would squash an insect.

"Why don't you go back in the house and let me worry about the men," he told McLain. "I'm the foreman, ain't I?"

McLain gave a hollow chuckle. "Yeah, but I'm the boss and don't you forget it." He peered at Garnet with rheumy eyes. "You think I'm crazy, but you should be watching for them, too. They're after you just the same as they are me. You're the one shot their daddy."

Nodding at the indisputable truth of what he'd just said, McLain shambled back toward the house. He was tired, so tired from all the nights of keeping watch, but every time he slept he saw that damn little bastard coming at him with that knife. He didn't dare even lie down in his bed anymore, but sat up in a straight chair so that if he nodded off he'd fall and wake himself up. He didn't get much sleep that way, but neither did he dream.

Disgusted, Garnet turned his back on McLain's retreating figure. "Hey, Tanner!"

Ben walked up. "Yeah?"

"The old man's got a bee in his bonnet about you. Stay out of his sight."

"Sure." Ben started to walk off.

"Wait a minute."

Ben stopped and again said, "Yeah?"

"You done any work with that gun?"

"What kind of work?"

"Don't play dumb with me. You know what kind of work. You ever killed anybody for pay?"

Ben took a drag off his cigarette. "I reckon I've faced a few for my own reasons, but not for nobody else."

"You willing to hire out?"

"Depends."

"On what? How much money?"

"Nope. On who'll be on the other end of my barrel. There's some men it just don't pay to rile."

"You yeller?" Garnet sneered, hoping to goad him.

"Nope. Just careful. Are you just making conversation or have you got somebody in mind?"

Rather than answer directly, Garnet said, "What do you think of Roper?"

Ben bared his teeth around the cigarette. "Like I said, some men it don't pay to rile."

"You don't think you could take him?"

"Let's just say I'm not sure enough of it to risk my life on a fight that ain't mine." Ben walked off, careful to keep his cold rage from showing on his face. The son of a bitch wanted him to kill his own brother! But why? He didn't dare let himself be seen talking to Jake, to maybe find out a reason. All he could do was worry and feel his anger grow. If Garnet kept asking, sooner or later he'd find somebody willing to go up against Jake. Likely as not, it would be a back-shooter, and that worried Ben.

Twenty years they'd waited, and now the waiting crawled on his skin like ants. For the first time in twenty years he was *home*, standing on Sarratt ground, looking at the house where he'd been born and where his parents had been murdered. By God, nothing was going to stop them now, not Garnet or anybody else on this ranch, not even the woman inside that house who ultimately held the ownership of the kingdom in her hands. She would marry Jake because they wouldn't allow her any other course of action.

Ben wondered what she was like. He hadn't even asked Jake her name. He didn't think much of her, though, marrying a man like McLain. He'd watched the house as much as he could without being obvious, but he hadn't seen any woman who could possibly have been her. Three Mexican women, two middle-aged and one young, had come and gone from the house; they were obviously servants. Another young Mexican woman who apparently slept out back of the bunkhouse had hung around all morning eyeing him like a buzzard waiting for a steer to die. He'd heard her name was Angelina and she was lushly beautiful, but Ben was too edgy to be interested in the sex she was clearly offering him.

In fact, there was no point in hanging around. He'd made contact with Jake, satisfied himself that his brother was all right, and they'd planned where and when to meet. He might as well saddle up and ride out, give himself a little extra time to intercept Lonny and make certain their men didn't blunder too close to the ranch and alert McLain. Just as soon as he managed to get word to Jake that Garnet was looking to hire someone to gun him down, he'd leave.

He walked around after supper, just wandering and smoking like he had the night before. Jake was nowhere in sight, but he hadn't expected him to be. He just waited, put out his cigarette, and wandered some more. When he paused under a big cottonwood tree, Jake murmured, "Here I am."

The shadows under the tree hid them from view, especially since Jake was squatting with his back to the trunk. It was another moonless night and some clouds had drifted in to blot out the stars, making the night dark enough. Ben leaned back against the trunk, too, lifting one leg to plant his boot against the wood. "Garnet tried to hire me to kill you," he said, making certain his voice was too low to carry.

Jake grunted. "I've been watching my back since the day I got here."

"Why is he after you?"

"He's got a bad itch for the little sister and I won't let him scratch it."

Ben grunted. He couldn't see getting that worked up over one particular woman, but he had seen it happen to too many men for him to be surprised.

"I guess I'll take myself on out of here tomorrow, then. We'll wait for you."

"I'll be there."

"Keep watching your back."

"Yeah."

Ben rode out early next morning, without saying anything to anybody. He hadn't done any work to speak of, so he didn't ask for any pay. He just saddled up and left.

Jake didn't watch his brother ride out or say anything when Ben's departure was commented on later. In two days he planned to follow him. Before he left, however, he had to see Victoria and tell her to stay in the house and make certain Emma and Celia did, too. But how the hell was he going to talk to her when she hadn't poked her nose outside in days?

He saw Emma the next day, late in the afternoon when she had stepped into the courtyard for a moment. He beckoned to her and she walked to the gate.

"How's Victoria?" he asked abruptly.

"Tired." Emma's face showed signs of strain, too.

"Why haven't any of you been outside?"

"It's safer inside." She gave him a wry smile, one that quickly faded. "You haven't found whoever shot at Victoria?"

"No. There's no sign. Is that why she's staying inside?"

"That, and to watch Celia."

"Why does Celia need watching? Any more than usual, that is."

Emma's eyes were black as she looked up at him. "The Major tried to get her alone in the barn." Once she would have been mortified at having to say such a thing to a man, but they had all changed in the short while they had been in the territory.

Jake cursed under his breath and didn't apologize. "I'm leaving in the morning," he said. "All of you stay in the house, away from Garnet—"

"Hey, Roper!"

Jake looked around to see Garnet walking toward them, looking suspicious. He nodded to Emma and walked away, leaving her biting her lip.

When Jake joined him Garnet jerked his head toward Emma, who was returning to the house. "Don't tell me you're gettin' sweet on *her!* But I guess she'd be the most grateful of the bunch, wouldn't she?"

Jake kept his face expressionless and didn't answer.

When there was no response, Garnet scowled. "What're you doing up here at the house?"

"Why're you asking?"

Dull red colored Garnet's face. "Because I'm the goddamn foreman, that's why, and everything on this ranch is my business!"

"Do tell." Jake walked away, his senses attuned to the man behind him, his skin crawling as he waited for the slightest sign that Garnet was reaching for leather. He was tense, ready to throw himself to the side and come up with his own hand filled with iron, but Garnet didn't move.

Emma kept her torment to herself all night. He was leaving. How on earth was she supposed to tell Victoria? It would break her heart, but she'd have to be told so she would know that they no longer had Jake's protection.

She was so angry on Victoria's behalf that she couldn't sleep and lay awake for hours. How *could* he leave after the things he'd said to Victoria, and the way he'd kissed her? Emma had instinctively trusted him and now she felt doubly betrayed, but knew that Victoria would feel even worse because she loved him.

Still, she couldn't stop herself from hoping that she had misunderstood him somehow, that his words had meant something else. That had to be it. She consoled herself with that thought and was finally exhausted enough to sleep.

Emma woke early and dressed without paying attention to what she was putting on. She would go down to the bunkhouse and ask Jake exactly what he'd meant. She hurried out of the house, not letting herself think how improper it was for her to go alone to the bunkhouse. But the hands always began work with the dawn and she didn't think anyone would still be abed.

The early morning air was cold, but warming rapidly as the sun came over the horizon. Emma hugged her arms to herself and increased her pace. When she reached the bunkhouse she knocked on the closed door, but couldn't hear any noise from inside. She knocked again just to be safe, then eased the door open. The big, dreary, low-ceilinged room was empty, though the floor and every surface was covered with the paraphernalia of the working cowhand. She turned, uncertain of what to do next, and walked swiftly to the stable in the hope that someone would still be about.

She was lucky. She found a lone Mexican, whose name she didn't know, idly pitching hay into an empty stall. She prayed that he spoke English.

"Do you know where Roper is?" she asked.

The man looked up, his round brown face blank.

"Roper?" she asked again. "Have you seen him?"

"*Sí,*" the man said.

"Do you know where he is?"

"He left, señorita. Early."

"Did he say where he was going? When he'd be back?"

The Mexican shook his head. "He quit, señorita. He left and took his gear with him."

Emma swallowed, feeling sick. It was true, then. "Thank you," she said, and walked back to the house.

Victoria, too, was an early riser. Knowing there was nothing to be gained by putting it off, Emma went directly to her cousin's room and knocked. Victoria opened the door with an anxious look as she shoved her last hairpin into place.

"What's wrong?" She knew something had to be wrong, or Emma would have waited for her to appear downstairs. "Has something happened to Celia?"

"No." Emma stepped inside the room and put her hands over

Victoria's, holding them and forcing her to stand still. "Jake has left."

The words were simple enough, but they didn't make sense. Victoria frowned, wondering what Emma was trying to tell her. "Has he found out who shot at us the other day?"

"No." Emma closed her eyes briefly. "Victoria, he's gone. He packed his gear and left. One of the Mexicans said he quit and rode out this morning."

It was like an invisible punch to the chest. Victoria stared at Emma and listened to her own heart laboring to beat. Her face was white. "He . . . *left?*"

"Yes."

Odd, how the very air felt dead, how it sounded dead, muffling the words.

Emma put an arm around her to brace her and somehow she found herself sitting down.

"I know we haven't left the house much lately, but now we'll have to be doubly careful," Emma said, trying to turn her mind to the most pressing matters. "None of us should dare set foot outside."

"No, of course not," Victoria murmured. "Not with Garnet . . ."

Not with Garnet uncontrolled, now. Only Jake had kept him in line. But Jake was gone.

Gone!

The light had gone out of the sunny morning. Victoria sat there for a long time, helpless to do anything more than absorb the combined battering of grief and betrayal, the emptiness of knowing herself not only unloved but unimportant to the point that he hadn't even told her he was leaving. He had meant everything to her, and she had been nothing to him.

He had said, "Trust me," and she had. She had remained and had endangered both Celia and Emma with her foolishness. They would have to pay the price and live like caged animals, just to survive.

It was all the more painful because he was the only man she had ever loved. The war had interrupted what would have been her courting years in Augusta, so she had never even had a chance to fall in love before. But she also knew that her reserve was so strong that it was likely those young men would never have gotten past that inner wall to the passion inside, as Jake had. She had risked everything for him, both socially and emotionally, and he had ridden away as easily as if she had been a whore like Angelina.

Emma had left her alone to deal with her agony in private, for which Victoria was pathetically grateful. What was pride? It couldn't put food on the table or clothes on her back; it couldn't protect the people she loved. Yet she clung to it as her last defense. No matter what it cost her, when she went downstairs she would show no hint of her agony on her face.

Perhaps sometime in the future she would take out her pain and examine it, but perhaps not. For now she had to deal with their survival because Jake's departure had endangered them all. They could remain within the protection of the house, but their safety even then was dubious. For the first time she regretted the Major's precipitous decline, for at least he might have made Garnet wary of breaching the sanctuary of the house.

She had seen the hate in Garnet's eyes when he looked at her, and the lust when he'd looked at Celia. There was nothing now to stop him from taking her sister; he would shoot Victoria down without compunction, should she try to stop him. She knew she would have to try, as would Emma. They would both fight like tigers for those they loved.

They would have to protect themselves until they could leave. And that would have to be soon. She quailed inside at the thought of venturing into the territory alone, but the alternative was unbearable. They would have to start planning immediately.

At last she stood and took a deep breath. Sitting in her room wouldn't bring him back. She looked at herself in the mirror and saw a slim young woman with a somber face, but she satisfied herself that she didn't look as if she were going into a decline. With her back straight and her chin up, she went downstairs.

It was almost lunchtime. She hadn't realized how long she had been sitting dazed in her room. When Lola served the meal, Victoria forced herself to eat. Personal loss didn't break the heart so much as affect the stomach, she realized, but heartache sounded much more romantic than stomachache.

There were only the three of them at the table, the Major having failed to return to the house. He had become so erratic that no one was surprised, or concerned. When they had finished eating, Victoria folded her napkin and looked at Emma. "We'll have to leave."

Emma nodded. "As soon as possible."

"Where will we go?" Celia's face was pinched. It said a lot that she didn't ask why or when, but only where.

"We'll have to go to Santa Fe so we can make arrangements to travel home. And there are soldiers there, so we'll have protection from them in case . . . in case we're followed."

Practical Emma began listing the things they would need. "We'll have to have horses and food, blankets, extra clothing."

"Guns and ammunition," Victoria said, grimly determined not to be caught helpless. She had learned a hard lesson in depending entirely on someone else for protection.

"How will we get the horses?"

"We'll have to leave at night, as quietly as we can."

"Tonight?"

"We'll try."

They spent the rest of the day secretly packing those few sturdy items of clothing they would take with them. Celia discarded her pretty new gowns without a qualm, taking her cue from Victoria and Emma. There was too much to do to fret about dresses.

Emma placed herself in charge of rounding up the cooking utensils and food they would take along. They would need only one coffeepot and one skillet, which she managed to filch from the kitchen. She made quick periodic raids, each time taking some small item such as coffee, sugar, flour, onions, tortillas, potatoes, beans, a sharp knife, three spoons.

Victoria slipped into the library intending to get the Major's guns, but stopped abruptly when she saw him sitting at the desk. He looked up, his eyes so bloodshot they reminded her of the pictures she had seen in church of Satan's eyes. He had made an attempt at shaving that morning, at least, but had missed several patches. Still, he got to his feet and said heartily, "Did you want a book, my dear?" in a ghastly echo of his former pompous manner.

"Yes, I thought I'd read for a while this afternoon," she said. She controlled her disappointment.

"Take what you like." He waved his hand. "Didn't think there was much here that would interest a lady, though."

She pretended an interest in the few books that lined the shelves, but she didn't even see the titles.

Behind her, McLain began to chuckle. Victoria darted a look at him and found him staring at her with gleeful malice. "Yep, you're a real lady. I got what I paid for. You're so starched and proper I'll bet even your drawers are stiff."

Victoria whirled and started for the door, but McLain kept laughing. "But them stiff drawers won't do you no good when Sarratt gets his hands on you. You thought you were too good for me, didn't you, you little bitch?" His breathing quickened as mirth faded and his malicious resentment came to the fore. "You didn't want me humpin' you, but what you want won't make a damn to Sarratt, he'll just shove it in no matter how hard you fight. But it ain't ladylike to fight, is it? No, you'd just poker up and lie there as stiff as a dead person . . . just like a woman who'd been shot in the head. . . ."

She bolted, closing the door on the vile stream of words that continued even without an audience to hear them. Her heart pounding, she ran up the stairs to her room. He was mad! But even knowing that didn't prevent the chill of fear that he was right. They had never found the bodies. Someone had shot at her. It was possible that one of the Sarratt boys had survived and returned twenty years later.

It took her a minute before she calmed enough to realize that it didn't matter. She would be leaving soon, with Emma and Celia, so it didn't matter if McLain was right. He would be the only one here.

She needed those guns, but she didn't get them that night. McLain sat in the room all night talking to himself and occasionally laughing, the bright lamps keeping the knife-wielding shadows away.

The next day Garnet came to the house and smiled like a wolf when he saw her. "How's that pretty sister of yours?" he asked, smirking because he knew he held the upper hand now.

Victoria looked through him and walked away without answering, but she was terrified.

She didn't have an opportunity to get the guns that day, either.

Before they went to bed, Emma hissed, "Maybe we should just forget about the guns and leave."

"We can't. You know what it's like out there."

The two young women stared at each other, at the stark mask of desperation and fear each wore. The task of getting to Santa Fe by themselves seemed almost impossible, yet they were driven to try it. Without any means of self-protection, it would almost certainly be suicide.

She couldn't get the guns on the third day, either.

On the fourth day a hot wind began blowing from the southwest, off the desert, eating at everyone. The men quarreled and three fights broke out, Lola and Carmita snapped at each other, Celia hid all day long, and the red stallion, Rubio, killed the Mexican Emma had spoken to the day Jake left.

The unfortunate man had become careless while putting the stallion back in his stall after laying down fresh hay. He turned his back just for a moment and the big animal attacked with his lethal iron-shod hooves, turning on the man with burning hate shining in his eyes. He reared again and again, the sharp metal cutting into the soft, twitching body, a thousand pounds of hate unleashed in destruction. The Mexican was unrecognizable when the stallion finally calmed enough for the other men to get a couple of ropes on him and lead him from the stall so they could get to the victim.

McLain snorted when he was told. "Damn stupid fool, he shoulda been more careful," he grunted.

But on the fourth day Victoria got the guns. Because she didn't know if they'd be able to leave that night, she didn't want the absence of their guns to be noticed. She took only one rifle, because McLain kept them lined up in the racks right behind him; one might not be noticed but three definitely would. To match the ammunition, she took one of the bullets out of the rifle and measured it against others until she found the right ones. She then hurriedly shoved the sack of ammunition into her pocket.

To her dismay she could find only one pistol. It didn't seem as large as the one Jake had given her the day someone had shot at her. As soon as the thought of Jake entered her mind she pushed it out, because she had found that was the only way she could survive. She repeated her search for matching ammunition and hurriedly left the room with the two weapons clutched in her arms, almost panicked lest someone should come in and catch her.

But they couldn't leave that night. Perhaps because of the wind, that hot, irritating wind, or perhaps because they were unsettled by Rubio's attack on the Mexican, several of the men roamed about restlessly all night. Victoria and Emma sat up in their darkened rooms until dawn, but always there seemed to be a small amount of activity around the barn and stable. There was no way they could leave without someone seeing them.

Late in the afternoon on the fifth day a cowhand rode in hard and fast, pulling his horse up so sharply that dirt and rocks were thrown in a cloud behind him. "Riders," he gasped, sliding from the saddle. "A damn big bunch of 'em, coming this way from Parson's Pass."

McLain went white. "Sarratt," he said in a hoarse voice, and ran for the house.

Garnet swore sharply. "You goddamn stupid fool!" he yelled at the fleeing man, but he didn't waste any more time on the Major. He turned back to the rider. "How many?"

"I don' know, boss. Twenty or thirty, at least." The rider didn't tell Garnet that he could neither read nor count, but merely used numbers he'd heard other cowhands use when referring to a large group. There were, in fact, sixty-three men heading toward the ranch.

Garnet thought about it. He doubted that the encroaching men were after the cattle; rustlers worked in smaller groups. But a force of twenty or thirty men crossing someone else's range wasn't exactly an act of friendship. On the other hand, he had enough men to handle a group that size. He didn't think for a minute that they might just be passing through.

But he didn't want to gather his men and ride out to meet them. For one thing, they might see him before he saw them. For another, the ranch buildings offered protection. Let them come to him. After all, they didn't know they'd been spotted. He had the advantage right where he was.

McLain burst into the library and jerked the rifles down from the rack, and made certain all of them were loaded. He didn't notice that one of them was missing. Muttering to himself, he carried them all up to his room.

He met Victoria on the stairs and laughed when he saw her. "He's coming, Sarratt's coming," he chortled. "A rider spotted him. Now you'll find out what it's like, you high-nosed bitch, and he'll make you wish you hadn't looked down on me like I was dirt." He brushed on past her and slammed into his bedroom.

Victoria hurried to the front door. Surely he was simply raving again. But outside she saw men hurrying about and her stomach clenched. "What's happening?" she called out to one man.

"Riders comin', ma'am." He pointed toward the south, toward Santa Fe. "From that way."

She withdrew and tried to reassure herself that just because riders were coming didn't mean any of those riders was a Sarratt. But against her will McLain had infected her with his terror.

She ran up the stairs and found Emma in her room. "We have to leave," she said. "Now, right now. Riders are coming. This might be our last chance."

Emma jumped up and got the pilfered foodstuffs from their hiding place under her bed. Victoria went along to Celia's room, hoping wildly that the girl was there instead of in some hiding place as she had been the day before. Her prayers were answered when she found her sister at her window, where she'd been standing watching the activity outside. "Why is everyone in such a hurry?" she asked.

"Riders are coming," Victoria said in a low voice. "We're leaving. Right now. Are you ready?"

Celia nodded, put an old hat on her head, tied a shawl around her shoulders, and fetched her own small bundle of things from beneath the bed.

Just in the short time that had passed since the rider had come in, dusk had fallen. The women made their way to the barn where their horses were stabled. Victoria carried the rifle, its barrel pointing downward and hidden within the folds of her skirt. The pistol was in Emma's pocket. Men were still moving around, but none of them seemed to notice the three women who walked purposefully across the grounds.

If anyone tried to stop them now, Victoria decided, she would shoot.

They saddled their horses. Sophie nickered eagerly at the weight of the saddle; she hadn't been out in days. Emma's gelding was similarly eager and even Celia's calm Gypsy danced a bit in anticipation.

They mounted while still in the barn, then spurred their horses forward, ducking their heads to clear the door. As soon as they were outside, Victoria wheeled Sophie to the left and plunged into the darkness, closely followed by the other two.

"Who's that?" someone shouted.

Quinzy, who had sharp eyesight, said in disbelief, "It's the women."

Garnet cursed, then said, "Let 'em go. Hell, they'll just get lost. We can find them later, when we've taken care of these bastards."

Victoria reined in to a walk as soon as they were away from the immediate vicinity of the ranch buildings, both because she couldn't see well in the dark and because she needed to think. If the riders were coming from the south, she didn't dare go in that direction or she'd ride straight into them. But Santa Fe, their ultimate destination, lay to the south. To the east and north, she knew, were the Comanche. To the west lay hard, unforgiving land. But they would have to go west, at least far enough for it to be safe to turn south later.

The Mexican scout, Luis, said in a soft voice, "They have seen us."

Jake swore softly and Ben spit. "Then we ride," Jake said. "Now. But we take it slow. Everybody wrap their bits and spurs, I don't want any jingling to give us away. When we get closer, we'll tie rags over the horses' hooves."

He looked up at the stars, then swung into his saddle. A savage anticipation welled in him. Tonight. It would be over tonight. McLain would be dead, and Victoria would be his.

11

The darkness and the strangeness of the land forced the women to keep to a walk when every instinct demanded that they hurry. If there was to be a moon it had not yet risen, and the hot, unsettling wind sent clouds scudding overhead and blocking out most of the starlight. The horses, sensing the nervousness of their riders, were skittish. It took all of Victoria's skill to keep Sophie under control and at the same time try to pick their way through the darkness. Though they could discern large obstacles well enough, the night obscured those small holes and ruts in the earth that could cause a horse to fall, maybe break a leg or even kill its rider.

Every sound seemed alien, magnified on the night air. Celia stifled a shriek when a hunting owl swooped overhead, then said, "I'm sorry, I'm sorry," so pitifully that tears stung Victoria's eyes.

She had never before sworn in her life, but she was so enraged at what this had done to Celia that the thought rang in her mind: "Goddamn them, goddamn them all!" She didn't mean it as a blasphemy but as a curse. All of them—McLain, Garnet, all of the gunmen at the ranch who had looked at them as if they were nothing but sides of beef, even Jake, for he had left them to face this on their own—she cursed all of them.

Celia would never be the same again. Her lighthearted innocence was gone and could not be recovered. When she looked at men now it wasn't with childlike faith that they would protect her; it was with full knowledge that there was evil in the world and the very ones she had always thought were her champions were instead those who would harm her.

Celia should have, in a few years, fallen in love with a strong, gentle man, married him, raised a family with him, and died at a very old age having known nothing but devotion from her husband. It was a dream of perfection which Victoria realized few women achieved, but it was the life Celia should have had. It wouldn't happen now. She had seen the ugliness the human spirit was capable of, and it had changed her.

War hadn't touched her, but the bitter, violent atmosphere of the West and Kingdom Valley had.

Sophie stumbled and quickly recovered herself. Victoria leaned forward to pat the satiny neck and murmur encouragement.

"Should we go on or wait until daylight?" Emma asked.

They couldn't have gone far, having been restrained to a walk most of the time, but Victoria felt as if they were a million miles from civilization. She started to say she thought it would be all right to wait until morning when the sharp retort of gunfire rolled through the night air.

It wasn't just one shot. It was a multitude of them, the sharp cracks of pistols, the deeper thunder of rifles, and it went on and on.

They all three looked back in the direction of the ranch, though there was nothing to see.

Emma spoke first. "It sounds like a war."

"It is. The ranch is under attack."

"But *who?*"

Victoria could barely speak, her throat was so tight. "The Major said it was Sarratt."

"It can't be. Why would someone wait twenty years for revenge?" Emma tried to sound soothing, but her own throat was tightening.

"Because the Major waited that long to get married," she answered, and swung Sophie's head around. She was so terribly frightened, but she had to stay in control. If it was Sarratt, would he bother coming after them? He wouldn't even know where they'd gone unless some of the men talked, if anyone was left alive to talk.

The Major had infected her with his maggot of fear; she could no longer convince herself that it was all just in his mind.

"We'll have to keep going," she said. "For as long as we can. The farther we are from the ranch come morning, the safer we'll be."

They didn't hit the ranch like a bunch of cowboys hoorahing a town, riding in fast and loud, shooting up the place. They left their horses back a piece and went in silently, on foot. Since it was going to be close fighting they all tied their handkerchiefs around their left arm for identification, so they wouldn't start shooting each other. It would identify them to McLain's men, too, but that couldn't be helped.

It started when one of the ranch hands stepped around the end of the barn and came face to face with one of the Sarratt men. The ranchhand reached for his gun and the Sarratt man's big Sharps rifle slug took most of the man's chest with it when it exited his back.

Jake and Ben fought their way side by side toward the house. It was hard to tell, but Jake didn't think any shots were being fired at them from inside the house and that gave him hope that the women weren't in immediate danger. His attention was centered on McLain, on finding him and killing him. It had to be; he couldn't afford to worry about Victoria until he'd taken care of McLain.

Someone shot at them with a rifle from the barn loft, the bullet zinging so close to Jake's head that he felt the heat from it and dived to the side. He looked around, saw Luis, and yelled, "Get that bastard in the loft!"

Luis grinned, his white teeth visible in the dark, and started his snaking run toward the barn.

All around them men were dead, wounded, or dying, and still the gunfire split the night from all directions.

"Where's Garnet?" Ben muttered.

"In a hole somewhere. He won't take any risks."

Wendell Wallace rose up from behind the hitching post where he'd been hugging the ground and drew a bead on Jake. Ben fired and Wendell fell back, his finger tightening convulsively on the trigger and firing a shot uselessly into the air.

Jake cautiously approached him, his .44 ready. When he reached Wendell, he saw that the man was breathing laboriously, with a frothing black liquid bubbling out of his chest.

Wendell looked at him and said, "Roper! Jesus Christ, why'd you do that?"

"My last name isn't Roper. It's Sarratt."

Wendell blinked, trying to focus on Jake's face. "Jesus Christ," he said again. "I thought we'd kilt you."

"No, but we've killed you. You're lung-shot, Wendell."

Wendell tried to take a deep breath, and the sound rattled in his throat. "Guess so." His voice was so weak it was almost soundless. "I'll be damned. Reckon I'm gonna die, then."

"Yep."

"Better'n gut-shot, anyways," he said, and his eyes became fixed in death.

Ben looked down at him. "That was Wendell Wallace?"

"Yeah."

"I remember him. He taught me how to whittle. Then he threw in with McLain and tried to kill us."

"Yeah," Jake said again.

They rushed the front door together, entering in a low crouch, hammers cocked and their fingers on the triggers. Nothing happened, no one moved. The lamps still burned serenely.

Ben's face was rigid. It was the first time he'd been inside his home in twenty years. He looked at the tiled floor where his mother had died.

They methodically searched the first floor, and found Carmita, Juana, and Lola huddled together in the kitchen. Carmita gasped when she saw Jake.

He didn't have time for explanations or reassurances. "Where's McLain?"

Carmita's eyes were huge. "I don't know, señor." She swallowed. "He was in the library."

They stood one on each side of the library door, and Jake

tried the knob. It was locked. He motioned to Ben, then stepped back, raised his foot, and kicked in the door. Ben went in first, diving through, rolling and coming up, but nothing else in the room moved. It was empty.

"Goddamn it, where is he?" Ben asked, frustrated.

"Like Garnet, looking for a hole." Abruptly Jake looked up and his entire face tightened. What if McLain was upstairs, using the women as cover?

He ran up the stairs with Ben right behind. He took the rooms on the right, Ben checked the ones on the left. They were all empty.

Damn him, what had he done with the women? Certain now that McLain had them, he swore that he would carve the bastard up alive if he'd even so much as bruised Victoria.

"Check the courtyard." It was the last place he could think of for McLain to hide without having to leave the shelter of the house and face the firestorm of bullets outside.

Ben nodded. "I'll go around the house and come in the back gate."

Jake waited in the kitchen to give Ben time to work his way around. The three servants were still crouched on the floor, huddled together for comfort. "What is happening, Señor Jake?" Carmita asked.

"We're taking back our ranch," he replied without looking at her, pistol in his hand as he eased the door open. "My brother and I."

Lola raised her head, her face strained. "Sarratt," she whispered as Jake slipped out the door.

Rectangles of light from the window splashed across the courtyard, illuminating some spots, leaving darker shadows in others. Jake could just make out Ben sliding along the wall, gun in hand.

"Major?" Jake called softly.

Hearing, Ben went motionless.

"Major?"

For a long minute there was no sound and Jake took another silent step around a bench, the very bench where Victoria had sat the day after she had married McLain.

"Roper?"

The whisper came from his right, close to the rain barrel. Every nerve in Jake's body tightened.

"Yeah."

"They said you'd gone."

"I came back."

Slowly McLain stood up from behind the barrel. The light from a window fell across his face, starkly etching the physical signs of his mental deterioration. He giggled. "I told 'im, but he didn't believe me. Sarratt's back, isn't he?"

Jake stared in disgust at the ruin before him. "Yeah, McLain. I'm back."

McLain giggled again. "No, not you. Sarratt. You're back, but so's he."

"I'm Sarratt."

"No, you're Roper. You've got to find him and kill him for me. You've got to—"

Jake moved another step forward, also stepping into the light. It hit him from the side, delineating the sharp planes of his brow, jaw, and cheekbones, making dark pools of his eyes. To McLain's fevered brain his face looked like a skeleton's head, a dead man come back to haunt him.

McLain moaned, shrinking back from him, and the sound swiftly escalated into a shriek. "You're dead!" he screamed. "You came back, but you're still dead. Get away, damn you! I need a lamp! *Someone bring me a goddamn lamp!*"

Jake felt his guts twist and a bitter taste filled his mouth. The man was a raving lunatic. The moment of revenge he'd waited twenty years for had finally come, the gun was in his hand, but the target was still eluding him, snatched away by madness. He wanted McLain as he had been twenty years before, not this slobbering fool.

Without warning, McLain jerked his hand up, the pistol trembling in his grip. Frozen in bitter disappointment Jake was caught off guard, and even though his pistol was already in his hand he had a split second of recognition that he wasn't going to be in time. Then a shot boomed from behind him, followed closely by another. McLain jerked from the impact of the two bullets, rising almost on tiptoe, the pistol dropping from his hand. He stared at Jake with virulent hatred.

"Die again, you son of a bitch, this time I'll kill you and make certain you stay—" He raised his empty hand, unaware that the pistol no longer filled it, and pantomimed the motion of firing. A look of utmost astonishment crossed his face, then it went blank and he died on his feet. He flopped, rag-doll loose, across the rain barrel.

Jake whirled, his eyes blazing, to confront whoever had snatched away his vengeance, whoever it was who had saved his life.

Juana stood with one of the Major's pistols held at arm's length, both of her hands clasped around the butt. Her face was expressionless as she stared at McLain's body. Then her lips twisted; she spat at the dead man and whispered, "Good."

Ben walked up, and he and Jake stood shoulder to shoulder looking at the dead man. Jake was aware of an absurd sense of regret. It was over, the driving force that had dominated their lives for twenty years, but instead of the wrenching battle he had needed and anticipated, he had faced a man diminished by insanity, and the final act of vengeance had been Juana's. In a way McLain had still won, for even though he lay dead at their feet he had robbed them of satisfaction by being less than he had been.

It left a hard core of bitterness, this unexpected defeat.

There was still gunfire outside the walls, but it was more sporadic now. It reminded Jake that it wasn't finished, not until Garnet's body lay at their feet, too.

And where in the hell was Victoria?

He and Ben stepped back into the house. Juana followed them, her face as blank as a sleepwalker's although silent tears tracked down her face. *"Dios,"* she murmured. *"Dios."*

From the way she was acting, Jake guessed at what McLain had put Juana through. He figured her need for vengeance might have been as great as his own and tried not to begrudge her. He bent down and lifted Carmita and Lola to their feet, assuring him that they wouldn't be hurt. "Where is the señora?" he asked. "And her sister and cousin?"

Carmita shook her head, looking frightened. "I don't know. They aren't upstairs?"

"No."

Carmita clasped her hands. "*Madre de Dios!* If they were out-side—"

She didn't have to finish the sentence. He turned on his heel and left the house. If they'd been caught outside, stray bullets could easily have hit any or all of them. It had been a firestorm of flying lead.

It was all over now. Those of McLain's men still left alive were coming out of their various hiding places with their hands high and empty. Jake and Ben searched the area, turning bodies over with their boots, kicking pistols away from outstretched hands. There was no sign of Garnet, or of the three women.

A cold sensation was freezing Jake's insides as he looked around at the vast, dark land. Had Garnet taken them? If he had, Jake knew he would never see Victoria alive again, because she wouldn't sit meekly while Garnet raped her sister. She would fight him and he'd put a bullet in her brain without a second thought. Despair congealed in a hard knot in his stomach at the thought.

He turned back to the small group of men huddled together and picked one out. He thumbed back the hammer, knowing everyone heard the small click, and pointed it at the man's head. "You, Shandy. Where's Garnet?"

Sweat began pouring down the man's face, despite the chilly night. "I seen him ride out, Roper. I swear to God I did."

"When?"

" 'Bout the time you went in the house. Him and a coupla others."

"Which direction?"

Shandy lifted a shaking hand and pointed east.

"Did he have the women with him?"

By now Shandy was shaking so hard his teeth were clattering together. "No, I swear he didn't."

Jake's finger tightened imperceptibly on the trigger. "I think you're lying to me, Shandy. The women aren't here. Garnet had to take them."

Shandy began wagging his head back and forth. "I swear, I swear," he babbled.

"He ain't lyin', Roper," someone else in the group said quickly. "I seen the women leave before the shootin' ever started. They lit out from the barn, ridin' west, in the opposite direction from Garnet."

Jake turned to Luis. "Get me a lantern." He lowered the hammer back into position, but looked Shandy right in the eye. "If you're lying to me, you won't see sunrise."

He, Ben, and Luis walked to the barn. Sophie was gone, as well as Emma's and Celia's mounts. The men used the lantern to examine the dirt floor of the barn, but too many people had been through it in the last half hour for him to be able to tell anything for certain. They walked outside, where he picked up Sophie's track with ease. He followed it for thirty yards, reading the sign.

"Just three horses," Ben said.

"Carrying light weights," Luis added.

Jake straightened, an incredible rage rushing in to displace despair. "The goddamn little fool, I told her to stay in the house." Now she had taken Emma and Celia out there, when none of them had the slightest idea how to survive or even find their way. Worse, Garnet was out there, too. Though he had headed in the opposite direction, he could have seen the women leave and veered around once he was safely away.

Ben rubbed a weary hand over his face. "We can't track them in the dark, Jake."

"I know." Even if he followed them with a lantern to pick out the tracks, a light would be visible for a long way at night. Not knowing who he was, the women would evade him; meanwhile Garnet could pick out his location. Every muscle in Jake was drawn tight, but there was nothing he could do. They'd have to wait until dawn before starting the search, even though that would give Garnet more time, too.

He was furious and his temper grew worse the longer he thought about it. If she had done what he'd told her, they would be safe right now instead of wandering alone in the wilderness. He only hoped she'd have sense enough to find shelter for the night.

"We've still got a lot of work to do," Ben said, interrupting his dark thoughts. "Like you said, this was only about a third of McLain's men. We might have some fighting still ahead of us, especially if Garnet joins up with them."

Jake grunted. "I don't look for him to do that. Garnet won't fight if he thinks it's anywhere close to an even match, and we pretty much evened it up tonight. But, yeah, some of the other gunnies might make a stand."

Ben put a hand on Jake's shoulder. "We'll find them tomorrow," he said, but he, too, wondered. A lot could happen to three women alone on the land.

Victoria was forced to call a halt for the night. Though her instincts told her to keep going, Celia was unused to riding very far even at a walk. Long before midnight the girl was in a great deal of pain, though she didn't whine about it. It wasn't until they stopped to relieve themselves that Victoria realized what Celia had been enduring, because she burst into tears as she slid to the ground.

"We'll have to rest," Emma said. "She can't go any farther." She rubbed her own bottom, wincing a little. "I think I'm going to be sore, too."

Victoria looked around trying to find some sort of shelter, but there was still no moon to aid her. All she could see was the black masses where trees grew. Well, at least the trees would shield them. She put her arm around Celia's shoulders. "Can you walk just a little way, up to those trees?" she asked, pointing to the right.

Celia nodded, fighting her tears. "Yes. I'm sorry. I know we should keep riding."

"So we should, but we're all tired and so are the horses. If we don't let them rest, they won't do us any good tomorrow."

They trudged slowly up the rock-scattered hill to the treeline and found a grouping of boulders that blocked off most of the wind. Victoria and Emma unsaddled the horses and gave them water, then tied them where they could graze. When they returned, Celia had arranged their blankets and divided up three small portions of food.

Victoria sank down on a blanket and gratefully accepted the bread and cheese, which she washed down with water. Now that she was sitting she realized how tired she was. Exhaustion washed over her; she barely tasted the food, but didn't dare sleep.

Fighting off the urge to lie down, she rested the rifle across her legs. "I'll watch while you two get some sleep."

Celia stretched out, groaning, and was asleep in only a moment. Emma came over to sit beside Victoria. "Do you really think it was Sarratt?" she asked, keeping her tone low to avoid disturbing Celia. "How could it be after all these years?"

Victoria sighed. "I don't know. It was just that the Major was so sure, and he was so frightened. He sat up nights watching for them, did you know? He didn't sleep. I'd hear him all night long, sitting in there talking to himself, and sometimes he'd come in my room and tell me what they would do to me—"

She broke off and Emma swiftly hugged her. "I know I shouldn't say it, but the Major *is* mad. You know that, don't you?"

"Oh, yes, I know."

"Then why would you believe anything he said?"

"Because he is mad, not stupid." Victoria stared out at the night. "Because someone shot at me. Because I couldn't think of any other reason—"

"Don't you think the Major has made more enemies than just the Sarratts?" Emma asked with the sweet voice of reason. "It could be anyone."

Victoria couldn't prevent a low chuckle. "Does it really matter? An enemy is an enemy."

"You're right, of course. It doesn't make any difference who shot at you, the intent remains the same."

"How comforting!"

They laughed quietly together for a minute, then Emma sobered. "How long do you think it will take us to get to Santa Fe?"

"I don't know. Surely we can travel faster than before, when we rode in the wagon."

"Unless we get lost."

"We'll turn south in the morning. We'll meet up with some-one on the way, and we'll ask directions."

"Do we dare?"

Victoria touched the rifle. "I'm willing to use this."

They were silent for a while, listening to the wind in the trees. Emma said, "The Major could come after us, you know. Or send Garnet. Whatever the trouble was at the ranch tonight, it's pos-sible they handled it."

That had occurred to Victoria, and she had decided she would not take Celia and Emma back to that ranch. "I'll do whatever's necessary." It was so hard to say that she shuddered, then quickly masked her reaction by saying, "I'm becoming chilly. Why don't you try to sleep, rather than keeping me company? I'll be fine."

"Will you wake me in a couple of hours? You need to sleep, too."

"Yes, of course."

Victoria thought of a lot of things, sitting alone in the dark-ness. She wondered what had happened at the ranch, because as Emma had said, it could have been anyone. She wondered if she should contact the authorities in Santa Fe to get help, and if any-one would respond even if she did ask them.

She worried about Celia. She should never have brought her out West. Now she could only hope that her little sister would eventually forget some of the awful things and learn to trust men again.

Jake . . . Her thoughts eventually, inevitably turned to him, and she almost whimpered aloud from the pain. Why had he left without a word after all that had passed between them? She remembered the way he'd kissed her, the times she had even allowed him to fondle her breasts. Was that why he'd left, because she had demeaned herself to him by allowing him those intimacies?

Did the why really matter? He had left, and she had to face the bitter reality that he hadn't returned her feelings at all. He had wanted to bed her, nothing more.

She meant to wake Emma, she really did, but she sat for so long with her harsh thoughts, and she was so tired, that she didn't notice when her eyes drifted shut.

* * *

"Victoria, wake up. It's after dawn." Emma shook her until Victoria sat up, yawning.

"Why didn't you wake me?"

"I meant to. I fell asleep." Alarmed, Victoria scrambled to her feet. She drew a little breath of relief when she saw that everything appeared normal. Emma and Celia had managed to build a small fire, and Celia was rather competently cooking potatoes and bacon. Coffee was bubbling in the kettle.

The sun was already shining, but the morning was still crisp and cool. She sought privacy to attend to her needs, then returned to freshen her face and hands with a dampened handkerchief.

They were all inordinately hungry and devoured the simple meal. Celia vigorously rubbed her abused rear when she stood.

"Will you be able to ride?" Victoria asked, concerned. Her own muscles were twinging, so she could imagine how Celia felt.

"Yes," Celia said, then added darkly, "but I won't like it."

Victoria laughed, but Emma grabbed her arm, cutting her off as she pointed to the east and said, "Look."

Victoria squinted her eyes, then saw the riders. They were silhouetted on top of a ridge by the huge red morning sun. She couldn't tell exactly how many there were.

Cold fear seized her. She whirled and kicked dirt on the fire. "Quick, saddle the horses!"

Distances were deceiving out on the land. The riders had looked so close only because the sun had been behind them; they were at least several miles away and couldn't have seen the women. Unless smoke from the campfire had given them away. . . .

Sophie chose that morning to be frisky, dancing away as Victoria struggled to get the saddle on her back. "Stop it!" she said sharply, fighting her panic. If Sophie sensed her fear, she'd never get her saddled.

They climbed on rocks to mount. Emma jumped down from her gelding and raced toward the fire. "I am *not* leaving the frying pan behind," she said. "It's the only pan we have."

Luckily, the frying pan had cooled enough that she didn't burn her hand when she snatched it up. She ran back to the rocks, and Victoria took the pan and stored it in her saddlebag while Emma remounted.

They didn't dare turn south now; that direction would insure that the riders cross their trail. Victoria put her back to the sun and kicked Sophie into a run.

Celia hung on with grim determination and her little mare tried valiantly to maintain pace with their larger mounts. Still Victoria and Emma had to rein in their horses to permit Celia to stay with them. Victoria cast several anxious looks over her shoulder, but the riders had descended from the top of the ridge and were lost from sight. She prayed that they weren't from the ranch at all, but were merely passing through and wouldn't pay any attention to their trail.

They gained the top of a crest and Victoria reined in, turning Sophie so she could watch the direction from which they'd come.

"Why are you stopping?" Emma cried, wheeling her own mount around.

"I want to see where they are. They might not be after us."

They waited, straining their eyes for sight of the riders. It was their ears that picked it up first, the distant rumble that sounded like thunder, though the sky was clear. Victoria waited, her mouth dry.

The riders topped another ridge, and her heart almost stopped. They were much closer than she'd feared, riding hard, and straight at them.

"Dear God. *Run!*"

She tried to think, but her brain felt numb. She knew it had to be either Sarratt or Garnet. Either meant death.

Celia was riding with her jaw set, though her face was pale. Victoria held back Sophie's long strides and positioned her on one side of Celia's mount, while Emma took up the other side. Better if Celia had taken another horse from the stable, but they hadn't thought of it. Now placid but slow Gypsy might well mean the difference between them getting away or being caught.

The landscape was changing, becoming gradually more dry and barren as the trees gave way to rock and shrub. A slight breeze picked up the fine dirt and blew it in their faces, covering them with grit. Victoria looked over her shoulder again, and again the riders were closer than they'd been before. She didn't recognize any of the men, but now she could see that they had pulled up their neckerchiefs to cover their faces against the grit. Their covered faces, even at a distance, were menacing.

She tightened her reins as they plunged headlong down a slope. Celia cried out and almost came off over Gypsy's head, but at the last minute Victoria reached out and grabbed Celia's skirt, hauling her back into the saddle. They slid and plunged to the bottom, and Victoria cried, "Stop!"

They reined in the horses. Poor Gypsy was almost blown, but Emma's gelding and Sophie were still strong. Victoria jumped down. "Quickly, Celia, change horses with me!"

"I can't ride Sophie!" Celia cried, appalled, though she obediently slid to the ground.

"You'll have to. I'm a better rider, I can get more out of Gypsy than you can. You take the rifle," she said swiftly to Emma. "Give me the pistol."

Emma, too, obeyed, but her face twisted. "What are you doing?"

"We have to split up." Victoria boosted Celia into Sophie's saddle, then she scrambled atop Gypsy. "Take Celia and ride east."

"East!"

"Yes, due east, along the base of this ridge. There's more shelter that way, and perhaps they'll follow me instead of you. Sophie is a strong horse, she'll keep going a long time."

"I can't leave you!" Emma shouted.

"You have to! You have to take care of Celia!"

"Then you go with her! I'll lead them away."

Victoria gave her a stark look. "It's me they want," she said. "It isn't Garnet; I know Garnet's horse. So it has to be Sarratt or—or—someone else who hates the Major. Now, for the love of God, hurry!" Without waiting, without allowing herself to look back, she touched her heels to poor Gypsy and rode west.

She had no hope of being able to outdistance the riders indefinitely; she only hoped to give Emma and Celia a chance to escape. Perhaps, even if Sarratt caught them, he wouldn't harm them. After all, they weren't McLains.

She rode as she'd never ridden before in her life, pushing the tired horse deeper into the barren, rocky land. It wasn't desert, but there were no trees, no crystal-clear rivers, no ripe meadow grasses. The sun rose high, burning her back through the thin fabric of her shirtwaist. Her arms and legs ached.

Gypsy stumbled. Victoria agonized, yet she knew she'd have to give the horse a rest or risk it dying under her. She stopped and dismounted, and walked Gypsy for as long as she dared before giving the animal a small drink of water. When the horse stopped blowing so strenuously, Victoria remounted and started her flight again, but at a slower pace. The mare simply couldn't manage more.

Victoria's throat was dry and caked with dust, but she didn't dare drink any of the water herself; she might need it for Gypsy. A wave of dizziness swept her, but she grimly concentrated on her balance.

Looking behind again, she blinked in confusion. She could see only one rider, steadily gaining on her—or was it a mirage? Where were the others? Her heart stopped in sickening realization. Her ruse had failed; he'd sent the others after Emma and Celia, but was coming after her himself, as inexorable as the sun. This was Sarratt. She knew it was Sarratt.

She kicked Gypsy, but felt no responding increase in speed.

They were nearing a huge outcropping of bare red stone when Gypsy began staggering. Victoria looked behind again and saw that he was only a few minutes behind. Her horse wouldn't go any farther. She reined in and jumped to the ground, then ran into the rocks. Her boots slipped as she scrambled higher and higher, searching for a cave or a notch where she could hide. The pistol was heavy in her pocket. Dear God, if she had to she'd use it. He was alone; just one shot was all she'd need if she aimed carefully enough.

She risked a quick look around a rock. He was below her dismounting from his horse with a powerful grace that frightened her, yet seemed dizzyingly familiar. The lower half of his face was still hidden by the neckerchief. He lifted his head and scanned the rocks, and she jerked back out of sight.

The hot rock was scorching her hands. She stared up at the relentless sun, glowing in a sky unmarred by clouds, and wondered if this would be the last time she would see it. She was more frightened than she had ever been in her life.

"Goddamn it, stop wasting my time and come out of there." The voice was muffled by the cloth covering his mouth, but the rage in it was plain.

Evidently he didn't think he had anything to fear from her. Victoria felt as if she had enough fear for the two of them, but somehow she steadied herself. She might lose, but not without a fight.

12

She fumbled for the pistol with shaking hands and for a frozen moment stared bemused at the glint of sunlight along the steel-blue barrel. What a strangely beautiful object, this instrument of death; it was so perfectly suited to its purpose. The only chance she had was to use it.

She held her breath, listening. When she heard a slight scraping below and to her left, she used both hands to pull the hammer back. She took two quick, deep breaths to steady herself, then she eased her head around the rock.

She saw him as he changed position, climbing to another section of rock. Her heart leaped and she fired wildly at him. The bullet chipped a little section of rock close to his head, sending the splinter flying. He dived for cover among the rocks, and she couldn't see him any longer, but she knew she hadn't hit him.

He would work his way in the direction from which the shot had been fired, and this time he knew she was armed. Victoria scrambled higher, scraping her palms on the hot rocks. A lizard stared at her with beady eyes, then darted into the protection of a cool, dark crack. She wished she could crawl in after it.

Maybe, while he was climbing up, she could work her way down. If she could sneak around him and get back down to the horses, she could take both of the horses and leave him stranded.

She sprawled out on her stomach and, keeping a weather eye on the rocks below her for any movement, began squirming backward. The rocks tore her skirt and scraped even more skin off her palms, but she barely noticed.

She thought she might make it. The horses were in sight and she was beginning to let herself hope. Then she heard the slight scrape from behind, her only warning before rough hands grabbed her around the waist and jerked her upright, startling her so much that she couldn't even scream. The man gripped her arm so roughly that her hand went numb, and he easily relieved her of the pistol. Despairing, Victoria stared up at the handkerchief-covered face of the man who was determined to kill her.

"You damn little fool," he said with quiet menace, tugging the handkerchief down around his neck. "Who are you trying harder to kill—me, yourself, or your horse?"

Victoria gaped up at him. The scorching sun was beating down on her bare head, and she thought perhaps she was hallucinating. But he was still holding her wrist painfully and his green eyes glittered at her from under the black brim of his hat. She hadn't thought she'd ever see those green eyes again. . . . "Jake?" she whispered incredulously. "I didn't know it was you—I thought—I thought you were Sarratt."

His expression was shuttered as he looked down at her, and a long moment of silence stretched between them, so long that she felt a chill of apprehension. His eyes were grim and cold.

"I am," he said.

He dragged her down from the rocks. "Sit down, and don't move even an inch. I'm going to take care of the horses. If you move, you'll regret it." He spoke in a very even tone. She didn't doubt him.

She sat in the dust and watched as he unsaddled the horses, then walked both of them around for a while. The horse he'd been riding was unfamiliar to her, a detail that made her bite her lip. If he'd been riding his own horse, she would have recognized it. Would she have still run from him? If she hadn't, would it have been a mistake? He was Sarratt, he'd said, and she still didn't know what he wanted with her.

Gypsy was so tired she could barely walk. Jake—if that really was his first name—gave some of their precious water to the horses and tethered them where they could get at the few succulent plants that grew in the shade of the outcropping.

Victoria felt shattered, even more so than when Emma had told her he'd left. It was a curious difference, but then she had hurt from the loss, the betrayal of her trust. Now she was terrified that the betrayal went much deeper than that. It wasn't simply that he didn't return her regard, but that he might have used her in the broader scope of revenge. Had he simply been hoping to satisfy some of his thirst for vengeance by cuckolding the Major? What was he going to do with her now? She tried to think of what to say to him, but her mind was blank, perhaps blessedly so. All she could do was sit and watch.

Jake himself was so angry he could barely speak. Not only had she disobeyed his order to stay in the house, but she'd led the others into danger. She had run their horses into the ground and shot at him. That alone made him so angry he didn't want to approach her again until he was more in control of himself. She looked exhausted, and dazed. It was a while before he calmed down enough to walk over to her, canteen in hand. She had to be as thirsty as he was.

She didn't look up at his approach, even when he was standing right before her with his legs braced, dusty boots nudging hers. She braced herself, but nothing happened; he continued to loom silently over her, dominating her without saying a word.

Finally she broke the silence. "It was you who attacked the ranch last night, wasn't it?"

Jake opened the canteen and shoved it into her hands. "Yes. My brother and I brought our men in and took back the ranch." He paused, watching her carefully as he said, "McLain is dead."

Victoria failed to react in any way because she still felt so numb. She tipped the canteen back and drank. It was refreshing, even though the water was warm.

Jake took the canteen away and drank from it himself. He recapped it and wiped his mouth on his sleeve, watching her all the while. "I said, your husband is dead."

She didn't look at him. "I heard you."

"Don't you care?"

"I don't mourn him, but I can't—I can't be glad anyone is dead," she replied.

"Juana killed him. He'd raped her."

Victoria flinched, and wondered if she had just lied. Perhaps she *was* glad that the Major was dead. He'd been a vile man. Would any living punishment have been enough?

"Ben and I control the ranch now."

A ghost of interest stirred in her, and she lifted her head. She hadn't truly understood what he'd said before. "So your brother survived, too," she said in a blank little voice. "I'm glad." She looked at the horses, a slight frown knitting her forehead, and asked the question she really didn't want to hear the answer to. "Where are the others?"

"I sent them after Emma and Celia."

"They—" She swallowed, and tried again. "They won't hurt them, will they?"

"Not if they don't try something stupid. Like shooting."

Victoria shivered, because Emma probably would shoot.

Jake rested his boot on the rock beside her and propped his arms on his raised knee. "Why'd you change horses with Celia?"

"Gypsy couldn't keep up. I thought Celia would have a better chance of getting away if she were riding Sophie."

He didn't say anything else, just stood there watching her. She looked at the ground; she felt so bleak inside it was almost unbearable. If anything happened to Emma or Celia, she would never forgive herself—assuming, of course, that Jake didn't kill her. But if he had been going to do so, she reasoned, he would already have done it.

She raised her head again. "What are you going to do with me?"

He smiled, not a particularly pleasant smile. *Make love to you until neither of us can walk,* he thought with a savage mixture of anger and need, born out of his worry and fear for her. The violent compulsion to mate was inborn, and he wouldn't be able to relax until she was well and truly his, until he felt her safe in his arms. For now, however, he still didn't dare touch her. Instead he said aloud, "Take you back to the ranch. After the horses rest."

She was afraid to ask any more questions.

There were four of them. Emma saw that much when she cast a desperate look over her shoulder. Celia was faring badly on Sophie. The horse seemed to be taking pity on her inept rider and was striding as smoothly as silk, but without reaching for the great depths of speed her steely muscles possessed. As a result, the four riders were rapidly gaining on them. Emma recognized her choices with agonized clarity. She could stay with Celia or she could save herself, but she couldn't do both. For Emma, there was really no choice involved. She held the gelding so that it matched strides with Sophie and awkwardly wrestled the rifle around. Riding sidesaddle wasn't the best position for firing a rifle and her first shot went wide.

Ben cursed and bent low over his horse's neck, asking the animal for more speed. It was tired, but with the other horses' hindquarters in sight it surged forward. Luis, beside him, did the same. Ben went for the wildcat who was shooting at them, Luis for the girl who was barely staying in the saddle.

It wasn't that easy. The dark-haired one shot again and this time the shot came uncomfortably close. The other girl somehow clung to the saddle and the big mare she was riding increased its speed. Ben angled his horse so that he came up on the right side of the one with the rifle, effectively taking himself out of her line of fire. His horse surged rhythmically beneath him, hooves pounding, lungs blowing; he pulled even with the gelding's hindquarters and his horse stretched out even more, driven by the need to get out in front. Inch by inch he drew even with the gelding.

From the corner of his eye Ben saw Luis reach out to grab the big mare's bridle. The little blonde screamed and began tearing at his hand, and the brunette tried to swing the rifle like a club, evidently not trusting her marksmanship enough to shoot with Luis so close to the girl.

Ben leaned out of the saddle and caught her around the waist, dragging her backward off of the horse as he reined in his own mount.

Emma arched and kicked, frantically trying to loosen his grip, but all she succeeded in doing was dropping the rifle. She reached backward, clawing for his face, his hair, any part of him that she could reach. Dangling in the air as she was, anchored only by his arm around her waist, she wasn't having much success, and in desperation she began hammering her heels against his leg and the horse's ribs. The animal snorted and plunged, and she heard the man curse as they both came off the horse, landing with a thump in the dust.

Emma kept kicking and tried to roll free. The man grabbed her foot and hauled her back, and when she kicked at him again he rolled on top of her, flattening her beneath his weight. He was cursing in a continuous if breathless stream, the words puffing out against her ear. He controlled her kicking legs with his muscled thighs and caught her flailing fists, then anchored her wrists to the ground above her head.

"Leave her alone! Get *off* of her!"

Ben lifted his head and saw the little blonde flying toward him, but Luis caught her from behind and held her, locking his hands around her wrists and then crossing his arms in front of her so that her arms were folded up and she couldn't twist or jerk free. Knowing that he didn't have to worry about her, Ben was free to give all of his attention to the squirming hellcat beneath him.

Emma rebelled completely against the heavy weight holding her down, arching and twisting, tossing her head in an effort to hit him in the face. She was too terrified to think straight, but she couldn't just surrender; it went against every instinct.

The man didn't try to hit her or hurt her in any way. He just held her and let her wear herself out struggling. But it had been a while since Ben had had a woman, and the soft, definitely female body squirming beneath him caught his attention. Blood pooled in his groin, and he began to swell and harden. Instinctively, he shifted his legs so that they were lying inside hers; when she arched again the movement thrust his erection solidly against her soft mound.

Emma shivered and went still, her brown eyes enormous in her pale, dusty face. She stared up at the hard face of the man lying on top of her, shocked at what she could feel happening to his body. She had never felt a man's weight before, and now that their battle had abruptly changed to a sexual one, she was frightened into stillness.

Though she knew there were others standing just a few feet away, in a strange way she felt they were utterly alone. She smelled his sweat, and his quick, hard breathing feathered her face. She knew hers must be doing the same thing to him, in a subtle exchange of their very breath.

She noticed his eyes were hazel, his eyelashes and brows black. He moved again in a slight shift of position that brought him even more snugly against her.

From a great distance she heard Celia sobbing. Emma rolled her head to the side, and the sight of the girl locked in another man's arms shattered the strange sensuality that had enthralled her. Hectic color rushed to her face.

"Please," she said in a stifled tone. "Let me up."

Ben propped up on an elbow, still keeping her arms pinned to the dirt with his other hand. "Am I going to have to wrestle you down again?" he panted.

"No."

He got to his feet and dragged her up until she was standing. Emma held out her arms, and with a small understanding smile Luis released Celia, who flew into her cousin's comforting embrace. The girl was terrified and sobbing in harsh, choking sounds.

Ben picked up his hat from the ground and slapped it against his pants, sending clouds of dust flying. He felt breathless, and though his erection had subsided there was still an uncomfortable tightness in his loins.

Emma stroked Celia's tangled hair and looked over her head at the men surrounding them. "What are you going to do with us?" she asked, instinctively looking at the man who had held her down as the leader.

"Take you back to the ranch," he said.

Emma ducked her head, hiding her alarm as she continued to soothe Celia. She was exhausted and wanted nothing more than to collapse, but pride held her erect, unable to show weakness to an enemy.

Ben looked up at the sun, estimating the time. "We'll have to rest the horses for a while before we head back. We won't make it to the ranch tonight, but we should meet up with Jake on his way back with Mrs. McLain."

Emma's head jerked up. "Jake?" she asked, her heart beginning to pound. Had Jake Roper come to their aid after all? But she was afraid to hope, because Jake was such a common name. Until then Emma had been determined not to say anything about Victoria in the hope that she had gotten away.

"Jacob Sarratt," Ben said. "My brother. I'm Ben Sarratt."

She stared at him, white-faced, because Victoria had been right after all.

"The—the Major?"

Ben walked over to snare Sophie's reins and gave Emma a dismissive look over his shoulder. "Dead," he said.

It was late in the afternoon when they saw two riders approaching. Ben grunted in satisfaction, glad that Jake had recovered the missing widow without any trouble. His plan to get legal possession of the ranch by marrying her would have been worthless if he hadn't been able to find her. Ben watched them ride up, more than a little curious about this woman Jake was willing to marry.

Emma finally recognized Victoria and stumbled forward with a cry, but she froze in her tracks when she also recognized the man riding beside her cousin. She shot a disbelieving look at Ben, then another at Jake. Jake Roper was Jake *Sarratt?* Understanding dawned. My God, he'd been playing them all for fools from the beginning!

When they reined in at the camp Victoria didn't wait for anyone to help her down. Unhooking her leg from the pommel, she jumped and stumbled, but recovered herself before Jake could reach out to catch her.

"Emma? Celia?"

Hearing the hoarse anxiety, Emma hurried forward. "We're both all right. Celia's stiff and sore, but we haven't been hurt. Are—are you—"

"Tired," Victoria said, her shoulders slumping. She allowed

herself the weakness only for a moment. Lifting her chin, she said, "I suppose you know?"

"About the Major? Yes."

"And about the Sarratts?" Victoria's face was expressionless. "Yes."

There was nothing else to say. They were all safe, at least for the moment. What lay ahead, they couldn't even guess.

Victoria sat quietly with Emma beside her. One of the men—the one they called Wylie—began preparing the evening meal. Victoria stirred enough to offer their provisions.

Jake was ominously silent, and Ben watched Victoria closely. She didn't know that he was admiring her quiet, dignified manner and the look of pride on her dusty face. He was even admiring the fact that she was obviously the cause of Jake's black mood, because no woman before had ever been able to get past Jake's wall of reserve.

They ate at sunset and turned in shortly afterward. Victoria was too tired even to argue when Jake dumped his bedroll beside her blanket, though she did wonder what the men thought. She decided that she was too tired to care and, curling up on her side, was asleep before Jake got his boots off.

When they reached the hacienda the next day, Victoria still didn't know what Jake intended to do with them. If he'd been planning to kill them, surely he would have done it and left their bodies out in the rocks. Instead he'd brought them back, to Carmita, who came running from the hacienda with glad cries and outstretched arms.

There were signs of the recent battle everywhere, from the multitude of new faces to the chips in the adobe walls. Several windows had been broken and holes peppered the black wood of the front door. Still, there were some things that were unchanged. Carmita was still motherly in her concern, and Angelina Garcia still lounged around.

The women trooped tiredly upstairs, with Carmita fussing around them while Lola and Juana began heating the massive quantities of water needed for them all to have a bath. Celia could barely climb the stairs, she was so sore; they decided she should have the first bath for the relief the hot water would give her muscles. Carmita also addressed the problem with a liberal application of liniment, despite Celia's blushing reluctance to bare her legs and backside.

The house was teeming with activity, and if there was one thing Victoria knew how to do it was run a household. She seized on the work to keep herself from screaming out her fears and uncertainties, because she still didn't know what was going to happen and was afraid to ask. The Major's room had been cleaned out as if he'd never been; even the furniture had vanished.

It was disorienting to open the connecting door between their bedrooms and look at the emptiness of bare walls and floor. Her husband was unmourned, and every trace of him had also gone. It seemed as if no one wanted to say anything about it. She wondered if McLain had been shot down in that very room. She backed into her own room and quietly closed the door.

When it came time for her own bath, she locked both doors and lolled in the hot water for a long time, soaking out the grit that felt embedded in her skin. She washed her hair, sighing with relief at the sense of being clean again, and leisurely brushed it dry. Eventually, however, she ran out of excuses to linger and was forced to dress and go downstairs for dinner.

The meal was a strange affair. Celia ate in her room, and the four people who sat down at the table were all silent for their own reasons. Emma, usually as self-assured as a Mother Superior, was pale and looked only at Victoria the few times she raised her eyes from her plate. Jake wasn't scowling, but his expression was dark nonetheless. He and Ben made no effort at conversation, but ate steadily. Victoria's own stomach was knotted in a mass of nerves and she only tasted a few bites.

Immediately afterward, the two men went into the library and shut the door.

Once they were gone, Emma came to life. "I'm going to my room," she said with heartfelt relief. "I'll have to read a couple of hours before I get sleepy, but at least I'll be able to relax."

Victoria nodded, equally relieved. "That sounds like a very sensible plan. I have some mending to do that will take an hour or so."

Very much in accord, they ascended the stairs together. Victoria sewed on loose buttons and mended torn hems, the mundane chore giving her back a portion of her lost reality. Many things on the surface looked as they had before, but the content had changed. Uncertainty was nerve-racking, she decided as she bit off the thread the last time and packed her sewing box away. The Major and Garnet were both gone, but her life was even more tenuous than it had been before.

At least she felt calm enough to sleep. She lifted her skirt to remove her shoes and stockings, then walked barefoot to the dresser to take the pins from her hair.

Her arms were raised, removing the last pin, when the hallway door to her bedroom opened and Jake stepped inside. Victoria went white. "What are you doing here?" she demanded.

For answer, he calmly turned the key in the lock and pocketed it. While she watched, horrified, he strolled to the connecting door and repeated the action. As casually as if he undressed in front of her every day, he then removed his boots and shirt. His naked torso was strongly muscled, with lean, hard bands delineating his ribs and stomach. She stared at him, mesmerized. A strange, warm sensation jolted her, and she jerked her gaze upward.

She stood frozen, her eyes huge as she searched his face. It was as expressionless as the day she'd met him, and she realized that this, then, was the final part of his revenge. She had been a complete fool about him; worse, even now she still loved him. It was a passion that twisted inside her, an ache intertwined with fear; she had never before known that a loved one could be simultaneously cherished and dreaded, but then she had never before loved someone who wanted only to wreak his vengeance on her.

"Come here," he said calmly.

Her heart thudded and for a moment pure fear pushed her to obey. Then her back stiffened and she put up her chin. "You think I should aid you in my violation? No. I will not."

He shrugged and a hard smile touched his lips. "It makes no difference to the outcome," he said, approaching to stand directly in front of her. "Neither will your next decision, but I'll give you a choice anyway. Take off your clothes, or I'll take them off for you, and I don't care about buttons or seams. It's your choice," he repeated, "but your clothes won't survive if I have to do it."

She looked directly up into his glittering green eyes, trying to read them, but his expression was closed to her. "Is there nothing I can say that will convince you to leave me alone?"

"No. I decided to have you practically from the first time I set eyes on you, and that hasn't changed. You can try to change my mind, though, if you insist."

She decided not to, because she was afraid she would descend to begging, and her desperate pride rebelled against that.

"You can even scream, if you want," he pointed out. "That won't do any good, either. It'll upset Emma and Celia, but they won't be able to help you. So what's your decision? Are you going to undress?" He lifted one brow at her, and hating her own cowardice, she lifted trembling hands to the buttons on her plain white shirtwaist. It seemed there was nothing else she could do.

She had never undressed in front of a man before, never dreamed that she would have to perform such an act. She unbuttoned the front, then fumbled with the buttons to the tight cuffs until he said impatiently, "Get it off."

The button at the waistband of her skirt eluded her, and with a muffled curse he pushed her hands away and unfastened the garment himself. It drooped around her hips, but was held up by the bulk of her petticoats. She removed the freed shirtwaist and dropped it on the chair.

"Now the skirt," he directed.

A fine shaking seized her legs as she lifted the skirt off over her head and placed it, too, on the chair. Now she stood before him in petticoats and shift, acutely aware of her bare shoulders and arms, and the fact that her nipples were visible through the soft, thin cotton.

He was only a foot away, so close she could feel the heat of his body. She tried to back away, but came up flush against the dresser.

His hard mouth twisted in wry acknowledgment of her action. "The petticoat," he prompted.

She untied the tapes and pulled the first one off over her head. He stared down in frustration at the almost identical garment that had been beneath the first. She hurried to release it, then closed her eyes in mortification as she let it drop to pool around her feet. Now she was clad in only drawers and shift, and hot color rushed into her pale face. Even on those two horrible nights when the Major had tried to consummate their marriage, he hadn't insisted on watching her remove her clothing. But this wasn't the Major, it was Jake. Paralyzed, she stared at his broad chest and naked, heavily muscled shoulders, the smooth skin gleaming in the mellow lamplight. Curly dark hair covered his chest, punctuated by two small, tight brown nipples. Oddly, she had never before thought about a man having nipples, and seeing his made her even more acutely aware of his half-naked state.

Jake stiffened against a surge of lust as he looked at her round breasts pushing against the thin cotton covering them. God, she was pretty, slim and ivory-skinned, delectably curved in all the right places. "Now the shift." The words were a little hoarse.

She turned white again and automatically crossed her arms over her chest. "No, I won't." But her voice shook, and Jake was almost at the limit of his control. He reached out and roughly jerked the garment up and over her head, forgetting about it even as he tossed it aside. His mind was on Victoria, on the pale, full globes of her breasts and the delicacy of her small, pinkish-brown nipples. He had wanted to punish her a little bit because of the worry and torment she had caused him by running off, but his patience and need for revenge had run out. More than anything, he now just wanted her naked and willing in his arms.

Victoria cringed as her breasts were bared. Not even the Major had ever insisted on seeing her naked bosom. She tried to cross her arms over her chest again, but Jake caught her wrists and held her arms down at her side as he leisurely looked her over.

"Don't hide from me." Heat was rising in him, swelling his loins with an intensity that made him shake, now that he was so close to having her. He'd never before known this kind of hunger, this overwhelming urge to have this particular woman and no other. "I'm going to see every inch of you before I'm finished."

"Why are you doing this to me?" she burst out, tears stinging her eyes. She blinked them back, not wanting him to see her cry. "What have I done to you?"

"You've got it all wrong," he said, his voice even hoarser than before. "I'm not looking for punishment. I want you, and you want me. It's time we did something about it." He released one of her wrists and put his hand on her waist, smoothing his palm up her rib cage, savoring the softness of her skin under his fingers. "You're going to enjoy it as much as I do."

She stared incredulously at him. "You're mad!"

Her disbelieving outburst told him a lot. He smiled and slid both arms around her, pulling her tight against him. "You'll see, sweetheart. I'm not McLain. I'm going to love you until we both go crazy."

Out of the confused, combined vortex of fear, shock, embarrassment, and outrage, only one coherent protest formed, and the words were a moan of despair. "But you—you shouldn't see me like this!"

"Why not?" he murmured, bending his head to nuzzle her ear. "You're so pretty and soft. We're both going to be naked before too much longer, and if you like to look at me half as much as I like looking at you, we may never put on clothes again."

She trembled at the very idea of lying naked with him; the thought was so foreign to her upbringing that her mind felt numb, unable to form the picture. She was pathetically grateful that at least she was still wearing her drawers, though she was afraid the garment wouldn't remain on her much longer.

"Kiss me," he said in a cajoling tone, but she couldn't. He cupped her chin and turned her face up to him. "Kiss me," he said again, whispering, and covered her mouth with his.

Victoria hung in his brawny arms, her toes barely brushing the floor. His mouth smothered hers, and she felt dizzy. Despite herself, she had to cling to his heavy shoulders. The raspy sensation of his hairy chest against her sensitive nipples almost took her breath. When she gasped for air, his tongue moved into her mouth, taking the deeply intimate kiss from her, penetrating her in that small way to help prepare her for the other. Despite her fear, his taste was warmly familiar, the scent of his heated skin so exquisitely tantalizing that she wanted to turn her face into his shoulder and inhale it more deeply.

A warm, heavy feeling was growing in her body, making her feel drugged. She pulled her mouth away but her head fell back, exposing her throat to his mouth. "That's right, honey," he murmured, sliding one hand down to her bottom and lifting her against the hard bulge at his loins.

She gasped again and moaned an incoherent little protest. He couldn't be doing this to her, she couldn't be feeling this way, as if she wanted him to continue kissing her, as if she wanted him to do more. It was a strange, hot madness, that she should want him to do the very thing she had found so repulsive when the Major had tried it. Her shock at her own lack of propriety made her squirm, an action that tore a groan from deep down in his throat.

He held her to him with one arm around her bottom, and with his other hand he pulled at the tapes that tied her drawers at the waist. When they loosened he closed his fist in the soft material and tugged it downward, baring first her buttocks, then her mound and thighs. Victoria gave a strangled cry and arched against the steel band of his arm, but he merely tightened it and lifted her higher, so the drawers fell to her feet, and then to the floor.

He picked her up in his arms and carried her to the bed. For the first time Victoria actively fought him, trying frantically to get away. She felt painfully exposed, so much at the mercy of his much greater strength and rampant sexuality that she lost control. She kicked and hit at him, trying to pull free and throw herself off the bed. He subdued her easily, catching her hands and pinning them over her head, controlling her legs with his powerful ones.

"Easy now," he said soothingly, his breath warm against her face. "Don't be afraid, honey, you have no reason to be afraid. I'm not going to hurt you." His voice was low and reassuring, and he bent his head to brush his mouth across the tender joint of her neck and shoulder.

The hot touch of his mouth on her bare skin made her jump, and with an incoherent cry she strained upward again. He held her down, wondering why she was so frightened. Surely she knew he wasn't going to hurt her. But maybe her experiences with the Major had been even more unpleasant than he'd thought, maybe she truly expected the worst of him. His body was screaming for him to take off his pants and enter her now, but relief wasn't all he wanted. Victoria was so much a lady, but she was also a woman of passion and he wanted her to give him that passion. He wanted her to cling to him, her body arching to receive him rather than trying to throw him off; he wanted to feel the soft internal clenching of her release.

"Victoria. Look at me, honey. Stop fighting and look at me."

"Get off of me," she cried in a stifled voice.

"No, I won't get off." He shifted control of her wrists to one hand, and with the other caught her chin and turned her head toward him. Her eyes were wet with tears, he saw, but she hadn't allowed them to fall. He kissed her temple in appreciation of her pride, then moved his lips to her cheek. "You don't have to be afraid," he repeated softly, and brushed a kiss at the corner of her mouth.

"Don't do this, please don't do this to me." The words burst out, and she was dimly appalled to realize she was begging. She'd sworn she wouldn't do that, but the stark reality of being stripped naked had also stripped her of pride. She would grovel if it would stop him from hurting and humiliating her this way. "I'll leave, I promise I will. We'll leave in the morning if you want—"

"Now, why would I want that?" he murmured, the corners of his mouth kicking up in amusement. He leaned over her and lightly rubbed his chest against her nipples.

The contact, light as it was, rasped across her delicate flesh. She inhaled with a quick, shallow gasp, her concentration splintered. Her nipples were burning, tightening. He did it again, this time increasing the pressure a little, and the traitorous warmth in her began to blur the edges of her fear.

He kissed her, opening his mouth over hers. He probed her mouth with his tongue, kissing her in the slow, sure, purposeful manner of a man who knows he isn't going to stop at kisses. She made a muffled sound of protest but he kept on until her lips softened, until he felt some of the tension ease out of her muscles and she began to respond to him.

She didn't want to respond; she tried to fight it, only to find herself undermined by her own emotions. When everything was said and done, she loved him. Even knowing he didn't love her, that his taking of her was part of his hatred for the Major, she couldn't stop the warm tide of feeling when he touched her. She couldn't stop herself from welcoming his small invasion with her own tongue and drawing his taste deep inside.

He stroked his hand in one slow motion from her chin to her throat, and downward to cover her breast. She jerked in shock, alarmed by the first feel of a man's hand on her bare breast. His palm burned her, and the tightening sensation in her breasts intensified. He gently kneaded, then rubbed his thumb around and over the nipple in a circular motion that made her moan aloud. She tried to jerk her mouth free of his, but Jake deepened the kiss, holding her while he transferred his attentions to her other breast.

She began to tremble, but no longer from fear.

He finally lifted his head and looked down at the soft, pale mounds of her breasts, at the tightly beaded nipples. His sinewy, darkly tanned fingers were a rough contrast against her delicate skin. "You're so damn pretty," he said, and bent his head to her breasts.

His mouth closed hotly over her nipple. Victoria cried out, the sound strangled in her throat. Pure sensation jolted her and she arched again, but was still held pinned by his controlling hand and legs. She had never imagined he would use his mouth on her in that way, never anticipated the searing wet heat, or the prickling pressure as he sucked strongly, his cheeks flexing with the movement. His tongue flicked and rolled around her nipple, and she began burning, the heat twisting downward to pool between her legs. She whimpered, aware of the shameful undulation of her hips but unable to do anything to stop it.

"That's right, honey," he whispered. "Let me feel you move."

He shifted his mouth to her other breast, awash in her taste, giddy with the sweet scent of her breasts and the feel of her nipples. She gave another little cry, the sound making him shiver with need.

He slid his hand down her belly and pushed it between her legs.

She jerked wildly, shock overcoming pleasure. "No," she cried, shaking. "Dear God, no!" Her hips bucked as she tried to dislodge him.

Jake caught her mouth with his, silencing her protest with long, deep kisses. She strained against him, but he kept kissing her until that storm of resistance, too, had passed. When she was limp and shaking, he lifted his mouth.

"You feel so good, sweetheart. Open your legs for me, let me touch you."

"No, it isn't right, you shouldn't do that—" She remembered the pain when the Major had shoved his fingers so roughly into her, and she shrank from the memory.

"Yes, it is right," he interrupted in a low, warm tone. His eyes were intensely green, burning, and—tender. "I want to touch you, I want to feel how soft and wet you are."

She shuddered. "You won't hurt me?" She wanted his touch. Her body was aching shamelessly for him, but the remembrance of her wedding night kept her from obeying.

His face tightened. "No, I won't hurt you," he promised, and wished bitterly that McLain could come back to life so he could kill him again for daring to hurt this woman. "Open your legs, Victoria."

She did, finally, her thighs relaxing enough to allow him to move his fingers. He did so gently, parting the lips of her sex and opening her to his caresses. Victoria shuddered again, acutely aware of the embarrassing moistness she knew he could feel as he lightly stroked her. But this wasn't like what the Major had done, she thought dazedly. He wasn't hurting her, he was rubbing her, exploring the sensitive folds with tender fingers, and he was breathing hard as if touching her there excited him beyond bearing.

"You're going to like this," he said, and brushed his thumb across the small nub at the top of her sex. An exquisite pleasure, so intense it was almost painful, shot through her body. She moaned, unaware that her legs opened wider as she arched against his hand.

He continued using his thumb, drinking in the small sounds she made, loving the way her hips were moving. The scent of her body was hotter, more intoxicating. There was fever in her now, the fever he had craved from the time he had met her, burning high to match his. Soon, very soon, she would be his. She was wet, he thought wet enough, but to make certain he slowly slipped one finger inside her.

Victoria stiffened when she felt her body penetrated, dazedly bracing herself for the pain, but instead the heavy, burning ache inside her intensified. No, it wasn't an ache, it was intolerable pleasure. She didn't know, didn't care. Her entire body was throbbing. She turned her head against his shoulder as he began moving his finger in and out, the motion enticing her hips into an undulating movement she couldn't control.

Jake groaned aloud. She was so small and tight he knew he'd have difficulty entering her, no matter how ready she was. She was so wet, trembling on the verge of satisfaction, that there was no point in delaying any longer.

Now, finally, he released her hands, but Victoria didn't think of fighting. It was too late for that. Fire was burning through her, her breasts were aching and there was a deep throb between her legs that she didn't know how to handle. Her body felt heavy and limp, curiously disobedient. She watched him without comprehension as he got up and stood beside the bed, his hands working at his waistline. Only gradually did she understand that he was unbuttoning his pants, and then only a fraction of a second before he pushed them down and off.

The lamplight was too bright to be merciful. A return to fear jolted her from her sensual daze, and she rose up on one elbow with one hand lifted as if to ward him off. He was plainly revealed, his strongly muscled body nude, his thick erection rising from the dark curls at his groin. She stared at him in terror. The Major hadn't looked anything like that. There was no way she could accept him inside her, he was too big, he would tear her apart—

"No," she said hoarsely, belatedly trying to twist away.

Jake hauled her back and mounted her, prying her clenched thighs apart and settling himself between them. Fear exploded within her, out of control, as his rigid shaft probed at the soft folds between her legs.

"I can't," she moaned, thrashing her head from side to side. "Jake, please!"

"No, everything's all right," he soothed. "There won't be a problem, you'll see. It'll slide in so slick and easy you won't be hurt at all. Just relax, sweetheart."

He knew she must be terrified because of what the Major had done to her, but he also knew that because the Major *had* done it and he didn't now have to break her hymen, she wouldn't be forced to endure that pain. No, he intended to make certain that this time would be all pleasure for her.

He kissed her deeply, and in despair she felt the rise of heat in her again, and the coiling tension that only he could relieve. With a sob she admitted defeat and lifted her hips against him, silently asking for his penetration.

"Please," she whispered.

"All right, darling," he murmured against her throat.

There was no way she could relax, no way she could be casual about what was happening to her now. He was going to do what he wanted to her no matter what she did, but accepting the inevitable didn't help. She was swept along willy-nilly, with no control even over her own body, which begged for his conquest. Her breath burst out of her in a shuddering sigh as he let all of his weight down on her and reached down between her legs, holding her open with one hand while the other guided his manhood. She flinched as he made contact again, his flesh smooth and hot.

"Jake—"

"Easy, easy," he whispered, and nudged the broad tip into her, following with a steady, relentless pressure that forced him past the restrictive tightness of her opening. Victoria pushed convulsively at his waist in an effort to repel the burning invasion of her body. Hot tears slipped down her cheeks, at last uncontrolled. He caught her hands and moved them, pinning them again to the pillow, then continued squeezing into her, inch by slow inch, until he was in her to the hilt.

"Oh, God," he groaned, fighting the waves of pleasure that swept over him. She was so tight that he almost couldn't bear it. To give himself time he held himself still, embedded deeply inside her, and began again the exquisite task of bringing her to pleasure.

"It's all right, sweetheart," he said, kissing her over and over. His penetration had been so difficult, he wondered for an instant about the Major. But he dismissed the thought; he hadn't felt the telltale resistance of delicate skin when he'd entered her. Still, she was crying and it wrenched at his guts. He wiped her tears away and began to slowly move his hips in the way that would bring her the ultimate ease.

She lay limply, her gaze fastened on his hard, intent face, accepting the penetration and retreat of his manhood in dazed muteness. When she had imagined this act of ultimate intimacy, she had thought of it in terms of pain and revulsion, unable to comprehend why men seemed to want it so. Now, as her breath caught, she began to understand what, beyond duty, prompted a woman to submit to the act. It wasn't submission as much as participation, although her body was only now beginning to learn that. The heavy thrust and drag of his maleness was bringing the heat within her to full flame again and concentrating it in her loins.

It began slowly because both her senses and flesh were still shocked by his invasion, but it was inexorable. The twinges of pleasure became sharper, and as her senses recovered they focused on her own body, bringing it alive in ways she had never anticipated. She smelled the clean sweat that made his body gleam, the musky maleness of his skin, even the new and exciting scents of their lovemaking. She felt his heat, enveloping her. She felt his hardness, the strength of his muscled arms enfolding her, the scrub-board flatness of his belly rubbing against her with each thrust, the powerful thighs that kept her own thighs parted, the hardness of his loins that pressed into her body with each recoil of his hips.

Her hands moved, slowly and without her awareness, to his shoulders; they were hot and smooth under her palms.

Her legs lifted and twined sensuously around his hips and thighs.

Her back arched, tilting her pelvis to receive him more fully.

And it grew in her, that heat.

Afterward, she never had any idea of how long they strained together, or when the heat shattered the last of her control. She clung to him, gasping at his strong hands on her breasts, crying out wordlessly when her hips lifted to meet him. His hair was plastered to his skull with sweat; her hands clenched in it, holding him to her. He groaned, too, with the inward thrusts that were driving them into their frenzy. She was liquid fire in his arms; her body burned him, and enchanted him. He took the full measure of her response and gave her his, caught and shattered in a way he had never been before.

And the heat became too much.

She clawed at his back, crying again, frantic for release from the incredible tension in her body. She was shuddering, lifting, straining toward him. He drove into her with a heavy rhythm that rattled the bed on its frame. She moaned, knowing that if she didn't find relief, she would shatter, her heart would burst. And then she discovered that the shattering was the relief. Her loins clenched convulsively around his manhood, then her senses exploded in great waves that lifted her entire body off the bed.

He caught her hips and pushed deeper into her, thrusting hard. He went taut and reared back, his powerful body arching like a bow as his climax shook him. A hoarse cry burst from his throat and together they died the little death that was a death of self, and an exaltation of life.

13

She awoke slowly, feeling a physical soreness and a certain malaise of spirit as she had to face the morning. She would have preferred it to remain night forever, for then she could simply lie in bed with him and push reality away.

She was alone in the bed, for which she was grateful. Despite the heated carnality they had shared during the night, she didn't think she'd have been able to blithely crawl naked from the bed in full daylight with him looking on. Nor did she now; she stretched cautiously beneath the twisted, wrinkled sheet. Though her thighs protested and her breasts and lips felt swollen and tender, the only real soreness seemed to be between her legs and to her relief even that wasn't severe.

Her depression wasn't brought on by her physical complaints, which were minor, but by her uncertainty that had, perversely, been increased by his lovemaking. Before, the situation had been that she loved him but wasn't loved in return. A simple, if painful, reality.

She still loved him. If she hadn't done so, she could have resisted him, but she had long ago admitted that she loved the rough, hard-eyed gunman. No matter if he called himself Roper or Sarratt, no matter if he'd sworn vengeance on everything and everyone bearing the McLain name, she loved him. She couldn't love by half-measures, holding back in self-protection; nor could she stop loving him just because he'd lied to her and betrayed her trust. Whether or not he wanted it, he had both her heart and her loyalty. The sense of honor that had kept her with McLain even when she despised him would keep her heart with Jake Sarratt forever. So she had lain beneath him in the night, shocked by the intimacies he'd insisted on, burning with the pleasure he'd given her, and she had become, irrevocably, Jake Sarratt's woman.

She had given him everything, her body and her honor, her pride. What deepened the shadows in her eyes was the inner certainty that he didn't cherish the gift. He had enjoyed her body, but she remembered with sharp pain that he had also enjoyed the body of the woman she'd seen him making love to in the barn.

The bright sunshine pouring in the window mocked her, but after another moment of lying in bed she answered the mockery by rising. Even though she was alone, her head was high and her back straight as she washed the evidence of the night from her body and methodically dressed herself in her usual modest shirt-waist and plain skirt. After she had picked up her scattered garments from the floor, she sat down at the dresser to put up her hair. It was a moment she had been postponing, because she dreaded looking at herself this morning, afraid the night's sensuality would show on her face.

To her relief, she looked much as she always did, although a little paler. Her face was grave and serene, and if there was a depth of new knowledge in her eyes, that at least was to be expected.

Facing herself in the mirror had been difficult; facing Jake would take every bit of backbone she possessed.

Jake brooded in the library, a cup of Lola's strong hot coffee in his hands. The night had not left him untouched, either. He'd known he wanted Victoria; he'd even admitted to being obsessed by her. What he hadn't known was how strong the obsession was or that now, after taking her, he'd want her even more.

All of his plans had seemed so simple, but now he was caught. Victoria was a temptation he couldn't resist, a complication he couldn't solve. He and Ben had the ranch back, the land that was theirs by birthright but not by law. McLain was dead; though Garnet had survived, it was enough that he was gone. Jake wasn't inclined to go chasing after him. If Garnet ever crossed his path again, he would kill him, but for now at least Jake was satisfied. Almost.

What was he going to do about Victoria? She threatened him in a way no one else ever had, because she threatened him emotionally. Last night had shown him his own frightening vulnerability to her. He was terrified of his weakness for her, of how close and raw she made his emotions. The only way Jake knew to deal with this kind of threat was to flee, to protect himself by being rid of her, but he couldn't do that without losing the ranch.

She had been McLain's wife; he should be disgusted at the thought of touching her, but the truth was that he ached to have her again and again. She was so fine that McLain's ugliness hadn't been able to coarsen her. The night they had just shared hadn't diluted the intensity of his desire; it had increased it.

He desperately wanted to fight that desire, to keep himself heartwhole. He could send her away, but the thought of some other man marrying her made him grind his teeth in rage. And with her went the legal ownership of the ranch. He was caught in her woman's web like some stupid insect, and damn if he liked that idea.

He couldn't let her go, so there was no sense in even toying with the idea. He and Ben had control of the ranch, but they didn't have ownership. Unless he married Victoria. Then it would be his, and he would deed half of it to Ben.

He could keep the ranch, or he could protect himself by letting Victoria go. He and Ben had been born in this house; the thought of coming back to it, reclaiming it, had been the driving force of their lives. He'd fought for it, killed for it, won it back, but still it legally belonged to someone else. He could try to close himself off emotionally, try to protect himself with the wall of ice that had served him so well until now. But physically and legally, he and Victoria were to be man and wife. He really had no choice.

Ben walked in, sipping his own cup of coffee. He sprawled in a chair close to Jake's and eyed his brother with sharp awareness, both of where he had spent the night and of what was on his mind now.

"She's a fine woman," Ben said.

Jake looked up. "I know."

"And a real lady. I'm not too sure about that cousin of hers, but Victoria is a lady through and through."

Amusement lightened Jake's frown for a minute, and he grinned at his brother. "Emma? She's even more proper than Victoria. What did you do to her to get her stirred up?"

"Me?" Ben snapped. "She shot at me, damn it, and tried to knock my brains out with the rifle!"

Jake shrugged. "Victoria took a shot at me, too."

"She fought like a wildcat," Ben said, remembering the way Emma had felt beneath him, the way she had gone still when she'd felt his hardness pushing against her. He shifted restlessly and changed the subject.

"Do your plans still stand?"

"What choice do I have?"

"We both know the choices." Ben knew Jake would never harm Victoria, but he wanted to jolt his brother out of his brooding, so he said, "Victoria owns the ranch now. You can marry her, or you can kill her."

Victoria had come downstairs just after Ben had entered the library, and stood outside the door trying to work up enough courage to greet them. Jake had seen her as no one else had, touched her as no one else had. The memory would be in his eyes when he looked at her, and knowledge would be in Ben's because the things that a man did to a woman were something that all men knew, and did. She hadn't intended to eavesdrop, but in her hesitation to enter the room she had. And what she'd heard had drained all the blood from her face.

So that was why he'd been trying to seduce her. From the beginning he'd planned to make her fall in love with him so she would be willing to marry him and give him legal ownership of the ranch. She supposed she could only be relieved that he'd considered that option at all rather than simply killing her outright, as he'd killed McLain. It appeared he hadn't yet made up his mind about her fate, though, and the knowledge stiffened her spine.

She stepped into the library, her entrance making both men look around at her. She was still white, but composed. "I couldn't help overhearing," she said in a tone that was calm, if a bit strained. She clenched her hands together to prevent their trembling and forced herself to meet Jake's narrowed green eyes. "Which should I prepare myself for, a wedding or a funeral?"

Jake scowled; he still didn't like the idea that she had so much power over his emotions, but the fact was that she did. Here she was as calm and cool as a nun, all starched and buttoned, as if she hadn't dug her nails into his back and all but screamed with pleasure while he held her convulsing body still for his thrusts. The memory burned through him and made him grow hard. Kill her? He couldn't ever form the thought in his mind. And how could she think it, especially after last night? Angered, he glared at her, his eyes icy green.

"The wedding," he said abruptly. "I've sent one of the men after Father Sebastian. He'll marry us this afternoon."

"Thank you," she whispered, and left the room.

At least there was no pretense between them, she thought with a bitter smile. He hadn't tried to lie to her and dupe her with romance. He hadn't even bothered asking her if she would marry him, but then, why should he have? She could marry him or die.

She sought out Emma, whom she found in the courtyard enjoying both the sun and their freedom from the yoke of constant fear. If for nothing else, Victoria felt gratitude to the Sarratts for getting them out of that.

"Jake is marrying me this afternoon," she said baldly, not knowing how else to state it.

Emma's mouth and eyes went round. "This afternoon?" she squeaked. Then she blushed and said, "Well, yes, of course, after last night—"

Victoria flinched. "You knew?" She was mortified.

Emma flushed even redder. "Not last night. But this morning . . . um, I saw him leaving your bedroom, carrying his shirt."

Victoria sank down on a bench and looked at her hands,

struggling with her embarrassment. It was foolish, really, after all they had been through. Even though Emma didn't know the shocking things Jake had done to her or the way she had responded, Victoria knew very well and couldn't prevent herself from thinking of them.

Emma sat down beside her and hugged her. "Please don't be embarrassed," she said. "You'll be married this afternoon, so I don't think it's so scandalous to have anticipated your wedding vows by less than twenty-four hours. Unless . . . unless it was awful?"

"No, it isn't that." She paused, then said, "He doesn't love me." Victoria sighed and watched a rose blossom swaying in the slight breeze. "Now that the Major is dead, the ranch is legally mine. The only way Jake can get it is to either marry me or kill me. I'm terribly grateful that he's chosen marriage."

Emma stiffened, shocked. "Then you can't marry him."

"Pride would say so, wouldn't it? But I like living. And he'd have to kill you and Celia, too, so don't be so hasty saying I should refuse his decision." She found that there was, after all, some amusement to be had. She smiled at Emma. "And it wasn't awful at all."

Emma blushed and looked away, but a smile tugged at her lips, too. "So it isn't that the act is awful, but sometimes the man is."

"Exactly. One's modesty is useless and it's painfully intimate, but not awful." She took a deep breath. "The opposite, in fact."

Emma shivered, but not from a chill. She couldn't stop thinking about the suspended moment when Ben Sarratt had lain on top of her, his heavy arousal obvious. She had given him the cold shoulder since then because his frank arrogance irritated her, but all she had to do was let her concentration slip and she felt the imprint of his body again, lying all along hers, pressing her down.

They sat together, each of them thinking of a different Sarratt. At length Victoria's empty stomach prompted her to the kitchen, since she had slept so late she had missed breakfast. There was work to be done, now that two men had moved into the house, and she had dawdled long enough.

The Major had always been out most of the day, until the end when his mind had gone; in fact, practically the only contact they had had with him was at mealtimes. It wasn't that way with Jake and Ben. Their presence was very much felt in the house; they were in and out all day, filling the rooms with their deep voices, the stomp of their boots on the tile floors, bringing the scents of horses and tobacco with them. Victoria managed to avoid Jake, but cornered Ben long enough to get him to point out to her which gear was his and which was Jake's. When she had it separated, she dithered about what to do with Jake's clothes. Should she put them in her room or in the adjoining room? Perhaps he planned on taking that room for himself, since he'd obviously given orders that it be cleaned out. It would have been simple enough to ask him, but she couldn't bring herself to do it. After all that had passed between them, now she didn't feel comfortable approaching him.

Jake noticed that his soon-to-be wife was avoiding him to the point that she didn't even look in his direction, and he grew more and more irritated as the day wore on. If she thought he would put up with this she was going to be sorely surprised. It was bad enough that she had gotten under his skin the way he had, but he was damned if he was going to let her sulk every time she didn't like something he did, especially when she was wrong. He was still angry that she'd thought he would kill her to get the ranch; more than angry, because that meant she put him in the same category with McLain. He felt wronged. But most of all, he still felt threatened, and he was glad of any excuse to feel angry, to hold himself at a distance from her. Damn her for the effect she had on him! All he had to do was see her and his heart started beating faster, he lost his concentration, and all he wanted was to take her to bed again. He thought of the night and his entire body shuddered with pleasure. It wasn't just that it had been good; it had been unique. Shattering. He had never before been so lost in a woman, so focused on her to the extent that the world outside that bed had vanished. There was a lot he'd intended to get cleared between them last night, but none of it had been discussed. He'd seen her standing there, he'd known that she was his for the taking, and he'd taken her. Nothing else had been important.

Jake and Ben, along with the foreman, Lonny, were discussing how they were going to handle the problem of the few remaining McLain men who were still out with the distant herds when Emma tapped politely on the open door and put her head into the room. She looked only at Jake, studiously avoiding the challenging, hooded examination Ben was giving her.

"Where do you want the wedding to take place, Jake? Victoria says it doesn't matter." That was a lie because Emma hadn't asked Victoria, but it was a small barb intended to sting. Emma hadn't forgiven him for his deception, and she wasn't above giving some back.

Jake scowled, just as irritated as Emma had meant him to be.

"In the parlor? That's where she married the Major." Emma smiled as she pushed the barb deeper.

Jake's face went rigid. "No," he said after a minute, his voice so flat and calm it took a good ear to hear the savagery in it. "The courtyard."

Emma smiled again and withdrew. Lonny stared at the closed door with a strangely satisfied smile on his face. "Thoroughbreds," he announced. "Yep, them women are thoroughbreds. It'll be nice, settlin' down with women around. They tend to make men act better than normal, don't they?"

"What would you know about it?" Ben asked with a snort of disbelief at hearing such a sentiment from their foreman, who was as tough and wiry as they came.

"Hell, I been around women!" Lonny snapped. "I reckon I know the difference atween ladies and whores, and these are ladies. They'll make you two watch your manners, iffen you got any."

Ben began chortling and after a minute Jake relaxed enough to laugh, too. Lonny was a veteran of more wars, shoot-outs, and brawls than the two of them combined. Their friendship with him had begun over five years before when they had hauled him, dead drunk, out of a burning whorehouse. For him to lecture them on the difference between ladies and whores was almost more than they could stand.

Father Sebastian arrived sooner than Victoria had anticipated, and she wasn't ready. Even given the circumstances of the marriage, she didn't intend to get married in the clothes she'd been working in all day. On her first wedding day she had brooded; on her second she didn't have time to do more than quickly freshen up and don one of her good dresses. On the first she had been terrified. She felt a lot of things on the second: sadness, because he didn't love her and was marrying her only for the ranch; innate fear, for her husband would still be very much a stranger to her despite their lovemaking, and he was a hard, rough man who had lived by his gun; relief, that he wanted her at all, that she would have a chance with him; excitement, very definitely. He would be her husband. Even if he never saw her as anything but a necessary nuisance, she would share his life, his name, and his bed, and she would bear his children.

There were other differences in this wedding, too. The people surrounding her seemed excited, even happy. Celia was still suffering from the effects of riding and was not as lively as before, but the look of strain was easing from her eyes and her merry laughter rang out several times. Emma was a whirlwind overseeing the rush and bustle of preparing for the hasty marriage, but her eyes were bright. Carmita chattered nonstop; Lola was singing in the kitchen; even Juana hummed as she rushed back and forth on errands. Men were in and out, bellowing, cursing, asking the pardon of any female within hearing distance for their cursing, cursing some more as soon as they forgot themselves, some of the bolder ones flirting with anyone wearing a skirt.

Only the bride and groom seemed less than ecstatic, though to be honest the men were interested only because of the chance for a party. Jake was tense, and therefore ill-tempered. Victoria was acutely sensitive to the reasons he was marrying her and became more and more nervous as the minutes passed. When she dashed down the stairs to the ceremony that would make her Mrs. Jacob Sarratt, she was shaking so hard she could barely hold her skirts up to keep from tripping over them.

"This way!" Emma said excitedly, hurrying her through the house. "Everyone's waiting."

Victoria hadn't asked and had vaguely assumed that the

wedding would take place in the parlor because it was the most formal room in the house. But Emma led her into the court-yard. Relief swept through her. The late afternoon sun bathed the courtyard in a mellow, golden light; the open space was crowded with, she supposed, everyone who worked for them now, men and women alike. The men far outnumbered the women, of course, and shifted back and forth on restless feet, awkwardly turning their hats in their hands. The women had decorated the courtyard as best they could with bright Mexican lamps, even though the sun was still shining, and colorful streamers that Carmita or Lola had saved from some long-ago festival.

Father Sebastian beamed at her as she stepped to Jake's side. A bit hysterically, Victoria wondered if he didn't find it strange that he should be performing another wedding ceremony for her so soon after the first. She had become a wife, a widow, and now a wife again with disorienting speed. If she had been at home, she would have worn black for at least a year and been secluded within her family. It would have been unthinkable for her even to consider another engagement for a year and a half, and here she was now remarrying only three days after her husband's death.

She fought back the urge to giggle, and jumped when she felt Jake take her hand. She looked at him with huge, startled eyes and was shocked back to reality by the cold green glitter of his. But his hand was warm, and when he felt how she was shaking he gently squeezed her fingers. The action steadied her, reminding her that, for all the violence and danger of this man, he had cho-sen to protect her.

She could remember little of her first wedding ceremony, but this one was crystal clear and she knew it would be engraved on her memory. Most of the guests were armed, but Victoria couldn't fault that when the groom was, too. The sun shone, the birds sang, men cleared their throats, the priest performed the ceremony, and she and Jake made the appropriate responses. All the while, her hand was clasped in his hard, strong one.

There were no rings, but she didn't feel the lack. She had removed the Major's ring on the ride back to the ranch, after she had learned he was dead, and dropped it in the dust.

Jake was also intensely aware of his surroundings, but even more so of the woman beside him. Now that she was becoming legally his, he was struck by the realization that by the laws of God and man he was now her protector; he had sworn to keep her from danger, to keep her warm, to never let her know hunger, to provide for her and any children they might have. He now stood between her and the harshness of life. Yet she was still afraid, because he could feel her shaking and her delicate hand was cold. Didn't she trust him to protect her? Then he realized that it was himself that she feared. How could she? But the fact that she did told him she was marrying him only because she thought he would kill her if she didn't.

The woman needed to learn some lessons about the man she was marrying.

Then the priest was blessing them, and it was done. There was a flurry of handshakes, hugs, and congratulations, and Carmita threw her arms around Jake's neck and gave him an enthusiastic kiss on the lips, then was mortified at her own behavior. "Welcome back, Señor Jake," she stuttered, and fled.

One of the Mexican cowhands produced a guitar and began strumming it. As the sun went down, the liquor was brought out. Whiskey and tequila ran down the male throats. A few of them grabbed the women and began whirling them around the courtyard, stomping in an enthusiastic fashion that had little to do with an actual dance, but a great deal to do with their high spirits.

Jake kept Victoria at his side. As darkness blotted out the sky the bright Mexican lanterns cast their magic over the courtyard and the laughter ringing out eased Jake's tension.

Without a word he put his arm around Victoria's waist and eased her against him, moving her into the slow shuffle that was all he knew how to do. She gave him a quick, startled look, then relaxed in his arms. Her head dropped onto his shoulder and she sighed, but he thought it was a sigh of contentment, or at least relief.

She felt so delicate in his arms. Her bones were as slender as a child's, her shoulders straight but still only a little more than half as broad as his. Her head tucked neatly under his chin, and the sweet, faint perfume of her hair elusively teased him. Her breasts were soft against him; he remembered how round they were, how pale and delicately veined, and how he had rubbed his face against them. Her slender thighs moved gracefully against his as they swayed together in dance; last night they had clasped around his buttocks in eager passion.

He had been half-aroused all day, unable to keep his thoughts from returning time and again to the night before. Now his erection pushed painfully against his pants, and he stifled a groan as he unobtrusively moved her in a hidden caress against his swollen groin. She looked up at him, and he saw her swallow. Her blue eyes were shadowed, but she made no protest, and after a moment she returned her head to his shoulder.

Ben leaned against one of the posts, watching Jake dance with his new wife. He liked Victoria, but then he should have known that Jake never would have planned to marry her if she'd been a shrill, condescending sort. He didn't know what they would have done, but marrying her would have been out.

He looked around the courtyard and caught sight of Emma dancing with Lonny, of all people. Ben would have sworn that Lonny had never even seen a dance before, but there he was, whirling and stomping and having the time of his life. Emma was laughing. Ben stiffened, his eyes narrowing as he stared at her. She wouldn't even look at him, but she'd dance with every clumsy cowhand who asked her.

Lola brought out refreshments, doughnuts and some squares of plain cake. The men swooped down on the doughnuts, which they called "bear sign," with yells of delight, and the dancing momentarily stopped. When it started again, Ben noticed that Emma laughingly declined all invitations in favor of some much needed rest. She found a seat on a bench at the opposite side of the courtyard from where he stood and contentedly watched the others dance. Most of the men were dancing with each other since there were so few women, but it made no difference to the mood of celebration.

Ben made his way around the courtyard and came up behind Emma. She didn't know he was there until he propped his boot on the bench beside her, and leaned forward to rest his arm on his raised knee. "How long are you going to run away from me because of what happened?" he asked in a cool, hard voice.

Emma didn't look at him. "Nothing happened, Mr. Sarratt." Her voice was as cool as his.

"The hell it didn't. You got me hard, and we both enjoyed it."

She hitched her shawl higher on her arms but still didn't look at him. "I think, Mr. Sarratt, that you must be used to a different type of female. I'm not responsible for your—your body, and neither do I enjoy being treated like a slut who would welcome your rubbing."

Ben's voice got even harder. "What *I* think, Miss Gann, is that your personality would be a lot sweeter if you had more rubbing."

Though Emma knew it was dangerous even to continue this wildly improper conversation, let alone make it even more personal, she couldn't prevent herself from sneering, "From *you?* You flatter yourself."

Ben straightened, a little shocked, then stepped over the bench to stand in front of her. Without a word he caught her wrist and pulled her to her feet, then dragged her out of the courtyard. Emma cried out a protest, but there was so much noise that no one noticed. When they were outside he whirled her around and flattened her against the wall, holding her there with both hands clasping her rib cage. Only a few inches separated them; he smelled hot and faintly sweaty, and she trembled with primitive response.

Out here it was dark, although light and music and gaiety were just on the other side of the wall. A peculiar bubble of silence surrounded them, broken only by the raspy sound of his breathing.

He bent his head. Emma pushed her hands against his chest and said sharply, "Don't you dare!" but her protest was useless. His mouth covered hers, and when she tried to turn her head away he shifted his hold on her so that her head was anchored against his shoulder, his hand clenched in her hair to hold her still. The hard pressure of his mouth bruised her soft lips. Desperately she bit him, her teeth sinking into his lower lip. He cursed and jerked his head away, and wiped at the blood that smeared his mouth.

"Do that again and I'll blister your bare ass," he snarled.

Emma found that she couldn't free herself from his tight grip. She threw her head back as she faced him defiantly. "You were hurting me! Was I supposed to do nothing?"

He paused, then said, "I guess not." He lifted his fingers to her lips and lightly rubbed them. Even in the faint light spilling over the wall he could see that they were already getting puffy. "I didn't mean to hurt you."

She could barely breathe, though she struggled to draw air into her constricted lungs. She wished he would release her, wished she couldn't feel his hard body pressing against her from breast to knee. She pushed against his chest again and found that the effort still had no effect.

He was still looking at her mouth. "We have to do something about this," he said under his breath.

"No, we don't," she quickly replied.

He gave a soft laugh. "That's what you think, girl." Then he kissed her again, claiming her lips with hunger, but no longer with violence. He moved his tongue into her mouth, penetrating deeply and drinking her taste. Emma jerked in his arms, then the tension abruptly drained out of her body and she sank against him.

A fine, heady madness welled up in her, born of the increasing pleasure she felt at his invasive kisses. She wound her arms around his neck and forgot about the protests she should make, forgot that no man could possibly respect a woman who let him kiss her like this unless they were engaged. Nor did she protest when he slid his hand to her bottom and arched her forward, nestling his hardness in the notch of her legs as he had done the day he'd wrestled her to the ground. Instead she whimpered, her head falling back to rest against the wall, and her legs parted even more in an instinctive yielding. Ben instantly took advantage, his hips moving in the slow grind and thrust of sex. He put his hand on her breast, kneading the soft mound through the barrier of her clothes. He felt her tremble, felt her legs give way, and caught her weight against him.

He kissed her jaw and the soft hollow below her ear, his mouth hot and wet. "Have you had a man before?" he asked roughly, praying that the answer would be yes.

But she dazedly shook her head. "No," she whispered.

He swore mentally for a long time, using every curse word he'd ever heard and coming up with a few new combinations. Damn, why couldn't she have done it just once before? As soon as he had the thought, his mind rebelled against it with angry possessiveness. He didn't want to think of another man sliding inside her, even though that would leave his conscience clear to do the same.

There were only two kinds of women: good women and bad ones. A good woman let no man except her husband enjoy her favors, but all it took was one slip to turn her into a loose woman. A good woman was both respected and protected; if a man ever forced himself on a good woman, he could expect himself to be hanged as soon as he was caught. That was the way it was, and Ben would have gladly helped hang the bastard who forced any woman, good or bad.

But other folks didn't see it like that; if Emma went to bed with him, she would automatically be stepping over the line that divided respectable women from the unrespectable ones.

The barrier was so black and white, so absolute, that Ben took a deep breath and stepped back. If he'd been thinking marriage it would be different, but Ben wasn't inclined to marriage. He wanted Emma, but the decision had to be hers because the risk would be hers, and he refused to seduce her into it.

"Then it's your choice, Emma," he said. The words were low and harsh; he could barely make his throat work. "We can go upstairs to my bedroom, right now, or we can stop. If you decide you want to go upstairs with me, I want it understood up front that I'm not a marrying man."

That was certainly honest, painfully so. Emma stared at him, bereft by the sudden loss of his touch, the pulse throbbing wildly at the base of her throat. In truth, her entire body was throbbing, hungry for more.

She hadn't thought of marriage, either. She had thought of nothing except first, the anger that had filled her, which she realized now was her protective response to the instincts he triggered in her, and then the wild urge to give in to those instincts. *Marriage?* No, that wasn't what she wanted, she barely knew the man. This was only the second time she had spoken to him. *And the second time she had felt him lying against her with heavy arousal.*

But his words were a slap of reality, showing her what she had been about to do. She could lie with him, but for no reason other than lust. And when she rose up from that bed, she would no longer be a respectable woman. If she ever married, and she hoped she did, she would have to explain to her husband why she wasn't virtuous. The only other alternative would be to go completely away from her family and anyone who knew her and begin a new life as a "widow," which would explain her lack of chastity.

She had so much to lose and so very little to gain. A few moments of pleasure, weighed against a lifetime of respectability. If she had loved him it would be different, but she didn't even have that.

With the inborn dignity with which she faced every hardship, Emma braced herself and gave him his answer. "Nor is marriage what I'm looking for. Thank you for giving me this choice."

Ben smiled crookedly at her. "What's the answer?" he asked, though he already knew.

"No," she replied, and walked away.

14

At nine o'clock Victoria excused herself and went up to her bedroom. She didn't know how soon he would follow, so she scurried like a madwoman to undress, wash, and cover herself decently in a nightgown. He had taken everything she had and she needed to regain part of herself, some small bit of modesty. She was only twenty-one and had twice been taken to wife, once for what she represented and now for what she owned, but not yet for love, for herself. She felt a need for whatever small defenses she could muster.

She was glad she hurried because the nightgown had barely settled into place around her feet when Jake opened the door and walked in. He eyed the nightgown. "That was fast."

She didn't answer, because it was obvious to him how she had hurried.

He stripped his shirt off over his head and dropped it on a chair, then bent down to untie the leather thongs from around his thighs. She watched as he removed his guns and realized that he hadn't worn them the night before. He had come to her unarmed, and she wondered if he had done so to prevent her from trying to grab one of his weapons and shoot him.

His powerful brown torso rippled with muscles as he poured

fresh water in the washbasin and bent down to splash it on his face. Victoria watched him, feeling her body already beginning to throb and come alive for him, and he hadn't even touched her. Her gaze slid over him, loving the hard strength of his body. He had several scars, she noticed, some of them so old they were nothing more than white lines, some of them still new enough to be red. She ached to touch them, to feel his heated skin beneath her hands.

He toweled his face and shoulders dry, watching her as she watched him. "Go ahead and take your hair down," he instructed, and she lifted her arms to obey.

Her hair reached her hips in silky waves when it was down. When she had all of the pins out, she went to the dresser and pulled her hair over one shoulder to brush it. Jake sat down to remove his boots and socks, but didn't take his eyes off of her.

"Good," he said softly. "Now take the nightgown off."

She moistened her lips. "I always sleep in a nightgown."

"No. You used to sleep in a nightgown. You don't now." He stood and began unbuttoning his pants. She watched without blinking as he shed his clothes, her gaze locked on his loins. He was heavy and aroused. By the time he was naked, she still hadn't moved.

He kept his voice soft. "Victoria. The gown."

She shivered, looking up at the determination in his eyes. The gown would come off, one way or the other. Slowly she reached down for the hem and began lifting it, revealing first her ankles, then her calves, her knees, the smooth columns of her thighs. He was as mesmerized as she had been watching him. The rising hem lifted higher, revealing the triangular patch of light brown curls covering her mound, then the gentle curve of her belly, the small indentation of her navel, the dip of her waist.

She stopped, her hands visibly shaking as she stared at him.

"Do you want me to do it for you?" he whispered, and she gave a small, jerky nod. He went to her and put his hands on her hips, but didn't immediately remove the nightgown. Instead he pulled her to him, and took her mouth with his. The kiss was slow and drugging. She dropped the hem and put her hands on his shoulders, letting the fabric drape over his arms and hands as he stroked her buttocks.

She was totally pliant when he finally lifted the garment off and carried her to the bed. His naked body was hot as he lay over her and covered her body with kisses. He tasted and nipped and licked, bringing both of her nipples to tight wet peaks. He tasted the underside of her arm, the curve of her waist, her belly just above her pubic curls. He rolled her onto her stomach despite her choked protests, and kissed her calves, the backs of her knees, up the back of her thigh, then gently sank his teeth into one rounded buttock, not enough to cause pain but to let her feel a slight sting. Then he worked up her spine, licking and kissing, sucking her flesh up against his teeth, and by the time he returned his attention to her buttocks she was writhing on the sheets, moaning with pleasure. One soft, fragrant location drew him to another, and he lingered over her like a bee over nectar, trying to sate himself on the taste and feel and scent of her.

He turned her onto her back again, noting the glazed look in her eyes and the flush on her breasts, the way her thighs naturally fell apart to welcome him. He took advantage of the invitation to bend and kiss her, his tongue making a brief foray that had her arching off the bed, and he saw the shock that wiped the sensual daze off her face. Before she could do anything more than sputter incoherently, though, he mounted her and stopped the protests with his own mouth as he carefully entered her.

It was a bit easier than before, but Victoria still flinched from the stretching as he squeezed inward. She couldn't decide if it was painful or so pleasurable that it bordered on pain. It didn't matter; her body was already so vibrant with yearning that it lifted, without conscious thought on her part, to his possession. He stroked her hair back from her face and kissed her, holding her until he had completed the penetration.

Victoria clung to him, wondering wildly if it would always be like this when he touched her. He did things to her that she had never heard of or imagined, and wouldn't have believed if anyone had told her. She was out of control, the gentility that was so much a part of her was forgotten in the tide of sensuality.

"God, sweetheart, you're so tight." He moved slightly and groaned aloud at the sensation. "Like a glove. Feel how tight you are around me."

She was panting, and her groan echoed his as he moved again. She dug her nails into his shoulders, her hips rotating as she asked, begged, for the relief she knew he could give her.

It was going too fast, but Jake couldn't slow it down. Her response drove him mad. He began thrusting into her in a hammering rhythm, rougher than he meant to be, but her hips thrust back at him with every motion in a frenzy that matched his. It happened fast, and hard, convulsing her in his arms and emptying him of both seed and strength. The satisfaction was shattering. Again.

Her body felt heavy and lifeless, so supremely sated that she didn't want to move. When Jake slowly withdrew from her she gave a wordless murmur of protest, but he rolled onto his side and pulled her into his arms, cradling her head on his shoulder. She opened her heavy eyelids for a moment; the lamp was still burning, but she was too tired to care.

He smoothed his hand down her body, slowly stroking her from shoulder to hip, reveling in her skin texture, in her graceful curves, everything about her. She drifted into a dream world brought on by exhaustion and pleasure, trying not to think, wanting not to think, even as the words escaped her lips: "If I hadn't married you, would I be dead by now?"

He went still. Desperately Victoria wished the words unsaid, because if it were true she didn't want to know it. He had married her, and even if it was to gain ownership of the ranch, she was still his wife. He had made love to her with care for her own pleasure. She hadn't intended to stir up the ashes and make trouble, yet now she had.

He heaved himself up so that he stared down at her. "I'll tell you this just once, then I never want it brought up again. I don't intend to have that thrown in my face whenever you start pouting over something. You were never in any danger from me. Understood?"

She was surprised by the anger she felt. "I'm not supposed to question your motives?" she snapped, trying to bolt upright. He tightened his arms around her to prevent the movement. "You lied to me from the beginning, you went off and left me to deal with Garnet on my own—"

"I told Emma—ah, *shit!*" he snarled, falling back on the bed in disgust as he realized what had happened. Garnet had interrupted him while he'd been talking to Emma, and he'd never finished his explanation. Victoria had thought he had simply deserted her. No wonder she'd taken the other two and fled! "Garnet interrupted me before I could tell Emma when I'd be back. I didn't abandon you, I had to go meet Ben. I'm sorry for that, but it can't be helped." He paused and gave her another hard look. "Now, did you understand what I said? I don't want to hear anything else about killing."

"I heard Ben say—" she began raggedly, and he held up a warning hand to stop her.

So he hadn't planned to kill her. That was nice to know, but what she really needed to hear was that he had married her because he loved her, not because it was the only way he could get the ranch. Her throat hurt with the strain of holding back the words, but she wouldn't beg. "Yes, I understand," she finally said. "You planned this from the beginning?" She swept her hand in a gesture that meant everything: the ranch, McLain . . . herself . . . everything he had done, even making love to her the night before. Had he thought that she would go more docilely to the wedding if he had already taken her to bed? If so, he had perhaps been right. She didn't want to believe that his passion had been calculated, but she couldn't deny that she felt irrevocably bound to him.

"Pretty much." He saw no reason not to tell her. "I was thirteen and Ben was eleven when McLain killed our parents and took the ranch. He thought he'd killed us, but we hid, and somehow lived. Ben was shot up worse than I was, and I thought he was going to die, too. We planned this for twenty years, working, saving money, practicing for hours and days and years with guns so we'd be good enough to take it back. Nothing was going to stand in our way."

"And nothing did." She added softly, "I do understand. The ranch is more important to you than anything else."

She waited, hoping he would deny it, that he would kiss her in that quick, fierce way of his and tell her that she was more important to him than any ranch. But he didn't, and she closed her eyes. It was a moment before she trusted her voice enough to speak again. "What would you have done if I hadn't agreed to marry you?"

He shrugged. "It didn't happen. No need to worry about it."

A cold wave swept over her, making her shiver. He misinterpreted the cause and pulled her closer, stroking his hand up her side.

"Cold?"

"No." Not on the outside. Inside, she felt frostbitten, but the words she needed still remained unsaid.

"I'll get you warm."

She heard the heat in his deep voice and her heart immediately began beating faster. Her body, it seemed, had already learned to anticipate the pleasure of his possession. She tilted her head back against his shoulder and gave him a pleading look.

"Jake . . ."

He didn't answer. He caught her thigh and pulled her leg over his hips, then angled inward. This time he entered easily, but her breath still caught in her lungs at the shock of penetration. The muscles in her entire lower body tightened and clamped down in eager anticipation, holding him, shaping themselves around him. She had no power to do anything else but cling to him.

Later, content, he lay on his stomach and went to sleep. Victoria stared up at the ceiling, the ashes of her very personal defeat bitter in her mouth.

The next day Luis entered the barn and caught sight of a bit of cloth as someone darted into an empty stall. He paused, waiting until his eyesight had completely adjusted to the relative dimness of the barn. Whoever it was had been near the stallion, Rubio, who was a fine-looking horse but also one of the meanest ones Luis had ever seen. Jake had big plans for that horse; he wouldn't take it kindly if anyone was foolin' with it.

Luis bent down and stuck a length of straw into each of his spurs to keep them from jingling. He silently pulled iron and eased down the center of the barn, cat-light on the balls of his feet.

He heard a sound, only the slightest of rustles, and moved toward it. His thumb eased the hammer back. He looked between the slats of the gate and stopped, puzzled. What was that patch of material? It looked like a skirt.

With a sigh he returned pistol to holster and walked forward to prop his arms on the top of the gate.

"Miss Waverly," he said politely. "Do you need help with something?"

The girl had been holding herself painfully still; he could see it in the taut lines of her body. Some game she was playing? But she jumped when he spoke, and the face she turned toward him was stark with fear.

"No," she said, scrambling to her feet. Bits of hay clung to her skirt. She stood in the middle of the stall, and the fear didn't leave her face. She was like a cornered fawn poised for flight.

Luis, though only twenty-two, had been earning his way with his gun for a long time. He was as lethal as a diamondback rattler, as too many men had found out to their cost. He couldn't remember, ever, any softness or love in his life, but in his early childhood there must have been a loving mother, one who had cradled her infant to her breast and crooned sweet songs to him, because Luis loved women. He loved the way they looked, smelled, tasted, walked, sounded, felt. Young or old, whore or spinster, slim or plump, from giggly schoolgirls to bawdy saloon girls to starchy matrons, he reserved for them, one and all, his sweetest smile and most liquid voice. He was used to all of them responding to him, even if it was only an involuntary softening of the eyes.

So why was this incredibly beautiful young girl staring at him in terror?

It piqued him. It hurt his ego. It softened his heart, because he didn't want her to be frightened of anyone or anything. Women, to Luis, were put on earth to be enjoyed and cherished.

He wanted to put his arms around the girl and swear to her that everything would be all right, that he, Luis, would protect her with his life.

Instead he smiled, exerting his considerable charm, and held himself very still. "Were you looking at the horse, *chica?* He's beautiful, isn't he?"

Her eyes were dark blue, like the deep depths of the ocean. Luis had been to California and had seen that wonderful color. His entire body tingled in reaction to her beauty. But still she stared blankly at him, not responding to the warm reassurance in his voice and smile.

Luis moved back a step, giving her more room. "My name is Luis. Luis Fronteras." He had no idea what his real last name was, but had chosen, when he was still a child, the name of the village where he lived in the streets.

Her eyes flickered a little.

"It was very brave of you to try to escape across such land," he continued soothingly. "Three women alone, and at night! I admired you very much. I wished to tell you that you were safe now, that we wanted only to protect you, not harm you."

"I wasn't brave," Celia finally said in a thin little voice. "I was terrified. Victoria is the brave one."

Ah, the older sister, Jake's new wife. She was indeed formidable, with her haughty chin and cool blue eyes.

"Yes, she is very brave," he said with real admiration. "Where were you going?"

"We wanted to go south toward Santa Fe, but we knew riders were coming in from the south so we couldn't. Victoria said that there are Indians to the east, so we went west and were going to turn south in the morning, when we were well away from the ranch."

A plan, Luis thought, that could well have worked if they had been more used to the land. He nodded his head and reached out to open the stall door, sweeping it wide and standing back to give her plenty of room. "And the other pretty lady, the one with the beautiful brown eyes—she is your cousin?"

He knew well enough she was, but he wanted to keep her talking.

Celia nodded, taking a couple of steps toward the open gate but halting before she got too close to him. "Emma. She came to live with us in Augusta several years ago, during the war. Uncle Rufus and Aunt Helen had died, and Emma's fiancé was killed in the war, and she had nowhere to go. Emma is brave, too."

"All three of you are very brave."

She shook her head. "I'm not brave at all. I was so scared and all I wanted to do was hide. Victoria and Emma said we must leave, so that Garnet and the Major couldn't . . . couldn't hurt me."

The blind look was back in her eyes and with a spurt of anger Luis understood. It was inevitable, really. She was so beautiful, how could any man look at her and not want her? Like everyone else in the territory, Luis had known McLain and Garnet by reputation, and he could guess what they must have put this beautiful child through.

Luis left his post by the gate, carefully walking off and showing her that he didn't intend to corner her. He paused in front of Rubio's stall, and the big stallion's ears went back as he watched the man. Luis was too smart to lean on the gate within reach of the stallion's teeth and hooves, but he couldn't help admiring the animal. "You magnificent bastard," he crooned in liquid Spanish, "you're not good for anything but the mares, eh? You're too mean to ride, but what a life you have! Nothing to do but eating, sleeping, and romancing the ladies."

Celia crept out of the empty stall and stood watching him, still half-poised for flight. Luis gave her a flashing smile. "I have never before seen a horse as beautiful as this one."

She nodded and at last her own smile broke out. Luis caught his breath, struck dumb. She looked like an angel.

"He's wonderful," she breathed. "I bring him things to eat, and now he lets me pat him on the neck."

He was alarmed that she would get so close to the animal, but he didn't scold her. Any hint of anger would send her flying.

"My name is Celia," she offered.

He already knew that, but he nodded as if she had given him a gift.

"I have a mare, Gypsy. Jake helped me choose her. She's really smart, but when ya'll were chasing us, Victoria made me swap horses with her because her horse is faster than mine and she wanted Emma and me to get away."

"Yes, a very brave lady, your sister."

"I'm glad that she married Jake. I like him, but he really should have told us his real name."

"He had his reasons, *chica*."

"I know." She sighed, and the bright light faded out of her face. "The Major was a horrible man. He killed their mother and father, did you know?"

"Yes, I know."

"Before I knew Jake was really Jake Sarratt, I used to pray that the Sarratts would come back and kill the Major. I know it's a sin," she whispered, "but I hated him."

"It's not a sin to hate evil."

"I hope not. I have to go," she said, suddenly taking fright again. With a swish of skirts she ran away, Luis watched her disappear out the front of the barn, her slender figure briefly silhouetted against the bright opening before she was gone from view. She was sweet and fey, and he wanted her.

The days after Victoria's wedding passed slowly. They had lived on edge for so long that the abrupt calm made them all feel as if the bright summer days dawdled along. Time didn't tick, it oozed. They were all relieved.

Celia began to giggle again, and the musical sound made them all smile. She dogged Jake's boot heels whenever he left the house, and although she was still shy with Ben, someone began playing practical jokes on him. Victoria strongly suspected Celia, because her sister had always had a penchant for that type of thing, but Ben *knew* it was Celia. He had seen her sneaking out of his room once, but he continued to pretend ignorance. She got such joy of it that he often exaggerated his mishaps, just to watch her try to act innocent while she was struggling with laughter.

But with Emma, Ben was held at a distance by a careful silence. She pretended he didn't exist, and he allowed her to do so. It wasn't easy, since they lived in the same house, but Emma's self-possession was such that it was possible. He wasn't sure how, but she could speak to him and still treat him as if he weren't there. It made him angry but he accepted it, because he knew the reason for it.

The days were busy. Despite their expectations of the worst, there hadn't been any trouble with the men who had been out with the herds. Some left with quick looks over their shoulders, some stayed. Jake and his men worked long, hard hours getting an accurate count of the herd and altering the brands on cattle and horses alike. Jake and Ben were often out of the house from dawn until long after dark. They would return tired and caked with grime, smelling of horses and sweat. To make it easier for them to wash they rigged up a contraption behind the bunkhouse: a small enclosure with two buckets of water balanced overhead and a rope tied to each bucket. Most of the men got in the habit of stripping, tipping some of the water over their heads, then soaping up and using the remainder of the water to rinse. Whoever used the water had to refill the buckets. At the end of each long hot day, there was always a line waiting to use the contraption, though a lot of the men still used the river if they were inclined to bathe. For some of them, that wasn't very often.

For Victoria, the slow summer days were filled with a deep sense of unreality. During the day she did what wives had always done; she mended, she made certain the meals were on time, and took care of the myriad and endless details of making a home. That was the way she had always expected her life to go, and the routine was as familiar to her as her own face.

At night, however, things changed. When Jake came up the stairs each night and entered her bedroom—their bedroom now—and closed the door behind him, nothing was as she had ever imagined her life to be. She spent the hours in a sensual daze, locked in his arms. She lost her privacy to dress or undress alone and had to accustom herself to his tall body in her bed. He touched her however and whenever he liked, and he liked it often. There wasn't an inch of her skin left unexplored. She drowned in the sensuality of the nights, her mind overwhelmed by the demands of the flesh, both his and her own. Sometimes when she awoke in the bright morning sunlight she was appalled at the carnal excesses of the night before and would swear that she would never let herself behave so mindlessly again. But her intentions never lasted past his first kiss, the first touch of his hard body against hers.

The more influence he exerted over her at night, the harder she tried to shore up her defenses during the day. If he had ever said those simple words, *I love you*, she would have abandoned herself totally to him, but the words he whispered to her were of lust. So every morning she tried desperately to isolate her heart from him, to wall up part of herself where he couldn't find her. It was pure self-defense, the need to keep a kernel of her being whole and untouched, a foundation on which she could rely if the rest of her life fell apart.

"A kitten!"

Celia's face was bright with joy as she scooped the tiny animal out of Luis's lean brown hands. She cuddled the ball of fluff to her cheek and the kitten gave a squeaky meow. "Oh, Luis, where did you find it?"

"In the tack room. Its mother must have died."

"Will it be all right?" she asked anxiously. "Is it old enough to eat on its own?"

He shrugged. "There's only one way to find out."

Together they trooped up to the house, where Celia begged Lola for a saucer of warm milk, which she placed on the sunwarmed flagstones of the courtyard. The kitten sniffed daintily before lowering its pink nose and beginning to lap.

Celia smiled. "It's old enough."

"It seems so." Luis watched her crouched there on the flagstones, her face intent on the kitten. She was so full of delight he wanted to snatch her to her feet and kiss her.

She looked up at him. "Where are you going to keep it? What have you named it?"

"I'm not keeping it anywhere. I brought it to you."

"You mean it's mine?" she breathed.

"If you want it."

"Of course I want it! I've never had a pet before." She lightly rubbed the kitten behind the ears and it arched up to her hand, but didn't lift its head from the milk.

"Lola said you'd found a kitten," Victoria said, stepping out into the courtyard. To Luis's surprise, she crouched down in a position identical to Celia's and stroked the kitten. "It's so pretty and soft."

"Luis found it. He said I can have it."

Victoria smiled. "What will you name it?"

"I don't know, I've never had a kitten before. What are some cat names?"

"Tiger?" Victoria suggested, then looked doubtfully at the kitten. She and Celia laughed together.

"What would you name it, Luis?" Celia asked.

He shrugged and sank down on his haunches to join the women. "I've never had a pet, either."

Victoria smiled at the slim young man, wondering if he felt a kinship with the little animal since he was so catlike himself. She liked him, even though she could look at him and see danger clinging to his broad shoulders like a cloak. But Luis's smile was always warm and gentle; he was never coarse around Celia, and he seemed to have appointed himself sort of a bodyguard for the girl. Victoria was glad and hoped Celia might lose some of her fearfulness around men. In general the men around her now teased her and watched over her, but never threatened her or gave her sidelong glances.

"First, is it a male or a female?" Victoria asked practically.

Again Luis shrugged, which piqued Celia's interest. "How do you tell?"

"You pick it up and look," Luis replied.

She did, holding the kitten on its back. The three of them solemnly studied its belly.

After a moment Celia said, "What are we looking at?"

"I don't know," Victoria admitted, laughter brimming in her eyes.

"Luis?"

He put his hand over his mouth and pretended to be considering the matter, but at last he was forced to admit, "It looks like a furry belly."

"That's what I thought, too," Victoria said.

Celia began to giggle, then they were all laughing. At the sound of booted steps, they looked up. Celia lifted the kitten. "Luis has given me a kitten," she explained to Jake. "We want to name it, but we can't tell if it's a boy or a girl."

Jake's face relaxed into a grin, and Victoria felt her heart turn over. He leaned down and took the kitten, his big, lean hand gentle as he held it up and looked. "It's a tom," he said, and put it down in Celia's lap.

"How can you tell?"

He wasn't about to get into one of those discussions with her, so he tousled her hair and said, "Practice. There were always a lot of cats around when Ben and I were young."

"Show me how to tell."

Victoria was watching with glee, waiting to see how he got out of that. Luis had turned his head to hide his grin.

"You'd need a male and a female side by side, so I could show you the difference."

"I suppose." She sighed with disappointment. "At least now we know to name it a male name."

"Call it Tom," he suggested. "That's a name, and it's a tomcat, so it fits."

"Tom." After a minute's deliberation she nodded, and returned the kitten to its saucer of milk.

Jake held out his hand, and Victoria placed hers in it for him to draw her to her feet. He guided her inside with his hand on the small of her back.

When they were out of earshot, she asked, "Can we trust Luis with Celia?"

"As much as anyone. She's too beautiful to expect the young bucks not to notice her, but he won't force himself on her, if that's what you're asking."

"It is, I suppose. It's just that she's so innocent. I don't want something awful to happen to her."

His green eyes gleamed. "Awful?" he asked in a deep voice.

Victoria blinked at him, realizing abruptly that he was escorting her up the stairs. She blushed hotly. "What are you doing?" she demanded in a fierce whisper.

"Taking you to bed."

"Jake, it's the middle of the day!"

"I know. What about it?"

"Everyone will know what we're doing."

"Do you think they don't know what we're doing when we go to bed every night?"

"People go to sleep at night. It's obvious we wouldn't be sleeping if we went to bed now!"

The pressure of his hand was inexorable. "We're married. It's legal." He was determined to break through her defenses, one way or another. He didn't know why, but she kept building barriers between them. When he came back to the ranch house every night, he always found an invisible wall between them, locking him out of her thoughts. Every night he would smash it down, but she would busily rebuild it during the day. He had come back to the house specifically to make love to her now, to see if he could destroy the barrier once and for all. He wanted all of her, every little bit of her, with the greediness of someone dying of thirst; he felt as if he'd been given a glass of water but told he could drink only half of it.

He locked them in the bedroom and stripped both her and himself. As he placed her on the bed, he saw the despair in her eyes. Despair filled his own heart. Why did she feel she had to resist him? Then she closed her eyes and twined her arms around his neck. For him, as well as for her, the why ceased to matter.

They came together in a rush of heated flesh, straining toward each other, already desperate with passion. The rest of the world was shut out during their lovemaking, but afterward, when she was trying to sort out her clothes, he saw the reserve in her eyes and knew he had failed.

15

Long after Jake had returned to work, he remained lost in thought. Victoria was *his* wife, but he couldn't say that she belonged to him. The knowledge ate at him. What was it that caused her to keep him that small, careful distance from her? Did she regret their marriage?

Her inner reserve hid secrets from him; he could sense their presence, even though he couldn't get inside her mind and read them. She was hiding something from him, and he was at a loss to know what it was. For the first time in his life a woman had gotten inside his emotional walls, stinging him to resentment by making him vulnerable, and doubling the resentment because he couldn't get to her as she had gotten to him. What was it? What was she hiding? Was it something about her marriage to the Major? Was there some lingering evidence of what he had done to her? It wasn't something she had done, he didn't think, but rather something that had happened to her.

The possibilities made him go cold. He was afraid to even ask her what was wrong, afraid he wouldn't be able to bear the answer. Every time he thought of her in the Major's bed he was filled with a bitter anger. He hadn't been able to bear seeing McLain's personal possessions and he'd had them all thrown out, but he couldn't throw out McLain's wife. She was *his* wife now—or was she? Was part of her mind still caught in a dark pit of memories? Was it more than that, something she couldn't deny or ignore?

There had been real fear in her eyes the first time he'd made love to her, but he brushed it aside thinking it was merely a result of the situation. He'd thought he'd won when she turned all sweet and hot in his arms. Surely she knew by now she had nothing to fear from him?

But it wasn't fear of him. It was something else, something that tormented her, and instead of coming to him for comfort she was locking it inside. Maybe she thought he wouldn't understand, maybe she thought he would blame her for whatever it was.

What had the Major done to her?

If he pushed her, she simply withdrew further. He had to teach her to trust him, and the only way to do that was to show her over and over how much he wanted her. As their intimacy deepened, so would her trust, and one day he would breach that wall in her mind. Whatever it was, he thought, he'd hold her and keep her safe and love her again. It wouldn't matter what it was, as long as he *knew*. He could fight dragons for her, but not ghosts.

Emma spent much of her time during those quiet summer days out riding. Their hasty flight had shown her how necessary it was to be in good physical shape in this country. Victoria rode out with her most days, and sometimes Celia would join them. On this particular day, however, she'd gone out alone because Celia had been off somewhere with her kitten and Victoria had been writing a difficult letter to her parents, informing them of McLain's death and her subsequent remarriage. They would be profoundly shocked no matter how she told them and she had been wrestling with it all morning.

Emma unsaddled her gelding. When she turned around to sling the saddle over the fence, she collided with a hard wall of flesh. She said, "Uummph!" and staggered back under the impact. Ben's hands shot out to break her fall. He steadied her, his hazel eyes intent as he looked her over. She was acutely aware of how disheveled she was; her hair was straggling down, she had gotten dirt on her white shirtwaist, and she suspected her face was dusty. A flush of embarrassment burned her cheeks.

Ben took the saddle from her hands and placed it on the rail. He took his time about it. She was usually so starched, but today she looked wonderfully tousled with her hair curling damply about her face. When he turned back to her she was still standing with her arms limp at her side, but now her face was tense. She felt it, too; he wished she didn't, because a one-sided attraction was much easier to resist than one that was mutual.

"Were you riding alone?" he finally asked, needing to break the silence between them.

She nodded. "I couldn't find Celia, and Victoria was busy."

"I don't like it. Don't do it again."

Another flush heated Emma's face, but this one was from anger. "You don't have the right to tell me what to do."

His brows drew together and he took a step closer. "Don't fight me," he said softly. "I said that for a reason. It's too dangerous for a woman alone, even when you're on our land."

She bit her lip, wishing her reactions weren't so swift and so close to the surface with him. "You're right, of course. I don't know why I snapped at you."

"Now you're lying, because we both know why." He reached out and trailed his finger across her collarbone, the light, delicate touch making both of them shudder. "You can always change your mind, you know."

She swallowed, her pale throat working. "And then what?"

"Then we can stop avoiding each other. We have an itch we need to scratch because it isn't going to go away until we do. Then we can sleep at night, instead of lying awake."

Emma whirled, turning her back to him. "Thank you very much," she said in a stifled tone. "I don't think I should waste my time on a man who thinks I'm no more important than a mosquito bite."

Ben put his hands on her waist and carefully drew her back until she was pressed against him, fitting her bottom into the cra-dle of his thighs. He rubbed his hips against her in a slow, circular rhythm. "I've never wanted to do this to a mosquito," he murmured, and bent his head to kiss the side of her neck.

She shuddered, and her head fell back against his shoulder. Her hands reached back convulsively and clamped on his thighs. His hot mouth raised chills wherever it touched, chills that raced over her and caused her lower body to quicken. "Oh, God," she whispered in despair. How could it be like this?

Ben smoothed his hands up her front until they closed over her breasts. He groaned aloud feeling the way they filled his palms. He wanted her naked, he wanted to lie naked with her. His hands were almost rough as he turned her around, his mouth hard and hungry as it closed over hers. Emma arched into his embrace, her arms twining around his neck. She was burning up, and the only thing that could give her ease was his bare skin against hers. She was wanton and knew she should be ashamed, but she wasn't.

Ben dragged his mouth from hers and pressed it to her eyelids, cheeks, and mouth with quick, hard, desperate kisses. "Lie down with me," he coaxed in a ragged voice. "I need you bad, Emma girl."

She could barely think. She was dizzy, clinging to his broad shoulders because her legs felt so wobbly. *Lie down with him.* She wanted to, she needed to . . .

"Where?" she asked. Dimly she noticed that her voice sounded as drugged as she felt.

Ben shuddered, and he actually took a step to push her toward an empty stall before he realized he couldn't just tumble her in the hay, right here and now. It was broad daylight. Men were constantly coming and going in the barn; it was a miracle that someone hadn't already interrupted them. He sure as hell didn't want some cowhand gaping at Emma's smooth white body. She was his, and no one else was going to see her.

It took every ounce of his control to drag his hands away from her breasts and cup them around her face. He kissed her again, fiercely. "Come to my room tonight," he said.

Her big brown eyes were dazed, and she licked her lips as if tasting him. Anguish stole into her gaze, along with reality. "I can't," she whispered.

He ground his teeth together. She had to leave this second, or he'd forget what few good intentions he had. While he still could, he released her and sent her on her way with a small push. She went without looking back, stumbling a little as if her legs didn't work right. Ben leaned his head against the top rail of the stall, breathing hard. It was five minutes before he straightened and left the barn, his face taut and pale.

In the loft Celia rolled over onto her back and stared at the dust motes floating above her head. Her eyes were both troubled and curious. Ben had been doing some bad things to Emma, but she hadn't seemed to mind. He'd done the sort of things that Victoria had warned Celia that Garnet and the Major wanted to do to her; thinking of them touching her like that made her feel sick to her stomach. But watching Ben do them to Emma hadn't made her sick; she had felt funny, sort of shaky and excited. Emma hadn't looked sick, either.

Maybe those things were bad only when bad people did them. She felt confused, but was also aware of a calm certainty growing in her. What she had just seen hadn't been wrong. It was new and a bit frightening, but not wrong.

The kitten pounced on her stomach, and absently Celia rubbed its little body. She lay in the dusty loft, staring at the sunbeams, and took the first step into womanhood.

Luis found her late that afternoon over a mile from the house, sitting under a tree and teasing the kitten with a leaf. She looked up and smiled when he rode up, but didn't speak. He swung down from the horse and let the reins trail on the ground. "Your sister is looking for you," he said, sitting down beside her. "Why did you walk so far?"

"I didn't intend to. I was thinking and ended up here. But it's pretty and peaceful here, don't you think?"

Luis studied the endless land around them; it housed so many dangers he never thought of it as peaceful. It was wild, big, but never peaceful. At this moment, however, it was empty and clear of any visible dangers, so he said, "Yes."

Celia lifted the leaf over the kitten's head. It reared up and batted with its tiny paws. She seemed content just to sit and play with the kitten.

Luis said, "We need to go back."

She sighed. "I suppose so." But she didn't get up. She hesitated. "If I—Luis, will you tell me something?"

"If I can, *chica*."

She turned her head and looked at him. Her face was pale, her dark blue eyes grave. "What men do to women—is it always bad?"

At her words he felt breathless, as if someone had hit him in the stomach. He didn't want to talk about this with her. She was so beautiful. Until now her youth had protected her from him; he had thought of her essentially as a child, despite the ripe swelling of her body. The look in her eyes now, however, was not that of a child.

He inhaled, long and deep. "No," he murmured. "It's bad only if the woman doesn't want to do it, if the man forces her. If they're in love, then it's a beautiful, loving thing for them to do."

She nodded and turned her attention back to the kitten. It rolled onto its back, grabbing at the leaf with all four feet.

"And it makes babies," she said.

"Yes. Sometimes. Not every time."

"I've been afraid of it, afraid someone—a man—would try to do that to me. Garnet wanted to, and so did the Major. They tried to catch me alone, and the thought of them touching me made me sick." It was easier talking to him if she kept her eyes on the kitten. But she could feel his attention on her; it was like the intensity of sunshine. "I thought it was bad. But it was bad only because of them, wasn't it? It isn't bad by itself."

"That's right." His voice was very grave and gentle. "It's people who make it bad. It's like this gun I wear. By itself it's nothing. But when someone holds it, it can be good, it can protect, it can feed—or it can murder. What it does depends on the person who holds it."

The kitten had tired of the leaf and spied Luis's spurs. Flattening itself on its belly, it crept forward in a slow, comical stalking motion. When it was close enough it pounced, batting at the star and making it twirl.

"I don't know anything about men, about their bodies. It seems frightening because I don't know exactly what they look like, or how they do it."

Luis concentrated very hard on the kitten. He knew what she was going to say before she said it, but he prayed that she wouldn't, because he didn't know what he would do if she did—

"May I see you, please?" she whispered. "I want to know. I don't want to be afraid anymore."

His heart stopped, and he closed his eyes. "*Chica,* no."

"Why?" Then abruptly her face flushed and she turned away. "I thought—because we're friends—but it's bad, isn't it? What I asked of you."

"No, not bad," he croaked. He, who was always at ease with women, who always knew the right thing to say and how to touch them, was at a loss and shaking with tension. "It's just— *chica,* this thing that men and women do, this lovemaking—I would like to do it with you. You're very beautiful and sweet, and I want you very much. But you should learn these things with someone you love, not with—"

"But I want it to be you, Luis," she said softly. "You're beautiful, too, and you make me feel safe, and warm inside. I want to see you, and touch you, and learn how you're made."

He was simultaneously numb and in pain. She wasn't asking for sex, only for knowledge. She wanted to examine his body. He didn't know how he could say no, when he thought he would die for the pleasure of her hand on him.

He slowly unbuckled his gunbelt. The kitten played around his boots, but he no longer noticed it. Celia moved closer, until she was on her knees beside him. The afternoon sunlight dappled her face and hair, washing her in a golden light. He could barely breathe. Dimly he noticed that she was breathing in soft pants, too.

He unbuckled his other belt and began unfastening his pants. He didn't wear a full union suit, preferring two separate pieces so he could remove the top during the summer when it got hot. He thought of all the times he'd so casually undressed in front of a woman. This time his heart was pounding as he peeled his garments off his hips and down to his thighs.

A slight breeze wafted over his naked flesh. Celia's lips parted and an expression of wonder lit her face. Very gently she reached out and touched him with one finger.

ally theirs, after all. But what else did she have that he wanted? He didn't need her at all now; if he wanted to, he could easily be id of her.

But she had also felt his passion; despite his roughness the night before, she'd felt it in him even then. He had been as much at the mercy of his body as she was to hers. If she truly believed that he could kill her after the nights she had spent in his arms, then she might as well put the gun in his hand because just the belief itself would be the death of her hope, her love. No, he wouldn't kill her. But neither did he love her, and that knowledge was behind all her fears and wild imaginings. Her body was safe with him; her heart was in mortal danger. It took all of her self-control to protect it and keep it hidden from him.

She sighed as she opened the door to Celia's bedroom, dragging her mind back to the matter at hand, which was finding her sister. She had had the embroidery hoop last, and Victoria couldn't find it.

It had been almost dark the day before when Luis had ridden up with Celia behind him. He'd found her under a tree over a mile away, he'd said, playing with the kitten. Now she had disappeared again, but surely she wasn't walking in the rain.

She went to the kitchen. "Has anyone seen Celia?"

Lola shook her head. Juana said, "I think she went to the barn. She took the kitten so he could play."

Victoria sighed. At least now she didn't have to worry about Celia's safety when she was out like that. She didn't want to find the embroidery hoop bad enough to get wet running down to the barn. She'd just keep looking for it in the house.

She began methodically searching every room and was on her hands and knees looking under the desk in the library when Jake came in. She glanced quickly away, feeling uneasy after the strange violence that had erupted between them.

He tossed his wet hat onto a chair and ran his hands through his hair. "What're you looking for?"

"The embroidery hoop."

"Under my desk?" he asked incredulously.

"Celia had it last."

He understood and reached out to help her as she got to her

His manhood began to stir. He'd prayed it wou[ld], knowing it would. Her warm little palm closed arou[nd]

She gave a soft murmur of delight as he grew t[o] cence in her hand. "You're so beautiful," she said lo[...] know it would look like this, or feel so hard and so[...] same time."

He closed his eyes, groaning with exquisite pain. "[...] You have to stop—*now*."

She didn't stop caressing him. "But I don't want to [...]

When his eyes flew open, she smiled at him, a war[...] very female smile. "I want to know everything, and I wan[...] teach me."

It was raining. Victoria thought the weather suite[d] mood, though she would have preferred the drama of th[...] and lightning to this gray, steady drip, drip, drip. The [...] before, lying in Jake's arms, she had thought she would die fr[...] the sharp ecstasy, but today in the gray light she wondered h[...] much more of herself she could lose before there was no[...] left. She had been drowning, mindless with sensation and [...] her last frail defenses wavering, when she had opened he[...] and seen him watching her with shrewd calculation. H[e'd] been gauging her response to him, deliberately taking her [...] and higher while feeling none of the giddiness himself. [...] been like a dash of cold water, and she had turned her fa[ce] from him.

She hadn't expected him to react with such violenc[e] had jerked her head back around to face him. His eyes [...] green with rage, his neck corded. But his rage had broke[n con-] trol and he had begun driving into her, hammering his [...] hers. Afterward, he had gripped her chin and said in a [...] voice, "Don't you ever turn away from me like that [...] forced her to lie close to him all night.

What was it he wanted of her? Why had he bee[n...] her like that? Her lips trembled before she could con[...]

He already had the ranch. As her husband, he l[...] everything that had once been hers. He had already [...] of the land to Ben. She didn't resent him for that;

feet. Victoria would have drawn away, but his fingers tightened on her arm. He closed his hands on her waist to hold her. His voice was low. "Are you all right?"

She knew what he was asking and somberly studied him in the dim light. He smelled of fresh air and dampness, she noticed, but his body heat burned through his rain-spattered clothes. "A little sore, but that's all. You . . . didn't hurt me."

"I'm sorry. You made me angry and I lost control."

If it got much darker, they would need to light the lamps. The rain pattered on and cool air blew in through the open window. She could feel her own pulse beating through her body. "I'm fine," she whispered. "It doesn't matter."

He drew her forward just a fraction of an inch, but he'd been standing so close already that the movement brushed her breasts against his shirt. She slowly inhaled, feeling her breasts tighten and swell. "I'll make it up to you," he said against her temple.

Her throat was tight, and her eyelids heavy. "You know . . . you know that there's no need." She had climaxed before he had, and he had groaned aloud at her inner contractions. Even in anger, he had been able to make her respond to him.

He pressed his mouth against her temple, his lips hot on the delicate skin. He covered her breast with his hand. "I think there is."

Her hand was on his shoulder, his powerful muscles firm under her palm. Without thinking she flexed her fingers, her nails biting through the damp cloth of his shirt.

"Jake." Her voice was low. "We can't. The door—not here."

Slowly he released her, his green eyes glittering in the dim gray room. He stepped backward until he reached the door, and with careful restraint shut and locked it. Then he began unbuckling his gunbelt.

Her lower body felt heavy. She watched him disarm himself, then looked around at the library. There were chairs, very comfortable leather chairs, but no nice long sofa where they could lie down. She ought not to let him do this—a lady never would—but they were locked in a shadowy world, surrounded by the smell and sound of rain, and her body was quickening. He reached for her, his hands sliding up her back to clench in her hair, his mouth coming down over hers in a deep kiss that filled her with his breath and taste.

He lowered her to the floor, and she didn't even notice that the dark wood was hard against her back. She felt his hands opening the buttons of her dress and sliding it off her shoulders. The soft straps of her chemise followed. Her pale bare breasts felt the wash of cool air, then his wet mouth seared her nipple and she moaned.

"You taste sweet . . . and cool." He gave the heat of his mouth to her breast, and the nipple puckered against his tongue. He sighed in deep, almost painful satisfaction, sucking in a rhythm that pinned the tight nub between his tongue and the roof of his mouth. Victoria moved beneath him, her legs shifting, her hips reaching for his. Her nails were digging into his shoulders, a primitive signal of passion that made his manhood surge against the restraint of his pants. He tugged at the buttons to free himself.

Her senses were so heightened that she could feel her own pulse as the warm blood pumped through her body. She smelled the hot musk of his arousal and shifted to aid him as he fought through the bunched layers of skirt and petticoats to find her legs. She wore the common, convenient open-crotch drawers, and his fingers went straight to the open seam, sliding into her soft folds. His touch burned like a brand, and she made an incoherent sound that could have been a plea.

He shifted his weight on top of her, opening her legs wider with his own thighs. The motion caught the fabric of her drawers and pulled them to the side, blocking his entry. He reached down, hooked his strong fingers in the opening, and ripped the garment from front to back. Victoria gasped, but didn't protest; she wanted him too much. She reached for him, needing the hot slide of his flesh into hers. She could feel him probing and lifted her hips in silent invitation, but he held back, cupping her chin in his hand and turning her face so he could look at her.

She knew that her soul was in her eyes, and desperately she closed them. It was the same act that had so enraged him the night before, but she couldn't help it. He would plainly see the aching tenderness of her heart, the silent yearning for more than he wanted to offer, and that was more than she could bear.

Jake looked down at her face, cameo pale in the gray, rain-washed light, and his chest tightened as he watched her close him out. Last night he had lashed out in anger, hurting her, but he wouldn't do that again. He murmured a soft reassurance, and slid his arms under her to protect her from the hard floor, as he slowly penetrated. The sensation made both of them catch their breaths, and against her will her eyes flew open.

His face was very close, his breath mingling with hers as he made a small movement that lodged him deeper. "All right?" he asked in a soft, guttural tone.

"Yes." The word was barely audible.

The reassurance was all he needed, and he pushed inward until she had accepted his full length. He watched every nuance of her expression, hungrily soaking in her response. Maybe she didn't trust him, but she wanted him. She was his wife; he was entitled to make love to her as often as he wished, strengthening the sensual bonds and seducing her into trust. Someday when he made love to her, he'd see only passion in her eyes, not the shadowed secrets that lurked there now.

He shuddered as a wave of pleasure washed through him. Not yet, God, not yet. He tightened his arms around her and rolled onto his back, taking her with him in a tangle of skirts and legs. She looked deliciously wanton with her breasts exposed and her dress rucked up to her waist, her eyes dazed with passion. He put his hands on her hips and guided her motion. He could feel her thighs trembling as they clasped his body, and she bit her lips to hold back a moan, lest anyone hear them.

The floor scrubbed at his shoulder blades, and would be doing the same thing to her knees. Her skirt and petticoats were bunched up, hindering her movement, blocking his view. Their big, comfortable bed upstairs was much better, but there was no way he could wait long enough now for them to get there. He lifted her off himself and got up.

"Jake!" She looked at him, her eyes dazed and bewildered.

"Easy, honey. I'll take care of you." He hoisted her onto the edge of the desk and pushed her skirts up again, then moved forward between her thighs. His entry this time was rougher, but she was ready for him and felt only relief.

His thrusts were harder and faster, his mouth hungry over hers.

Victoria cried out, the sound muffled. He was burning her alive and she loved it, loved him. Her body was screaming for release. How swiftly she had changed from the prudish young woman who had been horrified when he had seen her bare breasts! Now she would guide his hands or mouth to her breasts when she needed his touch; now she no longer even thought of putting on a nightgown, but crawled naked into his arms. He no longer had to coax her body into surrendering to every new sensation; she was eager for the hot, blinding pleasure of his penetration.

"God . . . I wish . . . we were . . . naked," he said with clenched teeth, his shoulders rigid with tension. He was panting, the speed and rhythm of his strokes approaching frenzy. She cried out, convulsing, and again he caught the sound with his mouth, holding her as she heaved in his arms and her soft internal muscles milked at his erection. He soared to the edge, and held back only because he wanted to feel every one of those small contractions. Even then, the timing was so close that she had barely gone limp in his arms when his back arched and he shook violently, spewing his seed into her.

What had begun with slow, dreamy sensuality ended with raw lust, and he felt drained. But he wanted more. He always wanted more. He slumped over her, and began kissing her again.

She moaned, her limbs heavy with exhaustion. He was getting hard inside her again, and she didn't know if she could summon enough energy to respond. Every nerve was tingling, her heart pounding. How could he push her like this? Always before he'd held her in his arms and let her rest before taking her again. This time he wasn't even pausing.

He loomed over her, his hands curving under her arms and over her shoulders to keep her from sliding on the desktop. His hips hammered and recoiled and hammered again, his shaft reaching deep inside her to her womb. She stared up at him, glassy-eyed; his face was so hard and intent that he looked brutal. His eyes were narrow and molten, the color a deep, hot green. Sweat ran down his face and matted his hair.

The edges of reality blurred and swirled. She heard a high, keening sound and knew it was hers, and he'd made no effort to muffle it.

She was burning, her flesh damp in the cool room. Her body shuddered under the impact of his thrusts. She tried to struggle up, but he pinned her down with his powerful hands. Her inner tension was already unbearable and getting worse. She began to fight him, sobbing with frustration. He controlled her, pushing her higher, his attention focused on her so intently that he was aware of nothing else in the world.

"Tell me," he rasped, wanting those damned shadows out of her eyes, wanting nothing hidden between them.

She was drowning, losing herself. The gray mists were crowding in, her defenses crumbling. The final victory was his, after all. "I love you," she whispered, and a small part of her was stricken even as her flesh shuddered at the climax of pleasure.

Jake crouched over her in writhing orgasm, his mind shattering. She loved him? Elation swelled in him; until that moment he hadn't realized how much he had wanted, needed, for her to love him. But the secrets were still there, because even as she had said the words he'd seen the sadness in her eyes.

Victoria heard both the echo of what she'd said, and the silence of what he didn't say.

16

She counted again, then a third time, ticking the days off on her fingers to make certain. She had waited each day for the beginning of her monthly time, dreading it because Jake would have to know; husband or not, she didn't know how to broach such a subject with him. But the day when it should have begun had passed without sign, and a sort of incredulous certainty had begun to grow in her. She was never late, not even by a day. Now, a week later, she had no doubt as to the cause of her body's failure to remain on schedule: she was pregnant.

She wasn't surprised, really, though she hadn't thought it would happen so soon. They had been married barely three weeks. But he'd made love to her every night, at least twice a night, and sometimes during the day, too. One of those times had borne fruit.

A baby. Victoria smoothed her hand down over her flat abdomen, then looked at her own reflection in the mirror. Outwardly, nothing was different. Inwardly, everything was changing. She was both frightened and elated. She carried Jake's child.

He didn't love her, but his child would.

The young woman in the mirror, sitting half-dressed in her petticoats and chemise with her long hair streaming over her shoulders and down her back, had an eerily serene expression on her pale face. Her eyes were calm, although darkened by her introspective mood. Victoria didn't feel calm at all; she felt shaky. She wanted both to cry and laugh. She wanted Jake's arms around her, now, in this moment when she first admitted and faced the fact that his baby was forming inside her. She wanted his strength and his passion. She wanted to lie with him on the white sheets and take him inside her in the act that had created this new life.

Her breasts throbbed, and she put her hands over them. Her eyes closed, and her lips parted. For the first time she didn't regret blurting out that she loved him.

He'd said he would be out all day. She would have to wait through the long hours until he returned home before she could tell him. Should she tell him right away, or wait until they were in bed together?

She would wait and see what his mood was, she decided, as wives had for thousands of years. If he was tired and irritable, she'd wait until after he'd eaten dinner and rested.

As it happened, Jake and Ben got back to the house earlier than expected that afternoon. The sun was a hot red ball low on the horizon and Victoria was helping in the kitchen when she heard the ringing of their boots on the tile floor. She stopped what she was doing, her heart going wild with excitement. She felt a little dizzy and smiled to herself; was it because of the child or the father?

"Victoria," Jake called.

"I'm in the kitchen." She wiped her hands and hurried out to meet him.

Both he and Ben were extremely dusty, their faces caked with mud where their sweat had run. She looked down in dismay at the clumps of dirt they had tracked onto the clean tile. They followed the direction of her gaze, then gave each other amused glances. They weren't accustomed to having to watch where they walked, but in the past three weeks they had been forced to adjust to the realities of living with three genteel women. Even Celia was growing up and becoming amazingly sedate, for Celia.

"We'll bathe outside," Jake said, trying not to smile. "Get us some clean clothes so we won't have to track mud upstairs."

"Certainly," Victoria agreed, giving their boots another appalled look before she went upstairs.

"I thought we were going to have a hot bath," Ben said.

"I haven't lived this long by being stupid," Jake replied, and Ben laughed at them both. They'd killed at an early age and lived the past twenty years by the law of the gun, but here they were, not daring to take another step because of the mud on their boots.

Victoria returned with clothing for both of them, as well as fresh towels and a thick bar of soap. "Supper should be ready by the time you're both clean," she said as she gave them their bundles.

There was already a line of men waiting to use the shower contraption. Cursing and mumbling under their breaths, they resaddled their horses and rode to the river, which was faster than waiting their turn. They stripped and waded into the water, catching their breaths at the chill.

Ben brought it up again. "We could have been having a hot bath."

"We could have been having a war, too." Jake whistled as he soaped himself. "Why didn't *you* tell her to have some water heated up?"

"She's *your* wife. It wasn't my place."

Jake grinned. As much as he would have preferred a hot bath, too, he didn't like upsetting Victoria. Like Ben had said, she was his wife. It gave him a pleasant feeling of possessiveness and of belonging. In the days since she'd told him she loved him he'd been treating her with a gentleness he'd never before imagined himself capable of. She hadn't said it again and the sadness was still in her eyes, but knowing that she loved him softened the hard inner core that had formed the day he'd seen his mother raped and killed. He was even more patient with her maddening reserve and withdrawals, knowing that she loved him.

Ben dunked his dark head, then came up blowing. He rubbed the water out of his face. "Ladies sure are a lot of trouble compared to whores," he muttered.

"But they make life more comfortable."

"Comfortable? *Comfortable?* We're freezing our asses off in the river instead of taking a bath in a warm tub the way we'd planned because you didn't want to upset your wife by tracking mud upstairs, and you call it comfortable? You've lost your mind."

"We have clean clothes, good food, and fresh sheets on our *real* beds every night; they smell sweet instead of like cheap perfume and stale whiskey, and they wait on us hand and foot. When was the last time you had to fill your own plate at dinner?"

"We have to watch what we say," Ben pointed out.

"As soon as we lose a button, it's sewn back on." Jake's green eyes glinted with wicked amusement. "Your problem is Emma."

"Ah, goddamn," Ben said in disgust. "That's another thing that's wrong with ladies. A whore rolls over easy, but a lady thinks the world will end if she lets a man in her bed."

"A whore lets any man who has the price get between her legs. Is that what you think Emma should do?"

Ben snarled in bad temper and splashed out of the river to stand on the bank. He rubbed a towel over his muscled body, his hazel eyes stormy. Finally he said, "No, I don't want her to do that."

Jake followed him, the crystal clear water sluicing down his body. He knew how frustrated Ben was feeling, because he remembered how he'd felt every time he had crashed against Victoria's rigid ideas of what was proper and what wasn't. Ladies were far more complicated than whores. A lady demanded more from a man than he wanted to give, but what they offered in return was a whole new way of life. They offered physical comfort, a warm sense of security, a sweet body in the bed all night, every night. Marriage was a high price to pay to get all that, but it was worth it. Even without the ranch he would have married Victoria, he thought, and looked up at the lavender twilight sky with a sense of shock.

After a minute he looked at his brother. "You could marry her," he said.

Ben pulled on his pants. "I'm not a marrying man, Jake. That hasn't changed."

"Then if it's just fucking you want, go to Angelina."

"I don't want Angelina," Ben replied curtly. "Hell, she's been had so many ways she can't tell the difference anymore."

"Exactly."

Ben scowled at him, then finished dressing without saying anything else. He wanted Emma, but not enough to offer marriage and that looked like the only way he'd ever get her. In a way it had been easier when he and Jake had just been drifting around, rootless, planning nothing but killing McLain and taking their ranch back. Well, now they had the ranch and there was no more riding out whenever they got tired of a place. They had a home and responsibilities. Ben wasn't sure he liked the sensation. It wasn't the ranch or the work of it; getting the ranch back had eased something inside him. It was the domesticity that was irritating him, the feeling of being hemmed in by rules. He wanted Emma, but he couldn't have her because of all those damned rules that governed respectable people. Ben realized that he wasn't quite respectable and never would be, any more than Jake would ever be just a rancher. They had lived too many years by the law of the gun. Under the surface the old instincts still ran strong. He just didn't know what to do with them any more.

Supper was ready by the time they got back to the house, and Victoria forced herself to be patient. Another couple of hours wouldn't make any difference; she would find the privacy she needed when they went to bed. She tried to imagine what he would say, how he would react, and found that she couldn't. They had never discussed having children. She felt a twinge of fear and gave him a guarded look, only to look away quickly again when she found him watching her.

She couldn't read him at all. He'd had too many years hiding his thoughts behind his hard face and expressionless eyes. She could see only what he allowed her to see. Sometimes she thought that open enmity would be less nerve-racking than passion from a man she loved but didn't know.

It was still early when he got up from the table and held his hand out to her. She felt the color rush to her face as she allowed him to help her up, and she didn't look at anyone as they walked out of the room. "Good night," Jake said, and Ben, Emma, and Celia each replied as his heavy hand on her waist ushered her up the stairs.

Emma watched them leave and bit her lip at the longing welling up in her. It wasn't just physical need that tormented her, but the need for what Victoria had found with Jake, the belonging expressed in the way he put his arm around her to escort her to their room. She wanted to feel that closeness, the partnership of marriage and a shared life. She turned her head and looked at Ben, at the hard, chiseled features.

He met her gaze and lifted his eyebrows in silent invitation. All she had to do to accept was to get up and walk upstairs. He would surely follow. Heat ran through her, and if he'd been offering more than a night or two, if it had been for forever, she would have gone and forgotten about marriage and propriety. But Ben wanted no claim on him, legal or otherwise. Her chest ached with the pain of having to deny both him and herself. She turned her head away and didn't move from her chair.

"Jake, there's something I need to tell you."

Her tone was troubled and Jake froze, his hands on the tiny buttons that marched down her back. He sensed that whatever it was she had been hiding, she finally trusted him enough to tell him about it, and suddenly he didn't want to know. She loved him; that was enough. He didn't want to hear about anything McLain might have done to her. McLain was dead, damn his soul. How could he hurt them now?

"I don't want to know," he said quietly, and pulled the pins from her hair to let it stream down over his hands in a warm flood.

She whirled to face him. She was pale, her eyes as huge as they had been the night he'd first come to her. "You *have* to know." She managed a shaky smile, one that faded as quickly as it had formed. "It isn't something I can hide or that will go away."

His stomach knotted. Suddenly Jake saw hell opening up at his feet. A flash of intuition told him what it was, and it made him sick. So that was why she had been so sad and withdrawn, why she had watched him so anxiously at times, why he'd sensed she was hiding something from him. God, why hadn't he thought of this? And how was he supposed to stand it? *He couldn't.*

Victoria began shaking as she met his hard gaze. "I'm pregnant," she said before she lost the courage to tell him. "I'm having your baby."

The bottom dropped out of his stomach and he stared at her, unable to believe what he'd heard her say. He felt empty, as if his heart and lungs and guts had all been torn out. And then in a rush he was filled with a bitter rage even stronger than what he had felt twenty years before, when he had watched his mother die.

Victoria's betrayal cut at him like a knife in the gut. How could she have said that, how could she have the gall to expect to pass McLain's child off as his? Did she think he was stupid? That he didn't know McLain had used her as his wife? She hadn't been a virgin the first time Jake had had her, and that was only three weeks ago. If she were pregnant now, the child could only be McLain's. Did she think he didn't know that? It was bad enough that she was carrying that son of a bitch's whelp, but if she thought he would let the little bastard have the *Sarratt* name, the name of the family its father had murdered—

Black fog clouded the edges of his vision. A dull roaring filled his ears. He saw her pale face, the soft lips that had just voiced a lie so monstrous he couldn't believe it, and without planning, without knowing he was going to do it, he struck her.

The full force of his arm was behind the blow. If he had used his fist instead of his open hand, it would have broken her jaw. Victoria saw it coming, had a split second of comprehension, but that wasn't enough to give her time to move. His hand crashed into her face, slamming her around and to the side. She thudded against the wall and slid to the floor like a broken doll.

He stood over her, his fists clenched and his eyes like green ice. The fires of hell would look like his eyes, she thought dazedly, seeing him through a fog. He was going to kill her, and she was still too numb to protect herself.

"Goddamn you," he said in a hoarse, violent tone. "There's no way in hell I'll let McLain's bastard have my name."

She let her eyes close as she gave in to the grayness rising in her. She wanted to let that blank world claim her; it would be much easier than facing what had just happened. Then comprehension of his words sank in, and she forced her eyes to open again.

She wet her lips and tasted blood. Her tongue felt thick and unwieldy, her lips puffy and numb. It was difficult to form the words but desperation drove her; how could he have drawn such a horrible misconclusion? No matter how hurt she was, she couldn't let him think that, ever. She tried to push herself into a sitting position. "No," she croaked. "Not his baby. Yours."

The rage flared up hotly, but he didn't move or speak. He'd never struck a woman before and part of his brain was horrified at what he'd done; when she had slammed into the wall he'd known an instant of sheer terror that he might have killed her. *But how could she keep saying it was his baby?* If she was far enough along to know she was pregnant, then it had to be McLain's.

He leaned down and jerked her to her feet. The pain made her gasp and try to pull away from him. He realized he was far from being in control and dropped his hands. She began to crumple and he grabbed her.

She took a deep breath, steadying herself, straightening her spine with the characteristic motion that wrenched at him. Carefully she stepped back out of his grasp.

He found his own control, but it in no way lessened his rage; it was in his eyes, in the rigid muscles of his face, in the harsh menace of his voice. "I'm not a fool, Victoria. I can count, and there's no way you could know yet if the baby were mine. We've only been married three weeks, not three months."

She was still so dazed that she couldn't formulate the words to tell him, couldn't explain that her menses were a week late and she'd never been late before, not even by a day, couldn't think of all the ways to convince him that the baby was his. The numbness was rapidly leaving her face and behind it came pain. Her cheek was burning like fire. Blood from her split lip dripped down her chin and she wiped it away, then stared in confusion at the red smear on her fingers.

"How far along are you? God, I knew you were hiding something," he said harshly, shaking his head at his own stupidity. "I just never thought you'd try to pass McLain's bastard off as mine." Abruptly his eyes narrowed as suspicion crossed his face.

"Or did you plan it all along? Maybe that's why you didn't kick up a fuss about marrying me. Too bad you weren't smart enough to keep this news to yourself for another month or so; I probably would have believed it was mine, then, at least until it came early. Or are you so far along you were afraid you'd begin showing before another month was up? That's it, isn't it?"

She could only wag her head back and forth, dumb with shock and disbelief at what had happened, what he was saying.

Jake watched her, waiting for an explanation or a denial. He felt caught in a nightmare, once again living through the destruction of his safe and comfortable life, and he desperately needed for her to give him some explanation that would help him understand what she had done. But she just stood there, the imprint of his hand turning from white to red to purple as the bruising on her face began to show, and her bloody lower lip puffing up. The visual evidence of the damage he'd done made his stomach suddenly twist with nausea.

But still she stood silent and frail. Her hair was straggling across her face and shoulders, her dress hanging half off. Despite himself, he reached out to push her hair away from her face. She flinched from his hand and he let it drop to his side. The heaviness of defeat was beginning to drag at his rage, sapping it away, but there was no way he could let her do what she'd planned.

"It can't live here," he said. "No brat of McLain's is going to be raised on this ranch or bear my name. When it's born, I'll send it back East somewhere. You've got until it's born to decide if you're going to stay here or go with it."

Except for the imprint of his hand, her face was paper white. She shuddered and tried to pull herself together. "You're wrong," she whispered. The words sounded mushy because of her thickened lip, and moving her jaw sent pain shooting along her skull. "You're the father."

"Don't lie to me!" he roared, the anger rushing back. "There's no way you could know you're pregnant if the baby were mine."

She twisted her hands together, racked with pain, at a loss as to how to make him believe her. "I—I'm not certain yet! It's just that . . . I think I am. My m-monthly time is late, and I've never been late before."

His eyes were like ice. "You're backtracking, and it isn't working. What you said was, 'I'm pregnant, I'm having your baby.' You sounded pretty certain to me, so don't try to change your mind now.

"But it couldn't be the Major's baby!" she cried. "We didn't . . . he couldn't—" She couldn't finish for the tears clogging her throat.

He stared at her incredulously for a moment, his eyes so cold she felt a chill run down her spine. "McLain humped every woman who'd stand still for him and some who didn't. You can't pretend he wasn't more than capable of doing the same to you. And if he 'couldn't,' why the hell weren't you a virgin the first time I made love to you? Maybe you didn't know a man can tell the difference, but we can. Don't tell me that he 'couldn't,' damn you."

The chill grew colder, and she felt as if the blood would congeal in her veins. She'd told him the truth and he didn't believe her; moreover, there was nothing she could say to change his mind. There was no proof she was even pregnant; she just *knew* she was. And she certainly knew the child wasn't the Major's, but how could she convince Jake of that now? She felt the death knell of her hopes in the heavy beat of her heart against her rib cage; if he had ever known her at all, if he had ever felt anything for her, he would realize she could never betray him in such a despicable manner. But now, in the most awful way, she'd learned once and for all that he had never even come close to loving her.

Her ears were ringing, her face burning. Shock and pain numbed her; she stared at him as if she didn't recognize him, her eyes shadowed pools in a bloodless face. She moved back from him another step. "Count the days," she finally said in a dull, even tone. "From the night you first came to me until this baby is born, *count* them, damn you! Then tell me if you still think it came early. I've been yours for three weeks now. You say I couldn't possibly know if I was carrying a child unless I was a couple of months along, so you think this baby must be the Major's. But I *can* tell, and I *do* know. I've known that I've been with child for one week, not four! So you count the days, and you wait and see if this baby comes in less than nine full months.

But, while you're waiting, while you watch the sixth, and seventh, and eighth months go by, remember this: Even if it has your face so that you can't deny it, I'll take it away from you, because you don't have anything except hate to give to a child!"

She pulled her sagging dress up over her shoulders and lifted her skirts, sweeping by him just as she had in the beginning, as if she would be contaminated if she touched him. His jaw set, Jake watched her walk from the room. He wanted to go after her, to shake her and vent his rage at her for harboring McLain's child in her body; her flesh that belonged to *him,* damn it! But there had been something in her eyes, a mixture of hurt and rage that gave him pause. Victoria had cursed at him; he'd never heard her swear before, never seen her so distraught. Uncertainty gnawed at him. Could she have been telling the truth?

No. McLain had been capable, all right.

But, somehow, Victoria had always seemed so innocent. The night he had first taken her, she'd been unmistakably shocked by the things he'd wanted to do, the things he'd done. All right, so she hadn't liked it with the Major; he could understand that. But there was no way he could believe McLain hadn't slept with her. The Major had been a lot of things, but impotent wasn't one of them.

Victoria went into one of the spare bedrooms and carefully locked the door, not because she thought Jake would try to enter but to insure that no one else did. What would she say if Emma or Celia came in? She was too shattered even to try to explain.

There was no linen on the bed, no fresh cool water in which to soak a cloth to press to her burning cheek. But at least there was a lamp, which she lit. She felt as if she might vomit, but a quick search of the room yielded neither basin nor chamberpot. She sank onto the bare mattress, her teeth clenched together to hold back the surge of nausea. The pressure made her jaw ache, and she probed that side of her face with cautious fingers. Her cheek was puffy and sore, but she didn't think anything was broken.

She tried to think, tried to sort out her rioting emotions, but no order presented itself. Jake didn't believe the baby was his. He had struck her. Moreover, he actually thought her capable of that sort of betrayal.

This would unavoidably affect everyone else in the house, like waves rippling out from a stone tossed into a lake. She regretted that, both for their discomfort and her own humiliation. Still, she knew there was nothing she could do to hide their estrangement.

She thought of packing in the morning and leaving immediately, and a harsh, bitter little laugh erupted into the silence. She was still in exactly the same situation she had been in as the Major's wife; she had no money of her own, and no way of leaving without Jake's permission and help. But while she had desperately yearned to be away from the Major, she didn't want to run now. She wanted to stay.

It grew slowly, a hard, bright little kernel of anger, as she realized she had meant every word she had said to Jake. She had asked why he had deliberately lied to her about his identity, but she hadn't really berated him for it. She had accepted it, accommodated him in marriage to give him back the ranch that had been stolen from him, given herself heart and soul to him. He had taken all of this and returned only hate. His hatred for the Major was all-consuming; even now, after the man was dead and buried, it still colored everything Jake thought and did.

No, she wouldn't make it easy for him by running away. She wanted to be right under his nose so he could see every inch she grew as her belly expanded with his child. She wanted him to count the days, and sweat. She wanted remorse to eat him alive, the same way his precious hatred had consumed him. Let him sleep with guilt as he had slept with vengeance and mistrust.

If she hadn't loved him so much, she would never have felt so betrayed by his lack of trust in her word, in her very integrity. He wasn't the only one who craved vengeance. She realized that she might not feel the same way in a few days, but right now she wanted to hurt him as he had hurt her. She couldn't take her revenge with a bullet, but he wouldn't walk away unscathed. She swore it.

* * *

The next morning after he'd left the house, she went into their bedroom and moved her things to the spare room. She made up the bed, carried in both chamberpot and washbasin, made certain the lamp was filled and that there was a supply of fresh candles if she needed them.

The injured side of her face was more stiff than actually painful. Her cut lip and the knot on the side of her head where she had slammed into the wall were more painful than her face.

Emma opened the door as she sat on the floor, putting her underwear away in a dresser drawer. "Victoria, what on earth are you doing?"

"Moving my things into this room," she replied calmly.

"So I see, but why?"

Victoria turned to look at Emma, inadvertently revealing the bruised side of her face. Emma gasped and rushed forward. "Your face! What happened?"

"I fell," Victoria said flatly.

Concern darkened Emma's eyes, then her gaze narrowed as she put two and two together.

"I don't want the household upset," Victoria said, her voice steady. "As far as everyone is concerned, I slipped and fell and hit my face."

"Yes, of course," Emma agreed blankly.

"Jake and I have quarreled."

Emma thought Victoria was understating that obvious fact. "Is there anything I can do?"

Victoria looked down at the soft cotton chemises folded in her lap and didn't answer the question. Instead she said, "I'm going to have a baby."

Emma gasped. "But that's wonderful!"

"I thought so, yes."

"Jake . . . doesn't?"

"He doesn't think he's the father. He accused me of trying to pass the Major's child off as his."

"Dear God." Emma sank down beside Victoria. It was so ridiculous she found it hard to believe. "Didn't you tell him that the Major couldn't . . . do that?"

"Yes. He didn't believe me about that, either. We both know

that the Major still visited Angelina, and evidently he was incapable only with me." *Thank God,* she mentally added.

"But why would he assume that the baby isn't his?" Emma was horrified at Jake's conclusion.

"Because we've only been married for three weeks. He says I couldn't possibly know I'm pregnant in such a short time if it were his. You know how regular my monthlies have always been," she said bitterly. "I'm a week late. What else could it be? I was so excited that I wanted him to know right away, so I told him. It's always been so convenient, knowing exactly what day my time of the month would start, but now I wish I had been so irregular that it would have been two months before I noticed!"

Emma put her hand on Victoria's arm. "I'm sorry," she said helplessly. "I don't know what to say."

"There's nothing left to be said." Jake had said it all.

"Perhaps if I talked to him—"

"No." She managed a smile and hugged Emma. "I know you're willing and I appreciate it, but he won't believe you, either."

"We won't know unless I try," Emma said gently.

"Even if he changes his mind, it won't change the fact that he thought me capable of such a despicable trick."

"But I want to do something!"

"You can. Try not to let this upset Celia too much, and carry on just as you normally would have. We have to live in this house; I don't want to embroil everyone in our argument."

"Do you think that's possible?"

Victoria managed a tired smile. "Probably not, but I'm going to try."

Jake hadn't chased after Victoria the night before because he'd still been so enraged himself. He'd slept very little, lying on top of the bed without even bothering to remove his boots, and was up before dawn. He pushed himself hard all day, doing the most physical work he could find, hoping to tire himself so much that it would take the edge off his anger. When he finally rode toward home, every muscle in him was protesting. He welcomed the discomfort.

He didn't see Victoria downstairs, though Emma was whisking about making certain the table was set for supper. Things looked normal enough, though he knew they weren't. He slowly climbed the stairs to their bedroom, his heart thudding in his chest. He'd have to apologize to her for hitting her; it had been tormenting him all day. It would never happen again, but he knew he would have to work hard to earn her trust again so that she could believe that. He opened the door, braced for his first sight of her since their fight, but the room was empty.

The reprieve left him feeling a little flat. He tossed his hat aside and stripped off his dirty shirt, then poured water into the basin and leaned over to wash his face. As he straightened, he realized that the room seemed different, not just empty.

His spine slowly stiffened as he looked around. His gaze lit on the dressing table, and he examined its bare surface. With two quick strides he reached the armoire and flung the doors open. His clothes remained, but there was only an empty space where Victoria's dresses had hung. He searched the dresser where she had kept her underwear, and wasn't surprised to find them gone. Now he knew why the room had seemed so empty; it wasn't missing just Victoria herself, but every sign of her occupancy. She had moved out of their bedroom.

17

Will Garnet had run fast, but he hadn't run far. He didn't go to Santa Fe; it was too likely he'd eventually run into one of the Sarratts, damn their black souls to hell. He'd gone to Albuquerque with the handful of men who had run with him, and hunkered down there to think things over.

All in all, he didn't much like his position. He could keep on drifting, change his name, and that didn't matter much to him if he thought the Sarratts would let the matter drop. Hell, they had their damned ranch back, didn't they? But he'd met up with Floyd Hibbs in one of the saloons; Floyd had been out in one of the upper ranges when all the fighting had gone on, but he hadn't much liked the way things had changed and had packed up his gear and left. What really worried Garnet was that Floyd said Jake Roper and Jacob Sarratt were one and the same, and that his brother was one mean-lookin' son of a bitch, too.

So, both of the Sarratts had lived, and the older one had been right under his nose for months. He'd always known there was a reason why he didn't like the bastard. The Major was dead, and damned if Roper—Sarratt—hadn't married McLain's high-nosed widow. Garnet remembered Jake Sarratt's cold green eyes, and he didn't think there was a snowball's chance in hell that he and his brother wouldn't be coming after him.

He could run, but he didn't think they would give up until they got him. He had put lead in both of them, something they weren't likely to let pass.

It didn't set right with him, letting Sarratt hunt him like he was a rabbit. So the thing to do was something they wouldn't expect.

He still wanted that little gal, Celia, more now than before. He dreamed about her at night, dreamed how close he'd been to getting her. He'd about been ready to put a bullet in McLain himself when the Sarratts had rode in, and if he'd just done it a day sooner, nothing would have kept him from having her.

He still wanted that ranch, too. It should've been his. McLain hadn't done nothing but shoot the Sarratt woman after humping her; it had been he, Garnet, who had put a bullet in Duncan Sarratt's head, and who'd shot up the two boys. The little bastards should've died. Hell, McLain had been right all along when he'd been yapping about not finding the bodies, that the Sarratts were coming back. He'd been crazy, but he'd been right.

Garnet thought about it a lot. He didn't want to rush into nothing; he wanted everything planned out real careful. But he wanted that ranch, and more than anything he wanted the girl. If he could get together enough men, he just might consider turning the table on the Sarratts one last time.

The situation between them had stretched into two miserable weeks before Jake sought her out. "Don't you think this has gone on long enough?" he asked curtly.

She didn't look up from the button she was sewing on to one of his shirts. "What has?"

"This situation."

"Actually, no. I expect it to go on for some months."

He clenched his teeth. He'd set his mind to apologize several times, but she always froze him out. Whenever he came near her, that patrician little nose would go in the air and she would leave the room. If she had to speak to him, she did it in tones so frosty that no one was left in doubt that the boss wasn't on good terms with his missus. And it went without saying that she never looked at him anymore.

His temper was frayed from the strain. He'd been infuriated when she had moved out of their bedroom, but at the time he'd decided it was better if they slept apart. His own rage had still been too close to the surface. But he was in control now and decided they should make the best of the situation. It would be easier on everyone in the house if they declared a truce.

"I want you to move back into our bedroom."

"Thank you, no."

With that cool dismissal she put the shirt in her sewing basket and got to her feet. Knowing that she was about to leave him talking to an empty room, Jake grabbed her arms.

"You're staying right here until I'm finished," he snapped.

She didn't bother to struggle. "You're hurting my arms."

He eased the pressure, but didn't release her. This close he could see the velvety texture of her skin, reminding him of the swelling and bruising that had so recently faded from her face. Every time he'd looked at her, the knowledge that he'd struck her that hard had burned like acid in his soul. "I won't ever hit you again, Victoria," he said in a low voice. "I give you my word."

She didn't respond; she was like stone, staring straight ahead. Her faint sweet scent teased him. He fought the urge to lean down and press his face to her neck in pursuit of that elusive fragrance. He began to grow hard but wasn't surprised. Hell, not even knowing that she was carrying McLain's brat could stop him from burning for her. He didn't know how far along she was, but her waist was still slender and she still walked with that provocative grace that drew him like a lodestone. That walk might turn into a pregnant waddle soon, but for now it made his heart pound.

He wanted her back in his bed, while there was still time. After the baby became obvious, it would drive him crazy to lie beside her and know it wasn't his, to be reminded every time he looked at her that she had belonged to McLain. Damn the bastard, even from the grave he had reached out to destroy his life.

"Did you hear me?" he asked.

Victoria looked straight ahead. "Yes, I heard you. Believing you is something entirely different."

His hands clenched again. "I give you my word."

"I put as much faith in your word as you do in mine."

Jake released her, dropping his hands as if she had burned him. He was fed up with the situation. It was time for it to end. "Move back into our bedroom. Tonight."

"No."

"I'll do it for you if I have to."

"Are you going to kick down my door?" she asked without interest. "Drag me screaming into your room? Because you'll have to do that, Jake. I won't walk back into that room as if nothing has happened."

"I'm not asking you to pretend nothing happened. I'd give a year of my life if I hadn't hit you, and ten years if you weren't carrying that little bastard—"

She slapped him, the sound sharp in the room. It happened before she realized she was going to do it. She had never felt such blind rage before and she had put all of her strength into the blow. Part of her was aghast that she had done such a thing, but another more primitive part was dismayed that she had done so little damage. The blow whipped his head around, but he remained solidly on his feet.

She was looking him in the eye now, as he'd wanted, but he didn't see any love and forgiveness in her face. She was white and trembling with anger, her eyes like blue fire. She went up on tiptoe to thrust her face close to his.

"Don't you ever call my baby a bastard again." The words were even and said through clenched teeth. She looked ready to kill him, or die trying.

Desire hit him in the gut. He'd seen Victoria bravely facing down Garnet, gentle with Celia, wild and passionate as he made love to her, an icy queen disdaining even to look at him, but this was new, this was a tigress ready to claw him to pieces. His erection pushed painfully against his pants as lust fogged his brain. He was reaching for her, everything forgotten but the burning urge to mate, when she suddenly turned even whiter and stepped back.

She clapped her hand over her mouth and swallowed convulsively. Astonishment wiped the rage from her face. She swallowed once more, then turned and ran.

She prayed she would make it to the privacy of her bedroom and not disgrace herself by vomiting on the stairs. Cold sweat broke out on her, and she staggered a bit on the steps. She should have gone outside; even if someone saw her it would have been better than the mess she was about to make. . . .

She made it to her bedroom, and the basin. Her insides felt as if they were coming up. She heard someone shouting, but she was heaving so convulsively that her ears were roaring. It had hit her with the force of a train, following immediately on the heels of that incredible, blinding anger, and she hadn't been prepared for either.

There was a strong arm around her waist and a hand on her forehead; without them she would have fallen. She was dimly aware of others rushing into the bedroom, of sympathetic murmurs. She sagged and was caught up in Jake's powerful arms. She knew it was him, knew it was he who had held her upright over the basin, but right now she didn't care.

"Put her on the bed, Señor Jake," Carmita instructed.

He did as Carmita put a cloth into Emma's hand. Victoria became aware of someone washing her face with a wonderfully cold, wet cloth. She saw it was Emma and was so relieved she murmured, "I've never been so sick before."

Emma murmured words of comfort as Carmita moved toward the door. "Keep washing her face, señorita, while I.get her something to eat."

Jake stared at the housekeeper as if she had lost her mind. "She doesn't need anything to eat," he told her. "She's sick."

Carmita patted his arm. "She is sick with the baby," she explained as she left to go to the kitchen. "It will settle her stomach to have something in it. Trust me, I know."

Sick with the baby. He stared at his wife, lying limp and pale in the bed she didn't want to share with him. He knew women were nauseated when they were pregnant, but from the information he'd heard tossed around in saloons it came real early in the pregnancy. Victoria should have felt it well before now, but she had sounded frightened by what had just happened to her. And if she'd been vomiting for the past month or so, he hadn't known.

He went to the bed where Emma was slowly wiping Victoria's face with the cloth. Victoria's breathing was slower now, but she was still deathly pale and her eyes were closed. "Shouldn't she be getting over this by now?" he asked, his tone rougher than he'd intended.

Emma didn't look up. "It's just beginning."

He stepped back. Either Emma was lying or Victoria had duped her, too. Once he would never have believed Victoria capable of such deception, but then he would never have believed her capable of the killing rage he'd seen in her eyes just a short while ago, either. He couldn't understand why she was so fiercely protective of the baby she carried, since she had hated its father, he felt as betrayed by that as he did by the fact that she had tried to give it his name. But a mother of any species was ten times more dangerous when protecting her young than a hungry male ever was. He had underestimated the strength of that instinct in Victoria. When he looked at it like that he could almost forgive her.

Carmita rushed back into the room with a plain tortilla and a cup of water. She sat on the bed and tore off a small portion of the tortilla which she pushed between Victoria's lips, despite her weak protest.

"You must eat it, señora. It will settle your stomach, you'll see."

Victoria didn't much care; she was beyond caring. But she chewed the flat-tasting tortilla and swallowed. To her vague surprise her stomach didn't revolt. Carmita fed her half of the tortilla, then gave her a small sip of water. "That's enough for now, señora. Rest and soon you'll feel much better."

Victoria willingly closed her eyes. She heard rustles of clothing and retreating footsteps, then the door closed and she inhaled once, deeply, and slept.

It was a short nap, but when she woke half an hour later she felt so well that it was hard to believe she'd been so violently ill less than an hour before. She lay still for a moment just to be sure, but her stomach was blissfully steady. She opened her eyes, sat up, and found Jake watching her.

She was shocked to realize he'd been sitting there the whole time. She saw a faint red mark on his tanned cheek. It was the only remaining evidence of her slap, and it astonished her anew. She'd never before in her life struck another human being.

"Why are you here?" she asked, sliding off the bed. With Jake anywhere close by, lying on a bed was risky.

"I wanted to make certain you're all right."

"I feel fine." She walked to the mirror and began repairing the damage done to her hair.

He came up behind her, dwarfing her reflection. "Come back to our room, Victoria."

She could feel the force of his will like an iron hand pressing down on her. He fully expected her to obey him; after all, his will had prevailed in everything from the very first. He had the power to enforce his orders and was willing to do whatever was necessary. She had been trained to believe it was a wife's duty to obey her husband; if the issue had been anything less important, she knew she would have given in without a struggle. But she couldn't give in on this. She gave her head a slow shake. "No."

He put his hands on her waist and drew her back against him. His head dipped and he pressed his mouth to her hair. "You need someone to look after you if you get sick during the night."

The heat from his body made her weak. What he offered weakened her, all the more so because it would have been so right for her baby's father to lie beside her during the nights and hold her while she was ill. But she couldn't go back into his arms knowing he hated the life growing in her, knowing that he wanted her back only for the sexual pleasure she could give him. It would be impossible for him to deny *that* charge, she thought, since she could feel his hard length against her buttocks.

It would have been so easy to let herself relax, to lie back against him and let his strength support her. Because it was so easy, she didn't dare let herself do it for a minute. She straightened and returned her attention to the task of pinning up her hair. "If I need anyone, I'll call Emma."

"Why disturb Emma when you could be in bed with me?"

"Why be in bed with you when I could disturb Emma?"

Anger darkened his face and drew his brows down. "I've tried to reason with you, but now I'm telling you. Put your things back in our bedroom and your ass back in our bed tonight, or I'll do it even if I have to carry you over my shoulder for the entire household to see."

"Maybe if you're violent enough you'll be able to make me lose the baby."

Her hissed words stunned him. For the first time he realized that if he did move her back into their bedroom he really would have to use force to do it. Until now he'd imagined that their estrangement had continued due to his own grievances, that when his anger calmed enough for him to tell her to return, she would do it. He'd expected her to balk, expected recriminations; expected to have to give her his sincere apology for having struck her and his equally sincere promise that it would never happen again, but he'd also fully expected to have her back in his bed that very night.

But now he saw that while he might be ready to end their estrangement, she wasn't. She wasn't about to forgive him. *She* was angry at *him,* and he had his stinging cheek to prove it. If his cheek was still burning, how had her face felt after his blow? Her slap had snapped his head around, but his had knocked her off her feet. A woman was helpless against a man, and he knew it. He'd never felt anything but contempt for a man who raised his hand to a woman, and now his contempt was turned on himself.

"No," he said in a tight, strained voice. "I won't do anything to hurt you or the baby."

"Then you'll leave us alone."

"Jesus." He was suddenly tired, as if he'd put in a long day branding calves. Victoria was as unbending as steel, and he didn't know what else he could say. He'd sworn he wouldn't hurt her, but it hadn't made any difference. Maybe he hadn't given her enough time, maybe her pregnancy was making her irrational.

He didn't know what it was, but he was wary of pushing her too far.

"All right, I'll leave you alone. When you decide you're ready to sleep with me again, all you have to do is open the door and crawl into bed. But don't wait too long. I might find some other woman who's willing to do what you won't."

She waited until he got to the door, then said, "Like the Major?"

He froze for a moment, his back stiffening, then left the room without a word.

Victoria dragged through the days. The symptoms of early pregnancy were upon her with a vengeance. Some mornings she was so sick that nothing seemed to settle her stomach. Even on the days when she thought the nausea would be mild, it took only a stray odor to send her stumbling for a basin or chamberpot. Her bladder seemed to be permanently and uncomfortably full; her sleep was so disturbed by her frequent trips to the chamberpot that she was dull and sleepy during the day. Most of all, her emotions were rioting. She cried easily, and lecturing herself had no effect on the endless tears.

The household was divided into those who knew and those who didn't. Carmita, Lola, Juana, and Celia knew only that Victoria was pregnant and were full of cheerful planning and advice on childbirth, childrearing, and names. They knew Jake and Victoria had quarreled, but didn't begin to suspect the extent of it.

Emma and Ben were the only other people who knew the circumstances behind Victoria's move to a separate bedroom. Ben was scrupulously polite to her, but there was a chill in his eyes. Emma didn't rebuke Jake by either word or deed, but she was cold to Ben because she felt he didn't have any right to pass judgment on Victoria.

The only censure Jake felt was from Victoria, and he endured it. What else could he do? She was too sick for him to press the issue, and as the days became weeks his biting anger changed to concern. Rather than gaining weight, she had lost several pounds. Her waist was reed-slender and her dresses were becoming loose. Her complexion was alternately pale, gray, and green-ish, and there were permanent dark circles under her eyes.

She should be showing her pregnancy by now, if everything were normal. He lay awake at night, tormented by the worry that something had gone wrong. Why wasn't the sickness going away as he'd heard it should well before now? He wasn't con-cerned for the baby, but about the possibility that he might lose Victoria, too. He began remaining close to the house as much as he could, so he would be on hand if she became seriously ill. God, if she would only stop vomiting so much. Almost nothing stayed down.

But being so ill hadn't changed her hostility toward him. It was in her eyes every time she looked at him, in the way she care-fully kept out of his reach and answered him only in a one-syllable monotone, if possible.

She hadn't forgiven him. He was the one wronged, but she hadn't forgiven him. For the first time he began to wonder if she really would leave after the baby was born, and how he would handle it if she chose McLain's child over him. The only alterna-tive, though, was to let her raise the child here on his ranch, and that he couldn't do.

"Victoria and Jake aren't happy," Celia told Luis, lying in his arms beneath a tree. They were in the middle of a copse, hidden from view by anyone who might happen by. They had become adept at finding places to make love, and Celia mildly enjoyed the intrigue. These past weeks had been the happiest of her life, as if all the pieces had finally come together and she was what she had been meant to be. Making love with Luis was so natural and perfect that she didn't give a thought to the rules and restric-tions Victoria had taught her. Celia was by nature a complete sensualist, and she had taken to lovemaking with guilt-free enthusiasm.

"No one is happy all the time," he said lazily. They were lying naked on a blanket, and he was sated from their loving.

"But they aren't happy at all now. Victoria looks so ill; I'm worried about her. And she won't speak to Jake at all unless he speaks to her first."

"They've just had a quarrel, that's all. They'll make up."

"It's been weeks now, and they haven't made up."

Luis acknowledged that Jake had certainly been in a bad mood for a long time now. He hadn't wondered at the reason, having more or less assumed it had something to do with Victoria being pregnant. Pregnant women could be hell to live with, he knew. And with Victoria being so ill Jake obviously hadn't been finding any pleasure in bed, which in Luis's opinion was enough to make any man bad-tempered.

Celia propped up on an elbow, her golden hair spilling to the side and covering his shoulder. Her dark blue eyes were sad. "I don't think Jake wants the baby."

"Why do you say that, *chica?* Most men are proud when their wives become pregnant."

"He doesn't like to talk about the baby. He doesn't seem excited about it at all, and a lot of times he'll get up and walk out of the room if we start talking about it."

It sounded to Luis as if there was very serious trouble with the boss's marriage, but there was nothing he could do about it. The delicate beauty of Celia's breasts drew him, and he circled one nipple with his forefinger, fascinated by the contrast between his brown skin and the milky fairness of hers. She stopped talking and drew in a breath, as he had known she would, her eyes getting darker and her lashes lowering.

"Perhaps they aren't happy, but I am," he said in the slower, deeper tones of arousal.

She smiled, the calm, confident smile of a woman that was new to her. She stroked her hand down his sleek, powerful body and closed it around his erection. "Yes, you look happy," she said as she bent to kiss him, but the real happiness was in herself.

He was so beautiful he took her breath away. She lived every day for the time when they would slip away and she would be in his arms again. Loving him was so wonderful she couldn't associate what they did together with what the Major and Garnet had wanted to do with her. Celia didn't dream of Luis in terms of marriage and babies, ideas that were alien to her because she had always lived only for the moment. She dreamed of him as he was now, naked and reaching for her, his dark eyes hot with passion.

Victoria was having a good day, finally, so Emma took advantage of it and slipped out to the stables. She quickly saddled her horse and rode out, desperate to get out of the house for just a little while. If all women got as sick as Victoria had with this baby, she didn't understand how a woman could bear to have more than one. If it went on much longer, Victoria would be dangerously weak.

The gelding had been feeling pent-up, too; she gave him his head and he stretched out in a full gallop. The rush of air cleared the cobwebs from her mind. She lost some of her hairpins and her hair came tumbling down, but she didn't care. For just an hour she was free.

Over the thunder of her own horse's hooves, she didn't hear the other horse coming up behind her until a bobbing head stretched out past her knee and a gloved hand reached in front to take her reins. Startled, she swung her riding crop before she saw who it was, and Ben flung up his arm to keep the whip from landing across his face.

"What the hell are you doing?" he yelled, pulling both horses to a stop.

Emma was stricken at what she had nearly done. "I'm sorry," she said, her cheeks losing their color. "I didn't know who it was. Why did you grab my reins?"

"I thought the horse was out of control."

She shook her head. "No, I was just letting him run. He's been as cooped up as I have." She gave him a quick glance. "It seems we both were mistaken, weren't we?"

Ben ignored that. "I told you not to ride alone."

She sat in the saddle and looked at him with an expression that calmly denied him the right to tell her what to do. She was too tired to fight, but she simply wasn't going to sit in the house like a child if she wanted to ride.

He sighed and kneed his horse away from hers. "If you want to ride, then let's ride."

She did, joyfully. She was surprised to see it was late summer;

the grasses were getting brittle and had a hint of yellow to them. They had arrived in the spring, but she didn't really remember much about it; the strain of surviving those weeks with the Major had taken all of her attention. It had been June, hot and dusty, when they had tried to escape. Now it was late in August, with only a few short weeks left before the first frost. She had missed the summer. It was disorienting.

She let the gelding run until he slowed of his own accord, blowing and tossing his head with joy. She patted his steaming neck as Ben reined in to keep pace with her.

She looked around at the broad meadow, with the craggy peaks bordering it to the north, and the tall grasses waving in the slight breeze. You could see for miles and she was amazed at the beauty of the land.

The horses slowed, then halted completely, lowering their heads to crop at the grass.

Ben removed his hat and wiped his sweaty forehead on his sleeve. His dark hair was damp, too, and his face was dusty. His hazel eyes were clear and penetrating. He said quietly, "Emma girl, are you ever going to come to me?"

A pang went through her. If he had tried to seduce her she thought she could have resisted him more easily, but it was incredibly hard to deny this simple invitation. "I want to," she said, the truth somehow easy to accept and admit out here in this high, empty meadow. "But how can I?"

"Easily. All you have to do is open my door. Or hold out your hand to me right now. That's all. I'll do the rest."

He saw the flicker of fear on her face and was puzzled. "I won't hurt you," he said in husky promise. "I won't lie and say the first time won't be hard for you, but I'll take care of you. I'll make certain you enjoy it, too. You don't need to be afraid of me."

"I'm not afraid, not of you," she quickly denied. Her brown eyes were as velvety as a doe's.

"Then what are you afraid of?"

She looked away from him, her eyes going to the mountains and the blue sky beyond. "All of it, I think. The act itself. It isn't the same for a woman as it is for a man. From what I can tell, for a man it's a few minutes of pleasure, forgotten as soon as he gets up, without meaning to him until the next time he wants to do it. For a woman . . .

"For a woman it's a huge step. It's trusting a man not to hurt her. It's taking a chance of pregnancy, which will ruin her life and the life of her child if she isn't married, and could kill her even if she is married. It isn't just taking a man into her body, it's taking him into her life, because the same act that means nothing to him can affect her for the rest of her days."

"It doesn't matter that much to whores."

"Is that what you want me to be? A whore? They do it for money, with any man who has the money. It's sad. They're sad."

He said harshly, "I don't want you to be a whore." He didn't want emptiness in Emma's eyes when he made love to her, he wanted to see wonder, and blind pleasure, and trust. He wanted her to see only him. "I wouldn't abandon you if I made you pregnant. I'm here to stay. Look at Jake; he didn't abandon Victoria, and it's not even his baby."

Emma rounded on him so fiercely he drew back, wary that she might use her riding crop on him after all. "Jake's a fool," she snapped. "Of course it's his baby."

He didn't take kindly to having Jake called names, and his eyes narrowed. "She told him just a mite too soon, don't you think?"

"She knew right away." Emma wasn't about to get into a discussion of how Victoria had known so quickly, but she wasn't finished. "It couldn't be the Major's child, because he didn't . . . do that to her."

"Yeah," Ben said cynically. "She tried to convince Jake of that. But why would any man *not* make love to his wife? Victoria's a good-looking woman."

She was flushed with anger. "He tried, but couldn't."

"Why couldn't he? It's common knowledge that he *could* with Angelina."

"I don't know why he couldn't with Victoria. He tried the first two nights they were married, but couldn't do it. He left her alone after that."

"How do you know? Were you in their bedroom watching?"

"She told me the next morning," Emma answered. "I know most women don't talk about things like that, but Victoria and I are very close. We've been together all of our lives. She was so frightened on their wedding night because she didn't know what was going to happen. She married him only because we were all starving and he said he'd give money to her parents if she'd marry him."

Emma's words were strong and certain. Ben frowned, thinking. What if Jake was wrong?

18

"You interested?" Garnet asked the man sitting across from him. The surface of the saloon table between them was pocked and gouged, and it carried myriad sticky rings where overflowing glasses had been set. The other man's face was almost as pocked and gouged as the table.

Bullfrog Espy took a long, slow drink of beer before adding another wet ring to the table. His eyes were the color of dingy water, and there was a cold, lifeless quality to them. "How many men you reckon it'll take?" he finally asked in a light, high-pitched voice that could have been a woman's. His voice had earned him his nickname "Bullfrog" because nobody in their right mind would call a man his size and temperament "Squeaky."

"Fifty, or thereabouts."

"That's a lot of men. Ain't fifty men I know that I'd trust."

Garnet shrugged. He didn't trust anyone. "It don't matter if we can trust 'em, just as long as they're willing to use a gun."

"And you ain't interested in the ranch?"

"You can have the damn ranch. It's the girl I want."

"Mebbe I'll want her too. It's been a while since I had a white girl."

"She's not the only white woman. Her sister and cousin are

there, too. They're young, good-looking women. But I want this one."

Bullfrog didn't fidget aimlessly the way most men did, and his stillness got on Garnet's nerves. But he was fast with a gun and didn't mind killing. Some folks even said he enjoyed it. "Jake Roper, huh? He's a fast son of a bitch. I seen him in El Paso one year."

Garnet smiled, a slow movement of his mouth that didn't ease the cold ruthlessness of his eyes. "Don't matter how fast a man is if you're behind him."

Bullfrog lifted the glass again. "That's true," he said.

The sunlight streaked across the tiles in the foyer, nothing like the night when the shadowed nightmare had taken place. But when the heavy front door opened and the shadow of some-one's head and torso spilled across the tiles, something flashed in Jake's head. It was exactly as it had been the night he'd looked down and seen his father's body sprawled on the floor.

Blood drummed in his temples. He stood frozen just outside the library door, his face twisting as the hot tide of hate con-sumed him. There, to the left of the stairs, was where his mother had lain with her face bruised and distorted by McLain's fist, where he had raped her while her husband's body lay only a few feet away. Her blood and brains had pooled on those tiles.

God damn McLain's soul to roast in hell! If he even had a soul.

He and Ben had watched him die, but they hadn't won. McLain still lived within these walls, within the home he'd fouled with his presence. His flesh and blood still lived in Victoria's body. The sight of her now, as she cast the shadow that had awakened Jake's memories, enraged him all the more.

She had been feeling well enough lately to get out of the house; the vomiting was gradually easing. Autumn was coming, and coming soon. It was September, and the aspens were golden.

She closed the door and stood still for a moment to let her eyes adjust to the light in the house. There was no movement to attract her attention, no sound, but suddenly the hair on the back of her neck raised up as a sense of menace chilled her. She jerked her head around and saw Jake.

His face was a twisted mask of hate, his eyes like green coals.

In that split second of recognition, she was terrified. He looked as if he wanted to tear her apart with his bare hands. Without thought, obeying some wild instinct, she ran.

Jake started, pulling his mind from the past as she bolted up the stairs. He started moving toward the steps, his warning call sharp. "Victoria! Watch the steps!"

By some miracle she didn't stumble. When the wave of dizziness hit her, she managed to grasp the banister with both hands and hold herself upright. Her vision wavered, then began to fade. She could hear him coming up the stairs at a run, his boots thudding, and she tried to haul herself up another step, but her legs were too heavy and wouldn't obey. With a dull sense of alarm and astonishment, she felt her body begin to sag and could do nothing to stop it.

Then steely arms were around her, arms that she remembered sometimes in her dreams that left tears on her face when she awoke. As the darkness became absolute, she wondered why he had caught her.

Jake swung her limp body up in his arms, sweat breaking out on his face at how close she had come to falling. She was in a dead faint, her head lolling back over his arm. He opened his mouth to yell for Emma or Carmita, but shut it as quickly as the impulse came. Victoria was his wife; he'd take care of her. He'd seen enough unconscious men to know how to handle a simple faint.

She didn't feel any heavier now than she had three months before. Just the feel of her in his arms struck him with a sharp, nostalgic pleasure, piercing and bittersweet. It shouldn't have been so long since he had held her; the chasm between them shouldn't have been so wide and deep and unbridgeable.

He started to carry her into their—his—bedroom, but changed his mind and went into hers; she would be less alarmed when she woke up if she wasn't in his bed. She showed no signs of reviving even when he placed her on the bed, and with growing concern he unfastened her skirt, then the light blue shirtwaist that was buttoned high under her chin.

He could feel the warmth of her soft skin, and the parting

edges of the blouse revealed the pulse beating gently at the base of her throat. His own pulse began to throb.

"Victoria, wake up," he murmured, stroking the hair back from her face. She still didn't stir. He lifted her skirt enough to remove her shoes, then took the pillow from beneath her head and slid it under her feet, slim and delicate in her white cotton stockings. His pulse beat faster.

She was his; her body was his. He put his hand on her stomach, searching for evidence of the life that had torn their marriage apart. Her belly was smooth and as flat as ever.

His brows snapped together. How far along did a woman have to be before her pregnancy began showing? The way he figured it, she should be more than four months along, certainly enough to be showing. But then, some women didn't get as big as others; he'd seen some who looked huge and some who didn't look very big the day they delivered. Maybe her clothing was disguising her shape.

He tossed her skirt up, his hand delving beneath the froth of petticoats, finding her cotton-covered thighs and sliding upward to her belly. She was warm and flat.

Her eyelids fluttered and struggled open. "Jake?" she murmured.

He leaned over her. "You fainted, but you're all right," he said in a low voice.

"I thought you were going to kill me." The words were a little slurred as she struggled to push the last remnants of unconsciousness away. She blinked her eyes and focused on his face. She saw no sign now of the intense hatred that had sent her running for her life, and in confusion she wondered if she'd been imagining things.

"No. Not ever." Jake's heart began beating heavily as he watched her. Her lips were soft and trembling slightly. Her wall of hostility was down; she was weak and disoriented. Before she could resurrect her anger he bent and covered her mouth with his, a muffled sound of pleasure coming from deep in his throat.

He used the pressure of his mouth to open her lips and slipped his tongue into her. A dizzying surge of delight went through him as he felt her arms lift and slide around his neck. He gathered her to him, deepening the kiss.

She had wanted him for so long, craved him for so long, that her whirling senses fastened on what he was doing. The taste of his mouth kept her from dying of thirst, his hands fed her in other ways. She moaned at the feel of his rough palm on her sensitive breasts, sliding inside both blouse and chemise and cupping the naked globes, then lifting them free of their cloth restraints. He left her mouth, his lips sliding down her throat and chest to close over one extended nipple.

The feeling was so electrifying that she almost shot off the bed. Her breasts were so tender that she could barely tolerate the pressure of her clothing, and his hot mouth fastening on her nipple was a maddening mixture of pain and pleasure.

She couldn't bear it. Tears sprang to her eyes and she pushed against his shoulders. "You're hurting me," she choked.

He lifted his head, his green eyes dark with passion. "Hurting you?" he repeated hoarsely.

"Yes . . . my breasts are sore. The baby—"

He drew back. The evidence of the child growing within her was here, in the larger swell of her breasts, the darkening of the nipples, the increased delicate blue veining running just under the creamy satin skin.

She scrambled off the bed on the other side and stood with her back to him as she restored chemise, shirtwaist, and skirt to their proper positions. "Thank you for catching me," she said in a tight voice.

He remembered what she'd said when she had first regained consciousness; she had thought he was going to kill her, and she had run from him in terror. God, what had they done to each other?

"I didn't mean to scare you." His own voice was gruff. "Be careful from now on going up or down the stairs."

"Yes. I will."

She was too slender. He watched her for several days, trying to handle his uneasiness. He counted the days just as she had told him to do, and tried to figure how far along she would have to have been before she knew she was pregnant. A month? Two months? He just didn't know, but he thought surely she would have been showing by now. On the other hand, if *he* had gotten her pregnant immediately, she would only be in her third month. And that would explain why she still wasn't showing.

The thought of it made him sweat as he remembered the things he'd said and done. Doubt, once admitted, gnawed at him.

He sought out Carmita and found her alone. Carefully he watched her reaction as he said, "I'm worried about the señora, Carmita. She's so thin. Shouldn't she be bigger by now? Is something wrong with the baby?"

Carmita beamed at him, shaking her head and making clucking noises. "You new fathers, you worry about everything! The señora has lost weight, she has been so sick, but the morning sickness is beginning now to go away."

"But her stomach—it's flat."

"It's just her third month, Señor Jake. It will probably be at least another month before the baby is big enough to begin showing."

Her third month. The pit of his stomach was cold. Jake counted the days again, but the numbers hadn't changed. If she were just three months along, that would mean that he—damn it, it just wasn't likely! That meant she would have known right away. She had been hiding something from him from the beginning; what else could it have been if not her pregnancy? And that absurd story about McLain not being able to have sex was a plain lie.

He sweated over it for a while, then decided to put his mind to rest about one part of it, at least. It was likely he wouldn't know the truth until the baby was born. But he went to Angelina Garcia's room behind the bunkhouse.

He realized that he hadn't seen her in a while, and he wondered if she had left. He would have run her off himself a long time ago, but Victoria hadn't mentioned it and Jake felt vaguely sorry for the woman, so he hadn't pursued it. How would she leave? Walk? So far as he knew, she owned nothing except her clothes.

But when he knocked he heard scrabbling behind the door

and eventually it opened to reveal Angelina, her hair hanging uncombed down her back, her eyes puffy with sleep. He ran his eyes down her opulent figure, and almost stumbled backward in shock. Angelina was visibly, undeniably pregnant.

The pregnancy hadn't changed her natural bent. "Well, if it isn't the *patrón*," she purred. "I knew you'd come to see me sooner or later."

He looked quizzically at her. In a mild tone he asked, "Why would you think that?"

She threw back her head and laughed. "Because of what I can do for you, why else?"

"Whose baby is it?"

She shrugged. "How would I know? Soon I will be too big for anyone to be interested, but right now there are several who like it. Men." She shrugged again, as if to say she would never understand their tastes.

"McLain used to visit you a lot, didn't he?"

A tiny, self-satisfied smile curved her lips. "He couldn't stay away from me. He came to me the night after his marriage. He thought he was a great lover, but he had nothing, I barely knew he was inside me."

"Then he never had any trouble having sex with you?" Jake's voice was expressionless.

Angelina laughed in his face. "No man has trouble with me, not even the Major. He couldn't get it hard with the señora because she was so cold—" Abruptly she remembered that the señora was now Jake's wife and she halted, her face turning sullen.

Jake felt as if someone had punched him. He had difficulty sucking in enough air to talk. "How do you know he couldn't?"

"He told me," she muttered. "I didn't tell anyone else because I knew he would have me thrown off the ranch, if he didn't kill me." She refused to say anything else. But she'd told Jake enough.

His face pale, Jake walked back to the house. *Victoria had been telling the truth.* It was his baby she carried, not McLain's. God, the things he'd said! He remembered the cold fire in her eyes, and for the first time understood the real violence behind it.

She had said that she would take the baby and leave; he'd

been so angry at the time that he hadn't taken the threat seriously. Now that he knew the truth he realized just how furious she had a right to be, and a cold fear grew in him that she really might do it. He would lose both Victoria and his baby.

His baby! She really had been that innocent about sex. He was the only man who had ever made love to her. And she was so angry even after all these weeks she hadn't thawed a bit, hadn't even begun to forgive him. Hell, why should she? Up until now he had still been insisting that the baby wasn't his!

He had to apologize, make it up to her somehow—but when he remembered the coldness of her face whenever she looked at him, he felt his stomach muscles tighten. He never would have thought that sweet Victoria could stay that angry for so long, but she had. Well hell, why not? He'd insulted her, slapped her, threatened her, and she was as proud as she was sweet. It wasn't just aristocratic breeding that kept her spine so straight; it was pure steel.

There was no point in putting it off. The quicker he apologized and got things straight between them, the better off they all would be. He looked for Victoria all over the house, and finally found her in the courtyard where the walls protected her from any autumn breeze that might chill her. She was taking advantage of the bright sun to stitch a tiny gown. The sight of that delicate garment in her hands made his throat tighten.

When she looked up at him, her eyes were carefully blank. "Yes?"

He squatted down in front of her, trying to think of the words he needed. He was painfully aware that these next few minutes might be the most important of his life. Finally it just seemed best to say it right out.

"Victoria—I was wrong. I'm sorry. I should have believed you. I know the baby's mine."

"Really?" she replied coolly after a moment of silence when his heart almost didn't beat. She bit off a thread. "How do you know that now, when you were equally certain a couple of months ago that it wasn't?"

Damn, she wasn't going to give an inch, and he couldn't blame her. She deserved her revenge. He looked at her delicate white skin, flushed with the sun's warmth and returning good health. Her breasts strained at her bodice, and he was suddenly consumed by a deep need to see just exactly how much this child of his had changed her body.

"I know I acted like a bastard—"

"Yes," she agreed, then returned to the question she'd asked. "What made you change your mind about the baby?"

"You haven't grown any—"

"The Major died only two days before you took me."

He got to his feet, furious that after all this she would throw McLain in his face when she knew damned good and well that bastard hadn't touched her, and now he knew it, too. Women were the most contrary creatures on earth; after the way she'd cried and begged him to believe her, now she was trying to convince him that the baby wasn't his after all! His hands knotted into fists. "Damn it, I know McLain didn't sleep with you!" he said. "Angelina told me that he couldn't—"

Victoria's head snapped up, and too late he saw the error that anger had led him to make. Her voice was frosty when she spoke. "Am I supposed to be happy that you'll take the word of a whore before you'll take mine? That you've been discussing *me* with that whore? You can take your apology and go to hell with it, Jake Sarratt!"

She surged to her feet, stuffing her sewing into the basket. Red spots of color decorated her cheeks.

"Calm down," he said, moving to catch her elbow in case she got dizzy. "You might faint if you move too fast."

"Whether or not I faint is my business, Mr. Sarratt. I'm none of your concern and my baby is none of your concern."

His eyes narrowed. Victoria had always pushed him further than anyone else dared, like a child who played with a tiger and never quite realized the danger it was in until it was too late. He watched her sail into the house, her haughty nose high, and the bright sun dimmed as he realized the truth in a paralyzing instant.

He loved her. He hadn't at first, but there had always been that strong sexual attraction drawing him to her. If he hadn't loved her, thinking she was pregnant with McLain's child wouldn't have hit him so hard. Had it been any other woman, he would have shrugged, sent her to Santa Fe, and he would have gone on with his life. Had it been any other woman, he wouldn't have been married to her to begin with.

But Victoria . . . he couldn't bear the thought of living without her. Now that he knew how much she meant to him, he panicked at the thought of losing her. He couldn't let it happen. He'd stop her from leaving even if he had to keep her prisoner in the house until he could make it up to her and she forgave him. He had already wasted three months with his stupidity. Three damn months!

But not one more day.

He strode quickly into the house after her, boot heels ringing on the tiles. His face was set in hard lines.

She had paused in the dining room to speak to Emma. Carmita was doing something at the table; he didn't pay any attention to what. He crossed the room, intent on Victoria. She looked up and saw him; a startled expression flitted across her face, followed swiftly by wariness, then naked fear. She dropped her sewing bag and took a step back. Emma's mouth opened with surprise, then she too got a good look at Jake's face and instinctively got out of his way.

He reached Victoria and bent, catching her behind the knees and back and swinging her off her feet. She gave a little cry of panic and struck at him, but he jerked his head to the side. Before she could try again, he shifted her in his arms and smothered her mouth with his. The kiss was deep and rough and hungry; he felt as if he could never get enough of her mouth, of the feel of her in his arms.

She pulled her head away, twisting it to the side so he couldn't kiss her again. She pushed at his chest. "Put me down!" She sounded frantic.

"I'll put you down," he said with hushed violence. "In my bed, where you belong and where you'll damn well stay." Leaving a gaping Emma and Carmita behind, he carried her up the stairs, taking them two at a time. She made no allowances for the possibility that he might drop her; she kicked and fought and arched her back, trying to squirm from his grip, but his strength was too overpowering. He simply crushed her tighter against his chest. He reached his bedroom and carried her inside, kicking the door shut behind him with a resounding thud.

She tried to bite him, fighting him as desperate pride had not allowed her to do the first time he had overpowered her in this room. "No you don't," he grunted, dumping her on the bed and throwing himself down beside her. He captured her hands in one of his and held them high over her head. "Calm down," he said sharply. "This can't be doing the baby any good."

Her hair was coming loose with her struggles, straggling across her shoulders. Her face was flushed and her blue eyes were almost throwing off sparks she was so angry. "What the hell do you care?"

"Such language," he mocked, wrestling her down when she almost succeeded in throwing herself off the side of the bed. When he had her secured, with her legs pinned by his and her arms once more anchored over her head, he used his free hand to search around her waist until he found the fastening of her skirt and opened it. The tapes of her petticoats didn't present much of a problem. He began shoving the garments down over her hips and thighs.

She made an explosive sound of rage and once again tried to sink her teeth into the muscled arm that stretched over her head, holding both of her arms captive. He laughed and jerked it out of reach of her teeth without even loosening his grip. His green eyes were very bright.

"Why don't you go to your precious whore?" she shouted.

"Because I'd rather be with you," he replied, not allowing her to make him angry. He buried his head in the soft curve between her neck and shoulder, inhaling her wonderfully sweet scent. It had haunted his nights, when he would wake up from erotic dreams and reach across the bed to gather her close, only to find it empty.

"I don't want to be with you," she said from between clenched teeth.

"You will," he promised, stroking his hand over her belly and breasts. "Remember the first time? You didn't want to be with me then, either, but you changed your mind. Haven't you missed me at all, sweetheart? Here? And here?" His wandering hand first touched her tender breasts, but lightly, so as not to cause her any discomfort, then down to her thighs. They were clamped together, but he still managed to slide one finger between them and find the open slit of her drawers. Inside was hot, damp flesh, and a shudder rocked him as he gently explored.

"No." The word was strangled. She turned her head to the side, away from him. "Please."

"You know I'll please you," he murmured, removing his finger to shove her skirt and petticoats completely off. Without their concealing bulk, her slender body was clearly outlined by the form-fitting shirtwaist blouse, shift, and the thin cotton drawers that clung to her thighs. She had very pretty legs, slim and well-formed. Her white stockings were held in place by plain white garters. He'd seen black lace garters and sheer silk stockings that hadn't excited him nearly as much.

Using the toe of his boot, he scraped her soft, flat-heeled slippers off of her feet and kicked them from the bed: "Don't want you getting the bedcovers dirty."

She didn't take kindly to the gentle teasing. "You've still got your boots on, you jackass!" She was seething, steam practically rising from her. He laughed low, inordinately amused at his very proper wife cursing at him.

"I'll take them off if you want me to," he offered.

"No!"

"Damn, you're a hard woman to please. Guess you're lucky that I'm a hard man."

She had no doubt what he meant, and if she had had one of her arms free she would have slapped him again. She was tiring rapidly; she hadn't recovered her strength from the long weeks of almost constant nausea. Devoutly, and without result, she prayed for one of the sickening bouts now.

She gathered her fading strength for one last desperate attempt at escape, tensing her muscles and surging wildly. He controlled her without effort, and Victoria was forced to the galling knowledge that there was nothing she could do. Hot, bitter tears slid down her cheeks, and she turned her head away as her body went limp.

"Don't cry, honey." Like the predator he was, he sensed her capitulation, and his voice was low and comforting. He released her arms, knowing she no longer had the strength to fight. "I'm sorry I didn't believe you, but it's over now. Let me make it up to you. It's been a long time since we've done this; haven't you missed it? Don't you remember how good I made you feel?"

She drew a deep, shuddering breath, fighting for control. "I remember everything you made me feel." Her voice was thick with tears.

He knew what she meant. He paused, his face tightening as the guilt over the pain he'd caused her almost overwhelmed him. Then he wiped the tears from her cheeks with his callused thumb. "Then hate me for it, but by God it won't make any difference. You're my wife, and your place is here with me."

She was tired, her muscles shaking. It was useless to fight him. She closed her eyes.

He rolled her to the side and unbuttoned her shirtwaist, then pulled it down her arms and tossed it aside. The shift went next, and she lay with her arms motionless, making no effort to cover her breasts.

The differences in them excited him. They were larger, firmer, readying themselves even now for the milk that would feed his baby. Her little nipples had darkened and seemed distended. He paused to remove his boots and shirt, his eyes never leaving her breasts. Without touching her anywhere else, he leaned over and lightly circled a pouting nipple with his tongue.

She gasped, her body arching. The touch of his hot tongue burned, and the heat gathered and pooled in her lower body. Her breasts became almost unbearably tight, just from that light touch. They were so sensitive that she almost burst into tears again, unable to decide if this was ecstasy or agony.

His breath washed over her wet flesh, making it tingle even more. He moved to the other nipple and subjected it to the same light, exquisitely gentle washing by his tongue. She trembled, fighting the blinding heat. Her hands gripped the sheet beneath her, twisting. No, no, she cried silently, he had to stop, she couldn't bear it—

With acute attention to her tender state, he sucked the nipple into his mouth and applied the lightest pressure.

A strangled sob tore from her throat, no longer in protest. Her hips lifted.

His hand went between her legs, and this time they parted easily. He rubbed lightly at her soft, exposed flesh, then slipped his finger into her. His memory of her tightness had tormented him, but he was amazed anew at how small her passage was. Sweat glistened on his naked torso.

"Do you remember, the time in the study?" he murmured, kissing her neck. "We were in too much of a hurry to take your drawers off, and I tore them so I could get at you better."

She moaned, her body twisting on his impaling finger. She opened her eyes but the lids were heavy, and her lashes fluttered. "Jake."

The sound of his name, uttered in that thick, helpless, wanting tone, made his heart leap. She was his. She was no longer fighting, no longer even thinking. Her hips lifted again.

He kissed her mouth, his tongue plunging deep. It was too late again to pull off her drawers. He tore the seam open, sliding down to explore the secrets revealed. Her woman's flesh was deep pink and glistening; he pressed his mouth to her in a deep, avid kiss, needing her taste, needing all of her secrets. She screamed, the sound muffled by the pillow she pulled over her face, and her cotton-clad thighs tightened convulsively around his head. He prised them open again, and held them wide. His tongue darted and dipped and circled, and continued as he felt the deep shudders begin. Her heels dug into the bed, both of her hands clenched in his hair, and she cried out again.

When it was over, her legs fell weakly open. She lay with her eyes closed and her breasts shining with a fine mist of perspiration, her chest heaving up and down as she fought for breath. He tore at the tapes holding the ruined garment about her waist, and stripped it away, then attacked his own belt and pants. Naked, he mounted her, and her eyes flared open at his slow, inexorable penetration.

She had almost forgotten the overpowering sensation of fullness. Her body had been preoccupied with its own gravity, but he had brought lust surging back. He grunted as he squeezed inward, the sound changing to a groan as he stopped. "Is it hurting you?"

Her hands were hot. She gripped his sweat-slick shoulders and twined her legs around his buttocks. "No. Don't stop. Don't stop, Jake, please—"

He gave a strained laugh, a sound of satisfaction rather than mirth. "No, I won't stop. God."

He didn't drive into her; he was too acutely aware of her pregnancy. He rigidly controlled his thrusting to a certain depth and rhythm, but it was enough. She convulsed again, greedily lifting her hips and taking the inches he had denied her. His senses exploded, and with a tight sound of defeat he gave her what she wanted as his loins pulsed and emptied.

Her white-stockinged legs remained locked around him. Her defeat, on this level at least, was shatteringly complete.

His breathing had steadied, his heart was once again beating normally instead of trying to burst out of his chest. Victoria, lying limp and unmoving at his side, seemed to be dozing. The sweat had dried on their bodies, and as he watched, the first faint chill roughened the skin of her upper arm. He heaved himself up and grasped the sheet, pulling it over them and tucking it around her shoulder. Her blue eyes flickered open, then she sighed and let them close again.

She seemed content to lie there, so close beside him. But he realized she was essentially alone. Before, she had lain in his arms, her head pillowed on his shoulder and her delicate hand sleepily stroking his chest. There was none of that mute intimacy now, no gentle touching, no lying tangled together and inhaling the other's scent. He hadn't known before what had made those drowsy hours after lovemaking so special, but now he did. The difference now told him that he may have won the battle, but he'd far from won the war. He wanted her willing touch, not this silent distance that told him she had been defeated, but not won.

Winning her back would take time, but he knew how to be patient. He'd been patient for twenty years, planning his revenge on McLain. He was willing to spend another twenty years teaching Victoria that she could love and trust him, if she would only allow him that much time.

He turned onto his side and pulled her into his arms, cradling her there whether she wanted to be or not. Closeness worked its own magic, and the sort of physical ecstasy they had just shared forged a bond he knew she couldn't easily ignore. He would use what weapons he had, because he dared not lose her.

"Tell me about it," he invited softly, nuzzling the fine hair at her temple.

"About what?" she asked in a cool, even little voice. Her eyes were still closed.

"About McLain."

The last thing Victoria wanted to do was discuss McLain; she was exhausted and wanted only to sleep. Even if she had been wide awake, however, she wouldn't have wanted to discuss the subject with Jake. He had forced her to a capitulation that deeply scoured her pride. What with her other grievances against him, she wasn't feeling very obliging.

She bit her lip, wishing that he would just go away. It was obvious that he had no intention of moving, however, so she said, "No."

"I need to know," he murmured, kissing the fragile hollow right below her temple.

Her eyes opened. "*You* need to know!" Her voice trembled with suppressed emotion. Her pregnancy had brought all of her emotions alarmingly close to the surface. "Tell me why I should care what *you* need! I needed my husband's support, and trust, and care; did you care about *my* needs?"

"I'm sorry, love. I'll do anything I can to make it up to you." He was completely sincere, and perhaps it was in his low voice because she gave him a quick, sharp look.

"How can you make up for something like that?" she asked, and closed her eyes with a weariness that was both physical and mental. "I can't think how it would be possible."

"Let me try anyway. We're married; we're having a baby." He smoothed his big hand down over her warm belly, wishing that he hadn't already wasted three months. "What does it feel like?"

Painful curiosity leaked into the words. "Can you tell anything yet?"

She gave a wry laugh. "Oh, yes, I've been able to tell a great deal. I've been deathly ill, so nauseated I could barely lift my head from the pillow. The smell of food is disgusting. I have an almost constant urge to . . . to wet," she said, stammering with embarrassment that she had said such a thing, but it had tumbled out without thought. "There is a sense of pressure, here." She laid her hand low on her belly. "I can scarcely bear for my clothes to touch my breasts, and I get dizzy if I try to move quickly. I cry several times a day, for no reason. I'm so tired I can scarcely get through the days, yet I can't sleep at night. I've really been enjoying myself."

He smothered a chuckle and planted another kiss, this one on her mouth instead of her temple. "When is it due?"

"Late in March." She found she couldn't deny him this knowledge about his child, now that he was asking.

His stroking hand smoothed over her belly, then down between her legs. She gasped, stiffening as his fingers leisurely parted and stroked. She would never have believed she could respond so soon after such explosive lovemaking, but her loins tightened.

"You feel wonderful; so warm and wet and tight. I want you so much I just couldn't understand how McLain didn't." His voice was muffled against her throat.

Victoria caught her breath, dazedly aware of the truth in his husky tone. He simply didn't understand it. She didn't know why McLain had been as he was, either, only how it had been.

"He tried," she whispered. "Twice. But he couldn't get hard, the way you do. It made him angry and he hurt me, but it still wouldn't work. After those first two times, he never tried again."

Jake closed his eyes, fighting the pain her words brought him. "How did he hurt you, love?"

She didn't notice the endearment. More and more of her attention was focusing on what he was doing. One long finger slipped into her and she moaned aloud. "He did . . . what you're doing now. But he hurt me, and there was blood. It was awful; I hated it, and I hated him. But when you do it . . . ah! Yes. Yes. It feels so good."

He leaned over her, increasing the brush of his thumb over her tiny nub. His heart squeezed as he thought how it must have been for her, a virgin ignorant of everything sexual, with a brute like McLain. Now he knew why she hadn't bled when he'd made love to her the first time. He didn't regret for himself the loss of that small membrane, only that she had been hurt and frightened.

He was the only man who had ever made love to her, the only man she had taken into her arms and her body. The knowledge flooded him with possessive pleasure. Whether she wanted it or not, she was irrevocably his. He would never let her leave him.

19

Jake had Carmita move Victoria's things back into his room. If he had thought Victoria would do so he was disappointed, but he knew well enough that their situation had improved to nothing more than a truce. She didn't again try to fight him physically, but her manner was reserved, her eyes still cool, and he knew he wasn't forgiven. It was enough, for now, that she was back where she belonged.

The next day Ben asked, "What happened?"

Jake tersely explained.

Ben shook his head. "Damn. I don't understand women. Whatever you expect, they'll do the exact damn opposite, even when you expect the opposite from what you first thought anyway."

Jake grinned in sympathy. Ben had gotten exactly nowhere with Emma. "Are you giving up?"

"Might as well. Yeah, I guess I am. Saloon girls are a lot simpler than ladies. I'm going to take a trip into Santa Fe before winter gets here, and have myself a good time."

Garnet had moved back toward Santa Fe, lying low and watching his back. Nothing was going to happen very soon, anyway. Winter was coming on fast, and spring would be a better time for what he planned. He had parted company with Bullfrog several weeks back; the other man was going to try to round up some of his old cronies in time to meet up again around the end of February. Garnet felt better with Bullfrog gone; he hadn't trusted the bastard not to put a bullet in his own back and carry on with Garnet's plan by himself.

He always sat close to the back door of a saloon, because you never knew when a quick exit might be needed. He was at just such a table when a tall, dark-haired man sauntered in and headed toward the bar. The well-worn pistol tied low on the man's thigh bespoke his ease with the heavy weapon, as did the easy, self-confident walk. It wasn't a strut; only hot-tempered kids looking to make a reputation felt the need for that, or for cutting notches in their guns. This man walked like he knew he could handle whatever got in his way. He had a presence about him that was strangely familiar.

Garnet peered at the stranger's face and a cold chill ran down his spine. For a minute there the man had looked like Jake Sarratt, but then Garnet saw that it wasn't. The resemblance, though, was strong. It was damn eerie.

A dark-haired saloon girl with a painted face and tired eyes perked up a little as she ran her experienced eyes down the stranger's tall form. She sashayed up to him, batting her eyelids and letting her hand trail down his thigh. He looked down at her and grinned, then nodded.

They turned away to go up the narrow stairs. Garnet quickly ducked his head so that his hat hid most of his face. He heard the stranger say, "What's your name, sugar?"

The voice was familiar, too, but not real familiar. It was like he'd seen the man once or twice, but hadn't gotten to know him. Damn if he didn't look like Jake Sarratt, though. Garnet kept his head down. It could be the other one, the brother. Wild elation shot through him. God, what a chance this would be! Give him five minutes to get started humping, then when he was going at it hard, kick the door in and put a bullet in the bastard before he knew what hit him. The only thing that kept Garnet in his chair was that he didn't know if Jake Sarratt was anywhere around.

Where had he seen the man before?

Then it came to him, and he turned pale. He'd had a beard when Garnet had met him, but there was no doubt it was the same man. It was Tanner, the gunslick who had ridden in late one afternoon and hired on, but only stayed a day or so before leaving as quietly as he'd come. But his name wasn't Tanner, it was Sarratt, and he would know Garnet on sight.

Garnet gave the room a good look, but didn't see anyone he knew. That didn't mean anything. The Sarratts had hired a lot of new men. There could be any number of Sarratt men in here right now, surrounding him.

There was no way he was going to go up those stairs. There'd be another time, and a better chance.

Being careful not to catch anyone's eye, he got up from the table and slipped out the back door. When he was in the sour-smelling alley he started running, slipped and almost fell, but caught himself at the last moment with his hands. His left hand was in something foul-smelling and squishy. Garnet cursed viciously as he got up and scraped the sticky crap off his hand the best he could, rubbing it against the rough side of the building. That was just one more grievance he had against the goddamn Sarratts.

He waited until he was a piece down the street before washing his hand in a horse trough, then he hurried to the crib where he was sleeping. It wasn't anything more than a lean-to built against a stable, and the walls were made of unfinished planks nailed across some logs. The cracks were big enough to shoot through, and it had started getting damn cold at night. He'd have to find something better soon.

He was sharing the crib with Quinzy, who was already rolled up in his blanket and snoring his head off. Garnet nudged him with his boot. "Quinzy! Wake up. One of the damn Sarratts is in town, maybe both of them."

Quinzy came awake without any of the mumbling and wiping his eyes that most men did. He sat up. "Is it Jake?"

"I didn't see Jake. It's the brother, I don't remember his front name. He's the son of a bitch who rode in calling hisself Tanner, and left right after that. Guess he came to talk to Jake about something. Goddamn bastards were planning it right under our noses!"

Quinzy was silent. This latest plan of Garnet's was stupid, but there was no talking sense to him. He had it in his mind that the little gal was his, and that he had a right to the ranch. Damned if Garnet hadn't gone as loony, in his way, as McLain had. Quinzy had drifted along with Garnet out of habit, but it looked like the time had come to part.

"Don't look like I'll be riding back to the kingdom with you, Garnet." Quinzy said. "Heard tell the land up along the Snake is mighty pretty and mighty lonesome, a good place for me to lay low for a spell. Reckon I'll do that. Twenty years ago I was game to take on the Sarratts, or anybody else come to that, but I'm twenty years older and twenty years slower. It's time for me to think about retiring."

"I hate to hear you're not going with me, Quinzy," Garnet said. "We been together a long time, but a man's got to do what a man's got to do."

"Glad you're being understanding about it, and all. I'll ride out early in the morning, before anybody gets a good look at me. Don't know if any of the Sarratt men know who I am, but iffen they don't I'd like to keep it that way."

Quinzy rolled back up in his blankets and listened to Garnet doing the same. After a while Quinzy began to snore again. He never heard the quiet snicking of a hammer being pulled back. If there was a fraction of a second after the trigger was pulled that he heard the explosion of the shot, it was too tiny a slice of time for it to do him any good. Garnet's bullet plowed into the back of Quinzy's head, splattering a big portion of the front of it across the wall.

Garnet rolled up his blankets and got his gear. There wasn't much chance of a single shot in this part of town being investigated, but it was best to clear out anyway. He looked down at the body. "Like I said, a man's got to do what a man's got to do," he said in an undertone. "If you ain't with me, you're against me."

It snowed early that year, a light dusting that barely covered the ground but gave hint of the coldness to come. That morning when Victoria left the bed to look out the window at the layer of white, she felt the child move for the first time She went very still, her hand pressed to her lower abdomen as she waited for it to come again.

Jake looked up from stamping his feet into his boots, noticing her stillness. "What's wrong?"

"The baby moved," she replied in a low tone.

He came over to stand beside her. She had donned a shift but nothing else, and he felt a surge of lust as he looked at her. She lifted her hand and his replaced it on her belly, while his other arm circled her and pulled her against his body. They stood motionless and finally it came again, a flutter so faint that Jake barely felt it. He caught his breath, his heart pounding at this evidence of life. Until now, the baby had been defined by symptoms, most of them unpleasant for Victoria. But this was different; this was *life*.

She let herself lean against him, knowing it would do no good to try to put distance between them. He made love to her whenever he wanted, just as he had before, with a searing sensuality that became more intense with time, rather than weakening. There was no part of her body that was sacred from his touch, and pregnancy seemed to have made her that much more responsive. Even her skin felt sensitized. Sometimes she felt she would drown in sensuality, but the loving playfulness that she had found with him before their fight didn't return.

Instead she resented his physical power over her, because he wielded it without love. Even after all that had happened, she still loved him; he would not have been able to hurt her so deeply if she hadn't. He cared for her, she thought, but she was carrying his child, so why wouldn't he feel some concern? And he enjoyed sleeping with her, that was plain enough. But not one word of love ever crossed those hard, chiseled lips.

She bitterly resented his lack of faith in her. It still rankled every day that he could believe her capable of such betrayal. His accusation had sprung from the legacy of hate he still carried around with him; even though McLain was dead, the hatred in Jake hadn't dissipated. Sometimes Victoria could almost feel McLain still in the house, with the ghosts of Jake's parents, keeping the hatred alive.

It would be best if she took the child and left. She didn't

want it to grow up surrounded by hatred; she wanted it to grow up happy, in a house without shadows. The idea of leaving teased her mind every day, but the difficulty of it defeated her. How could she leave? Where could she go? Moreover, neither Emma nor Celia would want to leave. Emma might watch Ben with great sad eyes whenever he wasn't looking, but the ranch had become her cousin's home. She wouldn't want to leave it or Ben, even if he had apparently lost interest.

Celia was growing up, rapidly leaving her helter-skelter ways behind. She was calmer, more dignified, more thoughtful. Her hair was usually neat now, her dress tidy, and she walked instead of skipping. She still spent a lot of time crooning to Rubio and trying to make friends with the great stallion, but she no longer seemed so obsessed by it. No, Celia wouldn't want to leave.

Jake turned her in his arms, his hand sliding up to cup her breasts. Victoria looked up at him, her eyes grave. He looked back at her with his intention plain. He'd just finished dressing, but the clothes came off as easily as they went on. He led her back to the bed, and it was another hour before they left the room.

The winter months came with a vengeance, with more bitter cold than snow, though there was enough of both. Victoria grew increasingly rounder, her pregnancy immediately apparent to anyone who took the time to look. Her mood changed, becoming both calmer and a bit dreamy as she was increasingly preoccupied by the changes in her body. Everything was out of her control. At least the last of the morning sickness had gone and physically she felt wonderful, though she still tired easily.

She would have thought that her increasing bulk would dampen Jake's carnal desires, but not so. He handled her with increasing care and made love to her in various positions that put none of his weight on her body, but he seemed to find her as desirable as ever. If she had thought about it she would have been reassured, but it never occurred to her to wonder if other men remained as attentive to their wives during pregnancy.

In the middle of December, Angelina gave birth. The woman had been in hard labor for over an hour before any of the men paid heed to the cries they heard coming from her small, cluttered room. Both Carmita and Lola were reluctant to attend the woman. Despite her own distaste, Victoria felt that she had to do something for her. Perhaps it was her own pregnancy that made her feel more deeply for Angelina's plight. For whatever reason, she wrapped herself in her warmest shawl and trudged across the yard to the far buildings. Carmita threw up her hands and followed.

Angelina turned her head on the soiled pillow as Victoria entered. Her teeth drew back in what was meant to be her usual insolent smile, but it became more of a grimace. "So! You want to see how it will be when it's your turn?"

The lack of cleanliness in the room was appalling. There was a small fireplace but the fire had burned down and Angelina hadn't been able to replenish it, so the room was decidedly chill. Despite that, sweat beaded on Angelina's grayish face as she suddenly contorted in another pain.

"Quickly, rebuild the fire," Victoria instructed. She wasn't herself too certain what to do, but warmth and cleanliness seemed a good place to start. With Carmita, she managed to get clean linens on the bed, though the mattress beneath was grimy. Carmita was the experienced one and took over with Victoria's blessing. The soiled negligee Angelina had been wearing was removed and replaced by one of Carmita's own, as hers were voluminous enough to fit over Angelina's swollen breasts.

The woman strained in labor all afternoon and into the night. Her lovely dark eyes sank back into her head and her lips were raw and bleeding from the scrape of her teeth.

Jake knocked on the door and tugged Victoria outside when she opened it. He pulled her within the folds of the heavy sheepskin coat he wore, wrapping her inside his own warmth. "Let Carmita handle it," he growled. "You don't need to be out here."

The wind bit through her skirts, and her breath fogged the air. "If it were me I would want all of the help anyone could give." She leaned against his muscled body, and his child moved strongly within her. "I think she's going to die," she whispered, strangely desolate. It wasn't just that she would be enduring childbirth herself in a few months, but that Angelina was so alone and would die so unloved.

If Angelina was truly going to die, Jake didn't want Victoria in there watching it. He tried to bully her back into the house, but she refused to budge. He was on the verge of physically carrying her when she lifted her wan face and said, "How can I expect anyone to help me if I'm not willing to help when I can?"

"Your situation is different. You have family—"

"Angelina doesn't. She has no one." She lifted her fingers to his lips, the first time she had touched him voluntarily outside of bed since the day she had told him she was pregnant. The light touch seared him all the way to his soul, and he trembled. He caught her hand and turned her palm against his cheek, cold and beard-rough.

"Shall I send Emma to help?" he asked in a hoarse voice. He could barely speak.

"No." Victoria's smile was wry. "She isn't married. It wouldn't do at all. But perhaps—if Lola will come. Ask, but don't order her. It should be her decision."

He let her go back inside the dingy little room with its coppery odor of hot, fresh blood and wished that she had just a little less the lady of the manor's ingrained sense of responsibility.

Lola did come, along with the news that she had prepared a light meal for them and left it in the kitchen; she would stay while they ate. Carmita took herself off for a hasty meal, but Victoria didn't feel that she could endure food right then. She was tired, and her stomach was a little queasy.

Angelina had been lying with her eyes closed for over an hour. She didn't open them now, but she said in a surprisingly strong voice, "You might as well eat. I would if I could."

"I'm not hungry," Victoria replied, sponging the woman's face. The time between contractions was short. For a while they had been almost constant, but nothing had happened and now they were spaced a bit further apart.

It was the last time Angelina spoke. Close to midnight she was delivered of a fat little girl with a crop of thick black curls like her mother's and the cord wrapped around her blue neck.

Victoria wrapped the small body in a towel, her heart breaking.

They couldn't stem the flow of blood and Angelina was too weak to fight. She was unconscious and never knew that her daughter had died while trying to be born. A few hours later she too died.

Carmita and Lola took charge of cleaning the bodies for burial and refused to allow Victoria to help. She was sent back to the house, her body weighed down with weariness. Her own child was merrily kicking her ribs, letting her know that it was doing well.

To her surprise, Jake was sitting in the kitchen hunched over a cup of coffee that was no longer steaming. He looked up when she entered.

"They both died." Victoria's voice was colorless.

Jake got up and held her in his arms. As he carried her to their room, she clutched his shirt and wept, her tears hot against his shoulder.

Neither life nor nature paused. Work on the ranch went on, and Victoria's girth continued to increase. Though she knew she would get much larger before it was finished, her shifting center of gravity made her feel constantly off-balance. Stroking her belly now during the baby's more acrobatic movements, she could discern a foot from an elbow, a hand from a knee.

"Jesus," Jake said one night, amazed at the force with which a tiny foot had thudded against his hand. "This feels like two wildcats in a sack fighting to get out."

"Thank you, how reassuring."

He grinned and continued stroking his hand lazily over her belly. "Do you think it could be two?"

"No. I've counted one head, two feet, two knees, two elbows, and two hands. In whatever position, there's only one baby."

He was relieved. The thought of her in labor with one child was scary enough.

Late in January Celia filched an apple from the storeroom and carried it out to Rubio. It was a beautiful morning, cold and crisp. A few inches of snow covered the ground, but the sky was cloudless. Her blood was singing through her veins; perhaps, just perhaps, Luis would be able to join her in her secret place in the loft. It was harder to find privacy now that winter kept the men close to the house. When spring came, she thought, she and Luis would ride out to a private place and spend the entire day making love.

Rubio was prancing around in the largest corral, snorting and shaking his head as he enjoyed his exercise. Dual trails of steam blew from his wide-open nostrils. He cavorted like a colt, and his red hide gleamed like polished mahogany in the bright sun.

Celia climbed on the fence, content just to watch him. He was seldom playful, so she didn't try to coax him to her to take the apple. In time he would work out his kinks, then he would come over to her for his treat. It had been weeks since he had tried to snap at her and he no longer shied when she patted his sleek, muscular neck.

He was beautiful, she thought, beautiful in much the same way that Luis was. They were both magnificent animals, dangerous and simple in their instincts.

Luis. Celia shivered. Just the forming of his name in her mind made her go soft and warm inside, the way she felt when they were making love. Her breasts tingled, and she thought of his mouth sucking at them. *Luis.*

Her grip on the apple loosened and it fell to the ground. She knelt and reached for it through the fence, but it was a good foot beyond her fingertips. Rubio was on the far side of the corral, his proud head lifted high. She was safe enough, she thought, and climbed over the fence.

Even inside the house they heard the piercing screams of an enraged horse. There were shouts and the sound of men running. There was another scream, only one, but this one was different. It went through Victoria's heart.

She ran. Emma tried to catch her. "Victoria, no!" Emma had a hard grip on her arm, but Victoria thrust her aside with violent strength. She didn't notice her unwieldy body as her feet flew over the snow.

"Celia!" she screamed. There was no answer.

In the corral a knot of men on horseback had thrown several ropes over Rubio's head and were fighting him to a standstill. Jake was one of the men. He dismounted and ran to a small crumpled heap on the ground. As he went down on one knee, he saw Victoria flying toward them, her face a white mask.

"Ben, grab her!" he yelled.

Ben ran, intercepting her before she could reach the corral. He held her by wrapping his arms around her from behind, locking them under her breasts. She kicked and heaved, but his iron strength held her.

"Let me go!" she shrieked, trying to claw his face. Tears streamed down her cheeks. "Celia. *Celia!*"

Jake shifted his body so that he was between Victoria and Celia, but she could see the blue of her shawl, matted now with mud. The tan of her skirt. The white tumble of petticoats. A small shoe, lying by itself in the snow. A silky blond lock, stirring in the wind. And a lot of red. Celia hadn't been wearing anything red.

"Get a blanket," Jake called sharply over his shoulder, and someone ran to do his bidding.

Victoria twisted, still trying to tear herself free. Ben was talking to her, trying to calm her down, but his words didn't make any sense. Emma was standing rooted to their left, her hands pressed over her mouth as if to hold her own screams inside. Her eyes were black in her colorless face.

The blanket was brought and Jake wrapped it around the small bundle. Luis rode up and a stark look tightened his lean face. Without a word he swung down and climbed through the fence.

As Jake started to lift Celia, Luis said, "I'll take her." His voice was tight. "You see to your woman and I'll see to mine."

Jake gave him a sharp look, seeing what was etched in Luis's eyes. He looked back down at the small, still girl and touched her bloody cheek with gentle fingers. Then Jake left Celia to the man who had loved her, and walked to Victoria.

She was no longer fighting Ben, but stood motionless in his grip with her eyes the only spot of color in her face. She didn't even have a shawl.

Ben released her and she stood alone, her body rigid. She searched Jake's eyes for any sign of hope and found none. Still, she had to ask, had to hear it said. "Is she alive?"

Jake wanted to sweep her up and carry her inside, have her warm and cosseted in bed before he told her what he had to tell her, but she was waiting, holding herself tight inside, and he knew she wouldn't leave until she knew.

"No," he said.

Victoria swayed and he reached for her, but in the next instant she drew herself up straight, her chin high. "Bring her inside, please," she said in a brittle but controlled voice, as if she would shatter if she let her control slip at all. "She'll need . . . she'll need washing."

Luis carried Celia inside, his face rigid as the wind blew her hair over his arm and teased his cheek with it. Victoria and Emma were behind him, their shoulders back despite their sudden haggardness. Jake and Ben followed, both of them watching the slender, unbending spines ahead. Jake wanted to take Victoria in his arms and give her what comfort he could, but held back. Comfort now would soften her, and she needed all the strength she could muster.

Carmita and Lola were sobbing softly into their aprons, while Juana had her hand stuffed into her mouth. "We'll need water, please," Victoria said softly as she directed Luis upstairs.

He placed Celia on her bed and knelt beside it, slowly wrapping a bright tendril of hair around his finger. The blanket covered her face, but her hair was free. "I love you," he said to the motionless girl, but there was no answer, and his heart was dying inside him.

Victoria put her hand on his shoulder. She hadn't known, but now she realized that she should have guessed. Celia had changed in the past months, since meeting Luis. "She loved you, too. You made her happy."

He swallowed and carried her hair to his face. It still smelled like Celia. "We were lovers," he said thickly. "It never felt wrong."

"It wasn't wrong." It went against everything they had ever been taught, but it wasn't wrong. Victoria was struck by how much their lives had changed, how much *she* had changed, since coming to this wild land. When she had first stepped down on territory soil, her life had been ruled by what society designated as proper or improper, but propriety no longer mattered to her when measured against love.

Love had changed Celia from a child into a woman. She had been content, no longer running from flower to flower as if in search of enough beauty and happiness to satisfy her need for it. She had found it in Luis.

Still sobbing, Carmita brought the water, but as she put it down she said, "I will wash the señorita, if you like."

"Thank you, but Emma and I will do it," Victoria said gently. It was the last thing they would be able to do for Celia.

Jake came up and took Luis away with him. Ben was overseeing the building of a coffin and having a new grave dug. Gently Victoria and Emma cut away Celia's torn clothing and began washing the mud and blood from her pale body. Rubio's sharp hooves had opened numerous deep cuts, but they were mostly on her back; she must have cowered with her arms over her head in a futile effort to protect herself. The back of her skull was flat and soft where the killing blow had landed, but her face was unmarked except for a small scrape on her forehead. They washed her hair and brushed it dry. Her eyes were closed like a child's in sleep, her long lashes resting on marble-white cheeks. Looking at Celia lying on the bed as they dressed her in her favorite clothes, Victoria thought that she looked as though she would wake if only they shook her, but the essence of Celia was gone.

Victoria didn't sleep that night. Jake insisted that she go to bed, and she did, but lay in his arms with her eyes open and burning. She had cried, but the tears hadn't brought a sense of release and now they wouldn't come at all. The pain clenched at her heart, sharp and unending. She had never been able to imagine life without Celia. Her sister had been as bright as the sun, and without her everything now had altered, become darker.

Her baby moved, and Victoria touched it. "She was looking forward to the baby so much. Now she'll never see it."

Jake hadn't slept either. He was too aware of Victoria's suffering, and his own sense of loss was acute. There would be no more conversations about riding astride or determining the sex of kittens, no more small shocks every time she opened her mouth, no more searches for items she had left in bizarre places.

He held Victoria close; he hadn't released her all night long and didn't intend to. "If it's a girl, would you like to name her Celia?"

Victoria's voice almost cracked. "I couldn't. Not yet."

An hour later she said, "She looked pretty, didn't she?"

"Like an angel."

"We'll have to take care of her kitten."

Dawn was a miracle of colors, gold and red and pink streaking across a lightening blue sky. Celia would have been entranced. Victoria looked at the sky and thought of all the dawns that would be less appreciated now, without Celia there to watch them. She got up and dressed. She had no black dresses for mourning, but out here it didn't seem as important as it had in Augusta. Grief was in her heart, not her clothes.

She twisted her hair into a careless knot, and Jake fastened her dress for her. She looked out the window again and said, "I want that horse destroyed."

Jake knew the need for revenge, knew how it could burn and fester. His hands tightened on her shoulders. "He's a dumb animal, Victoria. We had warned her time and again to be careful around him."

"He's a killer. He trampled one of the Mexican hands after you'd left that time, did you know? He should have been shot then."

The plans Jake had made for Rubio's get would never come to pass if he put the stallion down. Sophie was with foal, but he'd planned on buying other mares good enough to mate with the stallion. He wanted to produce a whole line of big, strong, fast horses. His heart ached, but destroying the animal wouldn't bring Celia back, wouldn't accomplish anything except Rubio's death and with it his outstanding blend of speed and strength. Victoria had been irrational about the stallion from the beginning, so Jake didn't expect her to make a rational decision now.

Still, it might become necessary to put him down. If no one could work with him without fearing for their lives, there would be no choice. Jake wanted to wait and see before he did something irrevocable.

"I won't order him shot," he said, and watched her face become even more withdrawn. He whirled her around to face him. "Not yet. I'm not saying I won't, I'm just saying that I'm going to think about it before I do something that can't be undone."

"Celia can't be brought back. Is that damn horse worth more than she was?"

"No, damn it, but killing him won't bring her back, either."

"It'll accomplish one thing, at least."

"What?"

"I won't have to look at the barn and know he's in there, safe and warm and well-fed, while my sister is in her grave."

They buried Celia with the sun shining brightly on her coffin, making the pale new wood gleam with a golden hue that almost matched her hair.

20

They all retired early that night, too dispirited even to try and talk. Emma watched Jake lead Victoria into their bedroom, his arm around her waist both possessive and tender, and the door closed to lock them in their private world where no one else could enter. Ben walked past her with a quiet good night and went into his own bedroom.

Emma carefully closed her own door, went about the nightly ritual of washing and getting into her nightgown, and then was totally unable to get into bed. She sat in a chair with her hands folded in her lap, rocking back and forth in a silent paroxysm of grief.

Death came so suddenly and it was so final, so indiscriminate. In a short time it had taken a nameless infant, an unloved whore, and a girl whose smile had made hearts break. They were promised nothing, any of them, not another year, another week, or even another day. Babies were born and every day of their lives after that was a risk. People could hide from life, but not from death.

Celia had lived life as if it were the greatest joy. She had reveled in its beauty and ignored the ugliness unless forced to look upon it. She had tried to hide from that part of life, but in the end it had found her.

In the end all they had was the moment, the everlasting now. One could plan for the future, one could try, but nothing was guaranteed.

Victoria was with her husband and their child was growing in her body. Celia had reached out with eager hands to embrace her love. But she, Emma, had turned away from the love that had beckoned her. Oh, she had had very good reasons and perhaps the love wasn't what she would have wished, but it had been offered and she had denied it.

How would she feel if *Ben* didn't survive the night?

A mighty hand squeezed her chest and tears leaked from the corners of her eyes. He might never return the devotion she felt for him, but that wouldn't make it one whit weaker. She had turned him away, and he hadn't asked in months now. She was alone, by her own will.

She got to her feet and blew out the lamp. Sitting here brooding wouldn't accomplish anything. She needed to get some sleep.

But she could not get into that bed. She paused, staring at its pale expanse in the darkness. A cold, empty bed, just as she was cold and empty.

She bolted out the door and down the hall. She jerked Ben's door open without pausing to think, her eyes wide and desperate, and came to an abrupt halt when he whirled around with his gun in his hand. The hammer was pulled back, his finger on the trigger. She looked down the unwavering barrel, dead level with her head.

Ben aimed the gun toward the ceiling and slowly let the hammer back down. "Don't ever do that again."

"No. I won't."

He wore only his pants, and the dark hair around his forehead was damp from his washing. Emma stared at the broad expanse of his chest, muscled and covered with dark hair, and felt her knees go weak.

"What do you want?"

"I want—" She stopped, her throat tightening. Her fingers dug into the wood of the doorframe. "Ben—"

He faced her, waiting.

"I want you to hold me," she whispered, one hand blindly reaching out for him. "Don't let me be alone tonight. God, I don't want to die without knowing what it's like to lie with you."

He sighed as he caught her hand, his rough fingers closing warmly, reassuringly around it. He'd given up hope that she would come to him, though he'd never quite been able to lose the dream. He had ceased to pressure her during the past few months, not because he'd wanted her less but because what he was offering wasn't fair to her. He still found the thought of marriage distasteful, and that was what a woman like Emma should have.

But his newly developed scruples didn't extend to turning her down if she came to his room wearing nothing but a thin nightgown, begging him to hold her.

Desire was already pumping through him, and he looked at her through narrowed, burning eyes. "You know that holding you won't be all I'll do, don't you? There's no way I can lie down with you and not be inside you, Emma girl."

"Yes, I know." She straightened her shoulders, though her soft, wide lips were trembling. "It's what I want, too."

He pulled her inside and closed the door. She was shaking as he gently freed her hair from its nighttime braid and spread it over her shoulders like a dark cloak. He lifted her hands and placed them on his shoulders, then bent and covered her mouth with his. Emma's eyelids fluttered shut, and she sank against him, against his wonderful heat and strength. Now that she had taken the step, she felt a deep calm underlying her sexual arousal, as if things had finally fallen into their rightful place.

He caught the hem of her nightgown and lifted it up and off. She trembled even more, and her hands made slight movements as if to shield herself, then she let them lie trustingly on his shoulders while he looked down at her slender white body. Ben felt breathless. She was so finely made that he felt coarse and clumsy, likely to hurt her with the lust that burned through him. He put his hand over one breast, marveling at the silky warmth of her and the contrast of his tanned, callused hand against the alabaster globe, then he lifted it and bent down to take the nipple in his mouth.

Incredible heat washed over her, more intense than anything he had taught her before. His taste and scent were achingly familiar; she recognized him by the primitive signs with which women have always recognized their mates. When he placed her on his bed, she went willingly.

"I don't know what to do," she whispered.

"I'll show you," he murmured in reply, kissing her neck and ear and then her mouth. He was achingly erect, throbbing with the need to enter her, but this first time control was crucial. "You taste sweet, Emma girl."

Emma moaned as he moved down to her breasts and began sucking at her nipples with a power that sent fire running through her veins. Time swirled and disappeared. His hands and mouth were all over her body, tasting her, feeling her. She received a jolt when he touched her between her legs, though the hot tide of pleasure quickly drowned her surprise. There was another jolt when he slid one long finger into her, testing both her response and the strength of her maidenhead. She winced away from the slight burning, but he rubbed his thumb across and around the sensitive nub at the top of her sex and with a whimper she returned, her hips rotating in search of more.

"Please." She clutched at him with wet hands. "Ben!"

He heeded her cry and stripped out of his pants, then spread her legs apart. He stopped to steady his breathing and regain his control. "It'll hurt just this once," he said roughly.

She lifted herself against the shaft that probed between her folds. "I know," she murmured as he let his weight down on her and settled his hips in the cradle of her thighs.

He entered her with care, pushing forward with slow pressure. She gasped, and her nails dug into his shoulders. Her body was opening for him, stretching painfully. She thought it was unbearable, but found that it wasn't. Her maidenhead gave way and he went deep inside her while tears burned her eyes. He lay very still, but she could feel his length throbbing as she tried to accustom herself to his penetration.

Then he withdrew, and she stared at him with dark, questioning eyes. He managed a tight smile. "No, it isn't finished. I'm just getting started, sugar, but I'm going to make certain you enjoy this as much as I will." Then he bent to her, applying mouth and fingers to the enjoyable task, and soon she was on fire. Just as she arched in her first convulsive climax, Ben thrust deeply into her, and there was no pain, only the intoxicating passion of their two bodies joined.

Two nights later Victoria slipped out of bed. Her eyes were burning from tears and lack of sleep, yet still she couldn't manage to do more than doze off occasionally. Every time she did, she woke with the sound of a single scream in her ears, and dreaded hearing it again.

It was after midnight now. Jake slept heavily, exhausted from the work he still had to do and his own lack of sleep since Celia's death. She didn't light a candle, knowing that it would wake him. His responses were still very much those of a gunslick, becoming instantly alert at the slightest noise or the light from a single candle. This was the first time she had managed to get out of bed in the middle of the night without waking him, which meant that she had awakened him a lot during her pregnancy.

She couldn't accept losing Celia, she just couldn't. Her older brother had been killed during the war and she had grieved, but it had been different somehow. He had been a grown man, and he had chosen to fight. Celia had been on the verge of blooming into full womanhood, a promise that would forever now go unfulfilled; she had not chosen to be stomped to death by a killer horse. Dear God, how she missed her!

And Rubio still stamped about in his roomy stall, healthy and vicious. It was just a matter of time until he killed again.

Unless she stopped it.

She didn't bother with stockings, but put on her slippers. Her shawl was hanging over the back of a chair, and she wrapped it around her head and shoulders. Jake's holsters were also slung over a chair, one sitting next to his side of the bed so he could reach them in a hurry. She tiptoed over and gingerly slid one of the heavy weapons free of the leather.

It weighted down her arm as she slipped from the room and down the stairs. She would barely be able to hold it steady if she needed it. She hoped she wouldn't.

The cold air blasted her in the face as she tugged the door open. New snow was falling, fat, fluffy snowflakes silently drifting down to cover everything in white. How Celia would have enjoyed it.

The walk to the barn seemed longer than it ever had before. The falling snow combined with darkness confused her depth perception and she stumbled several times. Already her feet and legs were freezing. It would be warmer in the barn with the body heat given off by the animals. Sophie was in there, her barrel swelling with Rubio's foal. And Gypsy, Celia's calm, gentle Gypsy. Several of the other mares had been bred to the stallion, but not Gypsy, and Victoria was violently glad.

She had to struggle to open the barn door, and a horse nickered in curiosity. The blackness seemed absolute. She left the door open, pushing it wide, then swinging the other door open, too. She knew that there was a lantern hanging just inside the right door and fumbled around until she found it and managed to get it lit. The warm yellow glow dispelled the darkness.

Sophie put her head over the top of the stall, and down at the far end of the barn Victoria could see the stallion's well-formed head, showing as a dark shadow rather than the red she knew it to be. How much better it would have been if the double doors at that end of the barn had opened into a free pasture rather than a series of corrals and pens, but they did, which meant she would have to drive the stallion back the entire length of the barn.

She knew she couldn't shoot the horse. As much as she hated him, she couldn't put the gun to his head and pull the trigger. Jake was right; he was a dumb animal. She could have shot him in self-defense or to defend anyone from an immediate attack, but not otherwise.

"You're safe from me," she whispered as she approached his stall, "as long as you don't start in my direction. Do you hear me, horse? Then I *will* kill you."

His ears went back and he watched her with unconcealed hostility. He began stamping, one hoof thudding down repeatedly. In her stall Sophie whinnied and kicked out, sensing the stallion's agitation.

Victoria gripped the pistol in her right hand and used both thumbs to pull the hammer back and cock it. She had to be ready in case he did charge at her. Then she unlatched the stall door and pulled it open, backing up with it, keeping the sturdy wood between her and the horse at all times.

He screamed and backed farther into the stall. "Get out," she hissed. She never wanted to see the stallion again. She had thought about it and in her exhaustion arrived at the truth: she couldn't live on this ranch if Rubio remained. The hate would fester, and every time she saw him she would remember that he'd killed her sister.

He reared, screaming shrilly again. "Go on, get out!" Victoria yelled. She grabbed a length of bridle from the wall, swinging it over the stall at him. "Get out!"

He bolted out of the stall and down the center of the barn, but halted midway, hooves stamping. His ears were still back and he reared, turning to face her. Victoria braced the gun on top of the stall door. "Come on, then," she whispered.

He screamed and ran for freedom, hooves thundering in the night. Other horses all over the ranch were awake now, kicking and whinnying. Lights were appearing as candles and lamps were lit, men were spilling out of the bunkhouse pulling on their pants and stomping their feet into boots. Victoria was half-frozen and wobbling with exhaustion as she left the barn after extinguishing the lantern. It was all she could do to push the double doors together again and fasten them.

Jake was running toward her with Ben right behind him. Both of them were armed, pistols in hand. When he saw her with his other pistol in her hand, he grabbed her by the shoulders and shook her. "What did you do?" he yelled.

"I let him go," she said simply, and handed Jake his pistol.

He shoved it into the empty holster. "You what?" Equal amounts of rage and incredulousness were in his voice.

"I let him go. I couldn't live here with him safe and sound in the barn and Celia in a grave. You'll have to make do with the foals he's already sired."

He swore violently, then shut up when he looked down at her. She was as white as her nightgown and shivering with cold; she had only a shawl thrown around her to protect her from the weather. She swayed, and he picked her up. "All right, darling," he said in a far gentler tone. "All right." He carried her back to the house and put her to bed. For the first time since Celia's death, she went soundly to sleep.

March came, bringing hints of spring that lasted just long enough to make them all start hoping. Victoria was awkward and slow-moving, unable to get up out of a chair by herself. She hadn't recovered her spirits, but was able to smile a little when Jake teased her. Her bulk had its own dampening effect on her moods; her back ached constantly now and she was unable to find a comfortable position for sleeping. The baby had settled so low that she found it difficult even to walk. If only this pregnancy would end! She found herself even looking forward to labor, for it would mean an end to this constant physical wretchedness.

Jake had never particularly considered himself a family man, despite the fact that he was now married and increasingly in love with his wife. It was with some surprise that he realized he was staying close to the house these days, just in case. He rubbed her back for her every night, and helped her out of bed for her numerous nightly visits to the chamberpot. The size of her belly alarmed him, for he knew how slender her hips were. Angelina had died in childbirth; he was terrified that the same might happen to Victoria.

The last of March came and went. Everyone watched her like a hawk. The third of April, it began snowing again and Victoria felt like screaming with frustration. Would spring and this baby never get here?

She couldn't sleep that night; she was more restless than usual, and the sheets kept tangling about her legs. Jake rubbed her back, but it didn't help. She got up to wash her face with cool water, and he got up with her. Since the night she had sneaked out to the barn and let Rubio go, she hadn't been able to stir without disturbing him. Neither of them bothered to light a candle; the snowfall filled the room with a pale, unearthly light and she was able to see quite well though everything was without color.

Suddenly Jake stiffened. She sensed his alertness and looked at him. He was staring out the window. She looked out the window, too, but could see nothing. "Get dressed," he said sharply, and reached for his pants. "Don't light any candles or lamps." He had barely buttoned his pants before he was out the door, buck-ling his guns around his lean waist.

He called down the hallway, "Ben. Riders."

Ben sat up in bed at the first sound of Jake's voice, disturbing Emma who had been sleeping on his arm. "Get up, honey," he said in a quiet, level voice. "We have trouble."

He was already up and pulling on his pants before she pushed the hair out of her eyes, but his urgency was contagious. She grabbed her nightgown and pulled it on over her head, shivering as the chill struck her bare body.

"Who is it?"

"Doesn't matter."

Victoria would need her. Emma dashed out of the room ahead of Ben, who was putting on his boots, and ran to her own room, which had been largely unoccupied these past couple of months. She didn't know what had kept her from completely moving in with Ben, because certainly no one had been censori-ous of their relationship. In fact, in the sadness following Celia's death, they had all pulled closer together, and Emma's happiness had seemed to cheer Victoria.

Victoria had never been more aware of her ungainly bulk than she was now, when she was trying to hurry. Jake was back in the bedroom a heartbeat after calling to Ben, putting on his boots, shrugging into a shirt but not taking the time to button it. He grabbed his heavy coat on the way out the door a second time. Over his shoulder he said, "Damn it, Victoria, get dressed!"

She was trying. She didn't bother to remove her nightgown, but pulled on one of her loose dresses over it. Emma came in, dressed herself, as Victoria was struggling to put on her stockings and shoes. "I'll do it," Emma whispered, going down on her knees and rolling the stockings up Victoria's legs. "What's hap-pening?"

"I don't know. Jake saw something and told Ben there were riders."

They listened, but couldn't hear anything. When they went downstairs they found that the men had roused the rest of the household, and the three other women were standing in their nightgowns in a terrified knot. Jake tossed Ben a rifle, then gave

Victoria and Emma an assessing glance. "Both of you get a rifle and find a place where you have plenty of cover but can see to shoot. I'm going down to the bunkhouse to wake up the men."

"I'm going down to the bunkhouse," Ben corrected, and both of them thought of Victoria, heavily pregnant. It was better that Jake stay with her.

Before he slipped out the door, Ben put his hand behind Emma's neck and pulled her to him for a quick, hard kiss. It wasn't until he was gone that she realized he had kissed her good-bye, just in case.

"What's happening?" Victoria asked calmly.

"I saw a light where there shouldn't have been one. Someone lit a cigarette, probably."

"What makes you think it was more than one man?"

"Experience." He shoved a handful of shells in each pocket and pushed the box toward them. "Fill up your pockets. Carmita, can any of you shoot?"

"Yes, Señor Jake," she said. "I can, and so can Juana."

"And I," Lola said.

"Good. All of you, get a rifle. It may be nothing, but by God if it's something we'll be ready for them."

"Indians?" Juana posed timidly.

"No. Indians would never have made that light."

White men. Raiders.

Emma watched the door by which Ben had left, willing him to come back through it.

The first shot made them all jump, except for Jake. He ran toward the front of the house and broke out a window with the stock of his rifle. "Find cover!" he yelled.

They scrambled for positions. "Coming in!" Ben yelled from outside, and the door burst open. He came in low, running, and was followed by five other men. "Thought you could use some extra guns in here," he said. Luis was one of them, his lean, dark face more alive than it had been in two months.

The women went upstairs, their hearts pounding as they chose windows. Following Jake's example, Victoria smashed the glass out with her rifle and cold air poured in. "At least I won't go to sleep," she mumbled.

The barrage of shooting opened all at once, and it seemed like it came from all directions. The house echoed with shots and the sharp smell of cordite burned her nostrils. She peered out the window, searching for a target. She could see dark shapes moving around and chose the ones on horseback; their men wouldn't be mounted, she reasoned.

A man on foot raised his head from behind a bush and aimed at the house. Victoria carefully aimed and pulled the trigger. The man fell back in a boneless sprawl.

She had killed a man. It left her surprisingly unmoved. Later, perhaps, would be time for reaction.

There were more shots from the upper floor now, and the others began picking their targets. Victoria shot at a man on horseback, but missed.

A cry of pain came from one of the bedrooms. Victoria started, but didn't dare leave her post. "Emma?" she called.

"I'm fine! Carmita? Lola? Juana?"

Everyone answered except Lola. Victoria heard a low moan.

Just then an orange glow flickered across the white ground. A man galloped toward the house, a blazing torch in his right hand. Terror struck Victoria's heart. They were trying to burn the house! She shot the man in the face and he tumbled backward off the horse, the torch flying from his hand and sputtering out in the snow.

Bullets struck the adobe walls and shattered what little glass was left in the window. Shards rained down on her ducked head. When she lifted it again, she saw another man carrying a flaming torch die before he could throw it at the house.

The adobe walls would be difficult to burn, she thought, as would the clay tile roof, but what if a torch came through one of the glassless windows?

She fired and reloaded, fired and reloaded, for what seemed like hours. Her entire body felt squeezed by a great fist. Terror ate at her, because she didn't know if Jake was still alive or if a bullet had found him.

Emma ran into the room, bent low. "Lola's dead, and Juana has been wounded, but not bad. She's still shooting."

"What about Jake? And Ben?"

"I heard Jake downstairs. I don't know about Ben." Agony was in Emma's voice. Victoria squeezed her hand.

"Who is doing this?" Victoria moaned. Every muscle in her was aching. She didn't know how much longer she could stay on her feet.

"I don't know. It should be dawn soon. At least then we'll be able to see."

Dawn. Had that much time passed? It had seemed like forever, but at the same time she would have measured it in minutes instead of hours.

She caught the acrid smell of smoke.

"Get water!" she yelled. "Fire! Get water!" She grabbed the pitcher of water from the table and ran out into the hallway. Pale smoke was drifting up the stairs. She ran down them, bending over as far as she could. Someone rose up in front of her, a face from hell. It was Jake, his face blackened with gunsmoke. "Get down!" he yelled.

"The house is on fire!"

He cursed and swung around. None of them had noticed the smoke, but now they could see it coming from the kitchen. He grabbed her arm and pulled her to the floor. "Stay here, do you hear me? Stay here! I'm going to get the others. We'll have to get out of here!"

How could they? They would run into a hail of bullets outside. But as Jake had said, they had to get out. They couldn't fight the fire and the raiders at the same time.

The smoke was getting thicker. She began ripping squares out of her skirt and soaking them in water from the pitcher she had grabbed. Ben crawled up beside her, grinning like a fiend. She hit him in the face with a sodden piece of material. "Tie that over your nose and mouth," she said. Her throat was burning, and she obeyed her own instructions.

"Is Emma all right?" Ben grunted.

"Yes. Jake has gone up to get them. Lola's dead."

Ben called the five other men together, and they pulled back from their positions as Jake came down the stairs with the three women. Victoria gave them all wet squares to cover their faces.

Jake hunkered down beside her as he tied the cloth over his mouth and nose.

"We'll go out through the courtyard," he said, his voice muffled. "It's the only way that'll give us any protection. I'll go out first, then another man, then the women. The rest of you come after the women and cover them."

Luis said, "We have to get word to Lonny, or our own men are liable to shoot us."

"We don't have time. Go, now!"

Jake dragged Victoria to her feet and down the hall to one of the courtyard entrances. "We'll take you to the smithy," he said. "It's closest."

The smithy was just a three-sided shed, equipped with the basic blacksmith tools, but it had the advantage of being directly behind the house. They would have some shelter there, but not much.

Jake went out first. He saw a muzzle flash as someone fired, the bullet singing close by his head with the sound of an angry hornet. He fired but must have missed because he saw a shadow dodging to the side. He fired at the shadow, and this time was rewarded by a howl of pain that swiftly disintegrated into silence.

Behind him he could hear Victoria breathing in hard, quick gasps as the smoke got thicker. Then he heard Luis, who came out after him, his dark eyes flashing in the light of the flames that were beginning to flicker through the roof. "Get your wife," he said to Jake. "I'll guard you."

Jake put his arm around Victoria's back and ran. She tried to stay up with him but stumbled, and he held her up with the sheer force of his arm, keeping himself between her and the most likely line of fire. "I can make it, just watch your back!" she gasped.

"Don't talk, just run!"

The men behind them were firing steadily, snapping off shots at anyone who moved. From the bunkhouse and stable came a furious volley, as someone spotted the women trying to flee the house and laid down covering fire so they could reach safety. Bullets zinged overhead, but they ran and ducked and weaved, never giving anyone a steady target.

Jake made it to the smithy with Victoria and placed her on

the ground at the back of the shed. He was already turning around to leave her as he said, "Stay down. Don't raise your head for anything." Then he took up position beside Luis, picking his shots and snapping them off, firing for effect rather than cover.

Emma tumbled into the smithy in a tangle of skirts, but she quickly got to her hands and knees and crawled to Victoria, swearing as the cloth tangled her legs again. Illogically, Victoria laughed at hearing those sort of words leaving Emma's proper mouth. Emma looked up and grinned. Most of her dark hair had come loose from its braid, and her pale skin was smeared with soot and gunpowder. "Well," she said, "there's no point in worrying about manners right now."

"I agree." Victoria laughed again, a bit disoriented. They had both killed tonight, so why worry about propriety?

Carmita and Juana scrambled in after them. Juana was bleeding from a cut high on her shoulder where a splinter of glass had sliced through the air. She sank down on the ground, still clutching a rifle in her hand.

Ben's left leg was suddenly knocked out from under him, and he went down as abruptly as if he had been tripped. Emma made a high, thin sound and despite Jake's shouted warning darted out of the shelter.

Ben was already rolling over, trying to get his good leg under him, when Emma slid into the snow beside him. She grabbed his collar and began dragging him, screaming and crying and swearing all at the same time. He was swearing, too, yelling at Emma to let go of him and get the hell back into the smithy, but she refused. Her strength amazed him. Though he far outweighed her, she dug her heels in and pulled and there was nothing he could do to stop her, no way he could break her grip. She dragged him into the smithy and immediately began tearing his pants leg open so she could see the wound.

"How is he?" Jake barked.

"I'll live," Ben replied for himself, though it wasn't by any means certain. The bullet had punched completely through his thigh. Still, if he didn't bleed to death and if he didn't get gangrene, he would be all right.

"Sarratt! Goddamn you, Sarratt, where are you?"

Jake's head came up, and an unholy look crossed his face, a cold glitter coming into his eyes. "Garnet," he hissed. A small smile of anticipation touched his lips, and he snaked a run across the yard. Now he knew who to hunt; it was what he'd been waiting for. This time Garnet wasn't going to get away.

Dawn was slowly turning the sky a pale gray. It was snowing again, the swirling flakes cutting down on visibility. Crimson and yellow light from the burning house illuminated the area in a strange, flickering glow. Victoria turned her head and looked at the house; the fire in the kitchen had burned through to the second floor. She could see flames breaking through the roof and licking out of the broken windows. It was dying, the old, graceful house that had seen both love and savage betrayal, birth and death. She hadn't been able to bring herself to pack away Celia's clothes, but now she wouldn't have to; the flames were destroying every memento, leaving only her own memories.

The fist tightened on her body. She lay panting, watching the flames, and when she could speak again she said, "The baby will be here soon."

Carmita gasped, too overwhelmed by the night's events to comprehend how she could deal with this, too. Emma looked up from where she was applying pressure to Ben's wounds to stop the bleeding, her face tight with strain. "Your pains have started?"

Victoria inhaled sharply, her fingers digging into the dirt. "Hours ago."

Garnet was desperate and losing control. It wasn't supposed to have been like this! It should have happened the way it had the first time, with them riding in and catching everyone off guard or asleep. Instead, those bastards had been awake and waiting for them. It didn't make sense, and it made him afraid. Only the thought of finally getting his hands on Celia kept him from running. This would be his last chance, because he knew that if he failed, Sarratt would hunt him down like a mad dog.

"Sarratt!" he bellowed. "Sarratt!" Even as he yelled, he changed position, working his way around toward the barn. If he could just draw Jake out, to hell with a fair fight. No way was he going to face Jake. Just one shot was all he'd need, a quick bullet in the head or back, and no more Sarratt. Someone had already gotten the brother. The kingdom would be his, and Celia would be his. He'd have to take care of Bullfrog in the same way he took care of Sarratt, but that didn't trouble him any.

Jake didn't answer. He remained where he was, watching. He saw someone quickly sidle into the corral. The light was too uncertain for him to recognize the man by anything other than instinct. Garnet was heading toward the barn, where he would have cover when Jake showed himself.

Jake didn't intend to show himself. On his belly he wormed his way from bush to tree to well-house, then to the bunkhouse. Bodies were sprawled all over the yard, dark, boneless heaps. A lot of men had died that night. He wasn't going to be one of them, but Garnet damn sure was.

"We need heat," Emma said calmly. "Can someone fire up the forge, please? And we need light."

Luis began stoking coal into the forge. "Heat, yes, but there's no lantern. It will be daylight soon."

Victoria didn't care about either heat or light. Every instinct, every sense, was focused inward. She was in the grip of a force that wouldn't be denied, a great squeezing force wrapped around her body and dragging her down. Even though she had witnessed Angelina's labor, she hadn't imagined it would be this bad. It was grinding agony, tearing her pelvis apart and forcing air from her lungs, and it went on and on with only spare moments of relief between the waves.

Ben lay next to the anvil, listening to Victoria's stifled groans. "Take my shirt," he instructed, keeping his voice steady with effort. "Twist it, and wrap it tight around a stick, then set it on fire. It'll give you a few minutes of light."

"All right," Emma said after pausing to consider the idea. "But not just yet. We'll need it more in a little while than we do right now."

* * *

Garnet worked his way around to the back of the barn and opened the door just enough to slip in. Fingers of light were beginning to show through the cracks as dawn progressed. He didn't have much time left. He ran to the front of the barn and opened those doors a crack, not enough for anyone to notice that they were open but enough for him to see and shoot. Now all he had to do was wait. Sarratt should be working his way toward the spot where Garnet had been when he'd yelled.

Garnet grinned. Just a few minutes. A few more minutes, and he'd have everything he'd ever wanted.

"Looking for me?"

The words were accompanied by the unmistakable click of a pistol being cocked. Garnet froze, sweat popping out on his brow despite the cold. He didn't dare turn around. Terror ripped through him as he realized that he was going to die. He had shot others with no more feeling than he'd have burst a melon, but the thought of his own death was paralyzing.

"You might as well turn around," Jake said softly. "I'm going to kill you either way. At least if you turn you'll have a chance to get a shot off at me, too."

The gun trembled in Garnet's hand. He'd die as soon as he turned, but he believed Sarratt when he said he'd kill him anyway.

"You should've kept going," Jake murmured. "As far and as fast from the kingdom as you could get."

"You'd have hunted me down," Garnet gasped. "And the girl—I wanted the girl."

Celia. Beautiful little Celia. Jake's mouth tightened with pain. "You'll never have her now," he said. Garnet threw himself to the side, turning and firing as he did. Jake was prepared for that and had positioned himself behind a bale of hay. Only his head and gun were exposed. He was calm as he fired, the first bullet hitting Garnet in the stomach, the second in the chest. Garnet crashed against the wall, his finger tightening reflexively on the trigger and getting off a shot that went through the ceiling before the heavy gun dropped from his hand.

Jake kicked the gun out of reach, just in case. The only way he'd trust Garnet was dead.

Garnet's eyes were open, his throat working convulsively as he tried to breathe. Red foam bubbled out of his mouth. Jake watched as his chest heaved up and down a few times, then stopped completely. Garnet's eyes glazed over.

There had been a lot of death on this ranch. Jake sighed, suddenly tired of it, but he automatically reloaded his pistol. It was quiet outside, he realized. Maybe it was over. He had to get back to Victoria.

"Boss? You all right?"

It was Lonny. Jake called, "Yeah."

"You better get back to the smithy. Luis says the baby's coming."

Jake had been frightened before; he'd been anxious, worried, tense; but now he felt pure terror. Victoria couldn't give birth like this, lying in a cold smithy, without blankets or anything. He ran, not even noticing the gun still in his hand.

Ben was propped up against the anvil now, shirtless, but someone had given him a coat. He was pale, but a quick glance reassured Jake that the bleeding had stopped. The forge was going full blast, giving off great waves of heat that fought off the chill in the open shed. Luis lighted a lantern and handed it to the back of the shed, which had been partitioned off by several skirts that were hung over a rope strung from side to side. Jake brushed past the skirts and knelt on the ground beside his wife.

Emma, Carmita, and Juana were all in their nightgowns, having sacrificed the clothing they had hurriedly donned over their nightwear for the makeshift curtain. Victoria's nightgown was rucked up to her waist, her knees bent and raised. Jake knelt beside her, his heart in his throat as he stroked her damp hair back from her face with dirty, trembling fingers. Her eyes were closed, her face paper white as she breathed in quick, jerky pants.

Carmita glanced up at him, her dark eyes worried. "Soon, Señor Jake. I can see the head."

Victoria's eyes opened. They were glazed, but fastened on him like a talisman. She reached up over her head, and Jake caught her hand in his.

"Hold on, love," he whispered. He was frozen with fear. He had brought her to this, endangered her life, reduced her to giving birth in the dirt like an animal, his sweet lady Victoria. He should never have married her, he should have sent her back East, where she could have had the sort of life she'd been born for, a life of comfort and gentility.

Her hand clamped down on his, and her teeth clenched. A low, raw sound built up in her throat, then erupted in an animal scream of pain, followed by another, and another. Her entire body was convulsing, bearing down, and her shoulders left the ground.

With a gush of blood and water, a slippery little body slid out into Carmita's waiting hands. The baby looked purplish and another sort of agony punched Jake in the chest as he stared wordlessly at the silent infant. Then Carmita thumped it on the back and a tiny, choking cry erupted that began building into a wail. She turned the baby, and Jake saw that it was a boy. Tightly clenched little hands jerked as his son expressed his upset at this unfamiliar new world.

Unbelievably, Victoria laughed, a tired, weak sound. "Well, he definitely resembles you," she said.

Jake looked at her in bewilderment, wondering how she could see any resemblance to anyone in the squalling, red, wrinkled scrap, still covered with the blood of his birth. Maybe in the dark hair, but it was wet and might not be so dark when it was dry.

She pulled him down to her, her eyes alight with mischief. Putting her lips against his ear, she whispered, "He's very *definitely* a male."

Then Jake understood what she meant. He looked at the naked baby and for the first time in his life, a blush reddened his cheeks.

She held out her arms for the baby. "Let me have him. He must be cold."

Carmita cut and tied the cord. The baby was quickly wrapped in someone else's shirt (everyone seemed to be giving up their clothing for the occasion) and placed in Victoria's arms. The baby stopped crying, slowly blinking his unfocused eyes as he responded to the warmth of being held by his mother.

Jake put his arms around both of them, resting his grimy cheek against Victoria's hair. "I love you," he said hoarsely. She was all that was good and strong and gentle in his life. Her hold on him had shattered the core of hatred that he had fed off of for so long.

Victoria tilted her head back, her shadowed blue eyes meeting his green ones. "I love you, too," she replied simply.

"I meant to give you better than this. We don't even have a house to live in now."

"I don't care." She was tired and leaned more heavily against him. "I'm glad the house burned. There was too much hatred locked in it, too much death. I didn't want all of that for him." She looked at her son and gently touched his downy cheek with a finger. He turned his head toward the touch, his rosebud mouth working.

"I can start over," Jake promised. "I'll build another house for you, if you'll stay with me. God, honey, don't leave me. You might as well shoot me if you're going to leave, because I love you so much I won't be any good without you."

He'd never before told her he loved her, never before looked at her with that expression in his eyes, so desperate and haunted and . . . and afraid. She couldn't imagine Jake Sarratt being afraid of anything, but it was there in his eyes that no longer looked cold to her at all.

It changed everything, his love. The hate was gone, and with it her reason for ever leaving.

"All right," she said, reaching tiredly for his hand. "You build your own kingdom and forget about the past, about that other Sarratt's Kingdom. It's really gone now, and we can start fresh."

Emma knelt beside Ben to check his leg. He grinned at her. "Do I have a niece or a nephew?"

"Nephew." She looked down, her face getting hot as she fumbled with his bandage. "And maybe a son of your own," she mumbled.

"What?" He stared at her in shock. "What?" he asked louder, sitting up straight.

"Hush!" she hissed at him.

He grabbed her arms, holding her still. "Are you sure?" he asked.

"It's possible. I'm not certain yet." She was just a little late, and her system had never been as reliable as Victoria's. But the possibility was there. She had spent too many nights in Ben's bed for her to think otherwise.

He began laughing and pulled her down for a hard kiss. "Emma girl, I haven't been able to think straight since I met you, and things aren't getting any better. I think we'd better get married, don't you?"

"Because I might be—?"

"No, because we love each other and we'll probably have a houseful of kids, so it would make things simpler if we were married."

Emma's dark eyes began to glow. "Ben Sarratt, I do love you."

"That's a yes?"

She nodded. "That's a yes."

Jake sat on the ground, holding Victoria propped in his arms. Unbelievably, she was sleeping and so was the baby. He looked at his son, all red and wrinkled and completely helpless, dependent on him for protection and food and everything else in life. He had to think about the future now, and his future was Victoria and the baby, as well as other babies that might come. The morning carried the stink of smoke and gunpowder, but the snow had stopped and the sun was trying to break through and shine on the new layer of white. There was something else new, something inside him, new and good. The future loomed before him, and he felt good about it.

He had Victoria, their baby was fat and healthy, and together they could build a life of their own without the taint of the past. The territory would see a new Sarratt's Kingdom, the one he and Ben would build, but this one would be as fresh as the snow that lay on the high valley.